DOMINATION DIARIES

Two Views of Lust, Lashings, and Love on a Historic Caribbean Island Plantation

By
JC Corbette

Follow on:
Facebook: JC.Corbette
Instagram: jc.corbette
Twitter: corbetteJc
Inquiries: jc.corbette@gmail.com

My man, on his knees and kissing my feet, is not just enchanting, it's proper.

Stefany Allain McCaskill

TABLE OF CONTENTS

notorious ancestor, Seumas Owen McCaskill. At *The Blue Calypso*, Mobley is promoted from filthy dishwasher to humble waiter - only to find himself at a table serving Stefany and her guests.

FUNGAL INFECTIONS AND FAT LIPS
Mobley discovers he has been getting more than just sleep in his closet apartment. Miles receives an attitude adjustment. A rum sodden Mobley takes a drunken roll in the gutter. Stefany has second thoughts.

RUM. RALPHING - AND REGRETS
Disgusted with herself for having pity on Mobley, a regretful Stefany makes clear her expectations. Leanne finds a new friend in Mobley while her two sex slave playmates, Joe and Heidi, attempt to show Stefany the wild side.

UNREQUITED LOVE - LEANNE HATCHES A SCHEME
Money troubles at the plantation multiply as Miles vows revenge. Leanne shares a BDSM book - Stefany is less than impressed. Leanne proposes a friendly wager - sexual slavery. Mobley, unsuccessful in

thwarting Stefany's morality rules, fears celibacy and is left to a loathsome self-reflection.

A BOTTLE OF TEQUILA AND FOUR FLAT TIRES

Stoney Brook begins to reveal a dark past. The property deed to Stoney Brook has been incomplete - there is much more (WITH taxes). Stefany and Mobley have a close call – and share something else.

PURVEYING A PIRATICAL PAST

Mobley comes up with a bold plan. Miles seeks reconciliation with Stefany. The foundation stones beneath Stoney Brook reveal a new surprise. Seumas McCaskill's ledger hints of a violent past. Constable Fillmore reveals a gory discovery in the aftermath of the Mill Property attack.

HIGH HOPES AND HORNY THOUGHTS

Mobley presents his plan as the investigation of the cave picks up. Heidi and Mobley each pay an evening visit to Stefany - with mixed results.

while Mobley recovers in a Caribbean hospital as he contemplates the possibilities of an ancient Voodoo legend.

Receiving a series of threatening letters, Stefany realizes what she must do. Heartbroken, Mobley returns to Chicago where a new revelation emerges.

Stoney Brook is reborn from the ashes. Miles at last grants Stefany a divorce. The Seumas McCaskill ledger reveals a final, shocking truth. Marisha Neita and Bhoki come home. Mobley graduates as a licensed architect and is later surprised.

CHAPTER 1
AS LUCK WOULD HAVE IT

Stefany: The city is alive with preparations for Christmas. My little business in downtown Montreal, Stefany's Coffee Shop, will be lucky to make it to the New Year. I had to let two of my employees go earlier this week. Bankruptcy looms. My jerk of a husband, Miles, has always said it was inevitable and running a vacuum would be a more appropriate challenge for me as I was bereft of any business acumen. I have not updated my diary in over 3 years, but I figured it was time. It's hard to sit down and write when there isn't anything positive to write about – but THAT has changed after this epic day. Spending most of the day putting up Christmas decorations, I decided to come home, wondering when I should just give up, both on the coffee shop - and my marriage. An hour ago, I got a knock on the front door. Now, I do have something positive to write about.

A guy in a business suit introduced himself as Gary Thomson, from some law firm in Scotland. Said he had flown all the way over here just to talk to me. He asked me if my maiden name was McCaskill, and I confirmed for him that it was true. And yes, I was now married to Miles Michaels (regrettably). After a few more 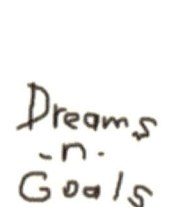 confirming questions, he then proceeded to name off my family members all the way back to the 1400s. When he finally got around to telling me what he wanted – I trusted him enough by this time to let him come in – shock is an understatement. He said I was the next in line, the "heir" to a historic sugar cane plantation on a remote, autonomous island in the Caribbean. It was built in 1623 by Seumas McCaskill, a Scottish Highlander, a direct ancestor of mine! The plantation is called Stoney Brook. It's hundreds of years old!

Of course, I thought it was a scam. It had to be. When I asked why it would only be me inheriting this property - surely there had to be hundreds of McCaskill "heirs" by this time in the family history - he explained it this way. The estate will was written in a way that allowed only one of the most direct heirs to inherit the property for each successive generation. Otherwise, over time, it would be fragmented and divided through disagreements, or whatever.

If I would not take the property, it would then fall to the next most direct heir. I guess I was the most direct by way of a bunch of my relatives dying in the trenches of World War 1, and then later, members of this same line of the family dying in the Spanish Flu Epidemic.

Thomson showed me an image of what looks like the ancient emblem for Stoney Brook. He said it is found throughout the plantation, including the front gates. It has a sword, and skull and crossbones on it. When I asked him why it had that, he said Stoney Brook is rumored to have been founded with money plundered through piracy by one of my Scottish ancestors!

~~~~~

After listing for just 3 days, I sold the coffee shop!!! I only made enough to pay off debts, but it's done. It's been a week since I met Gary Thomson, but assuming ownership of Stoney Brook is my once-in-a-lifetime opportunity I am NOT going to miss. Miles forbade me to even visit the property and left for the office. I am done this time. He will never change, and I have finally left him. This morning, I withdrew what little of my savings I own outright. As I write this, it's a week before Christmas, and I am in a hotel room wondering if I am soon to be homeless. All I can afford is the plane and boat fare for the trip down there and perhaps expenses for a month. Also, I have filed for divorce; yeah, it's been a long time coming.

~~~~~

Time for an update! It has been exhausting after arriving at Stoney Brook. I've been here now for two months. The bad news is my savings are gone, and everything is a mess. I can only afford peanut butter and jelly sandwiches. The good news? The potential is amazing! I love this place! It feels like it is truly mine. My saving grace so far has been some income from the current sugarcane harvest. The cane processor that accepted the harvest gave me a check! Cane harvest has been going on here for ages and provides a steady but small income to the estate which has enabled me to make the payroll and a small profit – and somehow keep me going. The workers are less than friendly at first.

~~~~~

Research time - I've decided to try and restore the property into a resort. The mansion is huge, and all the rooms can accommodate dozens of people.

~~~~~

I'm too busy to write anything. I'll try to add an update later!

~~~~~

I have come to the realization I can't do this alone. In addition to trying to get a bank loan, I need someone to help me. Beginning today, I will shop around for someone that has experience restoring historic buildings.

~~~~~

My online search for someone with experience as an architect went well. If I can start making a little more income, I should be able to make this work. I hired a guy today. His name is Morgan Mobley from Chicago. His profile seemed solid. He's something to look at too, I must say.

He seems legit; licensed architect, recently graduated, experience in historic restoration, worked as an apprentice in

Chicago. I confess, I did not investigate any of his references or double-check the honesty of his resume and credentials. Being truthful with myself, I admit his handsome features in his photo, curly blond hair, and his penetrating blue eyes had ~quite~ a bit to do with me deciding to hire him. That, and how he came across in his online interview. Wow. I justified it by making myself believe that his qualifications met all my needs and I ended up getting him cheap. Very cheap indeed. I was surprised he took my lowball offer. Maybe he was just interested in enjoying a bit of tropical island lifestyle. Should I be worried?

~~~~~

I finally met Mr. Architect earlier today. Morgan Mobley. Having been brought from the main island by water taxi, he only carried a backpack and a duffel bag. He looked capable and smart enough. Tall, probably over six feet one, in shape – muscular shoulders beneath a

Step 2: Regret over hiring a pompous ASS

tropical short sleeve shirt. Wearing tan cargo slacks, I could see that he has a flat stomach and long, strong-looking legs. His face was in several days of stubble which looks like his intentional style as opposed to just needing a shave after his long trip. Hmmm. Physically speaking, yep, he looks good. But...

As soon as he came to stand in front of me... okay... I began to have second thoughts. In-person, he emanates a college boy, beach bum vibe that doesn't settle well with me. He didn't exactly impress me on the drive back, either. His yapping was irritating and incessant, and he said some things that were just plain stupid. Plus, he smokes.

I know, I know. It's early and I'm being overly critical like I usually am with everything. Maybe he's all right. And after all, he just needs to do a good job! I need to chill. I guess I'll be able to know later if I made a good decision. Or not. Did I?

The taxi boat driver, after tying off, flailed his arms towards the dock, indicating Mr. Architect should promptly depart his company. The driver, spewing what I took to be a litany of angry curses in French, spat at his passenger's feet. Looking somewhat bewildered, Mr. Architect obliged, stepping off the boat. His backpack and duffel bag promptly landed on the dock, thrown without fanfare by the agitated driver. The mooring rope was cast off, more curses flew, and the taxi boat sped away into the distance. My Mr. Architect had arrived, for better or worse. I was hoping it would be for the better. Things couldn't get much worse.

Wondering what the hell could have happened with the taxi boat driver, I waved at Mr. Architect. He looked right past me. I may not be dressed to the nines, but I have never had the problem of catching the attention of men. The dockworkers and drunken regulars hanging over the deck rail at The Blue Calypso had certainly not overlooked me, the evidence being the usual rude whistles and catcalls upon my arrival. I again waved at Mr. Architect from outside of the dock barrier rope I wasn't supposed to cross. Again, he looked past me. I felt my cheeks flush with agitation. This wasn't going well. But I promised myself I would withhold judgment either way. For a while.

I was wearing cutoff blue-jean shorts and a dirty, sweat-stained t-shirt - my favorite attire since being here if I must admit it. With the constant work that needs to be done at the plantation and with the heat, I dress sensibly. At least it's sensible for me while the plantation is being renovated and restored. I could care less what anyone else thinks. I've done my time in business attire and I'll be damned if I put it on without protest and a good reason. Sure, maybe later when I must, but only then. These are the tropics and I'm not an ivory maiden that spends her day locked in an office, bent over a laptop and phone. Well, at least not since I moved to the island to take over Stoney Brook Plantation after I inherited the place five months ago from a relative I didn't even know existed.

Again, I raised my arm to catch his attention. Okay, yeah. I was getting pissed now. Judging by how he was ignoring me, he was anticipating someone better dressed.

How does a barely scraping-by, nearly broke, Canadian girl, turned newly minted plantation owner dress? To hell with that. It was hotter than Hades, I had just minutes before been mucking out a flooded cellar. Sorry, Mr. Architect, I'm not a fashionista, I'd left that lifestyle behind with my asshole lawyer husband in Montreal.

He was looking around the dock, puzzled. His eyes fell upon my battered Land Rover parked nearby, a painted Stoney Brook Plantation logo on the door faded and peeling. What was he expecting, a suit and tie entourage? A red carpet and limousine? He looked right past me and my opinions of him began to wane. There were maybe fifteen people on the dock, either workers or tourists. With my arm raised, frantically waving, I was the only person that looked as if I could be waiting for someone.

My irritation began to scratch its way up my sweaty back. Gritting my teeth, I wiped the perspiration from my eyes and swore I would not lose my temper just because I was hot and grimy. I should give this guy, Mr. Architect, a chance. He was a long way from Chicago, after all, and I had made quite a commitment to hiring him. Well, at least it was a commitment for me. For a licensed architect, he was relatively cheap. Still, it was quite a hit to my savings and my paltry operating expenses regardless of how cheap he was. I was going to have to turn a profit soon. Or else.

Screw it. I lifted the barrier rope and started walking towards him. A guy I took to be a dock manager began to voice his objections. After giving him just one look, he thought better of it and began attending to business elsewhere. I again raised my arm to catch Mr. Architect's attention. "Hello, Mr. Mobley? Morgan Mobley?"

Mr. Architect blinked and a gorgeous set of blue eyes fell on me, his best feature I noted. Well, one of his best features. Although he was sending out some irritating vibes.

"Yes," he replied, setting his backpack and duffel bag down. "You are from Stone Brook Plantation?" He reached to shake my hand.

"Um. It's *Stoney* Brook Plantation, Mr. Mobley. I'm Stefany Michaels." His eyes broke from mine and slowly roamed down my body, paused at my bare legs, then finally back up again. A slight smile broke out on his face. Was he passing *judgment* of how I was dressed?! There was something hungry and crude in his expression. Was he so rude as to be checking me out? Was that it? Not on the island five minutes and he was body scanning me? I was his boss, damn it. I would not tolerate disrespect or unprofessional behavior, a few things he would soon understand. I shook his hand and forced a smile.

I suddenly realized I was unconsciously tidying my hair. Catching myself and disgusted that he noticed, I dropped my arm. His gaze was unsettling - deep blue eyes washing over me like the nearby surf on our white sand beaches. It was a distraction to the mixed feelings I now had about him, and I was wishing I had instead hired the thin girl with horned-rim glasses from Seattle.

"Yes, well. Let's get you back to the plantation and I'll show you around."

"Thank you, Stefany. It's been a long trip and I'm looking forward to seeing Stone Brook. What a wonderful historic treasure you have there. I've got quite a few good ideas for you, and I'm ready to get started."

I cleared my throat. "Stone-*ee* Brook. If you are to work for me, you may as well use the correct name, eh? And it's *Ms.* Michaels if you please," I said, unable to help myself. He was so presumptuous.

"Um. Ms. Michaels?"

"Yes. Please call me Ms. Michaels. All my employees call me Ms. Michaels." Extended employment for this guy might be questionable, I suddenly thought, already finding myself wondering how I could get rid of him if necessary.

He paused. "Oh. I'm sorry. Yes, Ms. Michaels, it is, forgive me. I forget myself."

Yes, you effin did, Mr. Architect, I thought. He was cocky. Brazen and full of himself. The kind of egotistical

11

schmuck that fancies himself a ladies' man. Which he no doubt was. I took his duffel bag and when I turned my back, I rolled my eyes. I don't care how good he looked. It had only been a minute and this guy was already getting under my skin. I threw his duffel bag into the back of the Land Rover, and he tossed his backpack in with it. I took a deep breath as I slid behind the wheel and started the engine after he closed the passenger door behind himself. Maybe I was just grouchy because of the difficulties back at the plantation, the apathetic, uncaring staff, the flaming hot temperature, and high humidity. The pressure I was under trying to make this weird but lucky venture I was in successful. That must be it. Maybe this guy wasn't so bad. He did look a little nervous.

"So, what's the deal with the taxi boat driver back there," I asked, trying to navigate the Rover around several large potholes.

"That?" He waved his hand dismissively. "I think he was mad that I didn't tip him. Some kind of French gibberish he was going on about. No big deal. Like he didn't make enough off me just with the fare. I can't believe it costs that much to run me over here. Damn French you know. They'd squabble over a dime and lose a quarter."

The temperature suddenly got much hotter. I felt myself physically bristle. The nerve. And what a cheap fuck this guy apparently was. I may not be the best tipper, but whenever I took the boat taxi, I always tipped several dollars atop the regular fare, especially if there was freight involved. "Um. While I'm of mostly Scottish lineage, McCaskill was my maiden name, you should be aware I'm also part French, Mr. Mobley," I said, icily. "My mother's side. Quebec."

"Oh!" He looked startled. Like his big mouth hadn't gotten him into trouble before. "I just meant... they... about being worked up all the time. You know."

"Yeah." It was all I could say. He was making me ill with regret.

12

"I think I have a bit of French in my family line, also," he managed to blurt as I slogged into a pothole - on his side.

"Do say," I replied. He was showing himself to be an insensitive ass who would say anything to smooth out the rough patches his mouth was getting him into.

Weaving the Rover through scattered tourists, I stole several discreet glances towards my passenger. At least he had shut the fuck up. Nervous or not, maybe he had figured out he had better minimize the damage before I stopped the Rover and kicked his ass out. We hit the dirt road back to Stoney Brook, leaving the harbor village. He sat there peering out at the passing lush foliage nestled in among the distant mountains. He looked so arrogant. Was he? Was I reading him right? I don't mind confidence in oneself, but he exuded overblown ego, even with his mouth shut. I kicked the side of the door with my left foot, angry that I had hired him. But it wasn't like I was dating the guy, I reminded myself. I needed to be patient. It was his abilities as an architect I was hiring. He needed to draw up plans, fix and make stuff. That was all.

"So, you are of Scottish bloodlines, eh. You look very much like the lady lead in that teenage vampire movie series from back in the day. You could almost be her twin. Fair skin. Petite. Green eyes. A few freckles about the nose. Except your hair is darker, almost black. I can't think of her name now. She had a good Scottish name. Hmmm. Might have been Stewart. I don't know if she was actually of Scottish descent."

"I don't watch many movies. And those sound particularly irritating. Please don't make comparisons of me with people I don't even know, Mr. Mobley."

"Oh, I understand," he chuckled uncomfortably. "My apologies, of course."

We sat for a while, driving in thankful silence. Did he think he was complimenting me with that offhand remark about a movie star from some corny movie series that *might* have been Scottish?

"Ms. Michaels. Mind if I smoke?" He pulled a cigarette out from a pack in his shirt, tapped it against his wrist and withdrew one.

A smoker. Ugh. That was another strike against him. "Um. Sorry, yes, I mind. I don't smoke, and I won't have it in my car. And I won't have it at the plantation either, except in only a few designated areas. It's a fire hazard with all the combustible things we have around there, like cane chaff. The grass is dry. The buildings are old and would go up like a torch." I looked over at him, knowing I was not controlling my feelings very well. Odd I hadn't previously noticed, but just then I caught the subtle hint of stale cigarette smoke wafting from his clothes. "Frankly, Mr. Mobley, it's a filthy habit, and I'll be hard-pressed to tolerate much of that," I said sharply, the last few angry words catching in my throat. "Hard-pressed, indeed."

He smiled broadly and replaced the cigarette, patting it. "No problem. I agree, Stefany. I started two years ago and have been trying to quit ever since. Now sounds like a good time." The look on his face was, *oh, she's one of those.*

I downshifted hard to take a hill. "Ms. Michaels," I reminded him, the words unintentionally sounding like a hiss between my lips. "As I said, please call me *Ms. Michaels.*" I was getting the highest reading on my asshole meter since I had left my abusive husband. Regret flooded through me, wishing I hadn't been so swayed by this guy's looks. My knuckles were white on the wheel. I had hired him for all the wrong reasons and now I was stuck with him!

"Oops, sorry. My bad. *Ms. Michaels.* I need to get used to that." He resumed his gaze out the window, his eyebrows arched with what I perceived to be false humility.

I wanted to slap the living shit out of him. *My bad?* I absolutely hate that stupid urban teeny-bop phrase-ism. Few people had ever grated my nerves so quickly as this man. This was not going well. Not well at all.

14

I thought about my dilemma. He was hired, it was a done deal, at least for now. Me, patient? Maybe not.

Morgan: **This is not quite the paradise I imagined, even though it's a beautiful island and magnificent property. After a week of working at Stone Brook, I have managed to orchestrate quite a few improvements to the interior of the mansion. With Stefany, I was not so successful. What an unrelenting bitch. She is as cold to me as a Lake Michigan ice cube, and I feel sorry for the man who is married to this wench. She is quite beautiful, but that fact alone cannot hide the ugly reality of her wretched, dark, flavorless personality. Wretched! And in my book, one overrules the other.**

Never one word of thanks or job well done from her. She mostly gripes about why I am not doing more. I work my ass off. She is unmoved. And it isn't like I haven't tried. Something about me seems to really tick her off. I have no idea what it is.

~~~~

Today I became so badly sunburned I had to go to the village pharmacy for some

aloe ointment. Not a bit of sympathy from Stefany. Nada. She didn't even offer to go with me or compensate me for my expenses.

~~~~~

A positive note: There are quite a few gorgeous island girls with which to make friendly. So many beautiful, bronzed-skinned lovelies that make this gorgeous island even lovelier. The boys back at college would be envious beyond belief. The prospects of being laid on a regular basis by a multitude of island lasses are out of this world crazy good.

~~~~~

Stefany, after catching me taking one girl to my room in the manor yesterday evening, has forbidden me to bring any of the girls to the plantation! What, I guess I must be celibate now? She's not my mother. I'm an adult! She can blow me, for what I'm earning down here, a girl can come to my room now and then. That's a ridiculous rule. Fine. I'll just have to be careful and sneak the girls in. What a shrew.

"The knee wall project, Mr. Mobley. When are you planning on starting it?"

I was covered head to toe in plaster dust, miserable and itchy from repairing crown molding in the formal banquet hall. I leaned into the ladder, wiping the perspiration from my brow. Just a bit more and I would be finished. Stefany peered up at me with an expectant bitchy look that I was now all too familiar with. Gawd, how she could ruin a beautiful face. Her expression reminded me of a carp on the hook.

Setting the sanding block into the top tray, I stepped down off the ladder, admiring her form. Damn. If she just wasn't so... Stefany-ish. It would be interesting to see what she would do if I suddenly kissed those irritated, pursed lips of hers. I have no doubt, she would come unglued is what she'd do. Slap me probably. Maybe if she were getting some, she wouldn't be such the bitch. Certainly, she wasn't getting any, of that I was certain. I couldn't imagine who would give it to her! Her husband was thousands of miles away in Montreal and it was said he wouldn't come to Stoney Brook, opting to let his wife flounder with this little project she inherited. I couldn't blame him.

At least she was as sweaty as I was, with no air conditioning in the huge behemoth of a building that was the Stoney Brook mansion. It was too bad she didn't have any personality to go with her amazing body. The sweat was glinting off her exposed upper chest and legs. That personality, though. It could deflate my penis quicker than a five-alarm fire in a rendering plant.

"I've got one more room, Ms. Steph... erm, Ms. Michaels. The study. Then I can get to the southeast knee wall and get that new footing poured."

"Santiago and Miguel. What do you have them doing today?" she brusquely asked.

17

"Well, Santiago had some personal business to attend to and went to the village. Miguel, I sent to assist with renovations in the barn."

"Personal business?" she snapped. "What personal business does Santiago have that it was necessary to leave, and it was not passed on to me?"

"Well. I don't know, Ms. Stefany. It was... personal." I nearly chuckled at my own humor but thought better of it.

"Mr. Mobley. You do realize I have to somehow turn a profit here at some point? That's if I am to keep this plantation operational and keep employing ALL these people, yourself included. Time is of the essence. I have limited funds from a limited loan. We need to get these jobs done and move on to more important matters. This is taking entirely too long."

"This is a job that has to be done correctly," I tried to explain. "I'm doing the best I can. You must trust me; this is the process that we must take to restore this building to its original grandeur. It's why you hired me and why I'm here."

Agitated, she wiped several wet locks of hair from her brow. "An unfortunate circumstance that I can easily remedy, Mr. Mobley, should your pace not quicken sufficiently."

My jaw dropped and I found myself barely able to contain my rage at this insufferable pain of a woman. Of all the nerve... of all the bullshit I had ever taken in my life, this was the definitive motherlode. How *dare* she threaten me with termination when I was giving the last measure of effort in this sweltering, balls-scorching heat. I was trying to get the damn place livable once again.

"Yes, ma'am," I said, barely concealing my fury. My foot knocked over a bucket of plaster - a huge mess for me to clean up now. And with Miguel in the barn. My jaws clenched.

She smiled. It was a concealed smile... hidden, secretive, and mean spirited - a smile of self-satisfaction. Without question, I saw it. Just a bit. Then it quickly vanished. She was getting off on making me miserable! She

18

liked getting on my case, griping, riding my ass raw, day in and day out. What a rotten, sadistic specimen of a woman, I thought to myself. She probably wanted me to just quit, thus the hard tactics she had with me all this time. It made sense now. Well, two can play that game. I'm not going anywhere, I told myself resolutely.

"Will there be anything else, Ms. Michaels?" There was no mistaking the tone in my voice. I wanted her to feel my wrath. My hatred. My loathing. She stood there, staring at me as if I were some petulant schoolboy.

It was odd... and it happened at the most inopportune moment... but I erroneously caught my eyes dropping to the beads of perspiration visible on her exposed cleavage. It was just a natural thing - a moment of weakness. Unintended. My eyes darted back to hers which were a little wider now at having caught my regrettable indiscretion. Of all the things to do, this was the last on my list. Peering up at the ceiling in disgust, I imagined kicking myself. I would not. Could not. *Will not* be attracted to such an evil woman.

She blinked, clearly irritated, but let it go. "Get moving, Mr. Mobley! I'll be checking to see your progress in several hours." She pointed towards the spilled plaster. "More of my money wasted there. Get that cleaned up." She marched stiffly towards the closest door.

"Bitch," I whispered under my breath when she was a sufficient distance away.

She wheeled around. "What's *that* Mr. Mobley?"

I swallowed hard. How could she have heard? Does she have superhuman hearing? I couldn't afford to lose this job. After my last trip to what served as the village casino in The Blue Calypso, I had a total of forty-two dollars left to my name. Not even enough to pay that asswipe French taxi boat driver to get me back to the main island. "*Itch*, Ms. Michaels. I said this plaster is making me *itch*. When I'm finished, I'm going to have to shower." I smiled my best flirty, disarming smile.

She seemed to buy this, and her expression softened. "Oh. Well. We all have our crosses to bear, don't we? Get this room done." And with that, she was gone.

I sank into the closest sheet-covered luxury chair, propped my feet up on a similarly covered ottoman and unscrewed the top off a bottle of beer secreted in from my cooler. She could bite me. When I left, it was going to be on my terms. And there would be nothing she could do or say about it.

CHAPTER 2
BLUE BALLS, BRUISED BALLS

Stefany: The view is gorgeous out of my office windows this morning as I sit and drink my coffee - and think. Mostly about how my life has changed in such a short time.

The trees are swaying with a mild tropical breeze. The clouds that are painted in deep red hues around the rising sun are a stark contrast to the mountains that frame them through the valley. Yes. I love it here. I love the beauty. I love the freedom. If only I can make it work. Now that I'm here, I know this is everything I have ever wanted or dreamed of in my life.

~~~~

Leanne is coming today. Marcy prepared one of our nicest rooms on the third floor, with its own bath and parlor room. It's one of several so far that has all the amenities installed - a small fridge, microwave, and a nice large wall mount flat screen. It ate into my budget but at least that one is done. It has plenty of room and a fantastic view of the west side of the valley and the gardens. She should approve. I so look forward to seeing her, this most mischievous cousin of mine. But she will be a distraction and me with so much to do. She will want to drink, carry on, and want to tour everything, but I don't have time right now! Hopefully, she is not bringing any of her so-called "slaves." She is such an odd duck but maybe that's one of the reasons we get along so great. I don't know that I have a better friend in the world.

I have nothing left for me back in Montreal. I've been asked many times how I ended up here at Stoney Brook while my husband is back in Montreal. And every time I leave out the vital truth. I guess I do it because I just can't accept some of it myself. That fucking asshole, Miles. He's just sitting on the divorce I filed, and I know he isn't going to do anything. He knows everyone in the court, so he is going to try and screw me over, of that, I have no doubt. So, I stay married to the jerk for a bit longer.

~~~~~

Mr. Architect is doing a passable job, I guess. There is something I DETEST about him. I wish I had never hired him. What really pisses me off is he looks so damn good. I thought his application stated he was married but he's supposedly just recently divorced.  Or maybe separated - I don't know and I don't ask. In fact, I discuss nothing personal with him. Period. He has set about to man-whore on all the island girls and even those here on staff. Damn, I want to fire him, he is a complete asswipe. All men are the same and only think from what's in their pants. More and more I hate them. And that feeling doesn't bother me anymore.

~~~~~

Woe be to the woman should I catch her that is tramping about the hallways fresh out of the shower leaving wet prints!

They are a woman's small dainty tracks, so I know it's not Mobley and his galoot sized pontoon feet. Despite my warnings to the staff, this continues! It's a slipping hazard on these stone floors and I've almost fallen twice. I have no illusions that this is a continuation of the workplace disrespect Mobley has bred here.

~~~~

I got a phone call this morning from some guy claiming to be my distant cousin, Aaron McCaskill. Are people with my maiden name going to start coming out of the woodwork trying to claim Stoney Brook? This guy claimed that by way of his father, he was a more direct descendent of the McCaskill's that built Stoney Brook and therefore I needed to just hand it over to him! The phone call didn't go well, and I think my blood pressure went through the roof. He called me a fucking usurper and I'm not even sure how I replied to that, I was in such shock. I kept seeing visions of me on a flight to Montreal in tears, crawling back to Miles and begging him to let me back in the house. Please, Miles, beat the shit out of me some more, I'm a failure. After all this, would my dreams be trashed because there had been a mistake???? I didn't own Stoney Brook????

~~~~

After a quick and jittery call to Gary Thomson, that estate lawyer back in Scotland, turns out this guy is legit and an actual heir, just as I am! But - and here is where I'm dancing while I write this - he was written out of his father's will about 20 years ago. Turns out Aaron is a petty thief, drug dealer and even now is in a penitentiary in Ontario somewhere. Mr. Thomson says he tried to make a claim back when the will was being processed and Aaron McCaskill was refused any rights the first time by probate judges in both Scotland and Canada. Mr. Thomson assured me, for better or worse, I'm the owner of Stoney Brook, lock, stock, and barrel - along with the liabilities and debt as well. Wowwwwwwwwww am I relieved. Rock on, McCaskills, I got this... Your trashy, jailbird ancestor, Aaron McCaskill will not get his hands on Stoney Brook.

The incessant hammering and saws running is a constant reminder of all the work that the estate needs to get back to the gorgeous jewel she once was. Things are starting to shape up. And it is an exhilarating feeling.

My mobile phone buzzed atop my desk just as I was trying to figure out how far my $250,000 loan from my bank was going to carry me with getting Stoney Brook back up and running. After an audit and carefully looking over the books, it turns out the place is $1,065,000 in debt. The sugarcane harvest, the historic moneymaker of the place, after expenses, will not even be close to being any help. Tourism and operating the place as a resort was a great possibility, but as of yet, the potential was undetermined. There would be marketing required with travel sites and agencies - something I had not dipped my fingers into yet. Even with the debt, I still felt like I was living a fairytale dream. I just needed to make it work.

Sighing, I looked at the ID on my buzzing mobile phone of whoever it was trying to ruin my beautiful morning with me trying to be an accountant (which I am not). It was Rochelle at the front desk - one of several of my worker girls that was carrying on with Mr. Architect as chance would have it. She had already received two warnings and I was set to fire her and Mobley with the next infraction of any sort. I clicked the *accept* call button.

"Yes Rochelle, what."

"Ms. Stefany, your cousin, Ms. Leanne Tilden, is here."

A voice in the background on the phone sounded argumentative. Rochelle eventually came back on, hesitant. "Um. What should I do about your previous order not to bill her?"

"Yes, what about it?"

"She insists that she will only stay as a paying guest and has threatened to leave immediately and stay in the village, should you not comply and charge her the fair booking rate for two rooms. What should I do?"

"Ugh. I guess go ahead and bill her then. Stubborn woman. She always has been."

"Very good, Ms. Stefany. Also, she wanted me to let you know she is coming up to your office."

"Fine. Send her up. And it's *Ms. Michaels*, do you understand, Rochelle? I will not continue to be addressed by anyone on the staff by my first name! I really don't understand why I have to continually deal with such trivial matters."

"Yes, Ms. Michaels. I'm sorry. It's just that everyone seems to call you Ms. Stefany."

"Well, it's Ms. Michaels!"

"Yes, ma'am. Ms. Michaels."

This was the doings of Mr. Architect. That meathead, Morgan Mobley. He was the one that had started calling me Ms. Stefany and it had taken off with the staff despite my warnings. It was disrespectful and I would not have it! And in fact, the next time I saw Mobley, he would have some explaining to do. "Beautiful. Excellent, Rochelle. Then, let it be the last time I hear it. And have you again warned the staff of walking about the hallways dripping wet?"

"Yes, Ms. Michaels. But no one has admitted to doing it. And no one uses the shower in the staff room. Why would we? We just go home."

I thought about this. Perhaps it was one of Mobley's trollops roaming about after some sordid tryst. No matter, I should cover all the bases. "You tell them…" I sounded furious and didn't care. "If I catch them, it will be immediate termination!"

"Yes, Ms. Michaels. But… about Ms. Tilden…"
There was a hesitation on the other end of the line.

"What, Rochelle. Is there something else? Out with it, I'm very busy this morning."

27

"Ms. Michaels, she has brought with her several… friends. Umm. I think this is why she wanted to be billed for two rooms. One man, one woman."

Damn it. I had not been counting on her bringing her weirdo sex slaves, or whatever they were called, that she liked to keep around. I didn't need that strange kind of behavior going on in the estate when I was trying to get the place back to some level of respectability. I fingered the buttons on my mobile in thought. I couldn't tell her no, I suppose. But I could ask her to keep her strange proclivities confined to her room and not make a spectacle of herself around staff or public. Or me.

"Okay, Rochelle. Make sure Leanne and her guests have adjacent rooms. On the third floor, on the west end. If we need to get additional furniture, get Marcy and one of the men to help you."

"Yes, Ms. Michaels. Very good, right away," Rochelle said, hanging up.

Leanne could be irritating; there was no doubt about that. Bringing her guests and booking two rooms was her way of helping me out, I was certain. Every little bit was a help, though, and I couldn't argue with her that I needed the income.

After several minutes, there was a knock on the twin wood doors that opened into my office.

"Come," I said from behind my desk, smiling broadly, anticipating a warm hug from Leanne and loads of entertaining, animated stories.

The left door squeaked open. Morgan Mobley stuck his head in.

"Hello, Ms. Stefany. I was wondering if I could have a moment?"

Fucking shit fuck. Mobley, my first serious error in judgment since taking over and running Stoney Brook - not who I expected. I knew my expression was probably instantly hardening. With this guy interrupting my greeting Leanne, my morning was going to hell quickly.

"What, Mr. Mobley? I am expecting company shortly. Ask and go."

"May I come in?" He opened the door fully and stepped in.

"You are already in, Mr. Mobley. When we spoke earlier you said you were completely set in your duties for the week. What can you possibly need now?"

"I really need to go over these foundation repair estimates with you. I think they may be far over the amount that you discussed as being budgeted. And there are other material estimates for our other project lists that I believe are just too low."

Steam was coming out of my ears. He had already discussed these estimates with me, and he had assured me they were accurate and doable. I bristled in my chair.

"Mr. Mobley. I don't have endless hours in the day to micromanage what you have already agreed with me as being accurate numbers for various renovations. You assured me the numbers crunched."

He blinked, obviously trying to navigate the shallow waters of his limited intellect. "There was some additional damage that we have only just now discovered. I'm sorry, Ms. Stefany, but with old structures such as this, what is on the surface as needing repair isn't what always is the case once you get in and begin the work. If you recall, I did mention that those numbers were good, but they could change depending on what we found. And we found more. A lot more."

Mobley brazenly approached my office desk and leaned in casually on one arm. Seeing him drop his gaze to my exposed legs, I scooted my chair quickly beneath my desk. Self-conscious now and to ensure there would be no further view for Mr. Architect, I crossed my arms over my chest to keep him from leering down my casual t-shirt.

Another thing I noticed: I was again getting addressed as Ms. Stefany! This was getting out of hand. It was an opportune moment to bring up the issue of his instigating the staff towards disrespect of my authority. Yes, I would address that also now that this boob was in my office.

"Mr. Mobley, we are going to have a talk about how you address me. Yet again. For the umpteenth time. And, we are going to discuss how you have corrupted the rest of the staff in this regard. I've got everyone calling me Ms. Stefany. I have made it very clear to you that I am to be addressed by employees as Ms. Michaels. Have I not?"

"Yes, that is true, Ms. Michaels. My apologies."

"And you are an employee, are you not, Mr. Mobley? At least for the moment, I may add."

"Yes, Ms. Michaels. But we need to clarify these material costs."

I slammed my hand on the desk. "Look. Right now, I don't give a fuck about your changes! I've got my hands full with every other damned thing going wrong around here!" I stood to lean over my desk, my eyes narrow and angry, my impatience with this man now visibly paper-thin. "I'm… sorry," I caught myself. "I shouldn't have cursed at you. It's just…"

And that's when I caught his eyes darting for a quick peek down my shirt, only irritating me further. The nerve of this Man-Whore! "See anything you like?" I quickly re-crossed my arms over my chest. "Let me tell you something right now. If you wish to remain in my employ, you had better mind… where your eyes drift! Eh, Mr. Mobley?"

"Yes, my apologies, Ms. Michaels," he said with an imbecilic smile. He looked unfazed. Was he just being insubordinate? Or was he completely clueless?

"You will gather together all of the staff today. After lunch. And you will apologize to ALL of them for this little trend you have set, and you will take responsibility for it. I am fed up with all of this. This has gone on and on since day one. You will state for them the proper way everyone will address the owner of this establishment. That is *their* boss! It's Ms. Michaels! It's not hey you, hey lady, it's NOT Ms. Stefany. This you will do, that is, if you intend to remain under my employ. Have we an understanding here? You got it this time?" The veins were probably popping out on my temples and forehead. I wanted to strangle this man.

Mobley visibly swallowed, no doubt taking all of this rather harshly, which was, of course, my intent.

"Yes, ma'am. Ms. Michaels."

"You are dismissed, Mr. Mobley."

He leaned over the desk, his irksome but damnable gorgeous blue eyes locking onto mine. "But… Ms. Michaels, I still need to discuss these numbers with you. I must approve the work and people are waiting. You said yourself I must have your authorization first to pay for these things if there are changes. We need to do this now. If you want to keep to the schedule that you yourself have set for me."

I began considering where on the plantation it would be best to hide his body. "Mr. Mobley, you fucking mor-"

"A-hem! Excuse me, Cousin?" came the interruption from the office doors.

It was Leanne. Typically attired in a stylish, revealing summer miniskirt, custom white sneakers, toned bare legs gleaming and tan, she was leaning against the door frame.

Mobley's mouth dropped. The Man-Whore was visibly taken aback. I rolled my eyes in disgust.

A vision of smoldering beauty, Leanne strolled in, her eyes coolly assessing Mobley. She walked behind him shamelessly, her gaze taking in his ass. Stepping in front of him, she sat on the edge of my desk. I could not discern her expression, be it admiration… or revilement.

"Leanne! So good to see you get in. Umm, have you been standing there long?"

"I've been here the duration of the conversation, Cuz," she said, staring into Mobley's face. "This handsome fellow must be your Mr. Architect, eh? You should introduce me."

I sighed. Surely Leanne was getting enough action that she didn't need to flirt with Mr. Architect. What was her intention? If she had been listening, she could read between the lines. He was a pompous asshole, and not taking my position of authority very seriously. Leanne was always protective of me; was she laying an ambush for Mobley? I had seen such before, and it was not pleasant for those on the receiving end. Not pleasant at all.

"Leanne, this is Morgan Mobley. Of Chicago. Yes, he's the architect I hired to oversee renovations and improvements here at Stoney Brook. Mr. Mobley, this is Leanne Tilden, my cousin from New York."

Mobley extended his hand. Leanne left him hanging, simply eyeing him, a slight smile on her mouth. Finally, she took his hand. Mobley, uneasy and uncharacteristically out of his element – and possibly out of his league - looked a bit relieved.

"It's a pleasure to meet you, Ms. Tilden."

"I'm sure it is, Mr. Mobley. Get on your knees."

Mobley blinked. As did I. He and I were both wondering if we had heard Leanne correctly.

"Um. I beg your pardon?" Mobley asked, still holding her hand. He managed a nervous laugh.

"I said, get on the floor, Mr. Mobley. On your knees." Although soft-spoken, she maintained an unflinching glare.

Mobley looked over at me in astonishment.

"Leanne, ummm…" I began, trying to think of something to say on the fly. What, I am not sure. She held her other hand up to my face, indicating I should just ride this one out. I shrugged with a grin, not knowing what to think, partially terrorized, partially amused. I decided to let the uncomfortable scene play out to whatever conclusion Leanne had in mind.

Mobley looked bewildered but nevertheless dropped to one knee, all the while Leanne still holding his right hand.

"Both knees, Mr. Mobley," Leanne clarified. He put his other knee down, looking quite pathetic and comical in front of her.

"Okaaay." He said looking up at her questioningly, wondering what was going to happen next.

"Very nice, Mr. Mobley," Leanne finally said. "I appreciate a man that shows proper respect to a lady. You may kiss my hand."

Mobley hesitated. Then he decided, as I had, to just play along with Leanne. He leaned in and kissed her hand.

She smiled. "It is a pleasure meeting you as well, Mr. Mobley. I take it you are not used to such a greeting?"

Mobley smiled up at her. He tried to stand, and she placed a restraining hand atop his shoulder. "Well no. I am not... actually."

Leanne arched her eyebrows in amusement. "I thought not. Even if it is but a mild gesture." She drug the nail of her index finger softly around his chin.

"Um. Mild?" he asked, melting beneath her withering stare. He glanced across the desk at me nervously. I was just as amazed at her actions as he. She had nerve; I would give her that.

"Yes, quite mild. As a greeting, I could expect you to drop and kiss my feet, Mr. Mobley. Would you like that?" Leanne positioned herself slightly crossways on the edge of my desk, legs spread slightly, one angled over a bit more than the other. Mobley had to be getting a view right up Leanne's short skirt. Whether she was wearing panties or not, I didn't know. She had told me she oftentimes did not.

Mobley laughed. I, like him, was wondering what was going to happen next. I leaned over my desk, resting my chin in my hand. "Leanne? What..." I began to ask. Again, she held up a hand up to quiet me, never taking her eyes off Mobley.

"Well, Mr. Mobley?" she pressed.

Mobley shifted on his knees, visibly uneasy with this odd behavior, albeit by a beautiful woman. "I am unfamiliar with this custom, Ms. Tilden. Is this something that is characteristic of a particular culture?"

"Not really. But it is *my* custom of personal preference, Mr. Mobley. At least when I expect it. And with you, I think I will expect it."

Mobley didn't know what to do. I loved seeing him squirm, I confess. If Mobley had developed any understanding of Leanne in the few minutes since she arrived, he was probably getting the idea that she was a very dominant minded woman.

"I think I may have to talk to Ms. Michaels about this idea," Leanne continued. "I think she should be addressed with just such a respectful custom as that. By certain staff, anyway. Like you, say. Don't you agree, Mr. Mobley? It seems to me like she deserves the utmost respect. Having brought you all the way from Chicago to this wonderful place to work. Where else could you hope to utilize your degree to such a great extent? And license. As a certified architect. Eh, Mr. Mobley?"

I laughed out loud finally at the absurd comedy that Leanne was committing. A bead of perspiration dripped from beneath Mobley's curly blond locks, down his temple. As much as I detested Mobley, enough was enough. "Okay, Leanne. That's good. I don't expect Mr. Mobley to kiss my hands – or my feet - every time he needs to discuss where he intends to buy a box of nails."

Leanne tapped a finger softly on Mobley's lips. "Nothing to say, Mr. Mobley?" She laughed and shot an amused look at me. Running her fingers into his blond hair, she lightly pressed the back of his head towards her leg, bringing his face to one of her shapely and nicely muscled calves. Astonished, Mobley did not resist, simply looking at her wide-eyed. Perhaps my eyes were wider than his at this spectacle. Here was this cocky ass, on his knees, doing what Leanne commanded without so much as a whimper of a complaint or even questioning what she was doing. I knew she was a bold woman, but this was mind-boggling. Why was Mobley so compliant? Was this sexual harassment of one of my employees? I think it was!

Leanne pointed to her calf. "Right here," she indicated with her finger. "This time, I'll spare you to a

34

degree. Since I'm not out of my shoes, you may kiss me here, as a sign of respect and deference, Mr. Mobley. Go ahead."

Mobley, either thinking he was having incredible luck, or misfortune, I was unsure, planted a small kiss on Leanne's leg. She relinquished her grip in his hair and he sat back on his legs and looked up at her. I'm not sure I can describe his expression.

"Good boy, Mr. Mobley. We'll discuss proper respect towards Ms. Michaels later. I would suggest you gather the staff as she ordered and make your amends."

"Um. I'll do that." Mobley said standing. He grinned and laughed despite being nervous.

"Something funny about this?" Leanne asked him with a completely serious face.

"Oh no. Ms. Tilden. Nothing funny." Now the look on his face was one of sarcasm. Leanne looked unfazed.

"With Stefany's blessings, you are dismissed, Mr. Mobley," Leanne said with a smile.

Thinking Leanne had been joking with him, he turned to leave, glancing back questioningly at me one final time.

"Yes. With the foundation, just get it done, Mr. Mobley," I clarified, taking his meaning. "Try to keep the overruns to a minimum though, please. We'll figure it out… later."

"Yes, ma'am. And have a nice day, Ms. Tilden." He nodded with a smile to Leanne then to me. He turned and left the room. More than likely, he thought he would later be nailing Leanne on his own terms as just another of his sexual conquests.

"And there he goes, your wondrously handsome but somewhat wayward employee, Mr. Mobley," Leanne said again sitting on my desk, giving me a saucy smile. "Your description of him and his personality were spot on. Typical. But we'll work on that. I see potential."

We both laughed out loud. I walked from behind the desk and hugged her tightly. It was great to have her at Stoney Brook. Already the mood had lightened.

"Leanne! Seriously. You can't do that with my employees! I'll get sued! What would you have done if he didn't do what you asked? He would have left here angry and ready to make trouble. Or sabotage me or something."

"Harassment laws are much laxer here. I'm not an employee here, nor am I his manager." Leanne laughed. "So, after everything you have told me of him, I was more than happy to give him his first training lesson. He did what I said without complaint or objection, he wasn't going to get angry or say no. Take heed, Cousin. My experience has shown me that many men will comply with a scenario like this. I can usually tell which. And if I happen to try something like that with one that isn't compliant, off they go. Trust me, Mobley is down for more, he just doesn't know it yet. Right now, he's thinking he can turn this situation into something in his direction for an easy lay. As you so eloquently put it to me describing him on the phone, he is an arrogant, cocky ass."

"You never cease to shock me. You said the *first* training lesson?" I had to ask.

"Yeah. Shock and awe, baby. He'll need more. I'll handle it for you."

Whatever happened consensually between Leanne and Mobley was their business, but I didn't like it. And I didn't want any part of it. "No, please, Leanne. Whatever you have in mind, please leave my staff alone. Consider them off-limits to your twisted little ploys." I staged a forced laugh. She just smiled at me.

"We'll talk," she finally offered noncommittally, blowing me off. Her expression was amused but dangerous. Was she serious? She had just been kidding around I thought. Was she? I would need to make sure she would not harass Mobley any further, if for anything else, my own peace of mind. She could find additional playmates elsewhere on the island without raiding my staff. And with Mobley, she could perhaps be overestimating his ability to be compliant. He was after all a huge playboy.

36

Leanne fingered my t-shirt and stood back taking in my work shorts and sneakers. "This? This is how you dress, an owner of a multimillion-dollar island plantation? You aren't a peasant girl."

"It's who I am, I dress to get things done in this sweltering heat. And if things don't improve financially, I may be a peasant for life, sad to say."

Leanne kissed my cheek and squeezed me again. "Yes, you are who you are, Cuz. And that's why you are so lovable. The debt you will get through, I promise. You are much happier when you aren't kowtowing to that asshole husband of yours. I'm glad to see you have some spine."

"Spine?" I laughed, trying to object.

Ignoring me, she tried tidying my hair. "This isn't the place for college spring break attire, my little business protégé."

"True. But I have no plans to change now." I could not help but laugh. She would be in my closet soon, picking out clothes, trying to have me looking respectable, I knew.

Taking her hand, we walked out of the office to get her and her 'friends' settled in. I put out of my mind the entertaining yet worrisome scene of what had just transpired with Mobley.

Morgan: I'm making progress around here, but there is so much more work to do. Renovations are one thing but modernizing Stoney Brook while maintaining the historic appeal is another challenge altogether. I'm getting to know the hired hands, many of which have been here for years. It is a great place to work despite my boss, Stefany, who reminds me

daily that she is an overinflated windbag that needs a personality transplant. I am happy to say that my conquests of beautiful island women (including the staff lasses) continue unabated despite Stefany's fascist rules of the house.

~~~~~

A bit of research has been quite illuminating. Many of the inhabitants on this island are descended from Stoney Brook slaves. Built in 1623, the history of the plantation is very eventful and dark. Over the course of its existence, there have been murders, slave revolts, mass hangings, and even witches burned at the stake. Stefany's ancestors, the McCaskills who were from Scotland and rumored to be descended from Vikings, were unquestionably a cruel lot back in the day. Hardly a surprise that it runs in Stefany's genetics. Beatings and torture of the field workers and servants were commonplace here in centuries past. There are several cemeteries on the plantation, each with hundreds of headstones, some just simple rocks with some chiseled symbols, many of them slaves that died here under less than favorable circumstances. One rebellion took the lives of nearly all the McCaskill family members that were home at the time, said to be for their harsh treatment of the slaves. It was nothing compared to the resulting vengeance by the McCaskills that survived, which was said to have included hanging the dead perpetrators' upside-down from the ancient trees that line the long drive into the manor. There is even a dank stone dungeon in the basement of the manor where you can still see rusty iron manacles and leg chains attached to the floor and walls. One account stated that slave women suspected of being voodoo witches were burned at the stake here on several occasions. As a mix of Christianity and African religions, Voodoo was as much misunderstood in those days as it is now. I understand from several of native islanders that Voodoo is still practiced here.

For a place of incredible beauty, Stoney Brook Plantation has a very violent past.

~~~~~

The weirdest thing that has ever happened to me occurred yesterday. I was in Stefany's office trying to get her to understand that the materials lists are underestimated when her cousin, Leanne Tilden, came in. This chick was odd as hell, there's no doubt about that. Out of the blue, she insisted that I get on my knees and first kiss her hand, then her leg! Can't say I've ever had that requested of me. Truth be told, it kind of rocked to have a hot woman tell me what to do like that; this Leanne woman is beautiful. And even more significantly, it didn't hurt that she was going commando under that short miniskirt of hers, right there in my face! She was completely bare. If she was joking or not, she never let on, but I was down for that little sneak peek. I want those long legs slung over my shoulders. We'll see who gives who the orders when she's in my bedroom.

"Mr. Mobley, where do you want me to brace the concrete forms?" Santiago asked, tucking a wet rag into his back pocket after sponging his face.

Santiago was a good sport and a hard worker. After some initial hesitation to work with me, he and Miguel were turning into a reliable crew.

I wiped my brow with the back of my hand and peered up at the burning sun, pulling my white French Foreign Legion style cap down a little further. A brutal sunburn on my neck was all the encouragement I needed to find cover in the form of that little jewel of a cap down at The Blue Calypso gift counter. Soak the neck cover with water and you are good to go. The humid tropical midafternoon was sweltering, and it was taking its toll on my system that was still used to northern Illinois weather.

Pointing to several locations along the knee-wall concrete forms that we had erected, I indicated the additional bracing locations. "Here guys. Here. And over here. And be sure you add the same thing on the other side. We must make sure it is braced properly, or we can have the whole thing blow out. Then we are screwed."

"We will bring in the trucks and pour today, Mr. Mobley?" Miguel asked.

I loved their enthusiasm for this ongoing project. "No, we can do this first thing tomorrow." They promptly took several short pieces of lumber and went to work bracing the forms.

I had a strange feeling of being watched. Looking behind me back at the manor, sure enough, I saw Leanne Tilden standing on the second-floor balcony of one of the large conference rooms. Wearing sunglasses, she was leaning against the wrought iron railing, staring down at me. She smiled, so I waved. Ignoring me, she flipped her hair to the side and stepped back inside. It all gave me a high reading on my *teasing bitch meter*. The fact she had nearly shoved her bare coutchie into my face in Stefany's office had all but guaranteed I would be banging that hot number very soon.

After working several hours documenting the materials I would need to properly restore several stone out-buildings, I stopped by the estate kitchen, picked up a cup of ice, and poured a soda over it. I then strolled over to the next project on my list, the immense barn. At present, it served the plantation as a storage for equipment and supplies. Historically, the structure housed mostly carriages, wagons, horses, and mules. The building was magnificent in its own right: large hand-hewn beams, cobblestones on the main floor, with a second and third-floor loft. It even had a large cellar where a milking parlor had been.

Flipping my notebook to a fresh blank page, I wrote *Barn/Horse Stables* at the top and prepared to take an inventory of needs for repair and conservation. I walked into the building via the huge, massive front doors that were already open. Several workers were there during their business of operating Stoney Brook and keeping the sugarcane production moving along smoothly. After eyeing me, they turned away. I don't know if they avoided me because they didn't trust me or if they thought I was going to put them to some other work.

The barn was in fairly good shape, although there could be a bit of leveling in a few places. Inspection and good preventative treatment for termites would be a good idea with repairing any damage. We would need to replace a few siding boards here and there and maybe get some new stain on the old girl to spruce her up a bit. Much of the centuries old lumber had to be imported in by ship, I thought.

Scanning the massive beams supporting the second floor, I turned into a hallway that was supposed to have several offices and storage rooms.

"Ummpppffff." My clipboard ended up against my chest and my Styrofoam cup of soda crushed, its contents splattered before me. It was Stefany. My soda was now splashed all over her. Her hand wiped drops of the liquid from her face - then she stared. The servant girl that had been accompanying her quickly walked towards the front doors and disappeared into the gleaming sunlight; disappeared much as I wanted to at that moment. Stefany glared angrily.

"Mr. Mobley" she said, flinging drops of soda from her fingers, "why is it I am not surprised it would be you strolling around not looking where he was going?"

"I'm really sorry Ms. Steph- er... Ms. Michaels. I was just lost in thought trying to get an inventory of what I need to..." I cleared my throat. "To repair what needs... repairing in here." I gave her my best smile.

She was incensed. Maybe it was just the heat of the day taking its toll and whatever stresses she happened to be under, but she was about to meltdown, I could tell. The soda was doing a good job of making her little B cup bra stand out beneath her white t-shirt. I thought about how unwise it would be to laugh so I bit my tongue instead.

"And how did your apology meeting go with the staff, Mr. Mobley?" she asked brushing ice from her t-shirt. "That meeting you agreed to conduct two days ago when you were in my office? I understand you have still not done this. As I specifically requested."

"Um. I haven't had that meeting just yet, Ms. Michaels. I will later today. For sure."

She looked ready to slap me. The soda was running down her tan bare legs in little wet rivulets ending up in her socks, giving her the appearance of having wet herself.

"May I be frank with you, Mr. Mobley?" she asked, fuming.

I had no choice but to take what I knew was going to be some heated words. "Yes, Ms. Michaels. Certainly."

"I regret hiring you," she said bluntly.

This was going to be worse than I thought. I swallowed in the long pause that ensued. What could I say? "I said I was sorry about the drink, Ms. Michaels. It was an accident; I can assure you. And the meeting, I'll take care of it, I just have been very busy."

"I'm not talking about the fucking drink all over me! Or the meeting!"

I was taken aback a moment by the profane malice in her voice. She was nearly out of control with anger and my mind began spinning, trying to conceive a way of backing this conversation into some sort of civility that would salvage the afternoon.

"Um. Really, Ms. Michaels, it will all-"

"YOU, Mr. Mobley, are an arrogant shit fuck. You think I wouldn't find out about you still bringing girls to your room even after I EXPLICITLY instructed you not to?!"

Well, she had me there.

"Your progress around here," she waved her wet arms around for added emphasis, "is slower than an asthmatic snail! The work you do is… is… it's questionable at best! How do I know if it's even necessary? Or if it's quality or not?! It's all over budget! All of it!"

Asthmatic snail? Now that was hitting below the belt.

A car drove up outside of the barn at that moment, parking inside the door opening. The engine cut, the driver's door slammed and a middle-aged man that looked like an island native strode in. He had a wild look in his eyes that matched his hair, and even worse, a large kitchen knife in his right hand that looked to be at least 12 inches long.

Stefany blinked with alarm at this new development, momentarily forgetting about the tongue lashing she had been in the process of giving me.

"The workers say I find Meester Moblee here, si?" the man asked angrily in a thick accent. Everyone was angry around here, I thought with scorn. Was it the hot weather? That's all I needed was an angry man with a knife looking for me.

Stefany's eyes went from the man to me, then back again. "Sir, why do you ask?" Maybe Stefany had my back after all.

"He is here, si?!" he asked again.

"Um, sir, wait just a moment. Why are you here?" There was concern in Stefany's voice. My whole body was concerned!

"You?! Blond man. You are Moblee!" He pointed the knife at me. I instinctively moved in front of Stefany and took a step towards the man to get some distance for her, for which she seemed shocked. What, I'm not capable of gallantry?

"Yes, yes, I am Mr. Mobley. Whatever business you may have with me, I am certain we can discuss it without that knife, sir!"

44

"Nooooo! We discuss WITH knife, Mobleee." He walked over to me, and I had to wonder if I was going to get through the day without getting stabbed.

"Sir! I will call the police!" Stefany objected from behind me. She tried to move past me, and I blocked her with my arm.

"Sir, what is this all about?" I asked, unable to imagine what I could have done to so anger this man.

"My daughter! Maria! You despoil her!"

"What?" I blinked, caught off guard. Maria? I had to think. Who was Maria? Stefany resumed her hard glare at me from my side, looking as if she too would like a knife.

"You are walking balls of hound dog, everywhere to despoils our daughters, our women! Everyone talk about you! My Maria, she only eighteen! You! Hound dog of swinging horny balls. I cut off!"

"No. Wait. I not... um... I didn't *despoil*."

I scratched my chin, knowing there was a memory somewhere. Oh, wait. Maria. Yes, now I remembered her. A cute raven-haired girl I had picked up a few days earlier at The Blue Calypso after a hard night of drinking and gambling. I had brought her back for a wild evening in my room. She had left in the morning, a disheveled, albeit sexy hot, satisfied mess. Santiago took her home for me. I cringed. Yes, perhaps I did "despoil" her, although she certainly seemed to know what she was doing.

I put on my best innocent face. "Now just a minute, sir. I'm sure we can talk this out." What I could say to alleviate this predicament, I was unable to fathom.

"Did you despoil his daughter?" Stefany asked angrily. "Did you?!"

"What? No. I don't think I *despoiled* his daughter. No!"

The slight nuance was not lost to Stefany. "Don't *think*? Oh, I think indeed yes you did, Mr. Mobley!"

"No, there was no despoiling going on, I can assure you!" Hot wild sweaty sex with plenty of screaming and hair-pulling, yes, maybe there had been that.

He approached within several feet and made jabbing motions with his knife. "Now. I will cut balls off!"

Just at that moment, the passenger door of the car opened and the other heretofore unseen occupant stepped out and closed the door. It was Maria. She tentatively walked up to her father, her hands intertwined together, her fingers toying nervously.

"Father, no. He did not despoil me. He didn't." She looked at me with a pleading look, as if to say she was sorry for getting me in trouble. I wasted no time with the valuable out she had just given me.

"See? There. Even she says it. I did not *despoil* her." I eyed Stefany who looked skeptical. "I *didn't. S*he said it herself!"

"What then?!" her father asked furiously. "What you do with her all night?! You debauch her."

I shook my finger in denial. "No, no. I did not debauch her either, sir. No debauching."

Maria tucked her arm around her father and gently pried the knife from his fingers. "Father, we were reading. A new book that came out that he happens to have, and we were reading to each other. You know how I love to read the latest novels. That is all. He's a good friend. He reads well. Quite harmless."

Maria's father blinked, his strained face softening. Perhaps he too was looking to back away from the brink of the precipice we were all on. "Well. If you say so, then okay." He hugged her tightly and the two stood embracing.

He gave me one final glare. "But you stay away from this balls of hound I don't trust. Let us go." The two turned and headed towards the car. Maria shot me a discreet but subtle smile that Stefany certainly did not miss.

Watching them drive away, Stefany turned to me, her hands on her hips, still soaking wet from the accident from a

46

few moments before. "And just what book did you supposedly read with her? Please enlighten me."

"A new novel by Frank L. Pattenson. Flight of the Damned." Of course, that was entirely made up. The only reason I knew about that book was that I had noticed it as a new bestseller in the village bookstore window opposite The Blue Calypso. Flight of... something or other, it could have been ducks or geese. By a guy named Peters, or Patton. Maybe it had been Pattenson. I didn't know and didn't care. As long as my balls weren't on the floor.

"You expect me to believe that, Mobley?" She was still plenty angry, and she wasn't buying the story, that was clear.

Just as I was preparing an answer, Santiago rushed into the barn, out of breath. What now, I asked myself.

"Mr. Mobley. Please. A minute," Santiago said, out of breath. "Pardon, Ms. Michaels. Please." Santiago pulled me by the arm away and I had to wonder what the hell he wanted to tell me in private that he did not want Stefany to hear. Evidently, she wondered the very same thing.

"Santiago. What is it? What you say to Mr. Mobley you can certainly say to me."

Santiago did not relent. He brought his mouth up to my ear. "The concrete, Mr. Mobley. The forms. Failed. It's all spilled. All everywhere. I am sorry."

Any question I may have had as to what additional disaster could possibly befall me within the span of ten minutes was answered. Everything we had worked for, Santiago, Miguel, and me, had been ruined due to some mishap I had yet to discern.

"But. You weren't supposed to start without me. We were going to do that tomorrow! I didn't even know the concrete trucks had arrived. How?" My throat was as dry as the Sahara.

"What is it?!" Stefany again asked, now pressing hard. "What's happened?"

47

I eyed Santiago. The fear in his eyes was easy to see. He again leaned in to whisper. "It was my fault, Mr. Mobley. Miguel and me, we wanted to surprise you. And show you we could do it on our own. And I forgot you said to do the other side of the forms. I made a big mistake. I'm sorry."

It would probably mean his and Miguel's jobs. Santiago had been working at Stoney Brook for nearly seven years. He had a wife and several kids. Miguel was an employee of at least five years and similarly had a family to feed and house.

I turned to Stefany. It was turning into quite the afternoon for her as well, I knew.

"Ms. Michaels. I'm sorry to have to tell you this, but the crew has been pouring concrete over on the northeast estate knee-wall rebuild. It failed this afternoon. The mix is all over the yard. We must get the front-end loaders and begin cleaning up the mess. Quickly."

Shock slowly set in on Stefany's face as the enormity of the incident began to set in. "What? I didn't even know you were pouring this afternoon! You told me you were going to wait until morning?"

"Yes, well, they wanted to make some headway. Unfortunately, the forms failed while the men were making the pour."

"How much did we lose? Was the crew able to salvage anything? How much will the loss cost, Mr. Mobley?" Stefany's eyes were wide with panic.

"I'm sorry, Ms. Michaels. It will be a total loss. Perhaps ten thousand dollars or so."

Stefany's jaw was clenching in anger. "And why weren't you overseeing this as you knew you should, Mr. Mobley?

I looked over at Santiago. His fate was in my hands. If I told her that they had taken it upon themselves to do this, they would be fired.

"Someone screwed up here. Big time," Stefany hissed. "What happened, Mobley? Was this Santiago and Miguel's doing?"

I placed a hand on Stefany's shoulder. "It was my mistake. I didn't set the forms correctly. And I let them work it alone. I'm afraid the blame is mine."

Santiago's mouth dropped, and he looked at me disbelievingly. We both knew the implications.

She knocked my hand away. "It was such a mistake hiring you. Get out, Mobley," Stefany blurted. "I knew you were worthless. Absolutely worthless as fuck. Get out! You are fired. I want you off this property within thirty minutes!"

I wasn't sure why I took the blame for the mistake the boys made. And I wasn't sure she would fire me. But I did. And she did. What most surprised me was the harshness of her words stung far greater than I anticipated.

"Um. Ms. Michaels. I have no way to get to the village."

"Walk."

"May I please stay the night? It's late in the day. I won't make it to the village until very late at night. And I have my things to carry."

"Fine," she relented after a long pause. "But you are not staying the night. There's a village taxi, I will call it for you. My last charitable act for you, asshole. Don't expect another paycheck."

I didn't mention to her I only had thirty dollars to my name. With my latest gambling foray at The Blue Calypso, my entire paycheck was gone. I was nearly broke and now my carefree attitude and bad habits were coming back to haunt me. Without even a credit card and no savings, I would not be able to get off the island. Suddenly, I realized just how screwed I was. I had no idea where I could even sleep! Or how I would even afford to get a meal.

"Santiago?" Stefany asked. "Get the necessary equipment and additional field workers as we need. Get this problem cleaned up. Mobley, there will be a taxi here within thirty minutes, just enough time for you to get your crap packed. I don't want to see you around here for one second more than necessary." With that, she stormed off, her wet sneakers squeaking.

Santiago looked embarrassed. Yet grateful. "Thank you, Mr. Mobley. Thank you." He turned and walked after Stefany and turned towards me again as he strode. "Thank you."

Stunned, I started walking to the mansion. I had really done it this time. No job, no money, and nowhere to go.

Could I call a friend? Have them wire money? Could I call my ex? Maybe she would relent and be generous. No. I didn't even have a number for her, and I would be the last person she would help. There were no good options. None.

I trod up the back stairs to my room and began throwing my things into my duffel bag, not even taking time to fold my clothes. It didn't take long; I didn't own that much. Basically, I had just the clothes on my back.

I slung my backpack over my shoulder and picked up my duffel bag and made for the stairs. A sleek and shapely pair of toned legs met my gaze. It was Leanne sitting on the steps up to the next floor. She was leaning back on her arms, smiling.

"Leaving so soon, Mr. Mobley?" she asked, her voice dripping with sarcasm.

"Yes, Ms. Tilden. I'm afraid so."

"She just told me everything. She has a right to be angry, you know. She is trying to run this place on a very tight budget."

"Yes, I know," I admitted, agitated. Despite how sexy this woman appeared, she was getting under my skin.

"At least you were spared the indignation of her finding out you have no real degree, Mr. Mobley."

I swallowed. How could she know? Why would she know? "I don't know what you are talking about," I countered, making my way for the stairs.

"Sure, you do. I did some checking after she hired you. She is like a sister to me, after all, and I look after her. And imagine my surprise what I found." She stood up and faced me squarely.

She had me dead to rights. Somehow, she knew. She had found out. What I had dreaded Stefany finding out with a background check, her cousin had accomplished.

"Leanne. Look. I was only missing a couple of classes to finish my degree. I ended up getting separated from my wife and-"

"Save it. I don't need to hear it, and I sure as hell don't give a fuck. She fired you, it's a done deal. I think we both know there were laws broken with how you represented yourself. You should count your blessings." She reached out and painfully squeezed my dick and balls roughly through my pants. Surprised, I winced but tried to show resolve and that it didn't bother me in the slightest.

"Does that hurt, Mr. Mobley?" she asked, grinning.

"No," I chirped.

"Are you sure? Because it sure looks like it hurts. If you had stayed, whatever balls you do have would be under *my* control. You can believe that." She leaned into me, her lips nearly touching mine. My eyes were beginning to water. This woman was not going to intimidate me, no matter how good she looked.

"Do you *understand*?" she whispered.

What was it with this crazy bitch? I just needed to get out of the place, get back to the village and get my thoughts sorted out. This was the weirdest chick I had ever met.

"Aggghhhhh! Yes! Yes!" I was in agony. "Let go!"

"Yes, *Ms. Tilden*, is the correct response."

Whatever. I just wanted her vice-like grip off my junk. "Yes! Yes! Ms. Tilden!"

She laughed, finally relinquishing her grip, thank the stars. Despite her petite physique, she was not a weak woman by any means. I took a deep breath, my balls aflame.

Just as I was beginning to tell her to fuck off, I took the top step at a bad angle, stumbled, and fell. My duffel bag broke an uncontrolled decent when I hit the next landing wall. Everyone seemed to be after me this day, including Stoney Brook and Leanne. I heard the taxi honk its horn out on the circle drive.

I managed a final look back up the stairs at Leanne. She was smiling, leaning on the banister railing, evidently quite amused. Even though the crazy bitch had just nearly deballed me, there was something extremely alluring and sensual about her. She blew me a kiss.

"Buh-by, Mr. Mobley."

CHAPTER 3

MILES OF MONEY

Stefany: The staff seems forlorn as of late. It's been about a week since I fired Mobley. Everyone seems to miss Mr. Architect, but I can't imagine why. The whoring has all but come to a standstill. Some of the women no doubt have regrets as they had a continuous source of sex with Mobley. Lock up your daughters, wives, mothers, and grandmothers when Mobley is on the loose. The father of Maria had it right.

Mobley is a horny balls out hound dog. The workers miss his dash and bravado I suppose. He did cast a handsome shadow, I'll give him that much. I certainly don't miss his cocky attitude.

I have no idea where he ended up. The staff knows better than to discuss him around me as he is a sore subject. Rumor around was that he was broke and couldn't leave the island. HA! I have to laugh. Leanne says she knows where he is but respects my wishes and does not bring him up. Good riddance.

~~~~

Stoney Brook got its first two tourists' bookings! They are set to arrive later next week. Our master chef, Jellico, has the week off from the plantation kitchen, so he will be back just in time to handle the culinary delights for our new guests.

~~~~

It was an interesting phone call I got this week. And unexpected. The gist of it is this: I reluctantly agreed through my lawyer to temporarily suspend the restraining order against my asshole husband, and he is coming to the island. Shit. Miles is flying from Montreal in several days and is coming here. Leanne says I am making a mistake, but if anything, it will allow me to try to get him to agree to the damned divorce. I would love to arrange a deep-sea fishing trip for Miles - where he might have an unfortunate 'accident' and fail to return. It would be sweet justice, in my opinion. I would never do that, lucky for his worthless ass. It is a fun fantasy, however.

~~~~~

I suspect that what happened is Miles investigated Stoney Brook Plantation... and learned of the great potential it has. And soooo now he has taken a sudden interest in patching up our marriage! How convenient. When he thought I was inheriting a rundown shack on a couple of acres, he had NO interest. He didn't even want to hear about the details! He dismissed it all out of hand. Surprise! It's worth millions and it's in paradise, asshole. I'm glad he took no notice, because now with a divorce pending, he has no stake in any of it. My lawyer says I have no worries due to "intent to dissolve" before me obtaining the plantation, or some legal-ease reason. Miles has another think coming if he thinks I will ever let him get his hands on ANY part of Stoney Brook.

~~~~~~

Ever since I filed for divorce when I was back in Montreal, Miles has been carefully shielding our JOINT assets through shady legal maneuvering. At least it seems shady to me. How can it even be legal? I suspect that it is not, although I don't know what I can do about it. How can it be fair that Miles thinks that anything of mine... like Stoney Brook... can be partly his, yet a major portion of his assets are ALL his somehow??? Or are his with his parents and extended family? I hate them all, they are entitled assholes and greedy crooks. Sometimes I wonder if my lawyer is intimidated by Miles and his connections. Is he working for me, or Miles?

~~~~~~

Miles arrived. Fuck ☹

~~~~~~

It's unmistakable why Miles is here. There's only one reason he isn't being an asshole to me. It's his interest in Stoney Brook, which he is trying his best to conceal. His attempts at placating me and his compliments with trying to reconcile are all fake. I know it, and Leanne knows it. Fuck reconciliation. We are just biding our time until this asshole gives up and leaves. He's not getting me to sign any mutual ownership agreements with him for Stoney Brook. Period. I've been playing along listening to his proposals, but I don't let on that he has no chance. Leanne thinks I am not being forceful enough with him.

Why does he control me so? I have no courage when he is around, and I hate myself for that. Do I have "battered woman syndrome"? I don't know. Leanne would say yes, I'm sure, after all the times I went back to him. I can't count the times he beat the shit out of me. It makes me SICK. But I'm out on my own now. That should count for something!

He refused to discuss the divorce. I didn't press it as I told myself I would. So, I guess we are at an impasse. Leanne says I need to find a different lawyer, force the issue legally, and be done with him.

I still recall our last "disagreement." It was through his fists just before sending me to the hospital. Then I was victimized a SECOND time by his ass-boil of a lawyer who made me out to be the one instigating it in the court hearing. They are all just buddy-buddy good ole boys that scratch each other's back. All of them. I hate men. Every one of them.

Leanne has suggested that for dinner tonight we all meet at The Blue Calypso. I think she would love to shoot him. It's all she can do to remain civil to him whenever she sees him. At least he isn't staying at Stoney Brook and has instead agreed to rent at a fancy beach condo near the village. So far, he has behaved himself.

"It's a power trip, Cuz," Leanne said with a saucy smile, sipping a glass of wine while sitting in one of the recliner chairs in the second-floor reception room. "Wouldn't you at least like to try it, being in complete control sexually? It is something amazing that defies description."

I sat my glass of wine down on an end table and took a seat opposite of hers. It was late Friday afternoon and I had dismissed the staff early as a kind gesture for everyone's hard work and progress towards Stoney Brook being able to soon receive guests.

"I'm not interested in your kinky dominant, submissive romps, Leanne. I appreciate you wanting to share the concepts or whatever, but…please. Just keep it in the privacy of your suite?"

"Humor me, Stef. Let me show you a very mild demonstration. You've nothing better to do now and there's no one here in the mansion to cast aspersions."

"Ugh. You are ruining my glass of wine." I groaned as Leanne shot me an exasperated look. "Fine. Show me and get it out of your system." I sat back in my chair, prepared to be entertained at the very least. I took a loud sip of wine just to irritate Leanne.

"Stefany!"

"Oh okay. Sorry. Bring out the… whatever they are… Jell-O wrestlers." Of course, I wasn't sorry. I was in a playful mood, however.

"Stefany. And here I thought you were not a judgmental person."

"I'm not. Hey, Miles is still here, milling about somewhere on the estate," I realized as an afterthought. "What if he comes in here?" I asked.

"Who cares? He is useless and is the one person whose opinion is entirely irrelevant to me," she fumed. "He wouldn't make a decent slave and even raking leaves is beyond his ability."

I smirked. "Miles would never be submissive to a woman."

"No, he wouldn't. And he's not much of a man either, I can confirm for you, Cousin," Leanne quipped.

"So, are you dominant with your submissives all the time? These so-called slaves you have?"

"Oh, no," Leanne began to explain. "Now granted, there are some people that live in that lifestyle full time. That is too tedious and cliché for me, personally. My slaves all have normal lives. Outside of our playtime, we function as complete equals. But when I want them, they serve me.

Sometimes it may only be with tasks around my house. But mostly their service is sexual."

I blushed. I knew this was the case but to sit and discuss it so openly was embarrassing. "But why would they do this? Don't they get tired of being... used? Trained and whatever else you do with them?"

"Stefany, they crave it. They get off on being submissive to me, every bit as much as I get off on being dominant. We both serve a vital need to the other. I crave it for the power trip - and of course the incredible orgasms. They long to be controlled and used hard sexually."

"I'm sorry, Leanne, but it's weird. Weird as fuck."

"Say what you will, but it taps into human psychology. If you have an open mind and enjoy sexy fun, then it is something to consider. My slaves and I understand the rules and we agree to them. If they want out, I let them go, simple as that. I care for them deeply. And likewise, they care for me."

"Miles tried some of this stuff on me, tying me up, using handcuffs, that sort of thing. When we were still fucking, that is. It's bizarre and I didn't enjoy it."

"The marriage you had - and still have, unfortunately - with Miles wasn't a relationship. It was not healthy. You know as well as I do, what he did wasn't about good sex, it was abusive control. What I'm going to show you is different."

"Eh. Let's get on with the show." I flippantly tossed my hair and sat back in my chair, trying not to laugh.

"I am the dominant in my relationships. Whereas you, Cuz - and not to criticize - have always been submissive in every relationship I can think of, sexual or otherwise. Tell me, am I right?"

I thought back. I would have to say she was right. Was I just naturally a submissive person? "Yes. I guess so," I finally agreed. "I'm just not a dominant sort of person. Certainly not sexually. I never really thought about it."

"Miles, who is no kind of man - took advantage of your natural tendency to be submissive in relationships. To the point of being extremely mentally and physically abusive to you. To a criminal extent. We can both agree on that, right?"

"Yes." I was long past denying this ugly truth. "But I am better now. I walked away."

"Yes. You did. But would you have if you had not been offered Stoney Brook? This place came along like a miracle out of the blue."

"I would have left him, Leanne," I asserted firmly.

"Would you have?"

"Yes. He put me in the hospital. Again. Just before I found out about Stoney Brook."

"You were already thinking of going back to him. When I visited you in intensive care, you were making excuses for him again. Saying he was under stress, blah blah. Don't deny it."

"Okay. Maybe. I don't know." I took a sip of wine, trying to sort out my memories that were making a surprise comeback that afternoon. "I did escape. I am free of him, Leanne, regardless of what you may think. The marriage is by paper only. And I'll soon be rid of that as well."

She eyed me for a moment, perhaps considering her little demonstration a mistake. "To be clear, there are many nuances of submission and domination. They aren't all sexual. Other aspects of dominance... as in business... finance... you don't do too badly with those concepts." She waved her hand dismissively. "But we'll talk about those later."

"I thought you were going to demonstrate sexy fun," I chuckled, wondering what happened to the show.

"Okay. I'm going to show you what it is like to be the dominant. At least in a sexual relationship."

"Mmm kay." I took a big drink of wine to fortify my patience. "You aren't going to like... have sex here, are you? With your slaves? In front of me? If that's what you have in mind, please don't. I'll just leave. This had better be PG only."

"I'll spare you from anything too explicit. But I want you to get the idea." She snapped her fingers.

Immediately, her companion, Joe, came into the room and dropped on his hands and knees in front of her. Had he been standing around the corner waiting? I had to hand it to her, he was handsome, muscular, and very well built with washboard abs. The only thing he was wearing besides a pair of athletic shorts was an absurd, spiky leather collar with a chain. He handed the end of his chain up reverently to Leanne. I started to laugh but restrained myself with a hand over my mouth. Without saying a word, Leanne pointed to her feet, pulling his chain tight. On cue, one at a time he removed her high-fashion shoes. Propping one foot atop Joe's head, she pushed him down to her other foot, all the while keeping his chain pulled tight. His neck strained and it looked like an uncomfortable combination, yet he patiently kissed, licked, and massaged her foot without complaint.

Finally, I couldn't help it and broke out laughing. She looked at me sternly as if I were an errant high school student not getting the lesson.

"Go ahead, laugh," Leanne scolded. "It feels wonderful." She reached down and abruptly grabbed the hair atop Joe's head. Putting her other foot before him now, she continued the same procedure. "Now this one. Get my toes," she said to him, pushing his head firmly.

"I'm sorry, but it just looks ridiculous to me," I told her, getting up for a refill of wine from a bottle sitting on a buffet. It *was* ridiculous. "Leanne, what's the point? Getting some guy to slobber all over my feet? My feet are ticklish, anyway. I don't think it would do much for me."

Leanne snapped her fingers again. This time, the slave girl Heidi, came out. I looked around the room. Where were they hiding? This girl similarly dropped to her knees besides Joe, who never skipped a beat with his foot worship service. She presented an object to Leanne. I was unsure

62

what it was until Leanne took it. It was a riding crop. Finally. Some decent entertainment I thought with amusement to myself. Leanne smiled over at me as she slapped the crop into her open hand.

SWAP!

She leaned over, gently rubbing the riding crop along Joe's muscular shoulders and down his back. "Joe, you are allowed to speak. I want you to tell my cousin over here what you think about the duties I assign you. You will address her as Ms. Michaels."

"Yes, Ms. Tilden," Joe said, abruptly sitting up. Leanne immediately came down on his shoulder with the riding crop.

SWAP! Joe winced. I laughed again and hid behind my glass of wine.

"I didn't say you should stop servicing me. Get back to work. You can talk while you work," Leanne corrected before reclining in her chair. Heidi simply sat motionless, looking up expectantly to Leanne for some forthcoming direction. Hopefully, there would be some riding crop treatment for her as well. Although beautiful, she had the look of a petulant college girl.

Joe immediately returned to his duties at Leanne's feet. Sporting a noticeable hard-on beneath his shorts, he talked in between kisses and licks. It was comical. And yes, very odd. He gave the expected narration about how he loved serving his mistress and loved the taste of her feet, as well as the rest of her body. He enjoyed the sting of the crop, blah, blah. He was thankfully non-explicit. I thanked them and decided to head back to my room and enjoy a good book. She gave me an exasperated look when I left. I gave her my best toothy smile.

It was another day of surprises as Santiago left my office with further instructions on repairing the Mobley fiasco with the concrete. My phone buzzed and when I answered it, the woman on the other end identified herself as Marisha Neita, the overseer of the Island Historical Society down in the village. Their tiny museum is located several doors down from The Blue Calypso. She welcomed me to the island in a sultry, wonderfully accented voice that sounded like warm honey.

"I would very much appreciate it if you could pay me a visit soon?"

Thinking about this request, I immediately began to turn over excuses in my mind to put this woman off the scent of whatever it was she was wanting, which was probably a donation to keep her museum running. I was in debt over my head and with nothing to spare.

"Marisha, I'd love to, but as you can imagine, with trying to get Stoney Brook back into shape before tourist season, it's eating up every minute I have. I'm sure you have a very worthwhile cause there. Perhaps another time?" Like, another time far into *never*. There was a pause on the line while Marisha considered an appropriate response to my brush off. I tapped my foot on my desk waiting for the inevitable request to reconsider.

"Ms. Michaels. I'm not seeking money from you. I have something very interesting involving Stoney Brook that I think you would like to see. But if you are busy, yes, perhaps some other time."

Okay, this was intriguing. What was it? I decided to bite.

"Marisha, I'm not going to lie, if you have something that pertains historically to Stoney Brook, that is important to what we are doing here, I'll find time to meet with you." There. That sounded like a nice polite way of slipping back into her good graces.

"It is one of the few things we have here at the society that is directly from Stoney Brook," Marisha explained. "A fascinating artifact, quite well preserved. It is the original ledger of the founder of Stoney Brook, Seumas Owen

McCaskill, your ancestor. It has been handed down generation to generation through one of the first slave families of the plantation."

"A ledger?" This further piqued my interest. Especially if it was something directly from my long lost umpteenth great grandfather. "Please explain."

"It's an account like a diary. I've only tried to transcribe the first few pages. It's in Gaelic, but it's roughly written and hard to understand."

"Does the family who owns the book live on the island?"

"Yes."

"I'm stunned. I don't know what to say." I paused for a moment, thinking of the implications. It had never occurred to me that I would meet someone that had a lineage to the brutal past of Stoney Brook. The thought was an uncomfortable one, me being a descendant of the one that caused so much suffering. "Um. Could I see the ledger? And... do you think I could meet this person?"

"I think I can arrange that."

"Is 9:00 this morning okay?"

Walking down the worn boardwalks of the village, I passed The Blue Calypso from the opposite side of the street. It was early and the regulars weren't yet out for new iniquities at the bar. Suddenly, a disheveled figure shuffled out of the front doors whom I immediately recognized, even in his shabby state. My jaw dropped. It was Morgan Mobley in a grimy dish washer's apron, sweeping off the front porch. Looking gaunt, he needed a shave, and most assuredly, a shower. At least he had some type of employment. A scrofulous dishwasher was probably a very suitable job for his skill set and I didn't feel the least bit sorry for him. I started to catch his attention so that I could flip him off, then thought better of it. He was getting what he deserved, so I strolled on with an energetic bounce in my step, happy to see karma was alive and well, at least down on the village boardwalk.

Reaching the Island Historical Society several doors down, I turned the aged knob of a multi-paint layered, weather-beaten door. The latest color was a sky blue but was chipped to such degree the prior technicolor selections were discernable. It creaked open noisily on tortured, hand-forged, iron hinges, touching off a little brass bell. It all had a rustic, Caribbean charm, as did many of the old buildings of the village. A fat but adorable white and black cat immediately began winding its way around my leg.

Nudging the cat off, I walked in and closed the door behind me. The front room of the museum was strangely quiet. Evidently, it wasn't on the "must-see" list for many of the tourists combing through the streets. Numerous glass display cases contained items related to the early history of the island and village. Along the walls, antique, leather-bound books were neatly arranged on slumping, wooden shelves. Overhead, an unbalanced ceiling fan labored with soft, humming strokes.

A bronze-skinned young woman of probable island heritage suddenly appeared in the back from behind a doorway curtain of beads. Possessing hauntingly piercing eyes, she was incredibly beautiful. She smiled warmly.

"Hello. Ms. Michaels?"

"Yes. You are Marisha Neita?"

"I am. Welcome to the Island Historical Society, Ms. Michaels. As you can see, we aren't an affluent organization. We nevertheless maintain, store, and display many items that are of historical significance to our island."

Seemingly out of place, I pointed to a University of California at Los Angeles banner, hung incongruously over a display of old rusty tools. I noticed what appeared to be a volleyball with the university's logo sitting on a nearby shelf. "Are you a college fan?"

"I went there," she explained. "Earned several degrees. History."

"And the volleyball?"

"As an undergraduate, I was on a full-ride scholarship on their varsity volleyball team. How they found me, I can only guess. Maybe a scout. In high school here on the island, I attended several volleyball tournaments throughout the region, in the states, and Central America. They must have noticed me at one of those, they began recruiting me when I was a junior. I felt quite honored."

My gaze wandered the room, taking in the many wondrous items in displays, hung on the walls, or sitting on the floors. How had I not heard of this place before?

"Please, come back to my office. I will show you the Seumas McCaskill ledger." Marisha took my hand, which seemed odd to me. I had noticed that people on the island did this frequently and was a habit I too had picked up. She swept aside the curtain of beads to a back doorway, revealing her office. The only illumination in the room was a brass lamp sitting on what would have to be her office desk. The room was packed with boxes and artifacts lying about on the floor. Several odd items hung from the ceiling and lined the walls that looked distinctively Voodoo in origin.

Noticing my widened eyes, Marisha smiled, disarmingly. "I collect items that are also related to the early religion of the island. As you probably know, slaves, and later their ancestors, combined features of African religion or mysticism with aspects of Christianity. It is all part of our rich Caribbean history. And among some on the island, still practiced."

"Voodoo," I confirmed.

"Yes. And versions of it."

I had to wonder why the items took such prominent positions in her office. While I didn't know much about Voodoo, it seemed strange and ritualistic from my observations.

"Do you practice it, if I may ask?"

"I do. Yes. Does that bother you?"

"No," I quickly answered, thinking perhaps I had sounded rude for asking. "I'm not being critical at all. I just find the subject fascinating. I'm sorry if I sounded forward."

"Do not apologize, Ms. Michaels. You strike me as very honest and kind. I hope that we can be friends. And you should know my sentiments don't easily bruise." She motioned for me to take a seat next to her desk. Her smile was warm and disarming. "May I get you a cup of tea?"

"Yes, thank you. That would be nice."

"Anything other than the tea?"

"No, thank you. Just tea is fine." I wondered what she might have meant. Cookies?

From the back of her office, I could see her taking a pot of hot water from a stove. She soon arrived with two cups of tea. Taking mine, I nodded in appreciation and thought about asking her what was contained in the ancient, dust-covered jars on a shelf. They contained what appeared to be animal parts in some sort of fluid. I thought better of it.

Marisha sat down and gently removed a thick, aged book from her desk and positioned it among a pile of loose-leaf papers with scribbling. She opened it, revealing yellowed pages with nearly illegible writing in ink.

"And here it is, the ledger." She pushed it over to where I could see it. "It is difficult to make out. The writing is a mixture of the times, old English, Gaelic, and some other Scottish regional dialects I've picked up on. It is a sequential personal account of the founder of Stoney Brook Plantation, your ancestor, Seumas Owen McCaskill."

She took the stack of papers from her desk and handed them to me. "I've been transcribing it, working from the very first entry. This is a copy of what I have so far. I am writing his words as close to modern conversational English as I can figure it, but I will still try and keep the flavor of his own words. There will be misspellings and colloquialisms. Some parts are unreadable. As I know this must be of deep interest to you, I'll give you updates as I finish them. As you see… this is only a small amount so far."

"This is incredible," I exclaimed. "I never thought I would have a first-hand source of the founder, my direct ancestor. How can I ever thank you?"

"You are thanking me by taking an interest, Ms. Michaels. Everyone on the island is interested in Stoney Brook, it is a vital part of our history. I am every bit as fascinated as you, and we will learn together."

"How did it survive all these years?"

"It has been said that this ledger was a gift to the slave family by a later member of the McCaskill family. The descendants have had it all this time, keeping it safe."

"Can I meet this family?"

Marisha appraised me from behind her desk and slowly stood. She extended her hand which I warily took into my own.

"I am very pleased to meet you, Ms. Michaels. I am a member of that family."

Marisha explained that the ledger had been given to her by her father. Although she had many times thumbed through the pages, the contents were alien to her. The history of Stoney Brook and the ledger of Seumas Owen McCaskill were her inspiration for her college program studies. Only now, with two degrees and the aid of global networking and innumerable online resources did she feel sufficiently confident with trying to translate the book into something readable. She had never learned the identity of the first descendant of hers that was a slave at Stoney Brook but hoped the ledger may hold clues. She expressed hope that she would learn as much about her family as I may about the McCaskills.

Taking the pages of Marisha's first transcription, I was eager to start reading. The ride home was a somber one, wondering what I would uncover. I could barely keep my eyes on the road as they kept returning to the folder of papers sitting on the passenger seat. Marisha assured me that whatever we would find, she wasn't judging me by the actions of my ancestors. She promised to let me know when the next installment was ready, which she would be working on immediately.

That afternoon with papers in hand, I took one of the trails through the gardens and away from Stoney Brook to a secluded meadow near one of the plantation cemeteries. It was notable that I had not found a marker for Seumas McCaskill among any of the known graves on the estate, yet I was about to read his very thoughts from several hundred years ago. What was he like? Was he as brutal and hard-handed as what I had heard? Finding a suitable bench to sit on, I kicked off my shoes, reclined back and began to read what Seumas had to say.

> The Ledger of Seumas Owen McCaskill
> "It was sometime in the summer of 1607, me in Scotland, and I since discovered I had no mind for the hard-bitten labors of a hedgeman for the squire as I had been set about to do by my dear mother. It was on with my 12th year and happened upon a chance with a stranger of the name of Captain Peter Love that told me of adventure at sea. Further, he stated it would be well suited for just such a lad as I if I were to accompany him to the bay but to make no mention of said offer to anyone. Of which I complied, being soundly admiring of travels away and abroad.
> "I bade me mother and clan farewell, and my siblings not a shot of care, who knew not where I was going, took two days provisions and threw my lot in on a ship of brigands named the Priam. I was wee but was

70

set about by Captain Love hauling water, victuals, and such, and when taking a prize, I hauled shot and powder. All counted for my board, and I was to bear the older years of my betters as a good lad should or face the lash, which I did on occasion. To pass the idling time, the first mate Smith gave me a ledger, taken, he says, from the last prize they hove to and boarded and of which I used to continue my studies of the writ. Smith told me I would be home by the new moon, but it was not to be.

"It were in Loch Roag that we nearly met our end. After a well bounteous end, we were fine in Priam and even me, as a ship's boy, were set for a decent bit of pay for our troubles. Early one morning, we were nearly overcome by boats of the authorities and were nearly upon us, cutlasses in hand before we realized what was up and made sail. It were one of the closer of times with Love.

"Priam fairly well had its way, and it were no long after, perhaps a year, we took up with another that would be serving with Captain Love, it were N. MacLeod, a clan I knew of well. These two seemed as two of the same, but perhaps a year later, it would be MacLeod turned Love over to be hanged along with several of my shipboard brethren. Although I were no favorite to the either, yet it were Macleod paid me for my meager portion, which were nearly better than nothing. No more, I swore, were my labors be taken in vain if I had anything to do about it. November 1609

"N. Macleod gave me over to the Privy Council, along with Love, yet I was taken to the stay for my time at board, due my age, and told I had better give up pirating had I end up before the magistrate and tried, like Captain Love, who with a number of my shipmates went to the drop of a rope from a gibbet. They kilt him more than once, or so they tried, hung poor ole Love out to dry, the birds to clean and peck his bones as an eyeful to any that may take heed of the due rewards of being a pirate. It were a fearful sight to see, knowing the man who were now hanging there were the very man that took me to sea under his wing and learnt me the ways of a sail, hauled up as a warning they say, eyes gone, ragged flesh and showing bone.

Spring, 1610

"The privy cut me loose, saying I was just a lad that'd been led astray perhaps. And deserving of a second chance so they say and could find better company to find among my elders. I came to find out my mother died a year prior, so's paid my respects doubly so for my absence. And without my father, dead 11 years hence, I collected a few things from home against the wishes of my siblings that seemed none too joyed to see me return.

"Several villages from home, it were about this time I laid eyes upon Nancy McCullum. I had met her when we were both wee, but as it were, never considered her for what I found out to be more than a passing fancy. She took to me as well. It were not meant to be though, as her brothers threatened to run me through the first opportunity should I linger further. Then, I decided, if not for love or money be, it were time to head out for further adventures.

"My hands found their way around my father's Claymore, for sure, taken as it were, although promised to me long ago and rightfully mine. Off I went again, boarded a merchant bound for the Spanish Main.

"A full week at the doldrums took us to hell's keep from" ~unintelligible~ "that's when I decided to keep better to my ledger of sorts with no other company but a quill worth the wit. It be a hard night at it, with the storm and all, three hands overboard with the lash of the sea.

"ADDED WRIT - My first ledger was lost, so memories are thinner now, through the haze of time. I've filled 'em back the best I could, but truth told, I'm no ledger keeper. Nevertheless, to writ seems to set me at ease."

Marisha had done a decent job decoding the script. Even translated, I could capture the image and feel of the times of this man, my ancestor, Seumas Owen McCaskill. And shockingly, it sounded like Seumas had become a pirate at a very young age. The best I could determine, he had been a wayward child, subject to the vagaries of whichever way the wind blew. And it blew him into a life of early crime with someone that went by the name of Captain Love. Had he wanted anyone else to read his entries? Or were these simply notes jotted down for his sole benefit for the sake of remembering?

Gathering the papers together, I tucked them back into the folder and looked forward to the next update from Marisha.

Morgan: At least I still have my journal to keep me company. It's not much, but it's

all I have at this point. Looking back over the past week, all I can think is what a difference a day can make in one's life! One minute, I have a decent job, the next I'm without any money in a tiny island village with no way of getting back to Chicago. I could no longer afford my mobile phone and it is shut off. I have no way to even communicate with the outside world. That bitch of an ex-wife of mine would just love what has become of me. What the hell happened to my life????

~~~~~

If there is any good news to this predicament I am in, it's that the owner of The Blue Calypso, a guy named Eduardo, has agreed to let me wash dishes and work part-time as a waiter for letting me stay in a scroungy spare room that serves for storage on the third floor. Plus, he pays me a few dollars a week, which is ironic, given he has so much of my money that I previously gambled away in this joint. At least I can eat and get a roof over my head. I will have to keep looking for another job in the village. Maybe with two jobs, I could earn enough to leave.

~~~~~

I saw that asshole French taxi boat guy the other day, the one that brought me over the first time. He laughed when he saw me washing dishes and bussing tables. He informed me that no one else will hire me as he has passed the word around that I'm a cheap dickhead. Little fuck twat. Then he said my fare would be double, should I ever actually earn enough to leave. And he said the other taxi boats would be equally expensive. If I even look like I don't like it, he said it will go up three times as much. Maybe more. ASSHOLE! I spoke to the constable, or whatever it is that passes for the head of law enforcement on this godforsaken island. Some guy named Fillmore. He said he can't control what people say. I'm between a rock and a hard place.

~~~~~~

The amenities of my little storage room include a window out onto the alley. I have a nightstand and a three-legged chair that Eduardo drug out of the trash dumpster. Those serve as the only "furnishings" for my room. He said he heard I was a "three-legged" horny dog of man, so it should suit me fine. He seemed good-natured about it so I couldn't get too pissed and we both laughed. Hard to deny the truth, I guess. If I prop the chair against the corner, I can at least sit and not fall over. As for a bed, I have an old filthy mattress with no frame that must lay on the floor (I sprayed the hell out of it with germ killer from the kitchen). He gave me some spare sheets so at least I don't have to sleep on the stains. I use a washroom just down the hall. To shower, I must wear my swim trunks down to the alley where I can wash from a water hose. It's not a great set of circumstances, but at least I'm surviving.

~~~~~

I've cleaned the place the best I could. It will take some doing to convince cute island women to come back to this wretched hole for a romp on a stained mattress. It's a wonder I don't have crabs or some such of an infestation from sleeping here. Damned Stefany. Heartless cold wench. She could have shown a little bit of humanity and at least paid me severance for my last week.

~~~~~

I thought mightily on the subject tonight. It's not Stefany's fault that I'm where I'm at. Is it? I did take the blame for the knee wall failure, and she didn't know I was covering for the boys. I can't blame her for my fuck ups. Does that make me the good guy in all this? No, and she's still a heartless sinister bitch in my mind. I'm broke and living in squalor. Shit. Maybe screw being a good guy. It gets you in nothing but trouble. Santiago and Miguel still have their jobs. I have nothing. NOTHING.

~~~~~

Okay. It's been a few days. I have decided to make the most of this chapter of my life. Maybe getting fired and being broke is a good thing? I'm certainly not perfect. I hate to admit it, but I miss seeing Stefany. Did I write that? I almost want to slap myself for thinking it. If she just wasn't such a bitch. She sure looks good in those little shorts she wears around. Damned good. That sweaty, tight little body. Those muscular, tan legs. That sexy little crooked smile she has (never for me I recall) and those amazing lips. Beautiful face. Now that I don't see her, I guess I can appreciate her more. What a woman.

Wait. ~~~WHAT THE HELL~~~ I'm going insane, that's it. INSANE! Probably because I don't have her cratchety mongoose personality to deal with anymore. As for her cousin, Leanne, I still don't know what to make of the weirdness that chick was dripping all over the place. Hot, but a nut job weirdo in the third degree. I DO NOT approve of how she grappled my nards like a drunken fruit packer. I was sore for two days. Chick has a grip like a rock crane, for damned sure. She does look like she works out. Maybe she's a steak-knife psycho, I can't tell. Being a relative to Stefany, who knows. I'd surely give her some shake and bake if things were different. Leanne is no pushover, that's for sure. Despite it all, she's drop-dead hot. And no doubt a very successful businesswoman judging by the looks of her.

Leanne had the goods on me knowing I didn't fully earn my architecture degree though. If I ever get off this island, that's something I must fix. Finish those remaining classes I need. Somehow.

~~~~~

Stefany won't get out of my head. Odd, I know. If I could ever look past her wretched personality... I would have to say I like her natural look. She's gorgeous with no work. No fancy clothes, just a down to earth, authentic, woman.

Stefany has a lot of qualities that I find attractive. She strikes me as a woman that would rather wear jeans and sneakers, sip beer and watch a baseball game - as opposed to dressing up in high heels to the nine with layers of make-up. She's a naturally beautiful woman that is a bit of a tomboy. I have never met another woman like Stefany. What the hell am I saying! Again I'm obsessing over that shrew of a woman. I mustn't' forget her personality!! That alone is a deal-breaker. Good gawd, there isn't any denying it though – Stefany has the body of a goddess.

Here I am talking about two women that hate me and I have no chance with. I'm getting them out of my mind, NOW. At present, I have NO chance with any woman given my circumstances. I must laugh at myself, despite my predicament. Leanne nearly ripping my balls off may be the last action I get for a while. Ironic, I know. I'm not getting laid anytime soon. And I may never get out of here. It's late. I start my shift early tomorrow.

"Mobley put the dishrag down. You are out front tonight with Gloria and Lorena. You have tables 1 through 8. Okay? Don't piss off any customers! Don't get orders wrong. Don't spill shit."

Eduardo removed his black and white fedora to run his fingers through his thinning hair before adding cash to the front register. With his white shirt, black pants, and wingtips, he looked like a Latino Al Capone.

It would possibly mean a good night of tips. Something I desperately needed. He was doing me a favor as there were other waiters that he could have called into work.

"You got it, Ed."

"Good. Go change. Make me some money tonight, Mobley. Maybe I'll move you up to help out in the casino the way you are going." He looked me over appraisingly. "When you clean up, you look respectable. That's what we need here, respectable. And an added hand to toss out the bums when we need." He straightened his tie and stepped to the back to check on the kitchen.

Finally, I had a chance to start making enough money to get off the island and maybe get back to Chicago.

"Mobley, you have a party of six over at table 4," Eduardo yelled back into the kitchen where I was loading up my serving tray.

"Ok, sure thing," I acknowledged, already with over fifty dollars in tips to my name for the night. The evening was busy as hell, and I barely had time to serve one table before I was pulled away to another. I checked my bow tie, retucked my shirt, and grabbed six menus from the stack by the front door. I took dinner to table 2 and then turned to handle table 4.

My mouth dropped and I stared into a pair of green eyes. It was Stefany. She gaped at me right back, even as I stood paralyzed. She was with her sadistic cousin, Leanne, and two other men and two women I did not recognize. They were all quite well dressed, and the man sitting next to Stefany seemed to be her date. Given his sour expression, perhaps it was her long-lost husband, Miles, who I had heard about before getting fired from Stoney Brook.

Trying to regain from the shock and what was at least initially an awkward moment of silence, I gave them my best smile as if nothing were remiss.

"Good evening, all. Welcome… to The Blue Calypso." I cleared my throat, trying to find a more self-assured voice. "Um. Here are our menus. Would any of you be up for a pre-dinner drink while you decide?"

Stefany was still staring at me, unable to say anything. The strangers eyed first her then me with growing curiosity. Leanne, grinning, broke the uneasy silence: "Well. If it isn't Mr. Mobley! How quaint to find you here, waiting tables. I see you are doing well," she said acerbically. Seeing the other guests' inquisitive glances, she introduced me. "Everyone, I would like to introduce you to a *former* employee of Stoney Brook. Mr. Morgan Mobley."

I nodded uncomfortably. The strangers didn't seem aware of any controversy as they greeted me cordially, asking why I left Stoney Brook. They bought my explanation that I simply preferred working in the village for the time being as it was closer to the waterfront, with being an avid fisherman and all, which was a lie of course. I couldn't even afford bait, much less a fishing pole. I was glad they didn't ask any further questions about fishing because I didn't have a clue in hell what you could catch in the ocean besides sand in the ass. Leanne, knowing my deceit, continued to beam.

The man who was sitting next to Stefany may have heard of me judging by his reaction. His eyes narrowed as he surveyed me. Focusing my attention on Stefany who was still unable to speak, I held the serving tray in both hands and tried to think of something to say.

"Ms. Michaels. What a pleasure to see you. You are looking well." She continued to stare blankly, and my throat felt as if it were constricting. "This is not my usual assigned table," I lied, trying to sound smooth. "If you would prefer, I think we have another waiter that could better serve you, given your large number of guests. Um. If you would prefer."

She blinked several times, still evidently trying to come to grips with discovering that I could be waiting on her table. "I... I... think that... yes, I *would* prefer..."

"I think what my cousin means is that you will do nicely, Mr. Mobley," Leanne interrupted. "I'm sure you can handle the number of our party. Now, let's get those drink orders, shall we?" Stefany turned a fierce gaze upon Leanne.

Wondering what hell I just walked into, I pulled out my pen and tab and gave it a tap on the tray with a flourish. "Yes, ma'am, certainly. I am at your service then." Leanne gave me a taunting sideways look.

The strangers with them cast several glances back and forth, sensing the tension just below the conversation. They all gave their drink orders in turn, and I gratefully headed to the bar. Looking over my shoulder, I could see Stefany was watching my every move. She was holding back laying into me, at least for the moment.

CHAPTER 4
FUNGAL INFECTIONS AND FAT LIPS

Morgan: My life is a quivering mass of splattered goo on the windshield of fate. The mattress I've been sleeping on has given me a rash. I wiped the damnable thing down with a rag with bleach. The itching it gave me under my arms, up in between my legs and in the crack of my ass is enough to drive a man insane. My whole body became a red, raw rash. The only pleasure I now have in life is to drag my fingernails over the itchy areas and scratch the living hell out of them. That is what's become of my life. Laying on a festering mattress, scratching my ass, legs, and balls raw. Fuck!

~~~~

I couldn't take it anymore. People in the bar were noticing, the women laughing as I was caught a few times trying to claw my nuts off from the damned itch. The crack of my ass was an inferno of lava. So, yesterday, I went to one of the island doctors here in town. It cost me everything I made in a week, and he said he was doing me a favor, especially since he's heard of me as being somewhat of a "Casanova." Yeah, right. Even in my current state I still must suffer from the reputation that Leanne and Stefany gave me! Anyway, the doc tells me I have fungus or something. Oh, that's just great.

After making a few snide comments about me having disease ravaged balls, he asks me if I have slept with anyone, it could be contagious in my current state. WTF. I tell him I wash fucking dishes at The Blue Calypso, wear rags and sleep on a secondhand, flea-bitten mattress in a room with no furniture, does it look like I'm getting laid. What a fucking smart ass.

I thought doctors were supposed to maintain a professional air about themselves. I didn't get this shit from sex; it was from the crappy way I must live now!!! He kept piling it on though, getting a big laugh out my situation, which still makes me mad, even as I write this. The worst thing is, as I was leaving, he offered to set me up with some of the indigent old ladies down at the elderly care center he works at part-time, since, as he put it, "It will be some time for that cream to take effect and those old women don't expect things to work anyway. It will be your chance to get back in the game." I nearly punched his lights out, but with my luck, I may need more doctoring at some point in the future.

First, he gave me some spray to fumigate my room and possessions. And you can believe that damned mattress was thrown out the window of the third floor. It landed perfectly in the dumpster. Doc also gave me ointment I'm supposed to put on twice a day. Ohhh thank gawd the itching has abated.

~~~~~

I just got back from the Doc's house. That son of a bitch had me wash his car and sweep his garage for the rest of the payment I owe him for the medicine. The worst part is that several people I knew from Stoney Brook happened by when I was doing it. Shit. Can it get any worse??? Does hell have a basement???

The evening progressed, I managed to service all my tables and maintain my composure with Stefany's group. She continued to cast a suspicious eye to me whenever I approached but said nothing beyond what she wanted to order.

After taking orders for a second round of drinks from her group, I went to the bar and gave the list to the bartender. While looking over my receipts for the night I was surprised to feel a tap on my shoulder. I turned. It was Leanne.

"Stefany begged me not to come over here, but I wanted to tell you, you are doing a fantastic job, Mr. Mobley. At least with the first order of drinks."

"Oh, really, Leanne. Did she? Did she really?"

"Well… no. But I thought I would be polite," she said with a Cheshire smile.

I stood up straight, determined, facing her. Certainly, this woman was attractive, there was no doubt about that. But I didn't need to remind myself she was a vindictive, nasty bitch of a woman. She would probably be like fucking a cactus. My balls were clawing their way up the crack of my ass in self-defense just at the sight of her. "Does this excite you in some way, Leanne? Does my *humiliation* make you feel more like a woman somehow?"

"Why, whatever do you mean, Mr. Mobley?"

"Don't give me that," I hissed, trying to keep the conversation low so the neighboring patrons and the bartender would not pick up on it. "You know exactly what I mean. And you are a maniac, by the way. My last encounter with you told me that."

Leanne laughed. "You know, Mr. Mobley, during the conclusion of our last encounter, I do believe that you were in pain. Of sorts." She looked down at my crotch and then feigned a move with her hand, only coming to bring her hand up and push a strand of hair out of her eyes.

I instinctively tensed, holding my body away from hers. She laughed.

"My, we are sensitive, aren't we, Mr. Mobley?" She asked, barely managing the words from beneath the snickering.

"No! I just don't like some... some... psycho woman taking the polish off the family jewels." I tried to whisper this last, to which she laughed aloud, her head back, drawing the attention of all within earshot.

"Mr. Mobley," she began, "I assure you, if I had wanted to destroy your manhood, I would have done so. Like..." She again made a motion with her hand towards my crotch with which I immediately recoiled.

Her laughter was even louder. Stefany, from over at her table, looked our way with concern. The bartender gave me an inquisitive grin.

"Leanne!" I barked. "Please!" And then I just mouthed the word, "*please.*"

Her eyes roamed over me as if to judge my worthiness. Her expression finally softened, and she almost seemed to be sympathetic. "Oh, okay, Mobley."

"Just... please," I begged. "Let me just do my job and not torture me more than..." I paused, lost for the finish.

She answered for me. "More than you *deserve*?"

Irritated beyond explanation, I just nodded. "Fair enough. Whatever."

"Listen, Mobley. I suppose you aren't all that bad," she whispered, trying to sincerely be quiet. "Seems you working in this place has brought you a little well-deserved humility."

"Well, can we get on with the evening and make it through in one piece then go our separate ways?" I asked, hoping we could end the evening on a positive note.

"Maybe so," she said with a grin. "Mobley. You are a cocky ass, to be sure. A walking hard-on. An unqualified fraud. A liar. Charlatan. But you do have a few redeeming qualities."

"Leanne, I was quite capable of performing my duties at Stoney Brook and I was well on my way to getting that place ship-shape. Just because you found out that I didn't have a little piece of paper that signifies a final certificate of degree doesn't mean I'm incompetent."

Leanne waved her hand dismissively. "Mobley, I could hire some fucking deadbeat off the streets with your abilities, a novice, and pay them far less. Your fiasco with the concrete at Stoney Brook just confirmed all my suspicions. But... given your lack of qualifications, if I must say anything nice about you, there is one bit of news that left me in shock."

My eyebrows raised, waiting for this epiphany. More insults, no doubt. "Yes?" I finally asked, shaking my head.

"When you stood up for your workers. Nice. You took the fall for all that concrete mess. It really wasn't your fault and what you did, covering for them to save their jobs and never saying a word... I admit I was surprised. And a little impressed. As was Stefany."

I wondered who had confessed. I wasn't expecting Stefany to find out the truth. "Oh. Well. Thank you. They were my workers and I had to look out for them."

"Now Mobley, that unexpected example of gallantry makes no accounting for your *horrible*, bumbling, idiot, management skills that made the mess possible in the first place," she added quickly to disperse any belief this was an actual compliment.

"Right...," I said, gritting my teeth. When would this beat-down end?

She eyed me like she was trying to decide which box of cereal on a shelf to purchase. "There is... *one more* thing about you, I suppose if I must admit."

I nodded, waiting for this next revelation that would no doubt be another comment tinged with sarcasm. "Uh-huh. And what is that."

"Mobley, you are handsome, I'll give you that."

"Um. Thanks." I nonchalantly offered, not believing her. I tried to retain some composure and wondered if I should be angrier than I was.

"Shallow as a puddle of piss, mind," she added with a simper. "But handsome, nevertheless." She batted her eyes innocently, her smirk giving away her desire to see an angry, uncontrolled response from me.

Exasperated, I shook my head and looked away. I couldn't even tell if she was serious or if she was just messing with me. The bartender from behind the bar no doubt thought I was on my way to scoring, as I suppose the conversation could be misinterpreted as flirting. But I knew better. Leanne was grandly enjoying herself at my expense and regardless of whether it was an insult or not, I had to keep this job and not lose my temper or seem impolite. At least as viewed from my boss who was leaning in the doorway of the bar observing the course of the evening's business. He saw me and gave me a thumb up, smiling broadly, apparently mistaking the abuse Leanne was giving me for good customer relations.

"Okay, Leanne," I finally commented just as it looked like she would walk off, satisfied she had insulted me sufficiently. "But wait. Tell me. So, who is the guy sitting next to Stefany?"

She turned her body so that she was standing beside me, sort of as a co-conspirator, placing her arm around my waist. It was strange, almost like she thought of me as a friend and confidant despite our history and what was an obvious clash of personalities.

"Well," she stated grandly, emphasizing with her free arm towards her table, "*that* is her husband. Miles. And what a specimen he is. And I'm just going to say it. He's an abusive asshole. I hate his fucking guts."

Stunned by this revelation of animosity, I looked at her, disbelieving.

"By now, Mobley, you know me, to some degree at least. I say what's on my mind. I take no shit from anyone, and I can be a bitch. Especially to those that I think have crossed me. I'll lay this bit of wisdom on you. As men go, in comparison to Miles, you are a *stallion* of a man."

Was that a backdoor compliment? Or another insult? I wasn't sure. Was she now my *friend* of some sort? Was that what this whole conversation was about? Nothing about this dame could be taken at face value. I suddenly had a flashback of Leanne in Stefany's office, sitting on the edge of the desk, me on my knees, kissing her leg, getting a close look up her short skirt to see she was not wearing panties, her gorgeous pussy completely bare. Without reason or making any sense at all, my thoughts momentarily went to envisioning her naked. While I was trying to decipher all this confusion, she read my expression and slapped me on my ass, and I lurched forward, nearly causing me to spill the tray of drinks the bartender had just handed to me.

"It's a compliment," she said grinning, somehow reading my thoughts. "I like you, Mobley, pathetic as you are." I grimaced. She jokingly elbowed me in the ribs. "Nevertheless, if you want any tip at all, you'll get those drinks over to our table. The conversation is running a bit dry."

Stefany:
My friendly banker called yesterday. I can't say that it was a

particularly pleasant conversation. Grim would be more accurate. His assessment of my financial situation here at Stoney Brook is not a rosy one. My projected best-case income may not be enough to keep my head above water with the overruns we've had on everything. The repairs, the restorations. Modernizing the estate. The Mobley fiasco. Leanne has said she would loan me the money, interest-free, to help me keep things going until the place becomes profitable. Her payment back, she says, could be lifetime guest privileges. HA! I just can't accept that. At least not yet. She's incensed at my stubbornness, I guess. The problem is not that I don't want her help, as generous an offer as it is. She is quite wealthy, and I suppose she could do that sort of thing and not put too big of a dent in her net worth. The problem is…
it's that I want to do this on my own… be a success. Make something work because I have willed it.

I'm not sure what to do at this point except to keep plugging away. I have faith that this will work out. The bank says I'll run out of money in a couple of months and go bankrupt which they say, obviously, is a

serious concern to them. Yet I think I can make it work. Somehow. I will not take failure as an option.

The evening at The Blue Calypso was wild beyond my imagination. That is a certainty. I'm still sorting it out...

Leanne knew Mobley was working at The Blue Calypso and the evening was her idea of "entertainment." Initially reluctant to agree to come, I also knew Mobley was here, but I hadn't expected to see him waiting tables, recalling seeing him in the dishwasher's apron when I had visited Marisha Neita. Whether Leanne was just playing Mobley or stringing him along, I honestly couldn't tell. She almost seemed to be flirting with him whenever he would approach our table. Would she do that? Yeah, it's Leanne. Images of Leanne bringing Mobley to heel in my office, having him kiss her legs while on his knees came to mind.

I have very conflicted feelings about Mobley, given what I learned about him taking the fall for the concrete mess his workers had caused. I'm torn at calling it gallant. It was a mistake that cost me a bloody fortune, after all.

There is no question that I despise Mobley. But maybe there was more to him. Dinner was always good at The Blue Calypso, regardless of who the server was. I tried to brush any further thoughts of Mobley aside.

The conversation at the table was contrite at times, with my asshole husband dominating any conversation. He is such a jerk. And worse when he drinks. And he was putting away the mixed drinks furiously.

I excused myself and left the table for the ladies' room. Standing at the sink, I let the water from the faucet run through my hands. Looking into the mirror, I wondered what the alternate *me* would give in the way of advice. Why was I here? What was I doing, letting Miles come back and try to take charge of everything? I didn't even like him, I had to acknowledge. He hadn't changed a bit; he was the same old Miles. Except now he was trying to take over the one thing in my life that was giving me purpose. Stoney Brook.

Wetting my face a bit, I toweled off, tidied my blouse, and headed to the door. Just as I walked out, Miles stepped out of the men's room from the opposite door. I could tell by the arrogant scowl on his face he was in a mood to fight. I had seen that look many times before in our marriage. And I had seen it that night he had beaten me so bad it had sent me to the hospital. Whatever anxieties he was giving me, I was determined not to cower to this man.

"Your friends are all idiots, you know. Their stupid socialist ideas. You always did manage to surround yourself with such people."

"They are my friends, Miles. They are successful businesspeople from the island and I'm lucky to have them as neighbors. They have helped me immensely, with local laws and traditions… where to find what I need. Maybe you should ease off the drinks. You are starting to sound like you never learned a thing."

He shot me a dark look. "And what was it that I should have learned, Stefany?"

I was shocked he would even say that. "How about self-control? Not being an obnoxious shit?"

"Fuck you, Stefany. You are always the snarky bitch whenever we go out. You haven't changed a bit."

"Changed? I don't think it was *me* that needed changing. You promised me YOU had changed when you came here! You are rude and hateful. Everyone back at Stoney Brook is too afraid to even approach you, knowing you'll have some nasty criticism. Everything about you is the same. It just had to come out with a little booze." By now there were several tears streaming down my cheeks. "It wasn't you that ended up in the hospital from getting beat to a pulp. Never again. I want you to pack your things tomorrow and leave! There is no sense in you staying here any longer."

I turned to walk away. This wasn't going anywhere positive and better to just leave it be. Leave him be before he escalated any disagreement as he always did. Suddenly, I felt his hand grip my arm. He pushed me hard against the wall with a *thud*, bouncing several picture frames that were nearby.

"*No*. I am not going to go. Isn't it always just like you to try and take advantage of a situation. We are married, like it or not, and this plantation you have come into is every bit as much mine as it is yours. And I know what you'll do. It will be just like that coffee shop that never made any money. You'll run this place into the ground. It's already evident you are in way over your head."

He placed his arm like a bar across my chest as I struggled to leave. "We aren't going to be married much longer," I managed to whisper, seething. "And you'll never get Stoney Brook. You didn't want it before, now that you've seen it, you think you can just drop in and milk it for every dollar you can get out of it. I'll never allow you to take it from me. You try and…"

Pressing harder with his arm, he glared into my face. "Or what? What?! You think Leanne and her shabby legal contacts could stop me? No doubt that is what she has told you." He laughed cruelly. "I have an entire multi-million-dollar law firm at my disposal. I'm a major partner. One of the biggest, most powerful law firms in Montreal. You are out of your league as usual. A peasant girl from the Canadian countryside trying to suddenly play CEO. You can barely think your way out of a closet."

"You're wrong!" I struggled harder against his arm. "You can't hit me here. Hit me and everyone will see it and you'll go to fucking jail, asshole."

Taking the collar of my blouse in his fist, he slammed me harder against the wall, knocking the wind out of me. "No

94

one is going to see anything! We are going out this side door and you are going back, right now. In a cab. The only thing your friends will know is you didn't feel well, and you needed to go back. My advice to you is to shut your mouth."

"Miles. Fuck you," I mumbled.

His eyes wide and anger out of control, he moved his hand to wrap tightly around my throat. "You just never learn, do you?"

I stomped on his right foot as hard as I could, evoking a gasp.

"You fucking bitch!" The restaurant and bar were noisy, and I doubted anyone could hear this confrontation. I prayed Leanne would walk around the corner. Miles pulled his arm back, fist tight, uncontrollable anger reddening his face. He was going to beat the hell out of me again and there was nothing I could do. I had been in this situation many times before - I never thought it would happen again, not on the island. I closed my eyes, waiting for the impact.

Miles's hands were forcibly pulled off my throat and the sounds of a scuffle ensued in front of me. I opened my eyes just in time to see Mobley pushing Miles away from me. In what seemed like slow motion, I watched Mobley's fist slam hard into Miles's face. The blow sent Miles reeling across the hall and onto the floor.

It seemed odd, seeing Miles writhing around on the floor holding his face, blood soaking through his fingers. In my prior life, it had always been me in that position. It was... satisfying.

The chaos that followed seemed like a dream to me. Surreal. Miles regaining his feet, hurling curses and threats at Mobley. Leanne was suddenly there trying to usher me away from the conflict. Now, the hall was packed with employees and customers, all there, all caught up in this scene. I watched as several restaurant workers grabbed Mobley by the arms.

"You won't have a dime when I'm through with you, you fucking loser," Miles swore at Mobley.

"I don't have much more than a dime, so have at it, asshole," Mobley replied as he was dragged away, a look of shock on the manager's face.

Leanne pushed me back to the table, joined by our friends. "What the hell happened?" Leanne asked. "No, wait, I know damn good and well what happened." She took me by the shoulders. "Have him leave now, Stefany. It isn't going to work. Have him leave tonight." Our friends blinked, embarrassed for me, not knowing what to say.

Miles approached the table, straightening his blood-spattered shirt. His lips were swollen.

"That fool punched me. I'll see him in jail," Miles sputtered. He looked around the room to see that he was the center of attention. The scene was growing uncomfortable as everyone began to watch this new drama unfold at our table.

Leanne was angry. "And what were you going to do to Stefany? If that *fool* had not stopped you?"

"We were talking, that's all. It was an argument, yes, but nothing more. If it's any of your business, Leanne."

"It is my business," she crisply retorted. "She is my family as well as my friend. And I know all too well of your history, Miles." She turned to look me squarely in the eyes. "Did he hit you, Stefany?"

I looked down at my shoes, feeling shame. For what, I didn't really know.

"No," I answered.

She pressed on, determined. "Was he *going* to hit you?"

I stood in silence.

Leanne turned a hard gaze on Miles. Eyes shifted to me - the room was deathly quiet.

"Of course not," Miles answered for her.

Leanne turned to customers sitting at several of the tables that were near the hallway. "Did any of you witness what happened?"

One of them nodded solemnly to the affirmative, his eyes falling on Miles.

"Was he going to hit her?" Leanne continued.

"Yes. I had just gone around the corner for the men's room. That server stepped in and stopped him," the man confirmed.

"I think you better leave, Miles," Leanne said, taking the initiative and moving protectively in front of me. "Leave now. Go back, pack your bags, get a boat off the island tonight and leave."

Indignant, Miles finally turned sharply and walked out the front entrance, no doubt to hail a cab, the sounds of clapping restaurant patrons following him.

I remained with Leanne and our guests for an awkward dinner, and after an hour or so, we said our uncomfortable goodbyes. I strolled with Leanne back to our Land Rover, still a bit gun-shy and feeling tipsy from the drinks.

"It's good riddance, Stefany. Unbelievable that he was unable to control himself even for this little time he was here. Go through with the divorce. He will never change."

"It will be an all-out war, you know," I told her. "He has told me before he will never leave without taking everything I own. And he's got the connections and resources to do it."

"Let him try. There is too much baggage for him with what he has done to you. The courts have records of all of it. I took that man's name in there that was a witness. I'll have him give a video deposition before he leaves the island. Miles is not going to get Stoney Brook."

She was just trying to be positive. Miles practically owned the courts.

A light warm rain began to fall. I looked past Leanne, far down the street to the hunched figure sitting on the curb across from The Blue Calypso. "And him? What about him, Leanne. Mobley was fired. Kicked out… for helping me." I turned to walk to him, and Leanne caught me with a restraining hand.

"Wait, Stefany. He'll be okay. I made sure the manager knew what happened. I told him it was a mistake. Mobley will get his room back."

"And his job?"

Leanne shrugged her shoulders. "The manager said he could come back. If he wants." Leanne peered down the street at Mobley. "It's not a good time to talk to a man when he's like that. There's no telling…"

I moved her hand off my arm and started towards Mobley. "He saved me a fat lip. Maybe a broken nose, Leanne. I must do something. At least thank him," I told her as the rain fell harder. "I have to do this."

"Alright," Leanne relented.

I steadied myself and walked towards the forlorn, pathetic figure. As I approached, he did not acknowledge me. The rain was dripping off his face that was buried in his hands. He was soaked.

"Mobley? Um. Morgan?"

He slowly turned his head up towards me. He looked like he had been drinking. On second glance, he looked thoroughly drunk. "Stefany? What… are you doing out here… in the rain." He held the flat of his hand out as if to confirm it was indeed raining. His eyes blinked heavily.

"You've been drinking." I don't know why I said that and regretted it immediately. If everything that had happened to Mobley the past few months had happened to me, I probably would be drinking too.

He held up a nearly empty bottle of rum. "Yeah. I suppose I have."

"Why are you sitting in the rain… drinking?"

"To get to the bottom," he answered.

"Of the bottle?" I asked.

"No. My life. The whole damn thing. Tonight, I landed all the way. At the bottom. How can it go any lower? But you're right. I'm am gonna find the bottom of this bottle of rummmm." He took a long swig from the bottle. There was very little left.

"I see. Um. So…" I began, not knowing what I was going to say or why I was even standing there talking to him. "They fired you. For coming to my rescue." He made no reply, swaying a bit. The only sounds were the splattering of the rain, mixed with the loud raucous noises of The Blue Calypso across the street, which was in full swing in the late hour.

"I wanted to say thank you, Mobley. Er, Morgan. So. Thank you."

He laughed a bit, which seemed odd. He smiled up at me. "You're welcome. Miss Steffffany. If I may call you…. Miss Steffffffffaneeeeee."

"Yeah, sure," I agreed. He had not lost his sense of humor, it would seem. There was something very appealing about him at that moment, no matter how hard I tried to deny it. I looked back up the street. Leanne was waiting on me, making get-on-with-it gestures with her hand.

Again, there was a long uneasy pause. "And I wanted to say I'm sorry I got you fired."

He sluggishly waved a hand, dismissing me. "Ahhh. It's shokay. It's just another notch on the ole…" He looked confused for a moment, searching for a word. He picked up his bottle of rum. "Bottle? Jush another notch on the ole bottle… of *life*."

"Bottle of life?" I asked, amused at his analogy. "I don't think you can notch a bottle, Mr. Mobley."

He drug a fingernail across the bottle label then shrugged. "Eh. Whatever."

"But. I am sorry, Mobley. Leanne said she talked to the manager. She made him understand. Had him talk to the witness. He knows you were just helping me. They saved your tips, and you can go back to The Blue Calypso."

He stared down at the water swirling around his shoes. I leaned down; unsure he had heard me. "Um. If you wanted to."

"Thanks, Ms. Stefannneeee," he said finally. He looked up and wiped the water from his eyes. "You don't have to be out here. In the rain. Or say anything else. It's shokay."

"Ah. Right, then. Well. Take care." I looked again back up the street and could see even from this distance Leanne's impatient tapping of her foot on the pavement waiting for me. She was equally drenched as Mobley and me, no doubt. The difference is that I don't think Mobley really cared one way or another. He took the final drink the bottle had to offer and hiccupped.

"Look. Mobley," I began, knowing I had to do something. "Just… just come on back." There. I said it. It had probably been on my mind for a while, I just had been too much of a coward to act on it. "Come with me. Right now. I'll hire you back. We'll get you in some dry clothes and… you can have your old room back." Oddly enough, I did not feel any regret.

He looked up at me, his eyes glazed. "Wha?"

"Come on back, Mobley." He blinked up at me, not seeming to comprehend what I was saying. "I said *I'll hire you back*." I couldn't enunciate more clearly, yet he still sat there, silent. "Well? Come on, then," I finally said. It was time to just get him moving. The rum was hitting full force now and he was approaching a catatonic state. I reached down and started to pull him up.

"To Storny Book? Back?" he asked incredulously, seeming to disbelieve me.

"Yes, yes. Let's just go, okay? I'll send someone back for your things tomorrow."

100

"Thank… you. Ms. Stuff..aneee."

"You're welcome. Mr. Mobley." I put my arm around his waist to steady him and he nearly pulled us both over. The bottle of rum fell to the side and rolled down the sidewalk. Up the street, I could see Leanne making exasperated arm motions indicating I should NOT be bringing Mobley back.

"Ya know? Know what, Ms. Stufff," - he hiccupped again - "anny?"

"Um, what? Can you walk a little faster? I'd really like to get to the Rover."

"I know we have had a… rough time. You an meeee."

I felt a tinge of concern. He was going to say something obnoxious. "Yes. Right." Perhaps after he insulted me, I could drop him and move on without further concern, my guilt over him completely assuaged."

"I jush wanted you to know. Ta know…" He stopped as we shuffled along. Another hiccup. "Secret. A seeeecret."

"Secret?" I knew I shouldn't ask, but I did anyway. "What secret?"

"What?" he muttered in surprise, having lost his train of drunk thought. He looked around, dazed.

I rolled my eyes. The rum was hitting him like a sack of bricks. He must have started downing the bottle the moment he got tossed out of The Blue Calypso.

"God damn. You were saying, Mobley… You wanted me to know something!"

"Yes. I've always thought… you are so… very beautiful."

I stopped pulling him for a moment as this sank in. He looked squarely into my eyes, serious. It was odd because, in that moment, he sounded completely sober. Despite myself, he had melted my heart. At least for the moment. "Thas it. My… seecret."

I forcibly shrugged it off. Surely, it was just drunk talk. "And you won't remember *that* tomorrow, Mr. Mobley," I added laughing, continuing our trek. He would be

101

back to whoring with any woman that would have him in less than half a fortnight. And I would soon be getting pissed, trying to keep him from sullying the reputation of Stoney Brook with his scandalous behavior.

He pointed up the street. "Is... is that... is it... Leannnne?"

"Yes. Yes, that's Leanne. Can you just move a little faster?"

"Leannnne! Leeeee annnne... Tillldum!" He looked over at me matter-of-factly. "She hurted my balls something fierce, Ms. Stufff... any. Really... really.... bigly..." I laughed at this and could only imagine what was going through Leanne's mind as she watched us approach.

He swung his face close to mine, his breath ripe with alcohol. "Ack. Please."

"Shhhhe may not... be exACTLY happy... about me comin bakkkk."

Leanne stared at me hard before getting on the other side of Mobley to help drag him to the Rover. "Good gawd, what have you gone and done," she moaned. "Bringing home a stray? This evening has certainly been eventful."

"She'll be just fine with it. I'm sure," I told Mobley, looking across to Leanne. I would have laughed except that I was drenched and getting tired of dragging him. "Especially if she has your balls to squish again."

We pushed-lifted-rolled Mobley into the Land Rover.

"Yayyy." He fell over on his side onto the seat.

CHAPTER 5

RUM, RALPHING - AND REGRETS

Morgan: Morning arrived. Very late morning, evidently. After I opened my eyes, it slowly began to come back to me. The melee at The Blue Calypso. At the moment, I am hurting like a featherless chicken at the dog pound. At first, I didn't even know where I was. When I tossed the covers off and sat on the edge of the bed, I had to think - clean sheets, nice furniture, big room, large windows with a great view of the tropical mountains. I wasn't in my seedy little one-room rental over The Blue Calypso. Nor was I in my little bug-infested charity bed that has the chewed gum wads stuck all over the frame (the frame was a recent addition to the squalor of my room as I continued to move up in the world).

Now… my surroundings are much more opulent. Comfortable. And familiar. I am in my old room at Stoney Brook. On the nightstand, I even have a small pad of paper and pen to use for this entry for my journal. The only thing I have on is my underwear and a t-shirt. My jeans and shirt are hanging on the bedpost. Had I managed to undress myself? I doubted it.

I remember- I punched Stefany's asshole husband because he was getting ready to knock her lights out. Then the boss fired me because he thought I lost my cool on some innocent customer. He also kicked me out of my room rental as well.

I had bought a bottle of rum. My attitude was if I was going to be broke, jobless, AND homeless, by God I was going to get hammered. I certainly never thought that Stefany Michaels would be the cause of losing the Calypso job. She was like a tornado, tearing her way through my life.

The pounding headache is not going away anytime soon. Stefany had been talking to me about something. Something... Maybe bringing me back to Stoney Brook? Hiring me back? And Leanne had been there. Is this why I'm in my old room?

I am in for an uncomfortable conversation up in Stefany's office.

After showering and putting on the only clothes I had, I opened the door to the hallway and peered out. There were no armed guards. Stefany and Leanne were not waiting with clubs. What should I do now? It was time to pay whatever piper I needed to pay. And that would be Stefany. I started to make my way to her office.

One of the servant girls approached. She was new, carrying my travel bag and backpack that someone had apparently retrieved from my room at The Blue Calypso. She smiled knowingly.

"Hello, Mr. Mobley. On behalf of everyone, welcome back."

"I'm back?" I asked, just to be certain.

"Of course," she answered, seemingly perplexed that I would ask.

"I can take my things, thank you," I said reaching for my gear.

"I've got them. You had better go see Ms. Michaels." She brushed past me resolutely. I checked her out as she walked away. How long could she evade my charms? Perhaps later I could test the waters, I thought. She was quite cute. I stopped, thinking to myself. Had I learned *nothing*? I was insufferable! I was hell-bent on Stefany firing me before even getting over my hangover. I continued my walk-of-the-damned to Stefany's office.

Standing outside the large doors to her office, I took a deep breath and knocked.

"Yes, come in." The response was in Stefany's voice.

I opened the door and stuck my head in. "Hi. Ms. Stef... er... Michaels. May I come in?" I wanted to kick myself. Was I bound and determined to ruin my opportunity?

She calmly laid her pen aside that she was using on a pile of papers and apprised me inquisitively.

"Mr. Mobley. Yes, come in, I was expecting you. I see you survived the night."

After walking in, I closed the door and approached her desk. I felt like a little kid getting called into the principal's office. She motioned with her hand for me to take a seat in front of the desk. Casually dressed in a t-shirt and a mangy ball cap, she was as beautiful as ever. I couldn't tell what she was wearing behind the desk.

She brushed a lock of hair from her eyes, saying nothing. We sat in uneasy silence, looking at each other.

"Soooo," I finally said.

"Yes. So," she repeated, content to let me continue.

"Um. Thank you, Ms. Michaels. Thanks for bringing me back." My voice cracked. "I very much appreciate it."

"You don't remember a thing, do you?" she glibly asked.

"I punched your husband. Then I was fired. And then I got drunk. I vaguely remember seeing you. And Leanne. Um. That's about it."

"That's not too bad, Mr. Mobley. That's all *fairly* accurate."

"And... you brought me back here."

"Yes. Back here. I am in your debt, and I thank you for your intervention. He and I... are currently estranged."

"He was going to hit you. In the face. Hard. Estranged may be a little... easy on him."

"I appreciate your concern," she said, sounding slightly irritated. "But I'll handle him, Mr. Mobley. I don't need a rum-soaked lecture."

That was a bit harsh, I thought. "Right, sorry. He's... done this before, has he?" I asked, knowing I was probably treading in forbidden waters.

"Yes." She offered nothing more.

I rubbed my chin, uneasy under her gaze. "Did you... hire me back? Or. Is this just temporary."

"I did, yes. If you want the job again. At your previously agreed salary. Or you can go back to The Blue Calypso. It's your call."

"Then, yes. I would like my job back."

"If you get the urge to leave after making enough to get off the island, Mr. Mobley, I will want two weeks of notice. No sudden departures in the middle of something."

"Sure. I understand."

"Fine. It's all set then. Anticipating your answer, I arranged to have your belongings retrieved from The Blue Calypso and placed back in your room. Although, based on what I heard, I shudder to think of what may have crawled into your bag from your previous quarters at the Calypso. I understand there is a certain amount of earnings and tip money that goes to you as well. You'll find it in an envelope on the dresser in your room. Eduardo, the owner, sends his regrets at the misunderstanding and thanks you for your service. I believe that he also issued you a bar credit in appreciation of what you did."

I blinked in amazement. She hadn't missed a beat, talking like she was reading from a teleprompter.

"Eduardo also mentioned something about you being a better customer than a worker and would welcome you back, anytime. That said, the same rules apply here as previously laid out to you."

"Um. Now that I'm back, I was wondering if… possibly… you would consider a pay increase, um… if you could see fit," I began, giving her my best smile, wondering how generous she was feeling after having saved her from Miles. "I'm sure you could admit, my initial contract was low-ball, my responsibilities really warrant a bit more- "

"Wait. Did you… Are you," she was practically spitting out the words, leading me to believe I had made an error in judgment in asking. "Am I *hearing* you right that you are so unbelievably audacious… and shameless… and so out of touch with reality… as to ask for a raise after ALL that has happened? Correct me if I'm wrong. But that's what it sounds like. Am I right?"

Sitting uncomfortably, I wrung my hands and pretended to tidy my shirt, realizing it had been a bad time to bring it up. Oh well.

"It was just a… thought. My apologies."

"If you have a *thought* in that cavernous, empty vacuum of a balloon you call a head, keep it to yourself." She was losing her temper and I could tell she was trying to restrain herself. I feigned a hurt expression. She hadn't changed a bit; I could clearly see.

"I'm sorry, Mr. Mobley. That was… an unwarranted snide remark. I don't need to be insulting." She cracked several knuckles below the desk. "Despite seeing that you have NO better judgment now than when you first left. Let's move on." She took a deep breath, seeming to try and steady her nerves. "Okay. As for your duties here… and given your recent blundering incompetence in management… you are *more* than compensated justly. Do I make myself clear?"

"Yes, Ms. Michaels. Perfectly."

"Of all the fucking nerve…" she said under her breath as she glanced out a window. She was drumming her fingers on the desk, seemingly trying to find the patience to continue. "Oversee the work directly, Mr. Mobley, I can't afford another… *fiasco*… such as what happened with the concrete spill, gallant as you were, taking the fall for your men. Men who you should have been watching closely, I might add. It still cost me a lot of money. Money that we simply can't afford to piss away. And it pains me not to take it out of either your hide or your salary." She sat back smugly in her chair, satisfied she had been unable to restrain herself entirely from being nasty. She brightened suddenly. "In fact, if we are to come to terms here today, I will be docking your pay by… fifteen percent. Until such time as you can prove yourself. Now. Do you still want to work here? I can arrange for you to be driven back to the village immediately if you prefer."

Seeing that working at Stoney Brook paid much more than The Blue Calypso, I had little recourse but to accept. Now making less than even Miguel and Santiago, and most of the other staff, I chided myself for wanting more. "I understand, yes. Less fifteen percent agreed." I uncrossed my legs and clenched the armrests of the chair, thinking I could finally leave.

"*And...* no whoring the staff girls," she added quickly as an afterthought. "Keep your depraved knob wallowing off the estate."

I nodded in hungover humiliation and tried to hide my indignation. Evidently, she wasn't going to pull any punches - DESPITE my good deed. Her ungrateful haranguing was beginning to get under my skin, and I hadn't been back but a few hours. I stood and tried to leave.

"AND..." she added quickly stopping me in my tracks, evidently not finished with me. "...no committing lechery on any unsuspecting village women, OR guests... for that matter."

I couldn't help myself. "Am I to be celibate now, Ms. Michaels?" Upon hearing this unwise retort, her lips formed a narrow, scornful frown, thoroughly chilling any goodwill we had developed for each other.

"*Any* knot-holing is to be done far, far away from Stoney Brook and on your own time. Do we understand each other, Mr. Mobley? Should your decadent behavior be anything less than discreet, or if it reflects poorly in any way on Stoney Brook, I'll be more than happy to fire you. Again." She appraised me with a regretful, sour expression. "Off you go, then, and I hope this isn't a mistake on my part. See the crew and get back up to speed. You should know I have not the least bit of sympathy for a hangover."

Having managed to embarrass me despite the circumstances of me saving her ass from her abusive husband the previous evening, I nodded to her in acknowledgment. Again, I tried to leave. Stefany was still the shrewish, spiketitted windbag she previously was. She held up a hand indicating there was more.

"Um. Yes, Ms. Michaels?"

"First things first, I almost forgot. Last night, you threw up *twice* in the back of my Rover, Mr. Mobley. Rum. Copious amounts of rum. And the remnants of whatever disgusting thing that was your last snack, yesterday evening. I'm guessing chicken wings in bar-b-que sauce. There is a limit to my charity, you should know. I want it cleaned. Thoroughly. And deodorized."

"Yes, Ms. Michaels. Um. Sorry. I'll get right on that."

She nodded and resumed writing in her papers, indicating the conversation was over.

"Thanks, Ms. Michaels. For bringing me back. Really. I do appreciate it."

She was mumbling below her breath. "Wanting a fucking raise, indeed."

Okay, wanting a raise had been a bad idea. I turned and walked out, closing her office door behind me, finally free. She was so incredibly ungrateful after I had stopped her husband from using her face as a punching bag.

However, I would be making decent money again despite the decrease in pay. I would just have to be more careful and not gamble or drink it away. And I would again have a nice room. So, all in all, it was a win.

"Ugh." I rubbed my eyes knowing I had not escaped a monumental hangover. My stomach lurched and a headache was drilling its way through my brain. It was going to take an extra dose of ibuprofen this morning to get me going.

Staggering back to my room, I threw open the door and ran to the bathroom, my stomach heaving. I dropped to my knees in front of the commode, my head spinning, vision blurring. There was nothing left to vomit, I realized mid-way through a dry heave, the irony of having to clean Stefany's Rover not lost to me. Beads of sweat rolled down my face. "I'll never drink again," I mumbled, knowing I would probably be drinking again that very evening. It was a traditional chant.

Thoughts tumbled in my mind. How would I clean Stefany's Rover? What did one use to remove vomit from a car seat? My stomach heaved again at the thought.

"Mr. Mobley! Welcome back. I thought you might be... *up*, so to speak. Your door was ajar. Please do excuse the intrusion. No need to stop doing what you are doing on my account. Please. Do go ahead."

It was Leanne, of all people. And of all times to come in. She stood behind me, snickering.

"Leanne. Please... please just... leave." I sat up, trying to regain some composure, only having to return to the bowl for another dry heave. How could I have been so stupid to not close the door on the way in?

The water was running behind me in the sink. After a moment, she was kneeling beside me with a wet, cool washcloth. I was not so sick that I didn't notice she was wearing a very sexy mini skirt. It bunched up as she knelt, revealing her spectacular legs. Her top was equally enticing. Breasts, wonderfully luminous, bounteous orbs, restrained by a thin thread of fabric, mere inches away from my face.

What was I thinking!? I was incorrigible. Had it been that long since I was with a woman? The thought occurred to me that I was every bit the horny mongrel that Stefany and Leanne thought I was. Even as I was assaulted by a massive hangover.

She pushed me up to a sitting position, flushed the toilet, and continued to wipe my face. It was a surprising gesture, even if she was still smirking. She brushed several damp locks of my hair from my face with her fingers. "Should I have a few shots of rum brought to the room to celebrate your return, Mr. Mobley?"

"Nooo," I managed to reply, heaving again.

"C'mon, Mobley," she said, clearly amused. "You should get back into bed for a while." She pulled me to my feet and helped me walk back to the bed, which was fortunate as I was weak as a kitten. I fell from her grasp, however, landing flatly on the bed face first with the lower part of my legs hanging off the edge. I managed the strength to roll over and moan, reminding me of a similar move I made when I was a kid playing army soldier, pretending I had been shot. School mates would tend to my "wounds" until the bell signaling the end to recess. My performances were legendary on the elementary playgrounds, earning many encore requests. It elicited an uncontrolled smirk from Leanne. She wiped my face again with the cool rag, which was surprisingly soothing.

"Leanne. Is this some trick? You are planning on humiliating me in some way. Aren't you?"

"Why, no, Mobley. But it is a prudent suggestion," she replied. "Maybe worthy of consideration later."

Pouring a glass of water from a pitcher on the nightstand, she pulled me to a sitting position and held the glass to my lips. I managed several drinks. Letting me drop onto a pillow, she pulled a sheet over me.

I looked up at her while I held the sheet just up under my chin. "You are being nice to me. Why?"

"When have I *not* been nice to you," she asked dismissively, patting my cheek.

"Oh, I don't know, Leanne. It was such a rich history before I was fired here. Like. Maybe when you threatened to tell Stefany about me not having an architect's license. Or when you spilled wine down the back of my shirt and claimed you tripped. Or when you told several fathers of some of the girls I dated where I lived. Or when you took one of the condoms in my room and drew a picture on it and hung it on my door. Somehow you got a key and put itching powder in my bed, I know damn well it was you. Tabasco in my coffee. When you had one of the servant girls cut holes in my underwear down in the laundry room, again I know it was you. The nut grappling that last day. Or when-"

"Eh, we don't need to rehash ancient history, Mobley," she interrupted. "We are friends now. And that's all that counts." Her gleeful smile told me that I was in extreme danger. "Right?"

"Yeah. Okay. If you say so." I expected her to assassinate me at any moment.

She leaned down and kissed the top of my head. I looked up at her, shocked.

"What you did for Stefany… protecting her from that ass-wipe husband of hers. I appreciate what you did. And I have a whole new opinion of you, Mobley," she said, patting my stomach lightly through the sheet. "Not that I necessarily hated you before. You are a typical man, let's not forget. But I do have a new affection for you. I do think of you as my… friend. I'll tell Stefany that you are out with the boys, so you don't get in trouble. Get some rest before you go out for a new start."

With that, she softly ran a hand along my face as she turned and walked out.

I blinked in dazed confusion trying to sort out what just happened. My only remaining thought, of course, was when I could see her naked now that she might be into me.

Stefany: Mr. Architect is back at Stoney Brook. Ugh. The thought has me filled with mixed emotions: Revulsion  **on one hand, and an exasperated acceptance of circumstance on the other.**

He took out Miles for me, and I am grateful to him for that. Miles has deeply deserved that fist in his fucking face for

years. I would have most certainly had a black eye, maybe a swollen jaw if the abuse had been typical of what I usually received.

Leanne thinks Mobley is a hero, of sorts, and is worthy of a second chance.  Whatever. I suppose I do appreciate what he did. But it's hard to fathom her change of heart about Mr. Architect. She speaks of him now in almost friendly terms. Perhaps as one talks of their pet. Mobley as Leanne's pet???? I am at a loss.

Mobley looks good, in that, Leanne is certainly right. I've said it before and I'll say it again. Despite what I think of him, it is enjoyable to watch him and his pecs … and abs… and sensuous eyes… and amazing man-ass… and hot curly blond hair… back at work at Stoney Brook. As a physical specimen, Mobley has it going  on. All the things I WRONGLY hired him for in the first place. If only he didn't have the personality and intellect of an impudent, poxed toad. The empty head on his shoulders should be a huge turn-off to anyone of the female persuasion. And yet the women staff are all abuzz, thrilled that he's back. The men too are taken in by his manly-man charm and testosterone-ish charisma. The collective IQ of the plantation has fallen by about 50 points.

Now if I can just keep from strangling him.

It was nearly 9:00 pm. I poured another glass of wine and downed it, feeling sorry for myself.

Sitting alone in my office, I looked over the report the accountant sent along with several bank statements. At the current rate of growth in revenue with guests coming to stay at Stoney Brook along with all other sources of income, I still would not be able to overcome the interest payments on our loans. We were slowly sinking into insolvency. With the best-case scenario, it was uncertain if I could pay back my loans in a timely manner and still turn a profit. If Stoney Brook would begin having 100% occupancy, it would still be difficult.

My stomach churned, as I sensed the first indications that my dream was perhaps soon coming to an end. And after I had poured my heart and soul into it. I picked up my mobile to text.

Me: Are you busy? Can we talk?

I drank another glass of wine, waiting for her to text back.

Leanne: Sure, come on by the room! I have tequila
☺

Picking up the papers, I turned off my desk lamp and walked out of my office, heading towards Leanne's room. Her two "sex" slaves, Joe and Heidi had recently returned from the mainland, and she had no doubt been enjoying their company in the privacy of their adjoining rooms.

Arriving at her door, I knocked. Hesitating for a moment, I considered walking quickly away and around the corner. Perhaps getting her input on these statements could come later. Would I be interrupting some kinky sexual romp?

I tried to reassure myself. She had always been extremely open about her sexual proclivities but I'm sure she would not make me feel uncomfortable. I put my ear to the door, wondering if I would hear chains, whips, and moans. Nothing.

Giving my best resting-bitch-face expression, I had to ask myself - was I disappointed? I wasn't certain.

Slave Joe suddenly opened the door, catching me listening. I stood upright as quickly as I could, but it was too late. He acted like nothing was amiss, which was fine with me.

He was wearing only his underwear that featured his very hard erection that was stretching the fabric. That, and a leather collar that sported a dangling leash of about 3 feet.

"Good evening, Mistress Michaels. Please come in. We were expecting you." His accent sounded European.

His state of undress gave me pause. I forced my eyes to his face. "Uh. It can probably wait. Thank you!"

Just as I turned to walk away, I could hear Leanne calling me. "Nonsense, Stef, come on in. Don't be alarmed, he's harmless."

Reluctantly, I turned and entered, carefully navigating around Joe's welcoming pike to find Leanne relaxing on her sofa in a short evening dress, a slit seductively running up one side. Judging by her exposed hip, it appeared she wasn't wearing anything else. I had to wonder if she had thrown that dress on at a moment's notice. Reading a book by a floor lamp, the room was alighted with a dozen or so candles, giving a warm, sensuous glow. Jazz music on a low level added to the ambiance.

The slave girl, Heidi, lay on the floor in front of Leanne. If I were not under the effects of half a bottle of wine, I probably would have been more shocked. Unlike Joe, she was completely naked, again except for a leather collar and leash. The end of the leash lay on the sofa cushion, assumingly for quick retrieval. The riding crop that I had previously witnessed her using in the reading lounge was also within easy reach. Leanne, legs crossed, had one foot resting casually on Heidi's throat. I had to look twice, to be sure I wasn't just seeing things. Nope. She was using Heidi's throat to rest her foot on. Okay. I didn't anticipate that one.

Using some type of oil, the girl was adoringly massaging Leanne's legs and the one foot from Leanne's crossed leg that dangled over her head. She seemed not the least worried about Leanne's foot resting on her throat, although it didn't seem to cause the girl any discomfort. I assumed it had some sort of sexual dominant psychological intent. I had to wonder if I was in an alternate universe. I was sure I had seen this on Animal Planet with lions or wolves… or something.

"Doesn't that… *distract you*… from actually reading?" I was thinking maybe the jugular vein, pulsing. Maybe that was distracting. Or maybe the fact a little additional pressure and Heidi could be rendered unconscious. Did I have good guest insurance?

Leanne shrugged. "To a certain point, yes. In a good way, if they are doing their job well."

"Um. I see. I really could talk to you at another time…"

"No, please. Have a seat," Leanne countered, gesturing towards a chair. She closed her book and held it up to Joe, who promptly took it to a nearby table.

Weirder, more repulsive shit I had never even imagined. Leanne was a classy woman, yet here she was engaged in behavior worse than what chimps would do while foisting over each other at the zoo. How anyone could get excited by such trashy, shack-house perversions was beyond me. After checking for errant cushion stains, I grudgingly took her up on her offer and sat down.

Seeing Leanne pampered by her sex slaves wasn't really on my agenda for the evening, but maybe it wasn't that big of a deal. I must admit, I was a bit curious about what went on with Leanne's Dominant – submissive sexual lifestyle. Leanne informed me once that you always write Dominant with a capital D, submissive with a little s. Whatever, Leanne. Restraining an outward burst of laughter, I determined that I wouldn't judge. Unlike me, at least she was getting some, albeit in a stranger fashion than I would have.

"Bring us both a shot of tequila. Salt the rim and include a thin slice of lime on each," she ordered. Joe made a beeline for the suite bar. If only my workers around Stoney Brook would move that quickly upon command.

"I don't nee- "

"Nonsense. I was looking for an excuse to open that bottle," Leanne said, motioning for Joe to proceed. "The finest 100% blue agave tequila. Not to be beat. Pardon the pun." She laughed at her own joke.

He returned shortly with two shot glasses of chilled tequila. "Thank you," I said looking up into his eyes. He bowed courteously. He was quite a handsome man. If I were to see him on the street, I would never imagine that he would be a submissive sex slave. I would imagine him more in tiny work-out shorts, sweating away on a treadmill, the envy of every woman at a nearby gym. And he'd probably be gay.

My eyes briefly flashed over his nicely muscled arms… his mid-torso… His excitement had not abated. Sweat had formed in small beads over his abdominals, evidently from whatever exertions he had engaged in before I arrived. What had he been doing? Realizing that I was staring, I self-consciously averted my eyes, catching Leanne grinning. I held my shot glass up to her. "You do have good taste in tequila, Leanne."

"As I'm sure you do," she said amicably with a nod.

I have no tastes, I thought, bitterly. Especially in men. Look at that loser, Miles.

We didn't down our shots, but instead went slow to enjoy the fine quality, tasting a bit of salt with each sip. We finished the ceremony, sucking the small sliver of lime with a loud slurp. It was smooth and delicious. Just like Joe's well-shaped ass and thighs. She sent him back for another round as our conversation bantered back and forth for a few minutes around the latest gossip on the island. I was surprised Mobley's name didn't once come up.

After our third shot of tequila, I waved off any more as I had already been tipsy from the wine in my office when I arrived.

"Always the cautious one, eh, Cuz?" Leanne added, reluctantly letting Joe take our shot glasses.

"Moderation, Leanne." Although I'm not sure it was moderation on my part. I had already drunk far too much beyond my limit for the evening. By now I was feeling drunk.

"You are always moderate. I don't know that I've ever seen you rip-roaring smashed drunk. I'll have to put that on my 'to do' list," she said with a grin. "I challenge you to come out of your *moderate* shell, Stef."

"I don't have time for that," I replied defensively.

"Sure, you do. You just don't know it. *Yet.* I suspect that beneath that good-girl-next-door-facade, you may be far wilder than even me, Cuz."

With that, I scrunched my nose at her sarcastically to which she rolled her eyes.

Joe returned with his ever-vigilant hard-on to stand quietly, waiting for Leanne to command him. Was he on

119

Viagra? I had to wonder. Maybe that whole four hours and "call a doctor" was a needless worry for Leanne.

"Do you mind if I continue to keep them busy, Stef? If it makes you uncomfortable, I can send them to their rooms."

Busy? I had to wonder what would qualify as busy. Curiosity was getting the better of me this evening. "Err, no. I suppose not," I answered against my better judgment. I would blame any malfeasance on the tequila later, I thought to myself jokingly.

Leanne snapped her fingers and Joe immediately dropped to his knees on the floor. I started to regret my decision to let them stay when I saw Heidi open her legs so that Joe could orally service her. She made a whimpering little moan as Joe found his mark, apparently working with practiced skill.

Oh God, here they go, I thought to myself. Horning on each other like unrepentant alley cats. Considering leaving, the alcohol began to weigh me down, five-ton anchor style. Perhaps after a few minutes more.

Heidi's hips ground slightly up into his face with his ministrations. So, this was keeping them busy, evidently. I was not entirely surprised, although the scene was raising my heart rate. And why, I was not certain. Was it enticing? Shocking? Was I a closet voyeur? I nearly laughed aloud at this last thought. Even with me sitting there, they continued without the slightest of inhibitions. I'm sure my eyes were wide as sand dollars. I'm not so sure I wasn't getting turned on.

"What gives?" Leanne asked, looking at the papers in my hand as if everything going on was completely normal. I had to assume for her it was, although she doubtless thought it was amusing to see my initial reactions to how she and her companions carried on behind closed doors.

"Its. Um." I tried to gather my thoughts and ignore the hedonistic scene. I leaned over and handed the papers to Leanne. Damn, Joe looked like he knew what he was doing.

Heidi's magnificent toned, tanned legs framed his head. Her calf and thigh muscles alternately contracting and relaxing. The candlelight gleamed off the sweat that glazed their bodies.

The wine… and now tequila… were making me want to go out and dance, not talk boring numbers. And if not dance, then maybe not sit on the sidelines watching Heidi and Joe have all the fun. "Well, it's the statement from the accountant. And it still isn't looking good, Leanne."

"Even with the pick-up in new guest bookings?"

"No. It's my debt load. Perhaps I chewed off more than I should have to start things off. Maybe… I should have gone slower. Maybe restore only one part of the estate at a time." The booze for the evening was taking effect. I felt warm and relaxed and less concerned about the bad news from the accountant. My eyes drifted and caught myself watching the action on the floor beneath Leanne's feet. When was the last time I had a man doing that between my legs? I thought of Miles. Miles doesn't eat pussy; he would openly admit. He only liked to receive oral, not give it. Selfish shit that he is.

Leanne, seeing my expression, smiled down at Heidi, rolling her foot lightly across the girl's throat who was apparently orgasming… her legs now in spasms, her back arched. "She is a good girl, Cuz. I'm glad to have Joe and her back for a while."

It was just too weird, and I laughed aloud. Leanne arched her brows inquisitively, also amused. "What. You think this is odd, don't you, Stef."

"It's different. I'll say that. It's not something you see every day."

"True. Does it excite you?" she asked me bluntly.

I blinked, taken back by the question. "Excite? I don't know if I would say that, Leanne. It's just... different. I've never had anyone having sex in front of me."

"They wouldn't be doing this in front of most guests. I knew you would be open-minded. And not judge or be offended." She smiled disarmingly. I felt like a fly trapped in a spider's web. This was much more difficult to watch than Leanne's first demonstration in the reading lounge. Much more. This was enticing, I had to admit.

"No. I'm not offended." I squirmed in my chair slightly and tried to keep my eyes off Joe who continued to diligently perform cunnilingus. The muscles in his back flexed as he lifted her hips to his face. Heidi's strong legs likewise flexed and bowed, her feet on his back, pressing, forcing herself up into him.

"But... this does excite you, doesn't it, Stef?" Leanne slyly asked again.

"Perhaps a little. I don't know that I could ever... um... ever... use someone as a footrest," I clarified, laughing.

"You never know," Leanne smirked. "It's all in the mind. There's a lot more than just that, as you can see. Being a sexual dominant is a state of mind, just as being a submissive. It's about what gets us off. If everyone were to honestly explore their sexuality, they would find they prefer one or the other. Some prefer both. They are called *switches*. Heidi, for example, is a bi-sexual switch. Joe is a submissive. *And* straight as an arrow. He's only in it for the women. People's tastes are enormously diverse and varied. It is an erotic, sensual state of mind to engage in BDSM. I'm not a full-timer, nor are they. But we enjoy it fully when we get together. And I never make them do anything they don't want to do."

"Ahhh. Do you allow them to see other people?"

"Date? Yes, with conditions. They must first obtain permission from me. They are my subs, I'm their Dom. I can see whoever I want, and they understand that and accept it as part of their role in service to me."

"And Mobley?" I asked. "I'm surprised he hasn't come on to you."

Leanne laughed. "Mobley? Funny you should ask. No. Whenever I do see him around the plantation, he has been very well behaved. I do like teasing him though. A little flash here. A little flirting comment there. Make him sweat. Despite that, he has been a perfect gentleman. Besides. He has his eye on another."

"Oh, really? Who!?" This was a bit of news I had not heard.

Leanne smiled. "I don't know if I should tell you."

I felt my blood boil. That hairy-balled bastard, Mobley, was after one of the women staff members, even after being warned. "Tell me! I should have known he couldn't keep his pants up for long."

"He actually hasn't done anything with her, Stef. Not yet, at least. Settle down," she smirked.

"Nevertheless. I need to stay on top of this, so it doesn't get out of hand. Who is she, Leanne?"

"You," Leanne said with a grin.

I had to let this sink in for a moment before I could respond. "Er... what? That's preposterous!"

"You haven't seen the way he's looked at you? Come on, Stef. He has it bad for you. You aren't blind, surely, you've noticed."

"No! I have *not* noticed, and I'm sure you are wrong!"

Leanne gave me a mocking sideways look. "Am I? You had better get *on top of it*, Stef," she joked, using my own words against me. Heidi, moaning louder was apparently orgasming yet again, her hips thrusting more violently into Joe's face, who was redoubling his efforts to bring her to satisfaction.

Ignoring all of this, I kept my eyes off them and concentrated on Leanne's amused expression. "I'm quite sure Mobley hates me, Leanne. I'm not very nice to him. He is only staying on for the money."

"Stef. He's in *love* with you, *duhhhhh*," she said before rubbing her toes across Heidi's mouth as she orgasmed. Leanne's other foot remained on her throat, now pressing a little harder as she came. The veins in Heidi's neck were visibly swollen, pulsing beneath Leanne's foot. Heidi's tongue lashed around Leanne's toes, her breathing hard.

I wiped at the sweat beginning to bead on my forehead. It was bloody hot in here with these perverts, I decided. Couldn't they put on a damn fan or the air conditioning? I stared at Leanne, disbelieving that Mobley could be in love with me. "No. I'll never believe that. And... why do you do that?! That... foot on her neck... thing."

"For those that know, a beautiful woman's feet are a sensuous and erotic extension of her sexuality."

Leanne took the leash and gave it a little snap. Joe and Heidi stood up immediately, waiting expectantly for direction.

"Get the oil, Heidi. My cousin is next. Joe, you are to help."

The two descended on me before I knew what was happening. "Ha! No, Leanne, but thank you very much," I said, standing, then regretting the tequila shots.

"Sit down, Cuz. It will be mild, don't worry. You need to de-stress. And what's better than a little massage."

Joe took my hand with a smile and encouraged me to sit down. Reluctantly, I sat, and Heidi began untying the laces of my work sneakers. She pulled them off, then my socks.

"What are they going to do?" I asked Leanne with growing alarm.

"Nothing too salacious. Massage," she offered, watching me with amusement.

The two began kissing my feet and legs, massaging, rubbing, and licking me. Heidi began rubbing a warm oil over my legs. It must have been an edible oil because both licked it off as quickly as they had applied it. I wanted to leave. Sort of. "Leanne, this is massage?!"

"Massage, yes. The mouth is integral in a good massage, as are the hands. Open mind, Stef, open mind."

Heidi had my left foot in her hands. She popped first my big toe, then each of the others successively into her hot

124

mouth, one by one, making me squirm. It was so ticklish I felt like exploding out of the chair. I felt self-conscious knowing I had not showered since the previous evening. Were they sweaty? Did they smell? Neither consideration seemed to be of any concern as they continued like locusts on a crop of corn.

"You'll get used to it," Leanne commented, seeing that I was ticklish.

Joe was running his tongue along my right calve, his fingers simultaneously kneading. If there had been oil, it was gone, replaced by wet trails of saliva.

I looked back at Heidi, her mouth now completely on the ball of my left foot. "Leanne. But. She's a woman! I'm not. You know."

"Bi-sexual?" She laughed loudly. "Maybe not, Stef. But how do you know? Have you ever wondered? And anyway, there isn't anything too risqué here. She's just giving you a foot and leg massage. And using her mouth a little. No biggie. Just relax and enjoy it."

It did feel good. Amazing in fact. Both rubbing and massaging my legs was incredibly relaxing. Even their wet mouths, which I would have thought would be extremely uncomfortable to me, were soothing. And there was something else. It was powerful- their servitude erotic. It is hard to explain but having them on their knees in front of me, serving me in such a way... it was, as Leanne put it once before... a *rush*.

Leanne, intently watching my expressions nodded with a smile. "So. Not so bad, is it?"

"No. I suppose not," I managed to gasp as my fingers dug harder into the arms of the chair. Their ministrations were having a bit of a different effect by this time. Disgusted with myself, I found myself getting turned on. More turned on, rather. Maybe it had just been too long since I had had sex. Whatever the case, I could feel my breath getting shorter. I could feel the juncture between my legs getting progressively wetter. Very wet. Much more of this and I would spot the shorts I was wearing. A tinge of embarrassment crept in. Then left.

"If you want them to do more, it's no big deal, Stef. Just say so, and I'll step out of the room for a bit. Give you some privacy."

"No! Nooo. That's ok." Thoughts were swirling in my head, not the least of which was the idea that in addition to a man turning me on, I was also getting hot from being dog-lapped by a woman. It was all very confusing, having my ideas of who I was, morally, physically, emotionally, sexually… turned upside down.

Joe reached behind me, gently pulling my hips forward in the seat, his eyes looking up at me with a pleading subservience. He slowly spread my legs. Feeling increasingly helpless to desires I was not even certain I could identify, Heidi's mouth had moved further up my leg, now making little swirling motions with her tongue on my inner thighs. Joe spread my legs as wide as he could get me, now his own mouth on an inner thigh. Two heads bobbing about between my legs. I was lost in a sea of desire and lust, mixed with the need to maintain control. Whatever control I thought I had was quickly dissipating. Leanne, smiling, got up and left the room.

"Leanne! Wait! I don't…" I moaned softly as Heidi's mouth covered me through my shorts. Her hot, wet breath nearly sent me over the edge. Was she blowing hot air through my shorts?

Maybe I could enjoy what she was doing if she just stayed on the outside of my shorts. Yes. That was the ticket. That, maybe I could accept. Maybe? I tried to justify this all in my mind as just having been too long out of the saddle. This turn of events was certainly not what I had foreseen for the evening. Maybe it was just the wine. And tequila. Excuses. Bring on the excuses.

Ignoring my unspoken inhibitions, Heidi continued with her hot breath. Her mouth was separated from me by only a thin strip of fabric. She looked up at me with pleading eyes. Watching her work was incredibly erotic. Another woman. On her knees. Pleasuring me. It was not my idea of who I was. Her tongue began darting around the edges of my shorts, teasing me, playing for more. Joe reached up and gently began to massage my breasts from outside of my shirt. I bit my lower lip as my hips began to gyrate and thrust uncontrollably. Joe took my hand in his and placed it on her head, closing my fingers around a wad of her hair, indicating I should grip it tight.

"We like a firm hand," he whispered up to me. "Very firm." He returned to his work - his mouth just next to Heidi's. I could only stare down at them, breathless, my hips grinding harder against both of their faces.

Heidi stood up suddenly. She walked to the couch to pick up Leanne's riding crop. "Mistress Tilden commands us both," she said with a French accent, walking back over to me, looking visibly excited. "We are both her subs. But she allows me dominance over Joe. He is *my* sub. When she allows it."

"Oh..." I said weakly, as Joe continued to kiss my legs.

She appraised me with a deceptively innocent expression. "You will become more comfortable with this later."

"I will?" I asked, lustily.

She only smiled in reply. She straddled Joe's back and sat down. After affectionately stroking his face, she reached behind and smacked his ass so hard with the riding crop it made *me* wince. A visible red welt immediately grew around the edge of his underwear. I was in dreamland and any moralistic ideas I previously had were lost in the moment of lust. Joe's only response was to press his mouth harder against me and work more eagerly. Heidi brutally gripped a wad of his hair in a fist.

"You know what to do," Heidi said to him, leaning down. He began working his tongue around my shorts, proving he was every bit as talented as Heidi. His tongue

127

began to slip farther in, winding its way into me from underneath the side of my shorts. She took one of my hands and placed it in his hair, next to hers, indicating we should both control him. It looked as if she would rip the hair right out of his head. In a dreamy state, I joined suit and gripped his medium-length brown hair in an equally tight fist. We both worked his head together. My hips ground into his face as I grew more desperate with need.

SWAK! SWAK! Heidi whacked his ass, again and again, the effect was to drive his face into me. The sensation of his face pushing into me coupled with the visual image was nearly too much. *SWAK! SWAK!* She began savagely hitting him repeatedly while simultaneously shoving his head. He made little muffled wincing sounds against me, only adding to the sensations.

I felt the pressure rise… my legs taut with every sinew of muscle nearly to the snapping point.

I abruptly stood up. Where I got the sudden relapse of moral fortitude, I'm not certain. "Okay! O…. kay. Um." I took a deep breath, trying to regain my composure. "Thanks, guys. I think… I'll just call it an evening."

I moved Joe's head to the side gently so I could walk around him, away from the chair. Away from the orgasm of my life. The crotch of my shorts was visibly soaking wet… from their saliva… and from me. Joe looked disappointed that he was denied the full measure of his servitude. He didn't realize that he very nearly had taken me over the edge. And I still even had my shorts on. Heidi peered up at me with a slight, knowing smile. She knew that even though I was calling it quits, I was a project that had the first layer of finish on. From Heidi's expression, I could tell she thought it was now just a matter of time and circumstance and I could be a play partner. My fragile scruples had been severely tested. They were shattered.

Starting to make my way to the door, I paused, looking back. "Um. Not a word of this outside this room. Or else, I'll… or Leanne will…" Appraising their eager

128

expressions, it dawned on me, this was not an effective tactic. "Oh, never mind. You would both enjoy it too much. Just don't say *anything*."

"Very good, Mistress Michaels," Heidi acknowledged in her French schoolgirl tone. "We are very discreet. Would you like us to escort you out?"

"No. No, thanks. Tell… *Mistress Tilden,* I said good night. I can find my way to my own room." They both smiled up at me adoringly with a false innocence that made *me* want to use the crop on them. Okay, then.

I trudged awkwardly towards the door, the soaking spot of my shorts looking like I spilled a glass of water in my lap. As soon as I could get back to the privacy of my room, I would furiously work out the built-up sexual tension these two had wrought upon me. Repeatedly. If I didn't first encounter a stairwell railing… refrigerator handle, or the arm of a chair, perhaps.

CHAPTER 6
UNREQUITED LOVE – LEANNE HATCHES A SCHEME

Stefany: **What the hell happened???
Who am I kidding, I know full well what
happened. During what I thought would be
a very standard, boring evening discussing
finances with Leanne, I very nearly got it
on with her two sex toys, Heidi, and Joe.
And I'm sure Leanne had planned that for
some time. Damn her. I've no one to blame
but me, though. And a lot of wine and
tequila.**

**So I had a very restless night during
which I must admit, I had to take matters
into my own hands. Leanne will, of course,
act like it's nothing. Is it? I guess what
probably bothers me the most is my
reactions to Heidi. I almost let her get me
off. Another woman! Was I using them…
or were they using me??? I am not sure
about that one. If I were a little drunker,
how far would I have gone??? There was**

an unmistakable erotic power trip about that night in Leanne's room with Heidi and Joe. Yeah, it was hot. Damn hot. I felt like I was... a queen. A queen to be worshipped and served. To be given my every whim and fancy. Would I do it again? In the light of day, sober, I don't know. But I'm not going to think about that now. I won't because... I'm not sure I would say no....

~~~~~

My asshole ex, Miles, frequently visits now. I so want to snip both his balls off and shove them in his ears. He's still in his condo. Says he just wants to be close.  Learn and enjoy everything about the island. He's made this a chess game to get a piece of Stoney Brook. By hanging around and offering to help me financially, he thinks he will be able to claim some sort of mutual use when he next goes back to court. According to the lawyers, if I divorce him, he could still get a share of Stoney Brook. Those crooked assholes. For now, no divorce. The court will review it later, I'm told. How long is later?

Oh, and that pencil dick apologized for trying to hit me. Yeah, right. I hate him.

~~~~~

There's no question I'm running out of time. And money. Leanne has also offered financial help, but I don't want to accept it beyond payment for her room leases. I will do this on my own, succeed or fail.

Then there's Mr. Architect. Leanne, as if she doesn't have her fingers in enough pies around here... tells me he is in love with me. That's absurd. The only

person the arrogant Mobley will ever love is himself. I find I would still love to wedge my foot up his ass. Yes, I know he decked Miles for me. But who's to say any man walking by wouldn't have done the same. Am I being unfair? Maybe. I guess. I don't know?

~~~~~

Soooo… I started keeping an eye on Mobley. To see if there's any truth to Leanne's crazy notion. Does he have some sort of feelings for me? Good gawd, I hope not. I've caught him several times watching me when I am outside helping with one project or another. I've caught him checking out my ass… looking down my top… looking at my legs. Disgusting. I feel soiled. The only feelings Mobley has for any woman can be localized to the bulge in his pants. ~If~ Mobley had actual feelings for me, I think I would want to beat them out of him. Really.

Leanne Tilden was here!

~ And I approve this message ~

Leanne! Quit snooping in my desk!! AND Please stay OUT of my diary!!!

After thinking I would be successful avoiding Leanne and her weird sex minions following my indiscretion the previous evening, she waltzed through the doors of my office, a fashionable purse slung over her shoulder and carrying a book and a little box under her arm.

"Good morning," I said with my best fake, innocent tone. Trying to hide my embarrassment, I hid my eyes from beneath the protective shield of my hand which was set over my brow, hoping she wouldn't bring it up.

"Oh, you've got to be kidding me." She plopped in a chair in front of my desk.

"What?"

"You guilt-tripping about last night in my room. They told me all about it. They didn't even get you out of your shorts," she added laughing. "It was nothing, quit being embarrassed!"

"I'm not *embarrassed*. As you say, nothing really happened." Or… did it? Is having two people kiss and lick their way up your legs and offering you oral sex *nothing*?

"I'm just… occupied," I offered. "I do have other things to think about. You know? Financial matters. How I'm going to keep this place running." I looked at her squarely, seeing she was unconvinced.

"Here. This ought to cheer you up." Leanne set a box on the desk and opened the lid.

"Cigars! How thoughtful."

"Stef. Not just any cigars, they are Cubans. Remember when we would smoke my uncle's cigars out in the barn when we were teens?"

"Yes, I do. As well as the weed you always seemed to have."

"I have some of that too," she irreverently confessed. "Locally grown. Back in the room."

"Of course, you do. Please refrain from using it in front of the guests."

She handed me a cigar and took one for herself. I unwrapped it, bit the tip off and spit it into the trash can. She gave me an annoyed, emphatic look after showing me her cigar cutter.

Nipping hers carefully, she got up and threw the tip in the trash before producing a lighter. We lit up and began puffing away.

"I have a no smoking policy here, you know."

"Cigars are a refined delicacy, as you well know. Fine establishments of the past often had smoking rooms for cigars."

"Only for men," I affirmed. "The primary reason you like them, Leanne, is because you are out for a bit of shock value, in a *woman shoots up the galaxy* sort of way. Stick it to the man. Trample patriarchal tradition."

"Not all men are worthy of scorn, Stefany."

"Fuck men." I leaned back in my chair and plopped my feet up on my desk, dirty sneakers and all. I took a drag on my cigar and blew a puff of smoke up to the ceiling.

"And fuck women, too," Leanne joked.

"Unlike you, I meant figuratively, not literally," I confirmed.

"We'll debate your subconscious mind at another time." Leaning across my desk, Leanne grabbed my personal diary, which I had regretfully failed to return to its drawer following my latest entry. "Ah. You are keeping a diary. I recall you kept one when you were younger. It's therapeutic. I approve. You never did realize, when we were teenagers, I read them quite thoroughly during sleepovers when you were in the bathroom."

"What?!"

She began to thumb through the pages. "What untoward and tawdry comments have you made about me in here." She stopped at several pages and laughed. "Your artistic talents have not progressed beyond the first-grade level, I see."

"No matter. It's private." I reached across the desk and tried to snatch the diary, only to have her hold it out of reach. She took a pen off my desk and began scribbling her signature with a flourish, then added a comment. Smiling mischievously, she handed it back. "There. We are now officially diary mates. I expect full review rights in the future so that I may inspect it for any lapses in mental health. Or salacious content."

"There's never been anything too *salacious* in my diaries. It's always been standard fare," I explained.

"Oh, I beg to differ," Leanne chirped. "I recall one entry, your discovery of the joys of masturbation. With your electric toothbrush no less. While watching rock music videos."

"Damn it, Leanne! That was private!"

"You should know by now you can never keep secrets from me." Leanne pointed her cigar to me. "But on to my next point of discussion. Just look at yourself. Look."

I looked down, not seeing anything remiss. "What?"

"Grimy ball cap on backward. A nasty T-shirt that needs a wash. Haven't I taught you anything about being a woman of refinement and grace that befits your position as the owner of this business?"

"When I need to, I dress appropriately. I just don't need to right now. Have you just come in to irritate me today, Leanne?"

"I hope you realize, your mode of dress, in its current manifestation, is your subliminal rejection of the expensive sports car, tidy suit and tie world of Miles."

"What? Are you really going to ruin these great cigars by psychoanalyzing me? I'm just not the CEO type," I admitted. "I don't want to dress like that all the time."

"You have to dress for success and be a CEO type, Stef. If there's one thing I am going to teach you while I'm here, it's that you must know when and where to put on a presentable image. A pit-stained t-shirt is not suitable. What if someone needs to see you? Accomplishment is directly related to how you dress for it; all sorts of studies show that.

"I gotta be me," I said, drawing a look of ire.

"Yes, I suppose you do," Leanne said, admiring the rings float towards the ceiling. "I should make you a case study and put my psychology degree to good use. Stefany Michaels, the incurable tomboy. Tough as nails, yet you let Miles tell you time and time again he would not hit you again. And he always did."

"Those days are over, Leanne."

"Are they? You let Miles come to the island. You can see him try and wheedle his way back into your life. If it weren't for Mobley stepping in to save you at The Blue Calypso, you would have had another broken nose."

"It's complicated."

"Yes, it is. Part of it is called Battered Person Syndrome. With subsequent avoidance. The irony is, I bet if you fought back, you'd drop that limp noodle cold."

It was time to change the subject. "How about a discussion that won't ruin these fine cigars. What about the finances. Did you look over the statements I brought you?" I sent several more perfect smoke rings towards the ceiling. If only my finances were as tidy.

"I did. I won't lie. It's not pretty. But you can't give up. Stoney Brook hasn't met its full potential yet." She sat in silence for a moment, no doubt trying to sound encouraging with such a dismal outlook. "Something may come along."

"What can happen, Leanne? I'm going broke."

"We could reduce costs," she suggested. "Renegotiate the loans. No need to panic yet."

I admired my cigar, rolling it in my fingers. "I could do it, you know. Do it to save the place."

"Do what?"

"I could go ahead and take Miles' money. Let him be a partner like he wants. With his millions, it would be a done deal. He's offered to get me out of debt."

"And there it is. The real reason you let him come to the island."

"So, what if it is? He isn't granting me a divorce. So. If I can't leave him, maybe I should just go ahead and take the money."

"Once you sell out to Miles by letting him get a financial interest here, you'll never be rid of him."

I shrugged. "Maybe you are right."

"Of course, I'm right," she joked. "Just like I'm right you should start seeing someone."

"You are pushing that again? I don't want to see anyone. And if I did and his lawyers got wind of it, he could get an even bigger share of Stoney Brook in any settlement."

"Nonsense. You are both separated. I know for fact he's been dating. Be discreet and don't flaunt it. You'd be okay."

"You have all the bases covered, don't you, Leanne," I joked.

"Yes. I do," she admitted.

"Well, I'm not interested in meeting any new men, Leanne," I asserted. "Or women, should you have any doubts about me."

"So just like that, you are going to give up on any relationship? No one to share your dreams, your fears, your expectations with? And you are content - gasp - to go sexless?"

"I'm happy being by myself. No entanglements."

"Ah, the electric toothbrush must be wireless."

138

"That's not what I meant!"

"You aren't on some deserted island, Stefany. The world is full of hot, sexy, potential partners, you just need to open up your eyes to the possibilities."

I laughed. "Like Heidi and Joe?"

"You might really like that arrangement if you were to find the right person to serve you. Someone to bring you out of your shell."

"I like my shell."

"We just have to find you a sexual go-to guy. A toy. A sex *slave*. Someone to serve your every need, sexually, without question."

"Really, Leanne, that is just ridiculous." I leaned forward. "It's just not *me*, you know that. Is that your psychological analysis? You think I need some kind of dom - sex slave reverse therapy for the abuse that Miles put me through to bring me out of my shell?" I laughed, knowing that was exactly what she was thinking.

"It would be a mutually beneficial relationship between a submissive and a dominant," she explained. "It's not like it has to be permanent. Heidi and Joe can leave whenever they want. Or whenever I want. Experiencing being a dom would heal you, emotionally and sexually, I'm certain. It would clear up your perspective."

She eyed me over her cigar. "Be honest with me, Stefany. What did you really think of Joe and Heidi?"

"Okay. Take Joe. You can call him a slave or whatever, but he's quite clever. Typical guy. He's figured out that for the price of a few smacks on his ass, he gets to be the fox in the hen house. All the pussy he could ever wish for. Oh sure, he will need a few Band-Aids. Maybe some first aid cream. He gets what he's looking for. And he gets it aplenty," I noted with a laugh. "Heidi, the same. She digs it both ways, but she still gets what she wants. Sure, they are fine for your lifestyle." I blew another smoke ring. "But for me, Cuz? I'm not looking for anything. Miles beat any desire out of me to want to be in any other relationship. And I surely don't need a sex slave, of all things. The truth is Leanne, a person doesn't have to go through all this dominant and slave stuff just for sex. It's unnecessary."

"Maybe it's not for you," Leanne relented. "Even so. It wouldn't hurt you to learn a few new things." She took the book she brought in and handed it across the desk to me.

I read the title, shocked at her audacity.

Common Terms and Phraseology of BDSM
An Exploration and Discussion
By Dr. Franklin S. Moroney, PhD
Professor Emeritus of Sexual Psychology

"And what am I supposed to do with *this*? I bet it burns good, but I don't think the fireplace has been lit for hundreds of years."

"Read it when you get a chance. At least be knowledgeable about submissive, dominant relationships."

"I don't care about this crap, Leanne. This is your area of expertise, not mine. Really, I could care less." I tossed the book on the desk where it landed with a hollow *thunk*.

"You *might* find it interesting."

I laughed. "Let's say I do. Do you have any ready-made submissives for me, Leanne? I'm just curious. And I'm not talking about yours, Heidi and Joe."

"Um. No," she admitted. "But that doesn't mean you can't find one."

"Leanne, I'm not going to be a… torture chamber, whip-wielding leather-clad dominatrix. It just isn't me. It's not. No. I'm just… Stefany. Good ole, missionary position, wham bam, get some sleep, maybe fake an orgasm or two, boring sex, Stefany. It's all I need."

Undeterred, Leanne stood, walked around the desk, picked up the book and opened it, sharing the cover with me. "I met Dr. Moroney at a psychology convention in New York City. His theories of human sociology and behavior relating to sexuality are the definitive standard. See? Look, it even has pictures for the creatively challenged, such as yourself." She randomly flipped through the pages. "Hmmmm. Look, Cuz. This one. I bet you never heard of this one before." She held the book out to me as if nothing had sunk in.

I reluctantly took the book and looked at the picture which featured a blindfolded woman intricately bound in rope, suspended from the ceiling while orally fellating a man.

Shibari – The Japanese Art of Rope Bondage

There were several pages of pictures that followed, showing examples along with how-to diagrams.

"Gollicker jeeze, Bondage Man!" I commented in a vintage superhero pretend voice. I handed the book back. "It sure doesn't look like they are going to get out of those knots, my trusty sidekick!"

"You are sooo difficult. Here. Look at this one."

I sighed. "Femdom?"

"Yes. It's where the woman is in charge as a dominant over the man. The woman is worshipped by her partner, primarily in a sexual context. You'd love it."

"I bet Dr. Moron lives in a purple shack with pink curtains down by a set of railroad tracks somewhere." Taking the book, I flipped to the front and began to read off some of the terms in the table of contents: "Asphyxiation?"

"That one is done only with great care. Obviously."

"Obviously. Ball gag, blindfolds, caning, facesitting, face dildo, foot worship..." I laughed. "Wait. What the fuck is a face dildo?"

"It's where the submissive wears a harness on the face with a dildo attached to it. It's quite fun."

"Leanne, you are a lunatic." I could only imagine Heidi or Joe wearing such a device. I continued. "Handcuffs, hot wax, orgasm denial..." I paused and tried to control my laughter. "Pegging? What the hell is that? It sounds like what you do to tools in a garage."

"No. It's where a female dom fucks a male slave."

I shook my head. "Um. I don't follow you."

"With a strap on dildo."

I had to think about this for a moment before it dawned on me. I looked at her incredulously. "That's just *sick*. Do people do these things? I mean, really?"

"There are all sorts in the world, as you can imagine. No, Joe wouldn't go for pegging," Leanne chuckled. "But I'm sure Heidi could be convincing."

"Pegging sounds like it might be painful to the man," I added thoughtfully.

"In some cases, it probably is. It is humiliating more than anything."

I nodded approvingly. "You know? Maybe I might like pegging that fucker, Miles. That one, I might be down for. And for his lawyer pals as well. No lube." Leanne laughed so hard she nearly dropped her cigar.

"*Moving on.*" I continued with the list. "Speculums, water sports, whips, riding crops..." I looked up from the book. "Okay, wait. Water sports? What the hell is that? Sex in a hot tub?"

Leanne took a long drag on her cigar and exhaled. "Come on, Stef. You've never heard of that one?"

"No. Enlighten me."

"Pee."

"Oh, my gawd, some people are some trashy, twisted fucks."

Leanne shrugged. "Say what you will, but many of these milder things are found in bedrooms around the world."

"Mild? Sorry, but it's *all* bizarre... and disgustingly gross."

"I should tell you, there's actually weirder stuff in the back index. Things out in the fringe of behavior that may not be safe or healthy."

I handed the book back. "Noooooo, thank you."

"People experiment. They find things they mutually like." She took the book and slid it back to me. "Just have an open mind. Look at the mild stuff that could be fun." Leanne gave her cigar a deep tug. "Last night, you came in and had an open mind. At least for a few minutes."

142

"That doesn't mean it will happen again. My sex life is mine."

"Or lack thereof. Remember, your previous sex life only consisted of selfish abuse. If you got anything out of it, it was just a side effect. Miles destroyed your sex life. In part because he was an abusive asshole, and in part because he no doubt was a lousy lover. Am I wrong?"

"No. You are not wrong," I had to admit. "Miles was only into sex for his own enjoyment, period."

"That's why I am doing this," Leanne affirmed. "Get you to have some fun. Experience sexuality that is both fun and satisfying with *you* in control instead of the other way around. I want to help you bring it back. Just have a look through that book. Please."

"Honestly, I would be much more open to a nicely muscled, athletic, handsome, hot cabana boy. Maybe he's a college athlete. He'd give me a nice, warm oil massage. Then, just regular sex, no weird shit." I held up a finger to make a point. "And no talking! Then afterward, *BAM*, kick him the hell out and never see him again. Unless I wanted to, that is. But more likely, I would find another cabana boy. Now *that* plan, I kinda like."

"Quit it, Stef. Open mind. That's all I'm asking."

I took the book and plopped it into a desk drawer. "Yeah, okay, yeah. Quit hounding me about it, though. There isn't anyone I could *bondage* up anyway."

"Yes. There is, actually."

I dropped my feet off the desk. "What? Who?"

"Your very own Mr. Architect, Morgan Mobley."

I flipped the ashes off my cigar and gave Leanne a hard look before breaking out laughing. "Leanne. ABSOLUTELY not."

"Yes, Stefany."

"Listen. Let's look past the fact he abhors me. Contrary to all that crap you said about him being in love with me. He would be *the* LAST person to ever be submissive in anything. Especially sex. He would want ME to be the sex slave, knowing him."

"You think so?"

"I *know* so," I affirmed. "That egotistical, overbearing, hormone-driven, ball sack would never do such a thing. There's not a submissive bone in his body. You really are off the mark with that one."

"Care to make it interesting?" she coyly asked.

"Ha! Interesting? How?"

"If I get him in your office… anytime in the next four months, right here, naked, on his knees, ON your floor, with a collar around his neck, leash in hand which I would hand over to you… him FULLY prepared to serve you sexually and only you exclusively… and dedicated to taking whatever you dish out. Would you agree to terms?"

I snapped my fingers. "That's easy. And a stupid bet for you. He would NEVER agree to such a thing."

"But… would you agree to my terms? That's our bet, Miss Stefany Allain McCaskill-Michaels. No waffling and no getting out of it."

"Your terms?" I asked smugly, arching my eyebrows. So few times in my life had someone thrown me a sweet peach of a deal such as Leanne was offering me now.

"You would have to truly use him. You as the dom. Him as the sub. Your sex slave. Regularly. Pure sexual servitude. Hardcore. Using things that I suggest… but that you consent in good faith to try. I'll be your guide, to which I insist. You two would follow my directions, fully. Not watching of course, but guiding you both, nevertheless. Wholeheartedly and without complaint and without compunction. For a year."

"You've given this some prior thought, have you?" I asked with suspicion.

"I just thought of it," she said innocently. I laughed again, knowing she was lying. I leaned far back in my chair and inhaled deeply on my cigar before blowing a puff towards the ceiling. I thought about the proposal so I could ensure that I was shielded from any possibility that it could become a reality. This was Mobley we were talking about, anything sexual had to be well considered.

There was the fact he would have to stop man whoring and be in a "relationship" with me exclusively. That alone would be a reason that he would never agree. And he would never allow me to beat his cocky ass raw in a BDSM arrangement, of all silly things. He would never agree to be brought to my office naked on a leash, that was certain. Three huge points, all in my favor. I was safe, checkmate. Leanne had lost her mind.

"Haaaaa! And what do I get when you can't produce Mobley in all his cocky, egotistical glory and you lose this bet at the end of four months?" I asked.

"Dinner served any evening, in or out, for as many evenings as you want, all on me. For a full year."

"Hmmm." I nodded in approval at her suggestion. I looked at her thoughtfully, knowing that this was a great opportunity. "Okay. I like that. *And*… no more mention of my sex life. Everrrr."

"Agreed," she said.

"*And*…" I peered up at the ceiling, thinking. "I get that Victorian grandfather clock back at your home I have always wanted ever since I was a little girl."

"Damn you. Yes, agreed," she said reluctantly.

"*And*…" This was just too good to be true. She wasn't overly balking at my demands, so I could not resist adding more enticements. "I get a horse. For me to ride around here. Decently trained. Young, well bred. My very own. A way to bring some life back to those fancy stables I have here. You would have to get your own, given that you'll want to go riding around the island with me."

"Okay, yes, yes. But that's it!"

"*And*… feed for a year. No. Two years," I added as an afterthought, giving her a toothy grin.

"You are severely challenging my altruistic motives in this little affair. Severely challenging... Yes. Fine. But that is absolutely it! Nothing else. Are we agreed or are we not," she shot back testily.

I stood, spit in my hand, she did the same and we leaned across my desk to shake on it.

"Agreed," we both said together.

Leanne had bitten off far more than she could chew with this one. Despite all the bad financial news about Stoney Brook, this was going to be a win for me. And fun. I had just struck the mother lode and I was as gleeful as a kitten on a curtain.

I took a drink from my draft beer that came with my tuna sandwich at The Blue Calypso. Leanne, having proclaimed to be my financial advisor, sat next to me to hear the "amazing proposal" that prompted our trip into town for the lunch meeting.

"We are prepared to offer you market value plus a fifteen percent profit for Stoney Brook, Ms. Michaels."

Of the three men sitting across the table in expensive business suits, only one, a man introducing himself as Anatoly Pavlov, could speak English in a thick Russian accent. The meeting over lunch had been set up with a quick call, with assurances that it would be worth my time to listen to them.

"We are aware of your financial difficulties at Stoney Brook," he sympathized, lighting up a cigar. "You are over-staffed. The budget is bloated. Your restoration architect is a bumbling idiot. You have no marketing plan or any connections to major travel firms."

"How do you know who I have on staff? As for Mr. Mobley, I don't think I would characterize him as an idiot."

"We would. You have fired him once already, let's be realistic, Ms. Michaels, shall we? Expertise in properly restoring this historic property should go to someone that is at least marginally qualified. We have such resources. You could rest easy knowing that we would take care of your ancestral property with competent restoration. You will be proud of what we can do here. And you can make a profit, ease your financial burden, and get on with your life in a more meaningful way. We would give you a 5 percent interest in the estate, yours to keep forever."

"I want to know how you know so much about Stoney Brook?" I pressed, shocked at their insight.

"It is our business to know. Internationally, we seek high potential properties in tourist destination areas and renovate them. Stoney Brook, at least for the moment, has piqued our interest. With a degree of capital outlay and appropriate financial management, it could be a decent property."

"I am not interested in selling, Mr. Pavlov."

"Ms. Michaels. You are in debt with no means of climbing out. We understand that you may be in the process of divorce. That can not only be traumatic for a person, but expensive as well."

"That is a personal matter, sir. I would rather not discuss that if you please."

"Very well. But I can tell you this. As a person that has been involved in countless property transactions that count in the millions of dollars, I can see very clearly with my eyes. I have the experience to know. Where there will be failure and ruin. And I can see it with you and Stoney Brook. Please, be realistic. You have no background in managing such a venture and your funds have dried up."

"We are in a rough patch, but we will pull through with the tourist season," I objected.

"When you were a housewife, you ran a coffee shop, Ms. Michaels. Yes?"

Pavlov's tone was increasingly insulting. "Look," I tried to explain, feeling irritated and self-conscious of my background both at the same time. "I didn't just sit around my home waiting on my husband if that's what you are insinuating. I went to college; I have a business degree. I owned and ran a coffee shop in Canada."

"A small coffee shop is not Stoney Brook. You are near bankruptcy. We offer you a solution to save Stoney Brook and run it the way it should be run, preserving your ancestral heritage for posterity."

"Gentlemen. Mr. Pavlov. I'm not interested in selling Stoney Brook," I said finishing my beer. "If I should change my mind, I have your number and will contact you. Leanne? We really need to head back now, we have some other business to attend."

Both of us stood and I extended my hand to the three Russians.

"The offer may not be available later, Ms. Michaels," Pavlov warned. "And if it is, it may not be under such favorable terms for you."

"I understand. Good day and thanks for lunch." Leanne walked with me to the Rover. When out of earshot, she leaned to me, whispering. "I'm so glad you didn't let them talk you into anything. You are far from failing, Stef. You just need to catch a good break."

"Thanks, Leanne. They are right, though. Financially speaking, I may not be able to last the year. I'm not even certain I can make my next loan payment to the bank. There may be a time I wish I had taken their offer."

"Maybe. But that time is not now," Leanne declared.

Both of us climbed in the Rover. I started the engine and slammed my door shut. "If ever I've seen criminals, it would be those three."

"It's obvious they are used to throwing their money around and getting what they want," Leanne agreed.

"They don't give a shit about Stoney Brook. I do. And they aren't getting it. They'd burn the place down if it made them money. I wonder who they are getting all their inside information from? The bank? Some of our employees?"

"Maybe. They seemed to know a lot about your finances, so probably someone at the bank."

"They are right about one thing. We could do better than Mobley," I lamented.

Leanne laughed. "C'mon, Stef. I thought you were okay with him now?"

"True, I'm okay with him back working at Stoney Brook. In his limited capacity." I pulled the Rover out onto the main road and began heading back to the plantation. "But I don't harbor any illusions about him, Leanne. Even those Russian guys, as big of jerks as they were, could see the obvious. We could be better served by someone with more experience and knowledge. While Mobley *is* doing okay for us and getting stuff done, there's no getting around the fact that he is a complete bonehead."

"A bonehead that stood up for your honor," Leanne reminded me.

"I appreciate what he did. But don't lecture me, Leanne. I hired him initially for all the wrong reasons, you know that. Everyone sees it." I rolled the window down to rest my elbow on the door, disgusted with myself. "So, what did I do? I hired Man-Whore back again! I'm the idiot. I felt sorry for him and gave in."

"You are twisting this all the wrong way," Leanne counseled. "Don't let a meeting with some frauds wanting to purchase Stoney Brook and pressing all your buttons turn into a bash Mobley moment."

"Leanne. They were right. He's stupid as a shoebox full of blond hair. And I'm stuck with him."

Morgan: Projects at Stoney Brook have been proceeding on schedule. We continue to have cost overruns and Stefany continues to bust my chops.

All in all, she seems to be nicer to me although I would never think we will be friends. She remains cold and distant, even if more tolerant. My attempts at conversation with her always turn to work and she leaves it at that. We don't discuss what happened at The Blue Calypso when she brought me back.

Her rich asshole husband is staying on the island somewhere in an expensive condo. He stopped by the other day. Stefany looked none too happy, and they argued the whole time he was at Stoney Brook.

Miles came out to the barn where I was working, catching me alone. He told me we had unfinished business - whatever that means. I had to laugh, which just pissed him off more. He said he would never allow anyone to get away with what I did to him – punching him. He hinted around that he is "connected" to the mob or some such thing, he told me I may well end up floating in the Caribbean as fish food. Yeah, right. Get in line, pal. I've had plenty of people threaten me and I'm still around.

Further, the dickhead said if I so much as tell anyone about him threatening me, he will see to it that I'll pay for it, and Stefany will pay for it because she hired me back "for some reason." Why he would think I was somehow involved with Stefany to the point that he would include her, I don't know. I guess he figures since he's still married to her, she's subject to his abuse. Not if I can help it.

At any rate, I do not want to take a chance that her safety could be at risk on my account. Miles is a blowhard coward woman beater and I have no doubt he's full of shit. It is still very troubling and hard to believe that he abused Stefany as Leanne has told me. Regardless of how much Stefany may hate me, I would never tolerate that sort of thing by him to her. I may hit him again if the occasion should arise. More than once...

On a happier note, I am getting along great with Leanne. She is really a good friend now. I am yet to succeed in seducing her, however...

"No, no, Mr. Mobley. I cannot. I could lose my job. You wouldn't want that, would you?" Her right leg pushed in between both of mine, up into my khaki slacks, gently nudging my equipment. She ran both of her hands up my chest. Her lips were just a breath away. Her beautiful big brown eyes peered up at me expectantly.

We both were standing in the corner of the main kitchen, just enough out of sight that I could make nice if we were discovered. I looked over my shoulder. Nope. No one was in the kitchen. It was go time. Gisselle, what a lovely name. She was new and not yet overly encumbered by Stefany's Gestapo rules of keeping the staff from dating. For now, I could at least kiss this beautiful island girl. Then perhaps later, after sneaking her into my room, she could help ease me out of the horrendous case of chaffing blue balls that were beleaguering my every horny thought.

I slowly pulled her chef's hat off, releasing a locket of silky ebony hair to fall over her pretty face; a face that would be so hot to see in mid-orgasm. Judging by her shy demeanor and the sensuous turn of her lips at the corners of her mouth, I gauged her to be a passionate moaner - as opposed to the spasming screamer. Of course, I had been wrong with that assessment on numerous occasions. Both were welcome music to my ears.

"Mr. Mobley. We will be caught."

Oh, no we won't, my pretty little flower, I thought as I slipped my hand behind her back to bring her closer. Peering down her shirt, I could see that she had wonderful brown breasts... the sort that would shine up nicely with a baby oil massage for some pre-shower play. For several days, having seen Gisselle arrive early to work to change, I knew quite well she had wonderful, shapely, bronzed legs. I imagined her whole body oiled. I would pay particular attention to the cheeks of her amazing ass, sleek, slick, and slippery... ripe, twin mounds, just waiting for a teasing smack of the flat of my hand. I went in for the kiss...

Uffffff! She pushed me away with authority and took her hat from my hand. I blinked, knowing the growing erection in my pants was as startled as the rest of me. She determinedly lifted my hand away from behind her back.

She smiled saucily up at me. "I told you, Mr. Mobley. No, no. I need this job. Ms. Michaels would not be happy. I'm sorry, but you should let me get back to work." She tidied her uniform and carefully placed her hat back on. "If you get fired again, maybe then... I see you." She patted me on the chest before turning to walk away. She peered seductively over her shoulder at me once before engaging in some culinary necessity that involved lunch meat and cheese. I had to wonder. Was this a coup by the female staff: to flirt and cruelly lead me on, then suddenly refute my advances?

The virtuous shrew, Stefany, had practically ruined any chances for me of getting laid. The whole damned island seemed to have it out for me. I had struck out so many times, visions of my 5th grade rookie year in Little League baseball were coming to mind. If Stefany caught me outright "man whoring" as she called it, she would have my balls in a vice, and she would no doubt fire me again. It was a bitter reality. She was turning Stoney Brook into her own personal monastery with her medieval rules.

I tried to shrug off the failure to get to first base with Giselle. It was my day off. I could stroll down and see how the boys were making progress renovating the wine rooms in the cellar. No, surely, I could find something else to occupy myself given that sex was off the menu. I had a whole wonderful island to explore if I would just get some initiative and get out for a while.

I pushed away from the wall and decided to go sit out on the banquet veranda under one of the table umbrellas. One of the few perks of working at Stoney Brook was that staff could eat - and to a lesser degree, drink - for free. Maybe I would get a sandwich and a beer.

I strolled out into the brilliant sunlight. It was a steamy hot, gorgeous day with hardly any breeze. The raucous noises of tropical birds filtered in through the surrounding forests.

It would be the perfect day to lounge around a pool and admire any attractive female guests. If Stoney Brook had a pool that is. Stefany planned on breaking ground on a nice large pool and several hot tubs within the month. And yet she complained about money, I thought, shaking my head. Her argument was that she had intended from the beginning to offer such essential amenities to guests, and they were a vital marketing incentive. The completion of a pool and several hot tubs was a requirement in the provisions of her loans.

The veranda was occupied with several couples and groups. They were enjoying their lunch, sipping wine, coffee, and a variety of tropical drinks. I peered across the series of tables to see a very attractive woman in a bikini and sunglasses in the corner. She was sitting by herself in the sun, just outside the shade of her umbrella, cocktail in hand, reading a book, sexy legs propped up on a chair.

It was Heidi, one of Leanne's "friends." Leanne had thus far shot down every attempt I had made at going beyond flirting with her. Perhaps her companion would be more adventurous. I smiled to myself. Surely there was something kinky going on with that arrangement. A guy and a girl just traveling around with Leanne, "staying" with her... for... what purpose? The staff passed around rumors that they were with Leanne for sexual purposes. It would not surprise me, although I could not confirm it.

Yes, Stefany had warned me about "man whoring" the women staff. But if she never found out, there was no harm. The days were long and the nights longer, and any will power I had to honor that promise was quickly evaporating day by day. I thought back to the conversation in Stefany's office. Her rule of no "co-mingling" with the guests was outrageous. With a good dose of secrecy and discretion, I wouldn't mind getting to know Heidi to a much *deeper* degree.

The girl was a knockout, a sweet little piece of delicious female candy. I admired the sleek lines of her legs as I casually walked towards her. Like Stefany, she was not overly endowed up top, and like Stefany, the rest of her more than made up for any perceived deficiencies in the size of her tits. There's the old saying that any more than a handful is a waste, to which I vehemently disagree. However, B and C cups are just fine with me, I don't discriminate. There was no doubt in my mind that Heidi could distinguish herself quite well as a fantastic B cupster.

"Hello! How are you today?" I asked cordially.

Heidi pulled her sunglasses down to peer over the top. "Hello. Mr. Morgan Mobley, if I'm not mistaken?" she said, speaking with a thick French accent. She pulled an errant strand of strawberry blonde hair from her eyes and tucked it behind her ear. Her blonde hair stood in stark contrast to her tan body.

"Yes! I don't believe we've been properly introduced." I held my hand out to her. "Heidi?" She nodded in the affirmative, sat her book down and took my hand.

"It's a pleasure to meet the resident architect of Stoney Brook. I've heard so much about you to never have met you. Although I've seen you around here for some time."

"Very true. And the pleasure is mine. May I join you?"

"Of course." She pushed a chair towards me with a foot.

Issadella, the waitress girl on duty for lunch came over with several menus. Issadella had been my hot date on several occasions before I had been fired. Despite remaining friendly, she had taken no interest in resuming any romantic involvement, no doubt due to Stefany's rules. "Hello!" she said cheerily. "Ms. Heidi, Mr. Mobley. What may I get for you this afternoon?"

I looked at Heidi's drink, seeing that it was empty. "Would you like another drink?"

She eyed her glass and smiled. "Sure. That would be nice, Morgan, thank you."

"And a beer for me please, Issadella." I discreetly winked at her, to which she gave only a hint of a smile. Issadella turned immediately, returning to the veranda bar.

"So, it's a beautiful day," I began, starting off with a bit of safe small talk.

"All of the days here are beautiful," she further added. "Even the stormy ones. I love it when the storms roll in with the thunder and lightning. And seeing that over the mountains. The tropical smell of the rain and the flowers... wonderful."

Heidi was well slathered in coconut suntan oil, the sensual aroma of which hung in the air. Little beads of sweat had formed on her stomach, accentuating well defined abdominal muscles. Trying to keep my eyes focused on her face when she spoke was difficult. I wanted to devour her with my eyes.

I agreed with her assessment of the island's beauty and continued chatting her up. Contrary to my initial perceptions of her as stoically quiet, she was quite friendly and engaging.

Issadella soon returned with our drinks and handed me a receipt to sign. It was for Heidi's drink. I was being charged five dollars and seventy-five cents from my account. I looked up at Issadella, thinking it had to be a mistake. "I think this is an error," I told her. "Staff eats and drinks without charge, I believe. And all guests' expenses are generally inclusive, are they not?"

She clicked a ballpoint pen and handed it to me. "That is true, Mr. Mobley. But purchases by staff for guests are charged at a regular fee. Plus fifteen percent."

I coughed. Plus fifteen percent?! What the hell was this about? "I see," trying not to sound cheap to Heidi who was listening to the exchange with interest. The amount of a drink certainly wouldn't break me, but it was irritating that I was being nickeled and dimed from my paycheck. And for being cordial! "When did this become a rule?"

"Last week, Mr. Mobley. In fact, it's called the *Mobley Rule*. It's after you took two cases of beer from the bar without signing for them. To share with the three sisters that were here visiting from California?" I eyed Issadella. Was she trying to shoot me down here in front of Heidi?! Was she jealous? Perhaps Issadella did harbor resentment over our previous flings, after all. Hopefully, Heidi would not read between the lines of this embarrassing exchange.

"Ah, the sisters. Yes. Very nice people. Wonderful guests." I smiled at Heidi, hoping she would not get cold feet. "This receipt. It's probably the kitchen manager joking with me," I suggested, rolling my eyes for effect.

"Oh, no sir," Issadella countered. "No joke. It was Ms. Michaels. She said a lot more when she came to tell us about this new rule." Issadella batted her eyes innocently, visibly enjoying this moment at my expense.

"A lot more?" I had to think back. I could not imagine that two cases of beer had prompted this new hostile development. The Mobley Rule? Stefany had been short with me lately, but I thought all in all we were getting along. "And just what did she say?" I foolishly asked before realizing I was digging myself a deeper hole than necessary.

Issadella shot a mischievous glance at Heidi, then back to me. "There was… inappropriate language, sir. I really shouldn't."

"I see. Well, here we go then," I curtly replied, feeling my blood boil. I nonchalantly signed the receipt with a flourish and handed it and the pen back, trying to keep my cool. "No problem. A mistake, I'm sure. I'll take up this egregious oversight with Ms. Michaels later."

"I don't believe it is an oversight, Mr. Mobley. More of a… remedial measure."

"Yes, yes, Issadella. Thank you," I replied, seeing that I had been victimized yet again by head-nun Stefany and her monastery morality police.

"I'll be back in a bit to check on you two," she said cordially before walking away.

I tried to regain my momentum. "So, where are you from, Heidi?"

"I'm from Montreal. Although originally, I am from a small village in Quebec. My family is French-Canadian."

"And what do you do, career-wise, if you don't mind me asking?"

"Of course not. I am an art student at university there in Montreal. My senior year."

"Art, eh? Impressive. And what genres do you prefer to work in?"

"I do many, actually. I enjoy charcoals, watercolors, oils. Nudes are my favorite. Bronze sculpture is also one of my forte's."

We continued to discuss her interests in art. She asked me similar questions, inquiring where I studied architecture. The conversation turned personal. After a moment, I decided it was time to ask her out.

"So, Heidi. What would you say to you and me heading into town this evening? Dinner. Drinks. A night on the town."

"I'm sorry, Morgan. But I'm seeing someone."

I sat quietly for a moment, blindsided. Both of my engines were in flames, and I was headed towards the ground. She had seemed so receptive! And after $5.75.

"Oh. I understand, of course." At this moment, Leanne's other play toy walked up to our table.

"Joe, please have a seat with us. We were just talking of my art interests." She held out her hand indicating an empty chair.

"Ah. Hello," he said turning to me and extending his hand with somewhat of a scornful expression. "I'm Joe, Heidi's friend. You are Mr. Mobley, yes?"

I nodded and shook his hand, trying to guess the origins of the accent which was altogether different from Heidi's.

"You are German," I asked?

He nodded. "By birth, yes. But I am a Canadian citizen now."

I looked at both and made a motion with my hand. "So… you two…?"

"Yes, Morgan. Joe is my boyfriend." I was beginning to perceive a haughty air with Heidi I had not previously noticed.

"I see." I smiled at Joe, now hoping to extricate myself from this uncomfortable scene and go get a beer. If I wasn't in the hunt, why was I still on the trail. I made a bit more small talk looking for an opportunity to escape. They were quite talkative despite my moving to the edge of my seat. Getting away wasn't going to be easy.

"Joe, you are a very fortunate man. Heidi is quite a beautiful and evidently talented woman."

"Thank you! I would have to agree. And we have one other that completes our happy family."

"Um. Beg your pardon," I began, suddenly interested. "You said, *family*?" I asked this managing to keep a straight face.

"Yes. Miss Leanne. We are also… with her," Joe added nonchalantly.

Immediately I began to turn over the words "happy family" and "with her" in my mind. What was this I had stumbled into, a little hippie commune? So, the rumors were all true. Leanne was part of a hot threesome group and they traveled around together. I couldn't wait to press her on this topic later. Joe was earning my grudging respect. How was he managing this feat of juggling two women? He didn't look the type.

"And… what do you do, Joe? Are you also an artist?" I asked, thoroughly insincere. The thought that was crossing my mind was, *Joe, you bastard, you are banging two hot chicks at once, that is what you are doing*. I was envious beyond measure.

"No, we are quite opposite, Heidi and me. I am studying business management. However, I did meet Heidi at university. It is also at university where we happened to meet Miss Leanne. At a conference." I had to wonder what type of conference.

"And you've been friends ever since?"

"Yes. We see her, travel with her when we can. In between studies. As you probably observed, we were away for a brief period, both of us taking care of necessary business back in Montreal before we came back."

Sure enough, as if on cue, I saw Leanne strolling through the kitchen with a drink in her hand. She spotted us and came over to our table. I was a little surprised she greeted me so warmly. It was without insult or goading. At least for the moment.

"Ah. Mr. Mobley. Conversing with my friends Heidi and Joe I see. I'm glad you have made their acquaintance."

"I'm surprised you never introduced us before."

"Opportunity never seemed to arise."

After a few more minutes of polite conversation, Heidi and Joe excused themselves, off to go on a hike, leaving Leanne sitting across the table apprising me with amused suspicion.

"No doubt trying to make a move on Heidi, am I correct, Morgan?" I had to give her credit for being incredibly blunt and to the point with me.

"Yes. And I apologize. I didn't know she was… um…" I coughed trying to be serious. "In your *family*."

Leanne laughed. "Yes, they are family, in a manner of speaking."

"Leanne. You are every bit the horny pervert that I am. You know that, right?"

"I admit nothing, Morgan. I will acknowledge, however, that yes, you are an accomplished pervert."

I shrugged off this insult as typical Leanne banter. She never failed to disappoint and loved giving me a hard time. Occasionally she let me give it back.

"So… both of them!?" I asked incredulously.

"You don't have a clue," was her only response, brushing the question aside.

"Okay, so they are probably bisexual?"

"Heidi, yes. Joe, no. He is every bit a straight man like you, Morgan. Although your variety of straight is more born of the gutter than Joe's."

Leanne sat joking with me for nearly an hour. After several beers, I was feeling more reflective – if not a bit drunk. "Leanne," I started thoughtfully. "Do you think of me as… fake?"

Leanne pondered this for a moment, looking up at the sky. "Fake? Hmmmm. Morgan Mobley, do I detect a bit of rare introspection on your part today?"

"Introspection? I'm just trying to seek a bit of clarity. Am I a bad person?"

"No, I don't think you are a bad person at all," Leanne answered, smiling over her wine glass. "Quite the opposite. I would classify you as an undeniably good person. True, at first, I didn't think that. But I do now. And no, you are not fake, although you can be deceptive when you are out looking for a piece of ass."

"Am I thoughtless then? Selfish? Only out for my own gain?"

"Um. No, I don't think so."

"You said yourself, I'm more a person of the *gutter,*" I said, acknowledging her previous insult.

"Ha. I wouldn't want you any other way."

"But, what's wrong with me. I have no serious relationships. My ex, wherever she is at, wouldn't shed a tear if I were to die. Gutter is not what I strive to be! Look at you. You have… um… three."

"It doesn't hurt to look inward," Leanne encouraged. "You have no serious relationships because, by your very nature, you are a walking *hard-on*. And most men are at your age. You are too busy with the *chase*. And the fly-by-night

161

noncommittal screw that hopefully won't get you a sexually transmitted disease."

"I do chase women. I love women. I love everything about them. I admit it. I know that maybe I overdo that... Yes, yes. I'm a Man-Whore, as Stefany calls me."

Leanne smiled, amused with the change of subject this conversation was taking. She only nodded, sipping her wine, waiting for more. She could outdrink me, evidently, and she waited for me to further spill my guts.

"Leanne. I don't know. Maybe, I should seek something more meaningful... seek that special woman. That woman I would do anything for. Fall in love. But I've tried that, Leanne! I've failed every time." I hiccupped slightly, wondering if I should try a different type of craft beer. "Sorry."

Stefany appeared out by the barn, talking to several workers. She looked over and waved to Leanne who returned the gesture. Leanne swirled what was left of her wine in the glass. "Love. A conundrum, to be sure."

"How does one find true love, Leanne? Like... where?" I watched the sun gleaming off Stefany's hair. She began walking towards us. I needed an answer from Leanne before she came over to drip sour grapes all over our conversation.

"Digging out one's true emotions and feelings is tough. Love could be right in front of you, and you might not even realize it," she suggested.

The beer was making me overly chatty. "Tell me quickly before Stefany walks over here. Am I a *shallow* person? I honestly don't *think* I am. But I do things, and almost invariably I seem to get people angry or put out with me. Perhaps I am very flawed, I can see that. Is it because I like to date a lot?"

"Date? Is that what you call it, Morgan?" She laughed before downing the last of her wine. "It's your day off, what do you care if Stefany comes over here?"

"Because I want to hear your unvarnished opinion of me. Without the input of a woman that would just as soon see me castrated."

"Okay, here's the crux of it," Leanne began. "It is true that others often see us *far* differently than we see ourselves."

I thought about this for a moment, unsatisfied. "Yes, yes, Leanne. But do *you* think I'm shallow?"

She stood up and walked over to stand next to me. She patted my head playfully. "Yes. Indeed, you are quite shallow." Stefany was watching us both questioningly with her hands on her hips. Leanne turned to walk to Stefany, now going to meet her halfway. "An endearing, lovable form of shallow, nonetheless," she added flippantly over her shoulder.

The two women met in the front courtyard. I took a deep breath and wondered what Leanne meant by "lovable form of shallow."

CHAPTER 7
A BOTTLE OF TEQUILA AND FOUR FLAT TIRES

Morgan: I got a surprise going through my meager possessions. They were six printed text messages and post-it notes from my ex-wife, Trisha, hidden away in a copy of the magazine, *North American Architecture Today.* I had saved the magazine because it had an article on renovating old southern plantations, which was to be the model for me restoring Stoney Brook. I'm surprised it survived my stay at The Blue Calypso, but there it was...

I was getting ready to toss the magazine out, when the copies and notes dropped out, which I had totally forgotten. Why I kept them, I'm not sure. They are a sampling of the beginning of our relationship. Then they sequence further along until the last note. What a psychotic bitch. Before I shred them to pieces, here are some excerpts I have copied into this journal that should serve as a warning to me should I ever again consider marriage. Note - <u>she was away for school, just before we were married:</u>

"Morgan, I can scarcely wait until I am again in your arms. OMG I can't get you out of my every thought. Your eyes, your face, your lips, your touch, your kiss... Are you hard now, thinking of me? You better be. Have a good look at this picture I'm sending with this. You should know as soon as I get back, I will ~wear you~ out, buster. You make me so hot and wet when my legs are up over your shoulders and you are pounding me hard. Mmmm. I want you to think of that. Right now. Take care of business for me and send me a picture of it until I can get my own hands on you. Love you so very much. Always. PS Did I say how much I love you? I LOVE YOU! <3 T"

Note - <u>this was about a year after we were married:</u>

"Honey, I am at the salon, back in a bit. Also, I would appreciate you picking up your clothes that you left by your dresser. BTW, I don't really appreciate you off drinking with your friends yesterday evening. Think of the money you have spent on your so called 'friends.' They are no more your friends than the man on the moon. Is that what you want to do with your life? Love, T..."

Note - <u>midway towards the end:</u>
"I really can't get over how selfish you are. That money you spent on that motorcycle could have gone to other things, you know. But that's just how you roll, isn't it? All you care about is you. That's it. Just you. Really, I don't know what I see in you. Don't look for me, I won't be back this weekend. Up at my sister's place. I suggest you take a long hard look at yourself."

Note - <u>a little closer to the end:</u>
"Morgan, I'm going to be back late, me and the girls are going out to celebrate me getting my student loans paid off. BTW, there was a slight

mishap with your motorcycle earlier. I pulled in and nudged it with the car. It fell over. But how many times have I told you to park it out of the way? No one's fault but yours for this happening. I'm sure it's fine."

Note - <u>more closer to the end:</u>

"Morgan, the neighbor's kids came over. They were playing with my phone while I was in the kitchen, and I guess my access code was off. It would seem that one of your dick pics got sent to your mom."

Note - <u>the end:</u>

"Listen, fuckhead, it's OVER! I am so fucking sick of you and your shit. Just the sight of you makes me want to throw up. You will see that your things are out on the lawn, sorry about the rain. The locks are changed, and I will call the cops if you try and get in, and BTW, I have filed a restraining order. Don't ask to get back together again 'cause it aint happenin'. My lawyer is sending the papers to you. I HATE YOU and hope you choke on a big pile. BTW My lawyer is an absolute shark.

PS: Before we were married, I screwed your best friend over at his place. Three times! He was a LOT better lover than you, I can tell you. Chew on that one, loser!"

I reached up and grabbed a large, heavy steel ring, pitted, and encrusted with rust, hanging at about face height from a large bolt in the foundation. There were a series of twenty of them in the basement of the manor house, all set the same at about 5-foot intervals. Pulling my hand back, I surveyed the rust scale stuck to my palm. No one had probably touched those rings in nearly 200 years. I looked over at Miguel who was pushing a restored wine rack into place on the other wall.

"It is said those were for the slaves, Meester Mobley. Long ago. They were for punishments. Some to go to execution. That is what I was told by my grandfather."

Ugh. I had suspected they were used as such. I thought about cutting them out. No, Stefany would not approve, I knew. All the historical aspects of the manor and property needed preservation to the best of our ability. Even the unsavory slavery elements of the past. It was an agreement made with the authorities and was common to locations of significant historical merit. Guests would no doubt want to see the morbid curiosities of the past at Stoney Brook, of which there were many. The history was fascinating, I had to admit, despite the brutal implications on record.

My phone buzzed in with a message.

Stefany: To my office. Now.

It was a rather abrupt text, I thought. No "please" or anything else. Had I done something to piss her off lately? With that, I had to think. There had been no new sexual conquests of the female staff. Although that was not for trying, I had to acknowledge. Perhaps one of the girls had complained about my advances. Uh-oh.

I looked at the message again. Was I to be fired yet again? Taking a deep breath, I dropped my tool bag and set the laser level we were using on a stone ledge. "Santiago. Miguel. I must go up and see Ms. Michaels. Please continue with installing these new wine racks. Be careful bringing them in, don't scratch them on the floor or bang them on the doors. When you install them, keep them nice and tight, level and keep any anchor bolts well out of sight. I may be gone for a while."

Santiago pointed to the slave rings. "Cut those off, Mr. Mobley?"

"No, leave them, they are integral to the history of the building. But let's wipe all the cobwebs off, clean the rust off with a wire wheel and treat the metal with phosphoric acid to preserve them. We have a bottle of it up in the barn. Use a brush, don't drip it on the floor and be careful to wash your hands afterward. In fact, let's keep cleaning all these rooms down here after we get these bank of wine racks installed here."

"Si, Mr. Mobley," they both replied in near unity.

"Good luck with the boss," Santiago added with a smile.

"Thanks, I may need it."

First walking outside, I went over to a compressor in one of the nearest sheds and used the air nozzle to blow the rust and dust off my work clothes. If I were going to go up to Stefany's office to be fired, I wouldn't want to leave residue on her rugs. Who was I kidding, of course I did.

Approaching her office, I knocked on one of the doors.

"Yes, come in," I heard her reply.

I opened the door to see Stefany and Leanne poring over a pile of maps on her desk.

"Mr. Mobley. Good. Come in. I want you to have a look at these," Stefany said without any hint of the hostility I expected.

Okay, I had misread the intentions of her text. I should have known better. She was just a short and to the point kind of woman. There were legitimate reasons to call me up here and apparently, being fired was not one of them.

Walking over to their desk, I tried to make out the subject of their intense scrutiny. They were old maps - of the island, it would seem.

"Hello, Mobley," Leanne said, giving me a wry smile.

"Good morning, Ms. Tilden."

"How are things in the basement," Leanne asked.

"They are going fi-"

"Enough small talk," Stefany said, cutting me off. Her fingers traced over a boundary on the map that seemed to show the northern end of the island. "We are taking a trip today, Mr. Mobley," she asserted, never averting her eyes from the top map which was holding her attention.

"And it has something to do with these maps?" I asked.

"Yes." Stefany looked up at me for the first time. "It has come as quite a surprise," she hesitated. "We were notified today that the deed that was presented to me for Stoney Brook, which we have registered, was incomplete. On the northern side of the island…" She pointed for me to see. "Are over 3000 acres of land that is included with the estate property that we never knew about."

"That seems quite large to not have been mentioned before," I said.

"It is. It's been overlooked for more than 150 years," Stefany explained.

"It wasn't even on the tax rolls?" I asked, stunned.

"No. It's always been known as being off-limits by island inhabitants, and it just sort of went forgotten. The bad news is, yes, I will have to pay back fees and taxes on it. But this could be huge for me. Perhaps I could sell it off or use it somehow with operations here."

"And that is what we are going to go explore today," I said already knowing, leafing through the delicate, aged maps.

"Yes," Stefany confirmed.

"What is located there?" I asked, my finger pointing to a square structure drawn on the map, close to a beach.

"We don't know, Mobley," Leanne answered. "All we know is it encompasses a large stretch of beach, some forested and mountainous terrain. The only building on these old maps from the 18th century shows something labeled simply as a *mill*. Maybe that's what that square denotes."

"A mill. There are many possibilities with that," I added. "Lumber, flour. But more than likely a sugar cane mill, given the primary crop here at Stoney Brook. Are you going to go also, Ms. Tilden?" I asked.

"Regrettably, no," Leanne answered. "I'm taking Heidi and Joe over to the main island today for a little trip."

"So, Mr. Mobley. Pack a few supplies, pick up two backpacks from the hiking coordinator, some emergency items and be ready to go within the hour. Be prepared for a lot of walking overland through the jungle. I hear after we get through several small villages the roads are rough and the going will be slow. If we can get a move on, we can go see it, spend a couple of hours checking it out then be back by this evening. I've arranged the kitchen to pack us lunch and snacks. Gas up one of the Rovers. I'll meet you out front."

"Okay." The day would be spent hiking with Stefany – which would be interesting. Returning to my room, I packed a change of clothes and picked up my hiking boots.

Twenty minutes later and with our supplies packed, I pulled our Rover up to the front as directed. Stefany was waiting with the maps rolled up under one arm, her personal items in a carry bag in the other.

I got out and offered to help her, but she refused, throwing her own bag in the back of the Rover.

"You drive, Mr. Mobley. I want to look over the maps. I'll navigate for you."

"Right," I answered getting back in the driver's seat.

Heading out of the plantation drive, I noticed a dilapidated sedan sitting in the ditch. It was painted sky blue in what appeared to be latex house paint and polka-dotted with frequent patches of rust. It pulled onto the road behind us as we made our turn and followed at some distance back. Watching the interior roof fabric billowing behind the driver, I assumed it belonged to one of the field hands perhaps. As we began our adventure, it followed in the distance as we passed alternating scenes of sugar cane fields and dense tropical forests.

More than likely to avoid conversation with me, Stefany slipped in earbuds looking over the maps. She propped her smooth legs up on the dusty dash of the Rover, providing a ready surface for her to examine her maps – and eye candy for me. She looked wonderfully sexy in her khaki shorts and hiking boots.

"It looks like nice weather today for a trip, eh?" I asked, leaning over towards her, wondering if she could hear me.

She remained silent. I said it again - louder.

She apparently caught a bit of what I said. She looked over at me and pulled her earbuds out.

"What's that, Mobley?" She had to speak over the banging and clinking of the Rover, plodding through the potholes. Our windows were down, the wind rustling the papers she held against her legs, adding to the noise.

"I said..." my voice a little louder and trying to enunciate clearer, "nice day for a drive. The weather looks fabulous."

She blinked, irritated. "Mr. Mobley. I'm listening to my music, trying to make sense of these old maps. Small talk? Really? Is that all you've got?"

"I… was just trying to make conversation," I tried to explain.

"Do I look like I'm starving for idle, mindless conversation?" she asked testily. "Do I?"

"Um, I just thought…"

"Don't think, Mobley. Drive and don't irritate me any more than I can tolerate, please. Don't interrupt me with… *imbecilic* small talk."

She eyed me suspiciously but pushed her earbuds back in and continued studying her maps. After a few minutes I looked over at her, seeing she was distracted, a faint trace of her music was audible even over the ruckus of the drive. This could be fun, I told myself.

"Say there, Ms. Michaels. Hey."

Nothing.

"Stefany, can you hear me?"

Nothing. Perfect.

"You do have magnificent, sexy legs. Shapely, muscular calves and thighs. Very hot," I said quietly, feeling like a kid spying through a keyhole, relishing the idea of being able to quietly say what I wanted without getting caught. I looked over. Still no response, she hadn't heard a thing. "I bet you can kiss well. You are no doubt an expert kisser. And I bet those lips are good for other things as well."

I stole another glance. She continued to read her maps, none the wiser. This ROCKED. I felt like laughing aloud but restrained myself. "Yeah. I'd like to kiss those delicious lips of yours, Ms. Stefany. Maybe take a little of the ornery venom you have out of you that makes you such a harping shrew." I chuckled to myself, making sure she didn't notice. "You are quite a beautiful woman, Ms. Stefany. In fact, I'd like to kiss every bit of you, despite your cratchety, bitchy demeanor. You just need a good hard, deep kiss to bring you down to earth. And a lot more. A man to make love to you… good and hard. A man like… me, say."

Still nothing.

"I'd love to see you naked, Ms. Stefany. Oh, yes. Quite the woman, you are. One of the most beautiful on the island, I dare say. I'd bet you would be amazing in bed. Assuming I could work around that crabby, pickle-up-the-ass personality of yours. It's been a while since you've been laid, that's for sure," I said.

Looking angry, she pulled out her earbuds. "What the hell did you say, Mobley?"

I felt the blood drain from my face. "I was just talking to myself," I said smiling over at her. "I said been a while since the road has been graded, that's for sure."

"To Yourself?" she asked, unmoved. "Crabby, is it? Pickle?"

"As I was saying before. It's a *shabby* road. Rough and difficult... *fickle*. I'm sure it gets much worse." I waved my hand at the road as if to seek corroboration. Giving her my best disarming smile, I returned my attention to the road.

"Uh-huh." She put her earbuds back in, but not before shooting me a distrustful glance. Checking her with a discreet side squint, I watched her again return her attention to her maps. Crisis averted. My heart jumped, however, when I observed her sneakily slip her hand to the volume on her mobile, turning it down. She was trying to catch me! I could play that game. It was time for a song of my own.

"Soooooo, I'll be comin' round the mountain when sheee goessss, ohhhh I'll be comin' round the mountain when she goessss..." I finished the song as awfully as I could, adding extra nauseating pop style flourishes for effect. I looked over and she was staring at me incredulously.

"Gawd, Mobley. *That*... must be one of the most *atrocious* renderings of that song I have ever had the misfortune to hear. I'm sure you were the bane of your middle school choir instructor."

I watched her quickly turn the volume back up plus a little extra, and she returned her attention to the maps. I laughed aloud in my best evil villain laugh.

"Yes, but I was kicked out of choir after I was caught by the director making out with Sally Henderson beneath the bleachers," I explained to her quietly, loving the anonymity, popping in a piece of spearmint chewing gum into my mouth. "I almost had her pants completely off while they sang *There's a Great Day A-Comin'* during an assembly. The director discovered my absence during intermission and nearly pulled my ear off marching me to the office."

"And *that*… doesn't surprise me in the least, Mr. Mobley," Stefany abruptly said with disgust, never looking up from her maps.

I swallowed. Hard.

"Um. Ms. Michaels…"

"Just can it and drive, Mobley! You should know I have the right earbud turned completely off! My advice to you is to keep your disgusting mouth *shut* before it gets you fired again, and you are hitchhiking back to The Blue Calypso with my boot print on your ass! Your insolence! Your sexual depravity… knows NO bounds!" She turned and glared at me. "Beware, Mobley, lest you test me again. I have excellent hearing. And be glad I'm in a mood to tolerate your juvenile mischiefs." She rolled her eyes and looked out the window at the passing lush tropical foliage. "There's more in his nutsack than that empty head." She mumbled a few additional expletives below her breath.

Incredibly embarrassed, I realized she had just been stringing me along, listening to me the whole time, giving me enough rope to hang myself. I felt my face flush and decided it indeed would be best to stay silent. Busted. My mouth tasted metallic. She had me dead to rights but said nothing more. Perhaps Stefany had a sense of humor after all. Or… perhaps she appreciated the compliments. My guilt melted away and I smiled to myself.

I happen to glance up in my rearview mirror. Through the cloud of dust behind us, I could barely make out the old, battered car, which was still following. What the hell? Must be going to one of the small villages ahead. Still, it seemed odd.

After driving through several quaint villages, we took a remote and poorly maintained road that eventually took us to a dead end and a rusty gate, secured by an equally rusty heavy chain and large old-fashioned paddle-lock. The jungle was thick in this part of the island and there had been little if any recent traffic beyond the gate as it and the surrounding canopy hung heavy with vines and overgrown underbrush.

"This is it," Stefany confirmed. "I have no key. I guess we can leave the car here and walk around it."

I smiled over at her, ready to redeem myself. "Fortunately, I brought bolt cutters for just such an occasion."

I got out and rummaged around in the back, pulling a large bolt cutter from beneath the pile of supplies I had stowed. Walking to the gate, I cut an appropriate link of the ancient, rusted chain and unwrapped it from the gate. I prized the gate open and out of the way so we could drive through.

"Well done, Mobley," Stefany said. At least she wasn't holding a grudge, I thought.

I put the Rover in gear and drove through. Trees, brush, vines, and washouts made passage slow, yet we managed to proceed. Eventually, we reached a towering sheer cliff that was the base of the nearest mountain. Nestled up against the backdrop of the cliff was a huge four-story stone building of great age, beneath which a creek seemed to run. The structure had been long abandoned and was covered with vines and moss. Assorted tropical vegetation grew from the cracks and seams in the stone of the front façade. To the right and through the dense foliage, we could see a beautiful white sand beach. The property was a paradise.

"Wow," was all I could say as we took in the incredible scene.

"Yes, Mobley. I think "wow" expresses my sentiments as well. This must be the mill that is labeled on the map. As you suggested, it's probably a sugar cane press."

"Likely so," I agreed.

Stefany took a camera and began documenting the building and surrounding areas. After forcing our way through a door, a quick walk through the mill revealed that it had not been disturbed in many decades, perhaps longer. It was structurally sound, and a tile roof had kept most of the rain out. Of the extremely old glass windows, several were missing, and around these areas, the interior floor appeared rotted. There would no doubt be birds, bats and other creatures inhabiting the building. The damage could be mitigated, I thought, pondering the restoration effort.

The equipment, materials, and furnishings in the interior with its massive hewn beams and stonework were straight out of antiquity. For a person such as me interested in old buildings, it was a sight to behold.

After quickly exploring through several floors that seemed structurally sound, we decided to look at the beach area. For as far as I could see, a deep stand of coconut trees swayed in a gentle breeze off the sea.

After a long trek along the beach, we decided that we had documented everything we could during this first excursion. I paused for a moment, surveying the incredible scene. "Ms. Michaels. Stoney Brook and now this? You have incomparable luck."

"It's true. I still feel like I'm living some incredible dream. It's not been easy though. And I thought I could lose everything if I didn't come up with some money. But this. This could change everything for me, Mr. Mobley. I could maybe develop this. Or I could sell it. It's like a gift from out of nowhere. Another incredible miracle. Just dropped into my lap."

"You wouldn't sell it, would you? Look at this? The possibilities are endless. You could build a beachfront extension of Stoney Brook right here just by the careful renovation of this mill! Perhaps a restaurant with a tavern. You could offer guest stays here as part of an overall vacation deal."

"I never thought about that," Stefany admitted, pondering this idea. "But it would take funds that I don't have. Just think for a moment about how much I'm going to get taxed by the Island Tax Authority for this great windfall that they've overlooked for years. They are going to make me pay, big time. And I'm already in over my head in debt."

"Who knows at this point. You will have to put a pencil to it, Ms. Michaels," I said, again escorting her into the mill for one last look around.

Just as we stepped into the mill building, I vaguely became aware of a dark shadow behind the door. I began to turn - something cracked into the back of my head.

Small darts of light crossed my vision. I was dimly aware I was laying on the floor. In my dazed state, I managed to roll over to look up to see a person that had probably assailed me, a man who appeared to be a stranger.

Far away, Stefany screamed, "Noooo!" The stranger lifted a heavy steel bar over his shoulder, preparing to hit me again. As if in slow motion, I could see Stefany step over me and grab the man's arms, stopping the blow. Unable to move, I watched the ensuing struggle. She was holding her own, stomping his feet, hitting him about the face, all the while with one hand gripping the iron bar, keeping him from swinging.

With my consciousness ebbing, I blinked, struggling to clear my thoughts from within a black shroud.

Stefany: When I got the call from my bank on the main island, I could only assume it was some additional bad news. For once, I was wrong.

The idea that there were additional land holdings associated with Stoney Brook never occurred to me as a possibility. I'm

guessing it didn't occur to anyone else either, for at least several hundred years. How this additional land escaped the notice of loan officers, government assessors, and other island authorities is beyond belief.

There is a sizable chunk on the north end of the island that is a long-forgotten part of the Stoney Brook estate. The problem is now I owe back taxes and fees that haven't been paid in a century or more!

My New Carrot

Chalk it up to the highly inefficient and archaic records system of the island. The authorities claim this occurred due to a loss of records in a fire.

To take ownership, I must come up with the money for these fees and taxes, or at least agree on a plan to start paying them. Or I forfeit ownership to the island authority, which seems to be what they are betting on.

I don't have the money. How can I take out another loan to pay this off? Should I? The maps look like it could be an

amazing property. Is this a miracle or a curse?

Yesterday, I set out with Mr. Architect to go have a look at exactly what this tract of land looked like. And what was on it. And so began one of my more eventful adventures since arriving on the island.

Selling this land could save us," I remember telling Mobley, which turned out to be somewhat ironic. Maybe with what I could make on the sale, I could pay all the back taxes and loan fees, but still have money left over to help with my mounting bills on Stoney Brook.

These thoughts vaguely managed to cross my mind while I fought with some stranger that was trying to spill Mobley's brains over the ancient wood floor of the mill. I had the feeling I was fighting for my own survival as well.

Mobley had already taken one vicious surprise hit to the back of his head when we had reentered the mill building. The attacker was ready to administer the final blow when I grabbed his arms out of desperation. Mobley tried to get up but crumpled back down to the floor, losing consciousness. Or dying. I wasn't sure which, and I couldn't let go of the stranger's arms long enough to help or find out.

Who was this guy? Why was he attacking us? I assumed this wasn't just about Mobley because the guy seemed intent on getting to me as well.

I stomped as hard as I could on his foot. This had to hurt, and he bent forward a bit. With every ounce of strength I could muster, I punched him in the throat. This immediately resulted in him dropping the iron bar to the floor and making gagging sounds. As our feet shuffled in the contest, he kicked the iron bar back past me a few feet. Breaking off my grip on his arm, I stepped back and made a dash for the bar, tripping and landing on the floor. He lunged for me, his fingers gripping my shirt, tearing it just as I wrapped my fingers around the bar.

Standing, I swung the bar wildly, hitting him with a glancing blow that bounced first on top of his shoulder and then into the side of his face.

"Aghhhhhh!" He angrily ripped the bar from my hands. Now it was turnabout and he swung it at me in a wide arc, just missing my mid-section as I stepped back. If he connected with that bar as hard as he was swinging it, he would tear my rib cage out, I was sure. He tried once more, but I continued to back-pedal out of his range. I stumbled over an old piece of mill machinery as he lunged again. His last swing threw him off balance just enough for me to get around him and I made a run for it. He threw the bar to the floor and pursued, right behind me.

In making for the door, I knocked over a stand of loose boards that clattered behind me. At least for the moment, I was free. I ran out into the sunlight, unsure of my next move. Get to the Rover? Just flat out make a run for it?

Looking back, he had appeared in the doorway, tossing the boards aside, blood running down his mouth. Judging by how he was leaning against the door frame, he was in pain, which was fine with me. He began running after me, but by this point, my legs were already carrying me away from the mill as fast as I could go.

The quickest refuge seemed to me to be the trees of the forest. Then what? I couldn't count on Mobley to help. He could be dead for all I knew. How could anyone survive a blow like that to the head and live?

Adrenaline tasted metallic in my mouth, and I fought the urge to panic – maybe I was already! I could hear my pursuer mere steps behind me as I flung myself into the trees and brush. What could I hope to gain by running into the woods? It was only slowing me down. Sticks snapped. Leaves crunched. Vines pulled at my feet and arms. My breath was ragged, chopping at the air.

I froze suddenly, my heart thumping so hard in my chest I wondered if my attacker might hear it. I tried to listen, not only to get my bearings but discern where my pursuer could be. A twig suddenly snapped directly behind, and I knew he was there. A hand found its way onto my shoulder, curling, attempting to gain purchase. I yanked away and bolted again through the forest.

It must have been a vine that sent me headfirst into the moist, soft soil of the forest floor. As quickly as I could, I turned onto my back, and he was on me. His knee rammed painfully into my stomach, forcibly pushing the air out of my lungs.

I swatted his arms and tried to roll away, kicking, pushing, punching. It didn't work, he was much stronger than I was and certainly more capable. Somewhere, perhaps from one of his boots, he withdrew a knife. The shiny tip of this new deadly element was suddenly just over my throat.

"Now, you will die," he muttered, blood running from the corner of his mouth.

"Why!?" I asked loudly, with no other conceivable thought on my mind during this moment of survival.

"No offense. It's just business." He grunted, pushing the blade towards me.

I pushed and held his arms for all I was worth, but it would not hold him, I knew. This would be my final moment. This was my time, as unexpected and quick as it had come. No matter my determination, no matter my desire to live, no matter Stoney Brook, no matter my strained screams.

"NOOOOO!"

The blade came steadily closer to my throat. The tip pricked the skin and pressed. It went deeper. I felt the initial slicing of skin, the first wet, warm drops of blood that escaped to run down my neck. This would be the way I would die, I thought to myself trying to slow the blade. He was going to slice my throat open. A sudden calm came over me and I loosened my grip on his arms. Exhausted, I couldn't fight it any longer. The knife pushed deeper.

There was a confusing blur above me - an instant moment of incredible violence. Suddenly, I was seeing only the treetop canopy. No longer did the stranger peer down at me, preparing to end my life. He was gone. His knee that he had shoved into my stomach was gone. The knife was gone. If there were noises associated with this change of events, I couldn't discern them. At this time, the only thing I became aware of was the loud whooshing sound of my heart pumping blood through my body.

Slowly, the realization came to me. It was Mobley. He had launched himself through the air, smashing into the offender and knocking him clear of me.

As my senses crept back, my fingers dabbed at the small prick the blade had left on my throat. It was a cut, maybe the width of a finger with just a few drops of blood. Nothing more. One more moment and I would have been spilling blood from a severed artery.

I sat up, determined to help Mobley, a bloody mess who was no doubt fighting in less than his best capacity. The two men struggled, and Mobley managed to knock the knife clear of the attacker's hands.

I crawled toward the knife, trying to keep the stranger from getting it back. Both fingers from our hands closed on the handle simultaneously and I wrestled for it as he had to now contend with both Mobley and me. Mobley landed several hard punches to his face causing the stranger to relinquish his attempted grip on the knife. It was mine. The tables had turned, and I contemplated what I would do next. Stab him? At this point, I was prepared to do anything.

Suddenly rolling clear of Mobley, the stranger leaped to his feet and began to run back through the woods towards the mill and the entry road, where he would no doubt make his escape in whatever vehicle he was driving.

Mobley groaned and somehow regained his footing, but he staggered, his head injury and subsequent struggle almost getting the best of him. He extended his hand and pulled me up. We had both taken a beating in this strange and unexpected course of events. Regaining his balance, Mobley took off on a wobbly pursuit.

"Just wait here," he said over his shoulder to me.

"Mobley, no! You are in no shape to continue this! Let him go!" I yelled after him.

"I can't let him get away with this!" Mobley answered, crashing through the forest. "Stay there!" he warned.

I began running after them, not wanting to let Mobley face the attacker alone who looked in far better shape to continue the scrap than either of us. At least I had the knife. After chasing them for several minutes, I heard a car motor. It didn't sound like my Rover.

Coming into the clearing of the road by the mill, Mobley was standing out of breath next to our Rover as all four tires hissed loudly with escaping air. The bolt cutters laying in the dirt was the only evidence that the stranger had quickly rummaged through the Rover for something to flatten the tires. He had cut the valve stems off.

We watched helplessly as a car, down the road one hundred yards or more, turned around and drove away. It was a rusty, older model car painted in light blue.

After assessing the damage to the Rover and seeing that we would be going nowhere with only one spare tire, I began searching for my mobile phone. Fortunately, the stranger had not taken it as it was still tucked in on the side of the passenger seat.

Mobley dropped to his knees and took a sitting position leaning up against the hissing front right tire. He looked terrible with blood all around his neck and face.

Fortunately, there was enough signal to ring the front desk of Stoney Brook. I told them where we were and that they should contact the police immediately. I also told them to send out an ambulance for Mobley as well as Miguel and Santiago with tools and a set of spare tires.

It was going to be a while. Mobley seemed incoherent as I pulled him to his feet. I walked him to the tailgate of the Rover where I could see his head wound. Taking several rags and wetting them with some water from our cooler, I began cleaning him up.

He was a battered wreck. But even in this condition, I found myself impressed with his physique as I checked for broken bones. His pectorals were exquisite. My fingers paused slightly as I ran them over the muscled ripples before I caught myself. He didn't seem to notice, thankfully. I bit my lip, angry with my lack of control. Was I that hard up?

The gash on the back of his head was going to need stitches. After having him drink some water, I ripped a rag and bandaged his head to protect the wound. Despite his condition, there was a degree of rock-hard handsome dignity about him.

"You are bleeding from your neck," he observed, touching my neck with a finger.

"It could have been much worse," I acknowledged, wondering if he really knew how close I had been to death - if it were not for him.

Without any further word, he took a bandage from the first aid kit and gently applied it over my wound. "What do you think that was all about?" he asked, gaining coherence.

"I don't know, Mobley. No idea." Then a thought occurred to me, remembering the confrontation with the angry father in the barn back at Stoney Brook.

"Mobley, you don't think it was a pissed-off boyfriend, husband, father or… someone?" In his condition, I was trying to be as delicate as I could, but it was a question I had to ask.

"Honestly, Stefany. I… don't know."

I let it go for the moment, wondering if it was indeed the case. My eyes wandered away from his face, contemplating the possibilities when something caught my attention at the edge of the trees. I left Mobley and walked over to investigate this small object, discovering that it was a plastic sleeve such as one would find in a wallet. It was new. There was no doubt it had been dropped by the attacker while fleeing the woods.

It contained only two pictures: one of Mobley, and one of me. The pictures were of both of us at Stoney Brook, taken during indeterminate times and unknown circumstances. Was the stranger a hired killer? The implications were clear. The attacker had been after *both* of us. Maybe primarily me.

I looked over at Mobley, thinking of sharing the clue. Unaware, he was lying flat on the tailgate. I tucked the photo sleeve into my back pocket. I would keep this to myself until I could sort it out. At least for now.

He sat up as I walked back over to him. "You want something to drink?" he asked.

"No, thanks, Mobley. I had some water."

He reached into a bag in the back of the Rover and held up a bottle of tequila. "I meant something more celebratory. As in… celebrating that we are both still alive, that is."

"And why did you bring that?" I questioned, sitting down beside him.

He shrugged. "You never know. End of a day cap, after a beautiful trip. Maybe. You don't think it was a good idea?"

I took the bottle from him and pulled the cork out. "I didn't say that."

I took a deep swig and grit my teeth as it burned all the way down. He reached for it, and I held it away."

"Hey!" he objected. "What, you aren't going to share *my* bottle of tequila?"

"No."

"Umm. Why?" he asked, incredulous.

"Because, Mobley. You may have a head injury. And it's not advisable to drink alcohol if that's a possibility.

Sorry. I'm only helping you out at this point." I took another deep drink.

"Really?" he asked, doubting I was serious. "Are you sure about that?"

"Yes. Really. I'll reimburse you a brand-new bottle when we get back and after you check out as okay."

I looked closely at the bottle. "Although… I am fairly certain this is already *my* tequila from the bar stock." I peered up at him to see a feeble, guilty smile.

"Mobley. You sure work hard to fall below my lowest of expectations."

"But. I was going to pay fo-"

"Just shitcan it, Mobley. A bottle of tequila is the last thing I'm worried about at this moment." I took another deep drink, feeling the burning warmth from the intoxicating liquid all the way to my stomach. I felt better already. Shivering, my cheeks flushed suddenly, and I noticed Mobley curiously watching me.

After a moment, I took one last drink and stoppered the cork with a flourish. Handing the bottle back to him, I nodded approvingly. "Good idea to bring that, Mobley. Well done. Very relaxing."

"I'm *glad* I could help," he said sarcastically. He pulled the cork and took a drink.

"Mobley! I thought we agreed that was a bad idea for you."

"No, you agreed for me. Thanks, but I'm a big boy." He took another drink then threw the bottle into the back of the rover.

What was it about tequila? The steamy scene a few weeks prior with Joe and Heidi suddenly came to mind and I smiled. It had only been a few minutes, but I did feel more relaxed. Evidently, tequila was *my* kind of drink. While the attack and being in fear of my life had been traumatic, there was still plenty of good news for the day. We were both alive, I still had a wonderful new piece of property to consider in my future. What could be better?

187

We sat in silence for a while, letting the wild sounds of the forest wash over us. "C'mon. Let's go sit inside this amazing building and get out of the sun for a bit," I suggested. "My new building that I own. Me." I pulled Mobley to his feet.

"You are the fastest drunk I have ever witnessed in my life," he said.

"I am not drunk." I peered up at him as I pulled him along. His arms were like steel pipes. "Is that supposed to be an insult, Mobley?"

"Um. No."

I staggered slightly and he slipped his arm tighter around me. Which was just fine with me.

We reached the ancient door and pushed past the clutter of lumber the attacker had tripped over. Giddy now, I went in first and took his hand to pull him in. I caught the tip of my shoe on a board, and he pulled me from behind into his chest. I may have giggled slightly, which I regretted immediately.

My eyes caught his. "Oops. Sorry, Mobley."

"That's… quite alright, Ms. Michaels." In an instant, he turned me to face him and pulled me close. I gazed up at him, wondering if I was really going to go through with this. He kissed me. Softly. My lips gave tacit approval as I found myself reciprocating without voluntarily intending to do so. He pulled me tighter, bending me backward slightly at the waist over his arm, attacking my mouth. I kissed him back and wound my arms around his neck. His body was magnificent, and my need grew for this man I had despised only an hour before. I could feel his muscles rippling in his arms and his back.

What the heck was this? Was this because he had saved me? Again? The kiss grew more passionate, breathier, needier. There was an old rickety chair, probably several hundred years old. I grabbed his collar and pushed him backward, making him sit down. The chair creaked but didn't give way, astonishingly. He was as surprised as I was when I straddled his legs and sat on his lap, facing him.

Drawing on some pent-up energy I didn't even know existed, I again wrapped my arms around his neck and pulled him to me. He held me tight, kissing me deeply. Our tongues lashed, our mouths and lips wet and needy. Beneath me, I could feel his excitement pressing up against me, building in a noticeable bulge. I rolled my hips slightly back and forth on him, unable to help myself. This was going to progress beyond kissing very quickly.

I pushed away, perhaps sanity returning, catching my breath. "Enough. Mobley. Not a word of this. To anyone."

He looked confused. "But. Stefany, why… "

I brushed the mess of his wild curly blond hair out of his eyes that had escaped the bandage around his forehead. "You are an employee of mine. Nothing has changed. When we get back, don't expect any different treatment from me. None. This little… incident… never happened. A moment of temporary weakness. Only a kiss. That's all this is. And evidently too much tequila for me."

"I am so attracted to you, Stefany. Nada? Nothing for me? Because people that don't like each other don't kiss like that."

"As I said. Moment of weakness." He looked hurt. I almost felt guilty. So, I kissed him again - and again. Pent up passion rose now, nearly to the bursting point.

After several minutes, I again tried to take inventory of my senses and wonder what the hell I was doing. Should I feel guilty? What did this mean? How could I do this with Mobley of all people? I broke off the kiss and tried to get up off his lap, but he held me down.

"Mobley. I'm sorry, but let's be honest, you would be attracted to a knothole in a wall. I'm only a new conquest for you. And what I think of you is… that you are a good worker. And I'm grateful to you for saving my life today… *although* I'm pretty sure I saved your life, also! I am also grateful for you interceding against Miles for me at The Blue

Calypso. And… and… this… it was just… um. A kiss. That's all."

"Stefany. That's not true. It's not. I don't think of you like a conquest. What you mean to me is different. Somehow."

"You are an employee. I pay you. And we are absolutely *not* compatible." I snickered. "That's, for sure."

"I will work for free. No conflicts of interest. Would you see me then? See where…" He touched my cheek softly. "…this goes. You and me?"

"And what, you will be content with no money?" I laughed. What was he getting at?

"No. Maybe I could get another part-time job. Make some money that way. I would do it. I have never felt like this with anyone else. I'll do anything. I want to be with you."

"Be with me? Gawd. What does that even mean?"

He took my face lightly in his hands. I do have to admit; his touch was heaven. It would be all I could do to stop this right now. "I want to be yours. And for you to be mine. I want no one else."

I searched through his blue eyes, wondering what he was thinking. "This is all pretty sudden, don't you think?"

"Maybe. But it's a moment of clarity for me, Stefany. I won't ever let anyone mistreat you again. Ever."

"In the Rover on the way over, you said some nice things about me," I explained. "Yes, I did hear them. Nice compliments… if not a little salacious. NOT including the comments on my personality." He looked embarrassed.

"I meant them, Stefany. And no, not the bad ones, I was just being a smartass. You are so very beautiful." His lips again found mine and he kissed me. After a moment, I again regained control.

"The compliments were nice. I'll give you that. But that was all just about me, *physically*. What did you say about my personality, Mobley? Beneath the physical, let's be honest, you don't care for what you have seen. I don't blame you for that, I am what I am. And I admit, I've been a bitch to you."

"Stefany. I was wrong for saying those things."

"*Harping shrew*? Isn't that one of your names for me?"

"No," he said, trying to climb out of the hole he was in. "I said those things out of… spite. That's not what I really think. I often let my talking get ahead of my thinking."

"Yes. I can agree with that." Mobley had a sweet, soft center, evidently. Was he being serious? It was no wonder so many women fell prey to his charms.

"The point is, it's not how I feel about you. And I think… maybe if you knew me better. You would act differently. Towards me."

My eyebrows arched with suspicion. "In other words, not be so bitchy?" I was being difficult, crushing his ego I knew, but I was having too much fun watching him squirm.

He kissed me softly. "You will have no need to doubt me. I would do anything for you."

Just like that? An instant lover? Could he give up his woman of the week? Emotions swirled in my head as I tried to sort everything out through the tequila that had made me irritatingly weak. This was Mobley. Man-Whore Mobley.

"I trust NO man, Mobley. You should know that by now. I will be owned by no one. I will not be mistreated by anyone. Ever again. And I won't allow anyone to tear down what I have worked for. In some great miracle of fortune, I ended up with Stoney Brook. I am going to build it and make it successful if I must die trying. Leanne has warned me that I will have a slew of suitors at my door just for the fact of what I inherited. And I've never been too good with deciphering truthful intentions versus deceptive ones. Not that you are deceptive, Mobley. I just don't have any desire to find out. I don't need distractions."

"I would sign a contract. Anything. I will never make any claims against you, whatever it takes. I only want you."

Mobley, if he wasn't suffering from temporary insanity, could be quite sweet and persuasive, I was finding. I doubted his sincerity, yet when I looked into his eyes, he seemed truthful and straightforward. I sat there on his lap, stunned. Careful to avoid the bloody knot on the back of his head, I ran my fingers across his face then lightly over his amazing lips. My willpower was strong, but he had done a number on me. I imagined riding him just where he sat, seeing if the old chair would hold up with our exertions. I wanted him, bad, but I would never admit it to him.

I had practically insulted him, questioned his motives and his trustworthiness. And yet he was willing to do anything to be in some sort of a *relationship* with me. That was the first thing that was extremely unlike him. Where was his bravado? Cockiness? What the hell was going on with Mobley? I told myself it was horny desperation and nearly laughed out loud.

Outside, we heard a vehicle approach. It was probably Santiago and Miguel coming to pick us up. It pulled up close to the building and the engine cut out. "Helloooo?" It was indeed Santiago. "Ms. Michaels? Mr. Mobley?"

It was at this moment, staring into Mobley's eyes, that I realized perhaps Leanne had been right. Mobley had some sort of "feelings" for me. How deeply they ran; I couldn't be certain. But it was evident. It was there for me to read in his handsome face, and in his eyes that made a silent impassioned plea for "more."

A horn honked outside, and we needed to reply.

I kissed him one last time despite myself and stood up. "You are a good kisser, Mobley. Very good." I wiped my mouth on the back of my hand and smiled. "I'm touched by what you say you would be willing to do. I would never belittle that. But I can't accept it either. As for *us*, I'm sorry, but it's not going to happen."

"But what about this? What we just shared?"

"Yes. A kiss. Poof! It's over."

He stood, incensed and incredulous, no doubt in pain from the head injury - and the bulge in his pants that was rapidly deflating. "Poof?! That's all you have to say?!"

I had to laugh to myself as I walked to the door, relishing my cruel return to sanity. I looked back at him. "Yes. Poof."

CHAPTER 8
PURVEYING A PIRATICAL PAST

Stefany: There is no getting around the fact that I had very nearly been murdered. As was Mobley. My brief dance with my own mortality has left me contemplative, to say the least. The most important questions that remain unanswered were, WHY??? Were we still in danger? Would it happen again? Where had the attacker fled? Would he be back?

I went to the main island police station where I met the constable. He took my report of the attack at the Mill Property with skepticism until I showed him the knife and the prick point on my neck. He kinda looks like an asshole and I have my doubts about him really caring about any of this. I also gave him the photos of Mobley and me that I had found. And we certainly weren't imagining the gash on the back of Mobley's head, which was being treated at the hospital. The implications were clear to me: this was an attempted assassination.

I told the constable about my estrangement from Miles. I also told him about my increasing suspicions that Miles had something to do with this. His apathy and body language tells me he has dismissed my assertions the moment they left my lips. He said he would initiate an investigation "soon."

The constable says he's originally from the island but worked in the mainland United States and was a career investigator from the west coast. Whatever, just find the asshole that did this. So far, he doesn't have anything but our descriptions of the mysterious assailant and his car. How hard could it be to find that ugly car on this island?

~~~~~

Mobley was released from the hospital after staying the night for observation. Leanne volunteered to bring him back, as I wanted no part in it. He took a nasty hit, there's no doubt about that, and it took 12 stitches to close the gash on the back of his head. Yeah, I feel bad for him. But he is no worse for wear and back on the job. I am extremely relieved. Leanne has been in freak-out mode since all of this, worrying over me relentlessly.

~~~~~~

I have been careful to avoid Mobley since the Mill Property incident, sticking with short nods or a vague "hello" when I have chanced to cross his path. I can tell he wants more. He's like a hound that has been denied the steak bone and he won't give up on it. It's odd to think of myself as being on Mobley's romantic radar and I am not sure what to make of it. His eyes light up whenever he sees me, making me want to avoid him more.

Sure, we kissed. Maybe I initiated it. That fucking tequila is to blame. I admit, he is a specimen of a man physically, even after getting clubbed over the head. Just one of Mobley's biceps has more muscular sex appeal than all of Miles' body put together. But... personality-wise, Mobley is still Mobley, the Man-Whore. Am I reading him all wrong? Am I just misunderstanding him? Or perhaps I have placed too much emphasis on his more visible faults and not giving him a chance. Mobley did save my life; I have no illusions about that. But to ease my conscience, I am certain I saved his life first when the attacker was going to finish bashing his brains out! So, it all should be a moot point.

Do I feel something for Mobley? At this point in my life, I'm NOT going to get the feels. FUCK THAT. It's irritating as hell. I don't want to feel anything! If I do, it's momentary lust, nothing else! I am so disgusted with myself. Fuck men and cocky pricks like Mobley. It's been too long and maybe I just need to get laid. And after said laying, the man

gets the hell out. And surely, if I'm going to lust after someone, it can be someone other than Man-Whore Mobley! How did he even get in the position to be on my mind? I need to take the edge off again, tonight. Hmmm.

I suppose there's a time coming where I will have to talk about all of this with Mobley. Until then, I am content to avoid him - and make sure Leanne doesn't know anything about my indiscretion. If Mobley says anything to Leanne about the mill trip other than the non-kissing part,

he'll need stitches to reinstall his balls after I'm done with him.

~~~~~

So, my prime suspect in the attack is coming by to see me. Fucking Miles - the suit with hair. He is my main suspect because:

> **1- Despite what he says about a reconciliation, he hates my guts as much as I hate him, and I can see right through his lies. And I'm sure he only wants part ownership of Stoney Brook. And if I ended up dead? We aren't divorced yet. So...**
>
> **2- He despises Mobley after what happened in The Blue Calypso. Knowing Miles as I do, he is out for revenge at any cost.**

I'll play nice. For now...

"Are you sure you are okay?"

Miles sat across from me in a wicker chair beneath the shade of the east porch of Stoney Brook. The look he gave me at that moment I had seen numerous times before in our tumultuous marriage. It was one of false concern. He leaned over and touched my arm to better convey his fake worry.

"Yes," I replied, irritated I had to take this time out of my busy day to see him. "I wouldn't be here talking to you if I weren't."

"True," he said, taking a sip of his mint julep. Even in this tropical heat, he was dressed immaculately in a suit and tie, Rolex, wingtips – only the finest for Miles.

"Did the constable have any ideas of who may have done this," he asked innocently.

I eyed him carefully, gauging his reaction. He was a good lawyer, I knew, and he could win an academy award with his ability to act.

"No. Just our descriptions. And what his car looked like."

"Ahhh," he sighed, contemplatively. "Perhaps he will come up with something, then."

"Yes," I agreed, wiping a bead of sweat off my brow. It was an early afternoon and already hotter than Hades.

"Stefany?"

"Yes?"

"Let's get back together. It just makes sense."

I sighed. Not this again. He wasn't going to give up, that was apparent.

"No. It *doesn't* make any sense. We don't get along. I don't really want to get along currently. I just want you to leave me alone and grant me a divorce."

"It makes perfect sense to reconcile. I can protect you. Make sure you are safe. And I can also help you keep this place. With my resources and connections, I can help you keep Stoney Brook going… and at a healthy profit."

"I've told you, Miles. No."

"You told me it was *no* - for the time being. You said you would think about it. Sure, I made some mistakes and used bad judgment. I didn't control my anger and did some things I'm ashamed of. I hurt you. I am so very sorry for what I have done. But I am better now. Really. All I ask now is you give me another chance."

"I asked for a *divorce*, Miles. I don't want to give you another chance, I just want to go about my life, peacefully, and start over. Is that too much to ask?"

"I will not grant you a divorce. You should realize that by now. We will work things out," he said resolutely, sitting back in his chair looking self-assured. "Let me show you it can work. You owe me that much."

"I owe you? As you can probably already guess, after what you did in The Blue Calypso, I'm not ready to commit to anything like that right now."

"Then when, Stefany? When? When will you be ready to commit and let us get on with improving our lives? Our marriage?"

"I'll let you know," I answered, intentionally obscure, growing tired of the conversation. I was blunt and it nicely served up the effect I anticipated. He sat there like an impudent child, anger seething below the surface.

"Did you have anything to do with it?" I finally had the gumption to ask.

"What?" he asked, the incensed tone in his voice clashing with his prior pleas of reconciliation. "With what, the attack? Of course not! How... *dare* you. Is this what our relationship has been boiled down to, Stefany? That you would accuse me of sending someone to attack you?"

"I've got a lot to do today. I think you had better leave, Miles."

The expression on his face changed instantly. After a momentary uncontrollable relapse, he was back into character and he smiled, disarmingly. The smile of a snake in a suit. "Stefany. I will talk to the constable and see what he has. I'll do everything I can to help, I just want you to feel safe. And for us to get back together. Soon. I love you."

"As I said, I'll let you know." My patience was beginning to wear thin, but I tried to maintain my composure. At this point, I didn't know for sure if he had anything to do with orchestrating the attack at the mill.

"Okay." He stood up and came to me for an awkward kiss on the cheek. I flashed my best fake smile and stood up for a fake hug, hoping to quicken his departure. I don't know what I ever saw in this man to marry him in the first place. What was certain was that I hated him now and I wanted his lips off me.

Of all the times to walk through the front doors, Mobley had somehow managed to pick the current moment. His eyes widened when he saw Miles kiss me on the cheek.

Nowhere to go now but walk right by us, he approached, in his typical Mobley brash swagger.

"Good day, Ms. Michaels. Mr. Michaels."

"Hello, Mr. Mobley," I replied, hoping I wouldn't have to call security.

Miles, not saying a word, stormed off the porch towards his out-of-place, overly expensive sports car that he had specially shipped to the island. To his credit, he didn't threaten Mobley.

Mobley, watching Miles drive away, stood in anticipation of striking up a conversation with me. In no mood to rehash what I knew was on his mind, I was already on my way back through the doors.

I was surprised to see that one of the girls at the front desk had slipped a folder under my office door. It was from Marisha Neita of the Island Historical Society. She had deciphered more of Seumas Owen McCaskill's ledger. The note taped to the folder simply read:

"Here you go, Ms. Michaels. I would like to remind you we are not who our ancestors were, and as I send you these updates, please understand this is no indictment of you as a person or your namesake. You'll find in these latest transcriptions that Seumas McCaskill led quite a violent life. There is a lot more to go, I'll be in touch. Come see me for tea when you have time. ~Marisha"

Finding some time to myself that afternoon, I took the folder and walked out into one of the gardens. Outside by myself and immersed in the sounds of the noisy birds in the nearby forest, I opened Marisha's folder, ready to enjoy this latest excerpt in the life of my mysterious ancestor.

"The Ledger of Seumas Owen McCaskill (continued)

Several pages were unfortunately water damaged and portions of his ledger are unintelligible here - Marisha

Capturing the Bella Dama 1615

"It were off the coast of one of the isles in and around Hispaniola that we first sighted her. Spanish probably, armed, but looking a wee undermanned for some measure, gauging the lubberly manner of her sailing under flight, and nothing to turn our course, as we'd seen and taken far stouter. She flew no colors as to maybe set us off our wits as to who she could be, and perhaps we'd take the mystery as a warning. This were ill advised as her name were clear as day on her stern and not being on England's behalf. No matter, and half a deceit is a poor thing to pin ones hopes to on the high seas. The word from the long glass was that she was the Bella Dama and looked to be supplies and such. And there she were, laden rich and with no escort."

Note by Marisha: The ship and its captain at this point remain unknown, as their descriptions were more than likely lost in the damaged portions of the ledger. Further research may yet reveal more facts about this early period of the life of Seumas Owens McCaskill.

"After giving chase and a few bow shots, she hove to, we grappled and boarded, eager for close, hot action. The crew were hungry for some success and so it were without surprise that we were in no manner of bargaining. While it seemed that they were given to surrender and were willing, as it were, to try their lot to be left on some shore somewhere, it made no difference, for when the crew gained her decks, it were already over for their captain, crew, and passengers alike. Their captain fell by my own sword, my father's as it were, it were good to wet the polish. My measure of him and the others were that they were no much to speak of as fighting men. One man alone gave me sweat to exert myself, but I soon cleaved his head in two, down to the shoulders, and soon after to feed the sharks with his mates. It were the passengers that gave me pause, families, women, and children, and were all put to the sword and thrown overboard. It were at this prospect that I didn't find much peace, as an able-bodied seaman is a fair opponent, mind, and he'd better fight or die on my accord as a man ought to, but I never took to killing the fairer sex, the young or defenseless.

"It weren't long after, the crew turned against our captain and quartermaster, who were taken with shorting us with our just apportionment. We sent both to their own deep reckoning with lashed backs. The captain more so with a knife in his throat. The surprise were all mine as I were voted in proper as captain, the men noting my seamanship, knowing how to go about a proper fight, and fairness all around.

"From this point on, we sailed at my pleasure and crew were wholly in support as I did them fairly and open with apportionment. It were rated time at the mast and position, as to be honest and expected.

"Seventeen ships of varying size and compliments were earned through our travails over the course of about five years. They made us all rich men and truth be, somewhat lazy dogs. Now and then I showed the crew when to put a body on the sword. Word was out and a scrape or two were foretelling. The ship, hulled and taking it once to many times at the waterline were no good to us anymore. It were at this time, I decided I were done and left the men to their own to find a new ship and new captain.

"There were two that tried their hand of thinking I were too rum sot and favored the chance to kill me, relieving me of my apportionment. Neither were up to the task, and I brought their heads to the tavern should anyone else have a mind to cross a McCaskill.

"It were this time I decided to take up being a proper landowner and settled upon some property on an island far enough away from the Main, very peaceful and with a tavern and number of inhabitants. It were 50 slaves I first started off with for this task, to build and make what I had in mind. A sorry lot, they gave out more often than not, the lash not keeping them afoot. Three birthed, which were cause for hope of sustaining the workforce. Although eleven of these first died straight away and I had to wait 2 months until the next ship call, at which time I purchased an additional 30.

"One among these is a young slave girl that goes by the name of Bowkee." NOTE BY MARISHA: This sounds like a traditional West African name, Bhoki, which I'll use in these transcriptions.

"I bought her as a girl now going on three years ago, and presently appears to be about 15 and of age, decent enough at working and not found shirking as many others have, yet all improved by the lash. Bhoki has a comely look about her, and to quite a rare degree. I was told when I bought her, she were part white. She captures every eye that is set about, slave or white alike and has a jaunty spirit also, as would a laird even, which runs counter to her race by my reckoning. And her without even owning the stitches on her back. Nevertheless, has given me cause to bespeak a more respectful hand towards her despite myself.

"The land were soon turned and set about with a grand structure that I decided to call Stoney Brook. Situated over a caved natural spring, I found my true home and hearth.

"And so I have put Bhoki in at running the household with three others, set about in clothes and manner as one would expect of a finer household.

"It were also at this time I decided to take a voyage home and inquire as to the hand of my boyhood desires, young maiden of the McCullum clan, Nancy. Of course I

wondered, were she taken, her name now that
of another."

With trembling fingers, I closed the folder and stood,
terrified to learn that my own ancestor, Seumas Owen
McCaskill was a bloodthirsty, murdering pirate. Worse yet,
he was a brutal slave owner. The rumors and myths are true.
The horrific legacy of my namesake was a disgusting
montage of murder, robbery, and abuse.

A young couple approached, new guests, I
recognized, just having come to island the previous day.
Smiling, I greeted them with a bit of small talk before taking
their leave and heading back to the manor. The last thing I
wanted to do was talk to anyone after this latest installment
of the Seumas ledger.

I was thankful that Marisha did not seem to harbor
resentment that my ancestors more than likely treated her
own ancestors terribly. But what if it got worse? She said she
would not be judgmental of me. Marisha had given me sound
advice, I reminded myself as I walked in through the main
entrance, nodding to Acantrella at the front desk. I was NOT
Seumas, and his legacy was in no way mine. This was
history, nothing more. Despite trying to reassure myself of
this, the unease in the pit of my stomach felt like guilt.

Morgan: I will be able to get the stitches on the back of my head out in another week. The nut case with the pipe did quite the number on me. And I don't even know why. Stefany hinted around that it could be some angry husband or boyfriend, whatever. But the guy tried to kill her too.

I can't get her off my mind. Stefany. The "harping shrew." Except she is one of the most incredible women I have ever met.

I fall asleep thinking about her. I wake up - it's Stefany on my mind while I brush my teeth. Sleepless nights. Raging boners. Queasy stomach. Unable to concentrate. What has she done to me! She has burned through me like Sherman through Georgia. And when she sat on my lap - her writhing tight body – ohhh fuck. Out of the blue, she puts the moves on me, kisses me like she was ready to just fucking take me right then and there in that old mill. She rocked her tight amazing little ass on my lap as she sat. All of that and I had just very nearly had my brains knocked out which she made me forget quickly enough.

Of course, I would never tell anyone these things. It's really the first time a woman has ripped my soul wide open if I must admit it. If I had blue balls before, Stefany has cruelly made it much worse. I haven't had sex in... what, months? I don't really want any other women. I think I would do anything just to kiss her again. The sweet taste of her mouth. Those eyes of hers. What's wrong with me! I must be crazy to fall for someone so hard.

Anyway, I'm getting a grip. Right now.

~~~~~

NOTES: ~The Plan~ (or the project – haven't decided)

by me, MM

I have been very busy working on my secret "project." Making calls, writing proposals, emails, letters. Not much more leg work, and it will be ready to present to Stefany. Why am I going to such lengths with this "plan"? Is it my feelings for her? But I think I can make this work!

I really do want to help her save Stoney Brook. I want to save HER. She isn't saying much, but even with the increases in revenue, she is going to lose this place. Leanne keeps me in the know. Stefany isn't making enough to cover the bills and mounting expenscs. I think she's dead broke at this point. I've thought long and hard-on this, trying to figure anything out that I could to help her.

She must have incredible luck, with this whole Mill Property thing landing in her lap. Just like that, some long-forgotten

PRIME territory on this island is hers. It was every bit as unlikely as her first getting the plantation. One lucky woman, Stefany Michaels is. Although I doubt she would completely agree. It's kind of in her eyes. She knows she is going to fail. The taxes and back fees alone are astronomical – and growing. She'll lose Stoney Brook and end up back in Montreal.

But. I don't think it has to be that way.

~~~~~

After several more trips to the Mill Property with Miguel and Santiago, it is all coming together. I've made all the initial first contacts. I have the means, the materials, the methods - and most importantly, I've secured more than 3 million dollars in startup expenses for her. 3$^+$mill!!! And the commitments to secure it, with competing bids that will be coming in from four major fortune 500 corporations. All we must do is sign!

I have the plan that will save Stoney Brook for Stefany Michaels.

~~~~~

Putting it simply, this is the biggest thing I have ever done! And here's the kicker. It really doesn't do anything for me. So why am I doing this? She might not even like it! Or. She could get rid of me as soon as I hand it over to her! Is that my aim, to be the good guy? I do want to help her; I know this to be true. I don't really want anything out of this but her happiness – except maybe have her like me more - respect me more. Give me a chance?

My confession to myself: I think I have done this because I am deeply in love with her. And I would do anything for her.

I walked in and stood in line for a drink, admiring the early evening crowd. Every few nights, Stoney Brook features live music at the veranda. The dance area is highlighted with specialty accent lights and fresh arrangements of tropical flowers at each table. The staff sets up tables of delicacies and endless varieties of booze. While primarily for guests, native islanders are also welcomed with admittance for a cover fee. It didn't take long for these events at Stoney Brook to become the new hot spot for island nightlife. The crowds were big, and the money was rolling in. And so were the beautiful women.

I looked around, gauging the prospects. Not that any were going to be on my menu. Suddenly, just as my place in line paid off in front of the bartender, I noticed Stefany, standing alone on the plantation steps, simply watching the busy scene.

"Yes, Mr. Mobley? What will you have?" It was the cute staffer, Issadel.

"You. With nothing on but a saltine cracker," I half-joked with her, discreetly.

She smiled broadly. "Now, now. Mr. Mobley. You know the rules. I mean… what will you have to *drink*?"

I looked back over my shoulder towards Stefany. Yep. Still alone. Still standing on the steps.

"Two glasses of Champaign."

"Ah. You already have a young lady catching your eye, Mr. Mobley?"

"No. Of course not. I'm just going to go out and be… friendly."

With this, she smirked. "We all know you are very friendly. I will put this on your account," she beamed mischievously. She still enjoyed haranguing me over the bar tab issue I had with Heidi.

"Yes. Thank you, Issadel." Rather than try and redeem my reputation in her eyes, I nodded my respects and turned to make my way to Stefany through the shuffling crowd.

It was quite dark out, even with the accent lights. Stefany did not see me coming until I was halfway up the steps. She tried to act like she didn't see me and turned to go in the other direction.

"Ms. Michaels!" The live music was booming and now she tried to pretend she didn't hear me. I caught up, getting just behind her. "Ms. Michaels!"

"Yes, Mr. Mobley?" She was walking quickly away from me even as she answered. I hurried my pace to step in front of her.

"Ms. Michaels. You have been avoiding me."

"What? Avoiding? No. I am very busy, Mr. Mobley. As you are aware, there are a lot of things going on around here. What is it you need? How is your head?"

"Forget my head. I want to talk to you."

"About…? Bear in mind this conversation needs to be about something *work*… related."

I handed her the extra glass of Champaign, which she accepted reluctantly.

"This isn't looking like it's work-related."

"I wanted to talk to you about what happened at the Mill Property. Er. After I was hit on the head, that is."

"Um, no. Nope. I've told you, I will only discuss work-related subjects, Mr. Mobley. As for the events at the mill, the island police are handling that." She tapped the fingers of her hands together from around her glass. "Other than that, there is no need for us to converse this evening. Now if you will excuse me…"

She tried to get around me, but I stood in her way. I placed my hand softly on her arm which may have been a mistake. She stared at it with indignation. Surprised at the venom, I let it drop.

"Stefany. Please. Just give me a chance. Talk to me, at least?"

She looked up at me, growing angry. "Mr. Mobley. What should occasion that I am now on a first-name basis with you? I assure you, contrary to what you may think, *nothing* has occurred that changes that."

Hesitating, I swallowed. In my mind, the answer to this swirled around, with no intention of getting past my lips. *You sat on my lap and kissed me. Passionately. And now… I can't stop thinking about you.*

"Just hear what I have to say. Is that too much to ask?"

After taking a drink of Champaign, she leaned in conspiratorially to whisper. "I would suggest… that you watch yourself. I am not one of your little hussies that hangs on your every word, Mobley, I'm your boss. Irritate me any further with this and you can get your last paycheck. Hmm?"

The band began playing a popular slow dance tune, enticing couples to walk to the floor.

"Dance with me, then." I held out my hand to her. She stared in disbelief, and I wondered if I would, indeed, be getting my last paycheck that evening.

"Are you *really* that dense, Mobley? Is there so much air between your ears that the rushing noise blocked out what I just said? Should I have them call you a taxi at the front desk?"

"Take this dance with me. Please. And afterward, if you feel so compelled to fire me, I will accept my fate. I will pack my things tonight... with no further request of you."

The speed with which she set her glass down on a nearby table and held her hand out to me made me certain that she was going to call my bluff. She had found an excuse to fire me with ease and I had given it to her on a silver platter. Walking her down to the dance floor, her hand softly in my own, I had to wonder if this would be the last night I would see her. I pulled her close as we moved along between the other couples. She offered no resistance. There was no holding back at this point, if she was going to be rid of me, at least I would have my five minutes. I immediately began to regret my rash action.

I leaned down, my mouth next to her ear. "Stefany. Please listen to me."

"Say what you will, Mobley. You've made it worth my while."

"Do you really want to fire me? Just for how I feel about you?"

"Yes. The second time is a charm, I hear."

I softly pushed her chin up, making her look me in the eyes. I had nothing to lose. Again, she offered no resistance.

"Do I perform my duties well here for you?"

"You *did*."

"Have I stolen from you or committed any other offense?"

"You mean other than right now?" She laughed at her own wit.

"Come on, Stefany. Have I?"

214

She looked contemplative. "Well. You have called me by my first name when I have told you that it's inappropriate. And. You are an incurable man-whore. There are all the young ladies on my staff that you continuously bed, despite my warnings to you to keep it in your pants. You are self-centered. Arrogant. There's the knee wall concrete fiasco. You regularly pilfer booze from the bar stocks."

Ouch. The man-whore thing... well, there's the blue balls to counter that claim now. The young ladies. Meh. Self-centered, arrogant. Eh. Maybe. The concrete wall, I thought we let bygones be bygones. She had me on the booze one.

"That's... not what I mean."

"Oh? What do you mean?" She was smiling, very much enjoying herself.

I looked around. It was dark and crowded. No one was watching us that I could determine. Leanne was off with her friends engaged in conversation and wasn't paying any attention to us.

"Never mind that stuff. What I mean is. I... just want to kiss you. Again. And I'm willing to pay for it with it being my last night here. If that's what it takes."

I kissed her, lightly. She offered no resistance. I kissed her again, this time unable to restrain the pure desire I had for this woman. Whatever this was, this thing I had for Stefany Michaels, it was entirely new to me. She was on my mind, night, and day. Just a glimpse from her set my heart off at a racing pace. I wanted her more than I had ever wanted any woman. I wanted to spend hours looking into her green eyes... learning every little thing about her. And this simple act of kissing her as we slow danced was setting my soul on fire. It was probably going to truly be the last thing I did in my capacity as an employee at Stoney Brook. But at this point, I didn't care.

After a moment, her arms pulled me tighter. Her lips warmed against mine in a magical moment that I would never forget. It was every bit as intense as the kiss at the mill. I wanted to sweep her off her feet and carry her away. The song neared the final seconds, and I reluctantly withdrew from her mouth.

For the last few moments, her eyes locked with mine. The song ended and I took a deep breath, knowing this was probably going to be the end.

In silence, we walked back up the weathered, cracked stone steps to the table where our drinks were sitting. I waited for the inevitable conclusion of my brash request. Handing back her glass of Champaign, I waited. Unemployment wouldn't be that bad, I told myself. I had a little money saved and I could get back to the mainland at this point.

As if considering her options, she stood surveying me a moment from over the edge of her glass as she sipped her Champaign.

"So, are you going to fire me?" I finally asked.

"Not *tonight*," she said. And with that, she left.

"Si, Meester Mobley," Miguel said. "It is hollow, no?"

The wine racks in the plantation basement had gone in as I had directed, and they looked great. The accent lighting was perfect. We had preserved the historic flavor of the basement, even saving the slave shackles on the wall. Now Miguel, in an unused storage room, was using a crowbar to tap against one of the large square pieces of flagstone on the floor.

Miguel tapped it again. The stone seemed to have a resonance that the other nearby stones did not. This stone sounded hollow beneath it.

Santiago bent down, running his hands over the very old, weathered floor. "Should we lift it up? And see, Meester Mobley?"

I looked carefully at the stone. It appeared no different than any of the other floor stones. But it was huge, perhaps five feet by five feet. It had to weigh hundreds of pounds. I borrowed Miguel's crowbar and tapped several side stones. The stones that were adjacent and linearly aligned oddly sounded partially hollow.

"How did you find out about this?" I asked them.

"By accident," Santiago answered. "We were just here during break after installing the last wine rack and we have the crowbar in hand. Just tapping as we walk, you know. And we heard the difference in sound. Tap here, sounds hollow. Over here, no." Santiago emphasized his story by tapping two different areas of the floor.

I thought about the implications. The basement was what I had thought was the lowest point in the huge, old building. Was there more? It could simply be a fill cavity, albeit a large one. Perhaps the fill had settled over the centuries. If it were an intentional space that had been built hundreds of years ago, for what purpose could it serve? This was a tropical island, and it was hard enough keeping water out of the basement, much less something built at an even lower elevation.

If we pried it up, we ran the very real risk the stone would crack or crumble, or it could get chipped and damaged. What could we hope to find? I didn't feel like trying to find a replacement stone if we ruined this one.

I rubbed my chin, contemplating. "What do you guys want to do?" I finally asked. I would leave it up to my crew.

They both laughed. "Si! Let's pry it up, Meester Mobley! Up! Let's see what it is! If it breaks, we fix and we make it look good as new. No worries."

I loved their enthusiasm. "Fine. Go get some beams. Posts. Maybe a block and tackle and tri-frame. An armload of boards to safely set the stone on after we pry it up. And get those flat blade long prybars in the storage tool room. We'll see what we have, boys!"

The two hurried excitedly out of the room. Soon after, they reentered with everything that we needed to pry up the stone floor.

The three of us went to the most convenient end of the large stone floor piece and gently tapped our pry bars down in between the seam with mallets. When we were at a sufficient depth, I told the boys to hold.

"Okay. Each of you get a board by your foot. When we pry it up, use your foot to slide in a board under the stone, that way we have a good chance of getting it up and safely supported without it accidentally slamming back down and maybe breaking. Get on your bar. When I get to three, gently pull back. All three of us should be able to pry the piece up. Carefully. Even pressure. All at once. One… two…three."

The stone was every bit of several hundred pounds and probably a lot more. It took more than an easy pull to begin lifting the stone. Slowly, it rose, the slab probably being about 6 inches in thickness. After several inches up a blast of musty air puffed from around the sides. When the stone was high enough, we pushed our boards beneath it and let it rest on these for the moment.

If it was a void, it was a big one. Getting on my hands and knees, I tried to peer beneath the stone but could not see anything but blackness.

"Yes, Meester Mobley! It is hollow beneath!" Santiago said with growing excitement.

I pointed to a tool bag by the door. "Please. That little flashlight in the bag."

Miguel quickly retrieved the flashlight, handing it to me. I turned it on and tried to make out what if anything was beneath the stone. The hole dropped off out of my view. All I could see were sides that appeared to be hewn out of solid bedrock. From far below, I could hear what sounded like water running.

"You boys were right," I told them, congratulating them. "This is a great find. I can't wait to see what the hell is under here."

Just at that moment, my phone buzzed.

Stefany:

218

**Meet me at the front desk
in no more than 10 minutes.
Urgent. We have a police
visitor.**

I was excited to get into the hole, but I had my orders. Thinking quickly of what I needed for this new development, I took a notepad out and began jotting down a diagram for the boys.

"Santiago, Miguel, I have to go, so have a look at this. This is what I want you to do next. Get a couple of helpers from out at the stables. Get four guys to put wooden boards under the end we just pried up. Pry it up a little more. As soon as it's high enough, push a thick round wood post right under it, right in the middle, then gently let it back down. Be safe and stay well back from that hole. Don't stand on the stone either, it could break and send it and you down in that hole." They both nodded eagerly.

"Then, get two more round posts of the same size on this side that will be up. Gently have everyone pry that opposite side up so that it slowly comes to rest on the posts. Use wooden boards on that end to lift it slightly. Slide at least three more posts under that side. It will be up and well supported."

"Si!" Miguel exclaimed enthusiastically. "I see what you are doing. We will roll it right off and out of the way!"

"Yes," I confirmed. "But carefully! And no one is to go in that hole until I get back. I first must check the air down there and make sure it's safe for us to go in without respirators. There's a little confined space monitor I must use to probe the air. Make sure it's okay to breathe and there are no toxic gasses. Savvy?"

They both responded ardently, "Si, we savvy." They were grinning ear to ear, and I regretted leaving them alone to these first steps to an exciting new discovery, but I was also looking forward to informing Stefany of this potentially incredible new find - after I met her about her request to see a cop.

I made my way out of the basement, stopped for a quick drink at the kitchen and headed towards the front desk, nodding to the various staff and guests I encountered along the way. Sitting in the front room was a swarthy man, short curly black hair, thick, muscularly built, in a white-uniformed shirt with epaulets, navy blue pants with a yellow stripe down the sides and immaculately polished black shoes. He topped off his rugged look with a thin black mustache that curled stylishly at the ends. Bearing an attitude of thinly veiled impatience, he looked forcibly polite. Stefany sat across from him, her legs and arms crossed, looking uncomfortable.

She stood quickly. "Yes, Mr. Mobley. Thanks for coming so quickly, I know you are busy in the basement. This is Constable Fillmore."

I extended my hand in the introduction. "Morgan Mobley. Stoney Brook Architect."

"Pleased to meet you, Mr. Mobley. Now, if you both could accompany me, I am afraid I must ask you to come with me on official police business. It should not take more than an hour and a half, perhaps."

"But. What is this about," I asked.

Fillmore motioned with his hand towards the open front doors, where I could see a police cruiser parked in the circle drive. "Please. I will explain later."

Stefany gave me a sideways glance. "It's about the attack at the Mill Property, Mr. Mobley," she said quietly to me so that no one else could hear.

"Ah. Maybe they've finally found something!"

I followed Stefany and Fillmore out to his cruiser, opening the door for Stefany. She slid in the front seat and gave me a nervous smile. I briefly touched her shoulder. "It's okay."

Getting in the back, Fillmore took off without delay, practically flinging me into my seat. The interior of his cruiser smelled of a combination of sweaty body odor, chewing tobacco, and stale milk. Clicking my seat belt on, my work boots inadvertently crushed several empty fast-food boxes on the floor. With the windows up, he turned on the air conditioner which chugged out an artificially cool breeze, the vents set to blow directly in our faces. He drove down the road, leaving the estate to eventually get on a road that would lead us to a small village a few miles away.

The village was impoverished but nevertheless charming. Old people sat on their porches and little kids played stickball and hoops along the dirt streets. One impossibly thin man in white bellbottom slacks and flip flops stood in the doorway of a small grocery store, smoking a cigarette, watching us pass by with interest. Slowing down about a mile out, Fillmore took a turn off. Soon, the ocean was clearly visible from beyond a wide plateau of solid rock. He drove a little further, heading towards the coast. The road ended at a cliff that overlooked a remote beach. Parked here were several police cruisers, an ambulance, and a few unmarked cars. In the middle of this scene was an older car, which was the object of everyone's attention. It was the blue, rusty sedan of our attacker.

Fillmore parked his cruiser and shut the engine off. He flung his door open and stepped out. "If you two will please follow me."

Stefany and I got out and followed Fillmore to the attacker's sedan. He directed us to come close, where we could see a yellow plastic sheet covering something in the front seat. A body.

Several amateurish looking island police officers were looking through the vehicle, one dusting for prints, another picking items off the floorboards by tweezers in the grasp of latex-gloved hands.

"Ms. Michaels. Mr. Mobley. I want you to tell me if this is the man that you reported as having attacked you."

Fillmore pulled the yellow sheet back, revealing the head of a body, a man slumped in the seat behind the steering wheel. It was our attacker... with a gaping bullet hole in his left temple. The whole side of his face was caked with dried blood. Small bits of blood and what I had to assume was brain matter coated the opposite seat.

"Yes," I confirmed. "That's him."

Stefany turned away quickly, not wanting to see this gory development any longer than she had to. "Yes," she said in a strained voice. "What happened to him?" she asked.

Fillmore pushed a toothpick into his mouth and chewed on it, contemplating. "Well. We are still processing the scene, of course. There was a gun on the floorboard. We must send it over to the main island and check it and see if it was used. Suicide, I would have to say..." He pulled the toothpick out and stared at both of us, clicking his tongue behind his teeth. "But it could be murder. Not for sure. We don't get much of that here."

"Do you know who he is?" I asked, uneasy under Fillmore's stare. "Why he attacked us?"

"He is Francis Bellano. From Trinidad. Forty-two years old, no family. Petty criminal, out on parole. Most of his life in and out of court and jail. Violent offenses mixed with a bit of larceny. Known in the region to be a hired hand at times for noted criminal elements. I wouldn't want to set my sister up with him. Not exactly a pillar of the community. You know?"

Fillmore moved us back to his car and indicated that we should get in, the show was over. "Thank you for your help," he said, getting in and starting the engine.

"So. That's it?" Stefany asked. "Do you need anything else? Given he attacked us?"

"Oh yes," Fillmore answered without pause. "You will have to come sign some papers down at the station house and make some statements. We'll go do that right now."

"So, do you think you can find out why he attacked us?" I asked.

"I don't know. Maybe. Maybe not." Fillmore adjusted his seat back another notch.

Stefany looked back at me, questions in her expression. "So. But, it's over? I guess we don't have to worry about anyone trying to hurt us again. Right?"

Fillmore looked over at her and smiled, his toothpick back in position. "Oh no. I never said that. Lady, I used to live in Los Angeles. Twenty plus years on the force there. Crime scene investigator. I came out here to take this shitty little island constable job because this is where I was born. Giving back to the community, and all that, you know. Enjoy the beaches and the rum. Chill out with a girlfriend, watch sunsets and work a job where I don't have to constantly wonder if I am going to get shot in my liver by some punk. I can put my feet up and live the good life, maybe bust someone for stealing a carton of cigarettes or trying to cheat the house down at The Blue Calypso. Easy shit like that. This guy, Bellano. His background, him being over here, tailing you, attacking you. It all smells of something that is not easy shit, unfortunately. If he had a reason to come after you, there probably will be someone else for similar reasons. Could be." He again pulled his toothpick out for emphasis and smiled. "It would be safer for you two to get off the island. But I know you probably aren't going to leave. So. My advice is, watch your backs."

CHAPTER 9

HIGH HOPES AND HORNY THOUGHTS

Morgan: Going to see the dead guy in the car was, in the words of my best friend Sam from when I was a kid, a most grievous bummer. In addition to all the mental images that I'll never get out of my head, there were the pages of paperwork and questions we had to endure at the constable's station. Stefany was quite upset when we got back to Stoney Brook and quickly locked herself away in her office. Me? Maybe I'm a little relieved, despite what the fuzz said about "watching our backs." I think the guy just bit off more than he could chew, drug deal or whatever, and he got whacked. I'd like to feel bad, but he tried to cave my head in. Why he was after Stefany and me remains to be determined.

So, I've kissed Stefany twice now. Once (a lot) at the mill where she was the one that started kissing me, and once at an evening dance where I sorta forced myself on her. After the dance kiss, I honestly thought she would fire me. I could see it in her eyes, she was sorta pissed that I was so forward. But she seemed to change her mind at the last minute.

Why the hell am I playing with fire? Why? I like working here! Is it because I get off on the adrenaline kick? Kissing her was amazing and I don't think there has ever been any other woman that has come close to doing to me what she has. She seems like she could care less though. I see her in her office or pass by her somewhere at Stoney Brook and she can't give me the time of day.

She's all I can think of, damn it. I can't concentrate. People are beginning to think I've had a stroke or something, I walk around in a daze. Santiago and Miguel watched me walk off a plank and fall face first in the dirt. They thought it was a riot, they laughed so hard, bastards. How can this be? I play, I don't get played! No woman can play me, damn it. It was so much easier when I despised her.

~~~~~

I really didn't think I could feel like this about anyone. Shit. I've got it bad. If I wasn't so in love with her, I would hope I would get over all of this! I hate love! It's like… having the flu or something. I'm sick for her.

~~~~~~

I've completed my business proposal for her. It's all typed up and everything checks out. So far, she doesn't have any idea what I've been up to. No one does for that matter, not even Leanne. Today is the big day. I'm going to take it up to her office and give it to her. With this idea of mine, I can save Stoney Brook for her. I know it will work. I can give her everything she ever wanted. All she must do is say yes. She will need to meet with some companies, sign some papers and we are off to the races. Why am I so desperate to wonder if it is enough… for her to want me.

With a folder of my proposal papers under my arm, I knocked on Stefany's office door. She had no idea about my "plan." Or me coming to give it to her.

"Yes? Come in," I heard her say from behind the doors.

I swallowed and took a deep breath. I still didn't understand why I was so nervous about this. If she didn't like it, that was her business. Would she? What was I doing this for? I had put in a hell of a lot of time on it.

I opened the door and stepped in. Leanne happened to be in the office with her, sitting in one of the chairs in front of Stefany's desk. Leanne brightened immediately. "Mobley! Good to see you."

"Yes? Mr. Mobley, is there something you need?" Stefany looked disappointed that it was me. "Is this about the new discovery beneath the cellar?"

"No, not really. We will be getting to that soon, though. I'm inviting you both to join us. In about an hour."

"We'll come down, yes. Right now, we are kind of busy here," she said, hinting to me to leave.

"I was hoping... I could have a word."

The look on her face was plain. She was not overly thrilled with me interrupting whatever conversation they were having, which by the looks of it, was about finances.

"Yeah. Okay."

After shutting down the protests from my humiliated ego, I walked in.

Approaching her desk, it suddenly occurred to me I hadn't really prepared anything verbal to introduce my proposal. It was all written. They both stared at me, waiting. As usual, Leanne was dressed in an expensive, short dress, Stefany in her grubby attire.

"Um. Mr. Mobley. What? What is it?" Stefany asked, impatiently. "As I said. Busy here. Just deciding exactly when I'll be broke."

Leanne cocked her head inquisitively and smiled at me, amused, trying to read me.

"Broke?" I asked. My plan could not have been more perfectly timed, despite not being prepared. "More bad news from the bank?"

"I'm afraid so, Mr. Mobley. If we sell the Mill Property, perhaps we can put it off for a while. It all depends on what we could get for it. At this point, we are guessing."

"Maybe you won't have to sell it," I said quietly, catching both off guard. They were now peering at me questioningly.

"Okay, I'll bite. Explain," Leanne prodded. Stefany looked skeptical.

"Well. You see. I've sorta put together an idea for you. A plan. Sorta. Or a proposal. It's after we visited the Mill Property. And. Seeing everything there. And such. So. With how you could make enough money to… er… run everything. And save Stoney Brook. I've done all the research and you will see it is well considered. Quite thorough if I say so myself. I've made the necessary preliminary contacts and it can happen if all you do is make a few selections and approve it. Your existing sugar cane field hands workforce may be somewhat adequate for this with a bit of new training. In fact, you may well need additional employees. Especially if you want to continue the sugar cane fields. Which would be nice because they do add an element of historic authenticity around here."

Stefany leaned in on the desk and propped her head on her elbows, looking up at me, bewildered. Leanne had a somewhat worrisome expression that perhaps conveyed concern for my mental health.

"The hell, what?" Stefany asked, shaking her head in dismay. "I'm afraid I'm not following you."

"I've talked with a number of companies about my proposal." I held out my folder of papers. "Um. This proposal. They are very interested. The agreement I have tentatively worked out in our bid process is we would get over 3 million dollars of investment income to build the necessary infrastructure and processing. This would get us up and running but commit us to an exclusive arrangement with one company or corporate group. That's already a given. The bid winner would be awarded a seven-year deferential contract."

"Wait. What? Bid process?" Stefany asked.

"Yes. We have a bid process set up, where one winner from among the interested companies will be selected for a seven-year contract." I cleared my throat, seeing they were both thoroughly confused. "They are fortune five-hundred companies," I added, hoping to add credibility and impress them.

Stefany sat back in her chair looking astonished. "Mr. Mobley. I still don't know what the hell this all is about. Companies? Infrastructure? What, exactly is it they are bidding on?"

"Oh," I exclaimed, laughing uncomfortably. "Sorry, I guess I forgot to mention that straightaway. Sorta nervous, I suppose. I'll back up. It's probably the most crucial part of this."

"Um. Good idea, Mr. Mobley," Stefany added.

'It's coconuts," I said, beaming.

"Have you been drinking at the bar during work hours again?" Stefany asked acerbically.

"Please do go on, Mr. Mobley," Leanne encouraged, giving Stefany a reproaching glance for her underwhelmed expression.

"The Mill Property, it's a fantastic resource. All those coconut trees you have, many acres of them, they are of the species, Cocos nucifera, which is a bit of a story in and of itself. The short end of it is, there are two general types of coconut trees, basically, tall and short."

"Okaaay," Stefany said trying to make sense of where I was going with my proposal.

"The tall ones, Jamaican types, have bigger nuts, but produce less," I continued. "The short ones, that are Malayan types, produce more, but have smaller nuts."

"Wait, are we still talking about coconut trees," Leanne joked.

"Um. Yes," I confirmed. "However, there is a *third* type that is the most prized of all. Because it is a hybrid of both types and has all the best features of both and produces the most. It's called MayJam. It is a cross between the Malayan dwarf coconut and the Jamaican tall coconut. As luck would have it, Stefany, in addition to Jamaican and Malayan, you have an abundance of MayJam coconut trees at the Mill Property. Whether they were planted or somehow just got there naturally, I don't know. But the interesting thing is they are there in great quantities. Of all varying ages, too, so production is quite sustainable."

Both women looked stunned. Or perhaps just disbelieving and thinking I was joking perhaps.

"And... you can still maintain the Mill Property as a resort area, it won't negatively affect that at all. Maybe even make it more lucrative."

Leanne sat back in her chair, suddenly, looking satisfied, almost as if she had expected me to do this.

Stefany remained perplexed. "So, Mr. Mobley. We can produce coconuts at the Mill Property. What, exactly, is the significance of that? I do appreciate your enthusiasm, but I don't see how that helps me? What am I missing?" she asked after a long moment of silence in the room.

"Ms. Michaels. You have the raw ingredient of one of the greatest health foods. It's in demand and it brings in big bucks. Coconut juice. Essential for coconut water, health drinks, sports drinks, cocktail drinks. Coconut candy, granola bars, coconut oil. Even the husks can be recycled for use for pet bedding supplies. Companies that need these commodities are scrambling to make you a deal, ready to bid for what you can sell them. It's all those acres of coconuts you have. You are the provider of the raw resource. After a few years, maybe you could even produce your own finished product. It's worth a lot of money, as it turns out. Your workers can harvest them with a bit of training and equipment. Product is sent out for refinement by ship. With the income it can bring in, it can more than augment your operations both at Stoney Brook, and at the Mill Property. And as I said, there are three million dollars of initial investment just to get your operations started. This... can save Stoney Brook. For you."

I tentatively held out my proposal to her. She slowly took it and sat it on the desk, thumbing through it. After a minute, she looked up, the shock setting in on her face.

"Is this... for real, Mr. Mobley? Coconuts?" Stefany asked, the significance of my proposal hitting home.

"Yes," I answered. "Coconuts." Both women were silent. "With a bit of clearing of underbrush and establishing some trails, you own acres and acres of commercially viable coconut trees. You just need to send the bid out."

"Ah," Stefany finally said. Choking with emotion, her eyes turned watery, and it looked as if she was going to cry. "All I can say is, well done. Mr. Mobley. Very well done. Thank you."

"Very nice, Mobley," Leanne agreed. "This is amazing news and sounds quite possible. And very timely."

"You were thinking of closing down?"

"We were. We were considering selling the Mill Property," Leanne added, "but it would only be a stopgap measure over the long run. It wouldn't keep us in the black long, though. So. We were talking about finishing the year. Then sell Stoney Brook, and Stefany could perhaps walk away with some of her savings left."

"With how successful this all is? You are booked to capacity every night!" I could not believe it. The place is always packed now that renovations had largely been completed on the main building.

"Expenses and loans are eating us up," Leanne explained. "It is increasingly evident that we'll end up in bankruptcy. And now... you've at least given us an option; a reason for hope. You are amazing, Mr. Mobley."

Stefany slowly got up from her desk and walked over to me, her eyes red, cheeks streaked with tears. Slowly, she put her arms around me, hugging me. Touched, I reciprocated.

"Thank you," Stefany finally said. "It is very... nice... of you to do this, Mr. Mobley. Even if it doesn't prove feasible, I very much appreciate you. Um. What you have done. We'll look it over."

This was the most emotion I had ever seen from Stefany. In a word, I was shocked. But I was also elated with what I had conceivably done. Which was save Stoney Brook for Stefany.

"Okay. Let me know if you need any more details. Negotiations and the bid process could start this week. Today even if you would like. You'll find a list of the contacts in the proposal to get it going."

Stefany only nodded as she walked back over to her desk.

"Okay. I'm heading back to the basement. Will you both be joining us when we go down for a look?"

"Yes, Mr. Mobley," Stefany confirmed. "We will be there in ten minutes. We definitely want to see what is down there."

"See you in ten," Leanne said with a sly smile.

As I walked out of the office, I felt good about what I had done. Stefany had seemed so genuinely touched with my idea. Maybe it wouldn't get me into her pants any time too soon, but I would be happy with another kiss.

The air checked out safe down in the void. Twenty-one percent oxygen, no hydrogen sulfide, or any other harmful gasses. Santiago and Miguel had previously rolled the large slab of stone back and away on the posts.

An assortment of flashlights and lanterns were sitting around the edge. A journalist from the local island paper was also present with a photographer. With those guests, Santiago, Miguel and myself, there was an assortment of nine other employees eagerly anticipating this new discovery. We all stood, making small talk, awaiting Stefany and Leanne.

The hole was dark but from what we could make out, the stone steps that led down from the top were safe enough. By shining a flashlight down the hole, we could see that the steps ended at a rough floor of sorts. A small stream was also visible several feet away in the gloomy recess, bubbling and boiling towards a yet unknown destination.

"Are we ready, Mr. Mobley?" Stefany walked in with Leanne, the excitement evident on their faces.

"Yes, we are," I answered.

"I would like to go first," Stefany suggested.

I had to think about that one. There could be hidden dangers perhaps. A poisonous snake or two in hiding. Bats, maybe. I would hate to see Stefany rush from the hole, screaming and slapping away at a few thousand bats.

"I think it would be wise if I go first. Make sure it's safe then we can invite you and everyone else down one by one if it all checks out.

"I think not, Mr. Mobley," Stefany asserted, walking past me. "I'll lead the way. You accompany me, and *we* can see if it's safe."

"Um. Okay." If anything, Stefany Michaels was a fearless and courageous woman. And quite stubborn.

She took the lantern I was holding and proceeded to enter the hole. I snatched up a high-powered flashlight and quickly followed.

"Everyone just stays here for a bit while we make sure it's safe. Santiago?"

"Si, Meester Mobley?"

"When I call and if everything looks safe, please begin sending everyone down, one at a time, carefully on those stone stairs."

"Si. Will do."

Stefany was already at the bottom, peering around with her lantern. I hurried down after her, wondering if there would be snakes.

Shining the light up at the floor of the rooms above us, it was evident that we were in a natural cave that had been altered to some degree. The floor had been chipped and dug flat for passage. The path led deeper and soon the ceiling, walls, and floor became a completely enclosed natural feature. When Stoney Brook was first built, there was more than likely a natural entrance to this cave at this location. When I thought about it, the gentle rise of the topography that leads to where the main building sits would make such a feature possible. There were natural streams nearby. One of them was going subterranean somewhere close and was running here, beneath the foundations of Stoney Brook. This stream no doubt fed the water cisterns.

I tapped Stefany's shoulder, startling her.

"Oops. Sorry," I offered.

"That's okay. It's just kind of creepy down here. No one has been in here since near the time Stoney Brook was built, I'm guessing."

"I think you are right. Let's keep going." I shined the light beam ahead of us. The cave appeared to turn a corner and continue out of sight. "Everyone just hang on for a minute," I called up to the anxious faces peering over the side. "We are walking on for just a bit. I'll let you know. Hold on."

"Si!"

"Okay, let's go," Stefany suggested, beating me to the punch.

"Right. Let's watch for snakes around all these rocks," I suggested as she pressed forward without care.

Trying to keep up with her, I shined the light ahead on our path as the gloom closed in behind us.

We turned a corner. Then another. And still, the path led onward into the dark. Stefany strained to look ahead.

"What is that?" She asked, pointing to a mass of dark shapes arranged around a wider area of the cave that had been dug out and cleared to give the appearance of a large room. The stream continued in this area, right down the middle.

I shined my flashlight onto them. Stefany gasped and grabbed for my arm.

It was an incredible sight. Five skeletons glared back at us. They were of such immense age that the clothes that originally covered them were in small, tattered, stringy fragments.

An array of rusty cutlasses and ancient flintlocks lay against the walls. Tools, pickaxes, and shovels lay among the skeletons. Several old steel chests were also nearby as were several wooden barrels that were still managing to hold together.

"This is amazing," I gasped.

"These are... are... dead people! Just laying here. Beneath Stoney Brook! This is terrible, Mr. Mobley!" Stefany countered with rising alarm in her voice.

Her concern was a mystery to me. "Why? This is fascinating history, Stefany!"

"Mr. Mobley, I can't think dead people beneath Stoney Brook Plantation can be a good thing! I've got to call the police..." She turned to walk away.

"Stefany. Listen. This is a FANTASTIC thing! Believe me, it will only increase the interest in your property! Look at them. Whatever happened to them, it happened hundreds of years ago. We'll figure it out later. But just the historic appeal here is incredible! Look!" I pointed to the old muskets and cutlasses. "This... Stefany... is *amazing*."

"You think so?" She asked weakly.

"Absolutely," I confirmed. I pulled her close, hugging her. "It's fine. I promise. But. You are right, we do have to let the police know. And the authorities responsible for antiquities and such things as that."

"What about everyone upstairs?" She asked.

I looked around. Nothing had been disturbed. The only traces of anything for several hundred years were our footsteps.

"No one can touch anything. We can lead them down here, several at a time and quench their curiosity. And then back up. Then we need to restrict access to this until the authorities decide what to do. They may want to bring in an archaeologist or two, some experts on these types of antiquities, I would imagine. We'll see."

"Okay." She looked doubtfully again upon the bodies. "What do you think happened to them? Were they slaves?"

I shined the light on each one successively. They had bandanas around their heads and there was what I perceived to be jewelry on them, such as rings and chains.

"I don't know for sure. I don't think they were slaves, though."

I took her by her arm and began leading her out. "Let's show the others."

She stopped me suddenly, and I turned to her, wondering what she wanted. She pulled me down, kissing me. It was hard, needy, and unexpected. I blinked, enjoying her sudden initiative.

"Um. Thanks," I mumbled.

"No problem," she replied walking ahead.

Stefany: I thumbed through the photos in the envelope. Me with blackened eyes. Me with a broken nose. Me with my arm in a sling in the hospital. Me with broken ribs. Me with a respirator mask over my face. Me with intravenous fluid bags hanging from one of those little hanger things.

So, the lawyers representing me back in Montreal wanted me to look over the abuse photos and see if I would agree to have them shown in court. Sure. Why not.

Why not advertise to the world my every weakness, my dedication to a man that could do these things to me, time after time again. And I let him.

It would always start with anger. Then a verbal beat down. Then it would be physical. Get a beating, go to the hospital, he would apologize, whispers of counseling, and promises that he would change. His law firm would send counselors for each of us, or for both together. I would go back to him. Repeat. Repeat. Repeat.

And I never fought back. Even verbally, I was a marshmallow. Which just shocks Leanne, who seems to think I should have stood up for myself more... because I have this tough, tomboyish athletic persona she says. Whatever qualities I may have, the primary characteristic of my personality says... Please - beat the fuck out of me.

My lawyers tell me that Miles is contesting everything. And delaying. And he will not agree to any divorce. Not now. Not ever. It's going to take a long-drawn-out fight and there's not much my team can do. At least for right now. Of course not.

Tears are streaming down my cheeks as I write this, and I'm not sure why. Am I upset that Miles had beaten me to a pulp on numerous occasions? I wouldn't expect anything different from him. It's how he is wired, and how our marriage went almost from the day we were wed. But why be upset over it? It's history now. Miles, so help me God, will not do this to me again. I've changed. And whether he knows it or not, he is barking up the wrong tree if he thinks I will ever reconcile with him.

I let Miles and other men I have known in my life color my entire opinion of the male gender. In general, at least. My boyfriend after high school had backhanded me several times, verbally humiliated me until I would cry. All men are assholes. Am I wrong for thinking that? Leanne tells me that yes, indeed I am wrong. I have had "bad luck," she says. That, and for psychological reasons, I seem to seek such men out. The abusers I have had in my life, Leanne says, represents a very small minority of how men behave. Oh, really??? I am attracted to them subconsciously and seek that kind of man out. Bullshit. No one can be that self-deprecating and with such rotten luck.

Then there's Mr. Architect. Among his most recent heroic antics, he has perhaps single-handedly saved Stoney Brook Plantation for me. It's disconcerting that all my wonderfully low opinions of him clash so much with how he acts as of late. I love to dislike Mobley and he's making it very difficult to continue doing that. His plan of us going into raw coconut products production has every indication that it can succeed. I am grateful to Mobley. And yet, I still harbor some sort of resentment, despite my best efforts to exclude him from my unjust generalizations. Why? Can't I just accept him for who he is, the good... and the bad?

Is Mobley different? Maybe. But he still thinks mainly on a level that is in line with the zipper of his pants. He knows he is a disgusting, thirsty, sex-starved pig and doesn't seem to hide from it. He readily acknowledges all his flaws to me. That's a first, for sure. What more can he do? He may truly be in love with me ~ackkkkk~

~~~~~

Mobley - he has already done more for me than Miles ever did, or any other man for that matter, showing more  concern and even care. Am I attracted to him? Yes. Damn it. Will I ever give him a chance? I don't know. Mobley is a typical man with all his emotions tied directly into what hangs between his legs. I am as conflicted as ever.

I thought about Leanne's nutty proposal to have Mobley be my "sex slave." It was such a bizarre notion, but I get a good laugh out of it every time it crosses my mind. Of course, I am safe from worrying about that happening for real, but the prospect has a fantasy appeal about it, I must admit. What would I do under such circumstances???? Would I enjoy it???? Would I ever develop deeper feelings for Mobley, or would I just use him? What would it be like to just use someone sexually? With no judgments, no requirements, no guilt. No feelings???

Something that is just for one's own desires and satisfaction. I don't know if I could deal with that.

Yesterday, when I had complete privacy, I looked through Leanne's BDSM sex book. As I looked through it, I tried to imagine doing some of those things with Mobley. Some of it was oddly appealing. I would never admit this to her.

As I turned the thoughts of "sex slave  Mobley" over and over in my head, I find that they strangely excite me. I have caught myself several times squeezing my legs together and it irritates the hell out of me that my mind is so pliant to Leanne's suggestions. If such a thing ever would occur, Leanne would be all over it, coaching, demanding, and

advising. And there I would be…
missionary position Stefany. I must laugh. I
know that in truth if she didn't get
involved, I would no doubt be non-
compliant, as I would never have the
gumption to do such things with Mobley as
she described. Mobley would never enjoy
such an arrangement of being "in
servitude," even if it did concern only sex.

~~~~~

I hate thinking about this!!!!! The
Mill Property attacker, now dead, still
concerns me. It sickens me to think that
Miles may have had something to do with
it. And if so, I doubt it is over.

Constable Fillmore looks like
someone that could only be concerned with
how soon they could get home to watch a
ball game. The images of the dead man in
the old car are burned into my brain and it
is difficult not to think of that scene.
Leanne somehow came up with a variety of
firearms she wanted to be placed in various
places at Stoney Brook. I have forbidden
her to do this, and I assume she has them
all stashed in her room.

Am I still a target to someone? Who
knows? I don't say anything to Mobley

about this, but I am very worried about him also.

On an interesting and exciting new note, Leanne and I joined Mobley and his crew at the newly discovered cave beneath Stoney Brook. Complete with skeletons and everything. Which still creeps the hell out of me. It is an incredible development. It seems we have been having one every week now!

Also... I grabbed Mobley when we were in the cave. And - I kissed him.

After all the excitement of the day, it was good to get back to my room and just relax. A hot shower was in order, and I threw off my clothes and put on a robe. The secret cave with the creepy skeletons was incredible. I thought about Mobley. With kissing him, I had seriously encouraged him to remain on my scent. I had given the hound a bone. Did I regret it?

I plopped down in my recliner, wondering if I should get a shower first, or just watch a bit of television. The nearly imperceptible knock on my door startled me from my thoughts. It had to be Leanne. Who else would come knocking on my door so late in the evening?

I got up and walked to the door. "Yes?" Nothing. Then after a few moments, another soft knock.

Making sure the security chain was in place, I opened it and peered through the crack.

"Hello! Ms. Michaels?"

It was Heidi. "Yes, how are you this evening, Heidi? Is there something I can help you with?"

Carrying a shoulder bag, she was wearing shorts and a button-down casual shirt and her typical Converse tennis shoes.

"I just thought I would stop by and say hi, Ms. Michaels."

This was odd. I looked around her. Nope, Leanne wasn't anywhere nearby. Nor was Joe.

"Ahhh. Well. Good to see you," I said, trying to sound polite and wondering what I should do next. I held the top of my robe closed tightly.

She smiled. "May I?"

I wasn't sure I understood her. "Pardon?"

"May I... come in?"

I blinked, the implications suddenly running through my mind like a ticker tape machine. The image of her on her knees with Joe in Leanne's apartment was seared into my brain. I hesitated. I couldn't very well be rude. Putting on my best smile, I resolved to get through this interruption of my evening and go ahead and invite her in for a few minutes. Then I could excuse myself with needing to get up early and send her on her way.

"Certainly, Heidi. Please. Do come in." After letting her in, I wondered what I should do next. I had very nearly had sex with this woman, and I was taken aback with this visit.

"So, what do I owe the pleasure?" I finally asked.

"It's a beautiful tropical evening, Ms. Michaels. I just thought you might like a little company."

I had to think of a response. "Oh. Yes, indeed it is. Please sit down." We both sat on the couch, and I felt extremely uncomfortable and was hoping it wasn't showing. The image of Heidi's mouth licking and kissing my inner thighs flashed through my mind. I had made my intentions clear with Leanne, I had thought. I needed no "sexual servants," of either the Joe *or* Heidi variety.

"We have never really had a chance to talk. You and I," she said without pause.

"No. I suppose we haven't," I answered.

She opened her shoulder bag and produced a bottle of wine, the cork already pulled and slipped back in. Great. I already had a lingering buzz from the several drinks I had earlier on the veranda. She then produced several glasses.

I smiled. Leanne had put her up to this. Damn her.

"I thought we would enjoy a glass of white wine. Yes? It is chilled. For such a very hot day."

Tightening the belt on my robe, I knew I better nip this in the bud. "Oh, no. But thank you. You can certainly have a drink, though. I'll pass this evening. I'm afraid I have already had several glasses on the veranda earlier this evening."

Heidi smiled mischievously. "Ms. Michaels. I assure you. My intentions are quite well-meaning. Surely, you can humor me and drink with a friend, yes?"

Her French accent was very disarming. She was twisting my arm and I should have known better.

"Okay. Sure. I guess. Then maybe just one drink, Heidi."

She handed one of the glasses over with an odd but welcome addition of a sprig of mint. I would drink mine quickly, allow her time to finish hers, then send her on her merry way so I could get my hot shower.

Both of us engaging in various small talk, she set her empty glass down and took mine which was a quarter full. She poured another for her and topped mine off over my objections. I took a deep breath and set my now again full glass down on the table next to me, wondering when this woman would leave.

She held her second drink up to me in a toast, making me commit. "To the Stoney Brook Plantation. And may it long be fruitful under your guidance." I returned the toast, barely sipping it. Was she trying to get me drunk?

245

I stood, trying to give her the hint. "Well. It was certainly nice of you to stop by, Heidi. And bring me a drink, no less! Thank you!"

She also stood. Her eyes looked more assertive somehow. She walked over to me and put her hand on my shoulder.

"Ms. Michaels. I wanted to talk to you about... that night."

This was not good. No. I did NOT want to talk about that night. It was clear from her expression which night she was referring to.

"Oh. I don't really think we need to- "

"Yes," she interrupted. "*That* night."

Her fingers were softly massaging my shoulder. This was getting out of hand, and I wondered how Leanne would take me throwing her "sexual slave" out of my room. I tried to remain composed.

"Heidi. Really. I don't want to discuss that. I think it's time I turn in." I faked a yawn. "I have to get up early tomorrow and – "

"Ms. Michaels. I am rarely attracted to other people. But. I am very attracted to you." She moved so near to me I could feel her breath on my own mouth.

I laughed nervously. It was unintentional, but I couldn't help myself. "Heidi. Does Leanne know you are here? She put you up to this, right?"

Her hand continued softly massaging my shoulder. Now she was moving it up to my neck. Softly touching me. This was going critical. I had to get her out.

"No. Ms. Tilden does not know I am here. Nor does my slave, Joe. Does this suit you?"

Panic was setting in. What was this, Heidi was up to? "I don't really know if it suits me, per se... I just think that-"

"My Mistress Tilden has given me permission to see whoever I may like on the island. If it is discreet. And it is someone who I am very attracted to. And Ms. Michaels. I have kissed my way... *licked* my way up your legs, you may recall. And, I am very attracted to you."

She now placed her other hand behind my back. "I know you are uncertain. This is okay. I will not press you. But you should know. I want to taste you, Ms. Michaels. I did not make it, last time. But I.... want to. Very much so."

She made a move to kiss my neck. My mind was in turmoil with this sudden intrusion on my senses. I gently pushed her back. I was unable to formulate words at this point, and all I could do was look at her with a questioning expression.

She leaned over suddenly, rubbing her calves as if they were hurting. She made several little moans that would lead one to conclude she was sore, perhaps.

I rolled my eyes, looking at the ceiling. Would I ever get this girl who was obviously trying to seduce me out of my room!? "What is wrong?" I asked, glad to change the subject. "Muscle cramp... or something?"

"Yes," she acknowledged, looking up at with me with pleading eyes. "They are so sore. I hiked today. Ten miles. So sore. I really could use a bit of a massage."

I stifled a laugh. Was this chick really that shallow to think I would fall for this?

"Fortunately, Heidi, we have our talented hands at our spa. I'll give them a call! They will have you feeling better in no time. A good hot oil rub will have you feeling like new." I made my way over to the phone.

"I'm afraid that won't work, Ms. Michaels," Heidi said with what I perceived as false sympathy. "They are all away today. Closed. I checked the schedule."

Ignoring her, I called. After several rings, the spa room answering machine came on, announcing that all the masseuses and other staff would be available tomorrow and that they would be closed this evening for a prescheduled day off.

I frowned, forgetting when I had approved this bit of inconvenience.

Heidi ran her fingers softly along my face. "See? So, I wonder if you could help me, Ms. Michaels? Because I know you to be a good friend. This is all just as friends, I promise."

"What? Now, just wait a damn min-"

"This is good," she said, cutting me off. Smiling, she ignored me and proceeded to lay on the floor on her stomach. "Yes, thank you so much, Ms. Michaels. Soooo much." Heidi reached for her bag that was sitting on the coffee table and withdrew a bottle of massage oil and handed it behind her back up to me.

I looked at the bottle of oil. Lightly flavored with lavender, it was evidently also "edible." I peered down at her. She had already closed her eyes in anticipation of getting a rub down. "Really? Heidi? Edible?"

"It is a good option to have, with such a thing as massage oil."

"Heidi. I really don't think I am… up to ingesting any massage oil. Sorry."

"No, no. Of course not. Just massage. That's all."

"Ahh. Okay," I reluctantly agreed. Heidi was persistent and very scheming, I was finding out. "I see this has been warmed already."

"Yes, yes. I took the liberty. Because I know you could help me, yes?"

"Yes. I suppose so." I took a deep breath and knelt. Squeezing a blob of hot oil into the palms of my hands, I made for her calves and began rubbing. In the dim floor and table lights of my room, the hot oil gleamed off the smooth, flawless skin of her legs. Her muscles flexed and relaxed beneath my fingers. She had fantastic legs; I would give her that as my fingers kneaded first softly then more firmly. The oil had a definite warming sensation. God damn her.

After several moments, I thought I may yet get her out quickly. "There you go, Heidi. How is that?" I sat back on my legs, satisfied I had gone the extra mile for Leanne's sex toy.

"No. Please, Ms. Michaels. Please do continue. They still cramp."

"Okay. Fine," I mumbled to myself. I continued rubbing and kneading, feeling somewhat hypnotized by the repeated motions. I took the initiative and pulled off her sneakers and socks and rubbed her strikingly beautiful feet. I reached for my glass of wine and downed it. If I was going to do this, I may as well have a drink.

I sat and admired her sensuous body. All beauty and gorgeousness aside, this was a woman after all, and she was a temptation I had beat once before. I would ignore the fact that her mouth had been on the upper insides of my thighs. And I would ignore that very sexy French accent. I continued massaging her legs.

Heidi's ass slowly rose and dropped, grinding slightly with my ministrations. As my hands moved up her thighs, she spread her legs slightly, allowing me better access.

These events were like a blur... a dream... and I was certain it wasn't me that was massaging Heidi's legs. I watched, transfixed as her ass continued to rise and fall slightly as she began to moan almost imperceptibly. She spread her legs wider. My fingers lightly brushed the innermost junction of her legs.

Heidi turned over, stopping the massage, staring up at me. I sat back, intoxicated with the feeling I had just experienced with my fingers against her warm skin.

"Heidi. So. You should feel better. I think. You should go back to your room now."

She stood up. "It is your turn now, Ms. Michaels."

"What? Noooo. I'm fine. Let's just call it a night, shall we?"

She reached for me, pulling me to my feet, my robe sliding open to momentarily reveal my thighs. This was embarrassing.

Without pause, she kissed me. I blinked, surprised. Again, she kissed me, her lips soft and compliant. Her breath was hot on my mouth. It was different than kissing a man, softer, more sensual.

"I want you, Ms. Michaels. I want to satisfy you. As I almost did when you came to visit us that night."

"Heidi, it was just a momentary... lapse of judgment. I'm not into women. I'm not."

"No?"

"No."

"How do you know?" She untied the belt to my robe, and it slipped open, revealing everything I thought would remain hidden away. She slid her hands inside my robe, touching me in a melting little trail around my waist.

"Um. Heidi."

"That night. You did not get up and leave, Ms. Michaels. Not right away. Joe tasted you. I almost did."

"Oh."

"I am a submissive. I am Ms. Tilden's submissive. But I always get what I want. When I saw Ms. Tilden, I wanted her. And she made me hers. And tonight, I want you to make me yours. You need not do anything further for me. It is all I want. To satisfy you. And no one will know. Not Joe. Not Ms. Tilden. No one. Please. I beg you... to use me."

"Oh." I was in a trance. This had all been so sudden. I was losing my resolve to throw her out of my room and get out of this. She slowly pushed me back to one of my chairs. I sat down, wondering what she had in mind.

She slid her shorts down slowly, staring at me. She then unbuttoned her shirt and slipped it off, revealing her firm, small breasts. She picked up the massage oil from the floor. Her nipples were hard as small gumdrops. Her legs still reflected the oil from her massage. Although short in stature, she was a magnificently beautiful woman, flawless in every way.

She sat down on my lap, straddling and facing me, much as I had done to Mobley at the Mill Property. Her lips again found mine, hot and teasing. Heidi was seducing me, as much as I didn't want to admit it. But she was.

She slid her mouth around my cheek with small, deliberate kisses until she found my ear.

"Ms. Michaels," she whispered breathily into my ear, making me tingle all over. "I want to make love to you. With my hands. With my body. With my mouth."

"Oh," was all I could say in my dreamy state. I thought of the *Jungle Book* and the story of Kaa the snake entrancing Mowgli so that it could eat him. Tonight, I was Mowgli, except in a much more adult version.

I felt both of her hands now, inside my robe. She softly caressed my breasts, deliberately pinching my nipples just to the point of nearly feeling pain, bringing both to small, miniature erections. A minute later, her hands slowly dropped down my stomach to my thighs. She squeezed them, softly at first, then harder, almost painfully so. Her tongue danced lightly in my ear which gave me goosebumps all over my body.

"Your warm skin is like candy on my lips. And I do bet you taste so very good, Ms. Michaels."

"I... well..." I could manage nothing but incoherent utterance. Wherever she was taking me, I was about to go willingly.

Heidi now slipped one of her hands directly to my sex. She cupped her hand, squeezing. A small moan escaped my lips before I cut it off. I didn't need to ask her to know I was dripping wet.

"Will you feed me?" she asked moving her lips to my neck as one of her fingers entered me. "Feed me, please?"

Withdrawing her finger, she brought it up to her lips, staring into my eyes as she did so. It was glistening. Smearing it first on her lips, she slipped it in her mouth, sucking it.

"Mmmm. Ms. Michaels. Indeed, you do. You taste even more wonderful than I imagined."

She returned this same hand, again seeking the moist juncture between my legs. Again, she brought her finger up, again slick. This time, she moved in to kiss me, pushing her finger in between my lips and hers. Her finger smelled of a warm ocean beach after a rain - and she slipped it into my mouth, letting me taste my own slightly salty-sweet flavor with her. It was the first time I had tasted myself so directly. Heidi's tongue cleaned up any excess on her side of her finger before kissing me.

"It would be such a shame if you didn't share something so good." She went back for more, but now with two fingers. "Don't you agree?"

Her words were barely intelligible to me. I was in a transcendental state at this point and barely coherent.

I moaned, trying to find the words. "Heidi... I..."

"Shhhhhhhh."

Again, she wiped my wet essence all over her mouth before sucking her fingers clean. She then kissed me harder, more fervently. It was so strange, this kiss by another woman as I tasted myself on her lips and in her mouth. It was hungry, and full of passion, as a man can be. But different in some ways... her lips softer, more pliable. Her tongue circled my own, pushing deep, fighting for sensual control. Damn, she was good. Thirty minutes earlier, I would have sworn that these circumstances with Heidi would never take place. And here she was, her seduction of me nearly complete.

"I want to be on my knees for you," she whispered. She began backing off the chair.

A knock on the door broke the spell and jolted me to my senses. Heidi's eyes searched mine. "Don't answer it," she pleaded. "Just ignore it."

"Damn. Heidi, what if it's important? I have to," I said with genuine regret.

Again, someone knocked on the door, firm and urgent. Heidi got off me and made for her shorts and shirt, quickly putting them on. I stood up and tied my robe back together. "Hold on! I'm coming," I answered, the irony of the statement not lost on me nor Heidi, who shot me a slight smile.

Standing at the door, I looked over at Heidi. I pointed at her socks and sneakers that were still sitting on the floor. She quickly slipped them on. As for me, my robe was standard fare this time of evening.

"Who is it?" I asked first.

"Morgan."

"Ah, shit," I whispered. Heidi frowned, knowing her seduction had been sabotaged by none other than Man-Whore Mobley. Maybe the interruption was fortuitous. Did I really want whatever was going to happen with Heidi… to happen? Doubt was creeping back in. Heidi had skills. I tried to clear my head. The wine was taking its toll.

Unlatching the deadbolt, I opened the door a crack, peering out. There he was, but this time holding a bouquet of tropical flowers and… a bottle of wine. I closed the door and pressed my forehead against the door.

"Um. Ms. Michaels? Is everything okay?" he asked.

Looking up at the ceiling, I rolled my eyes. "He's got flowers and wine, Heidi," I whispered.

Heidi picked up her shoulder bag and sauntered to the door. I had pangs of regret as well as relief. I'm not sure any one outweighed the other.

"That's because you are in high demand, Ms. Michaels. Go ahead and see what he wants. I will be back. And we will start again from where we left off. When there are fewer distractions." She kissed me slowly. Then I opened the door.

Mobley blinked as he watched Heidi walk past him.

"Morgan! A good evening to you," Heidi said politely.

"And to you, Heidi." Mobley watched her walk away, sensuousness oozing from her every movement. His eyes swung back to me.

"Um. I didn't mean to interrupt. Anything."

"Oh, Mobley, get your mind out of the gutter. She came up to see me this evening to discuss how soon there might be new hiking trails on the Mill Property. She's an avid hiker, you know. She did 10 miles just today. I'm in a robe... because... I was getting ready to take a shower when she showed up. Unexpectedly. Just like you!"

Mobley stood in silence, not knowing what he should do. I helped him by taking the flowers, then the bottle of wine. "These are for me, aren't they?"

"Uh. Yes. Yes, they are."

I inhaled the scent from a variety of flowers, which were wonderfully fragrant. "Well. Don't just stand there, come on in, won't you?" I advised, peering over the flowers.

I made for my kitchen to get a vase. "Thank you, Mobley. These are very sweet." I returned and carefully placed the vase, now resplendent with the bouquet, on a sofa table against the wall.

"Please. Sit down," I said motioning to the couch.

Still looking uncomfortable, he sat as I appraised the wine. "How thoughtful," I said pulling several wine glasses from a serving cart. "Yet more wine," I said quietly, under my breath. "Just what I need."

"What's that?" Mobley asked, innocent and unaware.

"Nothing!" Quickly popping the cork with a puller before he could get to his feet and perform his gentlemanly duties, I waved him off. "I got this."

Pouring glasses for both of us, I left mine at a much lower level. Handing him his glass, I sat down on the opposite side of the couch. "So. What's the occasion? Why visit me..." I checked my watch. "At 9:53 this evening. Bringing me flowers and wine, no less."

"I just thought... Maybe we could celebrate a little."

"Celebrate?"

"Yes. Seeing how maybe things will now work out financially for you. And all the good things that have been happening. The Mill Property. The coconut groves. Finding the subterranean cave."

"Yes. All good, I admit. And mostly due to you. And I am very thankful to have you here at Stoney Brook. Quite thankful indeed. I am truly glad that I was able to resist my earlier inclinations to… send you packing. So to speak."

"That's a nice way of saying you wanted to fire my ass."

I shrugged. "Yeah. Pretty much." My eyes took him all in. Muscle by muscle. Mobley was one hell of a male specimen. "But I am very glad I didn't. You are one of my best decisions I have ever made."

He nodded off my assertion with false humility. He was still Morgan Mobley, after all. "But. It hasn't been without a bit of difficulty here and there, just in case your ego gets too overblown, Mobley."

"Should I take back a flower or two," he joked, making me laugh loudly.

"No. That's not necessary."

"Good."

"Yes. *Good.* And I should thank you, Mobley, for your timely interruption this evening. And for bringing me to my senses."

"Timely interruption?"

"With these wonderful flowers and delicious wine! That constitutes… a *timely* interruption, don't you think?"

"Yes. I suppose so."

I held up my glass to him. "So, here's to you, the timely… if not persistent… Mr. Morgan Mobley, Architect of Stoney Brook Plantation. And none better has ever been had."

"I'm not Man-Whore Mobley, tonight?" he asked, grinning.

"I *didn't* say that," I shot back, arching my eyebrows.

He laughed boisterously and held up his own glass to clink it to mine. "And to you, Ms. Michaels. Beautiful beyond compare. And one of the most incredible women I have ever met."

His toast left me blushing and embarrassed if that was possible at this point in the evening after everything that had happened.

As this set in, I smiled over at him, seeing that he had noticed my robe had slipped off, exposing my crossed, bare legs. He quickly looked up, seeing that he had been caught. Mobley, despite himself, or perhaps for all that he had done, was growing on me. Or maybe it was that Heidi had left me in a smoldering fire of need and it was all I could do not to jump Mobley right there and then. All I could think about was kissing him again. And cursing myself because I didn't have the nerve.

I sniffed, slapped the sides of my robe back over my legs and took a sip of wine. The robe sides slid back down. To hell with it. I propped a foot up on my coffee table, affording Mobley an even better view.

It was at this moment, a most devious idea popped into my head. Heidi's little ploy with the leg cramp! Why not have a bit of fun and pull that same scheme on Mobley?

His eyes about blew a gasket as I leaned over to rub my right calf slowly and deliberately. Oh, well.

"Bit of a cramp," I explained, kneading the muscles in my leg, delighting in his reaction, going a little above and beyond to tease him. Heidi would be proud of my deception.

"Ahhh," he mumbled, nearly choking awkwardly on a sip of wine. He tried to discreetly wipe away the dribble that made it down his chin to stain his sport shirt.

I nodded with a grin, acknowledging the gaff. It was odd to see Mobley look embarrassed. "Classy, Mobley." I flung him a tissue from the nearby table.

"Kind of went down the wrong way," he hoarsely admitted with a smile. Bashfully trying to recover, he dabbed at the stain with the tissue, having blown his normally suave and cool image.

I couldn't recall him being so flustered. And I liked him more already. As it stood, he was lucky I wasn't all over *him* this evening. Damn it all, let him have his look.

"I could help," Mobley volunteered, nodding to indicate my legs, still maintaining a cautious approach.

Oh, I'm sure he could. I thought about this for a moment, seeing that he took the bait beautifully. But what of the logistics? If I swung my legs up to him on the couch, I'd have an armrest to lean against and I would have difficulty keeping my robe closed. Nope. I could take a page out of Leanne's BDSM book on femdom, however. And I was just tipsy enough, and thanks to Heidi, horny enough, to not give a damn.

"Okay," I agreed. He brightened instantly at this. "But could you do it sitting on the floor? It would be more comfortable for me. You could lean up against the coffee table?"

"Of course." He was down on the floor so quickly I barely had time to blink.

He sat in front of me, ready to go.

I let him take my right leg first. I propped my other leg into his lap, intentionally resting my foot on the growing bulge in his pants. I innocently pressed, ever so slightly, watching him squirm. This was incredible fun. His position on the floor in front of me was a familiar sight, remembering Joe and Heidi working together that evening in Leanne's room.

"If you act one bit different once we are out of this room, I *will* fire you, Mobley," I teased.

He smiled up at me. "Understood."

I'd had more action in one night than I had in months. Was this just incredible luck, everything that had been happening to me? All of that didn't necessarily translate into getting laid, which would be a welcome addition at this point. Although with how Mobley's hands were working my legs, I probably wouldn't object if he tried. I decided to take more of Leanne's BDSM advice.

"Mobley. Remember this rule. Always work from the feet up. Okay?"

He laughed. "Okay." He began massaging my right foot per instruction. I leaned back and sipped my wine, feeling absolutely... *wonderful*. Watching him work was making me writhe in heated anticipation, which I tried to keep hidden from him. I closed my eyes and let the sensations roll over me. It wasn't too long afterward I felt Mobley plant a soft kiss along the arch of my foot. And then another up my ankle. And yet another up a few more inches on my leg. It wasn't hard to see that he had a distinct target in mind with those talented lips.

"Let's not get ahead of ourselves, eh, Mr. Architect."

That was all bluff on my part, of course. I was fully prepared to move ahead.

CHAPTER 10
WHAT'S LOVE HAVE TO DO WITH IT

Stefany: **Morning rolled around, and I could not ignore what had transpired the prior evening with first Heidi, then Mobley. What the hell was happening to me? Waking up, I had felt like a bitch in heat, having to peel off sticky panties and taking another shower. Okay. Gotta slow down on the drinking, it's getting me in trouble. Blaming alcohol seems prudent in this case.**

I suppose I had "awakened" sexually, only to find out what it is like to truly be frustrated in that way. Damn Heidi and damn Mobley. I've got sex on my mind all the time now,

Leanne is "Bi".

Am I!?

I don't think so...

which has probably been Leanne's plan all along.

Am I... turning into the female version of Mobley????

In asking that, I think I can safely say NO. Not at this point, anyway. Somewhere in the back of my mind, I've justified that response by the fact I haven't done the ~full deed~ with either Heidi or Mobley. Or anyone else.

One would have to say that I have still been faithful to – gasp – Miles. Gotta admit, it's been close, though. Why is that such a problem for me? So, what if I did? Is it that wrong? I don't have anything left for Miles. If he weren't blocking the divorce, I'd be done with him for good. And yes, I'd be back on the market and doing what, and ~whoever~ I wanted. At this point in my life, I think I would be naïve to think that love will have anything to do with any future relationships. At least on my part.

Uneasy and wondering what I could possibly say to Mobley after the activities of the previous evening, I headed downstairs. Maybe I should just get it over with and go see him. Talk about this... whatever it was that was darting in and out around the edges of our... friendship? Relationship?

Was it beginning to be a relationship? I had to think about that as I wound my way down the grand staircase. No, I told myself. It wasn't to that point. Despite the vibes that Mobley was throwing off with having "feelings" for me, as Leanne said. No. But, a friendship, however. Perhaps.

On my way through the front lobby, I stopped to check in on Lydia, one of my receptionists. Still a teenager and with a bubbly, outgoing personality, she had been handling the front desk admirably. She showed me the registry, indicating the several late evening arrivals with a finger.

"We are at capacity again?" I asked her, trying to sound cheery.

"Yes, ma'am. Through the weekend."

"Very good! Okay. If we have any early departures, please let me know at once."

"Yes, ma'am."

I turned and careened into Leanne.

"Wha hey, Cuz. My, my, you look splendid today," she cooed.

I didn't feel splendid. I still felt the tinges of a cheap wine headache. Mobley, I recalled, had brought up a questionable bottle of something that still had the remnants of a $4 clearance price sticker. Not feeling particularly introspective, I decided I would blame him for being hungover in a sundress.

"Oh. Well, just a regular morning, you know. Just regular... stuff. To do." I was horrible at trying to hide something. Did she know about Heidi? Mobley?

"I see," she replied, instantly seeing that she must investigate further and that something was suspicious.

"And..." She took me by the arm and led me over to a quiet sectional couch. "Did you have a good evening last night?"

"Um. Yes, yes, I did. Just a quiet evening in. Thank you for asking. And you, Leanne?"

She laughed. "Okay. What gives, Stef? Out with it. You were up to something."

"Just an evening of reading." I waved a hand dismissively, but she didn't buy it.

"Nope. Start spilling it. Details, let's go."

"Oh, shit. Fine. Well, you have to promise not to get pissed."

"Pissed? At you? I can assure you, there is nothing you can do that would make me get pissed at you. Please continue."

"It's Heidi."

"Heidi? How so?"

"She came to my room last night. She brought wine." I cleared my throat.

Leanne stared at me. "Heidi came to your room last night and she brought wine."

"Yes."

There was a long uncomfortable pause. "Um. So?" Leanne batted her eyes dismissively.

"So! Leanne, she came to my room! With *wine*..." I tried to emphasize the scandal by lowering my voice secretively.

Leanne sat quietly, appraising my expression.

"Well!?" I shot, seeing she wasn't getting the jist of my meaning.

"Well, what, Cuz? She came to your room, la tee da. I'm thankful you finally had some company up in that dusty hole. I hope she at least brought a decent wine. She does have good tastes."

I pulled her close by her shirt. "Leanne, she tried to seduce meeeeeee."

Again, she laughed. I tried to shush her as she was drawing attention to us.

"And did she?" Leanne asked maliciously.

262

There it was. How would I answer that without incriminating either Heidi or myself?

Leanne read my thoughts. "Stef. Please, like I care, come on. Knowing you as I do, I doubt very seriously that Heidi made it too far with you." She peered into my eyes, searching. "Anyway, nothing to be pissed about, I assure you. Heidi has my full permission to come rock your little socks off if you so desire." She smirked, and I could tell that she didn't think much happened anyway. Perhaps in her world, what did happen didn't amount to much. Reluctantly, I gave her a basic play by play.

"So, tell me something more about her," I asked as Leanne sat absorbing my story. "What is she like? With me, she seems quite... eager to please."

"She's in college, twenty-one years old. She is intemperate, immature and *very* aggressive."

"But I don't get it. You said she's a submissive. Right?"

"Yes, but she's quite forward and can be very pushy to get what she wants. Her libido is unmatched." Leanne laughed. "She would spend her entire day eating pussy if it were up to her. And she gets ultimate satisfaction from Joe to cap it all off. I have had to intervene on his behalf this week. He still serves me well, but she has left welts on his butt and his back to such a degree I've had to put him off-limits to her for a while."

"Wow."

"Yeah. Since I've known them, I have allowed her to dom Joe. But she is perhaps stricter than even me and she enjoys being somewhat cruel. She slaps him around like nobody's business. Joe strives to satisfy her, and apparently, he does so quite thoroughly. Yet she whips him even as he does so. She's a hot pepper, no doubt about that. I have told her she cannot whip him any further until he heals. And then later, she needs to tone it down."

"But. Joe must be enjoying this treatment. Right? Or he would have said something. Or just quit."

"You are correct. He is enjoying it. At least to the limits of his physical ability. Stef, some people don't know when they are going too far with this dom and sub stuff. Such is the case with Heidi and Joe. The idea is to have fun and enjoy it without going over the line. Use safe words. I'm still training them. They'll get it."

"It's just weird. Sorry, Leanne. But weird."

"Don't knock it until you try it. It could happen, you know."

"We've been down this road already. Umm, *no*, I won't."

"Don't forget. We have a bet in progress. Mobley turns up in your office, naked, on his knees, and you had better be ready to fulfill your end of the agreement."

The image of Mobley from the previous evening popped into my head. Mobley, handsome as ever, down on the floor in front of me, kissing and massaging my legs as I sipped his cheap wine. It all seemed to have gone against Mobley's domineering pushy "style." Yet, there he had been, not immediately scoring and seemingly ready to do anything I asked. The thought occurred to me for the first time- I could lose Leanne's bet. A tinge of panic suddenly swept over me. I felt nauseous.

"Leanne," I began, trying to find renewed confidence amidst my doubts. "I am quite safe in your little scheming bet. You will not get a womanizing playboy like Mobley to ever agree to such a humiliating role with me.

"Perhaps." Leanne laughed and stood, taking my hand. "Come on. I need to go up to my room and get my sunglasses. Then we can go to the kitchen and get a bagel and take a walk on one of the trails."

"Yes. I suppose so," I agreed, following her to the staircase.

"Did anything *else* happen last night?" Leanne suddenly asked, stopping at the first landing.

"Anything else?"

264

"You heard me. Anything else. Besides Heidi's little visit." She resumed her trek up the stairs after casting a speculative grin.

"No. That's… pretty much it." My morning conversation with Leanne was reinforcing my opinion of myself as a spineless jellyfish.

Leanne took my arm, appraising me. "What else. Stef, you are wonderfully transparent. You really can't keep secrets very well, you know."

After a moment seeing that she would not let the matter drop, I knew I had to fess up.

"Fine. I don't see why you must pry everything out of me so. It was Mobley. He came to my room… after Heidi. He brought flowers. And… more wine. Or something wine-ish, at least."

"You are quite the busy little beaver, aren't you, Cuz," Leanne remarked with a laugh.

"No! I'm not."

"So, details. Tell me everything."

I reluctantly told her everything that happened, and how Mobley ended up on the floor kissing his way up my legs.

"My, my! That does sound interesting, Cuz. First Heidi. Then Morgan. One thing is for certain, Stef. You have been quite influenced by the BDSM book I gave you! I'm glad I could educate you. I'm proud of you."

"What? No! I didn't even read your stupid book."

"I think you should read more of it."

"I'm not reading any more of it."

"Any more? So, you do admit reading some of it."

"No! I didn't."

"Let's review, shall we? Flirty, sexy fun. Very hot, very steamy. They were both decidedly submissive, sexually. Unlike your pathetic sex life with Miles where he is in charge and getting all the satisfaction, you were the one that Heidi and Morgan were lavishing attention upon. You were the one on the receiving end. Your satisfaction was their goal, not the other way around. You, my dear, are naturally becoming a dom. And you are liking it." She leaned over to whisper in my ear. "Even though you didn't actually get laid by either of them. The most problematic issue here is all that wine you drank last night."

"I didn't have all that much," I explained. "Just a glass or two from each. The bottles are up in my room if you'd like to verify I'm not a lush."

"I'll pass," Leanne smirked. Arriving at her room, she went in and retrieved her sunglasses as I waited in the hall.

I had to wonder if she were pulling strings somehow, influencing Heidi and Mobley. "Be truthful with me, Leanne," I implored as we went down the back steps. "Were you involved with either of them coming to see me?"

"I'm shocked you would think such a thing. I can honestly say, *no*," she cooed, still leaving me doubting her. "However, with how you tolerated Mobley coming to see you, I'd say you may be…" Leanne paused, appraising my expression.

"What!?"

"Er. Nothing. So, we get back from our walk, what are you going to do today?" Her evasion couldn't be more blatant. She knew damn well I would have to ask.

"Noooo, you tell me what you started to say!"

Leanne cleared her throat dramatically. "Well, okay. I'd say… you are developing deep feelings for our dear Mr. Mobley."

Of all the nerve. "I should say *absolutely* not! How in the hell could you say such a thing? Despite his slimy, lounge lizard vibe, yes, we are somewhat friends, I suppose. I really have no choice but to be somewhat nice, given everything he's done for me. But first and foremost, he's an employee here! I can assure you I am not developing… ugh… *feelings*… for him."

"Whatever you say, Cuz. Hmmm. Speak of the devil, here we are, walking by his room! Perhaps you should invite him to go to the kitchen with us."

266

"I don't think so, Leanne."

She smiled mischievously.

At that moment, Mobley's door opened. An attractive blonde woman in her early twenty's, long legs accentuated by a short skirt, came walking out, closing the door behind her. She nodded a polite acknowledgment to us and continued towards the stairs.

"That's unfortunate," Leanne casually commented. She pulled me along past Mobley's door. "Bagel. Remember, we are going to go get a bagel and go on a morning walk."

My teeth were clenched tightly in anger. It was an over-the-top jealous feeling that I couldn't shrug off... nor ignore. "That fucking bastard," I spewed. "He was just in my room last night! He couldn't even wait a day before finding another woman!"

"Stef, we don't know why that girl was there... exactly. A visitor that happens to be a beautiful woman doesn't have to have been there for sex. Or an overnight stay for longer sex. It could have been entirely... *innocent*."

"It wasn't innocent! We are talking about Mobley, after all. That... that..."

"Um. Man-whore?" Leanne finished for me with humor.

"Yes! And I'm not just mad because of... of anything! I'm mad because... because he is under... he is under *express* direction not to be bringing... *women*... to his room for nightly sleepovers! It sets a bad example, and he knows that! He can go rent a room down at The Blue Calypso for his scandalous hump fests!"

"Stef. You are stammering."

"I'm not stammering. I'm just... angry he violated..."

"What?" Leanne asked. "Your ideas of the relationship you were developing? Stef, maybe you should just admit, *that* hurts. There's nothing wrong with feeling that way," she consoled. "And, as I said, it may not have been what it seemed. Her coming out of his room..." Leanne cleared her throat. "In the morning. Well. Remember, there isn't anything formally declared… between you two. Right? I think you should talk to him about it before you crucify him."

"I'm not going to *crucify* him at all, Leanne. I'm… not going to say a thing about it. It doesn't mean a thing to me. He doesn't… mean a thing to me. Really, he doesn't. This is just serious for me due to his clear violation of the policy I set for him with how he is expected to manage his… his… *incorrigible* need to screw anything female on the island. But I'll not say a word about this, it would do no good anyway." Lost in deep thoughts of revenge, my fingers twirled a lock of hair. "But… I could *fire* him."

Leanne, detecting where I was going, quickly tried to intervene. "Whoa."

"No, I think so, Leanne. I need to *fire* his Man-Whore ass. Again. Today. Now. And not because I have any feelings for him!" I had lost all ability to think clearly, and I knew it. My reaction to this was confusing. What made me angrier was that I didn't know why I would be so angry in the first place.

Leanne stopped me at the kitchen doorway. "Now you just wait a minute. You need to step away from this anger and get ahold of yourself. Get a grip. You don't want to fire Mobley. Remember everything he has done for you. Everything he's done for Stoney Brook. He deserves far more consideration in light of this… *potential*… indiscretion. Don't you think? Really?"

"I suppose," I reluctantly agreed. I tried to take a deep breath and regain control. Dropping my arms to my sides, I tried another deep breath. "Yes. Okay. Fine now."

We stepped into the kitchen and went to the breakfast buffet table, where I took a bagel and rammed a blade through it sideways. Taking a dollop of cream cheese, I slathered it between the halves and slammed them together. The wait staff, seeing my mood, disappeared back into the kitchen.

Leanne, standing by the exit doors nibbled on her own bagel, watching my reaction as Mobley suddenly waltzed into the kitchen.

"Ms. Leanne! Ms. Stef! Good morning to you both. It looks to be a beautiful day out. I believe we are scheduled to meet a few of the archeologists this morning that have come out to inspect our ever-fascinating pirate cave." Mobley stopped, considering himself for a moment. "I say pirate cave. Which seems completely feasible as a name. The skeletons did seem to be attired and armed like typical buccaneers of the period. Having an actual pirate cave on the premises could be a suitable marketing draw after all. Don't you think, Ms. Michaels?"

"Mr. Mobley," I began. "I don't really give a fuck. Get to work and get something... *done*... today."

Mobley blinked, confused. "Um. Yes, ma'am."

No doubt bewildered with my reaction, he looked over at Leanne for guidance. She just shrugged with a grin.

I was irrational, I knew. I refused to face the reason why. Mobley had angered me no small degree. Was it jealousy? No! It couldn't be. I chomped angrily through the bagel. Yes, yes it was, I finally admitted to myself.

Jealousy over Mobley. Ack! The notion should make me more nauseous than I already was from his cheap wine. The thought of having any feelings at all for Mobley should require the wearing of a paper bag over my head. I will eliminate any such feelings as soon as I could muster whatever determination is required.

Mobley's soft caresses of the previous evening as he sat on the floor came back to haunt me. All his flirtations... the sweet sentiments... the flowers... the cheap but thoughtful wine. The soft kisses up my legs that had nearly sent me over the edge for him. His arm in the lower part of my back when he pulled me close before he left. The passionate kisses we had previously shared. I had genuinely been drawn to Mobley in a way I never anticipated.

269

And now. Now, I was angry beyond belief that with a little more goading, I could have slept with the notorious and false, Man-Whore Mobley.

I walked past Leanne as she was leaning against the wall, nonchalantly sucking cream cheese off her finger. "So. You just going to ask him? Or are you going to let this stew endlessly, like I know you are actually going to do." She chuckled at her own goading wit.

"I will not soil myself any further with that disgusting, walking, ball-sack, no matter what I previously thought of him. Or what he's done for Stoney Brook."

Leanne raised a finger to summon one of the nearby staff girls. "Um. Waitress? Please? One for the special, an order of self-righteous pride with a side of over-easy jealousy," she sarcastically chided.

The girl looked at her quizzically, confused with the strange request. "Ms. Tilden? Pardon, but I don't think we have that on the breakfast menu." Leanne laughed, further irritating me to the point of a boil-over.

Storming out of the kitchen and into the sunlight of the new day, I couldn't take it any longer. Despite my mood, Leanne was soon at my side as I walked stiffly towards the nearest trailhead.

Morgan: Okay, I paid an unannounced visit to Stefany last night. It was off the cuff, yes, but I did it anyway. She was in nothing but a robe, which totally rocked. The evening was amazing. And with unexpected results. There's something about Stefany that I can't put my finger on... She seems to like being "in charge" romantically. That's usually my role! After things were moving along, she ended up

getting me to sit on the floor in front of her. Seeing as how I thought I would have a clear view right up her robe, I agreed to this strange request, of course.

In what I took to be a serious case of a blue-ball teasing, she let me massage her legs. That turned into kissing her feet then moving my way up. She just looked down on me with this sexy, indescribable expression while I did all of this. It was an expression of... I don't know... of expectation maybe?

The sensations of the smooth, warm skin of her legs against my lips as I kissed my way up had the boner garage fully staffed. It's a wonder that Morgan Junior didn't snap in half against my zipper while sitting there in front of her. These things that happened with Stef last night, I would have never considered as a turn on for me. First off, I like being the one in charge. And what the hell, I don't think I've ever even kissed a woman's feet before.

And she scrimped on my view up her robe, always keeping herself covered. I couldn't even tell if she was shaved bare, with a landing strip or all-natural. Damn it. So there was no carpet munching after moving up her legs. No pole ride. None of it happened. And she made it clear that the massage and kissing were as far as she was going to let it go. We'll see about that later.

Even though I didn't get Stefany ankles up for the evening, she got me steamed like no other woman. "Not scoring" with Stefany was fucking hot. Another first for me.

I want to tell her I am in love with her.

~~~~~

Just like that, Stefany's attitude towards me has changed. And not for the better. I've never known such a moody person, friendly one minute, angry the next.

The last several days have been strange, that's for certain. Following the hot and steamy evening with Stefany, she has since ignored me daily, being as cold to me as she had during my first months of working at Stoney Brook. And here it was me thinking we had progressed. I am hesitant to discuss with her my latest ideas but decided to give it a go.

Checking for her whereabouts at the front desk, Marcy said she was doing something in the big barn, so I headed over to track her down. Entering through a side door, I could see her talking with several workers.

I walked towards her. "Hi, Ms. Michaels. May I have a word?" I began feeling strangely awkward. Why did I let this woman get to me so? And why should I care if she were pissed at me? Again. I should *not* care, I thought to myself, knowing I was lying. I had to face the fact that this whole being in love thing was seriously giving me a bad case of romantic derangement. I needed to get over it.

"Hello, Mr. Mobley," she said stoically, showing no indication that we had ever even moved past the professional stage of greeting. Seeing I wanted her attention, she already looked ruffled. "Yes? What can I do for you?"

The other workers, sensing the tension between us, quickly departed.

"May I update you on the status of our Mill Property and coconut contract? It has been a while since we spoke, and there have been many developments. I want to keep you in the loop."

Hints of a disgusted sigh escaped her lips. "I'm... busy... right now, Mr. Mobley. Perhaps another time."

"It won't take long."

"Fine," she reluctantly agreed after hesitating. "I'm headed over to the storage building to check on restaurant supplies. Let's walk."

Avoiding looking directly at me, she was as unfriendly as she had been when we first met. As to why, I had no clue. Several days before, we had seemed so close to a breakthrough in our relationship the evening I had spent with her in her room. Now... it was as if it had never happened. I had to wonder if it was that time of the month.

"The coconut contract is all squared away. The money is in the bank, so to speak. The tree groves are cleaned and groomed, and we have harvest paths now. And we are well on our way to refurbishing the Mill Property. Island Power has run the necessary lines and we now have electricity. Fresh water is not a problem, and as we discussed, the cisterns we installed should provide about one-hundred forty percent of expected use capacity. We have foundations completed for 15 bungalow units, and the mill itself is about seventy-five percent to a decent state of refurbishment. We could be ready to open within three months. And that includes the restaurant and bungalows."

"That's all real fine, Mr. Mobley. Very well done. Thanks. Now, if that's everything, I'll let you return to your du-"

"About the Mill Property," I interrupted, peremptorily cutting her off. "There are a few more developments, public relations wise."

"Oh?" she acknowledged suspiciously, still avoiding looking at me. "And what would those be?"

"With how we are preserving the natural habitat, leaving both the natural and historical aspects of the area preserved, we are going to be featured in a National Geographic documentary."

"What? Wow." With this news she stopped and finally looked into my eyes. "Well, that's a good thing, right?"

"It's a great thing. And we've had another request relating to this. Woods Hole Oceanographic Institute would like to partner with us, allowing them to have a research station on the property. If agreed, they will provide plans for a modest structure, built in good taste, that could house perhaps up to ten researchers with equipment and instruments. The architectural style will mirror our own bungalow designs and fit in nicely. They would like access to the bay to dock a research vessel and have even agreed to help with our finances for the dock facilities, maybe 15% or so of total initial costs. I've investigated it and it would in no way interfere with our operations other than we would need to add a bit of capacity to our utilities. Totally doable and a wise investment on our part. And... with helping and getting out there with conservation like we are, it would be great publicity. Our guests would be able to interact with their staff, ask questions. We could maybe even arrange some observation trips with them for the guests. Which could garner more donations for their cause. It's win-win for us and them. With that and National Geographic, Stoney Brook will get you into living rooms around the globe. I think it will be a great tourist draw here as well as to the Mill Property. All I need is your go ahead for these items and I'll let everyone know."

"Um." She looked shocked. "Mr. Mobley, just when I think I have you figured out or that I can expect a routine day, you blow me away with something else. Fact is, I don't pay you nearly enough. Yet another morning I have to let everything you do for Stoney Brook - for me - set in." She peered into my eyes, looking like she wanted to say something else. "Despite..."

"Despite?" I asked, lost to where she was headed in the conversation.

"Nothing." Whatever it was, she let it go. She turned and resumed her walk towards the storage building. "Absolutely, do it," she said over her shoulder. "It all sounds great, thanks, Mr. Mobley."

"Ms. Michaels. Wait."

I reached towards her, softly touching her arm. She kept walking.

"Stefany. Please."

"Mr. Mobley. I have told you... please, address me..."

"Tell me. Is it something I have done?"

"What? No." She stopped, immediately folding her arms in discomfort, considering my question. "*No*, Mr. Mobley. I just think... we need to maintain a professional relationship. It's not that I don't appreciate everything you have done. I do. Very much. But I regrct... that things moved past that point recently. It was a mistake on my part. It was my fault, not yours. I'm still married, after all. I certainly don't need a *boyfriend* on the sly to add to the complexity of my life. I need to get back to the business of why I'm here in the first place, and that is successfully running Stoney Brook."

"We are doing all of that. And your marriage isn't really a marriage, we both know that. There was something -

between us. I know you felt it too. I know I did. So. What's wrong with… more?"

"I think you have quite all the *more* that you need, Mr. Mobley," Stefany replied, her eyes darting away from my gaze.

"More?" I asked.

"Yes. *More.* Now, if you will excuse me, I'm going to check the inventory in the shed, then I must make a few important calls." She hesitated again. "Well done. Don't misunderstand me. I very much - appreciate you. Now, good day, Mr. Mobley."

After coming up from a meeting with several island authorities and the archeological team for an update on the cave, I took out my mobile and checked for messages. Stefany had brushed me off yet again.

Whatever chance I may have had with her in some sort of romantic relationship had evaporated. Unused to such rejection, I felt strangely miserable about it all. She had not made any moves to fire me, but I felt strangely unwelcome now, even though there wasn't anything tangible I could point to for that feeling. If I had to read her mind, I would bet that she would very much desire that I leave Stoney Brook for convenience sakes rather than outright hating me. Was there anything for me here? It was an idea I now seriously considered.

The renovations at the Mill Property were going as scheduled. The coconut groves were nearly all groomed and tidied up. The skeletons discovered in the basement cave were putting things on hold, but everything still looked promising with making that historic feature a major attraction to Stoney Brook.

I stepped out of the front door of the mansion and stood on the patio, bathed in the brilliant tropical sun, I took in the busy hum of everyday life as it now existed at Stoney Brook. People and vehicles moved about, set about to one task or another. The place had a new life, and I felt good about helping Stefany make it successful. There would be setbacks, no doubt. But at this moment, it was nearly perfect. Except for the fact that the woman I loved did not feel the same way about me.

I wondered. Did my desire to capture the affections of Stefany drive my obsession with helping her make Stoney Brook a smashing success? Maybe.

It seemed every time I happened by the front drive, there was an unpleasant reminder of the reality of Stefany's situation. Miles' expensive sports car seemed to be a regular sight. I had to wonder how he was spending his time with Stefany. Were they arguing? Talking about reconciliation? Or more?

A new message popped up.

Leanne:

> **Morgan, I have the pool
> all to myself. And Joe and
> Heidi. Come by if you get
> a chance. Good privacy
> today. I have a cold beer
> waiting for you. Let's
> talk... ♡ L**

Making my way through the manor house by way of the kitchen, I kept a keen eye out for Stefany. Miles was evidently on the premises for a visit, and she would be with him. I walked through the ballroom patio doors and took the short trail through a series of hedges to the pool.

Leanne, lounging in a recliner, sporting large mirror sunglasses, and sipping a Mai Tai, motioned me over. Joe stood behind Leanne, slowly massaging suntan lotion onto her shoulders and neck. Heidi sat on a side of the recliner, her job with the lotion was evidently Leanne's stomach and legs. My day was brightening, even if all I really wanted to do was be a voyeur for an hour or so. I paused for a moment admiring Leanne, her body gleaming and gorgeous in the sun, attended by Heidi, extremely beautiful in her own right.

And then there was the irritating schmuck, Joe. What a sap. My dislike for the arrogant Joe grew by the second.

"How goes it, Morgan?" Leanne asked. "You are getting the scoop on the bones in the basement cave?"

"Indeed I am. While it would be in poor taste to leave the skeletons out and exposed - and against island law, they can be reinterred into a marble crypt we'll build down there near where they were found. The artifacts, such as the firearms and cutlasses will all be returned, where they will best be preserved and displayed in a museum that we can set up in the basement near the cave entrance. It will all be done in excellent taste and be a huge draw to those that favor the storied past of Stoney Brook."

"Oh, yay."

"What, history isn't your thing, Leanne? That sounds like false enthusiasm."

"Oh, I'm enthused. Heidi? I'm enthused, right?"

Heidi paused from her ministrations to Leanne's right calf muscle. She placed a delicate kiss on Leanne's bent leg then gave me a mischievous smile, enjoying my reaction. "Yes, Ms. Tilden. Very enthused."

"Joe? You are enthused, yes?"

Joe leaned over to apply lotion to Leanne's upper chest, his fingers running beneath Leanne's swimsuit top, unabashedly massaging her breasts. "Oh, yes, Ms. Tilden," he said in his thick accent. "Very much so."

Nearly biting my tongue and cursing myself for my recent forced celibacy, I glanced around to verify that we were alone. We were. Leanne and her crew of Joe and Heidi were always well behaved in public, but they seemed to be relishing giving me a show.

"Aren't you worried you will be seen by some of the guests?" I asked. "Some are bound to head out here to the pool soon. I'm sure Stefany will give you an earful if you are caught."

"Mobley, you used to be so carefree, throwing caution to the wind. Now you are high-strung and uptight. What happened?"

"I'm not high-strung and uptight, Leanne," I protested. "I'm just... discreet. It's a necessary part of being employed here, Stefany tells me."

"Well, Mr. Discreet, if someone comes in, we'll go to the vanilla plan, quit worrying. And no need to worry about Stefany. She's busy up in her office still trying to convince Miles to divorce her. Which will again be to no avail."

I pulled a pool chair over and sat next to Leanne. My perfect positioning allowed a wonderful view down the bikini tops of both Leanne and Heidi. Gleaming, coconut oiled, superb boobies. Joe, evidently seeing my intent, attempted to intervene by parking his boxy ass directly in my line of sight. I wanted to kick him.

"Um. Pardon me, Joe?" I said, indicating with my hand that I was in a conversation that he was rudely blocking. "Can you hand me that cold beer on the table?" I asked. Joe's eyes darkened with hostility as he stiffly retrieved the drink for me. "Thanks." I moved my chair closer to block any further moves. The view was spectacular. Joe stood in his former position, pouting behind Leanne.

"So. Morgan. I have a bone to pick with you."

"Is that supposed to be a joke, Leanne? Very funny."

"I suppose it is a rather lame joke. I do, however, imagine you running around here using that very line on any unsuspecting beautiful females you may come across."

"I've cleaned up my act, you know that."

"Ah. Have you?" She said this with an interrogative smile that was both friendly and threatening at the same time.

"Well, yeah. Why? Did you think I was seeing someone?"

"No. Just curious as to the latest exploits of Man-Whore Mobley." Joe snickered vindictively at this. "Last we talked, you had me thinking you were... abiding by Stefany's establishment rules."

279

"Establishment rules? I don't know if I would phrase it exactly like *that*." I protested.

"Then you've been a good boy, Morgan?"

"Of course."

"Oh, come now. Once a scoundrel, always a scoundrel. You haven't enjoyed the company of any young ladies as of late? Like… say… back in your room? A few days ago? In the morning, a pretty blonde left your room. I just happened to be walking by."

I thought back, perplexed. "If I were getting laid, I think I would know it," I joked.

"One would hope," Joe quipped.

I wanted to flip Joe off. Maybe throw him in the pool.

"Joe, don't aggravate Morgan, he's had a hard time lately," Leanne smirked. "So, what of the blonde, Mobley?"

It suddenly came to me. "Oh. Yes, you must mean Annabelle. Tall? Indeed, quite pretty, and gorgeous legs, blue mini-skirt to match her blue eyes?"

"That would be her. Yes," Leanne confirmed.

"She's a tennis player. Quite bendy and wonderful. No, no action there, I'm sorry to say, although she is a genuine freak. We did have a thing back when I first arrived on the island. She stopped by that morning to see about maybe getting back together. It took a lot of self-discipline I didn't think I had, but I told her I couldn't. Now considering some recent events, I'm thinking I made a mistake sending her away."

"Eh. Maybe. Maybe not." Evidently satisfied with my answer, Leanne took a sip of her Mai Tai and leaned back in her recliner. "Beyond adhering to the house rules, I thought you were interested in Stefany? Have you already given up on that notion?"

I leaned over, trying to carefully select my words. Heidi was watching me over the tops of her sunglasses with amusement. Joe stood clenching his jaws, looking jealous. "Leanne. You are a very good friend. I can always tell you anything. Right?"

She took off her sunglasses, eyeing me at the prospect of new gossip. "What?"

"I mean. We can talk about things. Right?"

She pushed her glasses back on. "Morgan. We are very good friends, you, and me. In fact, you have come to be among one of my best friends. I like you and I enjoy your company, despite your shabby, low-rent quality of character."

I straightened my back in my chair, preparing to take offense.

"And... I trust you," she continued, trying to reassure me. "That is a rare feat indeed. You should feel quite honored."

"Shabby and low-rent?"

She waved her hand dismissively. "Let's not pretend to deny. Focus. Out with it, Morgan. Don't worry about Heidi or Joe. Just say what's on your mind."

"Okay. So. With Stefany. Why won't she give me the time of day? She's polite enough. She isn't hateful or anything. She just shut off like a switch. I thought we were building something, but I guess not. Today, she told me she just wants a professional relationship. In so many words."

Leanne sat quietly, evidently contemplating this statement. "And... what do you want, Morgan?"

"This is all new territory for me, and it's extremely frustrating. Yes, yes. I'm in love with Stefany. I think you know that." I glanced nervously at Heidi and Joe, but in true sex slave fashion, they acted immune to the conversation.

"I do," Leanne replied.

A brief pause ensued as we both sat, the warm tropical breeze flowing around us, imbued with the noises of the forest and the smells of new flowers.

"Leanne? So? What's going on?"

"I'm thinking, Morgan. Drink your beer."

"Leanne. I think I'm going to leave."

"Leave?"

"Yes. Leave. Maybe head back to the states. Find another job. Maybe go back to school. I don't think I can take... *this*... anymore."

"Ah. The pain of unrequited love." She laughed. "Poor Morgan gets his feelings hurt and he wants to take his toys and go home. Now you know how all the women have felt whose emotions you have so callously trampled in your sole pursuit of sexual pleasure."

"Leanne, I don't think it's very funny. And that's not true!"

"Oh, chill out, Morgan. It's *very* true."

"Do you think maybe she heard about Annabelle visiting me? Or maybe she saw her leaving the building? Or maybe someone said something to her?"

"Hmmm. Doubtful."

"Well then, what in the hell did I do, Leanne? You talk with her all the time, right? You would know?"

She mulled this over with a grin as she sat up. "Joe, Heidi, I'm going to take a little stroll with Morgan. I'll be back in a few minutes. Behave, should any guests show." They both nodded and went about their business, Heidi retrieving her drink from the table as Joe jumped into the pool. At times, their behavior was reminiscent of several loyal dogs, Leanne sending them this way or that. I wondered what they found appealing in demeaning themselves in such a mindless relationship with Leanne. Then I remembered; there was the sex.

"Come on, Morgan. We'll walk." She slipped on her pool sandals and wrapped her towel over her shoulders.

We took one of the trails away from the pool and soon we were among the lush tropical foliage. "So?" I finally asked.

"Patience, Morgan. I think I may be able to help you with your problem with Stefany. You know I'm a psychiatrist. Right?"

"You may have mentioned it if I recall. Usually, I just daydream while you carry on about yourself. I didn't know you were an actual psychiatrist. I thought you had studied it in a few classes, perhaps."

"No. I have a doctoral degree," she confirmed, ignoring my slight. "I was a partner in a practice a few years ago but opted out to pursue other avenues of interest. I may go back sometime. I have resources enough and I have invested well. For now, I just want to play for a while."

"Other avenues of interest?" I asked incredulously. "You mean cavorting around with your sex slaves Joe and Heidi?"

"Not just." She laughed. "I'm deeper than that, Morgan. You are so impudent. If you were mine, I'd punish you hard for that remark."

"Whatever. So, tell me how you can help me."

She placed a hand against my chest, stopping us both, facing me. "I have a *plan*."

"A plan? And it involves me?"

"Yes, you idiot," she cajoled. "Are you willing to listen to me? Have an open mind? You may as well tell me now, so if you are not interested, I won't waste my time on you."

"Of course! Tell me! If I could get back into the romantic groove with Stefany... or at least rebuild a friendship with her, I would try anything."

"Very well. You need some background information first. With Stefany, there is a lot of psychiatry at work. I don't know how much you actually know about her, but she has been an abused woman." Leanne peered over the top of her sunglasses at me. "*Severely* abused."

I had known this, but perhaps not the extent. "Um. Okay."

"This history goes far back into her past. And more recently into her marriage with Miles," she continued, again walking with me down the trail.

"I have a brand-new score to settle with that asshole," I hissed, clenching my fists.

"No. You don't. You'll mess up my plan, likely get fired, and you'll never get *anywhere* with her romantically. You are not to speak to Miles except in civil terms. Do we understand each other?"

"Fine. Understood."

"Stefany has been submissive all of her life," Leanne continued. "And she has allowed men to mistreat her since she was a young girl. Family men. Acquaintances. Past boyfriends. Miles. There's a pattern. She has a history of seeking out cruel, dominant men in her relationships. Boyfriends would start off okay, but then invariably show they were chameleons. It's no coincidence. Some people are magnets for abusers, and they subconsciously seek out these types. Stefany is this way. She did it again when she started dating Miles then marrying him."

"That's awful. But what can I do to change any of that?"

"I believe it would do her immeasurable good to experience the *other* side of the power dynamic. To be dominant, for once. A dominant woman... with a man sex slave... in a relationship that is not abusive, but consensual, sexy, romantic, and fun. And fortunately for you, that is just what I'm proposing."

"What? You've got to be kidding. You want me to be a sex slave? As in a BDSM sort of thing? Like you with Joe and Heidi? *That's* your plan?"

"Yes."

I laughed uncontrollably, sending several birds fluttering from the treetops. "Leanne. Stefany would *never*, EVER, go for such a thing. As for me, I have never been submissive about anything in my life. Especially sex. If anything, I'm like you. Dominant. I call the shots. And I've never had any complaints."

"I'm wasting my time," Leanne grumbled, walking ahead of me impatiently.

"No, wait. I will consider your "plan." Even if it has NO chance of working. What would I do? Let her tie me up, spank and slap me or whatever?"

"Thank about it, Morgan. This is Stefany we are talking about, not some tawdry one- night romp with one of your floosies. This would be long term. You would be under her control. Her getting off on it. Are you telling me that wouldn't crank your engine?"

I paused, thinking. It was such an unlikely scenario. But was I dismissing it too quickly? Anything with Stefany would be just my ticket, truthfully.

"Sexually, you would be in for a big surprise, Morgan Mobley." She grinned, seeing me mulling the possibilities. "No instant gratification for you as you are used to having. But… as her sexual submissive, you would attain levels of pleasure you have never dreamed possible."

"I can dream a hell of a lot, I'll have you know. And none of it with me as a slave."

"Fair enough. Could being a sexual slave to a beautiful woman be so bad, Morgan? It's *Stefany*. The woman of your dreams from what you have previously confessed to me. Think of the possibilities in that horny little mind of yours."

Leanne was sadistically twisting me around her finger. And she was right. It sounded exciting and arousing. But there was something else, too. Something at the base of my every thought about Stefany. "I know you are going to think I'm lying, but - this thing I have for Stefany. It isn't just about sex. I truly am in love with her."

"And that, my dear Morgan, is what makes you such an ideal lover for her. Who better to break this cycle of abuse she is in? Not every man is strong enough to submit to a woman. You are. If you don't understand the psychological implications of her as the dominant and you as the submissive, don't try. I'll do the thinking for you."

"Oh, really?"

"I am not guaranteeing what happens will be everlasting romantic bliss between you two. I can make an educated guess, however. What's certain is, I am offering you a chance to build a relationship with Stefany. With the likelihood of great sex, which I know must appeal to your whorish, base desires greatly."

I watched one of the birds overhead clean and fluff it's feathers. The birds about in the canopy seemed particularly raucous this day. "But how could you ever convince her to do this?"

She stopped me again on the trail to face me. "You have to leave it to me. My plan would give her power where she has never had power before in her life. It would *change* her life. For the better. You could be helping her become a better woman."

"Well. I would be all for helping her."

"Exactly what I thought. Let me see that pen and little pad of paper in your shirt pocket."

Curious, I handed over the paper and pen. She flipped the pad to a blank sheet and prepared to write.

"Okay," she began. "Tell me what you make here in a year."

"What? Why?"

"Just do it, you'll see," she urged.

I gave her my annual salary, less insurance and counting off the expenses. She laughed but quickly held her hand over her mouth.

"Oh. I'm... so sorry," she said. "I do recall you saying she got you rather cheap. But perhaps a reasonable price given you don't have an actual degree, eh Morgan?"

Now she was just trying to get under my skin. "Come on. That again? You are going to beat me up with that?"

"Nooo. You are right, Morgan. I was just being unnecessarily cruel." She grinned sarcastically, revealing her gleaming white teeth. "I can be quite wonderfully cruel, you know."

"I know good and well. What do you need to know my income for?" I again asked in protest.

"Because," she purred. "If you agree to my plan, right now, and you carry it out exactly as I say, I am prepared to pay you a bonus." She wrote down a number and signed her name below it, handing it back to me. "I will pay you that amount… an additional two years of salary just for doing this."

It was an incredible offer, and my mouth dropped open in shock. "What? Why would you do that?"

"I would do it because she is my dearest friend. If this is a chance to finally get her some help with how her past has damaged her, then it is a cheap price to pay. I would do anything to help her be happy. And I think this is the best way to do it. Do we have a deal?"

I scratched my chin. It was an interesting proposition, there was no doubt about that.

"And how long would I have to be in this submissive sex slave role to Stefany?"

"I require a year-long commitment. I'll write you a check later. She is to never hear a word of this payout."

Leanne could no doubt read the conflicted emotions on my face. "If I can't get her to do this, it's no harm no foul," she added. "You would give me my check back and I'll buy you dinner instead."

"But what if I don't like being a sex slave… or whatever?" I asked, honestly wondering.

"Morgan. I know you. You are a horny pervert. You'll love it. Eventually. Trust me."

I stared at her with suspicion. I couldn't help but feel that she was manipulating me.

"Either agree now to my terms, fully, or go about your business, Morgan, and not bother me any further with your ideas of sweet, dear love for our lonely Ms. Stefany." She extended her hand. "There will be no going back."

After a moment of final hesitation, I took her hand and shook it. "Agreed." For even a remote chance to try and win Stefany's love – and maybe get into her pants - this could be worth it. "But, sorry to burst your bubble, Leanne. She will never agree to this."

"She will. I'm sure of it." Leanne gave me a playful shove. "I know because several months ago, I made a bet with her."

"What? A bet? What kind of bet?"

"To get to the point, I bet her that I could get you into her office, naked, on your knees, on a leash, and willing to serve her every need as her sex slave, for a year."

"And? What did she say to that?"

"She accepted. The terms were, if I did indeed produce you in said fashion, she would be required to use you in a sexually dominant manner that I would be directing."

"I can't believe that! She agreed? And if you don't produce me in said manner, what happens then?"

"Oh, some paltry agreement that I would provide her a few horses and some dinners or something. I wasn't too worried. The bet is a sure thing, as I just demonstrated by obtaining your agreement."

"You tricked me! And you are a devil in a string bikini. I'll think about all of this, get back to you."

Leanne laughed. "Your thinking is done, my naïve, boyish friend. We have an accord. And yes, I will soon be taking you to make your previously described appearance in her office. I expect your full cooperation. No griping, no bitching, and no hesitation. You do what I tell you to do."

"But Leanne! I won't suffer an affront to my dignity and manhood! I mean, I won't be... *humiliated*, will I? In this plan of yours?"

"Morgan. Let's be real. You have *no* dignity. And your manhood is nothing but a pitiable extension of your solitary need for constant sexual gratification. I fear for any knothole in the walls of Stoney Brook. If not for this self-proclaimed *love* you say you have for Stefany, there would be no hope, whatsoever, of you of ever gaining any shred of manly decency and learning what a real relationship is all about."

She gave me a hard slap on my ass, surprising me, making me lurch forward. "Really, you should be thanking me right now. I have no doubt that in kindergarten you were one of the ones eating glue and plugging up the toilets with paper."

"I have plenty of dignity. And you didn't answer my question! Will this be… like… humiliating in any way? Because I don't think I could agr-"

"Yes. Some of it will most certainly be humiliating. Some of this will be addressed as a well-deserved crack of a whip on your arrogant ass, I can tell you that much. It'll be good for you." She began strolling casually back towards the pool, the *thwack thwack* of her pool sandals adding a strange rhythm to the squawks and squeals of the birds in the trees. "Gawd, I wish I were the one doing it. Maybe I could convince Stefany to loan you out."

"Wait!" I protested. "Leanne, now hold on." I caught up to her on the trail. She smiled knowingly, telling me I had been an easy mark for her dominatrix Stefany plan.

"As you already know, it would be most unwise to double-cross me," she warned, stopping suddenly. She turned to me, and squeezed my chin, making my lips pucker. "Which I know you would never, ever, do. Now that we've come to agreement, let's go back and have another drink. You can regale me with another of your pirate *bone* stories. Or some such. By the way, I think you have a dallop of fresh bird poop in your hair – may want to take care of that."

Standing in stunned silence, I watched her walk away.

"Not one question as to if it will be *painful*," I heard her mumble under her breath. "You are so cute, Morgan."

The telltale signs of something warm and disgusting wound its way through my hair and oozed onto my scalp.

CHAPTER 11
RIDING CROP ROAD RASH

Morgan: So, evidently, per Leanne's agreement, I am to become Stefany's sex slave. This is surely laughable, and I still don't quite know what to think. What the hell has Leanne got me into? For her part, she has agreed to pay me a sum that is twice what I make working at Stoney Brook in a year. It's the most money I've ever had or made.

I've had friends in the past that were into the "BDSM" scene. But I never asked them any questions and I didn't really look into it, as it has never interested me. Stupid plastic handcuffs and getting spanked, or something like that. Maybe that's not so bad, I guess. Whatever floats people's boats.

I have regrets over Leanne paying me in the agreement. Serious regrets. After hearing how Stefany has been abused in her life, it makes me want to help her even more. I love her despite what she thinks of me. I sure don't need to be paid to be with her. It makes me feel guilty, like I am profiteering off Stefany to trick her.

Leanne has not given me any idea when this is all going to take place. Supposedly, she will take me to Stefany's office, where I am to be "stark naked," wearing a leash, thus letting Leanne win a bet that those two had between each other. If Stefany abides by the rules, which I seriously doubt she will, I'll be doing the deed -of some sort- with Stefany for a year. I could think of worse things! What my future holds will be interesting.

~~~~~

The details of the "bet" are starting to sink in. I admit I am excited at the prospect of some sexy fun with Stefany, even if it is orchestrated by Leanne with me as a "sex slave." Leanne may be a beautiful woman, but she's weird as hell with her notions of turning Stefany into a "dominatrix." That just isn't going to happen, but regardless, I must wrap my mind around letting Leanne take me to Stefany's office – naked. I'd be lying to myself in this journal if I said I wasn't scared about what may happen, and most of it could be bad.

~~~~~

I've been thinking about what Leanne said about Stefany being abused. It makes me very angry. It's not much of a man that would abuse – or hit - a woman. I want to crack the skulls of the men – and especially Miles - that have abused Stefany in the past. If Leanne thinks this sex slave thing she has cooked up will somehow help Stefany, I guess I'm down for that. I WILL pay Miles a visit someday, I'll just keep that to myself. He has a lot of justice coming to him.

If Stefany does go for this absurd arrangement that Leanne has concocted, I'll be having a lot of fun with the most beautiful woman I've ever met. Yeah, that's a win. It will be embarrassing as hell, being naked in her office. I may get fired. But I agreed. And if she goes for it? So what, if she smacks me with a ping pong paddle while wearing a leather mini. Or puts fake, fuzzy handcuffs on me or some other odd domination thing. Big deal.

Whatever it is, if it's with Stefany, I'm all in for it.

Holding the small device up against the light for better inspection, it seemed to have all the features I was hoping for in a small compact unit. It was one of a hundred, the others all packed neatly in a box that I would take to the front desk for check-out and loan to our guests. The one sample I had in my hand, I would take to Stefany since she hadn't seen them or know what they were.

The wireless device, called a G-PupS, can be worn as a watch, on an ankle, around the neck on a lanyard, slipped into a pocket or clipped to the clothing of our guests when they hike the forest and mountain trails around Stoney Brook and the Mill Property. It doesn't just provide a real-time location of our guests out on these trails; it also provides such benefits as plant identification when queried and can run a location-specific narrative of information when used with an earbud. They can also interface seamlessly with any smart device.

G-PupS allows staff to monitor the location of our guests while allowing them to venture off on remote trails. The idea is it greatly improves safety. Should anyone get lost or injured, they could be quickly and easily tracked.

I texted Stefany with the good news and told her to meet me at the concierge desk.

She approached soon after, evidently having been mingling with the guests. Admiring her legs in a short dress with floral patterns, I had to wonder if Leanne was soon intending to implement her devious sex slave plan. Seeing Stefany sent a tingling feeling through my body in anticipation of being led naked to her office. The whole idea seemed so absurd. Yet it made my heart race thinking of it.

"Yes? What, Mr. Mobley. I was having tea with several of our guests," she said, visibly irritated at having been interrupted. "This had better be important."

"It is. I wanted to show you the G-PupS that I ordered. They are great. Personal mobile devices aren't reliable on our trails, and with these, they can help us locate any guests if the need arises. Guests can aim an optic eye at any plant, insect, or anything else and get identification and more if they are wearing an earbud. It's extremely small, unobtrusive and effective!" I handed it over to her. She looked angry.

"Um. Mr. Mobley. While I do appreciate such attention to *detail*, couldn't this wait for another time? I mean, really. I thought this was an emergency or something."

"Oh. Yeah, I just thought... maybe you would want to see them. I ordered one-hundred and they are preprogrammed with our terrain and information. We can start using them immediately. We can locate anyone right here at the concierge desk or take a mobile tracking unit out and find them on the trail. So. Maybe... you can have a look. At that one. Try it out, see what you think. Maybe even take it out on a trail, communicate with the front desk or ask a few plant identifications or history questions. Oh, it even updates our dining choices available here as well as island restaurant menus and entertainment options."

"Um. Fine. I'll have a look a little later." After a few moments of icy stare, she started to turn and walk away. She paused and turned. "Mr. Mobley."

"Yes?"

"When I say this - and I mean it in a completely inoffensive way, okay? I don't want to hear from you - for a while. Quit texting me about plugged up toilets..." Her voice began to rise with agitation. "Giving me unnecessary updates on broken fucking hydraulic hoses on the excavator... wondering how we can keep kids of the guests from peeing in the pool... Miguel's fucking genital rash keeping him on light duties, calling me on and on... AND ON... for

294

mundane crap that I don't need to hear about!" She took a deep breath, seeming to try and gain some control over her need to rant. "Um. Sorry. I don't mean to be… rude. It's just, I'm very busy, Mr. Mobley."

"Oh. Ms. Michaels. I totally understand. No problem." I hesitated to continue. "But…"

She turned sharply with this last. "What? But what?"

"There was one other thing I wanted to let you know. It's not mundane, I promise. It actually has great revenue potential."

"Ughh. What?" She was tapping her foot now, her hands on her hips, staring at the floor.

"It's a new idea I had. To use some of our sugarcane crops. The idea, which I already ran by some of our coconut partner companies, is to cut our mature sugar cane up and splice them into little coffee stirrers. Little sweet, chewable sticks. They are biodegradable and taste delicious in a coffee. I already have a contract ready to sign and we can give it a try. Who knows, it could go over big in the states. Is it okay to sign it in your stead? We can start immediately with what we already have harvested."

Blinking several times, she seemed to be trying to process my idea, despite her overall bad mood. "Uh-huh. Coffee stirrers?"

She looked at her shoes and muttered nearly inaudibly, "You are so fucking *exhausting*."

"I just thought-"

"Yeah. Yes. I guess! Go ahead. Thanks."

"Great! You'll see, that will be good for us."

She turned to leave.

"Um. Ms. Michaels. About the Mill Property restaurant…"

"Mobley, FUCKING WHAT?! WHAT NOW?! Helicopter rides?! Reusable toilet paper?!" Her outburst was loud and uncontained. Fortunately, her tea guests had stepped out of earshot and were on the front porch. There were several staff members present, however, and they stopped in their tracks, wide-eyed.

Taken aback by her angry response, I thought better of any further discussion. Stefany was yet again proving herself to be a woman of many moods. Still, she was cute and beautiful despite looking as though she wanted to hit me. "It's… not important," I said. "We can talk. Later."

"Great. Leaving nowwww." Stefany stormed off, even though I had just proposed an idea that could be worth several hundred thousand dollars of new income! Maybe more. How ungrateful! Perhaps she just didn't get the idea, I told myself. She abruptly stopped at the front door and faced me, holding her hands up. "I'm sorry. I didn't mean to yell." With that, she left.

The girl at the concierge desk snickered beneath her breath. "Mr. Mobley. Sounds like your tracker system didn't go over very well. Did she approve these? You don't want to anger the boss. I wouldn't want you to get fired. Again. Although, I did hear that The Blue Calypso has been looking to hire a new toilet swab."

"I'm not going to get fired! Just get these set up behind the desk, hook up the charger as I explained in the inter-office email. In several days, we'll start issuing them to the guests for the trails." I sat the box of G-PupS on the counter.

"Sure, Mr. Mobley. I'm sure Ms. Michaels will appreciate these, whatever they are. *Later.*"

She punctuated the last word for sarcastic emphasis. She was new, and no doubt got her disparaging ideas of me from the other staff girls. I would need to refute these whenever the opportunity arose.

She leaned over the desk, mischief in her pretty brown eyes. "Mr. Mobley. Guests, when they go on our trails, don't want big brother spying over their every move. They go to explore. Kiss. Make-out. Make love. Enjoy nature. Just because you aren't getting any, doesn't mean our guests shouldn't."

"What?! Whether I *get* any or not is none of your business, and I get... plenty. And I'll have you know we don't monitor guests' activities! These devices provide interesting, interactive information... and allow them an emergency way to contact us, if needed. That's all!"

"Yeahhhhh. And on this mobile monitor, we can't see their little red dot, where they are located? Moving along with their every step? Beamed from a satellite?"

"Yes, yes. But it's not like we have a video feed of what they are doing."

"But it is capable of video if the option is preferred, is it not?"

"Well. Yes, but we are not-"

"Mhmm. If you say so, Mr. Mobley. I am glad that is so. I would hate to think that you were doing this all because you are a *voyeuristic pervert*... of some sort. Such as I have heard." The last of this slipped nearly silently from her lips, but done so for effect, as I heard her perfectly.

"What!? Who did you hear that from?" I was barely able to contain my anger with this insolent, new staff girl.

"I don't recall who," she tried to answer, putting a thoughtful finger against her cheek looking up at the ceiling.

"You most certainly do recall. Who!?" I could not let this pass.

She smiled devilishly and leaned on her elbows over the counter. "So many have stories to tell of you, Mr. Mobley. What a lover you are. Always on the moves. They say you even tried with Ms. Michaels. You got your comeuppance and were shot down in flames. Now, you get nothing but a dusty latex glove and a sock in your room. Women here, they call you Sockman."

"Latex glove? Sockman? Whatever that means, you would do well to not worry about my love life. You are new here, Miss...?"

"Miss Acantrella. Ariana Acantrella. My initials are *AA*. Like anti-aircraft. I shoot things down." She held her hand out, which I refused, invoking her to laugh.

"And you are from this area?" I asked, barely restraining my anger.

"I'm originally from the Bahamas. Been on the island for about a year."

"Well, Ms. Acantrella. No. *None* of those stories are true. Whatever they are." Emphasizing my point, I waved my hands like an umpire indicating safe. I didn't know what was being said about me, but it had to stop. "I didn't get any *comeuppance*, as you say. And I would appreciate you not to follow in the footsteps of some of the other staff here, spreading falsehoods about me. Do you understand?" She was quite the pretty young thing, and any other time in my history I would have been on the scent. However, her impudent attitude clashed with my angry frustration.

"Oh, surely." She beamed; sarcasm alive in her eyes.

Turning to leave, I gave her one last finger raised in objection. "And I'm *not* going to get fired. Ms. Michaels likes everything I'm doing here. That other time... it was a misunderstanding. Ms. Acantrella. And you *shooting me down*, as you hint, is a misplaced fantasy. You'd do well to attend to work and quit sassing me."

"Ah. But you are not the boss of me, Mr. Mobley."

"No, I'm not! But I do have some pull around here! So. You'd best exercise a bit of respect. And quit spreading rumors." I was losing my cool with this girl, and she knew she was getting to me.

"Mmkay. I'll set up these little toys of yours, Mr. Mobley. And I can't wait to try one of your sugar cane coffee stirrers," she ended with a laugh.

Such outright insolence. And from someone so new to Stoney Brook. The entire female staff seemed to relish disrespecting me, as of late. Ariana had managed to severely get under my skin. Sockman?? Some truths are best internally ignored, I decided, grimacing to myself.

Having spent the day at the Mill Property, I pulled the Stoney Brook Rover around the circle drive and parked it into its designated stall next to the barn.

Going in the back way, I was looking forward to a hot shower and a cold beer. After reaching my room, I just managed to get my shirt off and was in the process of unbuttoning my pants when someone knocked on the door.

"Damn. Okay, just a minute."

I opened the door. It was Leanne. Looking gorgeous as usual.

"Leanne. Good evening!"

She walked through my arm, needing no invitation. "Good evening, Morgan. I thought I would catch you just coming in from the day."

"Yes. I was at the Mill Property, watching some of the crews put the final touches on the bungalows. The restaurant is up and running and everything should be ready by the en-"

"You can tell me all about the Mill Property later." Leanne smacked me in the chest with something, holding it there until I took it.

Looking at the item in my hands, I could see that it was a neatly coiled leather leash with a studded collar. "Um. Are we getting a pet dog mascot for Stoney Brook?"

"Yes," she said smiling, roughly squeezing my cheek. "You."

"Ouch! What do you mean?" I asked nervously, having an idea exactly what she meant.

"Tonight's the night, my dear Morgan. I've arranged to meet Stefany at her office to discuss *important* news. You. There on your knees. She has no idea. This is fun already, isn't it? Get your shower and meet me in my room in an hour. Bring a raincoat."

"A raincoat? You've been drinking, haven't you?"

"Yes. And yes. I expect you to be on time, Morgan. With the raincoat and that leash on. Nothing else."

It had been a week since we had discussed the "agreement." I had come to believe it was probably just a joke. If she wanted to push Stefany and me together, we could do it in more conventional terms.

"Now, wait, Leanne. Let's talk about this. Surely there's some other way we could go about your plan... other than me showing up at Stefany's office naked on a leash. I'm a bit tired tonight, anyway." She looked at me with an implacable expression, unconvinced.

"Morgan. Of course, I knew you would try and back out of our deal, you scared, pathetic little boy." She squeezed one of my nipples hard, making me jump.

"Ow! Quit that!"

"Let me give you a preview, Morgan. Since you *are* going to abide by the terms of our agreement."

"Um. Preview? What do you mean?" I asked weakly.

"Get on your knees."

"Why?" I asked, afraid of the answer.

She reached between my legs, grabbing my junk through my pants, and slightly squeezed. "Morgan. Do you remember when I gave you the little send-off at the stairs when you were fired?"

"Yes, how could I forget. But Leanne. Now we are good friends!"

"Oh, indeed, we are," she confirmed.

"Come on. Let's talk about this."

She squeezed harder. "Ow! Okay, okay." I pushed her hand off and away, then complied, getting on my knees. It seemed odd, yet also erotically charged, looking up at Leanne standing over me in her short skirt.

Leanne ran the fingers of one hand softly through my hair. "Morgan. We had an agreement. And despite your waffling, tonight is the night we embark upon our little adventure." Her grip suddenly tightened in my hair, pulling my head into her, my cheek against her leg. "You are going to get used to this view with Stefany. Right?"

"Uh. Leanne..."

300

Her grip tightened further, now painful. I would be losing a few hairs with this one. "Okay! Fine. Yes," I agreed, seeing that she was dead serious.

"Do you like the view, Morgan?" She ground herself ever so slightly against my head, her hard grip pushing my face into the fabric of her dress between the juncture of her legs. I was getting increasingly turned on despite myself.

"Yes," I admitted in a whisper.

"I can't hear you, Morgan."

"Yes," I said louder, muttering against her skirt, still looking up at her in astonishment. I had not envisioned such a situation with Leanne, as she was such a good friend. Aside from flirting, there was never any real indication there would be more.

"I bet you do. I knew I could convince you to keep your word."

"I didn't mean I wasn't going to keep my wo-"

"Morgan, just shut up. Get ready to serve, just as you agreed. You are not backing out of this, I don't give a shit how tired you say you are. Understand?"

"Yes."

"Good." She reached into her purse that was slung over her shoulder and took a slip of paper out. "Open your mouth."

I complied with the strange order, and I opened my mouth, now realizing it would just be easier to follow her direction. Besides, this whole scene was hotter than fuck, I decided.

She shoved it in between my lips and pushed my mouth closed. "Such a good boy. That's your check. Two years of pay. For my part of the agreement." I took the check out of my mouth, staring at it with regret. Guiltily, I folded it and laid it on the nightstand.

"Everything in order then?" she asked.

"Yes," I said, my mind a flurry of emotions.

"Yes, everything is… fine," she said, resuming her grinding against my face, harder now. The hem of her skirt slipped up and over my head, and any question of whether she was wearing panties or not became clear. She was not. Her wonderfully bare skin was soft and warm against my face, and I was having a whole new and unexpected appreciation for Leanne. Her hands pressed my head harder while my hands found the backs of her legs. My lips brushed softly over her juncture, finding that she was deliciously moist. I kissed her softly at first, then with more need, wet, deep, beginning to use my tongue, eliciting a soft moan.

"Damn you, Mobley. Damn. We shouldn't."

"No… we shouldn't…" was all I could manage to say against her, consumed.

Suddenly, she pushed me away, holding my head as she stepped back. She tidied the hem of her skirt down, then wiped her glaze off my lips with a tissue. "Wow. I wasn't expecting that. Thinking about this agreement has kind of revved me up. I envy Stefany. You are a very good plaything, I do believe."

"Um. Thank you?" I leaned back, suddenly miserable, and heated. Unable to help myself, I broke out laughing. She joined me.

Stefany: Miles, with his lawyers, has grown increasingly bold. And more assertive. He is now claiming that all our marital difficulties are due to me. While he will admit a small degree of "willingness to engage in mutual confrontation," he and his lawyers have come up with lies to put it

back on me, saying I initiated the fights, and I was aggressive and abusive. And I should be grateful that he would have me. What the hell? They said my injuries from our fights were either overexaggerated, self-inflicted, or were due to Miles defending himself. In their response to a court hearing on my divorce request last week, they said that I was "emotionally unavailable" and "romantically unresponsive" towards Miles. I kept a cold marital bed, whatever that means. They also said I showed "undue and inappropriate interest in other men" outside of our marriage. They somehow came up with a long list of men that I have known only as friends throughout my life, claiming they were lovers. What a load of total crap. Lies, lies, and more lies.

I feel so angry and enraged right now, I can barely walk about this place without a scowl on my face. In all of this, my lawyers seem to be leaving me powerless... helpless... to do anything. I think Miles has bought them off or intimidated them somehow. He has told me that it's just best we try and work our marriage out. I hate his patronizing, fake ass attempts to smooth things over. He flat-out told me divorce is out of the question. Every time he visits me at Stoney Brook, which is nearly daily now, he says he loves me and wants us to live together again.

He has made it all quite clear. Even if I were granted a divorce, he will get at least half of Stoney Brook. He has taken notice of the enormous income potential of the plantation. He seems to already know about some of the contracts and funding I've obtained. Financial details of operations at Stoney Brook are supposed to be confidential. Somehow, he knows everything.

As for all other assets in the marriage, his and mine together, he will get most of it through some sort of legal sleight of hand he has managed with his lawyers and the court. My lawyers, for their part, have done nothing but rollover. I must wonder if they were paid off or threatened. Miles and his cronies are quite capable of such things.

~~~~~

I have had a hard time focusing on taking care of business. Just a few weeks ago, I thought I had been on the cusp of romantic involvement with Man-Whore Mobley. Now, I barely take notice of him - other than the fact he continuously irritates me no end.

Truthfully, I have felt somewhat guilty about my treatment of Mobley. Time and time again, I must acknowledge to myself, the reason I am successful is due to him and his nutty ideas. Why do I have to be so cold to him? So, what if he did screw some blonde bimbo in his room the very night he tried seducing me? That doesn't bother me anymore… and it won't! He's such a typical shit-head male nut sack. It is his nature to be that way, and I was foolish for thinking he would only ever have eyes for me. I hate him! And yet, I still like him! Maybe. Or… it's just that I tolerate him. Yes. That's it. I tolerate the Man-Whore. I feel soiled just writing about him.

~~~~

Leanne keeps trying to soften my attitude towards Mobley. Good luck with that. From this point forward, I'm nothing but professional with him. Too bad. She

I prefer this...

hasn't said anything, but I know she has our "bet" in the back of her mind. Sad. She thinks she is going to convince the Man-Whore to agree to her weird sex slave terms – have me spank him or whatever. HA! Nope. She has lost her bet; she is just yet to admit it. If I had doubts, they are gone. I win! Now, I can write with enthusiasm that I look forward to my new horses! Fail, Leanne!!! I am excited at the prospect. I've put up a nice round pen and have been customizing several stalls in the barn!

~~~~

I had margaritas this afternoon with Leanne at the pool and then we had dinner. It was a great break from the crap Miles has been laying on me this week during his visits. Just to get away from  that scene and relax is much needed. We didn't do anything but joke, laugh, drink, and have fun. Just like old times. Not one mention of any irritating topics! I was even nice to Mobley, who happened by once. Nice as in I didn't flip him the bird in my inebriated state. But I thought about it. I'm glad Man-Whore took the hint and didn't hang around. After dinner, we went for a cool swim then hit the hot tub for more drinks. Odd, as I have never even tried my own pool or hot tub here at Stoncy Brook. It was fun dusting off my bikini and chatting with the guests.

Leanne kept ordering more margaritas. I think she was trying to get me drunk. It will take more than that, Leanne! She says she has a surprise for me

this week! Maybe it's my horses! I'm "giddy" up with anticipation!

After a nice shower and hanging my bikini up to dry, I slipped on my robe and wondered what I should do to cap off the evening. Margaritas and dinner with Leanne at the pool had been fun.

Feeling rather tipsy while walking into my office from my living quarters, I closed several files on my desk that I had left open. After tidying up the office for a bit, I admired the progress of my life and prepared to call it an evening with a good book. A soft knock at the doors startled me. Thoughts of Heidi and Mobley back for another round of tag team seduction ran through my mind. My mood was good, and my spirits were high. I honestly didn't know if I had the strength to send either of them out this evening.

I knew I would not have to worry about Mobley again after my recent treatment of him. Heidi, however, would probably not take no for an answer on a second attempt. I just wouldn't answer, I decided. But why would she be knocking at the office doors and not the door to my living quarters? Perhaps it was a guest requiring assistance? Or a staff member not realizing protocol to call the on-site supervisor first before disturbing me. Pausing at the door, I hesitated. Could it be Miles for a late-night visit to continue to try and convince me to get back together with him? Maybe he thought he could stop by for make-up sex? He had been hinting lately despite my firm rebukes. He was quite persistent though. I shook off these thoughts. *I had better just open it*, I told myself.

Cautiously, I creaked open one of the solid, large French doors and peered around the edge, hiding the fact I was in my robe.

It was Leanne. Having cleaned up from the pool, she was in a nice summer skirt. She looked primed for a night on the town. Holding a carry bag by the straps, she looked as if she had just returned from a shopping trip.

"Leanne! It's you! What the hell are you doing, I thought we were done for the evening?"

"Well, grandma, it's only 7:30," she laughed. "I thought I would find you in your office. Good guess, huh?"

"I suppose so. What do you need? I'm not sure I'm up to go out for more, Leanne. I've got a long day tomorrow and there's a meet-"

"Oh, relax, Cuz. I'm not here to drag you out for a late evening. But may I come in?"

I stepped back and opened the door for her. "Sure. But let's go over to my living room. No need to be in the office," I joked with a laugh.

As I started for the adjoining doors, Leanne halted me with a hand on my shoulder. "Actually, Stef, I wanted to talk to you in the office."

"The office? But why? Is there something wrong?"

"Oh no, nothing wrong. Listen, could you go get a bottle of Champaign if you have it? And several glasses? Believe me, I'll explain everything. You'll understand soon enough."

I was perplexed by this odd request. "But…"

"Please, Stef. Just go find a decent bottle of Champaign and two glasses. I'll wait."

Reluctantly, I began walking towards the door to my living quarters. "I really don't want any Champaign, Leanne. I've had more than enough to drink today. But you are welcome to further indulge your liver this evening if you so wish."

"Good," she answered. "I wish. Bring two glasses anyway."

"Fine. Okay." I shook my head at her willingness to overindulge. Champaign on top of the margaritas? The drinking that afternoon was still making me lightheaded. I would not be having more than a sip, and only that to appease Leanne.

Searching the pantry, among several bottles of wine, I found a solitary selection of Champaign. Just as with wine, I had no idea as to any merits of quality. Although my tastes weren't as cheap as Mobley's, if it were sweet and didn't give me a serious headache, whatever it was would be fine with me.

Making a quick detour to my bedroom, I tossed the robe off and slid into some old jean shorts with a grubby, suitably torn t-shirt. My shabby attire would irritate Leanne and further guarantee we wouldn't be going out.

Turning my attention again to the Champaign in the kitchen, I unwired the cork and slowly worked it out until it released with a pop. I held the bottle over the sink as the bubbles coursed from the top in rivulets, soaking my hand. Never a huge fan of Champaign, the only times I had it in the past was for some business occasions with Miles. Having a bottle was a fluke, a gift from a grateful guest several months prior.

With the bottle now open, wrapped in a towel and with two glasses, all on a serving tray, I shuffled back to the office in my fuzzy house slippers for this strange rendezvous with Leanne. She had piqued my curiosity. Perhaps she had some business or legal news for me? Maybe news of a new tactic to ensure Miles's legal defeat? Or one of her famous friends was going to book a visit to Stoney Brook and she wanted me to secure the reservation personally? And what was in the carry bag?

I threw open the door to the office with a grand gesture and presented the tray with a curtsey. "Okay, your royal highness, per your orders, your divine libations are at hand." Straightening, I sat the tray on the closest table. "How you can drink Champaign on top of all those margaritas is beyond me. Sometimes I think you're a bad influence, Leanne. Now if you will tell me why you… why… you… erm…"

Leanne was sitting in one of the office chairs, her legs crossed saucily, the warm hues from my desk lamp further emphasizing her typical appearance as a devious temptress. Cast across one of the small side tables was a full-length raincoat, no doubt used to procure our additional guest to the office without too much controversy in the halls. In one of her hands, she casually held a leather leash that loosely dangled back to the neck of Morgan Mobley, who was sitting on his knees beside her. Stark naked, he looked up at me with an excited expression of doubtful, almost apologetic anxiety. Fuck.

I'm sure any color in my face drained away. "Leanne? Noooooo." How Leanne's odd behavior managed to elude me from associating it with this possibility was maddening.

The room was so silent the only noise I could hear was my own stinted breathing. "Mobley. Nooooo." I felt sorry for Mobley to a degree, who sat quietly in palpable fear of my reaction.

Leanne, calm and nonchalant, twiddled the leash, looking entirely unfazed. "The Champaign is quite appropriate as we have a momentous occasion to toast. As you can see, Stef, per our bet, I present you with your new hobby. Your sex life is about to get more interesting. And I assure you, he is quite dedicated to his commitment of servitude to you. Aren't you, Morgan?" She gave the leash a little tug.

"Um. Yes, Ms. Michaels. I assure you, I'm… feeling quite dedicated to his… er… *my* commitment."

Leanne laughed with his bumbling repeat of the line she evidently told him to recite. "He's a little slow."

I didn't know what to say at this point. Leanne had me cornered. How would she react if I simply refused to honor the terms of our bet?

And what of Mobley, sitting awkwardly on my office floor without a stitch of clothing? He would be greatly embarrassed that he was somehow drawn into this scheme, and further, for agreeing to it. Embarrassment would abate though, I told myself. I could make it easy on him.

I could kick myself for letting Leanne con me into this. This could not be easily dismissed, I knew. Welching on our bet could drive a permanent rift between us, which I couldn't do. Leanne was my rock. She, above all others, supported me and could always be counted on to be there for me.

Perhaps I could fake it with Mobley. Go through the motions and trick Leanne that I was abiding by the bet. Was that even a possibility? What could Mobley stand to gain and why would he agree to this? Did he want to be a sex slave, of all things?! He was an incorrigible, wretched, disgusting, woman player, and as surprising as his compliance with this was, it was evidently a possibility after all. I should have known. Despite looking pitiable sitting there naked on the floor, anything to do with sex with a woman could be of interest to Mobley. Fuck. I wouldn't be getting my horses.

"Oh, the wheels are turning in your mind, Cuz," Leanne said, suddenly laughing. "I see them. The smoke is practically coming out of your ears as you try to think your way out of this one. Did you think I would forget?

"No. I just didn't think you would win."

"Well, win, I did. Here he sits, naked in a collar and leash, ready and willing.

"Mobley. You are telling me you are just fine with this ludicrous scheme?" I asked to make sure he wasn't drugged. "And *everything* this devious, shrewd, oversexed woman has planned?"

"Yes. I am," he confirmed following a moment of hesitation.

"Morgan? Please stand," Leanne asked. It all began to sound like a demented wedding of sorts.

Mobley stood, awkwardly holding his hands in front of his crotch. Leanne noticed this and whacked him on the butt with the end of the leash.

"Hands down, Mobley. I can't believe you, of all people, to have suddenly discovered modesty."

He hesitated, watching for my reaction. The whole scene was so unlikely, weird, and absurd, I suddenly laughed. Perhaps it was from still feeling tipsy from the earlier margaritas, but it felt comical. I wiped my hand over my mouth, visibly trying to restrain myself to not embarrass Mobley any further.

"Mobley. It's okay. Really. Evidently, the ship already sailed on you getting out of this one. Or me. So, let's see what you've got. C'mon."

Having Mobley stand there in abject fear of me and what I may do to him for this offense was amusing. I decided to enjoy the humor. Yes, I could get past my disgust for Mobley, I convinced myself. At least for now. I could still try and concoct a plan later to get out of all of this. Or. Perhaps I could blow up the whole thing right now.

Mobley dropped his hands away and my eyes fell to his package. My response was immediate and - unfortunate. I quickly slapped a hand to my mouth to stifle the snicker that I let slide past, to the detriment of Mobley's soon to be well-trodden upon feelings. Mobley, I decided, would have to take one for the team if I was to get out of this.

"What?" Mobley asked with alarm, quickly covering himself again with his hands. "Why are you laughing?"

"It's just that…" I began, trying to think of an easy answer.

"Just *what*? Tell me! Stefany, what were you going to say! Leanne, really, maybe this isn't such a goo-"

"Well. I thought it would be… *bigger*," I tried to explain, knowing full well I was being ungracious. Again, I snickered, throwing caution and manners to the wind.

Leanne, clearly put out with me, was not finding any humor in my attitude. "Stef! I can assure you, myself seeing

313

all of him, he is well within standard operating parameters for normal to slightly larger than average men. Are you saying that the pitiful excuse of a man, Miles, is bigger than Mobley?"

"Naw. Miles isn't any bigger," I explained. "Bout the same, I'd estimate. Mobley's may be a little wider."

"Now wait!" Mobley began to object. "I have never had any complaints and I know for a fact I am larger than most! When… you know… during stuff. Anyway, right now, I'm simply *uneasy* about tonight! Nervous! I didn't know I would be put under such *unkind* scrutiny. And objectified so. Leanne, this is NOT what I agreed to, I must protest this undue exa-"

"Mobley, shhhhh!" Leanne interrupted. "If anything, you get to learn what it means to be on the receiving end for once."

"It's like a frightened little turtle," I goaded, the grin on my face only further irritating Leanne.

"No!" Mobley countered loudly. "Noooo," he said, trying to sound calmer and in control.

Walking to him, I pushed his hands away. "Oh, don't get so bent out of shape, Mobley. I'm sure it's quite adequate. Although I'd hate to see it after a cold swim. And I'll say this for you. It's certainly none the worse for the wear you've given it, day in and day out."

"Stefany! That is quite enough, really…" Leanne objected.

Mobley tried again to cover and once again, I pushed his hands down.

"Mobley, I've seen it now, you may as well at least be proud of it. It's what you've been given by nature, and no one can help what nature gives them." An unkind snicker arose which I couldn't control. Poor guy. But it was Mobley after all. This was turning into riotous fun, and I decided to make the most of it. "So, Mobley. Turn around. I've seen under the hood. If Leanne is going to *force* me to comply with this agreement, I want to see the trunk."

I stepped closer and pushed his shoulder to turn him. He resisted. "Turn!" I ordered, gleefully caught up in the moment. "Am I not the Dom here?" I asked with dripping sarcasm. "I won't be sparing the rod on you, to be sure." Mobley's mouth dropped in shock as Leanne sat growing impatient with my antics. He reluctantly complied and spun in my grip. I stepped aside, hands on my hips, cocking my head, surveying him with a discerning eye as I would a side of beef. In truth, Mobley had a very fine, wonderfully shaped, muscular ass. A fact I would not reveal, I decided.

"Well. I suppose it'll have to do." I scratched my chin as if considering a used car. Leanne rolled her eyes, increasingly irritated with me.

"Leanne!" Mobley had had enough of my insults, evoking me to laugh yet again. "Clearly, Stefany has NO intention of actually taking this seriou-"

"Mobley, QUIET! Both of you! QUIET!" Leanne yelled, trying to regain control of the situation. She stood and walked to the service tray, poured two glasses of Champaign, and handed one to me. "Stefany, I would very much appreciate you discontinue your insulting attempts to *sabotage* these proceedings. I know exactly what you are trying to do. And it *won't* work. So now… it's time to face the consequences of our bet and comply with the terms." She took the second glass, filled it with Champaign and handed it to Mobley.

"And your glass?" I asked, suddenly losing my sense of humor.

"This is your moment, Stef. And Mobley's. Not mine. I want this to be the start of something great, just between you two. So now, without further ado," Leanne began, seizing on the moment, "A toast! To the two of you to celebrate a wonderful, fun, exciting, and sexy adventure."

Reluctantly, I held up my glass to Mobley and he softly chinked it against his. I caught his gorgeous blue eyes in mine. He looked like a deer in the headlights, I thought with amusement. It wouldn't do any good to fight it any further. If Mobley was down for this, now I had no choice but to go along with whatever was going to happen. "Okay, Mobley?"

"Yes." He took a deep breath as if girding himself in the face of our new reality. Leanne smiled with satisfaction.

We both sipped the Champaign, each of us eying the other with a renewed curiosity over the top of our glasses.

Leanne wasted no time in laying out her plan. I had no idea I had agreed to everything she began describing. I sat with the naked Mobley on the office sectional, Leanne opposite us in a chair. As she talked, Mobley took my hand, which was both unnecessarily reassuring and sickly sweet. I pulled it away and gave him a look, with the resulting expression of rejection and regret on his face making me want to laugh again. He was no doubt calling me an obnoxious shrew of a bitch in his mind and he was regretting letting Leanne talk him into this. Again, recalling the blonde bimbo slithering out of his room the morning after the very night he had tried to seduce me, Man-Whore Mobley deserved a good dose of rejection. *Maybe* this could be fun. I felt like a middle school kid taking stage directions for the annual drama club play.

"You both have to let me direct things. I'm not going to watch, no. But I expect you to go along with what I plan. No faking it, I'll find out. This agreement is for a period of up to one year. Morgan, when in a private setting with Stefany, you are to always address her as Ms. Stefany. Ms. Michaels is a bit too formal for this, so no need to say that. But nothing else, not Stef or some other name. Her title you use must be one of respect. Everyone understands so far?"

"Yes."

"Yes. But what will she call me?" Mobley asked.

Leanne laughed. "She can call you whatever she wants."

"What? Why can't I have a name of re-"

"Mobley. The idea here is YOU are the sex slave. It's no big deal, let it drop. Right?"

"Yes. Fine. I suppose."

"Can I call him Incorrigible Man-Whore?" I asked.

"Quit being a pain in the ass, Stefany," Leanne scolded. "Now, Morgan, you realize all the nuances of this. You will be in sexual service to Stefany. In whatever way I decide. There will be bondage. Humiliation. You probably aren't going to get satisfaction sexually any time soon. And if you do, it's dependent on Stefany. And me, through my direction. And later whatever she decides if I let her run the show."

"Now wait the hell a min-" Mobley started to object. Leanne shushed him with an angry finger. I laughed, thinking it was all sounding better already.

"Follow the rules. That's the *agreement* everyone has made. There will be some pain for you, Morgan, but it will be okay. Understood?"

"Pain?" Mobley laughed with what I took to be an insulting air. "Come on, Leanne, how bad could it be? Stefany is like… 125 pounds soaking wet. What pain can she possibly inflict, really? *I'm not worried*, believe me. I'm more concerned about the part where I don't get satisfaction any time soon. That doesn't sound fair."

"First of all," Leanne began, "don't be a disrespectful ass. And don't underestimate whatever pain she may dish out; you may well find it is all you can handle and then some."

"And then some," Mobley jeered, beginning to piss me off with his attitude.

"Hey. Are we going to have a problem," Leanne asked him threateningly.

"No. Sorry." He didn't sound sincere.

"A little bit of pain, I think," Leanne explained, "will end up being something you will enjoy, Morgan. It will certainly heighten your senses. And by proxy, hers."

"Okaaay," he agreed, looking up at the ceiling and sounding as if he were saying it to just move on.

He was so arrogant I wanted to slap him, right then and there. "Pain will be something you so richly deserve," I added. Mobley shifted uncomfortably on the sectional.

"Moving on," Leanne shot. "Morgan, you have to maintain a professional relationship on the outside with Stefany at all times. No matter what happens. Behaving, working, and acting normally with no word of this to anyone. I hear you yapping about this outside of this room, you will rue the day. You will still maintain due respect to Stefany as your boss, nothing changes there. Understood?"

"Fine," he agreed. "Yes, yes, yes. Can't we just get on with it."

"And you have to be committed only to this relationship. No other dating or seeing anyone. Except Stefany. Do you agree to this without hesitation?"

"I do. That sounds like a wedding vow," Mobley chuckled.

I glared across at him. The smile faded from his mouth. What an idiotic ass. It was highly questionable as to whether I could tolerate Mobley much beyond the Champaign toast. "Mobley," I began, "you can go out with whoever the hell you want." I was being unnecessarily short with him, I knew. But I felt like being short. "But I want you to take an STD test. Gawd knows you've been in every knothole on the island."

"STD test?" Mobley looked furious.

"Yeah," I confirmed. "I don't want crabs or venereal disease. There's no telling what kind of infestations you may be running around with, given all the whoring you've done."

"Stefany!" Leanne was approaching her limit with my attitude.

.

"No, that's fine!" Mobley objected loudly. "I always get regular check-ups and blood work. I take care of myself! But, if it'll ease her mind, I'll go get tested if that's what she wants. Far be it for me to make her fearful of catching *crabs*."

"Or venereal disease," I added, for clarification. "Or anal warts."

"Yeah. Or *venereal* disease or *anal warts*," he agreed, angry.

I looked inquisitively at Leanne. "Can we just do this in full-body suits of some sort? Latex things? I've heard about those. A full wrap of some sort for him?"

"Um, no, don't be difficult, Stef." Leanne took a deep breath. "Mobley, you can go to the doctor as requested. Great. No need for it tonight!" Leanne folded her hands over her lap. "Morgan. You will be faithful only to Stefany while in this arrangement so as to not incur any unforeseen ailments, such as Stefany has indicated she is concerned with."

"I meant what I said." He turned completely away from me in his seat and crossed his legs for added dramatic emphasis. "Ms. Stefany. I will only be dedicated to you. While we are doing this. And I *don't* have crabs or fucking V.D."

While a bit sarcastic, he did seem sincere. But I knew better. "*That* remains to be seen," I whispered under my breath.

"What?" Mobley asked, turning back to me. "I didn't hear that?"

"I said, mkay. Whatever." I rolled my eyes. "But you can go ahead and see whoever. I don't care," I added with a touch of venom. "You just better be clean."

"I'm sure he will abide by our agreement and will be faithful," Leanne added, shooting me an angry glance.

"Great. That's just great. Next thing, so we are clear, he has to do whatever I say, right?" I asked petulantly. "*Anything?* No matter what? He can't complain or argue? Or otherwise irritate me? If he does, the deal is off, I can tell you that right now."

Leanne looked concerned that it all may be slipping out of her hands. "Now, just wait a minute, Stef. We aren't doing anything *too far* off the beaten path. Yes, he'll do what you say, but it is through my direction, whatever it is you two end up doing. The agreement was that you will accept guidance from me. Let me run the show for you two. At least for a while. See how things go. Mobley knows full well he is to do what you request, and he has absolutely agreed to this." She eyed Mobley apprehensively. "Right, Morgan? You won't... *try*... and irritate Stefany. Agreed?"

"Yes, I said I won't aggravate her. And I won't. And yeah, I'll do whatever she asks. I already said I would."

"So, let's not start this all off by copping attitude? Both of you." Leanne stated with an edge to her voice, hoping it was an end to the confrontational atmosphere.

"No attitude here," he asserted, raising his hands defensively in the air. "What about her attitude? She thinks I'm a walking public disease menace." He leaned over to me. "Or maybe I have crotch mold. Or anal warts."

"Yeah. That's exactly what I think," I said insultingly, once again entering the fray. "You should be confined in a lab somewhe-"

"Shhhhh! Enough!" It was Leanne's turn to shoot each of us a look. At this point, doubt began to happily creep into my mind as to whether Leanne's plan for Mobley and me would come to fruition. Giving Mobley's naked muscular body another once over from the corner of my eyes, the thought oddly came with both joy and regret. I sat back and took a wait-and-see approach.

Leanne retrieved her carry bag. Reaching in, she pulled out an envelope and handed it to me. "Stef. Here is *Assignment 1* for you and Morgan this evening. I expect an honest effort. You'll note that Morgan's participation doesn't require *a doctor's visit* for any concerns, so you can put your mind at ease. Got it? This isn't meant to be quick, either."

I began to open the envelope and she stopped me. "We'll get to it in a minute."

"Where is my copy of the assignment?" Mobley asked.

"You don't need one," Leanne replied without hesitation. "Your job for tonight is to shut up and just do what you are told."

I chuckled, seeing Mobley's injured ego take another round of humility flak.

"Now," Leanne continued. "Let's have a look at what you will need for tonight." Reaching into the bag, Leanne began withdrawing a myriad of items. "First up, a riding crop." She laid this on the small table next to our chairs. "And handcuffs - and a section of rope. And finally, a ball gag with optional vibrator accessory."

"Now that ball gag looks promising," I chirped. "Could you wear that full time, Mobley?" Mobley eyed me but remained silent, despite my continued insults. I had to give him credit.

"Be nice, shall we?" Leanne scolded.

"You really expect us to use all of that tonight?" I asked, wondering how it was possible.

"Yes," she answered firmly.

"You are really enjoying yourself, eh Leanne?" I remarked. "Setting this all up. You are quite the pervo."

"Call me whatever you may. Yes." She eyed both of us critically, as would a painter over a work of art on canvas, still in progress.

"Tonight, is mostly about the intense visuals," Leanne began to explain. "Stef, even though Morgan will be actively involved, this is about him watching you. Up close. And you watching him *watch* you." Mobley looked at me, grinning widely.

I blinked, trying to take all of this in and whacked Mobley across the chest with the back of my hand for grinning. "Watch what?"

"You'll see. Now you can open your assignment, Stef."

I slid a finger under the envelope flap, opened it and withdrew the enclosed papers with a sarcastic flourish only to be shocked at the sheer volume. "Leanne, what the hell? This is several pages long! You can't be serious!"

"Pre-read your assignment," she ordered. "Silently. He'll find out what's on there soon enough. Refer back to it as often as you need this evening." Standing, she leaned over, tussling my hair like she used to do when we were kids. With no further word, she left.

I glanced across to Mobley. He raised his eyebrows and nodded with sympathy.

"Okaaaaaay. Here we go." I began to read to myself:

For STEFANY - ASSIGNMENT 1
In your room – You are to logon to the following account in mysexshowxxx.com for a video stream on your tv.
User: LeannesHotShows
Password: MakeItHurtGood69
Relax, have a drink with him if you'd like, or a snack. You will watch "movie 1" with him, which I have personally selected for this occasion. Yes, it is a porno, so he will likely get more out of it than you. But ya never know 😊 *It's a femdom movie. A woman dom using her male slave to get off on. About 30 minutes. It's a warm-up. Very hot. You'll get the idea.*

Next, kiss him. Go ahead, do it. Dive in. You two have done it before, go in deep and have fun. Make out. Enjoy yourselves. Keep your hands... and any other body parts off his cock, he will no doubt be planking at this time. That thing is not your concern for this evening, so leave it alone! But don't tell him it's not on the menu, FYI, these assignments are need to know basis only.

Have him stand up. You'll know when to move to the next stage, trust me. Tell him what you are going to do. It will excite him as much as it will you. Do it.

You are to use the rope to tie his ankles together. Not too tight, but make sure he can't get out either. <u>This is key: Leave about 4 feet of rope free.</u> Next, have him put his hands behind his back. Cuff him. Yeah, just like the cops do. The keys to let him out later are in the bag. Don't worry about the ball gag yet, we'll get to that later.

Take off your clothes. Do it in front of him. Yes, do it, that's an order. Do it slowly, let him see each item you peel off. Get naked. All the way. No cheating, I know how you are. You are seeing him completely naked, so get over yourself.

Bring him over to your comfy chair. This is going to be your area of operations for the evening. Have him drop to his knees, right in front of you. Yes, close in. Now use that extra rope to loop from his ankles up through his cuffed hands on his back. Tie it snug so it's not hurting him, but he can't move or stand up either. No, it's not pretty like shibari that I showed you in the book I gave you, but it works. If he hesitates or is insolent in the slightest, use the crop on his ass and legs. Do not hesitate. I'll know if you let him get away with anything.

Take a seat. He should be right in front of you by now, close. Okay, next, you are to order him to begin kissing your legs. Make him start at your feet, though. Since he is tied and cuffed, all he can do is kiss them. Make him use his mouth and tongue. Don't accept cheap work. Surprisingly, as you told me, you have already done this when you two fooled around the first time together. You followed my earlier advice, "always have them start at your feet." Very good, grasshopper, you are learning! Having him worship your feet is very symbolic… and satisfying. Your feet will be on the menu frequently. Tell him he better get used to it. Whack the shit out of him if he complains.

Next, have him work up. Up and up. Until he is working your inner thighs. Got it? If he is lingering somewhere too long and he needs to move on, whack his ass with that crop. He'll catch on. Believe me, he will be enjoying this every bit as much as you.

By this time, your oven is past the pre-heat setting and is baking at full temperature. He is seeing you up close by now as he is kissing your inner thighs. Very good. Let him get within a breath of you. But under no circumstances is he to touch, lick or otherwise taste your kitty. OFF LIMITS! Do NOT be tempted to let him go further.

You are to begin massaging yourself now. Use your fingers, work yourself slowly. Play with your clit. Expose it. Open now and then. Let him have a deep look. Tease him with how wet you will be. Good. Don't skip this thinking I won't know and don't pull any fake-ass modesty on me. At this point, you will be nuclear or else I will have to see about getting you hormone shots of some sort.

By the way, you are not to orgasm yet! Do not violate this order or you will incur my wrath, believe me, Cuz.

Okay. Now you can slip the ball gag over him. Position it so it's secured nicely, yet not yanking out any of his gorgeous blond locks. Got it? Now, with this ball gag, you will notice it has a very cool feature: It has a small vibrator on the outside surface of the ball. That's for you. Once you have him in position, you will see the small switch to the side of the ball that turns this thing on. Switch it on. (duh)

Scoot down further towards the edge of your chair. Your ass should be nearly hanging off the edge and you should be ON FIRE by now. Take a wad of his blond hair in your hand, make a fist, pull him in and get to work. This needs to be as hard a grip as you can - do it. Get one or both legs over his shoulders, step on his back for pushing leverage. He's a strong man, don't worry about it. Make his neck bend backwards, he can take it. Grind his face like he's the best amusement park ride of all time. As you do this, use that crop on him, moderately, now and then - on his ass and his back is good. It will be fun to feel him jolt into you as you do this. Don't worry about him, he's fine, just don't go overboard. If he asks later why you do this when he's doing everything he's told to do, tell him because you can - and to shut up. From here on out, you got this. Enjoy. Explode.

Don't do anything else, that's it for tonight! Nothing! Don't go too long with this first assignment, it's just a warm-up. Don't let him linger around or try and stay over. He'll have a monumental case of blue balls, that is if he hasn't spontaneously come all over himself. If he did, don't make fun of him or laugh, I know you too well. If he complains about not getting any, too bad, that's the breaks. Maybe he'll get some later. That's all you need to tell him. Get his raincoat back on him, kiss him good night and kick him out. This sets up known expectations I want you to instill in him. I'll expect a full report from you two in the morning. Nighty nite! ~L  *PS Sorry about not getting any horses, ha ha*

It was crazy. It wasn't me at all. How could this be happening? How I was even able to overcome my initial shy embarrassment is unfathomable. Against all my expectations, it was going just as Leanne had predicted it would go. I swallowed hard, unfamiliar with the horny bitch in heat that I had become, trying to maintain some degree of control.

Mobley had done everything I asked in the course of the evening, and he had done it eagerly. We had followed Leanne's "Assignment 1" to the letter. I felt like I was in a dream. A highly erotic, sex-charged dream.

I was close now, and everything pent up inside of me, many years of sexual frustration and failure, abuse, false love, all of it, was on the verge of erupting. With how I was feeling, I fully expected to die, succumbing on this first evening to a full-blown heart attack. Or an aneurysm perhaps.

And it wasn't even full-on sex. It was just half-way oral! Through a ball gag vibrator, of all things. Mobley's mouth wasn't even on me. It didn't matter. If I were pulling Mobley's hair out by the roots, I honestly don't think I cared. He had morphed before my very eyes into a simple sex toy, to be used fully. I knew it was wrong. I cared about Mobley. Maybe much more than I would admit. Even if he did betray me with a blonde bimbo. Later, I would restore his humanity

326

back to him in my mind. I would. I promised myself this. But for the moment, he was serving a much-needed purpose. It was a purpose that I suspect Leanne knew I needed to experience all along. Her and her damn psychology. Was I abusing Mobley? Abusing him as I had been abused? Was I? No, I wasn't breaking Mobley's jaw. Or his ribs. Or his…

A shudder ran through my body as every nerve tightened, the pleasure nearly too much to live through. If this wasn't even full sex, it evidently was more than I had ever experienced. It was *more*, somehow. Like a strong drug that was rendering me out of control. This whole scene that Leanne had concocted. It had cooked off in my mind in ways I couldn't even fathom. Poor Mobley. It didn't matter now. He would just have to take it like a man.

With my free hand, I now used the riding crop and lashed his back and ass with wild abandon.

WHAP! WHAP! WHAP!

"Mmmmmmmmpppphhhhh!" Mobley wincing from behind the ball gag only encouraged me. I wasn't sure, but I thought I saw tears.

WHAP! WHAP! WHAP!

"Mmmmmrrrrrrrwwwppppphhhh!"

With each brutal stroke, his head jarred the ball gag with the tiny vibrator forward, into me. The intensity was building to a point I had never before experienced. I don't know if he was trying to vocalize actual words or just moaning. His ass and back looked raw from my strikes - an angry red. And I didn't care.

I pressed one foot so hard into his back I was amazed it wasn't breaking his neck. Seeing his face in between my legs only drove my madness harder, further. One of my calves cramped and I powered through without pause. A range of emotions, memories, thoughts, and fantasies all played through my mind in a maddening jumble. I was out of control. I was angry, resentful, grateful, lonely, sad, happy… horny.

The orgasm that had been all my life in the making, teased into being this evening, exploded just as Leanne had commanded in her assignment letter. Exploding to such a degree my eyes rolled into the back of my head, my body twitching in nerve snapping spasms. Halfway through, I tried to push his face away, tried to get that damnable little vibrator nestled in the middle of his mouth away from me. I was too weak. Wave after wave flooded over me, and I fell to the side against the armrest in convulsions. I slipped down and fell from the chair entirely and I lay before Mobley, his eyes wide.

Exhausted, spent, and dripping sweat, after several relieving breaths I finally gained the strength to get back up on the chair.

"Mobley. I've never. And I mean never. EVER. Come that hard. Just letting you know. Maybe there's something to this scheme of Leanne's after all. Because wowww."

"Mmmmmrrrrppphhhhhhhhh!"

"I know, you want it off. Just a sec. I'll get it then get you untied."

I leaned over to him, switched off the tiny vibrator and began unbuttoning the ball gag. The whole thing, including his face, was glistening wet. From me.

"Mmmmrrrrmmmph!"

"Yes, yes, I'm getting it off, Mobley. Hang on. What is it, you gotta go pee or something?"

The ball gag dropped to the floor.

"HOLYSSSSSSSSHHHHHHHITTTTTTTTAAAAGGG GHHHHHHH!!!!!"

CHAPTER 12
THE PAINFUL EDGE OF ECSTASY

Stefany: Okay, so THIS happened. I lost the bet with Leanne. My first "assignment" as Leanne calls it, already went down last night. And... I have good news... and I have really bad news.

Leanne tells me I'll be using these on Mobley...

So. Leanne somehow managed to twist Mobley's arm and get him naked up in my office, and in so doing, winning the bet. Yeah, that was a shocker. An out of this world, unbelievable shocker. I really thought I couldn't lose, given what I know about Mobley – which is that he's an arrogant, overbearing ass that likes to be in charge. Anyway, she then proceeded to give me instructions for the evening that I had to follow. Surprise, surprise, Mobley is a sex slave. To me.

After grumbling a little about it, he played his part well, I have to say. And-

Oh MY Gawd! But... I screwed things up, I guess.

The setup involved Mobley getting tied up and basically giving me head with a ball gag. I know, weird, but whatever. I can't believe I agreed to it, but I had to... and so I did. I did it like the "loyal" friend I am, (damn that Leanne). And okay, yes. IT FUCKING ROCKED! (that's the good news).

Call me surprised. Whatever. All I know is having Mobley down on his knees, him all tied and cuffed up, his head bobbing between my legs as he shoved a little vibrator into me... I came so hard I thought I would die. And if not die, nearly pass out then. Miles never brought me that far and that hard. Or any other boyfriend of my past for that matter - and certainly not on my own! So… kudos to Mobley, the two-timing man-whore that he is.

Now, for the bad news. It's bad enough that it may potentially end all this bet business with Leanne. While in the "moment" - I got carried away with the riding crop on Mobley. While he was on the floor "servicing" me, the pain I was causing him only turned me on more???? I don't know why. Smacking his ass and the resulting little lurches into me were hot. I think I pulled a lot of his hair out??? There was a lot of it I had to vacuum up this morning. I think I also slapped his face, hard! And I don't even know why! Most of it I don't even really remember doing! Was I angry with him deep down? Just angry with men in general??? I would never think that causing pain, even to Mobley, would be me, or something I would ever want to do! It was like I turned into some other person completely different than me. And I did that to Mobley all the way until the finish. The big O. Which, yes, was nuclear and nearly killed me. Today, I'm sore just from the orgasm. Can't say THAT's ever happened to me in my life.

Anyway, when I took off his ball gag, he screamed like a banshee. That pulled me back into reality, and I suddenly realized I had taken it too far. Plus, he probably startled everyone that was a living soul in Stoney Brook. I quickly took off his restraints, and after a moment, he blinked it away and tried to say it was okay. At this point, he didn't even have a full erection! And this is Mobley we are talking about! I'll write more about Mobley's naked attributes later.

All I can say of Mobley is, afterward, he could barely slip on the raincoat that he arrived in. I tried to help him, but to say the least, he was sore. When he left my room, his arms were straight at his sides and immobile, he couldn't turn his head on his neck even! He walked like that monster from that old Frankenstein movie, OMG. Stiff as a board. Again, he tried to assure me he was okay, even bent down to kiss me goodnight, which was so sweet it made me cry as soon as he was out the door. I hurt him, badly, and I've never hurt anyone in my life. I feel terrible. Like, bad! But I digress...

For a brief period, I somehow lost myself in the dom and slave thing with Mobley. I became someone else, someone that was NOT who I thought I was. This is totally unexpected, and I'm consumed with emotions. Anxiety. Regret. Shame. Throw some guilt in there as well.

The most alarming thing is - I want it more! Even knowing what I did. Today, I will tell Leanne that I can't honor the bet any further, regardless of the consequences.

After getting changed, I decided to venture out and see what disaster awaited me after "Assignment 1." Hopefully, I wouldn't see Mobley. And hopefully, Leanne wouldn't ask too many questions and just let me get out of this and walk away with my head hung in shame.

After making a cursory inspection of Stoney Brook, no one seemed to look at me any differently. At least I wasn't projecting any weird vibe. All the service staff greeted me and treated me completely normal, several of them still irritatingly calling me by my first name, a lingering remnant of disrespect thanks to Mobley. I walked down to the basement where there were several workers fabricating safety handrails for the steps into the "pirate cave." An archeologist from the United States and an official from the Island Bureau of Antiquities were at the top entrance, engaged in a deep discussion about the recovered artifacts. Inquiring as to if they had seen Mobley that morning, they said no, and he hadn't answered his mobile phone when they attempted to invite him for their conference.

A jolt of fear shot through me. Was Mobley okay? Maybe I hurt him so bad he had to go to a doctor! Or a hospital! Perhaps his ass wasn't just beet red, but maybe I had removed some of the flesh and he required skin grafts! Was it that sore looking when he stood up? Maybe? Surely not? The gruesome possibilities began rolling around in my mind and I began to feel sick to my stomach. I had nearly killed Mobley.

Heading back to the front desk, I was just preparing to call Leanne on my mobile when I saw her bob her head up from a cabinet of first aid supplies in the small front office. When she saw me, she grinned and shook her head dismissively. It probably was no stretch of the imagination to think the bandages, ointments, and other medical items she was holding were for Mobley.

"Ah. Good morning, my difficult little dominatrix." She motioned me over to the lounge. "Let's go talk, shall we?"

Ariana was manning the front desk for the morning and probably overheard Leanne's dominatrix greeting. If she did, she didn't let on and only smiled.

I took Leanne by the elbow and lead her to a secluded corner where we could talk in private. "Shhhhhhh!"

"What?" she asked, dropping her medical supplies on a coffee table.

"I don't want you calling me such things, like "dominatrix" around the staff. She could have heard that!"

"Oh, you *are* paranoid this morning. Just as I predicted."

"Leanne! Listen to me! Listennnnn!" There was panic in my voice now and Leanne's eyes widened, seeing my state. "Are those medical supplies you just got for Mobley? Are they?" I didn't give her a chance to answer. I pulled her shirt, bringing her closer. "Leanne, I think I hurt him last night! Bad!"

334

"Stefany, *calm down*. You are acting deranged. More so than usual."

"But. Are they for Mobley? Have you seen him? Is he okay?"

"Stef. We need to talk."

"Ohhhh nooooooo," I moaned. I dropped into the couch. "It's bad, isn't it! Does he need to go to the hospital? Does he need skin grafts on his ass? Oh gosh, I'm so sorry!" I put my hand to my mouth, my eyes watering in pre-cry mode. "I'm bad, aren't I? I'm a very… *very*… *bad* person."

"Would you chill the fuck out!" Leanne was laughing now. "I've never seen you like this! I must say, the look of panic is unbecoming, Cuz. NO! You aren't a bad person. So just listen to me for a minute!"

"But is he hurt?" I pressed again.

"He's fine. He's a bit… um… sore. No biggie. Really."

"Sore? Bad sore? What do you mean, sore?"

"Let's just say he needs a break from any further whuppin' by you." She grinned and shook her head. "My, my, you little firecracker. I sort of expected this with me making you wade through years of suppressed emotions. I thought it was a *possibility* you might go all-in on this dominance idea if you were only given an opportunity. And boy, did you. What I wasn't expecting was for you to nearly skin him alive with the riding crop."

"I nearly skinned him alive? Oh my…" The alarm in my voice and look in my eyes must have been palpable.

"It's hyperbolc! No, I told you, he's not that bad. But I didn't anticipate this, so it's really my fault. I should have talked to you more beforehand."

"Your fault? It certainly is not! I'm the one who did it."

"Look. Stef. The past month or so, you have been angry with Morgan. Right?"

"I don't know. Maybe. I guess? Yeah?"

"You went off on Morgan, because… let's face it, he represents *all* men to you at this point. Much more so than I anticipated. So, let's ask ourselves, why would you get into this more than a moderate amount? You beat the shit out of him not just because you were getting off on it, but for a lot of other reasons. This goes further into your past than Morgan. So, let's look at the reasons." Leanne began counting off her fingers. "First of all, it's always been you taking the abuse. You've been hit on, used, beat up, hurt. And not with a *just for fun* riding crop. Fists. Kicks. Whatever Miles could get his hands on when he was in a rage with you. Or your old boyfriends. Second, you've been powerless. You never thought there was anything you could do about any of your abuse. Third, sex wasn't ever anything enjoyable for you. It was always for someone else. And fourth, you were jealous over Morgan."

"Jealous? I should say not. How do you figure that?"

"The blonde girl that came out of his room that morning after your evening with Morgan. It seemed like the relationship with Morgan was really taking off until that point. The blonde girl walks out. Boom. You were angry, hurt and quite obviously jealous."

I sat back. Was that it? Could it be true?

"That last point… jealousy… I'm guessing… is a big reason you took it out on Morgan and went *farther* than I thought you would. Down deep, you were very angry with him that you were taken advantage of, yet again. I didn't realize the degree this was true, and that's why it's my fault this happened."

"I don't know…" I began to counter. "Leanne. It's me that did this. I must square with it. And that's why I must back out of our agreement. I just can't risk doing that again. I'm sorry."

"Oh, get over yourself. Listen to me, Stef. He will be fine. There's something you need to know, and it will help you get through this."

"What?"

"The blonde woman? She had stopped in at Morgan's room that morning. He sent her away, telling her he was seeing someone. Which is *you*, by the way. Yes, they had dated when he first arrived on the island, but nothing happened when she came to see him, he was a good boy. You need to admit you were very jealous. It's because you have some deep feelings for *Mobley*. And you felt betrayed. You've got to own all of that."

This hit me hard. I acted out on Mobley because of jealousy? My deep resentment toward him was unwarranted – my cruel treatment to him this past month unjustified. Man-Whore Mobley wasn't so… whorish - or disloyal after all. And what, exactly, were my deep feelings for him? I didn't know and wondered if I ever would. I did know that the degree of guilt I already felt had tripled. "Damn it, Leanne."

"Yeah." She patted me on the back. "I know. But tell me this. Did you enjoy Assignment 1?"

"Yes. Oh gawd, yes, I did, I'm ashamed to say."

"Don't be ashamed. And quit feeling guilty. You just need to adjust your mindset a bit, and everything will be okay from here on out."

"No, it won't, Leanne. Like I told you, I'm not going to abide by our agreement anymore."

"Take your phone out."

"Why?"

"Just do it."

I complied, holding it in my lap.

"Now," she began. "Text him. Ask how he's doing. Explain to him why you overdid the riding crop." Leanne scooped all the medical supplies off the table and dropped them into my lap. "Then, go see him and help him through this. It will be a good bonding moment."

"But I can't, Leanne." A tear escaped down my cheek.

"Yes. You can. Now go."

"But. Have you seen him?"

337

Leanne laughed. "Yes, I have already seen him. He's lying on his stomach on his bed, practically immobile, acting like a big baby. Which is quite an undignified sight, I must say. Anyway, I told him I would help him, but it would be better if it's you to do it. I'll catch up with you later. If after you talk to him and you are certain you can't abide by our terms any further, I'll *reluctantly* let you out. But what this all tells me with what has happened, this agreement is more useful to you than ever. I will want you to stay with the plan and fulfill your end. Okay?"

I nodded solemnly. She kissed me on the cheek and left me to my thoughts. The first text would be the hardest, so I just forged ahead and sent it.

Stefany:

> **Hey. Are you there?**

Mobley:

> **Yes**

Stefany:

> **Mobley. I'm sorry.**

Mobley:

> **You mean about last night?**

Stefany:

> **Um. Yeah???
> Look. I went overboard.
> And I'm so sorry.**

Mobley:

> **I am a bit sore today, no doubt about that. But it's okay. I'll be fine. Other**

than that, it
was fun. Sure
seemed like you
had fun 😊

Stefany:

Yes. I did.
Quite a lot. It
surprised me.
But I want you
to know why I
went too far.
Why I kind of
raged on you. I
really didn't
even realize I
did it.

Mobley:

You don't have
to explain, but
Ok

Stefany:

I thought you
were still seeing
your old
girlfriends
when I kind of
thought we had
a thing going. I
saw a blonde
woman leaving
your room.
Leanne
explained to
me. I jumped
to conclusions.

Mobley:

Ohhh

Mobley:

> Listen. It's okay and I understand. I have a lot of reputation to live down, I know. This agreement we have, I entered it willingly, eyes wide open.

Stefany:

> I hate to admit it, but I was jealous. Of the blonde girl. And anyone else I thought you were seeing.

Morgan:

> You know what?

Stefany:

> ???

Morgan:

> It makes me happy, that you got jealous over me.

Stefany:

> Really? You've got to be kidding. Leanne tells me

I nearly took
your skin off.

Morgan:
Well, I'd be
lying if I told
you I feel great
right now. HA

Morgan:
But, yes, I like
it because it
tells me how
you maybe
think about
me. Maybe you
don't hate me
after all.

Stefany:
That's an odd
conclusion to
come to,
considering.
But I never
hated you,
c'mon.

Morgan:
Be truthful.

Stefany:
Yeah, okay.
Maybe just a
tiny teensy bit.
In the past. But
I don't now!

Stefany:
Morgan, I'm
thinking I
don't want to
do this again.

After how I
hurt you. I'm
telling Leanne
it's off.

Morgan:

I'm very sorry
to hear you say
that. Please
don't.

Stefany:

What? Really?
But I hurt you.

Morgan:

It's nothing,
I'm a little sore
is all. And even
so, I liked it. I
didn't think I
would, but I
did. A mind
trip. You are so
amazing hot.
And
BEAUTIFUL.

Stefany:

I don't know
what to say.
You really
want to keep
going?

Morgan:

Yes. It was one
of the hottest
things I've ever
done. Amazing.
Aren't you
curious as to

what else
Leanne may
have up her
sleeve for us?

Stefany:

Hmmm. Yeah.
I guess it does
have its
appeal. Let me
think on it
today. If we do
go on with
this, I'll try
not to hurt
you.

Morgan:

You mean
you'll try not to
hurt me "too
bad." Leanne is
writing the
script, don't
forget

Stefany:

Ummmm.
Right. I have
some first aid
stuff. Leanne
gave it to me.
Can I please
stop by and see
you? I want to
help. I caused
it, after all.

Morgan:

Great. Come
see me, the

            door is
            unlocked.
Stefany:
            BTW, I'm glad
            you don't need
            ass skin grafts.
Morgan:
            ????
Stefany:
            NM, I'm on my way.

Morgan: After meeting Stefany for
Leanne's Assignment 1, it feels like I lost
half the skin off my ass and my back. But
no, contrary to what Stefany had concocted
in her overwrought, guilty mind, I don't
need "skin grafts," which would be funny -
if - I could move off the bed. I'm just raw
and sore. Stefany beat the hell out me while
she was getting off. Let me clarify to myself
here. IT WAS ONE OF THE HOTTEST
THINGS I'VE EVER DONE, there is no
question about that.

        The problem is she kind of lost her
mind and reefed on my back like nobody's
business with a riding crop. It was like, the
more she got off, the more she whipped me.
To say I'm in pain now is the
understatement of the year. I've got these

raw, red streaks all over my back and my ass. I can't even sit on the john without pain -I have to "hover".

No, I didn't get off nor could I. It was Leanne's weird rules, so nothing for me. This time. But seeing Stefany get her rocks off right on my face was fucking hot and amazing. If it hadn't been for the pain, I think I would have shot my load just watching her. Damn it, I need relief. But I'm in too much pain to even think about rubbing one off solo. I'm horny and miserable.

Afterward, I could tell she hadn't meant to hurt me so bad. She is still really upset. I feel bad for her because she was so embarrassed that she had lost control. I don't mind her losing control, that is hot. I just don't want her to cart off half my ass to Timbuctoo with her when she does it.

I just discovered she must have scored several strikes with that damned crop over my back onto my nards because they feel like they have been reefed on with a pipe wrench – putting ice on them now. The woman can shred when she gets going, that's for certain.

Leanne just getting her to do this with me was a major feat. I would have said it would be IMPOSSIBLE. Yet she did.

It's weird. It's odd. I don't know why I feel the way I do. The fact I'm in love with Stefany is making the pain a little more bearable. I'll write more later when I am not so sore.

Several soft knocks on my door interrupted my thoughts of the prior evening. I knew it had to be Stefany. "Come in."

She walked in carrying a few first aid items. She closed the door behind her. Her eyes were wide as she surveyed her handy work.

"Mobley. Oh my god. Oh! I'm soooo sorry." She looked like she might start crying.

"Stefany quit it! I'll get over this. It's no big deal, really."

She came closer and sat her items down on the nightstand beside the bed. I was buck naked, laying on my stomach. But I couldn't help it. Moving around was pure hell. The welts and raw streaks on my ass were making me miserable. This is what other people that were into BDSM felt like that got whipped or cropped? To say I was surprised that little stick with a leather flipper thing on it - like what they use on horses - could hurt so bad was certainly a surprise. I made a mental note to myself to never again scoff at the notion that Stefany couldn't rain down a holy hell of pain when she wanted.

"Here. Sit on the edge of the bed." I motioned her to take a seat.

She sat delicately, her eyes still darting back and forth across my body. I reached over and took her hand. "Stefany. I'll be okay."

"Right. Sooo."

I tried to think of something to set her more at ease.

"So, when is our next assignment?" I joked.

She laughed slightly, much to my relief. "I can't believe you want another assignment."

"Yeah, I do."

"Um. I don't know. After you aren't as sore, obviously."

"Stefany. It was hot. I look forward to it."

"Well. It was for me; I can tell you," she admitted. "But other than pain, what do you possibly get out of it?"

"It's a build-up of sorts, I guess. I've always got what I have wanted right away. This is making me wait. It's different. And it's exciting. As for me getting mine, we have only been through one of her assignments. I'm hoping Leanne will write in something favorable for me. Soon."

She caught my smile and returned it. "Yeah. I bet she will. If not, I'll talk to her, as I don't feel right having all the fun. And I promise. I won't go overboard."

She sat pensively for a moment, caressing my face. "Morgan. Really? Please be honest. You can tell me. You don't mind being a… my… *sex slave*? I must say, I never thought this would be a conversation we would ever have or something to describe you."

I took her hand and kissed it. "It's all new to me, and honestly, yes, I like it. It was exciting and different, more than I ever expected. As weird as it sounds to say it, being your sex slave is something I consider an incredible stroke of luck. I thank Leanne's perverted mind. I want to do the job well. For you." Her breathing had visibly quickened. As had mine.

"Um. You were *quite* good for Assignment 1."

"And you?" I asked. "You don't mind being my sex goddess?"

She laughed. "No. I don't mind. Maybe Leanne is some kind of sexual genius. I'm… kinda getting off on it."

I grinned. "You already did, once."

"That, I did, Mobley. Incredibly so. We have your sore back and ass to prove it." We both laughed at this together. Sore back be damned, I wanted her now. Sexual tension began taking the place of her shy, initial panic. After a moment, she reached for the first aid supplies.

"We can't… um. Can't be doing anything in your condition. Plus, we have *no* assignment, our puppeteer Leanne wouldn't approve of us going off script," she joked nervously. "So, let me apply some medicine to your back. Okay? I think we treat it like a bad sunburn. That's probably what this calls for. Sorta."

"And on my ass?" I playfully asked.

"Be careful, Mobley. The cheeks of your ass, although red, look very spankable if you decide to suddenly be insolent with my charity."

"I won't be insolent. I promise."

"Then yes, I will treat your poor ass as well."

"So, what are you going to do?"

"First, I'll get a fresh washcloth from your bathroom and clean you up a little. Then I'm going to apply some first aid cream with aloe vera. And triple antibiotic. Okay?"

"Yes, please do. Can I do you as well?"

She laughed devilishly. "No. Here you are, laying on your stomach, you are sore as hell from me. And still, you flirt. Is there any circumstance imaginable where you aren't looking for a horny frolic?"

I didn't answer and decided to let her get on with it. Stefany cleaned and tenderly applied the lotion to each raw area on my back. It took her well over an hour for this extended procedure. During this time, we talked casually, continuing to enjoy each other's company. It was a marked departure from the tense discussions of the past.

Finally, she was done. "That's all I can do for you for now. I wish I could do more. But I can't."

348

"It feels much better already," I offered, trying to ease her conscious. "Thank you."

She bent down to my face, her hair sending wonderful cool tender sensations across my back where it touched. She ran her fingers delicately across my face then kissed me. First on the cheek. Then on my temple. I turned, reaching for her. Her lips found mine and we enjoyed each other this way for much of the rest of the morning.

"I've got to get back to my office and get some things done," she finally said, saucily wiping her mouth on the back of her hand. "I have an appointment this afternoon with some people that say they want to invest with us. At this point, luckily and thanks largely to you, we don't need investors. But I agreed to hear them out. Don't worry about work, Mobley. You can come back when you feel up to it."

"I'm ready now. I really feel much better, thanks to you. Where are these investors from?"

"They said Australia. It's just being polite to meet them, I think. They are here on the island, so it would be rude to refuse them." She paused. "Are you sure you are okay?"

"Yes, I'm fine. I can wear a loose button-up shirt. No biggie. Although I would appreciate it if you could treat my back again later. With that first aid cream?"

She smiled. "Of course. And make out more?"

"That's my primary interest in the request, yes." I admitted.

"You are incorrigible."

She started to get up, but I held her arm. "Stefany?"

She eyed me curiously. "What?"

I wanted to tell her I loved her. It was just on the tip of my lips. Almost.

"What?"

How would she take it? Approve? Disapprove? "I... er. It's nothing."

She bent down and kissed me again. "Careful now, Mobley."

She ran her fingers lightly over my lips, and I wondered what she meant. Did she know what I was trying to tell her?

"I'm glad you feel better. I'll check on you this evening." And with that, she left.

That afternoon, I managed to gingerly slip on a loose shirt and get dressed. My ass was every bit as sore as my back, so there would be no sitting down for the day. I had to laugh, thinking of my predicament. No, I couldn't have a normal relationship with someone. I had to fall in love with a woman that gets off beating the shit out of me. True, I was thinking in hyperbolic terms, but the humor was not lost to me.

Leanne met me in the hall, having been on her way to my room. "Okay, let me see, she ordered.

Taking her hand, I led her to an alcove out of view of the hallway security cameras. I lifted my shirt, showing her the welts on my back.

She suddenly broke out laughing. "Oh, my gawd!"

"Leanne! This isn't funny!" I rebuked. "This hurts like hell!"

"Let's have a look at the ole posterior." Leanne stepped behind me and pulled my loose-fitting shorts away to look at the similarly red streaks on my ass. "Wow. The girl has a cruel streak. Who'da thought."

"Cruel? You think? I must sleep on my stomach! I can't even sit down… you know… to even go to the bathroom. Sure, she feels bad. But you've got to get that riding crop away from her!"

"I'll see what I can do," Leanne agreed, still thinking the situation was far funnier than it was.

I pulled her close. "You've got to do something."

"I'm sorry. I just never thought she would do that."

"Well, she did!"

"Yeah, that's pretty severe for a newbie. She has had a lot of pent-up feelings. Evidently, she let them go. You should feel honored."

"I feel sore, Leanne. That's what I feel right now, fucking sore."

She laughed again. "Take an ibuprofen, you'll be fine. Look at Joe. He's had as bad at the hands of Heidi and he never whined about it. Quit being such a baby."

"Baby!?" At this, I just shook my head. My ass was hanging by a thread and she just called me a baby. If I wasn't careful, these women were going to kill me and laugh over my grave. And I'd enjoy it, evidently.

It felt good to get out of the room and get back on the job. The cream that Stefany had applied to my welts was doing the trick, keeping the injured skin moisturized so that it wouldn't dry and crack.

After checking in on the basement, I decided to take a stroll to the front grounds of the estate. It had been a while since seeing this part of Stoney Brook, and I didn't feel like talking with anyone. I decided to explore the old slave cemetery and some of the quarters. There had been little need for extensive restorations here as they were in decent shape.

A parking area was conveniently located near the rows of slave quarters, between the manor house and the front grounds. Many guests parked here as it was discouraged to park in the center drive. As I walked past the parking lot, I noticed a visitor sitting in a black four-door sedan. The front tags looked like those from a rental car facility in the village. He took no notice of me, his face buried behind a newspaper. I had the impression he was waiting on someone. I thought about telling him he could pull up to the front steps and wait but thought better of it since he looked immersed in his paper.

Winding my way through the slave quarters, I was impressed with the resilience those people must have had to endure early plantation life. Recalling the brutal stories of Stoney Brook, I had to wonder how many of the occupants of the small cottages survived. How many perished under hard work or brutal injustice? I ran my hand down the front door of the last cottage. Had one of the occupants done the very same thing, over two-hundred years ago?

Deep in thought, a car drove past on the main entry road. It was moving rather fast, certainly faster than the posted speed limit of 10 kph. It was the very same car I noticed in the parking lot, with the newspaper reader. I shrugged it off and headed back to the estate house.

It was nearly 3:00 and I hadn't accomplished much for the day other than to knock a bit of the sore off and loosen up. Looking up at the second-story window of Stefany's office, I wondered if she would be up for a cup of tea and some company. I couldn't stop thinking about her.

Walking in the front entry, I nodded to the desk staff, even the disrespectful Ariana. I thought about asking her if she had properly charged the GpupS locators. She smiled and I decided to go about my way, not feeling like a confrontation with her. I could check them later when her shift was over.

Heading up the grand staircase, I hit the second-floor hallway and headed to Stefany's office. The large doors that Leanne had just guided me through the previous evening were ajar. I stuck my head in.

"Stefany? Hello?"

No response. Her desk lamp was on. Several folders and papers were strewn about on the floor, which was odd. I stepped in. The scene in her office seemed strange with the disarray. Walking to her desk, a lump began forming in my throat as I then got a distinct feeling that something was not right.

Stefany's mobile phone lay on the desk along with her small purse. More papers and folders were strewn around her chair as well. Several books were knocked to the floor. It decidedly looked as if there had been a struggle.

I immediately took my mobile and called the front desk. Ariana answered. "Ariana. Have you seen Ms. Michaels leave this afternoon?" I asked.

"Why, are you in trouble again, Mr. Mobley?"

"Ariana, don't give me any grief, I just want to know, have you seen her?"

"Nope. I have not seen her."

"Okay. Thanks." I hung up and dialed Leanne. She answered on the third ring.

"Why hello my dear skinless Morgan. How are you feeling?"

Ignoring her question, I got to the point. "Leanne, have you seen Stefany this afternoon? She supposedly had a meeting, but I can't find her anywhere."

"No. I haven't seen her. But I haven't looked for her, either. Judging from the sound of your voice, you think something is wrong?"

"I don't know. Can you please come to her office and meet me? Quick? I want you to see this."

"Sure. I'll be right there."

While waiting for Leanne, I opened the cross-entry door from the office to Stefany's living quarters.

"Stefany?"

No answer. Entering, I checked all her rooms, confirming that she was not there.

"Morgan?" Leanne called from the office.

"Yes, right here, Leanne." I joined her. "Do you see why I'm concerned?" I asked.

"Yes. This looks like there's been a struggle. She is neat and tidy. She wouldn't leave her desk like this. Or her office." She had a look for herself behind the desk. "Anything in her living quarters?"

"No. It's undisturbed in there."

"And with her phone and purse in here. Have you checked with the staff?

"Yes. And nothing."

"Who was last to be with her?" Leanne asked, alarm growing in her voice.

"All I know is she mentioned an afternoon meeting with some potential investors from Australia."

"She didn't mention that to me. It's the first I heard of it," Leanne exclaimed. "And I think she would have mentioned that."

"She wasn't too serious about it," I explained. "She didn't think it was something she wanted to do, it was just being polite to these visitors who were already on the island, she said."

"We've got to get the police. Quick," Leanne said, dialing on her mobile phone.

I walked to the window and looked out at the last traces of sunlight across the tropical sky. Abduction was the only plausible answer. Someone had taken her, more than likely the people she was meeting.

After Leanne finished her call to the police, she came to stand by me at the window. "The police will be here when they can, they said. But that may be a while. Is this really what it looks like, Morgan?"

Thinking back to my stroll through the slave quarters that afternoon, I remembered the car sitting in the manor parking lot. The man at the wheel, purposefully ignoring my gaze as he read behind a newspaper. What if?

"She's been forcefully taken, Leanne. We can be nearly sure about that, just by the looks of the disarray in this office. She was likely led down the back way so that no one at the front desk would see her leaving. There was a car in the manor parking lot I noticed today. A guy was sitting at the wheel, and he looked like he was waiting on someone."

"Do you think he was waiting while someone else was taking her?"

"I think so! That was late in the afternoon. Whoever took her waited in her office for a clear opportunity to take her out when no one was about. No one has seen or heard a thing."

"Could this be related to the attack at the Mill?" Leanne asked.

"I don't know. It's getting dark, Leanne. I've got the feeling there is no time to waste. We can't wait for the police; we must do something. If she has been taken, every second she is gone increases the likelihood they will kill her."

"But what can we possibly do? We have no idea where they would even go."

Trying to determine a course of action, I took Leanne by the arm and began leading her out of the office. "Let's just get in one of the Rovers and get out and... drive. I remember what the car looked like in the manor parking lot. It was a black four-door sedan. Looked like a rental. Maybe we could get lucky and spot it somewhere."

"Morgan, that hardly seems likely. They will not be hanging around on the main roads. Without her having her mobile phone, we have no idea where she's been taken. She could literally be anywhere."

"But at least it's something!" I countered. "It's slim, I know, but..." We both knew this could be very serious.

Leanne touched my arm softly. "Oh, my. Let's go, then."

I closed the office doors, and we began heading to the front desk. I related the entire story to Ariana so she would know what to tell the police when she showed them Stefany's office.

"Send out a notice to the staff on the radios. Let everyone know that Stefany is missing and to get out and drive about. Report here with any news should they have any. Look for a black four-door sedan with rental tags. Call me on my mobile immediately with any news or if the cops need to talk to me. Ms. Tilden and I are going to take a Rover out and see if we can get lucky and find her."

Ariana was visibly shaken now. "Yes, Mr. Mobley."

Turning for the front door, my eyes caught an item on the desk in front of Ariana. It was one of the GpupS trail monitors. "Wait!"

"What is it?" Leanne asked, startled.

Picking up the monitor, I observed the small flashing red light, indicating it was turned on. "Ariana. Are these GpupS monitors working now?"

"Yes," she replied. "That one was just brought back a few minutes ago by a couple that went for an afternoon hike."

Thinking back, I recalled giving Stefany one of the units to try at her convenience. Was there any remote chance that she could have that monitor with her? And further, any chance the small device still had a charge?

Meeting Leanne and Ariana's questioning stares, I explained as the possibilities shot through my mind. "Some days ago, I gave Stefany one of these GPS locator monitors to try out, fully charged. As Ariana knows, they enable guests to locate certain landmarks and identify things they encounter on the trails. And…"

"They provide the location of guests," Leanne finished for me, her eyes wide now with the implications. "But would she even have it with her?"

"It's a long shot. But she was carrying it around in her pocket, telling me she would get around to trying it when she had time! If she has it…"

"And if whoever took her didn't notice it was in her pocket…" Leanne added hopefully.

"And if she turned it on now… to send a signal. Ariana, please pull up the tracking program on your screen. See if monitor number 1 is active."

Ariana typed several commands on the network monitor at her front desk. "Mr. Mobley. That was days ago. I have never seen number 1 active."

"But maybe she managed to turn it on this evening, hoping I would remember that she had it. She would realize that it would enable us to track her."

Drumming my fingers on the desk, I was growing impatient. Stefany having and activating the GpupS monitor that I gave her might be the only real possibility of locating her. Whoever had taken her did not have her best interests in mind, that was for certain.

"Well?" I finally asked, edgy.

"A moment, Mr. Mobley. It is initializing." Ariana, under the circumstances, was being quite tolerant of me.

"Sorry. I don't mean to be short. It's just that every second counts."

Ariana's face brightened. "It's on!"

Leanne and I both ran behind the desk to see the result. At the top of the screen, a box with active monitors showed only one active unit: it was number 1 - Stefany's. A map showed a small blinking green light indicating where Stefany's monitor was pinging to the satellite. The map had automatically scaled out, indicating the monitor was in the village.

"She has it! And it is working!" Leanne exclaimed.

"Ariana, quick, give me the hand-held field master. Is it charged?"

"It's plugged in with all the monitors. So yes, I guess. But it's never been used," Ariana explained. Rummaging below the desk, she retrieved a device with a small screen. It was a companion unit to the GpupS, intended for field use to track the monitors away from the desk if necessary. Taking it from her, I fumbled with it, trying to initialize it.

Unable to locate the power button, I grew increasingly frustrated. "Well, damn it! Why can't I find... You'd think they'd design these better! What the hell..."

"Here, let me, "Ariana offered. She quickly found the applicable power button, turned it on and handed it back. "There you are. Mr. Mobley."

"When the cops get here, show them where her device is pinging, Ariana! They can call me or Leanne, we've got to hurry and see if we can find her!"

Stumbling and hitting the edge of one of the front doors, I raced in a panic with Leanne out and down the steps. We quickly got into a Stoney Brook Rover, and we were on our way, Leanne directing me from the passenger seat.

"It's still pinging at the village," Leanne advised, intently watching the screen of the field monitor.

At times, I had the Rover up over 80 on some of the straightaways, flying over several rises and taking some of the corners on two wheels.

"Morgan! I know we have to get there quick, but it won't help Stefany a bit if we are dead, wrapped around a tree!"

I eased off the accelerator. "Yes, I concur." The potholes, washboard and general rough condition of the dirt roads had jarred the Rover, as well as our teeth and internal organs. Our sense of urgency only grew as traces of the setting sun in the tropical skies completely disappeared.

Finally arriving at the village, I glanced questioningly over to Leanne. "Okay, now where?"

"Take a left. I think."

We wound our way around the village roads, occasionally catching a curious stare from residents walking about or sitting on verandas. It was apparent that wherever Stefany was, she was moving, as we never seemed to catch up.

My mobile phone rang. I answered, trying to both navigate and talk. "Yes? This is Mobley."

It was the police. After confirming with them that I was tracking Stefany through the village, they assured me they would be joining me as soon as they could.

"Okay, now take a right," Leanne ordered with the latest direction towards the elusive blinking light on the field monitor screen.

Having made a circuitous trip around the whole village, we finally ended up at the docks. In the adjacent parking lot was a black sedan identical to the one I had spotted earlier in the day at the manor parking lot.

"This is it! I think that's the car over there, Leanne," I exclaimed, excitement in my voice building as I pointed it out to her.

"Her monitor is pinging right here, Morgan!"

Slamming the Rover doors behind us, we tried to determine where Stefany's signal was originating. The black sedan was empty.

Out of the corner of my eye, I noticed a boat at the docks revving its engines, backing away. Under the security lights on the dock, I could make out two men. One was at the helm, maneuvering the boat. The other struggled with a large sack or bag near the back. A large white cooler was also visible.

"There, Leanne! That must be them! They have her and they are leaving. We'll never see her alive again if they get out of our sight! Look! Look at that bag he's wrestling with! Look at the cooler. I think they are planning to throw her out at sea!"

I yelled at the top of my lungs. Jumping over the barrier rope, I ran down the dock towards them, Leanne hot on my heels. "Hey! You! Stop there!"

The men may not have heard me over the motor, but they did see me. The man at the helm gunned the motor with increased urgency to back and turn the boat towards the open sea. The boat cleared the dock and headed out into the blackness of the ocean, marked only by the running lights.

"Morgan, what are we going to do!? They are heading out fast!"

In desperation, I looked around for anyone that was in or near their boat that could quickly pursue. I glanced over my shoulder at the dock offices. They were all closed, the interiors dark. I thought about smashing the windows of the offices and rummaging about for a set of keys to a boat.

My eyes caught movement on one corner of the dock and a moment of hope grew. It was the French water taxi guy, the one that had vowed to never take me anywhere again after I first arrived on the island. There would be no time for niceties now. He had to take me and join in the pursuit, there would be no options. Stefany's life hung in the balance now, and every second counted. Even now it was getting hard to make out the running lights of the kidnapper's boat.

"Over there! It's the taxi boat, quick, let's get over there!"

We both ran through the maze of fishing nets, steel drums, and boat supplies. We arrived at the water taxi slip, panting and out of breath. The Frenchman's engines were still running, he had evidently just returned from hauling a fare to the big islands. His eyes widened when he saw me. Throwing down a tie line he stepped aggressively off his boat.

"Ohhhh, now lookee here, this cheap bastard American come to see me this late time of the evening... vous seau de chum de merde de mouette. Je ne t'emmènerai nulle part!"

I don't know what he said, but I didn't care. "See here. This is an emergency! The owner of Stoney Brook has been taken. There are two men taking her right now! On that boat out there, leaving the harbor! You must take us at once and pursue that boat!"

"De quoi parles-tu, imbécile, je ne le ferai pas!"

I looked over at Leanne. "What is he saying, what's that mean?"

Leanne shrugged her shoulders. "I have no idea. But I don't think he's going to take you."

"You take me now! Right now! Get your French ass in the boat, we are going! There isn't any time!"

He spat on one of my shoes. I punched him hard in the jaw, toppling the man to the worn wood of the dock. He laid there, dazed and silent, Leanne looking at me with a shocked expression.

Quickly throwing off the tie-up lines, I took the field monitor from Leanne and jumped in the taxi boat. "Leanne. Stay here, tell the cops what is happening. I will go after them!"

Regaining his senses, the taxi boat skipper regained his feet, looking as though he would try jumping back into the boat with me. I quickly reversed the engines and throttled them, ending the possibility of him joining me.

"Vous l'avez fait maintenant! Je vais couper tes coquilles!"

Coming out hot, I bumped the rear of the boat into the opposite dock. I gunned the throttle and headed out of the harbor well over the posted speed.

The Frenchman fumed, angry beyond words. "I keel you, cheap fuck when I find!"

"Morgan, be careful!" Leanne yelled.

"Yes! Yes, it's just been a while since I've driven a boat," I yelled back. The only time I had driven a boat was in my childhood when my uncle Herman let me take the wheel in Lake Michigan. I couldn't worry about details at this time, I had to catch up to the kidnappers. I poured on the throttle, full speed.

If the kidnappers could see me coming, they could just keep running. For good measure, I turned off all the boat lights after assessing the switches. The taxi boat had a large searchlight by the helm which was extraordinary luck. That could be handy, I determined.

Looking ahead I could barely make out the white stern light and the red and green running lights of the kidnapper's boat. They were almost out of visual range. A thought chilled me to the spine. What if they had seen me leaving the docks? What if they also shut off their running lights? They could go in any direction to lose me. Then, as if on cue, they vanished.

I had the field master, I thought, brightening. Setting the device on top of the helm control, I verified that I could still follow Stefany's ping. It was working!

The boat engines hammered on into the pure black of a moonless, calm ocean. Stefany's ping kept a relative distance on the screen of the field master. They were keeping pace ahead of me, but at least I wasn't losing them. I was driving completely blind; if I were to hit anything, I would never see it coming.

Several slight course alterations and a full hour passed. They hopefully didn't know I was pursuing them, but they also weren't slowing down.

What were they doing? Were they at this moment killing Stefany? Were they shoving her into the white cooler? What if they tossed the cooler at this time? I would go past it and never even see it!

Stefany's green blinking light began to move down the screen, indicating the monitor was drawing closer to the field master. Up ahead, a masthead light and running lights suddenly flashed on. The kidnappers' boat was just in front of me. I quickly throttled the engines all the way back. With no lights on, they would not have detected me approaching unless their boat was equipped with radar, which was doubtful given it looked like a recreational rental. They would think they were all alone out at this distance in the ocean.

Coming at them from the side, I edged the rudder to angle towards their boat. They were just coasting now. As I approached closer, I could see they were struggling with the sack at the back of the boat. The top slipped off and I could plainly see the brown hair of a woman. It was Stefany and she was still alive! She had duct tape over her mouth. One of the men withdrew a pistol.

My veins pulsed with adrenaline. Whatever I was going to do, it had to be now. Should I ram their boat? Yes! I would ram their boat and interrupt what looked like an impending execution. And if both boats sank? Life vests? There would be the inevitable struggle with both, one of them armed. I had no time to consider the possibilities. The man with the pistol leveled it at her head. I threw the lights on and gunned the engines, guiding the boat directly at their midship. The bow of the water taxi rose into the air with the full throttle, and I momentarily lost sight of the other boat. Hopefully, their attention was on me instead of Stefany.

A thunderous crash broke the stillness of the night. The impact threw both men and Stefany hard to the deck. In the process, it had nearly driven my own head into the instrument panel of the taxi boat. Running forward, I quickly jumped onto their boat and smashed my fist into the face of the man with the pistol. We both struggled for the gun, and I managed to knock it to the deck, just out of reach.

The other man, in the meantime, was attempting to push Stefany over the stern rail. My opponent quickly crawled on all fours and again gained a grip onto the pistol. Grabbing his hand just in time, I pointed the pistol to the sky. A shot meant for me went off up in the air as I tried to keep the barrel pointed away. Behind me, I heard a loud splash. Stefany was gone and the other kidnapper immediately came for me. After landing several good blows, my advantage was gone, and it would be only a matter of time before I was subdued as both men were large and powerfully built.

Gaining my feet, I took one final desperate sweep at the gunman's hand. The pistol flung away and clattered down the gunwale to flip over the side. At least that element was eliminated.

Tossing both men off me, I plunged into the ocean off the stern rail. I flailed at the water, not seeing Stefany. I swam just below the surface, my arms out, feeling for her. She could not have descended that quick! Unless they had attached weights. The idea was horrifying.

Just as quickly as this thought had entered my mind, the tips of my left hand glanced off a canvas surface. Wrapping my arms around this dark form, I pulled it to the surface. I could feel Stefany coughing beneath the canvas and duct tape. Yanking at the canvas, I loosened it away from her head and ripped the duct tape off her mouth. Gasping, she sputtered and coughed, choking in several strained breaths. With her arms and legs bound within the sack, she was unable to move and was flailing about in a panic.

"Stefany! It's me!" I yelled.

"Morgan!" She calmed instantly and began crying.

"I've got you!" I told her, trying to feel for a way to get her free of the bag.

Stefany gasped. "Look out!"

The two kidnappers had pushed their boat free of the water taxi. Although both were damaged, they were yet seaworthy. The kidnappers now put their boat into hard reverse to run us over and drive us into their propellers. There was no time. Stefany was completely bound and immobile in her canvas bag cocoon. With her under one arm, I pulled her away from the prop vacuum and kicked at the stern of their boat with both feet, attempting to get to the side and away. Their boat pulled past me. By this time, we were bobbing right at the hull of the taxi boat.

Seeing that their attempt to run us over had failed, they throttled their engines forward and drove away. Their lights gained distance as they headed away to the south-west, probably going to the big island.

She was crying against my shoulder in uncontrolled sobs intermixed with her struggles to breathe. "Morgan. I can't believe you are here! They were going to kill me!"

"You are safe now, Stefany. Let me get this bag off so you can move."

I tugged on the tape that bound the top of the bag. After clearing most of this away, I determined that her hands and feet were similarly bound. My fingers were nearly useless at this point. Finally, after several long minutes, I had her hands free.

"Let's get you into the boat and I can untie your feet."

Pulling her along to the stern, I realized the engines were idling. Unsure if the props were completely off, I kept Stefany and my legs clear of the back of the boat. Finding a pull ring for an access ladder, I gave it a tug and let it drop. Guiding Stefany towards the ladder, I let her get a hold. Climbing past her, I then pulled her up in the boat and onto the deck. Getting her to where I could see what I was doing, I unwound the duct tape from around her legs. I immediately fell back against one of the seat benches, utterly spent.

"Are you okay?" Stefany asked, herself leaning back and catching her breath.

"Yes. Just... so... glad... I was able to... get you in time. That was close. In many ways," I gasped. "We are just so lucky you had the GpupS with you. If we didn't have that?" Stefany nodded. We both knew the implications. She would be dead, certainly. No one would even know where her body would be dumped.

"I kept it in my pocket these last days," she explained. "I kept meaning to try it out and never got around to it. I was able to turn it on when they put me in the trunk of their car. You, procrastination, and that little device saved my life today. Thank you, Morgan. A thousand thanks."

I laughed. "You are welcome.

Getting up, she walked over and dropped to her knees next to me. She wrapped her arms around my neck and kissed me. Hard. After several minutes, she broke this electrical connection and smiled. "You taste salty."

"With that kind of reward, I would rescue you any day."

"Just a minute ago, I thought the only kissing I would do would be with the fishes." She pointed with her thumb back over her shoulder towards our hopeful destination. "Can you get us back to the harbor in one piece?"

"I'm going to try. You may want to locate the emergency life raft. And grab us a couple of life vests?"

"Sure." She helped me up, then softly patted my ass. "Are you still sore?"

I blinked. "I hadn't even thought about it. It must be the adrenaline. I don't feel anything, actually."

"You will tomorrow. I'll have to go easy on you for a week at least. As a reward for saving me. Yet again."

"Maybe just a few days," I joked. She nodded seductively and began looking about for a life raft.

The bow of the boat was badly damaged, but so far was holding its own and wasn't taking on too much water, at least none that was visible. There was a radio, fortunately. It hung off the lower helm. I pulled the mic off and pressed the transmit button. "Um. Hello? This is Morgan Mobley, does anyone copy?"

"Hello, this is the Village Harbor Master." He gave an authority location number, which meant nothing to me, I had no idea where I was even at, coordinate wise. "Mr. Mobley, the island police are standing by. Please hold."

"This is Sergeant Merata of the Island Police Department. Return that boat to the dock at once."

"Apologies, Sergeant, it was necessary to commandeer this boat to rescue Ms. Stefany Michaels. The owner of Stoney Brook Plantation. She was taken, I had to go after the people who kidnapped her."

"Are you returning that boat, sir? We are prepared to send out an armed patrol."

"Armed patrol? No! I'm returning it! You don't seem to understand, I had to take the boat, there was no time. There was a kidnapping. Is Ms. Leanne Tilden there on the dock? She can explain."

"Get that boat back here, immediately. Merata, out." It was a rather shocking exchange. The sergeant seemed more concerned for the boat than Stefany.

"Stefany! Did you hear that?" I called back. "Stefany?"

She looked unaware, evidently unable to hear the conversation over the roar of the engines as she searched for a life raft and life vests. I noticed water beginning to slosh about on the deck.

The helm console had a navigation panel and I fumbled through a series of switches. Not engaged during the pursuit, I had overlooked it. Now it lit up, ghostly green, complete with a compass heading, speed, conditions, engine specifications. More useful was the blinking icon that represented our position relative to the island and harbor, which were clearly shown on the screen. I eased the boat into the right direction and throttled the engine to a level I thought the damaged bow could handle based on the vibrations I could feel through the deck.

Stefany suddenly appeared at my side, thrusting a life vest into my hands. "You better keep it handy. There seems to be a lot of water coming in," she explained.

"Thanks. I spoke with the Island Police Department a while ago. They aren't happy with me, it seems."

"Because you took this boat to get me?"

"I guess so. They sounded quite put out."

"It's just a misunderstanding," Stefany tried to justify. "It's probably nothing. We can explain when we get back."

"Yes."

She put her arms around me again and kissed my cheek.

"You saved my life! They just don't realize."

I nodded, glad for the fortunate events of the evening. It could have easily been much different.

I could begin to see the lights of the island ahead after what seemed like hours at sea. The deck now had several inches of water on it and the bow was running low in the water. The engine was sputtering occasionally, probably due to the air intakes beginning to flood.

Arriving at the dock, I throttled the gasping motor back and ran the boat slowly into the Frenchman's slip. Unable to get the engine to shift into reverse, the damaged bow crunched into the dock with a horrible breaking sound, no doubt furthering the damage. A small crowd had gathered. I could make out numerous police, townspeople, and Leanne. The Frenchman was there as well, his arms flailing towards me to emphasize what I was certain a profane greeting.

The bow was nearly submerged at this point. Several bystanders took the tie-up lines and secured the boat. I cut the engine and it gave out with several loud clanking noises capped with a loud backfire. Dense, black smoke puffed from the engine compartment.

Tossing the life vests onto a nearby bench, I then took Stefany by the hand and led her off the boat. Leanne immediately embraced her in a crushing hug. A policeman grabbed me roughly by the arm. I tried to explain, but he could not hear me over the crowd noise.

The Frenchman I noticed, by now, was wiping tears from his eyes as he walked about his boat on the dock, surveying the damage, cursing.

"I should explain to him what happened," I tried to tell the policeman, who didn't comprehend. "See, I had to ram this other boat. It was the only way."

The Frenchman walked to me, his expression revealing a blind rage. Without warning he punched me in the face, bringing about a beautiful series of stars coursing through my vision. Falling back into the policeman's arms, I could vaguely hear cursing in French amid Stefany's vehement objections at my treatment.

"What are you doing to him?! He saved me!"

"He stole that boat and wrecked it, lady. Whatever else is going on here, he's going to answer for that," the policeman explained in a gruff voice.

"Morgan, just go along peacefully for now, we'll clear this up," I heard Leanne calmly coach.

The policeman, now joined by two other officers, allowed me to roughly drop to the deck where they rolled me over on my stomach. They pulled my arms behind my back and cuffed me. "It's off to jail for you," one of them barked. The Frenchman was kicking at me by this point, and I tried to turn to explain. This effort was rewarded with a strike on the back of my head from a police baton.

"Oww! I'm the good guy here! I saved her! What the hell…"

"Don't resist!"

Another unnecessary clunk on the back of my head with a baton sent pain blazing through my brain and more stars in my eyes. My consciousness was beginning to wane as I surmised that they were enjoying themselves far too much. Where was due process when you needed it?!

"Yes! The club for that stooopid Americahn thief," the Frenchman urged. "He destroy my beautiful boat! My livelihood! My career! I work all my life for theees and then theees cheap bum comes!" He scored a painful kick on my right leg.

"For God's sake, insurance will cover the boat!" Stefany yelled. "If not, I'll cover it! Quit hurting him! Don't you see he just saved my life?"

"Antoine, come to the station and file a complaint," one of the police counseled the Frenchman while nearly pulling my arm out of socket. Another strike of a baton crashed into my ribs.

"Ahhh! Can't you see! I'm not resisting!" And again, another whack on the head with the baton.

The crowd parted for the police as they dragged me off the dock.

"Yes! Antoine will come to file!" the Frenchman shouted. "I want to see theees bum to hannng! Slowwwwly!"

From this confused, chaotic, and painful scene, I could hear Stefany's voice. "Mobley! I'll get you out soon!"

CHAPTER 13

A LITTLE ROPE AND A FEW LASHINGS NEVER HURT ANYBODY

Morgan: I am back at Stoney Brook as I write this, preparing for a much-needed shower.

This morning, when my hands went to the back of my head, I confirmed there were two bloody lumps, generously incurred from a police baton down at the dock. Yes, indeed. When I woke up, I found myself in a filthy village jail cell.

The sheetless, tattered mattress and urine-stained pillow I slept on for the night were half stuck to my body from the blood. The sordid environment and scant furnishings brought back unpleasant memories of my days of boarding at The Blue Calypso. This was how island law enforcement rewards a citizen for saving someone's life?

Sore can't even describe how I am feeling. My back and my ass are still aflame from the cropping Stefany had given me just two days prior. There's that. Then, when I was struggling with the kidnappers (and the asshole French water taxi guy) I ended up with a busted lip, sore jaw, and a black eye. Add that all to what the cops did to me... cracking me on the head and seriously bruising several ribs. I've never been a fan of the fuzz.

Stefany and Leanne came in just after I woke up in my cell. They gave the officer on duty hell until I heard Constable Fillmore enter the office. Fillmore had been off the island during the kidnapping and so didn't seem to have a clue about any of the recent events. Stefany posted bail and they sprang me. I am eternally grateful to be out of that hell hole.

On a happier note, I saved Stefany. Every few minutes I remind myself of the relief I feel knowing she's okay. Stefany held nothing back with the kiss and hug she gave me when I stumbled out of the cell. Right in front of the cops and Leanne! On the drive back and out of view of Leanne, she discretely reached between my legs and squeezed my cock. Rather hard. Wow. It seems I have become her dirty little secret. Now that is what I call progress! (I'm so sore though, it hurt.)

~~~~~

According to Fillmore, given the circumstances, I would probably not get charged. Given the circumstances???? What the hell! I should think not! Those idiots. The police that responded to Stoney Brook and then the docks totally flubbed proper procedure. No shit. Of course, when I heard that one of the police was related to Frenchie the water taxi asshole, I understood their motives to arrest and beat the shit out of me.

Stefany claimed that her insurance would cover the boat, as I was an employee of hers. Frenchie had insurance, but it wouldn't be necessary. So, he reluctantly bowed out of any charges when he learned that he would be compensated for damages to the boat and the necessary repairs. Further, he would also be reimbursed for projected income loss while his boat was in the repair dock. That didn't stop him from cursing me upon sight at every opportunity.

I would have thought that finding the two goons that kidnapped Stefany would be an easy task. Where could they go??? Their boat was damaged amidships and needed repairs. Sure enough, the police found the boat at the big island, beat all to hell from me ramming it, just as I thought. And just like the sedan, it was a rental, with the address and names being fake. Both rentals were paid in cash, so no tracking a financial card. They didn't return to get their damage deposit, obviously. So, these thugs are still out there! Attempted murderers! The cops, including that Constable Fillmore, don't seem overly energetic about finding out who is responsible. I would think the prime suspect behind everything that has happened to Stefany and me would be MILES, the supreme dick of domestic abuse.

~~~~~

Afternoon update: The investigation continues. So far nothing more has happened, but we are going to take increased security measures here and around Stoney Brook. Stefany isn't going to venture out to the village or anywhere else for that matter without someone being with her or nearby. She doesn't like it, but it must be this way! Who knows when they could strike again? Obviously, someone is after her. She just barely escaped this last event with her life.

~~~~~

It has been touching, the way Stefany fawns over me. She insisted I take a week off, just recuperating. I was running a slight fever, so she made me go to the doctor and get an antibiotic shot. Every evening, she has spent several hours treating my injuries... in between making out with me. Damn, she is a great kisser. Kinda rough, though. It's a wonder I have any hair left; she always seems to be yanking it.

~~~~~

I think Stefany has suddenly discovered she REALLY likes being in control and she likes things rough. Kissing. Sex - judging from our one time. Can't say I ever thought THAT would be her style. Weird. It's like she's evolving, personality-wise. All that change and just from one assignment from Leanne? But whatever, she's hot as hell.

Stefany is the one initiating things. Out of the blue, if we are alone, she will just grab me and kiss me. It's so strange. And exciting. At one point, she took me by the collar and pushed me up against a wall to kiss me. She took me to my room, slammed the door, made out with me a bunch more, and unbuckled my pants for some hands-on fun. I'm still in shock. She said I deserved some "relief" outside of Leanne's plans and it wasn't a violation of the agreement! Mind Blown.

Stefany is like a totally different person now. This whole BDSM adventure and her new attitude... it's a shocking transformation. And it's also fucking HOT. This is like nothing I have ever experienced with a woman. Behind closed doors, she is completely uninhibited with me. I think this is the first time in her life she is doing whatever she wants.

There is something different in Stefany's eyes now. It's hard to explain. It's very sexual, but also needful. And maybe dark? Whatever happened to us in

Assignment 1, for whatever reason, it opened a sexual Pandora's Box for her it seems. I'm impressed with Leanne's psychological theories, that's for sure. It almost makes me want to read some psychology books. Almost.

I love Stefany more than ever.

Constable Fillmore drummed his fingers on the veranda wrought iron table. With him, our meeting consisted of Stefany, me, Leanne - and Miles. "You have been taking precautions?" Fillmore asked. "Not venturing off the estate grounds alone? You are being careful about admittance through the gates and who you meet with?"

"Yes," Stefany and I replied in unison. One of the wait staff brought out iced tea as a cool breeze rustled the table umbrellas. The evening was beautiful with a dramatic, scattered sunset in the west over the mountains.

"Constable, I would like to know who is trying to kill me," Stefany remarked, growing increasingly impatient with the status of the investigation. "Surely, you have some idea."

"Unfortunately, Ms. Michaels," Fillmore began, carefully choosing his words. "We don't have any solid leads. While we think the events are related to the assault at the Mill and the kidnapping, so far, we don't know who may be orchestrating these events. We don't have identification yet for the two men that kidnapped you and we don't know if they were working for someone else, although I think that is highly likely. You should know, if you haven't already surmised, we are a small department. We have limited resources. While we are doing everything we can, our investigation isn't on the same caliber as you may expect in

Canada or the United States. We've asked for assistance from our neighbors, but we can only expect so much."

"So, really? That's the best you can do?" Leanne snapped. "What are they supposed to do, just hope it doesn't happen again?"

"No. Ms. Michaels needs to take the precautions that I've already lined out for her. And Mr. Mobley? You as well, as we are still not sure if you are being actively targeted, which does seem to be the case based on the attack at the Mill Property and the photos left at the scene. However, you could have been targeted there by mere association with Ms. Michaels. We may not ever know for certain."

"Because that attacker is dead," Leanne added.

"Right," Fillmore confirmed with a menacing glare. "Were you aware that before you were the owner here, there have been arson attempts to burn the mansion down?"

"No!" Stefany gasped.

"Yes, several times recently that I know of from the records. They failed, fortunately. Likely disgruntled workers, angry family members. When you assumed ownership of Stoney Brook, Ms. Michaels, you were stepping into a hornet's nest, to be sure. You should realize that, now."

Miles immediately sat his drink down and glared. "I think, Constable, you should further consider the potential of some employee being involved. Look at this bungling idiot," he said, suddenly pointing at me. "For all we know, he orchestrated this whole thing as a means of trying to deceive Stefany. Morgan Mobley is a con artist, everyone knows that."

"Con artist!" I pushed my chair away to stand. This direct afront to my character would require a bloody nose. Soon.

Constable Fillmore held a hand up to symbolically restrain the contention. "Let's just all stop it, right there. Please sit, Mr. Mobley."

I reluctantly complied.

"I'll handle who is on my suspect list, thank you, Mr. Michaels." Fillmore took a deep drag on his cigarette. "Allow me to give you just a brief overview of the situation. Ms. Michaels, your distant cousin that tried to lay a claim to Stoney Brook, Aaron McCaskill, was paroled several months ago, he is residing in Ontario, Canada. We've located some other McCaskill's none too happy with your inheritance and believe they were unjustly disqualified like Aaron. There are three Russian businessmen that contacted you for a proposed purchase of the plantation - we are unable to locate them. There is a group of disgruntled field workers that were dismissed from the plantation before you owned it. There is a degree of resentment by some on the island; people that don't want Stoney Brook to return to prominence, due to the simple fact some of their ancestors were murdered here. There is organized crime on the big island that has their fingers into everything. And most recently, men claiming to be from Australia that ultimately kidnapped you."

Stefany looked increasingly worried. "I had no idea there were so many possibilities."

"Unfortunately, we do have to look at back door engineering for crimes like these. Such as Mr. Michaels suggests. Mr. Mobley, even though you rescued Ms. Michaels, as an investigator, I must look at the possibility that you could be staging these events or working with others. Even though, rest assured, I don't think that is the case."

Miles smirked. "There you go. Something that makes sense."

"What!? That is outrageous," I spewed, barely able to contain myself. "I'm a suspect? I saved her both times, risked my own life, and paid the price this last time with a beating by your cops that threw me in jail! One of them happened to be related to Frenchie, down on the docks!"

"Yes, Mr. Mobley, anyone and everyone can be a suspect," Fillmore said.

My anger suddenly shot through the roof. I felt like lunging across the table and grabbing Miles by his expensive shirt and tie. "And what about this guy here? Her husband, Miles, the newfound resident of the island that is suddenly interested in Stoney Brook? And suddenly he wants to fix his estranged marriage? Have you had a good look at him, Constable? If you want means and motive, there you go, look no farther."

Stefany instantly bristled with my outburst. "Mr. Mobley! That is completely out of line."

"I'll not have my integrity questioned by some half-assed frat boy," Miles seethed angrily.

"Enough. All of you. I am formally requesting that none of you leave this island. Not until I entirely clear you from suspicion. And that's going to be a while."

"But I travel frequently back and forth, here to the mainland for business," Miles complained. "I can't stay here indefinitely!"

"Any of you will make an arrangement with me prior to any needed trips," Fillmore asserted. "Mr. Michaels, I will need to coordinate with you where you are going and when you plan your return. Each time."

"Fine. Just make sure you check out the frat boy here," he added, pointing to me. "Look at his background. As I have, which I make a habit of doing for any employee of mine or Stefany's. He's making quite the name for himself here. His only interest, I believe, is to skim what finances he can out of my somewhat naïve wife. If she'd just admit it, she has already had to fire him once. He's a fraud. Just some loser that never finished college." Miles chafed behind his expensive sunglasses, no doubt staring at me with hatred.

From beneath the table, I felt Leanne's restraining hand against my stomach. She shot a glance at me, letting me know I needed to remain calm.

"Miles, he's not skimming money and he's no fraud," Stefany objected. "He's my employee, not yours, so leave him out of your nasty little witch hunt. Mobley was fired early in his work here out of a misunderstanding."

Miles sat back his chair. "A misunderstanding? Bullshit. His blunders cost you thousands of dollars."

"I can vouch for Morgan," Leanne offered, looking back at me with sympathy. "At least with him, I know who has honest intentions."

"But you can't vouch for me, though, right, Leanne?" Miles asked angrily. "You've never liked me, and you don't have any right to insinuate anything here."

"Who says I'm insinuating? Perhaps I should just say it outright. Eh, Miles?" Leanne said, growing angry.

"As I was going to say," Fillmore added, visibly irritated. He took a long sip of his iced tea and flicked a bug off his arm. "We are on the case and will let you know if we hear something."

"Surely, you have something more you can share with us now?" Stefany proclaimed.

Fillmore took a deep drag off his cigarette. "We recovered the sedan you were taken in, Ms. Michaels. It was a rental. The registry information was all fake and the transaction was in cash. The boat that you were taken in was located on the big island. Again, it was a rental with fake information. That's about it."

"What about fingerprints," I asked. "Items left behind or dropped. Forensic stuff. Anything?"

"We tried lifting prints. There were hundreds of different prints on the rentals. We have some decent complete prints, but they don't match anything in Interpol."

"What about physical descriptions from witnesses?" Leanne added.

"Yeah. We have them. But no one that we can find matches the descriptions. Witnesses don't know who they were. They seem likely to be from outside of the islands. Someone will have to come forward, hopefully, with some new information that can lead us in the right direction."

"That's it!?" I stood, angry that this supposed law enforcement official had made no more progress than this. "You've got nothing! You are no closer to finding out who is behind this than you were the first day we contacted you. Meantime, Stefany could be attacked again at any time! I can tell you; you need to be looking at this prissy asshole right here," I fumed, pointing to Miles. "I'd lay money he is behind all of this." I barely managed to restrain from saying he was physically abusive to Stefany.

"Sit down, you fucking idiot," Miles hissed. And with that, I resolved to beat Miles's ass to within an inch of his life whenever opportunity should arise.

"Mr. Mobley," Stefany began. "I will fire you right now if you don't sit down, close your mouth and control yourself."

Leanne nodded to me, indicating I had crossed the line and should just shut up. I swallowed and complied, somewhat hurt that Stefany would threaten me in such a fashion. I was only worried about her well-being, she had to know. I had been the one to save her from every threat. Why would she protect Miles? He was the obvious suspect in all of this! She seemed to be protecting him, I thought with dismay.

Fillmore stared calmly at me, blowing smoke up into the air. "We continue to build evidence. We continue to interview potential witnesses. We've shared what we know with Interpol as well as with other departments in this region. It's all we can do right now. I can't pull a miracle out of a genie's ass. Island police here make less than what fast-food workers do on the mainland. We are geared more towards finding someone's missing pig or a stolen spare tire. While we will do our best, murder and kidnapping are at the extreme limits of our investigative abilities. I do have investigative experience from back in the United States, but I am only one man. I have a budget that would be less than what is annually spent for cocktails at this place."

Stephanie, by this point, was holding her face in her hands, at least symbolically blocking everything out. Miles had his arm around her and was leaning over whispering encouragement. Seeing this undoubtedly false sympathy, I wanted to throw up. Not to mention it was causing me no small degree of jealousy. I was the one that should be holding her, comforting her.

"Look. Just take the precautions we've already discussed. And Ms. Michaels, I can tell you this," Fillmore continued. "It's a damn good thing you had that GPS device with you. Without that, you would be deep in the Caribbean Sea. Be careful. Keep your head about you." As he finished saying this, he shot a look in my direction.

She ordered me to my knees as I tried to catch my breath. I looked up at her. She was a stunning beauty, I acknowledged to myself, wondering how she seemed to largely hide this fact when out in public. Several bangs of sweaty, errant hair hung down over her eyes. Somehow, Stefany had been hiding all her life in psychological camouflage. Standing in front of me, she radiated sexual power and confidence. Mentally, she was amazing - complicated, but amazing. She was quite simply the most incredible woman I had ever known.

The way she was acting, one wouldn't know she had just barely escaped death after being kidnapped in a case that was still open with no one in custody. Stefany was very good at compartmentalizing her thoughts, I was learning. And when she was with me alone, such as she was now, she focused on making out - and sex. Her transformation was stunning. She didn't want to discuss business, her near scrapes with death, Miles, or anything else that wasn't related to her newfound appreciation of the sexual "lifestyle" Leanne had introduced us to. She was fun... yet intimidating at the same time.

Going from a businesswoman to boss, concerned friend, passionate lover, or strict sexual dom, she could turn her different personalities on and off like flipping a switch, which was startling to a degree. Was this due to her abusive past and emotional damage she had incurred at the hands of men in her life, like Miles? I wondered. Her personality had fractured now, into many different versions of herself that would pop up as the situation she was in may demand. Maybe this is what Leanne had wanted all along of me, to somehow help Stefany find herself? Regardless of how weird our scenario was, I was grateful for my part as Stefany's romantic interest, be it as a sex toy, sex slave, or whatever the case may be.

After getting me off with a hand job that ended with me blowing my load onto her legs, she insisted that I "thank her" for my relief. She kicked her shoes off, peeled off her socks, then slipped out of her shorts and panties.

"Lay down. Flat on the floor." Straddling my head, she sat down and fucked my face with wild abandon, coming as hard as she had in Assignment 1. I could taste her for real this time, with no damned ball gag in the way. She was delicious... and I was ecstatic.

Running her fingers through my hair, she smiled seductively while looking down at me. "Well, I know I feel much better, Mobley. Your tongue is everything I had hoped for. You? You feel better?"

"Yes. Thank you," I managed to mumble from between her thighs against her pussy, as she caught her breath, still sitting full weight.

"You are welcome." Her muscles tensed and she closed her eyes, her body spasming slightly, a lingering remnant of her prior orgasm.

"But what about Leanne," I asked. "We broke the rules, didn't we?"

She patted my cheek. "We didn't go all the way. It's our little secret. And I'm sure she would be thrilled that I can finally sing of the joys of cunnilingus. As for the hand job, it didn't seem right, me having all the fun. Making you wait. I'm not that cruel."

"You have very soft hands. You aren't too cruel."

"Not *yet*," she said, moving to sit back on my chest. We both laughed.

"You weren't really going to fire me again, were you? As you suggested when we were talking with Fillmore?"

She roughly tussled my hair. "Yeah. I would. If you can't keep your mouth shut."

"I rather thought we were past that, and on to a more... stable relationship." I took both her hands, kissing them for emphasis. "Both professionally. And personally."

"We are. But you should know, I have limits. I can't burn the house down around me because you don't know how to control your emotions about Miles."

"It seemed like you were favoring him."

"I was. I think the world of you, Mobley, you are the reason I'm successful. You are some amazing fun that I never even thought possible, but let's be real. Miles can't even get a hint at our relationship. He's bad enough about everything as it is without him suspecting I'm having a BDSM fling with my main employee. He will collect any dirt on me he can. You ran your mouth at the worst time. Unlike just a minute ago, which was the proper way to use your mouth."

Thinking about this, I had to admit she had a valid point. "Fine. I'll strive to be more in control of my emotions. Although I still think he is an asshole beyond compare."

"I agree with you, but there's nothing I can do about him, and he is not granting me a divorce. So, this all needs to be handled delicately. And discreetly. Miles can know nothing of this if you want to continue seeing me. And to continue in Leanne's little sex assignments."

"I do. Yes."

"Mobley, you know, if not for Leanne and her weird ideas, we would never be experiencing this. I wouldn't be having so much incredible fun with you. Who'da thought. I feel so... *alive*."

"I would say you are thoroughly enjoying it. Ms. Stefany." I laughed at the continued forced formality of having to address her as *Ms. Stefany*. I pulled her forward, lifted her shirt, and softly kissed her stomach just below her belly button before returning to the wonderful creamy object of my desire between her legs. She wound her fingers tighter in my hair and moaned softly. "I love pleasing you," I said with my lips against her warm skin.

She soon came again, thoroughly wetting my mouth and face. Falling off me to the side, she trembled with the aftershocks.

"Damn, Mobley. What have I been missing." She stood and extended a hand to me. "C'mon. Get up."

As soon as I regained my feet, she wrapped her arms around my neck and kissed me again. I reciprocated, pulling her tight to me. Finally pushing her hands against my chest, she stepped back and surveyed the slick streaks down her legs. "A man's semen running down my legs. Something else that's new for me. You expect me to walk down the halls and back to my room looking like a large snail has been climbing me?"

"I'll get you a towel."

"Please do. My newfound appreciation of kinky behavior does have some limits."

I went to retrieve a fresh towel from my bathroom.

"Thanks," she said, dabbing it around on her legs. When I get back to my room, I'll shower and wash off any remaining traces of your devotion."

"A touching sentiment."

Looking at me, she dabbed the towel around my face. "Looks like maybe I returned the favor, just for you. You look like you were out in a rain."

"I was. And I loved it," I confessed.

"Did you, now." Swirling the towel, she suddenly whipped it into a rat tail, snapping it just inches from my sore ass.

"Hey! That almost got me! I'm still sore," I objected.

"Oh. You are sore?" She snapped the towel again, this time landing a painful strike directly on my ass.

"Ow!" I immediately began chasing her around the room, to her delighted giggles. Catching her, I threw her onto the bed, covering her with my body. Slipping an arm beneath her neck, we made-out for a few minutes until I felt a hand in my chest.

"Mobley. Get the hell off me. Now." Her stare told me I had violated some form of agreed behavior. I quickly got off. She got up, the expression on her face serious.

"Um. I'm sorry, I shouldn't ha-"

She immediately snapped me in the ass again, making me hop. She laughed jubilantly, having successfully tricked me.

"Owwww! Hey!" I quickly wrapped my arms around her, lifting her off the floor, confining her from any further strikes.

"You are soooo easy, Mobley."

We kissed, hard, yet again. I couldn't get enough of this woman.

"I can't believe how fun you are," she mumbled against my neck, softly biting me.

"I'm looking forward to Assignment 2," I confessed, whispering in her ear. "You think it will be soon?"

"I'm assuming so, knowing the hot, over-sexed mind of Leanne as I do. Now that she has us bound in agreement, she will be wanting to pull the strings and make her puppets dance again. Your back and ass going to be able to handle me, Mobley?"

"I'm okay. But you are going to go... *easier*... on me, right? Please?"

"Because, why? Because I feel soooo *sorry* for you being in such pain?"

"Wait, I'm not asking you to feel sorry for me," I laughed.

"Why then? Because you saved my business? You made me lots of money? Saved my life? Twice? Or should I just go easier on you because I'm a nice, sensible girl?"

"I'm not making any lists," I retorted. "Maybe just ease up using that riding crop? Or cane, or whatever else Leanne may give you. I'd like to be able to walk the next day."

"Eh. We'll see. To be honest, I find I get off on it. Poor Mobley. It seems so... appropriate... for you. I rather like the pathetic whimpering sounds and hard breathing you carry on with when you are in pain."

"I was afraid that you did."

"Oh, I do," she said against my lips.

"I'll up the limits on my life insurance."

"You do that," she giggled, patting me on the cheek. "I will never forget everything you've done for me. However, all those considerations are outside of you being my sex slave... and just aren't part of this game, Mobley."

"Is this a game?"

"In a manner of speaking, I suppose so. A very fun game." Her eyes were radiant with mischief. "You are thinking you've helped Leanne in creating a sexual monster, don't you? I've been let out of my cage. Unleashed. Really appreciating sex for the first time in my life. Horny as fuck." She reached between my legs with her free hand and squeezed me only to discover that I was regaining my appreciation for her. She delicately stroked me several times, her eyes seductively gazing into mine.

"Um. I wouldn't phrase it like *that*, really..."

"Actually, it is rather truthful. But don't worry, Mobley. I'll cause you no permanent damage."

"That's reassuring to know. I think."

She wrapped the towel around my neck, pretending to choke me. I made a fake gagging sound and rolled my eyes, eliciting a laugh from her. Contemplating, she ran a finger over my lips. "Such a gorgeous, handsome mouth. A very talented mouth. When it's not off and about, insolent. I hope to be putting it to proper use, soon."

"Didn't you just put it to proper use?"

"Not enough. Get some pants on. If you recall, in forty minutes we've got the ceremony with the island officials to inaugurate the plantation museum. I'll meet you there." She put her clothes back on, kissed me again, and left.

Having just given a toast in a show of gratitude, Stefany announced a twenty percent pay increase for everyone. Stoney Brook had gone from fourteen employees to over one hundred fifty. They, along with the Island officials, tourists and a good number of locals were in attendance for the evening at the grand opening of the Mill Property.

"I'm not going to lie," Stefany declared, returning to her seat, wiping beads of moisture off her cold drink. "I've lost sleep knowing someone is out to get me. I've had nightmares. Anxiety attacks. But you know what? I'm not going to let it ruin my life."

"You can't just live business as usual, though," Leanne argued.

"No, you are right. We'll take precautions, be careful, Mobley and me. We'll take Fillmore's advice. And hope the island cops figure out who is behind the attacks."

I nodded in silent agreement. Behind us stood the impressive stone and timber beams of the Mill Property, now restored and fully functional, resplendent as a restaurant and inn. It was the grand opening. Musicians regaled the crowd with a lively repertoire on an ancient loading dock which now served as a stage for performing arts. The property's spectacular beach lay only several hundred yards away. A wonderful salty aroma of the ocean hung in the air.

The day before, Stoney Brook hosted a ceremony with island officials and the opening of the Stoney Brook Museum. The event was televised worldwide. The basement museum, now tucked in alongside the racks of wine, was becoming a major draw to the plantation. Opening the pirate cave to tourists was soon to follow.

With the amazing historic attractions of the soon-to-open pirate cave, the museum, and the Mill Property, Stoney Brook was now on the map of top Caribbean tourist destinations. Stefany had every room booked out for over a year.

"That was a nice toast, Cuz," Leanne said, just loud enough to be heard over the music and the raucous, loud crowd. "Now I want to propose a toast of our own." She held her glass up. Stefany, Heidi, Joe, and I, followed her example, hoisting our drinks in the air. "Here's to Stoney Brook Mill!" Our glasses clinked and we each took a drink.

After a few minutes of small talk, Heidi and Joe left the table to go mingle among the crowd.

"Now that we have some privacy, I need an update," Leanne announced. "Are you two still on board with Assignment 2? Stefany? Morgan?"

We answered in unison with a *yes*.

"Do Heidi and Joe know?" Stefany asked.

Leanne looked over at Heidi and Joe, engaged in conversation several tables away. "I haven't told them anything about it. Even if they guessed what is going on, they could care less. Although Heidi may be a bit jealous of you, Morgan, for getting in good with Stefany." She laughed, then considered our expressions carefully. "There hasn't been any… *cheating*… on the terms?"

I looked across at Stefany. We hadn't *really* cheated. Not too bad, at least. A little hand job there, a little taste here, a towel snapped on my sore ass. The nuance of degree would suffice to ease any guilt. "No," I answered for both of us.

Leanne eyed us suspiciously. "Do we need to review any bad behavior that violates our agreement?"

"Leanne, we haven't cheated," Stefany confirmed.

Sipping her drink, Leanne contemplated this, looking for the telltale signs of a lie.

"Yet," Stefany tauntingly added, taking a drink of her Mai Tai.

"Just a few weeks ago, Stef, you could barely tolerate being in the same room with Morgan."

"Yep. True," Stefany admitted.

"Wait, really?" I asked, my feelings a little hurt. "It was that bad?"

Glancing up at the night sky, she smiled. "Relax, Mobley. I've had a change of heart, to be sure."

"And professionally?" Leanne continued. "You two are getting along normally outside of what you are doing behind closed doors?"

"He hasn't let his work suffer if that's what you mean," Stefany answered. "He still treats me respectfully outside of our agreement as he always has, maybe better. No sarcasm or snide remarks. He does what I ask him, and he does what is expected. It's a win-win."

"I was never sarcastic or made snide remarks," I protested.

"Um. *Yes*, you did," Stefany forcefully countered. "Little nasty comments under your breath. Disrespecting me with the staff. Man-whore mongering. Being generally irritating."

"Now wait, I nev-"

"All water under the bridge!" Leanne interrupted, trying to head off the passions of the past that she had inadvertently stirred. "Right?" she asked Stefany.

"Right," Stefany answered sheepishly, visibly ashamed she had relapsed into a moment of Mobley bashing, her once favorite amusement.

"Let's stay focused on what is good in all of this; the fun you two are having." After a moment of silence, she eyed us thoughtfully. "I must say, with this agreement, you both seem much more openminded than I ever imagined possible."

I jumped slightly as Stefany's hand found the crotch of my cargo shorts from beneath the table. I grinned knowing that Leanne was aware.

"Obviously, *despite the past*, he is my knight in shining armor," she replied. "Being with him in these assignments of yours is what has given me a new lease on life. It's what I look forward to. Um. I never thought I would say that," she admitted with a laugh. "I never knew your weird notions could be so fun. Call it an epiphany if you'd like."

"You two have ventured outside the realm of vanilla sex. I'm so proud of you," Leanne jested. "But discretion in public, please?"

Stefany grimaced and withdrew her hand, much to my regret.

Leanne leaned over the table to whisper conspiratorially. "You two are suddenly acting like over-sexed rabbits. One never knows who could be watching around here or anywhere else. In your little naïve and inexperienced minds, you may think you are getting away with something… when in fact you are not. Someone could see you. Like Miles."

"Miles can't just come here and destroy my life," Stefany complained.

"He isn't giving up anytime soon," Leanne said. "So, don't get caught, which would just give him ammunition against you." She considered us carefully. "I had *no* idea it would go this well with you two in these assignments. It almost makes me a little… worried."

"Worried?" I asked. "Why in the world should you be worried?"

"Like with anything. To become addicted to something is usually at the exclusion of other things; other essential parts of life."

Stefany shook her head with disagreement. "Leanne, we aren't excluding anything. Or overdoing this. We are just having fun. That's all."

"Need I remind you that you very nearly skinned Morgan alive with that riding crop?" Leanne smirked. "That is the very definition of overdoing it. Stefany, you have alarmingly shown that you are over-eager to administer pain."

"C'mon, Leanne. I'm not over-eager," Stefany countered. "I'm just learning this whole dom thing. It was probably just the subconscious jealousy. Who'da thought, such a little thing like that crop. It's so small." With a mischievous glint in her eyes, she made a whipping motion over my head.

Leanne took a drink. "I thought about taking it away from you. At least for a while. Until you are better able to control yourself."

"Yesssss," I gloated with a fist pump.

"What? I was just inexperienced," Stefany countered. "Look at him, he's fine now. I'll be easier next time. Right, Mobley?"

During the blazing hot events of the evening of Assignment 1, that riding crop, in Stefany's impassioned hand, had reigned down hell. A hell I wasn't sure I could handle again without skin grafts. She seemed to hold the crop with an uncomfortable degree of reverence. Seeing her enthusiasm, I reluctantly agreed, hoping she would be more moderate. "Um, right."

Leanne sat appraising us for a moment. "I thought I would have to prod you both more; try and get you two out of your shells."

"I finally see what I've been missing all of my life," Stefany explained. "I regret ever passing judgment on you, Leanne, for your weird sexual notions."

Leanne laughed. "You are forgiven, Cuz. Glad I could help."

"So, let's talk about Assignment 2," Stefany suggested, shooting me a seductive smile. "When is it?"

"Soon," Leanne teased.

Stefany sucked a cocktail cherry off a toothpick. "Mobley almost pre-ruined Assignment 2."

"I did no such thing," I countered, immediately knowing what she was talking about. It was my blow up at Miles during the meeting with Fillmore.

Leanne looked puzzled. "Refresh my memory."

"I had to nearly fire him yesterday when we met with Constable Fillmore. His mouth is more suited for some things than others," she said wryly. "Leanne, I'm hoping you will take advantage of that fact as you compose Assignment 2."

"Oh, yes. I think you will be pleased," Leanne confirmed with a laugh. "But I can make a few adjustments to better honor your request."

"Wait," I said. "Don't I get to make some requests?"

"No," both women answered together. Seeing and hearing Leanne and Stefany talk about sex so freely was leaving me with an uncomfortable, raging hard-on.

I leaned across the table to whisper. "I sorta thought I might play a more active role. Soon."

Stefany sat back and eyed me. "You mean, when will you get to fuck me?"

I was taken aback by her explicit question. Things had certainly changed. Seeing my expression, she laughed. "Maybe you won't, Mobley. I'm the dom, after all. Maybe I'm going to fuck you. Like, with one of those big black strap-ons. Pegging, I think it's called?"

"Now wait a minute! I never agreed to that sort of thing!" Surely, they were joking. "She's just kidding, right, Leanne?"

Leanne balked at this momentarily. "Eh. We'll see what's in the cards for you."

Panic began to set in. "I said I would do about anything. But not that, come on."

Stefany whacked my chest, laughing. "Relax. Yes, I was just kidding. Sort of."

I sunk back into my chair; my fears only slightly relieved. "Look. Leanne," I began, fidgeting with a drink coaster. "These initial assignments you are giving out. We have to follow them to the letter?"

"Yes. For a while," Leanne declared.

"Why, you have other ideas, Mobley?" Stefany cooed. "Let me guess. Afraid of the crop?"

"Um. No, it's not that," I answered, even though it certainly was. "I am just not used to having such matters laid out in a strict sequence of events and controlled like this. And I have a request. Of sorts."

Leanne smiled broadly. Amused, Stefany purposefully turned in her chair to look at me. "Please share."

"I know that BDSM people wear different types of outfits during sex. Leather, latex, that sort of thing."

"Sometimes. What's your point?" Leanne asked calmly.

"I would like to request that I don't have to wear any of that stuff. Those weird straps, or leather things. Plastic pants. No fruity, fluffy tutus. If that's what you are planning. Please, no. Just normal clothes, okay?" The request may not have been well phrased, but I hoped that it was well-received.

"I'd like to see him in a cocktail dress," Stefany blurted. "I would like to request that."

"No!" I exclaimed to Stefany's laughter.

"We aren't doing anything too weird," Leanne affirmed, rolling her eyes. "Even I'm not a big fan of dominatrix costumes. Anything else, you two?"

"I think that covers it," I confirmed, meeting Stefany's knowing gaze with my own, wanting her right there.

Beneath the table, I took one of Stefany's hands, risking a reprisal from Leanne. Her fingers softly enclosed around mine. Glancing around to first ensure no one was observing, I raised her hand to my lips, kissing it. "I will do anything for you, Stefany." Short of telling her how madly in love I was with her, it was all I could do.

"Awwww," Leanne crooned. "He really is so very sweet."

Stefany rested her head on her free arm, appraising me from the corners of her eyes with humor. "Anything? I'm touched."

"Yes. Anything."

"Did you hear that, Leanne. He said *anything*."

"Yes, I heard," she confirmed. "I'll start working on the revised Assignment 2 script."

Stefany smiled roguishly, her white teeth gleaming. "Hot wax it is. On your balls."

Leanne choked and dribbled some of her drink onto her shirt.

Stefany: Things are heating up with Mobley. I never thought I would write THOSE words.

He's been wanting to tell me something, I can tell it's just on the tip of his tongue. I'm just hoping he keeps a lid on it. As Leanne has

told me before, she thinks it's the "L" word. Whatever. While I do like him, I'm in this for fun, not love. I have convinced myself of this quite thoroughly. So, I won't dwell on it.

I've read Leanne's zany BDSM book. It's interesting to see what she has been

picking and choosing for Mobley and me. There are quite a few things I want to try. What has happened to me? I've become a sex maniac.

~~~~~~

I've begun reading several other books. Some erotica novels, stuff like that. Leanne probably thinks I've gone insane, in taking such a liking to her assignments. The thing is, I imagine that Mobley is the only man on the planet I would ever do these things with. It just seems so "doable" with him. Hard to explain. It's comfort, attraction, lust, friendship, just getting off on beating his ass. A lot of it has to do with his personality. I get off on the fact it is Mobley... and I'm in charge.

To make things look legit with the staff and not to raise suspicions, we decided to stay in separate bungalows at the Mill Property. It was my first overnight visit to this amazing place. Mobley and his crew have done a fantastic job renovating and updating the place.

I looked at my watch. It read 7:00 PM. Sitting in a much too revealing miniskirt, I bobbed my foot from crossed legs, barely able to contain the anticipation. Leanne had gone over the details of Assignment 2, and I was excited to the point I could see my heart visibly beating beneath my shirt. I was startled to hear the knock on the bungalow door, even though I was expecting it. Opening the door, my guest stood on the stoop with a handful of tropical flowers, his favorite way to meet me, which he offered with a smile.

Taking them, I inhaled them deeply, then invited him in before anyone might notice.

"These are beautiful, Mobley. Thank you."

"Beautiful flowers, for the most beautiful woman in the world."

I swung my arms around his neck and kissed him, passions pent up to the breaking point. It was finally Assignment 2 and we had waited long enough.

Morgan was undoubtedly a great kisser. Every occasion I had kissed him, he never left me anything but thrilled despite my early opinions of him. Kissing Miles was like tonguing a cold oyster on the half-shell. Kissing Morgan was a hot, evening bonfire on a tropical beach.

His fingers wound their way through my hair. I softly bit his lower lip. He ground uncontrollably against me, and I reciprocated. Already, it was hot, sensual - needy.

"You think I have changed, don't you?" I asked breathlessly, breaking away from his amazing lips.

"Have you?"

"Yes."

His gorgeous blue eyes wandered through my soul, making me wonder if I could feel more towards him than I had previously accepted as true. "You are... confident," he said. "You are taking from life what you want, rather than letting life take from you."

"An astute observation." My fingers on the back of his head tightened in his blond locks, pulling his head back, allowing me to softly kiss his neck. Mobley was the only man in my life that had allowed me the freedom to find out who I was... to discover passion and sensuality. Mobley had given to me the greatest gift - confidence.

"You know what I think, Mobley?"

"What?"

"You make me want to live."

Telling him what to do and commanding him didn't seem weird anymore. With him, it felt natural and fun. It was an amazing feeling that I'm not sure I could share with any other man. He allowed me to have power. No one had ever done that. And I feasted on this new energy. Mobley was the apex of my newfound sexual freedom.

My mouth found his again, our breathing heavier, more urgent. After a long period of enjoying him, I broke away, circling him, admiring what would be mine for the evening. My hands roamed his body, over his chest, across his stomach, over his muscular ass. I softly squeezed him between his legs, seeing that he was as excited as me.

"You have the look of a predator," he remarked jovially.

"I am, Mobley."

"I'm yours. Use me as you please," he teased.

I smiled disarmingly while pushing a finger up against his chin, which had the intended effect of making him somewhat uncomfortable. "You should know, I plan to do just that this evening. Hard." His expression turned somber as my hands caressed his jawline and neck. "I've very much looked forward to this."

"Me too."

"It's such a turn on, knowing you are so willing to be my sexual plaything." Undoing his belt, I whipped it from his slacks evoking laughter from us both. He watched, amused as I slipped it around his neck. Leanne had given me a regular collar and clip-on leash, but it had a shag carpet, lounge lizard aura about it. A thick leather belt was much more to my liking, to the point and genuine. I put the end through the buckle and tightened it, almost to the point of discomfort. I gave it a precursory tug. "Yes. That'll do. Get on your knees."

Perhaps surprised that Assignment 2 was proceeding without delay, he obeyed, dropping to his knees.

"I suppose you want a rundown of events tonight. What Leanne has in mind for us?"

"Yes, I would like that," he admitted.

"Too bad. You'll just have to be surprised." My top was as short as my skirt, exposing my midriff. I roughly pulled his leash, forcing his face up against my bare stomach. "Is this what you want, Mobley?" Adrenaline was already coursing through my veins, and we hadn't even started yet.

"Yes."

"As much as I do?"

"Yes."

"I'm glad to hear that. Because I'm going to put you through your paces tonight."

Keeping his leash taut, I ran the fingers of my free hand through his blond hair. His mouth brushed across my belly button, his breath hot against my skin. He was being reserved, waiting for my cues. I never thought of Leanne's assignments as training - yet they were. Mobley was allowing me to go in whatever direction I wanted. It was exhilarating.

"Kiss me, Mobley. It's one of the few times I'll let you use your hands this evening."

Holding me by the backs of my legs, he brushed his handsome mouth across my stomach in a flurry of soft kisses. Growing bolder, he lifted my skirt and leaned down, kissing the insides of my thighs. I pulled him tighter to me with the belt leash, and I threw one leg over his shoulder. His mouth found the cotton panties at the juncture between my legs, nearly making me want to explode all plans for the evening and just let him do his thing. It was early in the evening, and I had to take my bites of Mobley in small portions and make him last. In Assignment 1, I had never actually enjoyed Mobley's mouth directly on me. Breaking the rules, that was a treat I later enjoyed in his room, riding his face after a hand job. His tongue had been amazing, and I wanted more. But that had to wait. There was a method to Leanne's madness, and I reluctantly decided to abide by her instructions. I took a deep breath and pushed his face away.

"That's good… for now." I pulled him to his feet. He was every bit engulfed in the sexual flames of the moment as

I was. Letting him loose, I walked to the nearest chair and sat down, leaving him puzzled and wondering what he should do. His cock was a conspicuous bulge in his slacks now and he was no doubt miserable in a good way. He started towards me, and I held up a restraining hand to keep him in the middle of the room. "No, stand right there. Strip. Get your clothes off. Slowly. So I can watch."

He obliged, peeling off each item of clothing until he was only wearing his belt leash. Morgan Mobley, both cute and handsome at the same time, was a sculpture of a man, there was no doubt about that. I sat back, admiring his naked form for a while, keeping him guessing. It wasn't odd anymore, now that we had seen each other naked in the most intimate of ways. He had literally seen every inch of me in Assignment 1. Yet I still felt I was discovering who Mobley was. And I savored memorizing every delicious inch of his body.

"Come here," I told him. "On your knees in front of me. And hand me your leash."

He complied, his expression eager and anticipating. "Get started. You know the drill. Start at my feet, work your way up. And down."

He pulled off my shoes and began with tiny kisses on each of my toes. Showing good patience, he took his time. Using his tongue, he wound his way around my feet and legs with little wet trails. I leaned back in blissful enjoyment. If not for the highly charged erotic element of what he was doing, I could fall asleep.

"So, Mobley. You recall the pull-up bar I had in my living room? It was positioned in a closet door as part of my workout regimen. I do pull-ups on it whenever I get the notion. I don't use it as often as I'd like, I admit."

"Um. I don't think I ever noticed it. My attention was on something much more pleasant and amazing to look at."

"Why, Mobley. Are you trying to flatter me?"

"I'm just speaking the truth. Ms. Stefany," he mumbled against the sole of my left foot.

400

In learning to look past the Man-Whore persona, I had discovered there was a very adorable side to Mobley that I never imagined existed. He was submissive to me in this fun, sexual adventure, yet he was more of a man than any I had known. I leaned forward, pulled his head up and kissed him.

"Damn, you are so sweet; you could give me pause to ease up on whipping your ass."

"Ah, I'm glad you want to ease up some." He raised his eyebrows hopefully. "You are planning on easing up? Right?"

Letting him try to find the answer in my eyes, he looked slightly worried. Playfully pulling his leash, I again brought his face close to mine. "Back to the pull-up bar. Look over there in the entryway to the kitchenette."

Puzzled, he noticed my pull-up bar, neatly positioned high in the entryway. "Oh! You brought your pull-up bar. That's dedication, for sure. Good idea."

"I didn't bring it for me."

He cocked his head inquisitively. "Um. You want me to do pull-ups?"

"You are ruining my previous estimates of your intelligence level, Mobley. Really." I got up and walked to a nearby chest of drawers to pull out a shoebox of neatly wrapped cotton rope sections. The pieces were soft and forgiving, yet capable of strong restraint. "Leanne gave me these for Assignment 2." I nearly laughed as the reality dawned on his face. "Over you go. Under the pull-up bar."

He looked at it intently, trying to determine what purpose it could possibly serve in any kinky plan. "Okaaaay. I don't see what we can possibly do with that. And I thought I was imaginative!"

"Maybe we will *jump start* your imagination."

"I thought Leanne would have something more challenging, to tell you the truth," Mobley commented.

"That's good to know, Mobley." Moving him in a position directly beneath the bar, I first tied his wrists together. Then brought the long trailing end down and tied his ankles and back up for several loops just above his knees, effectively immobilizing him. I hooked my foot under a small step stool that sat next to the entryway for guests to use to reach the upper cupboards of the kitchenette. I pulled it over, next to Mobley.

"Well, this is different," he happily remarked. Something in his voice exposed a degree of skepticism for Leanne's idea.

"Yes. It is. It took several lessons, but Leanne was eventually able to show me how this works." I took an additional section of rope, ran it under both of his arms. I chuckled to myself, eager to dash yet another level of Mobley's ego to pieces. After several loops, I took the double end and ran it beneath his legs. This configuration of rope went down on either side of his cock and then back up the crack of his ass to be secured across the shoulders. With plenty of slack remaining, I tied him together at the elbows. He was now bound securely in a net of rope.

"Stand on your tiptoes," I told him. He raised his heels slightly. "Mobley. Quit trying to chump me and get the hell up on your tiptoes. Up! Waaaay up." He gave a better effort, standing much higher up on his toes. I then brought the trailing end up, pulled it tightly. Stepping up on the stool, I secured the two ends of the rope firmly to the pull-up bar.

Now face to face, I took the opportunity to kiss my way up and down his neck several times. "You taste good," I said huskily against his skin. Momentarily satisfied, I stepped down to admire my work.

Bound and immobile, he could do nothing but stand in the entryway. His arms were pulled back and drawn up by the bar and would keep him well behaved. With a good degree of his weight supported by the pull-up bar, he could turn and twist at the most. Any attempt to drop down from his toes and the rope would draw painfully around his balls and up through his ass crack. Trying not to laugh, I had to give Leanne credit for creativity. In an emergency, if he struggled for all he was worth, he could eventually dislodge the pull-up bar. Maybe. But it would cost him a serious rope wedgie.

"Mmmm. You do look good, Mobley. You have a stylish belt leash." I gave his leash a small tug. "Ankles, legs, and arms tied. Looks like you are all dressed up and nowhere to go." I laughed at my own joke. "You are all mine, tonight." Encircling him, I allowed my fingers to roam over his body. I stopped occasionally, slow kissing his chest, his arms, and his back. He was hard.

"As I learned in Assignment 1 and later in your room, you are very well endowed, I must say. More so than any of my men before. My, my. Nice," I cooed. "Seven and a half? Eight? And as big as my wrist. Nice package, indeed." Barely contacting his skin, I ran several fingers against the ropes that were climbing up his ass. It evidently tickled and he shuddered, struggling to maintain his balance on his toes. He would be getting tired standing like that, yet there would be no drooping for fear of the nuclear wedgie. Ever so lightly, I drug a fingernail along the full length of his erection. Recalling some of the things I learned in my research, his slight involuntary forward thrusts told me he was in a good place sexually and mentally.

"Does that feel good?"

"Oh, damn, yes," he mumbled. "Yessss."

"You want more?"

"Ohhh yes! Please, yes."

I gripped his erection firmly, and slowly stroked the full length, as I found he liked when I jacked him off back in his room. He moaned softly, and his eyes were closed in ecstasy. "Just think, Mobley. Imagine what it must feel like to have my mouth on you. Or get you balls deep into my pussy."

"Please! I want it soooooo bad," he begged, all hints at dignity now vanquished. "Please, please."

"I like your enthusiasm. We'll see how things go tonight." I played with him a few minutes more, noticing his increasing struggles to stay on his toes. Yet his cock looked as though it were on a hair-trigger. I placed my finger on a clear drop of fluid that had formed on the tip of his cock. Moving my finger away, it drew out into a tiny, clear string. Yep, he was excited.

"Um. I've heard about using rope in BDSM, of course," Mobley innocently commented, entirely unaware of what the immediate future held for him. "While this is interesting, I fail to see what possible use we could have for this arrangement. Perhaps we should... try something else? Somewhere else? Um, right? Ms. Stefany? This is a bit uncomfortable between my legs. I'm rather drawn up... by this rope."

"I don't think so." I could see right through him with his poorly disguised attempt to move the activities to a favorable change of venue. He was hilarious, I was learning, whenever he tried to be tricky or deceitful.

"What? Please. It really is getting... rather difficult... to stand here." Several beads of sweat were now forming on his forehead and his temples. Perfect.

I walked back to my drawer of supplies. Twisting on the rope and craning his neck, Mobley tried to turn and see what I was doing. Just out his vision, he struggled to see. "What's that you have there? What did you get?"

"Quit talking, Mobley," I admonished. "You yap way too much. We are going to have to work on that." I returned, approaching him from his back with what I had retrieved from the drawer.

Mobley, his frame cast in warm hues by the lighting of the lamps in the room, was an impressive male specimen, tall and muscular. Mounting the step stool, I gazed into his beautiful eyes, face to face, still hiding the object behind my back. I stood in close to him, grabbed his hair with my free hand and roughly pulled him into a kiss. He relaxed after a moment and his own passion fueled the kiss. Our tongues mutually explored, each of us breathing harder with anticipation.

WHAP!

"Mmmmppppphhhh!" Mobley lurched against me in the middle of our kiss, surprised by the strike of the crop I landed on his bare ass. "Owww!" He blinked, attempting to process what was no doubt a sharp pain across his left ass cheek. "You brought the riding crop?! I thought you were going to go easy on me!"

"I'm going to go easy-*er* on you. Pick up on the nuance there, Mobley. I enjoy this far too much to leave it out of our fun time."

"But I thought Leanne was going to take it away?! For a while!"

"She left it to my discretion after I agreed I wouldn't abuse it any further. So here it is. And your brief, harmless pain brings me... *pleasure*. So, tell me what you want."

"What I want?" Mobley exclaimed. "I want you to put that damned crop away, that's what the hell I want!"

WHAP! WHAP!

"Aghhhhh!" Mobley jerked and squirmed against the ropes. "Ohhh, son of a..."

"Evidently, you aren't getting the message here. Get used to the crop. As I said, it gives me pleasure. So again. Tell me what you want." My hand made its way to his hard cock which was suffering no loss of enthusiasm with my questioning. I stroked him with purpose, the alternating stick and carrot technique confusing him.

He blinked, searching my eyes for the correct answer. He was in the middle of both passion and pain. His expression betrayed a mix of newly discovered sensations within himself. I softly kissed him to give him encouragement.

His eyebrows raised with a new possibility. "I want... you to... *please*... put the crop away? And... quit spanking my ass? Ms. Stefany."

WHAP! WHAP! WHAP!

"AGHHhhhhhhh! My gawwwd! Oh, holy mutha..."

While he languished in this new agony, I twisted him around to where I could see his ass. Several angry red streaks were dashed across his amazing muscular cheeks. It was minor league so far, no antibiotic salve needed. "Let's try again," I suggested, returning him to face me. I moved in close to his ear to whisper. "You can do this. I have full faith in you, so listen to me carefully. It brings me pleasure. Sooooo. What do you want?" I bit the lobe of his ear gently and kissed his cheek.

"I *want*... you to use the crop. Because it brings you pleasure. And... I would do anything for you."

I pressed my nose to his and smiled. "There! See, you do get this, Mobley!" I kissed him, our lips a maddening union of lust. "The last part was very sweet. I wasn't expecting that," I said against his lips.

"I mean it," he whispered back. "Some of this may take some getting used to. But I would do anything for you. Anything."

This reignited our kiss. His oath of dedication to me was so heart wrenching, I almost wanted to melt all over him. Half-hanging, half-standing there, tied up, completely at my mercy, totally naked - he was adorable. Considering the one emotion that seemed to have betrayed or eluded me in life, I wondered if I could unknowingly love him in secret. While it was a remote possibility, it did nothing, however, to lessen my desire to use the riding crop.

The crop was my wonderful newfound toy. I loved how it felt in my hand. I loved the little threatening and somewhat military whapping sound it made against my leg. It would be meeting with Mobley's arrogant, albeit wonderful ass, whenever the occasion might warrant. If he thought being sweet to me would save him welts on his ass, and anywhere else I deemed appropriate during these assignments, he better think again.

With both arms around his neck, crop dangling in one hand, we kissed until I could feel him beginning to falter. His legs were cramping, and he was not able to stay on his toes as high. The result, of course, was the initial pangs of the atomic wedgie. As I gazed into his eyes, his expression became one of silent pleading. He wanted to say something but was holding his tongue. A real trooper.

Rubbing the end of the riding crop across his back, he flinched several times in anticipation of my strike. The crop tip gently glided down his body to his cramping legs. I didn't hit him, although he was surely expecting it, judging by his stiffening reactions. "Do you trust me, Mobley?"

"Yes."

"Completely?"

"Yes."

With this, I returned to my desk drawer of toys to retrieve a blindfold. Climbing back up atop the stepstool, I then wrapped it around his eyes and tied it at the back of his head.

"How's that," I asked. "Can you see anything?"

"It's fine. I can't see anything." He hesitated. "What… what are you going to do?"

His question was so fraught with fear I had to laugh. Ignoring him, I reached between my legs and moved the thin strip of my panties to one side. This next move was reminiscent of what Heidi had tried with me, so perhaps it was a Leanne trademark, I thought with humor. I was juiced. Wet, slippery, and sticky would be a suitable description. Dipping a finger inside me, I curved it upward and withdrew. That sensation alone almost threw me into an orgasm. I placed this same finger tenderly on his lips, glazing them. He figured out rather quickly what I had done, sucking my finger clean despite the fact he was in agony.

"How do I taste?" I asked suggestively.

"Like a crisp ocean beach on a cool morning. Please, give me more." Despite his request, his face grimaced in pain. He was reaching the end of his endurance and I would need to get this show on the road soon.

"What do you want, Mobley?" I asked, wondering where that question would lead him.

"I want more. I want you to feed me. I want to suck and lick you to get every drop. I want you to come in my mouth, over and over."

Now using two fingers, I got them slick. I needed relief so bad I was near the point of explosion. I held my fingers near his lips, barely touching him, taunting him, making him lean towards them despite his discomfort, but keeping him from sucking them into his mouth. Instead, I wiped the glistening reward across my own lips.

"You can have it off my lips this time." I kissed him, letting him consume me. As he did so, I repeated the process, bringing my fingers up to wedge them between our kiss. We both sucked and played our tongues in and around my glistening fingers.

"Ms. Stefany, please. I want to dine between your beautiful legs for hours, drinking you up. They are the twin columns into the cathedral in which I want to worship. Let me worship you."

I was in awe, if not outright impressed with his ability to fashion a corny line. I would try and remember that later.

Hopping off the stool, I kicked it to the side. Moving in behind him, I untied the release ropes, freeing Mobley from the pull-up bar.

He tried to stand but his legs gave out and he dropped to his knees. "Sorry," he said, breathing hard. "That was a lot harder to do than I thought. But a hell of a lot of fun."

"Indeed, it was," I agreed. Leaning down, I kissed him on the side of his mouth. Beginning the task of untying the ropes, I paused midway through to rub his shoulders and chest. Once free of the ropes, I pulled him to his feet. "Come on. You aren't out of the woods yet, as far as getting tied up goes. But at least next you can lay on the bed." Still blindfolded, I had to nearly drag him to the bed. I then went into the kitchenette, returning to give him a cold glass of water. "You okay? Need a break?" To ask was proper according to Leanne. I didn't want to kill him, after all.

He swilled the water down. "I'm fine. Can I take the blindfold off now?"

"No, that is staying on. Lay down in the middle of the bed," I ordered without explanation. "Arms out, legs spread."

Mobley did as I asked. He was still quite hard, I noted. After retrieving the ropes from our previous play session, I began the task of tying his hands and feet to all four corners of the bed.

"What if I have to pee?" he asked suddenly.

"Um. Do you have to pee, Mobley?" I asked, exasperated. "That should have been covered when I asked you if you were *okay*."

"Yes. Sorry, need to pee. Can you take off the blindfold now?"

"No. I'll escort you." I reluctantly untied what I had begun with the ropes and helped him get off the bed.

"But. I don't want you to see me pee."

"Oh, gawd, Mobley. Here you are naked, I've seen every inch of you, as have half of the female residents of the island, surely. I've even seen you ejaculate back in your room at Stoney Brook. And now, suddenly, you are a modest man? About peeing, of all things?"

"Well. I would really rather you not see me."

I shook my head in disbelief. "Fine. Come along." Grabbing him by the arm, I led him to the bathroom and indicated where the toilet was. "Here it is. Feel it?" I directed his hand toward the toilet seat. Sink is to the right. Door behind you." Stepping out, I closed the door behind me and went to sit on the bed to wait, thinking maybe I should have just taken the blindfold off for this interruption.

After a minute of hearing what sounded like the Fountains of Paris, the toilet flushed, then more sounds of him knocking about as he washed his hands. Mobley was apparently a germaphobe, which didn't bode well for him, considering some of our play activities. The door opened, and he walked out, hands in front in the style of a mummy, fresh out of the crypt and nowhere to go. Before I could reach him, he tripped over the leg of the nearby sofa table. Destroying the table, both he and a lamp went crashing to the floor.

"Mobley! Are you all right?" I asked, running over to him.

"Oh. I guess I misjudged the direction to the bed. Yes, I'm fine. But I think I broke something."

Pulling him to his feet, I began picking off the pieces of ceramic that were stuck to his skin. "Yes, you broke the end table and the lamp. I was coming to get you!"

"Oh. Lessons learned, eh? Sorry about that stuff I broke."

"Right. Well, follow me, the bed is over here." Guiding him back to the bed, he returned to his sprawled position. I laughed quietly, seeing he was now limp as a noodle. It was going to take some work to return to the flash fire state we were just in prior to the peeing episode.

"What's funny?" he asked, his head angled towards where he estimated I was standing.

"The welts I'm going to put on your ass for breaking my stuff," I joked, returning to the task of tying him down.

"What?" he asked with growing alarm. "I said I was sorry. You are going to crop me for that?"

"The correct question would better be, am I going to crop you *more* for that." Hiding my intent in a serious, stern voice, he evidently could not detect I was enjoying this immensely.

"And... are you?" The trepidation in his voice was real, and I loved it.

Pulling the last knot tight, Mobley was securely immobilized and drawn out, spread eagle on the bed. Grabbing him roughly by the jaw, I squeezed. "Yes. I am. But since you are laying on your ass, your legs and stomach will serve nicely for the reminders I am going to give you to listen to me and not wreck my room."

"Oh." It was the only shaky response he could come up with, evidently. Covering my mouth, I restrained a snicker.

With Mobley secured to the bed, he could wait. I went about the task of cleaning up the mess he had made with the lamp and table. Finding a broom and dustpan in the kitchenette, I began sweeping everything up and getting it in the refuse container. It wouldn't be pleasant to step barefoot on a broken piece of ceramic.

"Where did you go?" Mobley asked from the bed.

"Cleaning up the federal disaster you created," I answered from across the room.

"Are you just going to leave me here?"

"Mobley. I may leave you there for hours. I may run some errands. Take a short stroll over to the bar for a drink. It's my decision. You'll never know when I may come back. Good thing you went pee, huh? Hopefully, there aren't any more pressing concerns by nature for a while." This jab was pure gold, and I could imagine the concerned expression he was painting from beneath the blindfold. He made several exploratory tugs on the rope to no avail.

"Wait... I... um. Hours?! Ms. Stefany? Please. I'm not sure-"

"Shhh! Quiet. The more you complain, the longer I will leave you laying like that."

"But I thought we were-"

"Shhhh!"

Finishing cleaning, several ideas popped into my head, and I began to savor further teasing Mobley. These fun adventures didn't have to be entirely about sex! I congratulated myself silently for having such a devious mind. Clicking on the television, I began scrolling through the channels for something good. *House Plants with Fran*, a two-hour special. Perfect. I turned up the volume to a decent level.

Retrieving a juice drink with a straw and a bag of tortilla chips from the kitchenette, I returned to the couch and kicked my feet up on the coffee table. Crunching the chips loudly in my mouth, I added an occasional loud slurp of juice. Mobley began impatiently tapping the seconds off with a tightly bound foot. I picked up my book I brought for the trip and began reading where I left off, with no intention of listening to Fran describe how to clean the leaves of a *Ficus elastica*.

Several chapters into my book, Mobley began trying to gain my attention with rather loud sighing noises, which weren't going to work, of course.

After a few more minutes, Mobley looked as though he were going to expire from boredom. Snapping my book closed loudly, I clicked off Fran's rambling diatribe on proper misting and casually made my way noisily to the front door. I opened it. I closed it. Then silently tip-toed my way over by the bed to sit in the nearby chair and enjoy the results of my newfound sadistic side.

"Um. Ms. Stefany? Are you there?" Mobley finally asked after several minutes. It would be hard for him to find any answer in the steady hum of the overhead ceiling fan.

"Shit," he finally exclaimed. "I can't believe she just fucking left me like this. Fuck."

Restless, he tossed and twisted a few minutes more. "What the hell am I supposed to do now?!" he asked himself. "This might take fucking hours. God damn it."

It was all I could do to keep silent and somehow restrain my urge to laugh. Mobley talking aloud to himself was a new revelation.

"Well. At least I peed," he commented thoughtfully. "*That* could have been bad. Have her come back here… and finding pee all over the bed. Holy crap, it's a good thing I don't need to dial up number two. Now *that* would be embarrassing." He laughed at this, then rolled his head side to side, bored. "She may damn well skin my fucking hide off with that riding crop when she gets back." He sighed loudly.

This served a good reminder, and I silently got up to retrieve my favorite toy which I had left in the kitchenette. Standing by the bed with my crop in hand, I waited for a select moment.

"Damn it! C'mon, Stefany, shit. C'monnnnnnnn."

That would be it, I determined. I aimed for a particularly sensitive portion of his stomach, atop a nice, shapely, abdominal muscle.

WHAP!

"Aghhhhhhhh!" Mobley nearly elevated the entire bed with the surprised jolt he gave. "Holy shit! I didn't think you were here!"

Climbing onto the bed, I straddled his chest and sat. I caressed his face with the riding crop. "I see that."

"You... um... were here the whole time?" he asked nervously.

"Yep."

"You listened to everything I said?"

"Yeah. And you are right, you better be glad you didn't pee on my bed."

These revelations were turning around in his head, no doubt, and he remained silent as I ran the crop over his cheeks and lips.

"My, my," I said. "Such a filthy, insolent mouth. But I've got something I think will help with that," I suggested.

"What?" While he was trying to hide it, again there was unmistakable fear in his voice. Looking back over my shoulder, I could see a nice red welt was forming over his stomach.

"I have dinner for you tonight, Mobley," I revealed, still softly caressing his face with the crop. "I know you are probably getting hungry. Right?" I patted his cheek with a little more force than might be expected from a tender touch.

"Er. Yes. I am. That would be... great."

He truly thought I was going to make dinner for him, the dolt. I stood up, still straddling his chest. "It won't take long to prepare." With this, I slid my panties off and dropped them onto his face with my foot.

"Is that... is that your panties?" he asked through the fabric.

"Yeah," I said, now shedding my skirt and peeling off my top. "An appetizer." Slipping my right foot through the

413

panties, I pushed them roughly over his mouth and nose, rubbing them over his face.

"Is it good?" I asked. I was now completely naked, not that he could see. "Smell good?"

"Oh. Yesss," he answered enthusiastically. It hadn't taken Mobley long to get back into action.

The crotch portion of my panties was slick with a thick, wet streak of my cum, a result of excitement from our previous activities. Positioning myself with my hands against the backboard wall for support and using my toes, I pushed the soaked crotch into his mouth. "There you go. Your appetizer. Suck it clean, Mobley. Thoroughly." As he worked, I added an occasional toe into his mouth for fun. Once again, his cock was hard as a rock.

We played like this to the point his whole face became a wet mess. Finally satisfied he had cleaned them well, I slung the panties off to the floor. Alternating feet, I slid them across his face, enjoying the sloppy wet, tickly sensations. "Tongue out, Mobley," I ordered, letting him finish his appetizer while lapping my soles.

It was time for dinner, I finally determined, seeing we were both now ramped up and again eager. Dropping to a kneeling position onto his shoulders, I lowered myself, my pussy now just a breath away from his handsome, needy mouth. He intuitively ascertained what I was doing, craning his neck to taste me, yet I denied him, momentarily fighting my own needs.

WHAP!

"Aughhhh!" The strike of the crop across one of his legs surprised him and made him jolt and pull against the rope restraints. I did it just because - and offered no explanation. I considered it progress that he didn't ask - a little pain for my pleasure.

"Did you like your appetizer, Mobley?"

"Yessss."

"And you are ready for dinner?"

"Yesss, please," he pleaded. He had been tormented and teased all evening and he was putty in my hands at this point.

I slipped off his blindfold, letting him finally see. "What do you want?" I asked, a repeat of my previous question he had now come accustomed to hearing.

"I want to worship you. Please. I want you to come repeatedly on my tongue, in my mouth, on my face. Please."

"Wish granted."

His face was already wet, but he was going to get a refresher directly from the source. Never in my life did I think of myself as a woman that got overly wet. My assignments with Mobley had changed that thinking. Over the past several weeks, rare was an evening that I didn't peel off my panties to find them soaked and sticky. Simply thinking about Mobley was enough to slick my panties. Each time I got off on his mouth, I discovered I was giving him my version of a torrential downpour.

I laid the crop to the side and ran my fingers through his hair, softly, playfully at first before culminating into a tight fist. It had to be mildly painful, yet he offered no complaint. Spreading my pussy with the fingers of my freehand, I lowered myself the remaining few inches onto his mouth, effectively sitting on his face. Finally, I had Mobley's mouth again, skin on skin, servicing away. It was blissful and erotic as hell, enjoyable as I had remembered from our first time with him doing this.

Prior to the *new me*, I would have been worried about smothering him too hard with such a position. Oddly, with renewed confidence in myself, that was no longer a concern. He could handle it, I told myself. While he could breathe through his nose when it wasn't smashed against my clit, the panting noises he was making indicated he was struggling. I ground in a slow rhythm, lifting occasionally on the upstroke, letting him gasp for breath between the cheeks of my ass.

"Tongue out. All the way," I instructed. "I want it in deep."

His struggle to breathe only excited me more, I discovered. The air in and out of his lungs was oddly cool against my wet skin. Leaning back on my free arm, my hips found a slow, curving, thrusting rhythm as my thighs flexed around his head, fucking his tongue, alternating it into my pussy then into my ass. The scene reminded me of a movie I had watched once, where a woman slowly and sensuously rode a mechanical bull.

I simply couldn't wait and in the span of a few minutes, my impatience and greed won out. I needed to come. Bad. The evening was young, and I could enjoy Mobley as long as I could take him. With increased urgency, I ground his face faster. What built up in my loins was an intensity perhaps even greater than in Assignment 1 or in his room when I had stroked him off.

Mobley worked hard for me, lapping, licking, sucking, using his mouth and tongue like a true champion. At this point, I used his whole face, hard sliding full length, from his chin, tongue, over his nose to up and over his eyes. His eyes probably burned with my juice that was coating his face. I didn't care.

As I reached the final, explosive, nerve-shattering, muscle-snapping moment of an incredible orgasm, the half moan, half groan that escaped my throat sounded more animal than human. Wave after wave broke over my body and my legs spasmed and cramped uncontrollably around his head. I could only ride it out. Mobley gasped for air when he could, for which I was grateful because his breathing was not my concern at the moment.

As I wound down into a warm, sleepy state of bliss, I became hypersensitive to every touch and sensation. Still quivering, I fell to the side and rested my head on his arm, completely and utterly spent.

Eventually managing to regain control of my senses after several minutes, I righted myself and brought my face close to his, touching noses. Still struggling to regain his breath, he smelled like me. Thoroughly wet, he looked like he had come from the shower. And unlike all the other men I had known in my life, he had done it all for me. All of it. He hadn't even got off. My heart pinged. But this time I didn't shake it off. I swiped the wet hair from his forehead then caressed his face. How lucky was I, this remade woman I had become? For me with the former men in my life, receiving oral sex had been iffy at best, and usually lackluster with little or no results. It never occurred to me how much I could enjoy it.

"Thank you," I whispered, knowing I was like a kid just off a death-defying roller coaster. I would let him – and me – catch our breaths. Then I'd be running to get back in line for another ride. I kissed him, tasting light traces of my musky, earthy flavors on his mouth.

CHAPTER 14

THE NEW STEFANY

Stefany: I just got back to Stoney Brook after spending an amazing night at the new Mill Property. The highlight would have to be completing Assignment 2 with Mobley. O M G. It was HOT, it was INCREDIBLE. I played it out as Leanne instructed and Mobley did his part to the letter. There were plenty of laughs in it too, and I had many opportunities to tease and joke around with him. The result is... today, I'm SORE.

After spending the whole evening with Mobley for Assignment 2, I was spent. EXHAUSTED. How many times did I come? I lost count. I had to feel sorry for him at the end, as it was just like the first time in Assignment 1. Mobley wasn't written in for getting any of his own gratification. Why Leanne is writing these with only me getting satisfaction, I'm not sure. It no doubt has to do with some of her weird psychology stuff. Anyway, long story short, I invited Mobley to spend the night in my bungalow, which he did. Poor guy, he had a hard-on the whole night. I know because he was jabbing me in the back most of the time. No doubt, if I hadn't been there, he would have already taken matters into his own hands and obtained some "relief." HAA. Soooooo, this is where things get a bit "sticky."

We woke up the next morning and Mobley got down on his knees by the bed, kissed both my hands and feet before

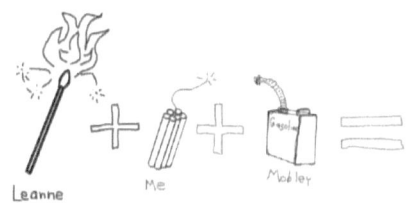

letting me up! Ummm, okay. Sweet, and a turn on. But, wow, he sure is into the part. I didn't even ask him for that. So, we got up, brushed our teeth, etc. I was in the kitchenette of the bungalow getting a glass of juice when Mobley pulls me back to bed! Okaaaay. So, we are back in bed, he wants to make out some more. And we do. Like for… over an hour! The sun was well up, but he pulls me with my back against him and just holds me. I was already feeling guilty that these assignments of Leanne's are kinda selfish for me, but this was really getting to me at this point. He was hard as a rock while we were cuddling - his cock was between my legs, pressing and sliding around the outside of me from behind. It felt so damn good, so I know Mobley was also getting tortured.

Yes, I agreed to follow Leanne's rules. She has told us to follow her assignments to the letter. No satisfaction for Mobley. This is henceforth a top-secret entry and Leanne had better not find my diary! So… I turned over to face Mobley. Kissed him. And told him I wanted him to fuck me. Hard. We would just keep it to ourselves and not mention it to Leanne. I must give him credit, he hesitated, because he was really trying to follow our agreement with Leanne. After a lot more kissing and me stroking him with my hand, me telling him it would be all right, and that we just wouldn't "mention it," he gave in. He rolled me on my back, hiked my legs up over his shoulders and slowly entered me. The look on his face was indescribable. I thought he might have a heart attack or something, he had been so wound up. I was still wet from the excitement the previous night! I haven't been fucked in a long time, the last pathetic episode being with Miles. THIS... was a jackhammer session that defies any description. Somehow the bed held together.

It wasn't a BDSM thing, what we shared. I wasn't telling him what to do or being dominant. It was just "regular" sex, I would have to say. But wowwwwwwww.

Mobley, in his tortured and miserable state, went slow – at first. Since I haven't had full penetrative sex in ages, I needed to get things back in the groove with him, so slow and easy was just fine with me to start off. Mobley's no pencil dick, and I must admit, it hurt at first. Hurt like HELL. How he maintained control, I'm not sure. But the pain gradually gave way to amazing ecstasy. He filled me to the brim when he finally got in balls deep, holding himself there for a minute. I never imagined Mobley would be a sweet lover, but he is. I needed gentle and easy at first, and he was. I had to continue to coax him for more and I finally got him to just let us enjoy it hard.

Throughout this, he kept kissing me, taking my legs, and kissing them as he fucked me. Finally, he pressed his face against my calf, moaned and blew his load. I think he came for over a minute and I could feel him pulsing inside me. By the looks of him when he came, it must have been soul-rending.

He was so tired afterward, I had to laugh. We were both covered with sweat and he was like a bag of wet flour at this time. After holding him for a while, I had to just push him the hell off and tell him to try and go back to sleep. Which he did while I went to take a shower!

It's called a "cream pie," Leanne told me once, letting the man come inside. In Leanne's world it no doubt enables all sorts of kinky behavior. With Mobley, it warranted a shower. This was a dripping, epic, oozing down my legs cream pie, to say the least, and hours later, I still feel like I'm "leaking" a little even as I write this. Mobley power-washed me with his orgasm.

Good thing I'm still on the pill, to be sure. He could inseminate a village of women.

~~~~~

I feel better knowing Mobley got to have some fun just for himself. It was no doubt some much-needed relief for him, long in the making. It was hot as hell for me, and I came again just with him fucking me. Now, what if Leanne asks either of us if we are abiding by the rules? I can't lie to her. I don't think Mobley will either. Maybe she won't ask?

This is crazy, all this hot, wild sex stuff with Leanne's assignments. I would never have thought, in a million years, this would be my life. Sex was never anything more than a chore. Not now!

Mum is the word and bring on Assignment 3!

I ran my hand along the glass top of one of the impressive new displays in the basement of Stoney Brook. The display cases and related exhibits were all situated near the stairs that led down into the subterranean cave. We called it the "Pirates Cave," as an aid for an effective tourist draw, and a name that seems fitting.

"There is something of specific interest I want to show you, Ms. Michaels," the lead archeologist, Ben Miller, informed me. "A sword that was recovered with the bodies in this cave is a style called a Scottish Claymore. This item was stored in a box and covered in a unique mixture of tallow and wax. It is remarkably preserved, given the humid environment. It cleaned up quite nicely and shows an incredible degree of craftsmanship and artistic detail. It is a masterpiece, and it's priceless." Using a key, he opened the glass top then handed me a pair of conservator's white gloves. "You will want to use those."

I slipped on the gloves, amazed that I would be holding something so old and a part of the history of Stoney Brook. Miller delicately lifted the sword from the case and handed it to me as Mobley looked on.

"Wow. It's so heavy," I remarked, turning the sword over to admire the various engravings and artwork.

"Yes," Miller agreed. "This is a Highland sword, estimated to be from the late 15th, early 16th century. About sixty inches, overall. Quite long."

"Wow."

"Wow, indeed. Now. I want you to look right here, where I am pointing." Miller indicated a spot on the blade near the hilt with his finger. "See? Right here."

Barely visible, there was some writing. "What is it?"

"It reads your surname, McCaskill. This is the sword of your ancestors. It was no doubt passed on through several generations until it ended up here."

I stared at the sword with reverence. "Wow." Holding such an intriguing historical artifact of my family was overwhelming. This very sword, I realized, had been wielded by Seumas McCaskill, handed down from his own father.

"Has any of the DNA information come back on any of the bodies we discovered in the cave?" I eagerly asked.

"It has, but none are a match for your lineage," Miller replied. "Based on how the bodies were attired, the weapons and artifacts found, we can fairly conclude they were sailors, and more, they bear all the telltale clues of having been pirates."

"If my family built Stoney Brook and this sword belonged to the founder, Seumas McCaskill, why would it be left down in the cave, with bodies that may have been pirates?"

"That, I don't know," Miller said. "We may never know, most likely, unless more evidence surfaces."

"I have one more item I would like for you to see," Miller said, reaching for one of the smaller items near the sword.

It was a necklace with a silver charm. It appeared to be in the shape of a cross yet had markings that gave it the overall appearance of the shape of a skeleton.

"This," Miller began to explain, "was found among some of the other small items in the case with the Claymore. It was in a small, deteriorated wood box full of rose petals."

"Any idea what it is?" I asked, fascinated.

"It appears to be a Voodoo charm. It is a fascinating piece. There's some writing on the back, we could barely make it out until we cleaned it," Miller said.

"What do you think it says?"

"A name, perhaps. It's spelled B-o-w-k-e-e. It seems to be an early African name."

Shocked, I realized the significance of the piece. "I read about this person!"

Miller was confused. "How? Who"

"She was a slave of Seumas McCaskill! I read about her in the Ledger. Marisha Neita thinks the name would be more properly spelled, B-h-o-k-i, today. *Bhoki*."

"Incredible," Miller exclaimed. I will want to read these ledger accounts later as Marisha finishes them. Will that be okay?"

"Yes," I confirmed, feeling uneasy about Miller seeing some of the more brutal accounts of Seumas McCaskill."

I rolled the necklace around in my hand, amazed. "Why do you think it was wrapped in rose pedals?"

Miller smiled. "We can only speculate. But I think you could guess as well as me. I would suggest that it has the hallmarks of a tender memorial. Some sort of remembrance of someone dear. A loved one, more than likely."

I nodded, deep in thought. Who exactly was Bhoki to Seumas McCaskill?

After looking at the ancient relic a few more minutes and considering the potential stunning revelation of how it was stored, I laid it back into the case. Miller locked it and gave me the key.

"I think you'll find people will want to come to visit here just to see all these amazing artifacts. This cave showed us a moment frozen in time. Thank you, Ms. Michaels."

After a bit of small talk, Miller and two other archeologists and a representative from the Smithsonian Institution said their goodbyes and left. They had worked on the cave project for several weeks, culminating in the Stoney Brook Museum. It was small, nestled into one end of the basement, but it was spectacular. The stairs down in the cave were now safely bordered by a rail.

Alone in the cellar, Mobley took my hand. "C'mon. I'll show you the new tomb and the display where we found the artifacts." He led me down the stairs at the entrance of the cave as the sound of trickling water from the stream echoed off the cave walls. While left in its original condition, modern amenities such as electric torches and safety ropes would now guide tourists along the walking trail. The recently installed lights added a warm glow to the shadows on the walls.

"We have security cameras installed down here for the safety of our guests. But they aren't powered on yet," Mobley explained as we walked.

Turning a corner, Mobley suddenly stopped. "Slavery. Pirating. Murder. Your ancestors were a brutal, cruel lot," he remarked, peering down at me with mischievous blue eyes. "A trait that you have undoubtedly inherited. They would be proud that the raven-haired beauty of Stoney Brook is following in their traditions."

"Is that a fact." He was joking, I knew.

"Oh, that's a fact. Ms. Stefany."

"Have I told you I found a new leather cream conditioner for my riding crop? It makes the end very supple. Bendy. More whippy."

"Um. No. I thought it was rather whippy, already. I never thought Leanne would give you equipment that wasn't fully effective."

"Mobley, you make me want to go the extra measure. You can give me a full report after Assignment 3, to be sure." I flipped my hair back over my shoulder and resumed my walk toward the tomb. "I have just realized that I've been far too generous with you."

Mobley grabbed my arm, halting my progress. "Wonderfully generous. Wonderfully cruel."

"That "cruel" remark is going to cost you several layers of ass epidermis," I remarked, staring threateningly at his hand on my arm.

"Promise?" With that he suddenly pulled me close and pushed me against the cave wall, pinning me. He kissed me.

Surprised, I hesitated, not knowing if I should be pissed or reciprocate. The latter seemed prudent, and I wrapped my arms around his neck. "Sex slaves aren't supposed to assert themselves over their master," I remarked through the kiss.

"Call it a sex slave uprising. You kissed me down here before, recall."

"I recall."

"Want me to quit?"

"No," I admitted, kissing him back and pressing my knee up against him suggestively between his legs.

After a few minutes, he relinquished the lock on me. "I want you, every hour. Every day," he whispered against my lips. "These assignments are too far in between."

"You can still come and see me. Or I could come to your room," I suggested.

"Every night?"

"Mobley. Whoa. It's hard enough to not go full out on you when I see you, much less torture ourselves every night. The rules."

"Yeah. The rules," he lamented. "But we already broke the rules. When…"

"I let you have a mercy fuck?" The term just popped into my head, and I laughed even as I said it.

"Wait. It was a mercy fuck?" Now he sounded hurt.

"Nooooo," I consoled. "Maybe it wasn't a… *mercy* fuck. After all, I wanted it too. And I enjoyed it immensely. As for the rules, I'm sure we'll break them again," I said with a duplicitous smile.

"We will?" He sounded surprised.

"I'll say this. Let's just play this the way we have been and not overdo it. Keep it real and on the downlow. We can't be letting anyone get suspicious. Especially Miles."

He looked sad and disappointed. I ran my fingers up into his blond hair. "Hey. It makes things more intense, later. What's that old saying, absence makes the heart grow fonder?" Reaching between his legs, I squeezed him. "Or it makes Mobley grow harder, as the case may be."

We both laughed, he kissed me again and we resumed our trek.

"What if Leanne asks if we broke the rules?" he suddenly asked.

I shrugged. "We tell her the truth. No biggie. We aren't machines, ya know."

"Yes. I like that," he admitted. "Not machines." I had to laugh out loud at his juvenile eagerness to frame the excuse in advance.

Reaching the tomb, I was astonished. My worries that the display would be in poor taste were unfounded. "It's beautiful," I gushed. "And the exhibit is magnificent."

428

Built of black and white marble, the airtight tomb featured a strip of thick, clear glass which allowed the visitor to view the skeletons lying in repose inside. I leaned over, peering in. Wearing the clothes they were discovered with, they were neatly arrayed, full length on silk shrouds, illuminated with small LEDs from the marble top. The inscriptions on the outside explained the circumstances in which they probably died, with dates and other details. In a glass case adjacent to the tomb, a Smithsonian forensic artist had recreated the faces from studying the skulls. The faces of long ago peered out from the case, giving life to the adventurous feel of the display.

The exhibit next to the tomb provided additional information, documenting the discovery and subsequent historic interpretations of the site as well as acknowledgments of the archeologist, historians and conservators involved. As with the museum back at the cave entrance, several display cases showed off many of the artifacts found with the bodies. It was all nicely done and wonderfully informative. Anything concerning authentic, historic pirates of the age is a huge draw for tourists as if Stoney Brook needs any additional allure. Here, visitors could see real pirates, what they wore and the items they carried with them.

I turned toward Mobley, who bore the beaming, proud expression of a father whose son had just hit a home run in baseball. "Once again, you have shown me that I have every reason to adore you. It's neither gaudy nor disrespectful. Outstanding job. Well done."

He put his arm around me, hugging me tightly to his side. Gazing up into his eyes, I gave him an approving smile. "But you can still expect to lose your hide in the next assignment."

"You are raising my taxes forty-two percent?!" I was yelling at this point. "This is total bullshit!" Slamming the paper down on my office desk, the men jolted from the outburst. I stared across at the two island officials that were visiting. Leanne, sitting to the side of my desk remained silent with a grim expression.

"Think of it this way, Ms. Michaels," one of the nervous men tried to explain. "You have grown to such a degree, and are so successful, a good portion of our island infrastructure now goes to support your enterprise here at Stoney Brook. It's only fitting you share with us some of this success. Help us fund better roads and services."

"I already do! I pay wages, I hire people! Tourists and visitors come! Besides Stoney Brook, they also patronize businesses - OTHER than mine - on the island! They buy souvenirs! They rent stuff! Eat at other restaurants! Stoney Brook is the reason more people are coming to the island in the first place! It's the reason the island economy has grown to where it is now, better than it has ever been! It's the reason you now have more revenue than you have ever had!"

Largely thanks to Mobley and several incredible strokes of luck, Stoney Brook was successful beyond my wildest dreams. Money was now not a problem. I cracked my knuckles, staring at the men. I had a burgeoning bank account and had the resources to do whatever I wanted to do. Free of all debt, I was 29 years old and had become a multi-millionaire in the span of months. I was now wealthier than Miles.

"Ms. Michaels. Be reasonable. We think it's only fair," one of them tried to explain. "You have the means…"

I abruptly stood from my chair. "Fair? Oh. I'll show you fair." Enraged, I kicked my chair away and made my way around the desk, with every intention of getting my hands on the two tax weasels to physically throw them out of my office. Leanne quickly intervened, grabbing me around the waist, hoisting me up in mid-air, my legs kicking, hands reaching for them. It wasn't necessarily the most dignified way to end a meeting.

"Perhaps we could consider adjusting our numbers down as an appeal of sorts. We'll return later, Ms. Michaels," one offered as they hastily beat a retreat from my office. "Perhaps when you can discuss this with more objectivity."

"Yeah? You do that, bloody grifters. And I'll make sure my foot is handy to plant up your ungrateful asses."

The door closed, and the men were gone. Leanne shook me by the shoulders, restraining a laugh.

"What?!" I asked, still angry and shaking.

"It's just. I've never seen you like that."

"Like what? And don't tell me I'm being unreasonable. If ever there were two jackasses that needed ejections off my foot, it is those two."

"Maybe," Leanne agreed. "In the past, you would have just taken their crap. Rolled over. You probably would have written a check."

"No. I wouldn't have," I said weakly, realizing that she was right.

She offered me a glass of water. "Stef. You have changed. And personally, I think it's a good change."

I stood for a moment, revelations of self-awareness suddenly dawning on me like a veil lifting over my eyes. "I… have."

"Yes."

"But, how? What is this?"

Leanne wrapped an arm around my shoulders. "Ah, my young, beautiful, but naive apprentice. It's called… confidence."

I thought about this for a moment and could see that she was, indeed, correct. I was supremely confident. In everything.

"Next, we'll work on self-control," she added with a patronizing pat on the head.

"I've said it many times, now. I don't want to reconcile," I told Miles in as steady a voice as I could muster. "I want a divorce. Let's face it, it's over. We both should be able to move on, see other people."

"And you know my feelings on that. We've been around and around on this. I will not grant you a divorce. Plus, the court has *mandated* that we try and work it out. Can't you do what is best here? Give me a chance, Stefany. I have changed."

No, he hadn't. I drummed my fingers on the balcony rail of The Blue Calypso, angry but hiding it well, wishing I were spending the beautiful mid-afternoon with Mobley rather than Miles. We both were standing on the outside balcony, leaning against the rail, watching tourists stroll the sidewalks, milling about like mice exploring a maze, popping in and out of stores. It was odd that we had chosen the village bar as a place to meet. It wasn't that long ago that Miles had tried to punch my lights out in this very place.

"Your lawyers have done a good job. Dragging this out. And just what does reconciliation mean to you, Miles?"

"I want to be a part of your life again. I want to see you more. Maybe move in with you at Stoney Brook."

This last request was over the top. Immediately I began to roll over the consequences in my head. That would squelch any happiness I could have with Mobley. Leanne's fun assignments would certainly be out of the question. Miles would be all in my business in every way. And he would want to be intimate again. I shuddered. This last thought made my skin crawl. Not a very auspicious beginning to any reconciliation.

"No, Miles. You moving in is out of the question. I couldn't take that, after everything that has happened. You know that." I tried to sound as convincing as I could.

Miles pondered this rebuke for a moment, sipping his expensive imported wine. "Perhaps it is a bit too soon," he finally agreed. I was shocked. "I'll agree to remain at my condo on the island. For now."

"But," he began, reminding me that Miles always had a fallback plan. "I want us to see each other, privately. And I want to be able to go to dinner with you, do things together. Maybe travel, go on vacations as well as business trips."

Sticking my thumb into the top of my bottle of beer, I withdrew it.

SPLOP!

His demands were not entirely unexpected. It was a standard routine for Miles to parse his primary interest within several other minor considerations. His main desire would be forthcoming next.

"But I also want to be a part of operations," he added, making it sound as if it were an afterthought. "Put me in charge of something. I want to help. I want to contribute. The court said as much, in their last decree. That I should participate with you in this." He slipped his hand over mine. "It will be good for us."

I turned to appraise him, this man that I felt no connection to and only wanted out of my life. The man that had beat the shit out of me, literally, beginning soon after the honeymoon was over. There was no way, legal way at least, of keeping him from getting involved to some degree in Stoney Brook. Which is what he wanted all along. It was why he was on the island in the first place. He sniffed money. The court ordered attempt at reconciliation allowed him a shot at it. Life never offers a clear-cut victory, I well knew. You manage the frayed edges. You roll with it.

Sipping my beer, I smiled. "You can manage the Mill Property. But you must do things my way. It's my vision, and it works. You manage it, *as is*. You must tolerate Morgan Mobley and all other staff. And Leanne. Understand I'm in charge. If it gets out of hand and I ask you to leave, you go. And I want all of this in writing."

Miles thought about this offer for a moment, visibly taken aback by my quick response. It wasn't optimum for either of us, but it would mostly keep him out of my hair and busy. It would engrain him into the fabric of Stoney Brook, which I deeply regretted, but I didn't have any choice. The divorce wasn't happening any time soon, so it had to be done. The Mill Property would work. He could get involved there and hopefully wouldn't wreck the progress.

"Agreed," he said finally. His dark eyes reminded me of those of a venomous snake, such as I had seen in zoos. Calm, searching, emotionless - dangerous.

Touching the side of my face, he used a finger to loop my hair back over my ear. "You are so beautiful. No one can ever deny that." He tried to kiss me, and I extended my hand instead.

"What's happened to you, Stefany," he asked flatly, tentatively taking my hand. "You seem… different. Surer of yourself."

I gave him a fake, disarming smile. For once in my life, I knew I could handle Miles. All of him. All of his bullshit. Or anyone else's bullshit for that matter. I felt like punching him in the mouth. "I'm just the same 'ol Stefany."

Morgan: It is said that diaries are therapeutic. They help us with introspection and maybe if we are lucky, we can improve ourselves. I hope I can improve who I am. Not overnight, but maybe a little at a time. There are a lot of things I know I could be better at as a caring, thinking human being. In the past, I've been a selfish asshole. Only thinking of myself. Arrogant. Self-consumed. I know this. And it's not who I want to be. I'm just being honest with myself here.

~~~~~

I suppose as most men go, I've had my share of gorgeous, beautiful women. Women have told me I'm quite handsome, which is always an ego boost. Now, I don't know about that. But whatever I do have, I admit I have not used it with any ethical standard, that's for sure. Truthfully, I could be called a "player." When people on the staff here and around on the island call me by my nickname, "Man-Whore Mobley," I suppose it is an honest characterization.

I love everything about beautiful women. When I've had my friends ask me if I'm a leg, ass, or boob guy, I have always replied - no. I am an ALL OF THAT guy. I love all aspects of a woman, including her mind. I like smart women. And if they are smarter than me, that's just fine. I like athletic, in-shape women. Pretty tomboys... Country girls. Nerds, but those that have tight bodies. Goth girls if they aren't overly weird. The sexy lawyer type with the high heels and glasses on the tip of her nose is good too. Love 'em. I'm not into any gnarly body parts. I don't like glamorous women. Give me a woman in a pair of Chucks over high fashion fake-ass glitter any day. But I do like my women to be able to dress up to that standard if needed. I'm shallow, I know. But whatever. I have standards of beauty from head to toe that I consider essential. That goes for personality, too.

Now, with all of that said, there are outliers. Once, I met this hot chick, but she had a prosthetic leg. She was still sexy and beautiful. Cute as a button and a wonderful personality. Could I go for her? I think so. But not sure how the sex thing would work out. Probably not a problem. Thought-provoking. It could be awesome and incredibly kinky. Maybe.

Another example was this woman I knew that was deaf and had difficulty speaking. Would slur her speech all over the place. Could I go for her? Yeah, I think so. For some reason, I think it would be hot to hear her talk while giving me oral.

Evidently, there are variables in my desires that even I am not fully able to explain. But whatever. The body can be great, but the mind is a universe all unto itself.

~~~~~

More introspection. I love sex. No, I'm not attracted to every woman, only a few, actually. I don't get into dim-witted attractive women, although I admit I might fuck them if I could get them to leave quickly afterward - and not try to call me. Yeah, I'm selfish, I know. Again, just being honest with myself.

~~~~~

The whole love thing - I failed miserably at that. When first coming to the island, I would have said love SUCKS - without question - and I'll never dabble in that bit of malarkey again. After my ex, I really didn't think I could "love" any woman. Ever. Now, let me clarify. I can "like" a woman, certainly. Be friends? Sure. LUST after her - oh, most certainly. Take Leanne Tilden for example. She has become one of my best friends. I can tell her anything, and she is knock-out gorgeous. Do I lust her? I suppose. She has a lot to lust about, that's for sure. But at this point, it would feel weird being more than a friend with her. Oddly, I guess I do sort of love her, in a weird plutonic friend sort of way.

And then there's Stefany. Without really knowing, I started falling for her soon after several months working for her here at Stoney Brook Plantation. That's even though I absolutely detested her at first. DETESTED! And here is the weird part. After falling in love with her and having that kick my ass, the lust part came. So, it's a love AND lust sort of thing. But yeah. I fell in love with Stefany, and it was the big deal. To me, anyway. Far more so than any other woman I have ever known. She fried me like an egg. Done. Never thought that would happen to me again, much less the degree.

~~~~~

Stefany has taken to being a sexual dominant like a duck to water, and she may well destroy me in Assignment 3. I think she is looking forward to whipping my ass with that crop again and I wish Leanne would just take it away from her. Stefany is getting off on the control and power. The worrisome thing is, turns out she's a chick that digs giving pain. Leanne's little experiment unleashed all sorts of things in Stefany. And that, in

turn, makes me feel two things.
Excitement. And fear.

~~~~~

Even though Stefany is sometimes rough, other times she is tender and delicate as a flower. It's like two sides of a personality. She truly cares for me, I believe. She says she does. She says I'm the only man that has ever made her think and feel the way she has! And that is huge. Even Leanne is amazed at all of this. She doesn't talk about Miles at all with me. That's a good thing. As for me? Does she know how I really feel about her? Although I have almost blurted it out several times, I have managed to keep it to myself.

~~~~~

This last weekend, I spent the night with her at the Mill Property. She worked me over, to say the least. Tied me up, teased me, whipped me, got off on me orally. I didn't get any relief out of it for me until the next morning - I loved every minute. There's no doubt about it, she challenges me physically with that bondage and whip stuff. Afterward, I was sore for two days.

So, before we left, we made love. Maybe it was just sex for her, but for me, it was making love. Leanne doesn't know we broke the assignment rules yet, and I don't know how she'll react to that. It wasn't BDSM style - just vanilla straight up if I had to describe it. Just the way she kissed me and held me makes me think that it's possible… maybe… she could feel towards me the way I feel towards her? She was so tender towards me. Soft. Unusually so.

I think about sex with her all the time now, it is driving me crazy. I can't wait for each assignment to come out. And it's not just sex. I want to be with her, see her, hold her, kiss her. I want more.

I would never have thought that sex that included me getting my ass whipped with a riding crop or being tied up would constitute the best sex I've had. But there you go, it's true. Maybe some of it is the anticipation. Some of it is letting someone else have complete control, which was hard at first. Giving Stefany oral, which seems to be the main element of these assignments, is brain-melting, nut-rupturing hot. She loves it, that's for sure. Being dominated sexually by a woman -

440

there is something to that, gotta say. And oddly, there is something to the pleasure with pain thing. All of it is an amazing new trip for me. BDSM - who would have thought.

~~~~~

There have been a lot of great things happening at Stoney Brook and the Mill. I think Stefany is fully out of debt now! She has been wanting to show me the books for a while, but I never seem to get around to it. She said she wants to share with me all that has happened, financially. With the coconut production in full swing and the sugar cane stirrers, plus regular operations with the guests, I think she is making a lot of money. She is as happy as I've ever seen her. Except when Miles is around, she is always in a good mood.

I love Stefany so much, it hurts. I think about her, and I just want to blow up. Like from a land minc, maybe. If not for that asshole Miles, I would marry her in an instant if she'd have me. I'm talking "marriage" - the thing I most despise. That's how serious I am about her. There isn't anything I wouldn't do for her. I would happily die for her.

Leanne watched me intently from behind her large, mirrored sunglasses as we strolled on the beach at the Mill Property. Normally, I wouldn't have accepted a call from the states, but noticed it was from the bank that once held my student loans. I could barely hear the nasal-voiced woman over the crashing waves and seagulls. "We are sorry, sir, but we need a payment today." The woman read my account number, old address, and phone number back to me for confirmation. "We have determined that given your status with living out of the country, you have been identified as a substantial default risk with your student loans. The bank has been quite lenient with extending your credit, but that has now reached its limit. Payment in full on the remaining balance is immediately due. While we could accept a partial payment, that will not keep us from seeking restitution such as garnishment of wages or seizure of assets. Full payment will be nine-thousand three-hundred, twenty-seven dollars, and seventy-eight cents. We accept credit cards or bank transfers. How would you like to pay?"

"The balance last I checked before I paid it off was only around three-thousand dollars!"

"We received no pay-off for this loan, sir. The last payment was two-hundred-fifty dollars, made nearly two years ago. How would you like to pay?"

It was that bitch ex of mine. She had sabotaged the payments to the bank, somehow, so I would get into trouble. "If I pay that, it's everything I've managed to save," I objected.

Reluctantly, I pulled my wallet out from my back pocket and slipped out the one credit card I owned. "I'll pay with a card," I replied. Just recently obtained, I had applied for the card over the last month for emergencies only. I read off the numbers for nasal woman, confirmed the payment amount in full, and ended the call. I had traded one debt for another, would end up paying hundreds more in interest, and was virtually penniless again. "I've got fourteen dollars left until my next paycheck," I remarked sourly.

"Morgan. What happened to the check I gave you for your part of the agreement?"

"It's back in my room. I've not cashed it, Leanne."

"What? Look. I told you, I can cover this for you right now beyond your agreement check that you refuse to cash for *some* reason. I'll give that bank my debit card number and be done with it. This is a minor amount for me, and I would be happy to do it for you. Consider it a bonus."

I thought about her offer for a moment, only because I was in such a poor state. "No," I finally said. "I'll not be sponging off my friends, that's never a good idea. I can manage until my next pay. Stefany did give me a raise, so that helps. But I thank you though, Leanne."

She smiled. "Fine. But go cash that check! And you know you can always come to me whenever you need help. I will always be here for you, Morgan."

"Thanks. That means a lot."

She stopped mid-stroll and took my arm, turning me to face her. "Morgan. I love kidding and teasing you. But listen to me. Despite your shortcomings, each of which I adore by the way, you are among the finest men I have ever known. You remember that. The fact that we are such close friends is a treasure to me."

"Is all of that... why you have encouraged me to form a relationship with Stephanie by means of these BDSM assignments?"

"Absolutely. You are perfect for her. And she is perfect for you. You've both saved each other, and you don't even realize it. I love you both and want happiness for each of you."

I put my arm around her, kissed her on the cheek and we resumed our stroll. "Leanne. This relationship that I'm in with Stefany. With her as the dominant and me the sex slave."

443

"Yes. What about it," she asked, stopping to pick up a particularly beautiful example of a seashell. She showed it to me, and I nodded in agreement that it was indeed a spectacular find.

"After several assignments, I think I'm getting a handle on this BDSM stuff. Stefany loves it, which is hot. If I had to describe it, it seems like it almost always consists of stuff like… a lot of oral sex, getting tied up, foot worship, using toys, being made to wait to get off. A little bit of pain with the pleasure."

"As far as you two go, I suppose that's an accurate depiction," she remarked, still engrossed in the features of the seashell, putting it up to her ear to hear the rushing sound of a faux ocean."

"At first, I was skeptical about the whole thing. I didn't think it was any big deal. Now? With Stefany at least, it's a hell of a lot of fun."

"I'm glad you have gotten over your initial reluctance," she absently replied.

"So. Is it what you call living in the lifestyle? With Stefany and me?"

Leanne laughed suddenly. "Noooooo. You aren't living in the "lifestyle." You two are just having a little orchestrated, mildly kinky fun, that's all. And that's great. There's nothing wrong with that. It's still mostly vanilla sex, with a little strawberry cream on top, perhaps."

"But Leanne, you are in the lifestyle, though, right?"

"No. I just dabble around the corners, actually. I'm not in a full lifestyle sort of arrangement and don't want to be in that level of commitment. People that are into bondage, submission, and domination 24 – 7, hardcore, those are the ones in the lifestyle. They do the master and slave thing full time. Often in public even. That's not for me, I am much more discreet. They believe it and live it; they live it like it's a marriage vow. And some of the things they engage in are *much* more extreme than what you two do or even me."

"But Heidi and Joe are your sex slaves."

444

"Yeah, they are. But they are just in it for the momentary sex, as I am. Mostly for behind closed doors. They can leave any time they want. See anyone they want. It's only for fun play. Who knows, I could have totally different playmates next year. It's roleplay, Morgan. I'm a woman that enjoys not-so-vanilla, good, hot, rough sex."

I thought about this steamy revelation. Leanne was a sexual firecracker and I wanted to know more. "You're a dom. And Stefany is a dom. How did you figure out that is what you two are? Why not submissives?"

"It's all personality, Morgan. I don't have the personality to be submissive. I never have. Now, Stefany, she's a different story. As I told you before, she has disastrously lived her life in submission to others, not just sexually, but in *every* way. Abused even in that role. Now, with you, she has a chance to experience other things. And she has, in a spectacular fashion. I think we can both agree she seems to be naturally dominant, particularly with sex. She has just never had the chance to explore that side."

"Why did you think I would make a good sex slave to Stefany?"

"Just a hunch. We obviously couldn't have two dominants trying to get along in these assignments. I thought you could handle moving into that characterization because first off, you are a strong, confident man. It's not every man could handle being a sex slave, let's face it. Most would feel threatened. Not you."

"I guess that's a compliment," I quipped.

"Oh, it is. Morgan, you love women. And it's obvious you love sex. Most importantly, you are in love with Stefany. That's huge in something like this."

We reached a beach table and chairs with an umbrella. Pulling out a chair, I let Leanne sit first. After a few minutes, a server came by, inquiring if we wanted anything to eat or drink. We both ordered beers.

"With Stefany," Leanne began to explain, "you are the perfect sex slave for her. The submissive. For you, she is

445

the perfect goddess, or whatever you want to call her. The dominant. When this is over, I doubt either of you will ever find anyone that will be compatible like you two are for each other in these roles."

"You think it will someday be over!? I hope not."

"Enjoy each other while you can. Nothing lasts forever, Morgan."

Santiago, sitting in the passenger seat, looked across at me. "Why we are stopping at here, Meester Morgan?" Miguel, in the back, leaned forward, also curious.

The little convenience store was on the way to the Mill Property, our destination to work for the day. "I want to get a cold drink. I forgot to pack a cooler. I'll get you each one, what would you like?"

Santiago's face brightened immediately. "Orange Crush."

"Miguel?"

"Same, except the grape one!"

Heading towards the door, I began pulling out my wallet to make sure I had cash.

A shiny object in the road gravel near the store steps caught my eye. I stooped to pick it up. It was a necklace with a religious medallion. It looked to be made of silver and in the rough configuration of a Christian cross but had the overall appearance of a stylized skeleton.

At that moment, one of the front wooden posts of the store ripped to pieces sending fragments flying over me. I abruptly straightened. A sharp crack echoed across the fields from far down the road. Momentarily shocked and unsure as to what had just happened, I peered into the distance towards the source. The reality dawned on me as I saw the glint off a rifle barrel several hundred yards down the road. It had been a bullet that shattered the post, and my head would have been in the direct path of where it hit had I not bent down!

Someone parked alongside the road was using the juncture between their door and the car body to steady their next shot. I immediately ducked and dove for the front of the Stoney Brook Rover.

Bits of metal and plastic flew off the Rover by the back taillight as another shot echoed. Worried one of the shots could enter the vehicle from behind, I shouted to Santiago and Miguel. "Get out and take cover here at the front! Do it quick, hurry!"

The two men both bailed out of the Rover and joined me at the front as another shot shattered the back window.

"Meester Mobley! Someone is shooting at us," Santiago yelled as panic began to set in. Miguel squinted his eyes tightly shut as another round tore through the Rover, penetrating through several layers of body metal, lodging into the engine block.

"Yes, I know, guys. Keep your heads down."

Several curious faces peered from the windows of the store. Another shot sent them scurrying away.

Whoever it was shooting at us had missed their opportunity by mere chance. If I hadn't ducked when I did, I would most certainly have a bullet in my head. "Okay, listen. Here's what we are going to do. After the next shot, we are all going to run for the side of the store. It's better cover. Okay?"

The two nervous men nodded, uncertain. We waited for a moment and another shot hit the right rear tire, causing it to emit a loud hiss as it lost air.

"Okay! Go!" We all immediately bolted for the store. Miguel, with adrenaline no doubt surging through his veins, slipped on the gravel, and dropped right in the line of fire. Santiago hesitated.

"I've got him! Get over there!" I bent down to grab Miguel's arm as he was struggling to his feet. Another shot careened into the store porch. Another pinged through the frame of the car. Pulling Miguel, we made a hasty exit out of the line of fire to the side of the building.

Pulling out my mobile, I dialed frantically for the island police - the call wouldn't go through. I had to hope the store owners had managed to place a call. The scene turned strangely quiet, and we realized the shots had ceased. Looking around the edge of the store, I could see the assailant had given up and was back in their car. With the engine revving high, the car swung around in the road, spun out on the gravel, and headed off in the opposite direction.

CHAPTER 15
SOLO PERFORMANCES

Morgan: Another harrowing event. This time, someone taking a shot at the boys and me with a rifle. I can't help but believe this has to do with the previous attacks. Maybe by getting rid of me, Stefany would be more isolated, perhaps more apt to sell out and leave. It's a possibility, I think.

Who would benefit? The list is long. There are islanders that are resentful of the plantation. There are foreign interests from all corners of the globe that approach her near daily, inquiring about buying her out.

Then there's Miles - Stefany's asshole estranged husband who refuses to grant her a divorce. He had no interest in Stoney Brook NOR his wife until the place started becoming profitable. I don't trust him, yet now he is rooted into Stoney Brook because Stefany relented and gave him managerial control of the Mill Property. He's despicable, and could be capable of anything.

The assailant at the Mill Property had been murdered sometime after his attack. Was it because he knew too much? And what about the two men on the boat that abducted Stefany? I thought about both scenarios, and the more I reflect on this last attack on me, the more I'm uncertain.

~~~~~

Stefany's transformation seems nearly complete. She still has a weird multiple personality vibe, but I'm just used to it now. These last few months with her have been incredible. I've literally watched the creation of a celebrity right before my eyes. She now graces the covers of numerous magazines as one of the most rapidly successful businesswomen to come up from practically nothing. Of course, it doesn't hurt that she is extraordinarily beautiful.

~~~~~

A few weeks ago, Stefany was interviewed by a UK news outlet on the success and history of Stoney Brook. After a few photos and videos of her were circulated, they went viral. She is a rising star as a multi-millionaire businesswoman on a tropical island. Publishers, producers, and others are constantly contacting her. It's weird, all this attention that is lavished upon her. She never wanted this, but she is handling it well.

~~~~~

Stefany's latest adventure is to be invited to New York for a photoshoot and interview by a leading business journal. She hasn't mentioned it much to me, and it doesn't sound like she will take me with her. I confess a part of me is jealous that she will be spending her time with others that will be flattering her for her intelligence, success – and allure.

With all this free advertising and her celebrity, Stoney Brook is more popular than ever. We never have a vacancy. Everyone wants to meet Stefany, have dinner with her, drinks, get an autograph. The coconut business, the Mill Property, and everything else we touch turns to gold. This has all happened so suddenly, it could make me think I'm living in a dream. Am I?

~~~~~

This, for me, is unexpected as it is odd because I've never known anyone famous. She hasn't let it go to her head and insists nothing has changed. I asked her yesterday if she was getting the big head with the increasing fame and she said, "no, but I might take off an extra layer of skin in the next assignment just because you asked that question." HA! She is different from when I first met her, there's no question about that. Sure, in some ways she still acts the same. But when I'm "in service" as she likes to call our time together, she's a totally different woman.

Some women have a talent for exuding a smoldering, sensual, erotic personality. They can seduce with a glance. Or just by the way they may talk, walk, sit, how they toss their hair out of their eyes, hold their mouth, their expressions. Fashion and makeup have nothing to do with this inherent quality, and people who believe this are sadly mistaken.

I can honestly say Stefany could seduce a stone. What she has become - I can't entirely put my finger on it – is a mixture of confidence and attitude. Whatever she has done to herself, the combination is a lethal one. She surpasses even Leanne with this "new" quality, element, or whatever "it" is. Everyone that meets her sees it. She kills and burns every heart she comes across. She has new suitors at every turn, and with every phone call, it seems. Miles can only sit back and watch, knowing she doesn't give a care in the world for him anymore. He had an amazing woman and lost her. It's a partial justice for him, in my opinion.

~~~~~

The one quality, above all others, that can take a woman over the top... is confidence. Stefany didn't used to have confidence. She certainly has it now. It is NO act. Thinking back about Stefany's journey in confidence, when I first met her, my impressions were completely wrong. I overlooked her simple beauty, as it was hidden away and nearly imperceptible beneath the grime on her face she could barely be troubled to wash off as we restored Stoney Brook. She was a roughhewn tomboy, naïve as hell, with little knowledge of the world and who seemed bent on business failure. She didn't truly believe in herself and no one else did either, except Leanne. She had just lucked into inheriting an old broken-down plantation. But she grew. Leanne gradually fixed her presentation with tactful guidance here and there. She taught Stefany how to look and act the part of success.

~~~~~~

My initial plan had been to make a little scratch, milk the job for a while, enjoy some island ladies, and work on my tan until she went under with Stoney Brook, which seemed inevitable. That was all shallow and stupid, to say the least. So, in discussing who has changed the most, Stefany or me, I guess I would have to say it's been me. That's what I think, anyway.

Stefany tells me I am all she needs - if I obey and don't piss her off. Obey??? Granted, she said this mostly in jest. However, in my past, that word alone, "obey," would have pissed ME off to no end. I can't imagine any women I've previously known ever saying that to me. Now? I want more, and I would do anything she wants. Hell yeah, I'll obey. I'm grateful. I'm in love. Even if she doesn't have the same feelings for me. She

jokes around so much with me, it's hard to tell when she's being serious. She says I make her laugh as hard as I make her come. It's odd because most of this "humor" is lost to me.

Through all of this, I am still her dirty little secret. I could be that forever.

Yet again, nothing from the so-called "investigation" into why Stefany and I were being hunted. Constable Fillmore didn't even bother coming to brief me and instead sent a "subordinate detective" who turned out to be some beach-bound eighteen-year-old kid that took a criminal justice elective class in his high school. His ability to use the English language was limited at best.

"I narrowly avoided being shot in the head! The only reason I'm here is that I just happened to bend out of the way of the bullet at the last minute! You don't even have any ideas who could have done this. I think you can understand my *concern* here."

"Please, sir. We have limited resources; we do everything we can dat find the person dat does this."

I rubbed my eyes, tired of the excuses. "While I can imagine you are doing your best," I began, "the efforts of your organization on our behalf do not set me at ease. I assume that at the most basic level, it has occurred to Fillmore that it's obvious there is more than just one person involved in this? Since the first attacker was found dead, and now this, this must be an organized effort? Maybe the first guy that attacked us at the Mill Property was silenced because he knew too much?"

"Yes, sir, we have considered this facts varrry closely. Varrry closely, yes. Amongst our investigators."

"Investigators?" I pressed, my impatience slowly growing. "You guys are just Fillmore and a few island cops; some didn't even graduate high school. Does anyone actually know how to conduct a real criminal investigation?"

"Of course. We know how to do all dees things... fingerprints... collect the hairs... blood splatter... stool swabs... all dat. We look at photos... such things. Surely."

I now had no doubt this kid was making it all up as he went. "Look. Have you thought about getting help? From some of the other nearby islands? What about Interpol?"

"Yes, sir, we are getting much helped. Much."

Seeing that the discussion had concluded the minute the young "detective" finished taking my statement, I politely shook the boy's hand. It wasn't his fault, after all. In some impoverished shanty on the island, a mom and dad were extremely proud of their son's achievement of gaining employment on the police force. Fillmore, however, was the one culpable in this obvious display of incompetence and for the lagging progress of the investigation. Despite Fillmore's experience as a big-time detective on the west coast of the states, he seemed entirely ineffective and even apathetic to our case. There hadn't been a murder on the island for over 30 years, and the island cops weren't equipped to handle anything more than the occasional drunk or speeding ticket.

The boy detective departed from the front porch of Stoney Brook, and I strolled back into the lobby, which was deserted, the staff apparently taking a break. Standing at the front desk, I noticed the complimentary edition of the local island newspaper. The headline read, *Plantation Employee Shooting – A Near Miss*. How comforting. Reading the story, I could see that details were short, other than someone had shot at me and my crew at a convenience store. Police were on the "hunt" for the lone gunman, yet unidentified. I laughed. No doubt, he would remain unidentified. Unless he showed up somewhere with a bullet in his own head.

Suddenly, a hand slipped into mine and pulled, surprising me. It was Stefany. She towed me behind her towards the closest empty conference room.

"Hello. I didn't see you standing there, Stefany. What is it?"

Not answering, she closed the twin doors behind us. I began to wonder what I had done. Standing in front of me, she peered up into my eyes. "What? What is it, Stefany?"

She moved in close in front of me, pressing her hands against my chest. "You could have been killed!" Her eyes were watering, and she was quite visibly upset.

"But I wasn't."

"Only because you just happened to bend down! This could so easily have been a very different outcome." Her voice choked with emotion. "I could be arranging your funeral right now."

She had been upset before, but not like this. Tears were streaming down her face. "It's okay, it didn't happen," I consoled, taking her by the shoulders.

Pushing away, she pointed to a nearby chair. "Go sit. Over there."

I sat, wondering what she had to tell me. I was stunned as she sat across my lap and wrapped her arms around my neck.

"I don't know what I would do without you. And I'm not just saying that because of the *play fun* we have. You are much more to me than just… *that*. You are simply going to have to be more careful. I mean it. Do you understand?"

Wiping away her tears, I held her face between my hands and kissed her softly. "Yes. I'll be more careful." I was touched, and maybe a little surprised that she was so upset at my near miss with death.

"Stefany, it wasn't that long ago that you wanted to throw me off the plantation," I said jokingly, trying to lighten the mood.

She slapped my chest with fury and buried her face into my neck. "I never wanted you hurt! Even when I did think you were a scurrilous pest."

I lifted her head and trailed a finger beneath her hair, tucking it behind an ear. She was so beautiful, even when upset and crying. "I'll try to be more careful. And this goes for you too, you know," I added. "You have been a target as well."

"Fine, yes. Just take precautions, Mobley. If you need, take me with you."

I laughed. "Oh. Ms. Stefany, will you protect me then?"

Put off by my remark, she clenched her jaw. "You know what I mean. At least we can be watchful together. You know better than to underestimate me, Mobley." She softened suddenly, tidying my shirt collar. "Despite the fact that it has been you that has saved me again and again."

I held my hands out in a wide gesture. "I would never underestimate you. But look around. We are still here. Both of us."

"Nevertheless, I would feel better being with you when you are out and about, driving to the Mill Property or... whatever. You need looking after."

Kissing my way down her neck to her shoulder, she involuntarily moaned softly, reacting to the touch of my lips. "And you, Stefany. You need looking after. A task I am most happy to accept."

"Mobley. Please be serious for once in your life. I don't think... you... you are understanding my concern here! I want you... to be... to be safe."

"Concern noted. Are we due soon for a new assignment from Leanne? I feel particularly *useful* to you today. Let me relieve some of your stress."

"You are incurable," she mumbled, pushing my jaw up for a kiss. "That mouth needs to be put to proper use. Yes, we have new assignments, I'll let you know when. Patience."

The tropical midday sun was beating down with a particularly harsh vengeance and I was looking forward to a cold beer at the end of the day. Every now and then, a particular memory from one of my latest sexual adventures with Stefany would jump into my mind, evoking either a smile or a secretive erection. It was often both, which I had to hide from my present company.

Sweat was dripping down onto my face as I helped Miguel push a large stone into position in one of the front gardens we were improving. "There, that looks good. A few more and this is going to look great with the new plants," I observed, stepping back to admire our work.

"Stoney Brook. This is the prettiest place in the Caribbean, Meester Morgan," Santiago said from behind me, adding the finishing touches to a circular reflecting pool around a spectacular fountain.

"Indeed, it is," I agreed.

"Mees Michaels. She was upset with you, no? We have heard from the kitchen staff, she does no like you to drive alone anymore. We must go with you always." Santiago laughed. "We usually goes with you always anyway! And shooting, it still happens." Santiago rattled off something in partial French, partial Spanish, the roots of which formed the typical island dialect. If I had to guess, it had something to do with Stefany not wanting me to get my balls shot off. They laughed.

"A woman, Meester Morgan," Miguel began to explain. "They think many times with their hearts, yess monn."

"I suppose that is true, yes," I agreed, straightening my back. What was Stefany's heart telling her? Was she developing feelings for me such as I had for her? Perhaps she did think of me beyond just being a sexual play toy. The degree to which she was concerned for me was touching.

Stefany had hinted that Assignment 3 would be soon, yet it had been two days. I couldn't wait. I wanted her and being forced to maintain a strict professional relationship with her as of late was excruciatingly difficult. Even a kiss would be great.

My mobile suddenly buzzed from my back pocket. Slipping it out, I could see that it was Stefany. My heart involuntarily skipped a beat. She didn't text me often, and seeing her name was always a dose of adrenaline.

Quickly, I opened the message.

Stefany:
Please report to my office immediately.

Reflecting on this, I realized I was disappointed. What was I hoping for? A declaration of love? A lewd sext or raunchy comment? Yes, I thought, laughing to myself. That was exactly what I was hoping for, rather than this official-sounding request that reeked of being a typical work-related subject. It was probably to do with one of the new contracts I had recently helped arrange.

Taking a moment in the lobby to visit the washroom to clean up a bit, I made my way to her office. The doors were closed, so I knocked.

"Yes, come in," I heard from within.

Opening the door, I stepped inside to see Stefany sitting alone in one of the lounge chairs situated in a sectional arrangement towards one side of her office. Resting her chin in her hand while surveying me, she was resplendent in an a short, but elegant black dress, her legs crossed. Wearing expensive white, custom sneakers—a gift from Leanne—her legs were magnificent and bare.

"Did you want to see me? About something?" I asked, puzzled.

"Yes. Close the door," she answered flatly.

I walked over to her with the primary intention of getting a good look at her in that sexy dress before she turned the discussion to whatever business she had in mind. Hopefully, it didn't concern the finances. Accounting was never an interest of mine and I didn't care too much about the numbers if we were making good money. She now had several professionals for such things. I was just the idea guy, and I liked it that way.

"There's a bottle of wine in the kitchen," she explained, surprising me with this unexpected direction. "Go open it," she continued, "and bring it out with a glass."

"You mean, glasses?"

"No," she corrected. "One glass, Mobley."

Evidently, I would not be joining her. Thinking better not to ask why she only wanted one glass, I went to the kitchen. Returning as requested, I handed the single glass to her and stood with the bottle in hand.

"Right. Pour, Mobley," she finally said, somewhat irritated with my hesitation. I did as she asked, and she took a slow sip and sat back, looking up at me with an odd, appraising expression.

"Is this… one of Leanne's assignments?" I finally asked, excitement suddenly coursing through my body.

"No," she answered. "It is one of mine, though," she added after a pause.

Reality began to dawn on me. Whatever she had in mind, this was her idea. "Ohhh. But I thought tha-"

"Mobley, you are on what we have agreed to call, *service time*. That seems a suitable term. Please recall, it was my term, not Leanne's. And during *service time*, you will not talk unless directly questioned. Despite all the progress you have made, you still run your mouth far too much. Don't be a buzz kill."

"Um. All right. It's just that I didn't realize it was serv-"

Stefany held a finger up to her lips. "Shhh."

I looked down at my shirt, with large wet rings of sweat around my neck and under my arms. My back would have a similar sweat mark. Surely, she could let me clean up first. I was in a disgusting state, she had to know that. "But this is unexpected. I'm just in from working outside and I'm all swea-"

"Mobley. Shut up," she interjected. "I know quite well you were out working in the heat, and you are filthy. Let's reinforce your understanding of what it means for you to be my sex *slave*, per Leanne's agreement." She paused for a moment with a smirk. "I still can't get over saying that. Sex slave. It sounds so... seedy and contrived." Collecting her thoughts, she shrugged it off and continued. "Look. I might call on you at any time. And you will not talk during *service time* unless...?"

"Um. Questioned," I confirmed. Every time I heard her use the term, sex slave, I wanted to laugh except for the fact I knew she would beat my ass with that riding crop for being insolent.

"You are learning. so am I. It's understandable. Now, set that bottle of wine on the table here by me and go over to my desk, open the top left drawer, and bring me my riding crop. I'm going to enjoy this wonderful afternoon and reinforce your education should you need any reminders."

Not the crop, I thought to myself. The one thing I could do without. "Shit." I said under my breath as I retrieved the crop.

"What's that, Mobley," she asked.

"Nothing. Just doing as I'm told."

She smiled as I handed her the crop. "Thank you."

The change in her attitude from earlier in the day was startling. Standing in front of her, I waited for whatever was next. She was so beautiful I wanted to scoop her out of the chair and kiss her - before fucking her brains out.

"Strip," she finally said.

I began to question this but wisely caught myself just as her jaw set firmly, her eyes narrowing. Unbuttoning my shirt, I started to oblige. The scene was strangely stimulating. She sat evaluating my every move, looking the part of the powerful, in-charge, executive woman, albeit an extremely sexy and attractive one.

"Slow down. Slow." Her crossed leg bobbed rhythmically. "Think, Mobley. What does a woman want to see? She doesn't want to see a man quickly throw his clothes off like in a post-game locker room. She wants to savor it. Slowly. Work it. I thought you were smoother than that, c'mon."

Feeling somewhat insulted, I obliged, slowing my progress. I tossed my wet shirt and khakis to the side in succession. Finally, down to my underwear and socks, I searched her face for direction. These too, I questioned with just my expression.

"Yes. Those too," she added, sipping her wine, reading my mind perfectly.

Entirely naked, I stood in front of her, somewhat self-conscious as her eyes roamed up and down. Why I would suffer modesty now, I couldn't say. At this point in our relationship, she intimately knew every inch of my body. If my deodorant was still working, it was questionable.

"Now, go get a towel out of the bathroom and get back here."

It was an odd request. Complying, I then returned from the bathroom, holding a towel to her. "It's not for me," she clarified. "Spread it out on the floor in front of me."

After placing the towel as she instructed, I stood back up, waiting, and wondering what she would do next.

"Turn around."

Complying, I turned around, eyeing her nervously over my shoulder.

"Don't look at me, eyes to the front, Mobley." I did this, embarrassed knowing she was staring at my ass.

WHAP!

Jumping forward from the hard strike of her crop, I couldn't help myself. "Ow, fuck! What did I do!"

"First of all, you aren't listening well. And second, you are talking. Would you like another?"

"No!" I caught the urgent tone in my voice and tried it again. "I mean - *no*, Ms. Stefany." I swallowed. My ass would no doubt have a new red streak. Leanne could probably discuss the psychological particulars of that development, but it mattered not to me except for the sting I was currently feeling.

"Face me," she calmly ordered.

I was beginning to get an erection, but she made no mention of it. I searched her gorgeous green eyes for further direction.

"I love it when you don't listen. Don't you?"

"I... will try to listen better."

She smiled behind a sip of wine. "Either way, we can make it work. Read my mind. What do I want you to do now?"

I hesitated, not knowing. "More... wine?"

"Mobley, sometimes I have to wonder how you made it through grade school. On your knees. When in doubt, just get on your knees. It's probably what I want anyway. And who knows. Remember that and maybe you'll save yourself a strip off your ass if I happen to be in a bad mood." I quickly dropped before her and she laughed, gently caressing my face with the crop.

This order of activities was quite familiar I noted, managing to keep from smiling. If I appeared the least bit sarcastic, the crop would find its mark on my shoulders I knew. Reaching behind, I massaged the painful welt that had formed on my left ass cheek.

"Stroke yourself," she said after another sip of wine.

Questions were evidently all over my face. Seeing this, she relented. "Oh, what? You can go ahead and ask me. This time."

"But. You just want me to... do myself? Right here?"

"Yep. That's it. That's what the towel is for. I don't want your jizz on my legs this time, nor on my rug, Mobley."

"And that's... all... you want me to do?"

"Yes." Thoroughly enjoying herself, she ran the toe of her sneaker over my cock. "Stroke."

Doing as she asked, I began stroking my own cock. The strangeness of the situation and awkwardness began giving way to a smoldering lusty need. She sipped her wine casually as I worked, watching me intently but never moving from her chair.

I raised a hopeful, questioning finger.

"*What* now."

"Can I ask one more question?"

"I'll indulge you, Mobley. What?"

"Why just this… with me doing… me?" I asked, knowing I was pressing my luck and risking the crop.

"This is all about a good show." She again caressed my cheek with the crop. "Continue. You asking a lot of questions is not the best use for your talented mouth, which I *will* remedy at another time."

Complying with her wishes, I returned to stroking myself as she watched, nonchalant, occasionally sipping her wine as if this were something we did every day. After a few minutes, her mobile phone buzzed on the end table next to her chair. She picked it up and answered.

"Oh, hello, Leanne. Yep. I'm in my office with an employee. Sure. Come on down."

I very much wanted to ask if I could stop, but Stefany made no indications. Leanne had seen me naked, but not in any active scenarios such as with our assignments. To this point, everything had been private and only with Stefany. I hesitated, hoping that she would let me go back to her room for privacy.

"I didn't tell you to stop. Keep going," Stefany ordered.

This was adding a whole new element to our relationship. Would she let Leanne in to see me in this compromising position? A few minutes later, a small knock broke the silence, and I would have an answer to my question.

"Leanne? Yes, please come in."

Leanne strode in casually after closing the door behind her. "If you are discussing something pressing with one of your people, I can come ba-"

Her eyes immediately widened with shock at the scene. Despite my best attempts to just play it cool, my cheeks flushed with embarrassment.

Leanne held out an inquiring hand towards me. "My, my. What have we here, Cousin? I didn't realize you were in the company of Mr. Mobley. Who is… *naked*… and evidently pleasuring himself? I don't recall *this* in the latest assignment I sent you, Stef."

"It wasn't. This is on my own. I mean, come on. Can't I begin doing what I want? In addition to your assignments, of course."

"Um. I guess. It's just…"

"Just what, Leanne?" Stefany asked, her eyes never leaving me. "Mobley. I didn't tell you to stop."

SNAP!

Having to tell me to continue one too many times, the strike on my shoulder with the riding crop had a bit of extra effort. I quickly returned to my duty.

The two women continued to talk around me as if I were solely there for entertainment. It was odd, yet exciting at the same time. For the time being at least, I was just sexual theatre, the prospect, while new to me, wasn't entirely objectionable.

"It's… I never imagined you would be into this to the *degree* you are," Leanne continued. "Maybe I'm just surprised?"

"You opened this Pandora's Box, Leanne. I'm all in now. Get used to it."

Seeing Leanne at a loss for words was new, too. Her eyes went from me and back to Stefany. Her expression was a multitude of emotions; shock, amazement, alarm - and to some degree, excitement.

"So. Can I watch, too?" Leanne finally joked.

"Of course," Stefany said without pause. She motioned to one of the adjacent chairs. "Have a seat. Mobley was just demonstrating his masturbation skills, something he no doubt frequently practices."

Leanne laughed, taking her designated seat.

"Mobley," Stefany interrupted. "Stop, go get another glass and some wine for Leanne."

I complied, rising to go get another glass in the kitchen, walking uncomfortably with a raging hard-on. Leanne giggled from behind me. "He is rather well endowed. I didn't realize."

"He makes Miles look like a toothpick," Stefany joked. "Not that size matters."

"True," Leanne agreed. "But it is better than a tiny alternative."

"A talented tongue, though, is worth at least as much as a nice dick."

"You've discovered," Leanne declared, "a woman could conceivably live by a talented tongue alone."

"Indeed. If Mobley were to have an accident tomorrow and lose his cock, I would be sad, certainly. He'd probably have to have a prosthetic of some sort sewn on. They do that, you know?"

"So I've heard," Leanne acknowledged.

"Of course, he'd have to work that tongue double-time to my satisfaction. Which is fine. He seems to enjoy it as much as me, mind you. I could be perfectly happy with that. Everything else is icing on the cake. This may sound crass, Leanne, but Mobley's face was made to come on."

"Evidently, by you, Cousin."

Stefany brightened with a sudden idea and turned to Leanne. "I could loan him to you."

Leanne laughed at this notion. "At the current time, I am getting plenty of talented head. Maybe some time, though, yes." Leanne eyed me from her chair. "With everything that you say he is, he has piqued my curiosity."

"Let me know," Stefany casually affirmed, sipping her wine, slipping off her shoes and ankle socks, looking very comfortable.

Red-faced now and shocked at their erotic, albeit joking banter, I filled Leanne's glass with wine and handed it to her without comment. She wanted to question me, I could tell, but we both kept our silence. She glanced at my erection then threw me a sly smile, her eyes full of humorous derision. Was Stefany joking about loaning me?

"Back on your knees, Mobley," Stefany instructed. "Continue."

I dropped and returned to stroking my own cock, oddly aroused at this strange notion of performing in front of two beautiful women who were content to sit in front of me, sipping their wine as they watched.

I was getting close as they chit-chatted small talk between each other. What should I do? Hesitating, I stopped, trying to maintain steady breathing.

"Why are you stopping, Mobley," Stefany asked.

Embarrassed and failing to answer, she pushed my chin up with a big toe. "Why?"

"I'm... close," I explained.

"Close?"

"Yes."

"Ah. You are right to wait," she said, leaning forward in her chair. "Thanks. That reminds me, you are never to come without me saying so first. While you compose yourself, get up and refill our glasses."

I did as she asked, taking the bottle from the table, erection in tow.

At this, Leanne chuckled. "I had no idea you had him so well trained. How did you manage to get him to just shut up? We all know Morgan has quite the gift for incessant gab."

I began to offer resentment at this remark before Stefany again shushed me with a finger. Needing no further persuasion, I poured their wine and returned the bottle to the table.

"The riding crop can be quite persuasive," Stefany explained jokingly, flashing me a knowing smile. "And he *agreed* to do everything I asked, so he's being good and keeping up on his commitments. A right proper sex slave. Yes, Mobley?"

"Yes, Ms. Stefany."

"Good." She leaned back in her chair. "Back on your knees. Continue, Mobley. All the way. You may finish."

"Stef, you seem to be doing quite well on your own," Leanne remarked. "You don't have to do my Assignment 3 later this week. I think you are ready to do whatever you want on your own."

"Oh, yeah, I'm doing Assignment 3," Stefany confirmed. "I read it and it's great. I just wanted to do some of my ideas as well. How do you like this one?"

"I've created a monster," Leanne joked.

The whole scene Stefany had concocted was unbelievably erotic and raunchy, and yet it was an exercise in control and visuals - even though it was just me doing me. It was voyeuristic, which is something I never thought I would engage in, much less like. And it had me on the verge of blowing my nuts right there in front of them. Perhaps still nervous, I closed my eyes and continued to stroke for them, oddly excited.

"Mobley. Eyes on me. The whole time, don't close them. And scoot forward on the towel."

Wondering what she had in mind, I obliged, moving in closer to Stefany, my face now at her knees, keenly aware both women were intently watching my every move.

"Keep going," Stefany said, propping her right foot onto my shoulder like she was simply relaxing during a typical day. I could plainly see her exposed white panties beneath her skirt that had bunched up around her hips. "You are to look at me and don't turn away. You may kiss my legs for inspiration."

Accepting my reward, I caressed her calves with my free hand, kissing her, leaving little wet trails up and down her legs, all the while looking up into her eyes. I had to wonder if she had any idea just how deeply in love I was with her. Did she know my secret? She did know I would do anything for her, which she was learning to use to her full advantage.

Drunklike and moaning, I leaned in against her left knee, kissing it as I began to come. Creamy streamers gushed out onto the towel as they both watched as I struggled to keep my eyes locked on Stefany's as she had instructed.

"Nicely done, Mobley," Stefany complimented when I sat back on my heels, spent. She casually sipped her wine and softly ran the toes of one foot across my lips. I tried to regain my breath.

"Get dressed. Put that towel in the bathroom hamper," she said, pushing me back with her foot against my chest. "You can go back to work, now."

Leanne, still amazed at the newfound kinky talents of her cousin, sat in amazement at the sight, wearing a lusty hungry look that I had never seen on her. "That. Was. Fucking. Hot," she managed to remark hoarsely.

"Same time Friday every week?" Stefany asked her, still watching me as I pulled up my underwear over my depleted cock.

"Yes," Leanne agreed.

Stefany: Good gawd, I'm having so much fun with Mobley. On sooo many levels. He's reached down and touched something deep in me that I never knew existed - essentially, the ability to enjoy sex. His magic mouth - and amazing tongue - and his incredible cock - are driving me

CRAZY. Maybe this is unintentional on his part, who knows. If it weren't for Leanne's "contract," my life would be much different. I give her credit, of course. But Mobley keeps it going and he hasn't complained once. Except maybe about getting cropped, which he better damn well get used to. He seems to enjoy what we do every bit as much as me - and that makes it even more exciting.

The bad news is someone shot at Mobley while he was away with Santiago and Miguel. They had stopped at a little grocery and gas station. If he hadn't ducked just at that very moment to pick up something off the ground, he would more than likely be dead from a head shot. That Constable Fillmore and his "department" are clueless. They have absolutely NO idea who may be behind this, nothing. Mobley thinks it's Miles, but I don't think Miles would be that stupid to hire someone to kill us.

When all of this happened and I got the full story, I realized some startling things about myself. Even though Mobley and I have a very unusual relationship - and it certainly started off rough - I've learned to "feel" something about someone again. I wasn't just upset upon hearing his near-death experience, I was wrecked over the thought I could have lost him! He means so much to me now. To be blunt, he's not just a blond-haired head between my legs eating my pussy. What is mysterious to me is I am not sure how Mobley transitioned from sex toy to someone that I care very deeply about.

~~~~~

One thing I must acknowledge is, I wouldn't be where I'm at without Mobley. He made me a success. He saved this business! This is one thing that is with me every minute of every day. I don't talk about it much, even with Leanne. But there it is. Funny thing is, Mobley has never tried to make hay of this - AT ALL. He doesn't even ask for a pay raise! I'm still getting my head around this, the enigma of Morgan Mobley.

Of all people, I never thought it would be Mobley to tug on my heartstrings. I don't tell him this, but I used to RELISH hating him. Now, I can barely stand to be without him. What the hell. Now, he is closer to me than anyone in my whole life apart from Leanne. I don't mind exploring myself with him. No matter what, he accepts me and wants even more. There could be no better lover for me, that I have come to realize. In all of this, I must remind myself his needs are as important as mine.

As far as sex goes, I've had a whole new universe open. I feel bold. I do what I want. I get what I want - and I find myself wanting more and more. Am I addicted to sex??? Something I used to think applied to Mobley??? It used to be just having an orgasm with anyone besides myself was nearly impossible. Now? I'm a multiple gal.

DECISIONS

The power and control I have over Mobley

is a constant, EPIC turn on. And I don't even know why!

I'm not the least bit shy around him. Having sex and being naked in front of him is as natural as breathing anymore. That, in and of itself, is earth-shattering considering I've never wanted anyone to ever see me naked.

~~~~~

Okay, so I'm putting my thoughts together, trying to figure this all out. Everything before Mobley was horrible sex. Old boyfriends were lame, now that I know what good sex can be like. Miles doesn't even qualify as a man by comparison and a cheap vibrator is more desirable, sexually, and intellectually. A soggy ham sandwich would be a better lover than Miles.

What have I done to myself? I've changed so much. I think and look at things differently. All because of this BDSM thing of Leanne's twisted little mind that she cooked up with Mobley and me. I will not allow the "feels" I have for Mobley to wreck my fun with him. I haven't gone THAT far down the fucking rabbit hole. And no matter what, I vow, here and

FOREVER, I will not allow these new feelings I have for him to morph into "love." I won't allow it! Yes, I care for him. We are great friends, I like and lust him, and that is ALL. I may crop his ass extra just because of these "feelings" I think he may have for me.

As I just wrote this - I regretted it. The words sound awful and mean. What has happened to me! Leanne would have a psychological field day with this.

~~~~~

Asshole Miles has somehow managed to insert himself at Stoney Brook, and it's my fault. But he's helping to run the Mill Property, so he is largely out of my hair. He's no doubt over there flirting up every woman that will return his advances. I caught him so many times being unfaithful, I think it probably started nearly the day after our wedding. At least Miles is conveniently away from being anywhere near here during my playtime with Mobley.

~~~~~

Tomorrow, I'm going to hire a security professional to evaluate Stoney Brook and the Mill Property. We'll add

more security cameras and do some training. I'll also put some measures in place just to make sure Mobley stays safe. He'll be stubborn about it and say I'm overreacting, but it will be mandatory. I could threaten him by saying I would withhold sex from him, but who am I kidding there.

"Look. Look here," Mobley implored.

Making sure no one was looking, I reached down the back of Mobley's sweatpants, feeling about on his butt cheeks. I could have died laughing but managed to keep a straight face.

"Yeah. So?"

"So? It's sore and welts are raised! You still whack on me with that crop, and damned hard at that. And after being all worried about me getting shot from a sniper. Feel that. Feel the raised welts." Mobley angled his butt towards me to better facilitate a feel. I now knew that we were just about as close as any two people could be, considering this whiny narrative Mobley was giving me about one of our latest unscripted trysts. We were every bit... a couple? The irony was not lost to me.

I withdrew my hand. "Mobley. I'm going to give you an extra lash or two in the next session just because you are griping about it."

"What? Remember when you came to my room after stripping the skin off my ass in Assignment 1? *You felt bad*, you said. You were going to go easier, you said."

"Quit exaggerating. I certainly did NOT strip the skin from your ass in Assignment 1. It was a little red is all. Cry baby."

"But now, it's sore. I can't impress on you how sore! Very, very sore."

"Were you not satisfied? Did you not enjoy yourself? Please do tell me if you didn't. Because it sure looked like you *were* enjoying yourself."

"Well. Um. Yes. Yes, indeed, I did enjoy myself."

"Ah. So, it's just a bit of residual pain you are regretting now? Is that it? Well. You can't see it, but I'm crying on the inside for you, Mobley. I am. I'm soooo sorry." I fake wiped a tear from my eye.

"What? You are?"

I smacked his butt hard, evoking a wince and sudden lurch forward. I laughed, realizing yet again that Mobley was gold-medal gullible. "Gawd. It was sarcasm, Mobley. It gives me pleasure. Which is *your* main purpose in life. Right? "

"Er. Yes."

I batted my eyes in my best innocent schoolgirl imitation. "You better just learn to roll with it. For me?"

He pulled me to him. "Really?"

"Yeah."

He kissed me, hard.

I pushed away from him after a moment, conscious that privacy was limited. "Better close it down, Mobley. Miles is supposed to be arriving soon for a meeting with me in the office. Not to mention there are too many prying eyes about."

He looked disappointed. "Later?"

"We'll see." I peered up into his handsome face, lost in the deep ocean blue of his eyes. Never in my life have I had a man so into me. It was both powerful, exciting and in some ways, terrifying. Before we both turned to go to our respective tasks, I jabbed him in the ribs. "You better hope I forget this conversation. Complaints about the crop only get you more."

"You are kidding again, right?"

"I'll rub lotion on it for you," I joked.

"So, when is our next assignment? Can we work on it tonight?"

"Here you are complaining about being a little sore, and you want another assignment already."

"I do feel better."

"Great. But we are going on a little break for a couple of days. I was thinking let's just do movie night together. No assignments. You come up tonight. Say around 7:30?"

He grimaced. "Just a movie? I don't understand. Can't we-"

"It's *that* time, Mobley. Of the month? Just come up and let's enjoy each other sans sex for once. Let's see if it's even possible."

"Oh, that. I see. Listen, that doesn't scare me off from you in the least. We could... you know... in the shower? In case you didn't know, for a guy, it's called getting your *red wings*. I don't know what women call it. Have you heard of that term?"

"No. What an incorrigible and disgusting pervert you are. Truly. What does it say for me that you no longer shock me, Mobley?"

"7:30?"

Later that evening, the soft knock on the door to my quarters told me that it was just about time to start our movie night date. Opening it, Mobley stood with a large, covered bowl. He ogled the short house robe I was wearing, as usual. "I brought popcorn. And..." He slipped his hand behind him and withdrew a beautiful tropical flower from his back pocket. "A flower for you, my beautiful goddess."

I laughed again at the notion of him calling me a goddess. I would never get used to that. Just *Ms. Stefany* works for me, but I'd roll with it. Here he was with yet another thoughtful, sweet gesture from a man I used to think was shallow. Taking the flower, I delicately smelled it in my best ladylike fashion, enjoying the wonderful aroma. It was so fresh; he must have just cut it from one of the gardens. Laying it on a nearby bureau, I similarly took the bowl from his hands and sat it next to the flower. I then reached out, clenched Mobley's collar and pulled him in, shutting the door behind him with my foot. I immediately pushed him against the wall, wrapped my arms around his neck and kissed him.

"Wow. I'm glad to see you too," he grinned when I finally let him up for air.

"It would seem I can't get enough of you, Mobley. Imagine that."

"Nor I of you." With that, he again pulled me close, bit my lower lip, and this time initiated a session of passionate kissing that left me weak in the knees.

"Damn you. You insolent thing," I said, gasping, finally pushing him away.

"I am. You should do something about that," he suggested, obviously wanting more than the movie for the evening.

"Oh, I will. You'll pay. Another time."

"Why not now? I think you know I would do anything for you."

"I do know that." I pulled him again to my mouth. "And believe me, Morgan Mobley, as long as I breathe, I'll never forget that. But for now? No."

At that point, I wanted him more than anything else in my life. Even more than Stoney Brook. Unable to put into words what I felt about this man, all I could do was slide the palm of my right hand softly down his jaw. Through our weird relationship, he had somehow rejuvenated my heart and soul. I couldn't explain the dynamics or psychology. Leanne perhaps could do that, but I doubted it.

I thought about this for a moment. What if I were in love with Morgan Mobley? Would I even know it? It was a question I didn't want to examine too closely. Avoiding the question and answer was something I had perfected throughout my life, and I knew even with this situation, I would look past it and ignore it – just roll with it.

"You should know, Mobley, I reserve the right to kiss you at any time during the movie. Is that okay?"

"Yes," was his only reply. Even after months of an ever-growing relationship, Morgan Mobley was something totally new to me in every way. His humor. Passion. He was both goofy and gullible. hEverything about him was perfect for me. I knew life better than that. The only thing left would be when he crushed my heart like fistfuls of dried leaves in his strong hands. Wasn't that the inevitable conclusion to this?

I took his hand and pulled him towards the couch. "Let's go, Mobley. The movie is ready. Please sit on the floor. I'm so used to using your hair for a handgrip, tonight, I just want to enjoy running my fingers through it while we watch. You have such soft hair. It's sort of a girl thing. You know?"

"What? For the whole movie?"

"Yes. Why, do you have a problem with that?"

He smiled. "I guess not. Go ahead."

Morgan sat down on the floor, leaning against the couch. I sat behind him and wound my bare legs around his chest, my crossed feet resting in his lap. If not for the pledge of abstinence, I would have acknowledged his persistent erection which I could feel. His chest rose and fell, and I felt more intimate with Mobley than anyone else in my entire life. Leaning back and enjoying myself, I ran my fingers into his wonderfully soft locks of blond hair. It wasn't quite long enough to braid, but that didn't stop me from trying. He seemed to be enjoying himself, but his eyes soon became droopy with my ministrations. Having grown quiet, he didn't seem to be following the movie, instead enjoying the sensations of my fingers in his hair.

Kissing the insides of my knees at one point, he suggested I rethink a romp in the shower to which I declined with some hesitation.

About three-quarters of the way through the movie, Mobley was out cold asleep, his head leaning against my right knee. How he could sleep even as I was tracing the outline of his jaw with my fingers was amazing.

Several times I leaned down, running my lips over his ears, planting small kisses along the sides of his face which made him squirm, revealing that he was somewhat ticklish. The overall effect, however, was to continue to put him to sleep. Just watching him warmed my heart.

Locking my fingers beneath his chin, I pulled his head back and leaned down, blowing lightly in his face. Other than a slight mumbling sound, he remained asleep. I had to laugh. Evidently, he could sleep through anything.

After a while, I too found myself dozing off. The movie ended, and I changed the channel to something innocuous for background noise and leaned back, enjoying the warmth of Mobley's body. After one final caress across his cheek, I too succumbed and allowed my eyes to drop closed just as I heard a knock on my door.

After disentangling myself from Mobley, I walked to the door and cracked it open with the safety chain latched. It was Leanne. I let her in.

"I thought I would find you two together."

"What's up," I asked seeing the worried look on her face.

"Miles is here. He's on his way up and will be here any minute. You've got to get Morgan out."

I thought about this for a moment. Mobley made me happy. Now, I was going to have to change my plans for the evening for someone that did the opposite of making me happy. "Maybe I should just tell him tonight, I'm seeing Mobley. Get it over with. Maybe then he'd agree to the divorce."

"No! You can't let him catch Morgan up here. It will only make things worse for you in court, and probably worse for Morgan." She caught my hesitation, alarm growing on her face by the moment. "Look, we can talk about it later! Get him out, Stef. I'll go run interference. Hurry!" She stepped out and closed the door behind her, leaving me to wake Mobley.

Leaning down, I lifted his head and kissed him. Stirring, his eyes fluttered then focused on me. "That's a nice way to wake up."

"You've got to leave; Miles is on his way up. Sorry."

This thought rolled around in his head, just as it had mine. "Let's just tell him. We can't keep running around in secret. You are separated, damn it!"

"Not right now. Come on." I pulled him to his feet. At the door, I gave him a goodnight kiss then swatted his butt before I sent him into the hall. "Take the second-floor hallway all the way around to the back stairs."

He grinned back at me. "Thanks for a great evening. Even if it was *milder* than usual. Good night."

"We'll resume your regularly scheduled duties soon." I blew him a kiss and closed the door.

Miles had just missed seeing Mobley leave my room, which would have made for some difficult explaining. He did mention with suspicion that he had seen Mobley on the back stairs. I simply shrugged it off and said there is no telling what Mobley is up to after hours.

I reluctantly let Miles stay the night and sleep on my office sofa. His argument for needing to stay over was that he stayed late making arrangements for restocking the Mill Property. Again, I had to deflect his requests for reconciliation and his desire to sleep with me. It was a relief to send him away after an awkward breakfast.

Returning to my office, I found my thoughts again drifting to my favorite subject: Mobley. Turning over the confused jumble of conflicting emotions in my head, I had to ask myself, where was I going with this strange relationship I had with him. A depressing thought occurred to me. What if Mobley tired of our playtime? Or he became bored with me? And how would that affect our ability to work together in the future?

As I mulled these discomforting thoughts over, I noticed a folder had been slipped under the office doors. Quickly walking over to pick it up, I was pleased to see that one of the front desk staff girls had brought it up. A sticky note on top told me that Marisha Neita had sent me her latest transcription of the McCaskill ledger. Every four days or so, I could expect just such a folder from Marisha, and I had now read enough of the ledger to determine that my ancestor, the founder of Stoney Brook, was no angel. Despite the brutal nature of Seumas McCaskill, I eagerly devoured every new revelation from his ledger.

I called the front desk and told Lydia to hold my calls and visitors for a while unless it was an emergency. Getting comfortable at my desk, I propped my feet up and flipped open the folder to begin reading Marisha's new revelations.

> The Ledger of Seumas Owen McCaskill
> (continued)
> > April 20, 1622
> > "I wed Nancy McCullum, in doing so, uniting two proud ancient families of my homeland. Me being back home caused some disagreement but it all went over after a fashion, and the McCullum's came around to the idea after they discovered I was a right and justified landowner, even if it were across the ocean. My earlier seafaring with Captain Love was mostly forgotten and none knew of my time later at sea and being on the account, and

none needed know anything of it, my career being known as a merchant man to both families.

September 24, 1622

"Having arrived with Nancy at Stoney Brook, she is overwhelmed by its size and complexity, all running smooth by the overseer's hand during my absence. Bhoki were rightly set out, having not yet learned to temper her tongue and manner, even with the lash, and being a bad influence on the others. The household runs better with her though, and I'll bring her back in several weeks after she learn some degree of humility at the hands of the overseer, as he has no hesitation to mar a smooth, she-slave's back, one as pleasing a sight even as Bhoki's may be, with all her fiery charms that catch the eye. I've instructed him I'll have no permanent marks made, nor will I tolerate him to make her cause of pregnancy or otherwise ruined to excess before she is again set back at the house.

"The overseer, he are a right strict man, as much as myself perhaps, and he tells me he beat to death two of my slaves while I was gone, which caused me some degree of anger, as it's money out of my pocket and with no recompense. Another brace he set to the irons in the cellars without food and water, losing another two before letting them out. Yet he says it were necessary as a lesson to all. Births are up and so I have hope the work force will be sustained over time without need of additional purchases."

Recalling the wall-mounted steel shackles in the cellar where Mobley installed the wine storage racks, I sat

484

up, feeling ill to my stomach. In its early history, my beloved plantation, Stoney Brook, had been built on cruelty and murder, there was no question about it. Despite vowing that I would not let this negative energy derail what I was building, none of it sat well with me. For the first time since reading Marisha's transcriptions of the McCaskill ledger, I hesitated, wondering if I really wanted to know more. What would it change?

Steeling myself, I decided to press on. I did need to know these things, regardless of how distasteful they were. There was no gilding the lily with this account, and it had taken some of the luster off my romantic idea of the plantation and my ancestors. Again, I reminded myself: I was not Seumas McCaskill. I had nothing to do with how he obtained or built Stoney Brook.

January 8, 1623
"The production of our primary crop is well underway, with a sizable portion of our land set to growing sugar cane. I've also set a crew to begin work on a sugar mill to better process what the island can produce, furthering my profits as my neighbors were also in need of such.

"Nancy has fallen in love with Stoney Brook and is taking up her rightful place among the everyday here. She has made friends of other ladies of the island and frequently has them as guests which makes the evening hours wile away.

June 17, 1623
"Nancy is with child, and I could not be happier.

December 22, 1623
"I am the proud father of a healthy son, Arlon Carrick.

May 3, 1624

"It were quite a surprise, when five of my old shipmates came a calling but not for social means it would seem. A low lot, rope and sail shakes that were in general of poor service if memory served. They had discovered my whereabouts by word of mouth of Stoney Brook and all I had built in such a short time. Having squandered their own lives to this point, they further meant to take from me whatever they could, figuring they were more entitled to what was my share of earnings when I was captain. Their presence has brought about several questions by the gentry of the island; our neighbors and friends, those that have seen them about here, them making port here as a shady refuse aboard a merchant and seeking me out and being the appearance of less than common sailors. There are now questions as to my past, as already the case with Nancy and I find they have caused me a considerable degree of discomfort. They paid a call here at Stoney Brook and threatened my family and my livelihood if I didn't send them on their way well paid with what I have kept as my own share and what I have used to build my fortunes here at Stoney Brook. Taken with her beauty, one met his fate with Bhoki's knife when they meant to have her, when first they came while I was away. The commotion was made aware by all, and so in the process, another, shot by my overseer. The remaining bilge rats by my own hand, although I were stabbed and shot through in the doing.

"It were at this time it came to my attention that these five were under a Letter of Marque from the Crown, and their deaths will come to my account for murder, putting me at risk of being sent back and tried for piracy. It is for this reason, the fate of these five will never be known, and it is only assumed they have gone missing, vanished. Several made inquiry but were assured they seemed bent on departing on a ship that left 3 days prior.

"Despite my injuries from the fray, all minor to my luck, I'll recover, but they will not, they safely be awaitin' hell and no longer will they bother me or anyone else for that matter. Given they were under a Letter of Marque, no one can ever know their fate or discover their whereabouts lest I risk a dance at the gibbet. Aye, and I've taken the safest recourse I know. They will serve out eternity beneath the foundations of Stoney Brook, as will the means of which they meant to use to bring me low, being their firearms and personal arms. As the two that fancied to take me by sword were cleaved thoroughly through by my family's Claymore, I've hidden it also with this lot, well tallowed in the sheath to keep, although I know not what proof could be made I killed these men with it. Perhaps it be prudent caution is all my own mind, and I intend to retrieve it later to pass this on to my own son."

I continued to read the ledger transcript for the better part of the afternoon. Each page delivered more shock than the last as more and more pieces of the Stoney Brook puzzle came together.

Bhoki, the beautiful slave girl, was evidently not a young woman to be trifled with, slave or not, yet she had obviously been abused by the "overseer" for having a defiant, rebellious nature. Had she also been abused by Seumas? It was a possibility, judging by the somewhat lewd way she was described in the ledger. The injustice and cruelty made me cringe.

Additionally, I had a cryptic hint at the pirate cave in the cellar by Seumas himself. He had killed members of his old crew that had come to look him up and rob him. To cover up his past and keep anyone from asking uncomfortable questions about piracy, the dead men had been interred into the bowels of Stoney Brook, sealed up and eventually forgotten.

And now, I finally had an answer as to which ancestor of mine had assumed ownership of Stoney Brook after Seumas: Arlon Carrick McCaskill.

CHAPTER 16

A TALENTED TONGUE IS A TIRED TONGUE

Stefany: I met Marisha Neita in town again today. She had more of Seumas' ledger transcribed. We read it together,

The Charm That Marisha Gave Me!

completely immersed in the early life of Seumas' young son, Arlon Carrick McCaskill. Despite the joy of having a healthy child, the times were rife with violence and cruelty

at Stoney Brook, with slave hangings after uprisings, beatings, and other atrocities I could barely stand to read. Truly, I am ashamed of my namesake. They were brutes. I know Marisha is as shocked as I am, yet she holds it all in very well and has withheld passing judgment on me for my ancestors.

~~~~~

I've been having Mobley report to my office daily for the purpose of him providing oral servitude. I have to say, it is a great way to top off an afternoon, seeing him on his knees beneath my desk, face between my legs while I enjoy myself. We were even interrupted several times with people coming into the room to see me! None were aware of his presence, thankfully. It was sort of a turn-on discussing business while he lapped away in secret.

Another element I have permanently added to Mobley's repertoire is having a cup of ice ready for him while he's giving head. Leanne's BDSM book mentioned the various sensual uses of ice and I love him occasionally using a piece of ice between his lips, lightly rubbing it over my inner thighs. And when I'm about to come, the amazing sensations of a piece of crushed ice in his mouth is indescribable.

He loves everything about these head sessions except him not getting any action in return; a marked departure from his sexual dalliances with all the women in his past when it was ALL about him. Not so with me. He's learned not to complain, and I like to see his tortured expressions when he leaves, blue-balls ala mode. It's fun to make him wait. He gets his reward when the time is right.

~~~~~

I have an idea and some new plans for Mobley. Plans that go beyond the regular assignments from Leanne or his daily oral service. During his last office performance in front of Leanne, I mentioned to her that I would be willing to loan him out if she would like. There's something hot about the notion of "making" him service other women at my direction. She dismissed it, of course. When I said it, I wasn't sure how serious I was being. Was I? I think I am.

This was another idea I gleaned from a story in Leanne's BDSM book. It was about doms sharing their subs with other doms, and the power rush and pure hot sex it could be. It continued to roll around in my mind after I read it, and the more I thought about it, the hotter it got. I think it's the excitement of controlling him in such a manner that is so compelling in this.

So, here's the idea… what if I made him service Leanne? And Heidi, even? While I watch and give him directions. It would sorta be like what Leanne did with Heidi and Joe when I visited her in her apartment. Maybe lash Mobley's ass cherry-red to make sure he is "doing it right"? Then to cap it all off, take my turn with him. I've certainly never considered having anything to do with sex in front of any other people. That was strictly *ewww*, I've always thought. But now? It wouldn't *really* be sex with anyone else. It's only watching Mobley being used by them at my direction. Holy shit… it sounds fucking hot. Should I?

Have I changed that much over these last months to even consider such a thing? Am I that much of a horny maniac now??? Leanne certainly doesn't have any problems talking about her sex romps in front of me. Am I going over the limit?

Mobley has granted me the freedom to consider such things. Okay, decision time. I'm going to do it. I'll have to figure out a time to tell him. I suppose he could back out of it if he chooses to. I won't make him do it if he's absolutely opposed to the idea. But he's dedicated to me and what I want. Plus, it's Mobley, the walking hormone. So, I am betting he will be "down" for it. Where is Leanne when I finally come up with a good pun???

Ariana handed me my mail as I walked past the front desk. "Thanks. Hopefully, these aren't all bills," I joked.

"Ms. Michaels, do you know where I might find Mr. Mobley? Miguel and the boys were looking for him to discuss a project they are supposed to be starting down by the barn."

"Hmmm. He's probably just tied up," I explained.

"Okay, thanks," Ariana shrugged. "I'll tell them to see him tomorrow morning if he doesn't show up."

"Right." I took the back stairs and began reading the mail. Several letters were handwritten notes from guests thanking me for their wonderful visits, which were always a welcome surprise. I loved reading letters from satisfied guests. More and more, it seemed that the amenities of Stoney Brook were receiving recognition in magazines and travel shows.

Getting to the last letter, I arrived at my office door which I pushed open with my foot as I read. Closing it behind me, I set the mail on my desk then checked my phone for any messages. Nothing pressing, which was good. Having just spent an hour going over inventory with the kitchen manager, the afternoon was getting late, and I was looking forward to a glass of wine.

Mobley, I noticed, was still nicely bound and completely naked in the doorway to my living quarters. The ball gag I had shoved in his mouth before I left to alleviate the griping and complaining was still in place. He was probably a bit sore, but none the worse for wear. His arms were behind his lower back in handcuffs and pulled up slightly by a rope to the top of the door jamb – at just the right height to keep him on his tiptoes. By using my workout pullup bar, it was a repeat of what we did at the Mill Property bungalow. His ankles were bound together by a smaller piece of rope. It looked uncomfortable and I was glad I was the dom and not the sub. He tried to mumble something to me, but I ignored him for the moment.

I poured my glass of wine then walked over to my office bureau, took my crop out of the drawer, and set about dealing with Mobley. Dragging my finger slowly across his chin, I was reminded that he was still Mobley after all, and he was quite prone to irritating back talk, which is what got him tied to my door jamb in the first place.

"My, my. You are an insolent one, aren't you, Mobley? Has this last hour tied up in the door jamb taught you anything?"

"Mmmmrfff!" Whatever he mumbled against the ball gag, judging from the look on his face, it was yet another insincere apology. Typical.

"Let's go over the list of offences, shall we?" I began. "First, telling me I'm… and I quote… *just one step away from being a vengeful, spurned shrew of a nag*? And second, going on to say I'm working the staff like Stoney Brook is a gulag work camp. Oh really?"

WHAP!!!

"Mmmmrfff!"

494

"Then third, telling me I don't know what the hell I'm doing when it comes to demonstrating good leadership? Fourth, and most egregious of all, telling me I don't know how to drink a quality beverage like Scotch. What the hell!? Where did that all come from!? Are you in such a bad mood and so assuming you think you can come up here and unload on me like this?"

WHAP!!!

"Mmmmmmmrfff!"

"Mr. Mobley. I know full well what good Scotch is, you arrogant ass. *And* had you bothered to ask before you burst in here in your accusing tone, I have increased benefits this year to three weeks of vacation for everyone. Even you, although you hardly deserve it after this tirade of yours. You really should get all your facts straight before you go letting your mouth get you in trouble. *Again.*"

I pulled the gag off.

"That sharp tongue of yours is useful to me in only one capacity, do you understand that, Mobley? You assume too much with our familiarity with each other. I'll not have you come up here disrespecting me, throwing insults. Have you learned your lesson?"

"Yes! Yes," he breathily answered. "Cramps… leg cramps! Please!"

"And now, are you prepared to make up for your impudent transgressions? What was going to be a simple business discussion with you this afternoon turned into a huge fiasco. Now, I'm in the mood for something else. And you know what? You had better not expect any return gratification. What say you."

"Agreed! I'll… do whatever you ask. Just untie me from this fucking do-" He caught himself just as he realized how he was sounding. "Um. *Please* untie me from this door. And I won't volunteer any more… inappropriate comments… just because I'm in an… intemperate mood. As you say."

WHAP!!!

"OWWaahhhhh!"

"Good. I should say not. Seems you have been getting quite brave with your grousing comments and opinions of late. And you have no problem telling me all about them. Should I release you from the door? Honestly, I don't think you've learned a damned thing."

"No, I have, I promise. Please, *please*, release me from the door. Ms. Stefany."

"When I call you up here, I don't expect the cranky, irritable and brazen version of Morgan Mobley to show up. And ruin my mood, for either business... or pleasure."

"No. You are right. I just felt like... crabbing... I suppose. I won't do it again, I promise." His eyes were pleading. I managed to restrain a devious smile. Truthfully, I couldn't be happier he showed up at my office in a bad mood.

"Oh, we both know you will do it again," I remarked acidly. "It's who you are, after all. I guess I shouldn't have expected a complete personality transformation with you. Although, you are much more tolerable than when you were first employed here. Good gawd, you couldn't be made to shut up come hell or high water. At least now, with our agreement, I have the crop to remind you - a tool that has proved most useful in improving the quality of our conversation. Not to even mention the ball gag. Where has that been all my life for the men I've known?"

"Stefany, can we just move past this and let me off this damned door before I die of old-." His eyes went wide, realizing that he had again run his troublesome mouth. "Ah, shit." Evidently, he *hadn't* had enough. He began swinging his butt away from me to avoid another painful strike. I wished he would come up insolent every time he visited; he was making it so much fun.

"You just can't help yourself, can you?" I asked, unable to keep from laughing.

"No! I mean, yes! I didn't mean to say... *that*. I'm just in a foul mood, today. I'm sorry."

I ran the end of the crop over his manhood teasingly. "So. You are ready for me to let you down, insolent man?"

"Yes."

Pulling on the release knot, the rope came loose from the pullup bar in the jamb. His arms dropped and he looked visibly relieved. He began arcing his shoulders back and forth to ease the apparent stiffness from being tied for over an hour. I took off the handcuffs, then he bent down and untied his own ankles. When he handed me the small piece of rope, I almost thought he would make another smart-assed comment. He was wisely silent.

Taking a good magazine, I then sat down in the closest chair with my glass of wine and a cup of ice for Mobley. I was going to enjoy relaxing – and getting off – for the next hour or so.

"Mobley, get over here, it's floor duty. Let's see you use your mouth for something other than insolent backtalk."

He dropped to the floor before me, pulled off my shoes and began kissing the tops of my feet - standard procedure.

"No griping or complaints, Mobley?"

"Well, to be truthful, this kind of work does put me in a better mood."

"I'm glad to hear that. Just remember, nothing for you today."

"Um. Fine," he mumbled with a slight tinge of disappointment as he started kissing and sucking each of my toes.

The man needed to remember his place, and he was doing a magnificent job of it, letting his tongue lap away at my soles, then wind its way around my ankles - it became increasingly difficult to concentrate on my magazine. Deciding to let him take the initiative this time, he eventually kissed his way slowly up my legs, stopping at strategic points to work, such as the sensitive spots around my knees. The relaxing feeling I was enjoying eventually turned into something much more needful. The magazine became nothing more than a prop in my hands. Mobley had been through this drill enough to know what I wanted. After due diligence, I pushed off my panties and slid down in the chair to give him easy access. After a few soft, sweet, little kisses on the insides of my thighs, he pushed the hem of my skirt up and I opened my legs for him. As I absently turned the pages of the magazine, he dove in, for the most part softly, at other times more forceful, depending on my urgency. He was masterful with his lips and tongue, occasionally using ice, kissing, licking, and sucking away on my clit much as he had just done with my toes. With his whole mouth over me, he would repeatedly push his tongue as far into me as he could, all the while looking up into my eyes. I loved this so much, I think it was something I could enjoy nearly full time - I felt sorry for women that would never experience the joy of such an arrangement as I had with Mobley.

Numerous times, he brought me to the brink, made me wait in agonizing need, then pushed me over. I don't know how many times I came on his wonderful mouth; I didn't keep track. As usual, he didn't complain about what had to be a painful grip I sometimes had in his hair - always extra credit for that. A little over an hour later, it was time to release him so he could return to work.

I had to laugh. He always wanted to get his own satisfaction after getting my rocks off. Hearing him beg for relief, even a hand-job, was a huge turn-on. Begging was good, griping and bitching was not. But it wasn't going to happen for him this time. He couldn't just come up to my office and unload his insolence on me. There was decorum to consider, after all.

His hair was a mess and his knees were as red as his glistening, wet face. Tidying my skirt, I then helped him get dressed, patted his face lightly with a towel, and walked him to the door. He hesitated for a moment, no doubt thinking of trying a bit more begging. I grinned up at him knowing he would lose his load with a mere breath on my part.

"I was thinking-"

"Nope."

"But I was good! Right? And thought-"

"No."

"But-"

"Nuh-uh."

His lips began forming yet another appeal and I held my hand up to stop any further juvenile back-and-forth. "I SAID… noooooo, Mobley. Let it be a lesson to hold your tongue… well, not hold your *tongue* per se. I'm rather partial to your tongue. I meant… the never-ending backtalk."

He looked utterly miserable. "Fine. Okay," he agreed, sulking. He turned to go.

"Wait," I said, taking his arm. I wrapped my arms around his neck and kissed him. He reciprocated around my waist, pulling me in tight. After a moment, I let him go. "Feel better now?" I asked.

"Yes," he replied with a smile. "And no. I am sorry about being such a grouch."

He turned to go. I swatted his sore butt without warning, making him lurch his hips forward, eliciting a laugh from us both. As an afterthought, he turned back. "Hey, how about we go to The Blue Calypso and take in a bit of dancing tonight?"

"Sounds like fun. See you at 7:30," I suggested.

"Maybe after…?" His hopes were not entirely dashed, it seemed.

"We'll see, Mobley. Who knows? Maybe it will be your night."

As soon as I closed the door, I laughed, happy as a schoolgirl in love. I poured another glass of wine. Whatever would I do without Morgan Mobley?

A soft breeze whipped through my office windows sending papers fluttering off my desk. The small silver Voodoo talisman on a necklace chain that Marisha had given me months earlier fell to the floor. Picking it up, I stared at it, mesmerized by the idea that it was supposed to hold some protective charm over my life. Was it, in fact, a protective charm? Or was it just a figment of Marisha's imagination, an indoctrination of superstitious beliefs?

I let it spin on the chain in front of my face. It was remarkable in that it was identical to the one that belonged to Bhoki that was discovered in the cave with the Claymore sword. Perhaps it was a traditional island design, started by the slaves of Seumas' time. It was roughly cross-shaped. Marisha had been so thoughtful as to even put my name on the back. Looking at the back, I nearly misread it, thinking it said "Bowkee," just like the piece in the basement museum. I rubbed my eyes. The script was clear - "Stefany."

It had been only several days prior that Marisha had invited me to attend a "Voodoo" service for one of her friends that had died. The experience had been vivid. It seemed to be a mixture of Christian beliefs and traditions that appeared distinctively African in origin. At one point, Marisha invited me to participate in a dance, which I did to the best of my ability. I have no idea what was going on, but it was weirdly interesting. An odd thing about it was, some of it seemed almost erotic. Seeing Marisha and some of the other island women slowly writhe and move, their bodies sleek with oil and scantily dressed was mesmerizing. The music emphasized drums and other percussion instruments that seemed to emanate from inside me. All in all, it was a remarkable experience. They have invited me to regularly attend their other meetings, which I think I will. It was a chance to meet more of the native islanders and they seemed to appreciate the outreach and interest in their culture.

Was Marisha's trust in charms and talismans misplaced? While it was true I had not been harmed in several close scrapes with someone bent on killing me, it could have very easily gone the other way. Marisha had all the outward appearances of a modern, sophisticated woman; college-educated, well-adjusted socially, an accomplished athlete. And yet she still believed in such things. I tenderly placed the talisman back onto my desk by the pen holder. It gave the impression it was "looking" at me.

"I should get Mobley one," I said absently to myself, thinking about his own close brushes with death. But I knew Mobley would immediately dismiss any talk of magic charms as mystic rubbish.

Deciding to take in a bit of ambiance to read Marisha's latest ledger transcript, I snatched it up and headed downstairs. "Lydia, please hold my calls for an hour or so unless it's an emergency," I said, walking past the front desk. "I'll be in the basement looking over some of the additions to the museum display."

"Yes, Ms. Michaels."

I smiled, liking the proper address. It had taken months to correct Mobley's insolent influence on the staff.

Once in the basement, a cold chill ran through me as I scanned the ancient artifacts sitting silently in glass displays. I could imagine the great violence that these items had witnessed – from pirating on the high seas to swashbuckling sword duels that occurred on the very floors of Stoney Brook. Seeing where Seumas had committed his five attackers to eternity along with the sword that played a large part in this conflict was rather spine-tingling. I reprimanded myself silently for having such a macabre sense of curiosity.

Running my hand over the display case that contained the Claymore sword of Seumas McCaskill, I had to ask myself; did I need to fear the evil traits of my own ancestry? The cruel manner of treatment by Seumas towards his slaves was indescribable. While I was proud to be the heir to Stoney Brook, it still gave me pause to consider that it was built on the backs and blood of men and women that never shared in its wealth or glory. I couldn't deny it, on some levels I was ashamed of my long-ago ancestor, Seumas.

Flipping on the breaker to light the cave, I took the stairs down to find a suitable quiet place to read Marisha's transcript. Why I would read it down in the cave, I wasn't quite sure. To perhaps get a feel for what Seumas was really like? Or maybe glean some idea of the times in which he lived? Or maybe I was just a sucker for the spooky atmosphere. Whatever it was, I made my way along the path that eventually led back to the pirate tomb. It was eerily fascinating to me that those very men were contemporaries of Seumas – rogue pirates and thieves.

Even though the historic cave was now safe for the public, it remained one of the creepiest places on the plantation, particularly when visiting it alone. I would pat myself on the back for my plucky courage except I knew that I was in fact scared to death of the place.

The subterranean lighting was somewhat dramatic I thought. Although well done, it gave the cave an additional mystical feel. The only sound was the bubbling of the small stream as it made its way along in the cool air, next to the cave path.

There were several benches added to the trail. Selecting one, I took a seat and began to read.

The Ledger of Seumas Owen McCaskill (continued)

October 13, 1624

"Nancy has shown me daily her displeasure with Bhoki and my insistence she remain a servant of the house. With no other recourse than to send her to the fields, little was accomplished as she has set the whole lot of slaves to a barbaric religion of sorts that can only be described as having erupted from hell. Whilst some seems to be taken from a proper Christian upbringing, there is much that seems to fly in the face of righteousness.

"Deep into the night, the overseer has disbanded these ungodly rituals that more oft than not are conducted with mysterious objects made of bone, plants, pots or cups of blood, and various dead animals. There seems to be use of a type of root as well, that is said to induce spirit visions.

"With the finding of numerous strange amulets and other hellish objects about the house, the overseer held a punishment day, with the main supposed actors taking their lashes along the front entry with the rest to watch for a-warning. It were Bhoki who were also taking the lash for which I was unaware, and she were marked as worse as one could have the rest. I held the overseer accountable for full payment of this offense, as he were not to mark her, and it caused bad words about the manor. I am considering sending the overseer out.

March 8, 1625

"Healed and about, Bhoki remains sullen and unlike before, she speaks not to me unless only answering. Her eyes betray a contempt of me that weren't there before. Nancy wants her sold away entirely, as well as several others that have taken on a more rebellious role among the other slaves.

"The strange items continue to appear in the house and must be of demonic origins. The overseer has since hung two slaves for this offence he claims were involved, but confides he know not, but is done as a warning of sorts. Bhoki takes this action to be of my own. Again, I expressed my displeasure at thinning the workforce, and on my lost investment which is no small measure. The overseer is to leave at sight of first sail back to Ireland and shall never return upon pain of death.

April 25, 1625

"Bhoki is with child."

With trembling hands, I closed the folder, headed up the stairs and shut off the lights. Stunned, I didn't know what to make of the account. Certainly, it was a brutal story.

And what became of Bhoki and her child?

Morgan: **The last few days have been very eventful here. Stefany has a friend who is a native islander. Her name is Marisha and is quite intelligent, beautiful, and well-spoken. Stefany tells me she attended a funeral after an invitation by Marisha. Everything I've heard tells me this woman is likely involved in Voodoo. I am not familiar with the religion, but I have the feeling there are two sides to it, both good and evil. I could be wrong. Stefany seems deeply fascinated by Marisha and her beliefs. I can't help but notice that Stefany seems changed somehow by the experience. It worries me, and I'm not even sure I know why.**

Stefany can't seem to soak up enough new experiences or dive deep enough into her newfound ocean of freedom. I shouldn't be anything but happy for her with this, yet I am hesitant. Maybe I'm just overthinking all of this. Could she be going

too far in this new lifestyle she has made for herself? She continues to evolve. As I write this, I am confirming to myself that while this is okay, I don't want her to lose what it means to be "Stefany." I love her more than ever. Will she ever return these feelings?

~~~~~

Today, we made an astounding discovery while thinning some dense brush perhaps half a kilometer from the manor. It was a small cemetery, previously unknown. And the most distinctive feature? The crypt of Seumas and Nancy McCaskill. Of course, I was shocked. Long before I ever came on the island, many people had wondered where the first McCaskill's were buried, or if they were even on the island at all. Many thought they had either been returned to Scotland or been buried at sea. Now we know, and I'm surprised it's taken this long to discover the site. Even though it was heavily camouflaged by trees, brush, and vines, the crypt itself is quite a prominent structure, standing at least fourteen feet or so in height and excavated below to a similar depth.

Another odd thing about the tomb is that it looks to have been frequently visited. There were several strange items placed around the crypt. Additionally, there were symbols on the outside of the tomb itself, which to me appeared to be drawn in blood. Very weird and it all looked like Voodoo activities. Another Stoney Brook mystery.

Although this may not be the spectacular discovery that the pirate cave was or the Mill Property, it is quite significant to the history of Stoney Brook. Truthfully, it is quite a beautiful addition to an already incredible estate. The cemetery of her earliest known ancestors must be quite meaningful to Stefany, although she received the news quietly and seemed reserved to hear of the discovery.

The crew and I have commenced cleaning and restoring the newly discovered cemetery, augmenting it with attractive paths and landscaping features, as it will be on the list of must-see places for visitors to Stoney Brook. The strange symbols and graffiti on the main McCaskill crypt have been washed away after considerable effort.

"Mees Michaels. She is so happy these days," Miguel noted at my side as we strolled through the kitchen, in to take a break from the late morning heat. Stefany was across the room talking with several of the staff girls laughing and conversing. It was true, I had never seen her happier.

"I agree, Miguel," I said, making a downward motion with my hands to let the boys know we needed to talk very quietly. "She is a different woman than the one I first knew when I started here." The staff seemed to like her more these days and enjoyed chatting with her, not just about work, but their lives as well.

My group of workers and I continued to walk through the kitchen, ultimately headed to the patio. We stopped briefly to sample several pastries and get a drink. Unlike the men, I elected to go against the wisdom of cool hydration and poured a cup of coffee.

"That Meester Miles, over at dee Mill," Santiago chimed in as I stirred in creamer, "I no think he ees married no more to Mees Michaels. The workers, we all say he jus' tryin' to get dee money, monn. Yes, Meester Morgan?"

Thinking about this carefully, I decided to avoid any landmines. "I don't know. True, they are separated. But at this time, I wouldn't venture a guess about his motives, Santiago."

"It ees said, Meester Morgan," Miguel continued, now whispering so low I could barely hear him. "Mees Michaels... well... it ees said... she has a boyfriend. I think this must be true, no?"

Admiring the sugar cane coffee stirrer that I had inspired into existence, I slipped it in my mouth and enjoyed the slightly sweet flavor. I could tell from Miguel's expression that he did not suspect that he was speaking more truth than he knew. This, I needed to head off as quickly as possible. With any luck, the men would spread a rebuttal of this around if I sounded convincing enough.

"Oh, I don't think that's it," I replied disarmingly. "Lucky be the man if it were true, though."

The men nodded vigorously in agreement. "Lucky yes, beyond all else," Miguel confirmed. "I think that man would be very wonderfully busy, Meester Morgan."

"Yes, indeed," I offered. "But I think she's happy because Stoney Brook is so successful now. We are no longer in danger of going bankrupt. She is making a good profit now. It is a great relief to her."

"Yes. That must be it, Meester Morgan," Miguel offered.

Santiago raised a finger. "But with a woman like that, it is fun to think about the alternative, mon."

"True. She does capture the imagination," I suggested.

"She captures many imaginations," Miguel laughed. "That husband of hers, Meester Miles. He must be a crazy man, no? To not bed dee woman every day he has dee chance."

"He doesn't seem up to the task, Miguel."

The men laughed. "And that, Meester Morgan, only makes the thought more eenticing," Miguel noted.

"Ah. I would never sleep," Santiago explained.

"Your wife, mon. She will fix you gooood," Miguel joked. "Put you to sleep forever, mon."

The men snickered among themselves. Fortunately, it didn't sound like it was *me* that anyone suspected as being *the other man* among the staff. Miguel and Santiago would have certainly goaded me with their suspicions if this were the case. The image of me on my knees in her office "performing" the day prior came to mind. I smiled to myself. If they only knew the half of what it meant to truly be in service to Ms. Michaels.

We were just nearly out of the kitchen. "Mr. Mobley," came the familiar voice across the room - lively and spirited, hopeful even. A beaming smile spread across her face much as the sun had broken in on the new, tropical day.

"Yes, Ms. Michaels? How are you today?"

She approached, a playful glint in her eyes.

"I'm doing great. You and the boys?"

"We are enjoying a beautiful new tropical day. We were just on our way to tune up a garden with a bit more landscaping."

She paused, eyeing me thoughtfully. "I was wondering if I may have a word with you?" She extended her hand towards the entrance to the staff hallway.

"Of course." Indicating to the men I would catch up with them later, I followed her through the kitchen to the hallway. She looked about for a moment, making sure we were alone.

Putting both her arms around my neck, she pulled me to her mouth and kissed me. She held it and so did I. Her fingers wound their way into my hair as I lifted her partially off the floor.

When she finally let up, I gazed into her beautiful green eyes and ran a finger over her sly smile, wondering what new mischief she was conjuring.

"I do so like it when you need to "have a word with me," I whispered against her mouth.

"Oh, so do I."

After a moment, puzzled, I had to ask. "Um. Is there anything else?"

"No. This is it," she answered, continuing to ply my hair with her fingers. "I just wanted to kiss those amazing lips of yours."

"These are the best kinds of breaks," I added.

Placing her hands against my chest, she then pushed away and started to walk off to some other duty.

"Stef?"

"Yes?"

"Can I ask you a question?"

She laughed and returned to give a playful tug on my belt. "This technically isn't service time, so I suppose so. What?"

"The other day. When you wanted me to… um… do myself - on your floor?"

"Ah," she smiled. "How could I forget. It was another wonderfully entertaining afternoon thanks to you. What about it."

"Well. You said it was going to be a regular occurrence?"

"Maybe. Although I like oral service days just as much. I guess it depends on my mood."

"But. About Leanne. You let her in to watch… erm… what you were wanting me to do."

"Yeah. So?"

"You offered to "loan me out"? Would you really do that?"

"Why? Does that bother you?"

I ran my hand along her arm. "I just thought. It was you and me."

"For the most part, yes."

"The most part?"

"Yeah. I reserve the right to… *play*… with you however I want to. Within reason, of course," she said with a voice of honey. The slightly upturned smile that played the corners of her mouth always drove me crazy. We both knew damned well I'd do anything she wanted, even if it was getting "loaned out."

"But I don't get it. Back when we were just starting out in our assignments, remember when you thought I was still having a fling and seeing that girl in my room? The blonde tennis player?"

"Yes?"

"You seemed so jealous. You were mad at me!"

"I was, yes. But, as we both know, I was mistaken in the assumption you were returning to your old ways of Man-Whore Mobley."

510

"But now you are willing to "loan" me out? Why would you be jealous about the blonde woman and not about this?"

"Hmmm. Good question," she began. "You are already mine, by way of the agreement. I can have you any way I want, whenever I want. And I want you all the time."

"Good to know," I grinned. "Please. Continue."

"Just using you hard gets me off... *because* you are mine. It's the control."

"I get that. And true, I enjoy it, too. But why would you enjoy watching me with another woman?"

She looked up, searching for the words of her explanation. "It's weird. But... it's just a continuation of the idea. It's hot to think of... *me making*... you do it."

"But. You aren't *really* going to do it, right? You are joking, c'mon."

"Mobley. I know this is a little outside of the agreement. I won't force you to ever do anything you absolutely don't want to do. So. If I were to ask you to do it, would you?"

"If it gets you going... well, okay. When?"

"When I tell you to."

"And this is something that you want?" I asked, just to make sure I was understanding her correctly.

"I'm exploring the thought of the idea. I think so."

Her expression was resolute and determined, even though her response was less than decisive. Again, the *new* Stefany. She was both exciting, mysterious, erotically sensuous, and scary, all at the same time. What she was telling me would no doubt have been a dream fantasy for me and for nearly every other man on the planet. To "service" several beautiful women at once, under the direction of another beautiful woman. Now, however? Oddly enough, even considering my past, I wasn't sure. Stefany was more than enough for me. I didn't know if I should be excited, jealous, or hurt that she came up with this idea for a new play theme.

"When we first met, I would have never guessed you had such a kinky side."

"It's a new intrigue, Mobley." She kissed me to cap the point.

"So. This other woman, it's undoubtedly Leanne?"

"Yes. I decided it's going to be a girls' afternoon. Drinks, music, conversation. *You* will be the entertainment. And I am going to invite Heidi as well."

"What? Stefany! She hates me! I don't kn-"

Stefany put a finger over my lips to halt the objection mid-sentence.

"Let's just see what happens. And Mobley, I expect you to do a good job." She walked away, shooting me a glance over her shoulder, one side of her mouth in a slight smile. She often teased me, playfully threatening me with things she would never really do. I still wasn't sure if she was serious.

It was later Monday afternoon when I managed to catch Leanne coming back from town. Stefany was away for the moment at the Mill Property, so I knew I could talk in confidence. After Leanne parked her car in the lot, she cast a curious smile as she strolled up.

"Morgan. And what do I owe the pleasure of your company? Coming out to welcome me back, how nice."

Much to her surprise, I took her hand and pulled her to the side of the large porch, out of sight of the eyes of any staff or guests.

"Leanne, Stefany says she's going to… you know. Loan me out! During the… you know!"

Leanne about rolled with laughter. "You must mean your performance you are scheduled for tomorrow afternoon? Ah, yes. I do seem to recall an offer of letting me sample your skills. You have such a sensual mouth for a man. Full lips, an obviously energetic tongue. It's a wonderful idea, I think."

"Leanne, this is not a joke. She is deadly serious! She is going to invite you... *and* Heidi, she said. Said she gets off on it, ordering me to do it, seeing me get *passed around* or whatever. What the hell, Leanne. C'mon. You've got to do something!"

Leanne ran her fingers across my cheek finding much amusement in my situation. "Well, I have always wanted to try you out, Morgan."

"Leanne, please. Be serious."

"Oh, come now, Morgan. Am I that reprehensible?" She playfully flipped my lips with a finger. Irritated, I grabbed her wrist to try to talk some sense into her.

"Quit that. You know I think you are the farthest thing from reprehensible. There have been times... we almost..." I stopped for a moment, realizing where I was going with the conversation. I looked around, confirming that we were alone. "We are *friends*, Leanne," I forcefully whispered.

"And are you not friends with Stefany?"

"Yes! But I thought we were... that she maybe... viewed me as more than a friend."

"Hmmm. I do think that's true. To a degree. I would have thought this little scheme would perfectly suit your natural *tendencies*?"

I hesitated.

"You crack me up, Morgan. Oh, how the mighty have fallen."

I pulled her closer, whispering with urgency in her ear, trying to get her to take me seriously. "Think about where this is going. And truthfully, this wasn't the agreement."

"The agreement was, you'd do whatever she wants."

"Within reason!"

"Eh. It's unexpected, certainly. But I think it's within reason."

"So, you are fine with this?"

"Morgan, I am kidding you to a degree about this, I admit. Look. Honestly, I don't really think she'll go through with it."

"And if she does?"

Leanne thought about this for a moment, then smiled. "We'll cross that bridge when it comes."

"Leanne. I thought she was... you know. Into me. She seems to really like me. Likes my company. Beyond the sex stuff. You know what I mean."

"Yes, I know. I won't bore you with what I think the psychology of this is, but she's a new woman, in many ways. She's transformed before our eyes to a degree I didn't anticipate."

"And I don't mind that. It's just. When I agreed to this, I thought it was just going to be only with Stefany."

"So did I. But you must give the girl her due, Morgan. She's into this far more than I ever thought she'd be."

"If this were to happen, it seems like we would... I would... be breaking the rules or something."

"Rules? There aren't any rules in this except you have to obey Stefany for her pleasure."

"What about you? We are too good of friends for this. It would feel weird. It could ruin our friendship."

"As I said, I don't think she will do it. It's a long time until Friday. Who knows what will happen between now and then?" Leanne softly stroked my jaw. "But if she does, it wouldn't bother me, I can tell you. I promise, I'll still be your friend," she cooed. With this, she laughed fully, enjoying the teasing she was giving me.

"What about Heidi? Heidi doesn't even like me! Who knows what she would do! She'd probably kill me."

"Morgan. Getting head from someone you *don't* like can be thrilling, let me tell you. You use the hell out of them, even rougher than normal. It's very satisfying. Heidi would be in for a real treat. And the rest? Well, it's all an intriguing prospect."

514

"Rougher than normal? Wait, it can get rougher?! Could you convince her not to come if Stefany invites her? Maybe that would help discourage this whole thing, too."

"No. This is Stefany's idea. If Heidi comes, it's of her own free will, I won't make that decision for her. Why, I am surprised at you, Morgan, for hesitating at a shot at Heidi. I seem to recall you were interested in adding her to your "bag collection" when she first came to the island."

"Bag collection? I don't recall any such-"

"Yes. Don't act like you can't remember what that means, it was your term, "Bag 'em, then let 'em go." Really. Whatever happened to Man-Whore Mobley? Has Stefany rehabilitated him to such a degree he doesn't recall all the women he seduced then sent packing the next morning? Many no doubt with broken hearts. If not wishes for vengeance." Leanne clicked her tongue against her teeth.

I had to laugh at Leanne's perceptions of me. Sadly, they were an accurate characterization of the old me, even if it did hurt my feelings. "You vilify me, Leanne. As usual. I never sent any woman packing. I cared about them."

"Bullshit. It's so cute when you fish out that tired, old denial. Morgan Mobley, you were a true cad in your past." She leaned in close for emphasis. "*Cad.*"

"We can argue about that later. This is different."

"Different? Morgan, I remember a time when such a scenario as this would have melted your horny little Man-Whore brain," she laughed.

"Look. It's embarrassing enough just having to… you know. In front of you!"

Leanne provocatively slipped a hand inside my thigh and moved it up, softly bumping my package. "And you performed *admirably*, Morgan. Take my word for it. I was impressed. And I'm not easily impressed. Just thinking about this has me looking forward to Friday. Leanne removed her hand and smiled mischievously, no doubt feeling my involuntary growing erection that was taking off despite myself.

"So. You won't just stay away for my sake? As a favor? Please?"

"Sorry, no. If she invites me on Friday, of course, I'll be there." Leanne's face brightened. "Having your face between my legs would be enjoyable, I have no doubt." She playfully pinched one of my nipples from beneath my shirt.

"Ow!" I moved her hand away.

She flashed a devilish look before walking away. "I can't wait to see what our naughty little protégé has cooked up for you."

CHAPTER 17
LUST AND SEX VERSUS LOVE AND SEX

Morgan: There's still no word on the investigation into who was trying to kill Stefany and me. Nada. Nothing. I must wonder if Constable Filmore has ever really investigated anything like murder. He says he is an experienced cop from his days back on the west coast of the U.S. I'm not sure I even believe him.

Stoney Brook continues to have soaring profits. Stefany is quite secure with her finances at this point. I get the impression she is genuinely grateful for everything I have done for her, but I only want to see her happy. I've never known a hornier woman. I get the impression she is further testing the boundaries of her own sexuality. That's fine with me, as long as I'm always in her plans - and there aren't any other dudes involved.

The Stoney Brook Museum is finished now. Not only are the guests enjoying the incredible displays, but many tourists are coming from nearby islands just to see it. Some people come to the Mill Property for the restaurant or the nightlife. Having these diverse draws is only making us more well-known and successful.

The crypt we had built to contain the bodies down in the cave has tempered glass viewing portals so that visitors can view the remains in a respectful manner yet see their attire. It creeps some people out, but it doesn't stop them from visiting the site. Stefany was opposed to the viewing portals, but she was eventually talked into it, if it was done in a sensitive manner. The weapons and chest of valuables remains within secured displays next to the crypt and up in the cellar part of the museum next to the wine rooms. It is one of my favorite places in Stoney Brook, and it has an "aura" all its own, bespeaking of ancient times and lives lived long ago.

If I had to name one favorite artifact among those that we discovered down in the cave, I would have to say it's the Claymore sword that belonged to Stefany's ancestors. It clearly has the name McCaskill engraved on the blade. Why it would be down in the cave and not have been handed down is a mystery. It is in nearly perfect condition despite the elements and is prominently displayed in the cellar with a case all its own. The good condition was no doubt due to the waxy lard, or whatever it was that someone long ago smeared over the metal of the blade to store it. It was odd to see Stefany hold it when she first learned it had been in her family. She almost seemed frightened to touch it.

~~~~~~

Stefany has some new plans for me at the end of this week. She mentioned that she may "loan" me out, but I didn't take her seriously. Perhaps I should. Is she experimenting with voyeurism? If so, I would be surprised. It just doesn't seem like something she would ever do, knowing what a private person she is. When I first met her, I don't think she would have even approved of a kiss in public, much less be involved in a sexual scenario with a group.

Stefany told me I had better be prepared to do whatever she asks. And when she talks like that to me - it kinda turns me on too. Hopefully, she'll never want more than me for a guy. Everything else she has cooked up so far has been hotter than hell. I imagine the time is coming where Stefany will tell Leanne she doesn't need any more assignments; she can come up with her own ideas. So. Yeah, I'm down for it (except the damn crop). She seems excited, even more than usual about whatever this playtime may incur. I'll do what she asks, but I would be more than happy with just her as my one and only play partner.

Friday afternoon rolled around as my anxiety steadily built waiting to hear from Stefany. She was supposed to let me know when I should prepare to arrive at her office for my "solo performance" - and whatever *else* she had in mind. My jitters were getting the best of me when I heard a text pop in.

Stefany:
Mobley, sorry for the late notice. We are having a business social this afternoon in conjunction with a pool party and dance. Buffet dinner. Clean up (obviously) and wear your finest suit and tie. Give the boys the rest of the day off. Please arrive at 3:30. Representatives from our business partners will be there, many others at the pool party.

Come prepared to mingle and tell them how our operations are going here. Thanks ♥U ~S

This was interesting. Evidently, there would be no "performance" today - and everything that would have potentially included. A part of me was disappointed. Sure it would be hot and fun. Stefany would probably enjoy it, and by proxy me as well. Another part of me was relieved, as my only desire now was for Stefany, which was very much against my former character and mode of operation. She was everything I ever wanted, I had discovered. This brought about deeper considerations. If she got off on "sharing" me, what did that say about how she felt about me? Did she have any feelings for me at all beyond *plaything*? I shrugged these conflicted thoughts off and helped Miguel and Santiago put away the tools we used for a sidewalk repair.

After showering and putting on a fine black tuxedo with white bow tie I had scored in a bet with Eduardo down at The Blue Calypso, I headed to the pool area behind Stoney Brook at the appointed time.

The gathering had commenced, and many guests were already present. A live salsa band played, and I wondered where I missed the notice for this festive event. I rebuked myself for not reading my company calendar more often. Everyone was dressed formal, and I was glad that I had the tux option.

Stefany had evidently invited numerous locals to the event as well as a cadre of our business partners. I even noticed Eduardo, who had several weeks prior talked me into taking the line against him with a basketball playoff game. I made the spread and won the tux, which he had to have altered to my size, much to his displeasure. In a profane litany of insults, he had threatened to stop the courtesy of running my bar tab next time I came for a drink. He managed a somewhat guilty apology with a wink when I left the

Calypso, my tuxedo in hand. Eduardo was a decent guy. He just hated to lose.

"That's a nice tux, Mobley," he commented sourly after approaching. "You almost look like you deserve to wear it." He patted one of the lapels. "It was quite expensive. Who is this Morgan Mobley? He doesn't win anything. What happened."

"Don't ever bet unless you are prepared to lose," I coached with a grin.

"And don't come back to *The Blue Calypso* unless you want to pay full price for your drinks. And maybe a little extra for you. Because you irritate me. And you are cheap."

With this indictment, I had to laugh. Such was Eduardo's personality. Seeing someone else he recognized, he began to trot off, but first turned with a smile. "Mobley. I do hope you'll give me the opportunity to make my money back with a new bet soon. College playoffs."

"I doubt it, I don't gamble anymore." With this, his smile instantly faded. He cursed me quietly as he walked away, leaving me laughing. Eduardo had a heart as big as the Caribbean Sea, but his personality was as prickly as a cactus.

Among the guests were many familiar faces. From across the pool, I noticed Leanne conversing with some men who would no doubt be flirting with her. I caught her eye and she smiled, probably disappointed that she wouldn't be enjoying my "performance." Miles was noticeably absent and upon inquiry to some of the staff, I heard he was organizing a beach party at the Mill Property. Stefany had arranged for buses to transport the guests to this event later in the evening. Again, I thought about the value of reading my calendar.

"Um. Excuse me," I heard in a familiar voice behind me. Turning, I was surprised to see Heidi who was attempting to slide by me with two drinks in hand to head off deeper into the crowd.

"Heidi, good to see you," I said, trying to fake sincerity, though I did admire her splendid figure.

"Whatever, I'm sure," she said in a condescending tone as she quickly began navigating the crowd. No mention of anything with Stefany. I was going to ask her why she wasn't with her sidekick, Joe, but she was gone in a flash. She appeared to be heading towards an attractive woman in an elegant purple evening gown. My suspicions were soon confirmed when I noticed the two discreetly stealing a kiss. Heidi was seeking additional entertainment for the evening it would seem. At least it wasn't me. That was both good and bad, I decided.

Soon after, I felt a hand slip beneath my arm. It was Stefany, resplendent in a short black dress and medium length heels. Her eyes went over my full-length several times, as did mine over her.

"Wow, Mobley. You look *amazing*. Where did you get the tuxedo?"

"It's a long story." I leaned down to her ear to whisper. "Miss Stefany. You are the most beautiful woman to ever grace the planet. Just so you know."

She peered up into my eyes. "What can a girl say after a compliment like that."

I laughed. "Thanks?"

"We'll discuss your pay raise later," she joked.

"I mean every word."

"I know you do. It's why I rent out such a big piece of my heart to you, Mobley."

"I don't want to rent. I want to own."

She shrugged noncommittally. "Nuances."

I wondered about this strange phraseology but became lost in her green eyes and the way the setting sun gleamed bronze through her hair. I took her arm, wanting to pull her in to kiss her.

"Not now, there are too many eyes," she advised. "I want you to talk to some of our partners. You have formed most of these relationships. I want to show you off for several hours, come on."

After a busy late afternoon meeting guests and talking with our business associates, I went to the bar to get a refill on a whiskey and tonic on ice. Stefany had disappeared during the evening and the only familiar faces were those of the wait staff circulating around the pool and among the guests.

Many of the guests were tipsy, evidenced by the increasingly loud laughter and talking. The sun was down, and the lights were on, giving a spectacular, lively aura to the old girl, Stoney Brook. This was the place to be, *the* Caribbean hot spot. Thinking about the progress made with the restoration, I was proud of my contributions.

A few of the more solitary minded guests began to depart for other activities such as the trails or garden walks. Many boarded the several buses chartered to the Mill Property for the beach dinner and after-party.

My mobile buzzed in with a text.

Stefany:

> **Good job with the guests today. I'm in the office, come on up.**

This jolted me awake. I had been so busy during the afternoon, the "performance" was out of mind. It was late, so likely it was off. Maybe she wanted something else. Some other play fun? My heart raced for a moment considering the possibilities.

Me:

> **Should I change? I'm still in my tux.**

Stefany:

> **I like the tux. Wear it.**

Me:

> **Are we going out? If we go to the beach party, maybe we should change, yes?**

Stefany:

> **Mobley. Get up here.**

She wanted to see me in my tux. Fine. I thought about goading her further just for fun. Perhaps we were going to do Assignment 3. The excitement built as I chugged my drink, handing the glass to Rochelle who happened by with a bussing tray. I tried to say hello to her. The loud, raucous pool party drowned my words and she only nodded with a smile, unwilling or unable to engage in any further greeting.

Making my way up to Stefany's office, I passed a few inebriated guests. While parties weren't unusual at Stoney Brook, this one seemed larger than usual.

Reaching her office door, I knocked. After a moment, Stefany opened the door and told me to come in.

I felt a surge of adrenaline. When I stepped in, I was surprised to see that my day had been planned after all. Music videos played amidst a pall of cigar smoke. Three office chairs were rearranged into a circle around the center of the room. Leanne and Heidi, both looking inebriated, were engaged in conversation. Evidently, their poolside activities had taken a backseat to whatever Stefany had planned for me.

Stefany looked quite sober and directed me over to where the women sat.

"Look. Our bartender has arrived."

Heidi eyed me maliciously from over the top of her drink. Leanne was smiling broadly, the implications of the evening playing in her mischievous eyes.

"Um. Will I be joining you… or…"?

Stefany put one of her hands behind my head, grabbing a fistful of my hair and pressed her mouth into mine. I wrapped my arms around her, and we stood like that for a long moment, kissing passionately while Leanne whistled.

"Tongue, anyone?" Leanne quipped.

"I've been waiting all day for that," Stefany remarked, finally letting go, wiping her mouth with the back of her hand.

"Me too," I added.

"But to answer your question, you won't need a drink, Mobley."

"This is… service time?" I was honestly wondering as it seemed no one was particularly paying attention to me except for Stefany.

"Did you think I forgot about our plans today? Quit asking questions, take our glasses and go into the kitchen and get us fresh margaritas."

After refreshing their glasses from a pitcher of margaritas, I stood to wait for Stefany's next direction. The women, wearing short dresses, their shoes off and thrown a in pile by the door, eventually ended up seated in the circle. They continued to chat, laugh, smoke cigars, and drink as if I were not even present. It was an odd scene and I nervously wondered where this was all leading.

I thought about walking back into the kitchen to make myself a drink. Taking the first step towards such an end, the women suddenly stopped talking. Only the music played loudly in the background on the office sound system.

"Mobley. And where are you off to?" Stefany asked. "Did I say you could go?"

"Um, no." They sat curiously appraising me, puffing away on their cigars. The room seemed to fill with electrically charged sexual tension. A drink in hand would have been calming. "I… just thought… I'd fix myself a-"

"Come over here. Stand right in the middle." Stefany pointed to the center in their circle of chairs. I obliged, nervously walking in.

"Off with the tux, Mobley," Stefany ordered. "And you know the drill now well enough. Slow. Only leave your tie and underwear on. For now."

I did as ordered, slowly slipping off each item of clothing, starting with the jacket and finally ending up only wearing my tie and underwear. I had to slip the bow tie back on around my neck as it had to come off with the shirt. The women chatted casually the whole time, smoking their cigars and laughing. If not for their hungry eyes fixated on my every move, I would have said they were uninterested.

Stefany changed the music to upbeat new pop. "Dance for us, Mobley."

This was new, and I no doubt looked perplexed. While I could dance, I never considered myself a strip-club style of dancer. I had to laugh.

"It's a compliment," Stefany explained with a smile.

"We want to admire your gorgeous body, Morgan," Leanne added. Heidi remained silent and looked as if she wanted to serve me up on a platter with an apple in my mouth.

The women all sat in their chairs, chatting, and sipping their drinks, their eyes on me, waiting for me to start. Not usually self-conscious, this would take a bit of mental stamina to force myself to drop my inhibitions and gyrate and dance as these women wanted. I started off slow and simple, with some basic moves such as I'd do in any nightclub, but with a partner. As the drinks went down, and the energy went up. I began hamming it up and the whistles got louder and longer.

Working the circle of these three women, I began pulling them up in succession, dancing with them. When it was Stefany's turn, she grinned and pulled me in close. "You seem to be enjoying yourself," she whispered in my ear.

"This was your idea, let's not forget," I replied.

"Yes, it was."

The next song was slower, and I pulled her closer. Her hand found its way into my underwear. She squeezed softly, evoking a growing, enlivened response. For better or worse, Stefany had pulled the trigger - things were definitely heating up. Leanne whistled and Heidi clapped.

In mid-dance, Stefany bent down and slowly pushed my underwear down, freeing my now semi-hard cock. I stepped out of them, and we resumed our dance, her hand now constantly between my legs, stroking me. Fully erect, she began pushing and grinding against me. Stefany encouraged Heidi and Leanne to take turns dancing with me, and each dance grew more sexually aggressive than the last. All three were sliding and grinding against me, caressing, and stroking my cock at their pleasure. For my part, I tried to restrain myself the best I could.

Finally, Stefany pushed me to the side. "I think it's time for a show, Mobley. She smiled over at Heidi, who was now visibly turned on and barely able to sit still. "Heidi, we are glad you could make it to our little party. This is the second Mobley performance for Leanne and me. What do you think so far?"

Heidi's eyes fixated on my cock, which was erect from the excitement. "I'm happy you invited me," she answered. "You do say he's trained?"

"Yes, very much so," Stefany answered. "He does need frequent work, though."

Leanne's mischievous smile caught my eye. She gave no indication she would delay any plans Stefany may have.

"We need several accessories for him tonight, I think," Stefany suggested. "Mobley. What is the one thing that is my favorite accessory for you?

"The crop," I answered flatly.

"And you like it, right?" she purposefully asked.

"No," I answered truthfully, the afternoon booze making me slightly difficult. She glared at me.

"Yes. You *do* like it," she informed me as the other two women snickered.

"No."

"Yes."

Her eyes narrowed, and I knew I had agitated her to the limit.

"Um. Yes," I obliged.

Leanne and Heidi laughed. Stefany placed her hands on her hips and tapped her foot, seeing how far I would go with teasing her. "And what else might you also like, Mr. Mobley?"

I thought for a moment. Stefany loved having my belt run through the buckle and left loosely cinched around my neck. She enjoyed pulling at strategic times, or just holding it while having me do whatever she wanted in the heat of the action. It wasn't too uncomfortable, but she could get it quite tight at times, making my face turn beet red.

I reluctantly walked over to where my pants lay and withdrew the belt. "You must mean this?"

"Bring it here."

I walked over and handed it to her, and she promptly looped it around my neck and through the buckle. She smiled knowing that my playful moment was over. She pulled the belt tight, and I could feel the veins throbbing beneath my neck.

"As usual, that will come in handy. Obstinate man."

"As will his hair," Leanne added.

"Or his ears," Heidi added, getting into the moment.

"Yes, both of those options are great," Stefany agreed. "Mobley, go to the drawer, you know where; bring the crop." The women took their respective seats.

Apparently, I would not be spared that damned crop. And it was Heidi I was more afraid of than Stefany or Leanne. Heidi had a look that hinted she would try very hard to skin me alive.

Retrieving the crop, I handed it to Stefany, who was playing this whole scene incredibly cool. She blew cigar smoke into the air then smiled, letting me know I was going to be in for it this evening.

"Go get the towel in the bathroom."

The towel, I knew, was useful in preventing any messes on her floor, a consideration I learned during the last "performance."

Retrieving the towel, I took the initiative and spread it out neatly at Stefany's feet.

"That'll do for now," she affirmed. Leanne let escape a small laugh. Heidi continued staring transfixed yet was still engaging in small talk.

"On your knees, Mobley. Let the show commence," Stefany said, sitting back comfortably in her chair, crossing her legs, and taking a drink of her margarita.

Dropping to my knees, I began to stroke myself per orders and with a prior understanding of what my performance would entail. Stefany had to remind me with the snap of the crop to maintain eye contact with her the whole time, which I several times neglected, probably more out of embarrassment than the lapse of memory. The women continued to chat among themselves as I worked. Several times, I was asked to get up and refill their glasses, their hands roaming up and down my legs and over my cock, each time more boldly than the last.

After a while, it was too much, and I was about to explode. While trying to maintain eye contact with Stefany, I finally realized I couldn't hold back any longer. "Um. Ms. Stefany. Do you want me to continue?"

"No. Not right now." She stood up, took my belt leash, and pulled it taut. At this point, the sexual tension in the room could be cut with a knife. Belt leash in hand, she slowly walked me on my hands and knees over to where Leanne was sitting, parking my head between her legs, and handing me over. She gave Leanne the crop.

"Here you go, Cuz. He's had enough fun for now. It's our turn, I think. Would you like to try him out first?"

Looking up at Leanne, my eyes met hers and I could not help but feel embarrassed. She smiled devilishly and we both felt the odd sensation of knowing that this was going to happen. As with the previous "performance," there was a hungry look in her expression, and now after Stefany had used me to stoke up a nearly uncontrollable fever of need, she was quite ready to see what I could do.

Stefany slapped the side of my face surprisingly hard, leaving my cheek stinging. "Mobley, I expect you to do a good job. Start with her toes first." She then roughly pushed my head down with her foot.

"I'll do the best I can," I mumbled against the toes of Leanne's left foot. I would have laughed but knew better. That, and my throbbing cheek.

Stefany returned to her chair, and I began kissing Leanne's toes as ordered.

"That's good, Mobley. Don't just kiss. Use your tongue. Both feet, don't miss a single spot. Then do her legs."

After a few minutes, Stefany walked back over, roughly took a fistful of my hair and lifted my head. "Enough of that. It's time to *really* feed our pet. What do you think, ladies?"

Heidi by now was using both hands to squeeze herself beneath her skirt. She huskily mumbled something beneath her breath in French.

"He does have… such a pretty mouth," Leanne quipped suggestively, standing up.

A pair of delicate, lacy panties dropped past my head – evidently Leanne had decided against going commando that afternoon. She stepped through them and kicked them to the side. The belt tightened, pulling me up to where I was eventually sitting back on my haunches. She looked down at me with an intentionally disarming, playful smile that conveyed only one thing – I was in for it. Running the leather tip of the crop across my face, she patted it softly on my cheek that Stefany had just slapped. She then sat back down on the edge of the chair and pushed the hem of her skirt up around her hips and out of the way. She gripped the belt leash right at my neck and pulled me into her. I wouldn't ever again need to wonder how rough Leanne could get as a dom.

"It does look like you are going to be busy this evening, Morgan."

Stefany: Mobley's performance with my "sharing idea" in the office was in a word, blast furnace hot. And I am left with the need to square with it as I now write this.

After Mobley had taken care of Leanne, I then sent him over to Heidi. She ended up pushing him onto the floor and riding his face cowgirl style. This went on between the three of us for most of the evening in between cigars, margaritas and soft jazz. We took turns getting off on Mobley and it was crazy... and it was nuclear. Much later on, it became clear Heidi and Leanne were finally ready for more than lip service and wanted a different kind of ride from Mobley. Of course, they were both quite well satisfied by this point through who-knows-how-many orgasms. And that's when it happened - I put an end to it. Sorry girls. It was a great idea, but I decided I'm not sharing Mobley any further. I guess it was an "epiphany." Been there, done that. Enough. Yes, I did enjoy it, immeasurably. But I also learned a lesson. I was fighting guilt and jealousy the whole evening, trying to suppress those feelings. Yep, there's something deeper I have with him. I'm not sure I can even define what it is.

I probably looked like an idiot after I had invited them up. I simply told them I had changed my mind about going full in on this idea and asked them if we could call it a night. Leanne seemed pleased about it all like she had attained some sort of psychological goal with me by forcing me to realize Mobley is more than just a sex toy.

I think Heidi was pissed, although she tried to hide it. She was by no means finished for the night. The nice thing is they didn't press me any further. They both agreed to gracefully bow out for the evening and let me come to terms with why I had changed my mind.

Poor exhausted Mobley. As soon as Heidi and Leanne were out the door, I had my confessional with him. Mobley asked me what happened. I realized I had to be truthful with myself. And him. So I told him. It was because he was mine. I had never had anyone before that was totally just mine. I ended that talk with a soft kiss on his lips and a vow I would never share him out again.

Then... he paid for it hard. The evening had keyed me up so much, I was a walking sexpot of need. First, I had him drop to his knees for yet another bout of oral service. I think I almost strangled and suffocated him. Oddly, I was so wound up, I felt like being rougher on him. I don't know why. Mobley finally got relief from an hour of jackhammer fucking me on practically every piece of furniture in the office – including my desk. I'm sure he has my ankles well memorized as they were up around his head often enough. He was so tired afterwards, he could barely walk. Before he left, he kissed me. He is more dear to me after all this than I can barely stand to admit. Ignoring my growing feelings for him isn't working.

~~~~

Leanne has given me Assignment 3. I can't wait. It again involves ropes, so I've been practicing on the ottoman in the office. It's rodeo cowgirl stuff - face riding - some of my favorite Mobley fun. I'm getting wet again just thinking about it. Ideas, ideas. I am going to make a few changes to Leanne's itinerary and make sure Mobley gets a much more satisfying role. He deserves it.

The morning sun was gleaming brightly into my windows, promising a spectacular new day. I immersed myself into the pillows on my bed, contemplating the jealousy I had felt with Leanne and Heidi. Sharing Mobley out didn't sit well with me, even if it had been incredibly hot, and he had been willing to do it just because I asked.

Having finished writing my conflicted thoughts on the evening in my journal, I closed it and tossed it in the drawer of my nightstand - where Leanne would hopefully not snoop - and pulled out her Assignment 3. She had been very basic, leaving me to fill in the details. That was not going to be a problem.

For STEFANY - ASSIGNMENT 3

Okay, my horny little protégé, this assignment features a change in venue – different sights, it's a more public area so caution must be taken. For this assignment, you will be using the barn. You need to make sure when you are using it, it is locked and secured, with no worry of being interrupted or discovered.

Of the items I'm giving you in your assignment bag, you'll find the standard supplies: rope, ball gag, baby oil, vibrators, dildoes, blanket. You'll find some additions that you can use if you want, like candles (for hot wax), a small electro-shocker, and various lubes to try. You bring your riding crop.

As you know, you and Mobley have been quite busy lately with your little schemes, so I think it would be best to wait for this assignment for a week or so.

I'm going to be brief - here's the basics:

- *When you get Mobley in the barn, make him strip. Make him get on his knees and show due appreciation. Make him tell you all about why he is glad to be on his knees. Some crop is good here.*
- *When he is suitably ready, you are to pull a square hale bale*

out of the stack and move it away a few feet. Place the wider side on the floor.

- *Get about 3 sections of rope and run them beneath the bale at both ends and the middle. Leave slack both sides.*
- *Place the blanket on top of the bale. Have Mobley lay down on it. Position him so that his head is just barely hanging off one end.*
- *Use the rope and tie him onto the hay bale. He should be thoroughly lashed onto the bale. Then tie his hands to his sides. Tie his legs and ankles together, lashed to the bale. When you are done, the only thing Mobley should be able to move is his head. Get the idea?*

Here, I'll leave you to your own devices; you know what to do. Riding things out on a haybale in this setting is visually different and stimulating. He will feel helpless and be very obedient and compliant. If not, use the crop. While this assignment is also a lot about you receiving oral pleasure, I also want you to go all out for the cock ride. You decide when. It will also be a good reward for him for doing a good job. Make him earn it. Go back in for some oral for a break if you want - don't hesitate to pause for a while. Make it burn. He's your sex slave, use him like one (something you don't seem to have any problem doing). Be creative, I'm turning you loose with this one.

Here's to getting a leg up! ~L 💙 I'll expect a full report!

536

I heard a soft knock on the door. It was still early, so perhaps it was one of the staff coming to inform me of something that required my attention.

Dropping Assignment 3 back into the nightstand drawer, I slid out of bed and tied on a robe. Opening the door, I was surprised to see Mobley standing there with a tray of breakfast. I no doubt looked confused. He was the first to speak.

"May I come in?"

"Of course. I just wasn't expecting you."

"You were thinking that after last night, I might be sore, perhaps?"

"Something like that," I answered with a laugh. I stepped to the side and as soon as he was in, I closed the door behind him. Careful to avoid upsetting the breakfast tray, I put an arm around his neck and pulled him into a kiss. "Good morning, Mobley. What are you doing here so early?"

"I wanted to bring you breakfast in bed."

"You never cease to amaze me. And even after I mistreated you so harshly last night."

"I suspect you don't feel too bad about that."

"Not in the least," I convincingly lied.

"I thought so. Go get back in bed."

Giving him a smile, I complied, jumping back in bed, stacking the pillows behind my back so I could sit up.

"Okay, so what do you have for me?"

"All the essentials, my beautiful lady." Sitting on the edge of the bed next to me, he positioned the tray over my lap. "Coffee. Orange juice. Two eggs, over easy. A slice of ham. Toast. And a piece of chocolate, to top it all off."

"All wonderful selections. Thank you!" Finding myself hungrier than I expected, I started in immediately, sharing with Mobley.

Taking a bite of toast, I then took a drink of juice, watching him from over the glass. "So. About last night. When I sent Heidi and Leanne out?"

"Yes?"

"Can you be honest with me, Morgan?"

This sudden question threw him off, and his expression turned serious. "Of course."

"Are you... disappointed in me? About this sharing idea I came up with?"

"No. Surprised, maybe." He reached for my hand, comforting me, seeing I was uncertain.

"I'm glad you feel that way. Because. I overlooked your feelings about it, I think. And. I'm sorry."

"It's okay."

"I won't do it again. I don't want to share you. You aren't who you used to be. And I'm not, either. I got carried away. Maybe I'm... getting oversexed or something."

He laughed. "No, you aren't. You are just trying new things. Some things you like, some you don't."

"You forgive me?"

"It's unnecessary for you to ask. All I need you to know is... you are all I ever want." he said, kissing my hands.

I hesitated for a moment, wondering if I was going to cry. "Good." I sat the tray on the night table, slipped my legs by him and got up to walk to the bathroom.

"Where are you going?" he asked.

"Brush my teeth."

"Oh," he said, confused by this impromptu revelation.

After a moment, I returned to still find him sitting on the edge of the bed. Slipping off my robe, I pushed him flat onto my bed and straddled him, surprising him. "I like the tangy feeling of having fresh breath. So I can do this." Leaning down to him, I began kissing him, feeling a heated need for him once again building to an explosive point. Reaching between his legs, I could feel that his level of excitement was growing as well.

Jumping off, I undid his belt, unsnapped his pants and yanked them to his ankles. With no fanfare, his underwear was next. His erection stood straight up, demanding attention.

538

Mobley had been quite busy the previous evening - I wondered if he were as sore as I was after the pounding he gave me.

Sitting on the bed beside him, I wrapped a hand around his shaft a began slowly pumping him, eliciting a soft moan. I loved how he felt in my grip.

A small bead of clear fluid soon appeared at the tip of his cock. Leaning over, I let my tongue draw up his full length. I paused at the top, sopping up this little treat, savoring the slightly salty flavor.

Giving head was not something I had ever considered one of my talents, as there had been so few men I had ever wanted to do it with. I probably wasn't very good at it, I had long ago admitted to myself. Mobley, however, was inspirational. For him, I was willing to learn.

He was on a hair trigger, even with this brief treatment. I decided to risk it and I ran him into my throat as deeply I could push him. Withdrawing, I repeated this for several minutes, using my lips to tightly encircle him like a sliding ring. He began working with me, synchronizing a hard thrust into my throat each time as I took him. Gagging several times, I had to be cautious, pausing occasionally to catch my breath. His need was growing, making him impatient - his hands soon found the back of my head, pushing me harder and deeper with each thrust. He was close.

Plans for the day required a hypersensitive Mobley. My objective had been achieved. It was cruel and teasing, I knew, but I'd make it up to him later. I abruptly stopped and sat up.

"Why are you stopping," he asked, breathless and desperate to resume.

"I want you primed," I taunted, "and I also want you ready. For later."

"Ready? For what?"

I climbed back up to him, first kissing his chest, then working my way up. "I've got some good news," I managed to say between kisses.

"What?"

"I've got Leanne's Assignment 3. It involves us going out to the barn. How about… later this afternoon?"

"Yes!" he lustily agreed. "But can't we… continue what we are doing now? I'll still be fine for later. I promise."

"No. I want you to wait." I mumbled against his lips. "I want you ready for a nuclear meltdown this afternoon."

"You are killing me! I'm already nuclear now!"

"Yes. Yes, that is true. But who's in charge?"

"Um, you," he admitted with anguish in his voice.

"And who gets to arrange our itinerary?"

He grimaced in misery. "You. But-"

"That's right. If I were to let you have too much fun right now, it wouldn't be as fun later."

"But. It will! Just think of it as *more* fun." He wrapped his arm around my neck and pulled me closer. "It won't lessen one slightest bit of need; I can promise you."

I sat up and put a finger to my cheek in deep thought, further teasing him. "Hmmm. I don't know."

"Stefany. Please." He was ready to beg any way he could into a romp, I noted with humor.

"I do like the pleading. Let's see how it looks on the floor. On your knees."

Complying, he quickly dropped to the floor, looking so cute as he again asked for relief. I almost changed my mind.

"That's a good start, to be sure." His stone hard cock gleamed with my saliva. "Nooo," I said with sudden resolution. "I don't think so. Your time is coming this afternoon in the assignment. I promise I'll see to it."

With puppy dog eyes, he looked so flatly disappointed, I had to laugh. "But I tell you what, Mobley. If you can handle it, I'll give you a morning taste. But *only* if you can be happy with that until this afternoon. Or… we can both wait. Either way. Those are your options."

"So, you get off again?!" he asked, incredulous. "And I still have to wait more?!"

"That's corrrrrrect!" I confirmed, teasing him with a finger down his nose and across his lips.

Looking thoroughly disconsolate, he suddenly brightened. "Okay! Yes, a taste then!" he immediately answered with such a turnaround of attitude, he caught me off guard. I had assumed he'd pout, and we would both wait until that afternoon. Mobley was an old west gunslinger… but with his tongue.

"Are you sure?" I cooed, playfully dragging it out. "With all you had to eat last night, I am surprised you are wanting more. Hmmm. You have to promise you won't spontaneously burst your pants."

"I promise I'll *try*."

"That wasn't an entirely satisfactory answer." I ran my fingers through his hair. "Do you think I'm being cruel?"

"Yes. Of course, you are being cruel," he admitted. "But I want more anyway."

By this point, my stomach was hurting from laughter. I patted his cheek. "Oh, you are such a good, devoted, sex toy."

He immediately positioned his head between my legs the moment I spread them, shocking me with his need. I ran my finger lightly over my panties. After all our time together, Mobley undoubtedly knew my pussy better than I did. "You seem so eager this morning, Mobley. Surely your tongue is sore?"

"It is. I'll power through it."

"Very well. You brought me breakfast. And now I'm going to give you yours."

"Great," he mumbled against me, beginning to kiss my legs.

I was finding it hard to be serious. He was having as much fun as I was, even though he was miserable with need. "I think you'd say about anything to get what you want. Am I wrong?"

"No."

"Ask me nicely, then."

"Please, damn it!"

"Well. Okaaay." Smiling, I slid off my panties and tossed them off with great drama, arcing my legs high on either side of his head.

"How's the view, Mobley?"

"Beautiful. I want more," he moaned. Going against our standard rules, he resumed kissing my inner thighs, not asking permission. I put a restraining hand against his forehead, stopping him.

"Nope, Mobley. Not just yet." My free hand went to work on my clit, rubbing slowly, dipping an occasional finger.

"But... god damnit. Stefany! You said I could taste," he was sounding in pain.

"I did." And with this, I drew my knees up to my chest. Withdrawing my now soaking wet hand, I ran my fingers over my calves. "You can taste me... this way," I explained, guiding his head towards the slick little trails on my legs. "There you go. Lick. Breakfast is served." He took to the idea immediately and he wasted no time running his tongue along the little paths I made for him to follow. I repeated this, eventually adding my toes and the arches of my feet for his ministrations.

Mobley dutifully lapped and sucked away each new slick streak. The action in between my legs was close, right in his face, yet I would not allow him there, letting him only watch me work, tasting me indirectly.

Despite how I was joking and playing with him, the scene was incredibly hot, and I silently congratulated myself on having a filthy, kinky mind. It was quite a workup for Mobley considering he was still exhausted from the prior evening. I noticed his hand rubbing up and down between his legs, which was not allowed. "No cheating."

After a few minutes, I could take it no longer and held his head tightly in between my legs, letting him work the source directly. I was very sore, but it did not matter, I powered through it. Orgasming hard, I rode the waves as I rubbed my clit, bumping my finger against his nose as his tired but talented tongue wound its way into me. I gave him one final treat, dipping for his reward a last time, slipping my fingers into his eager mouth.

"Did you enjoy your creamy breakfast, Mobley?" I asked, spent.

Trying to stand, he had to steady himself against the wall. He was so tortured I thought he would just fall to the floor and erupt in spasms. His hair was a mess and his erection awkwardly stabbed into the air. "Oh, yes. I... Um. Yes, I do. Did." was all he could mumble incoherently.

"Remember. You can't *self-serve*. Not even *accidently* humping the edge of your dresser or doorknob or something, which I totally wouldn't put past you. Nothing. No getting off in any way. Until I let you, later. Understand?"

He wobbled a bit, then scornfully pulled his pants back on. "This..." He cleared his throat, trying to gain his composure. "This afternoon, then," he finally said in a zombie-like voice, beginning to walk towards the door.

"Don't forget the tray," I reminded him.

"Oh. Yes. The tray."

"Thank you, Mobley. For a wonderful breakfast."

"Um. Yeah. I'm. You're... Um." Taking the tray, he left, softly closing the door behind him, intoxicated with need. If even a slight breeze swept by him, he would spontaneously blast a hole through his khakis. Perfect. Mobley would be *more* than ready for Assignment 3.

Reaching the bottom of her iced coffee, Leanne slurped the final drops through a straw, the loud bubbly noise drawing the attention of several nearby hikers.

"You seemed to *thoroughly* enjoy that iced coffee," I chided as we walked through a Stoney Brook garden trail.

"It's your boyfriend. I'm trying to refuel," she explained with a final gasp off the straw.

"What do you mean," I asked, instantly regretting the question.

"He's a vampire, you know. He *drained* me of all energy."

I looked off towards the mountains, again feeling regretful. "Glad you enjoyed him, but sorry, Leanne. As I explained last night, it was a one-time ride."

"Oh, I do wish you would reconsider ending your little Mobley share circle. I can only imagine what it would be like to play with his gorgeous cock. I fully understand your greedy desire to keep him all to yourself."

"Well. I've already seen Mobley again this morning," I confessed.

"What? Really? And is he okay with everything? And your sudden lapse into monogamy?"

"He was okay, yes. I... explained it... clearly, I think."

"Any nuances of this *explanation* you'd care to share?"

"This morning, he brought me breakfast in bed!"

"Wow. That was sweet of him," Leanne admitted, stopping to smell a large, red tropical flower. "That is definitely a major relationship goal. Nice."

"I know, right? But he didn't go without reward. I fed him a creamy breakfast."

Leanne paused mid sniff and eyed me.

"And should I take that with how it sounds?"

"Yes."

"How can he even chew food this morning? His tongue is probably like a tow rope. You on the other hand, are insatiable. Let me guess. Afterward, you left poor Morgan without any satisfaction."

"Right. I'm prepping him for Assignment 3 this afternoon."

Leanne looked concerned. "I thought you were going to wait a few days! You just had Mobley make the rounds last night, then again this morning, and you are ready for *more*??"

"He's fine. Everything is fully functional, I can attest. Yeah, I am ready to enjoy another fun day with him. Assignment 3 *rocks*!"

Leanne stopped in midstride on the trail. "Look, Stef. You've got to go a little easier on him. He is a man, not a machine, after all. And it's Morgan Mobley we are talking about. He's not a man accustomed to such torturous waiting periods. I'm getting concerned. This is way too much, way too fast. You are overdoing it, my little protégé."

"No, I'm not overdoing it," I asserted. "I am quite confident he got everything he needed this morning. I want him in full appreciation mode this afternoon. We are very much looking forward to your Assignment 3. You may feel earthquakes today. I know I will."

The assignment was amazing. I could only wonder what Mobley thought about it. After staggering back into the lobby of Stoney Brook, I decided to see if Leanne was in her pre-agreed position of reclining by the pool. She was.

Failing to notice me with her nose in a book, I walked up to her and pulled it from her fingers. I pulled the nearest chair in close and took a seat.

"Ah! You are back from your adventure! You may want to run a comb through your hair before the guests and staff get suspicious of you."

"Why? What could they possibly think? It's 2:30 in the afternoon. I look totally legit, having been out *working hard*."

"Yeah, you've been working hard all right. You bad girl. Okay, go ahead and tell me how it went. Is Morgan still among the living?"

"I should tell you, you are a cruel mistress, coming up with such ideas," I admitted to Leanne approvingly. "And your kinky imagination knows NO bounds."

"True," Leanne nodded matter-of-factly. "Give me some juicy details. Did Morgan like it as much as you obviously did?"

"It was… *indescribably* hot. Leanne, each assignment is better than the last. I don't see how you do it."

"Hmmm. Well. We all have a talent of some sort," she glibly explained.

"I feel like I'm going to spontaneously catch on fire." I leaned in close to whisper. "Leanne, I can't get enough of him," I confessed. "Is this normal?"

"Normal? That horse left the barn quite a while ago, Stef. However, you should know that this is a lot like a fine dinner. After a while, all this intense sex can become old. The staging. The same lovers. The sheer effort of imagination. People inevitably get tired. Or lazy."

"I'm not tired of it now, I can tell you."

Leanne laughed. "So far, you do seem to be an exception to the rule, my horny little dominatrix in the making. So where is Morgan, getting a shower and recovering?"

"He's still out there, strapped to a hay bale."

Leanne's mouth dropped. "Um. What? You are kidding, right?"

"It's no big deal. I'm just giving him a little lesson in patience while we take a break. He's okay. I'm not finished with him yet. I'm going back for seconds." I peered down to inspect my nails, wondering if I should later visit the salon.

Leanne pulled her sunglasses off. "How long has he been out there strapped to the bale!?"

"Oh. I don't know. Forty minutes maybe. An hour."

"Holy shit! What!?"

"It's good for him." I laughed and bumped her shoulder with my fist. "He thinks I might not come back for hours."

"How do you know someone won't find him in there? That would raise all kinds of questions you don't need!"

"The barn is locked, and I've told all the crews that there is maintenance going on and to stay out. It's all good, Leanne. Quit worrying."

"Um. Yeah, I'm worried! And even more so about you! Where did you get the idea to do this? Not from me, I can tell you!"

"I read about it in your book. Doms often tie up their subs for extended periods, leaving them alone in isolation. It builds patience and is good training. I've actually tried it several times with him."

"Now, Stefany, just wait a minute! I never intended you to take that book so seriously! Most of the things in it, I don't even do! It was just to sample a few things!"

"And that's what I'm doing. I'm sampling a few things. With Mobley."

"I think you are going too far! I don't think it's a good idea to just leave him like that!"

"Despite our short time together, I've got to know him pretty well. More than any other man I've known in my life, including Miles. Like me, Mobley's discovered things about himself he never knew existed. Namely, patience. As you know, I've kept him on low sexual broil all day long ever since I fed him *breakfast* this morning. Assuming he hasn't spontaneously creamed himself, I'm going to let him finally get a little relief. So quit worrying."

"What, you are *still* teasing him?"

"Yeah. I could just touch him with my pinky finger, and he'd explode."

"But... He thinks you just left him there to be found by anyone that might stroll in?"

"Yeah. Pretty much. Genius, right?"

Leanne looked increasingly agitated; an uncharacteristic strain of worry having come over her face.

"C'mon, Leanne. Believe me. He had fun. And I'm going to go give him… and me… more fun in a few more minutes. So chill."

"Okay, I have to say this. You are scaring the hell out of me with how you are so into these assignments. You have, like… changed. A lot! And I'm not sure if I haven't made a mistake! Maybe I have sorely underestimated the psychology involved here between you two… I thought I had considered all the varia-"

"Leanne. I love my life. I feel great," I assured her, seeing how suddenly worried she had become. "You have helped make me a new woman. And thanks to your assignments with Mobley, I'm finally enjoying sex in my life. I love being dominant. And in charge. And having confidence. In the end, it's all consensual fun, by both of us. He's into this as much as I am. Ask him later if you want."

Leanne stood up from her pool lounger, contemplating this for a moment. "Stef, h*e's by himself strapped to a hay bale out in the barn.* What if he has to go the restroom?!"

"Oh, he's fine. Before I left, I pushed him and the bale over on the side and told him to have a go at it if he needs to pee. It's a livestock barn, after all. There's a good storm drain in the floor."

I had never seen Leanne look stressed like this before. "And… he's okay with that?!"

"Why wouldn't he be okay with it? Guys don't mind going pee anywhere, you know that. And anyway, he's gagged. It's irrelevant what he thinks."

"Irrelevant? He's hanging on his side tied up! And you left him gagged!" Her voice was loud enough to catch the attention of a couple swimming at the far end of the pool.

"Yes. isn't it ironic," I said with a laugh. "I finally have Mobley to where he will shut up - unless I tell him to talk. And I gag him anyway."

"Oh. My. Gawd!! It was never my intent to create an unhealthy addiction!"

Leanne was evidently not finding the same hilarity in the moment as me. She began looking about with a regretful expression, chewing a fingernail, something I had never seen her do before. "This has to stop! What have I done," she exclaimed to herself.

I stood and massaged her neck, finding her muscles stiff and tense. "Leanne. Relax! Assignment 3 is going great! It's all good."

CHAPTER 18

A HAY BALE TALE

Morgan: The boner status is DEFCON level 1. Stefany was in particularly good form with Assignment 3 from Leanne. She left me bound up in the barn, and to be honest, I thought she was just going to leave me for hours on end. It was completely within the realm of possibilities with her. She had loved leaving me bound at the Mill Property, pretending she would not return anytime soon. I should have anticipated a repeat of this. Whenever we find an occasion to talk about it, she can't stop laughing and seems to relish this prank. I expect it will not be the last time. It would seem she has grown to love her role as a dominatrix.

Being tied up notwithstanding, the afternoon with Stefany in the barn was hot beyond anything I could imagine. I've always thought I had a very sexually overcharged imagination, but this day was unbelievable.

The "first" part of the assignment was very fun, and Stefany got off more times than I can count. I think one reason it was so intense for her was for the reason I was bound up on that damned hay bale. She had complete control. If I talked too much or complained, she would just gag me. I could only move my head, and by default, my tongue. She could do what she wanted. It was VERY uncomfortable, and I still have a rash on my neck and back from where the damned hay pricked my skin for hours. Despite the discomfort, it was freaking amazing for me, too. Yes, she was cruel, it was hard to endure being bound that long, yet it was also sexual lava.

When she finally came back to the barn after leaving me, I was unquestioningly relieved. I thought it was over - until she propped a foot in the middle of my chest and began untying her shoe. It was not over, not by a long shot, and she kept me tied up for this "second" part of the assignment. The damned ropes were binding and hurt like hell, and so did that infernal, prickly hay bale. Yes, I would happily do it again. Thinking back, it was just pure, flaming, otherworldly sex of a sort I have never experienced, even with the other assignments.

She stripped her clothes off and teased me – to a point at which I thought I would finally suffer a fucking stroke. After some hot preliminaries, she went through the standard fare; making me beg (by using that damned crop) to kiss her feet and various places on her legs. I thought she would be done with me after this, considering we were now hours into this assignment.

She straddled me, sitting on my upper chest and it was then I knew my duties were far from over. She was so close I could almost taste her, but she kept a grip in my hair to keep me from this. She loves this repeated scenario, keeping my face just an inch or so from the action between her legs. It serves to taunt - yet also please. This time she surprised me, using a toy she had brought for the occasion. I had to watch what she was doing with it, which is so wonderfully cruel I can't even explain it. I couldn't do a damned thing about it.

It was similar in some ways to Assignment 1, she only let me watch for a while as she worked herself. First, I wondered if I would survive the afternoon. Then second, I wondered if I would depart this world without ever having fully achieved my own satisfaction, which she had now drawn out to a full, miserable day. I guess I shouldn't have worried - my neck is still sore from her pulling my head up to "finish" her with my mouth several times. She continued to enjoy using that damned crop while doing this, claiming it made my face jolt into her, increasing her pleasure. How the hell does she think of this stuff? Somewhat painful, yes, but mind-melting.

So Stefany finished the day riding my raging cock like I was a wild bronc. Seeing her writhe and arch her back atop me was something I'll never forget – it was rough… and it was unforgiving. And I loved it. When it was all over and ended with a balls-full explosion that I thought by all rights should have sent her through the roof of the barn, she leaned over, her sweat dripping onto me to the point I could taste it. She softly put her hands on either side of my face and kissed me as passionately as I have ever been kissed.

When she finally untied me, I was beginning to see spots in my eyes. I tried to stand but fell over, which didn't even seem to shock her as she dressed. When I told her she might well have damaged my balls permanently, she only laughed, told me to toughen up, and slapped my ass. Two days of mind-blowing sex and I don't think she even wants to take a break. Truthfully -will I survive much more of this?

Stefany is an insatiable goddess.

Walking back from the barn, our feet dragging, we were silent. It had been surreal and exhausting - and incredibly hot and fun.

Her hair was going in every direction and looked as though she had been run through a washing machine. Ruffled and visibly tired, she limped slightly.

"Ow!" I yelped.

"What?" She asked, concerned.

"Cramp. Back leg." After straightening my leg to ease the discomfort, she looked at me with humor.

"We look like we are refugees, returning from a war," she remarked.

"I have a question for you," I asked as I massaged my sore jaw, stopping her before we began our ascent up the front entry steps to the lobby.

"Yeah? What, Mobley? I'll entertain just one question. It's all I have the energy for."

"Um. Why do you pinch my nose off so that I can't breathe very well? You know… when you are riding my face."

"Why? You got a problem with that?" she asked saucily.

"Nooo. Just wondering. It's something new."

"It turns me on," she stated matter-of-factly. "I like you gasping for breath from your mouth and struggling when you are going deep - just before you make me come. I learned about that in one of Leanne's videos. Knew I had to try it. Glad I did."

"Yeah. Me too. Oddly." I found myself almost wishing we were back in the barn.

"Mobley," she began. "Seriously. Is there anything I could try that you wouldn't like?"

"With you? I don't think so," I admitted. "Although less of the crop would be okay."

She laughed and pulled me close, kissing me softly, her hands over my ears. I pulled her tighter into me, arching her back over an arm, our kiss growing in need. And just like that, we were nearly ready to go at each other again.

"Are we crazy, Mobley?" she asked, still dazed from the intensity of the kiss.

"Yes. I believe that we are," I answered letting her up. I still felt dumbstruck from the whole afternoon.

"Is this what it's like to be a sex addict?" she asked with a wince. "Exhausted, barely able to walk? Sore, day in, day out?"

"Maybe," I admitted. "Or the aftermath of a rugby game. Whatever it is, I'm not ready for rehab."

"Me either." She grinned and took my hand, pulling me up the front stairs.

"Lydia, please cancel my 7:00 dinner with the Robierres," she said after walking through the front doors with me. "Convey my regrets, something came up. We'll try to reschedule tomorrow." She dropped her arm from around my waist. Previously, shaking hands was the extent of any public displays of affection with me. At this point, she just didn't care. I was stunned.

"Yes, ma'am. But... what about Mr. Michaels? He phoned and said he is coming later this evening to see you."

"Cancel that as well. Tell him I've turned in for the day and have no time for him."

"Um. Yes, ma'am."

Leanne was in the lobby, and I had to wonder if she had been waiting on us. She looked very worried. "Stefany, you are *that* tired? It's only 6:00!" she exclaimed. "We were going to get together later this evening after your dinner. Remember? Talk over *things* while relaxing with a drink by the pool?"

"Oh. Well, nonetheless, Mobley and I have worked hard today *restacking* that hay in the barn. I intend to keep my appointment with a bubble bath and a glass of wine. Before turning in. Perhaps another time."

Stefany looked as though she had just run a marathon and yet a playful smile teased the corners of her mouth for all to see. She seemed to be flaunting the risky behavior, unworried she had entered with her arm around me. Whether the staff accepted her explanation or not didn't seem to be a concern to her in the least. They surely had to wonder why "restacking hay" wasn't the duty of the field hands that normally handled such chores. No further explanation was proffered, and no one dared to ask.

Stefany bit the side of her bottom lip and looked like she would nearly break out laughing. At that moment, she was at her most beautiful, more so than ever, I realized. She pulled back several raven strands of wild, wayward hair from her face and looked back as she began to take the steps up to the second floor.

"We'll talk later, Leanne. Good evening, all." She nodded to Lydia then shot Leanne a knowing glance. "I'll see you tomorrow, Mr. Mobley. Outstanding work in the barn."

"Yes, Ms. Michaels. Thank you," I replied nonchalantly, and in so doing ended up walking into a lobby chair, falling, knocking the side table and lamp over, then awkwardly landing on my back on the floor with a loud *thud*. To my horror, everyone was staring. Was I that disoriented? Lydia snickered uncontrollably and several of the guests gasped. Stefany covered her mouth but couldn't help but laugh.

Leanne offered me a hand, pulling me up. "My, my," she said. "That must have been some really heavy hay bales. Eh, Mr. Mobley?"

Embarrassed, I tidied my shirt. "Whoops," I offered with a stiff, fake laugh. "Guess I'm really tired. There were quite a few bales... to... um... restack."

Leanne continued to stare. "Oh, I'm sure. Your shirt, Mr. Mobley?"

I looked down at my shirt. "Yes?" I asked. "Ah." It was then I noticed I had buttoned it crooked. I quickly shoved the tail back into my pants and hoped for the best.

Stefany resumed her trek up the stairs. Turning to the hall, I slogged back towards my room under the suspicious glares of all who had witnessed the awkward scene.

Closing my door behind me, I took a deep breath and fell face first onto the bed. I heard a text message signal on my mobile.

Stefany:
> **You Ok??? What the hell???**

Me:
> **Yes, I just wasn't looking where I was going.**

Stefany:
> **No kidding. We didn't make a very graceful entry, I guess.**

Me:
> **No, we didn't. And maybe I'm just kind of dazed is all. You worked me over hard.**

Stefany:

I enjoyed every minute of it.

Me:

I know I did.

Stefany:

I could use a bath partner.
There are a lot of soap
bubbles in the tub. Nice and
slick.

Me:

Will I be able to fit?

Stefany:

If I sit up on the edge, there's
room for your head between
my knees. You could further
explain to me how much you
enjoyed today. While I have a
glass of wine.

Me:

You are unquenchable. You
might well kill me.

Stefany:

Maybe you should get a good
evening of rest. I can see you
tomorrow.

Me:

Make it a double funeral. I'll
be up in 30 minutes.

I walked into the bathroom and pulled the aspirin
bottle out of the medicine cabinet. I took off the cap and
bounced several pills into my shaking hand then tried to
stretch the cramps out of my shoulders. I opened my mouth
and looked in the mirror. My tongue felt like the Famoso
Raceway, races run daily. It was so sore I couldn't extend it
all the way. If someone were to offer a million dollars to
whistle, I wouldn't be able to do it. Deciding to add one more
aspirin, I tossed them into my mouth. I thought about

washing them down with a drink of whiskey, which could also help with the aches and pains. Going for the more sensible glass of water, I heard a soft knock. Opening the door, I was surprised to see Leanne.

"You clumsy fool. May I come in?"

"Leanne. Of course! Come in." She hesitated. I took her hand and pulled her in, closing the door behind her. "I may be clumsy, yes. *You* though, are a very naughty woman."

"So. Glad to see you aren't *weird* with me about last night. We are yet friends, I see," she purred. "Joyous moment. I thought I might have to schedule you for a session of therapy."

I felt embarrassed. "I'm okay. I admit, it was hot. You certainly seemed to *enjoy* yourself."

"Oh, I did. I have a newfound respect for you," she said, squeezing my cheek. "I was sorry it ended so soon, though. Heidi was also ready for a lot more."

"I'm fairly certain you two left satisfied," I reminded her.

"Oh yes, that we did," she admitted. "But alas, I fear your Lady Stefany has put an end to such group events. Sad, but perhaps for the better."

"Yes, probably," I admitted. "She decided that she does not want to share. I'm happy with that, actually."

Leanne nodded. "I get that and I'm glad you feel that way. You should be hers alone."

I peered into her eyes. "That was quite the assignment you gave Stefany today," I said, changing the subject. "I think she almost killed me," I joked.

"Yes, and she certainly took the full measure of the assignment to heart, I see. She added her own touches. It was supposed to last under an hour - not all afternoon. I've come to see if you are okay. Her and that damned BDSM book I gave her," Leanne mumbled with a grimace. "I'll be honest with you, Morgan. I'm coming to regret all this now. She wanted to experiment, and now she's like a little kid in a candy store, running around to sample everything."

"So, Leanne. Is it bad for me to get my hopes up?"

She cocked her head, uncertain with the direction of the conversation. "What do you mean?"

"That she really cares for me? There must be something there. Something more. It's more than just sex, right?"

She took a deep breath, looking tired to again revisit the subject. "Morgan. I've told you before, I don't want to give you false hope. She likes you because you are a fun sexual plaything. I'm not sure if there is more."

I tried to mask the disappointment that was on my face. "That's it?" My eyes dropped to the floor, unable to hide my feelings any further. "When I'm with her, it just seems like it's more."

"Have you forgotten she parceled you out to two other women to enjoy you last night? Not that I'm complaining."

"No. But she regrets that now," I emphasized.

"She thinks the world of you, I'll not deny that. But is she in love with you? I'm sorry, Morgan." She hesitated. "I don't think so. I think she's only in this for the fun. But. I mean, there's always a *chance* I suppose. I can't predict the future; I have painfully realized. The woman has changed, that's for sure. I Just want you to keep your head about you, okay?"

"Okay."

Leanne ran a playful finger along my jaw trying to lighten the mood. "So, let me guess, Morgan. You are preparing to go see her again tonight? And after everything you two just went through? You look as though you can barely stand."

"Yes. That's the plan. Why?"

"You two are going to *kill* each other. With sex. Are you okay with what happened today? Her leaving you alone out in the barn, tied up?"

"I was worried at the time, true. But she was just playing around. I'm sore, but fine. We both had fun."

Leanne stepped in and pulled up my shirt, revealing rope burns, hay rash, and several angry red stripes from Stefany's crop. "And this?"

"Yes. It hurts a little, no question about that. It's all in the fun, it gives her pleasure - and me. I'm fine with it. This type of play oddly heightens the senses."

"From a meek little bird, I've created a true freak," Leanne muttered with reluctance. "The degree of this is something I did *not* anticipate. Knowing Stefany as I have all my life, I'm shocked, frankly. I should have known better than to play with her emotions and feelings. And yours. Now in retrospect, I think I should have just left both of you alone."

"But everything you wanted to happen has come to pass," I explained. "Stefany is happier. Look at her. She's the most confident woman I think I've ever met - in addition to you. Be it sex or business. She's moved to a much better place in her life thanks to you."

"Let me ask you a question. Would you be participating in these assignments as a submissive or sex slave with as much gusto with another woman? Or would you instead go back to the old Mobley, you calling the shots, you being the dominant sexual partner, doing whatever you please, using women like potato chips?"

"I never used women like potato chips," I objected. I thought about her question. True, it was exhilarating and different, being on the receiving end of sexual domination by a beautiful woman. But how much did it have to do with it being Stefany? A lot, I knew. "I do like it. But to answer your question, I can't imagine doing this stuff with any woman other than Stefany."

"Just as I already knew. Let's forget the sex and just talk about Stefany's life for a moment. We don't even have any idea of how Miles will play into any of this. Yes, she's separated, but he still hasn't granted her a divorce. If he caught on to these assignments, which you two are more less advertising now, he could have extra ammo against her. Have you thought of that?"

"Miles has never been faithful to her, you know that, Leanne. To hell with him. I have no intention of *moving on* from her."

Leanne faced off with me, suddenly serious, her hands on her hips. We stood looking into each other's eyes, attempting to comprehend something neither of us truly understood.

"You've missed the point, Morgan. *When this is all over, and it will be over some day,* then what? What will be the collateral damage? Can either of you even function in a future relationship? I never meant for this to be so serious. Look. I've underestimated her. I'll just say it. I think I've made a grave mistake pushing you two together like this."

"No, you didn't. Leanne, I love her more than ever. Why would I fall out of love with her? I won't - not ever. In fact, I've been meaning to give you something." I walked over to my dresser and pulled open the top drawer. I took out a small piece of paper and held it up to her.

"That's the cashier's check I wrote you for your agreement to terms of being Stefany's sex slave. For which you have met beyond my wildest expectations," Leanne observed dryly. "Why won't you cash it? I know you need the money."

I tore it in two and handed it to her. Stunned, she took the pieces and looked at me questioningly.

"I don't want any payment for anything that has to do with my relationship with Stefany. It… taints it," I explained. "She is the only reward in this that I ever want."

Stefany: My playtime with Mobley has been incredible. The barn assignment left me barely able to walk afterward. Words really can't describe what he's done to me

insofar as waking me up sexually. I suppose I could feel guilty or ashamed - I don't.

Just a year ago, I would never have imagined myself doing anything with a man such as what I did with Mobley for Leanne's assignment in the barn. Teasing him, I left him tied up on a hay bale for over an hour and he never even got mad! He only wanted more.

When I returned to the barn for round 2, I decided to give him a drink from a bottle of water I brought in my tool bag to keep him hydrated. Leaning over on him, I pressed down on his throat with the sole of my foot. It wasn't too much, but enough that his face turned red – and he didn't complain once. To the contrary, judging by his reaction, I think he got off on it. I poured the water into his mouth - more or less - and I would let off the pressure for him to swallow. Feeling the arteries in his neck throbbing beneath my foot was a power trip. It was hotter than hell, and I'm not even sure why.

Mobley - my "submissive sex slave" - so appointed by Leanne in some crazy bet. It was laughable and weird at first. And sort of ironic. As my sub, he has shown more strength and character than Miles or any of the macho guys I used to let beat the shit out of me. Different women are empowered in different ways, I suppose. For me, Mobley is more to me than just a sex toy. I don't know exactly what.

~~~~~

I feel like Leanne has been "analyzing" me lately. While we do share a lot, I am not going to discuss with her my deeper feelings for Mobley. That's my secret - I'm entitled to a few. Not everything has to be slung out  for public consumption. She can be very prying. And irritating!

~~~~~

HUGE NEWS! I've been selected as Businesswoman of the Year by a prestigious group in Europe! Their invitation includes an all-expenses-paid flight for me and a guest to Paris where I am to stay in luxury accommodations for three days! I never heard of such a thing and thought it was a scam, but it all checked out.

While it is spur-of-the-moment and it will disrupt my plans for a few days, it's a significant enough event in my life that I have no choice but to be thrilled. I am told the awards event will be attended by hundreds of the top business leaders of the world!

It's all over Caribbean regional news, and even back in Canada. When Miles heard of it, of course, he demanded to go, even as he attempted to diminish the significance. I flat out told him no, it was going to be a brief trip and I needed Mobley to attend with me since he was the one largely responsible for my success. Miles was furious. After threatening me a few times, he relented. I'm done with the part of my life where I'm intimidated by Miles - or any other man, for that matter.

Mobley was genuinely surprised – and touched – that I chose him to accompany me to Paris to attend the awards ceremony. Who else would I take?

The truth is, regardless of any other considerations, it is Mobley that I must thank for my achievements. He is the only reason Stoney Brook the astonishing success that it is.

Leanne has agreed to watch everything for me while I'm away. I'm excited beyond words!

Extremely sore from Mobley the prior day and having left my phone in the office, I trudged to the front desk to check messages after helping update inventory in one of the storage sheds. Lydia was manning the desk this morning. I wiped the sweat from my forehead and leaned on the desk. I probably looked hungover, which in a way, I suppose I was. It was a Mobley sex hangover. I had to wonder how he was doing.

"Ms. Michaels?"

"Lydia. Yes? Sorry, I'm just a little under the weather today."

"Sorry, ma'am. You received a call, which was said to be most urgent."

"Who was it from?" I asked, curious.

"It was the woman from the European Council of Outstanding Business Leaders. She said she sends her hope that you will plan to attend the proceedings in Paris. If possible, she would like to know if you can commit to this today."

"Lydia, please call her back and tell her I very much appreciate the tickets and orientation packet she sent. And yes, I will be attending. With Morgan Mobley."

The flight to Paris was long and we were both tired. Despite this and after several cups of coffee, we decided to spend some time enjoying the lovely Paris evening. After checking into our room at our gorgeous luxury hotel, the Le Meuricel, we took a cab and headed out to the shops and little cafes of the neighborhood known as the Butte Montmartre.

We held hands as we strolled along, and I was as happy as I had ever been in my life. That was saying something, given the amazing turns my life had taken over the past two years. Stopping him suddenly, I stepped in front of him, took hold of his shirt with both hands, and looked up into his blue eyes that were glinting with the nearby light of a streetlamp.

"What?" he asked, wondering what I was doing.

"Nothing. I just like looking into your eyes."

"Do you, now? I guess it's mutual then." Smiling, he pulled me close, swept me off my feet, and deftly made several spins. Several pedestrians, evidently approving of us validating Paris as a city for lovers, stopped to clap and whistled. He kissed me in the glow of the lights of a nearby café, amid the steady flow of passing tourists. We were oblivious - and free.

The evening grew late, and we returned to our room, bleary-eyed and desirous of nothing more than sleep. No one back at Stoney Brook needed to know our room only had one bed. Mobley managed to kiss me once more. The last thing I remember was his arms around me as we both surrendered to exhaustion.

My eyes fluttered open, and I woke up to my regular, sweet kiss from Mobley as the morning sun streamed into our room. It was time for the big day, and I flung myself out of bed.

"Mobley! Let's go!" Groggy and in the fog of not being fully awake, I panicked, looking at the bedside clock.

"I've already been up for an hour," he said with a smirk. "I let you sleep in. We have plenty of time! We can go to eat breakfast, get dressed up, then take a cab. The beginning presentations don't start for several hours."

Relieved, I sat down on the end of the bed. "Oh."

Mobley nodded with amusement and handed me a cup of coffee. "Relax."

After a breakfast fit for royalty in the hotel restaurant, we changed into our best clothes; Mobley in a black tuxedo and white bowtie, me in a blue, floor-length dress. In the lobby, Mobley pushed me in front of a huge mirror and held me from behind, ignoring the attention we were getting from onlookers.

"World, I would like to present to you the talented, incredibly intelligent, *most* beautiful woman in the world, the owner of Stoney Brook Plantation - Ms. Stefany Michaels."

I laughed at his audacity. "Keep going," I goaded.

"The woman," he added, "that owns all of me. My heart. My soul."

We looked at each other through our reflections in the mirror, suddenly serious. I didn't know what to say or how to respond. Mobley was all but telling me he loved me. And all I could do was hesitate. "Morgan…" I turned with blurry eyes and straightened his bowtie as a tear managed to escape down my cheek.

I'm not sure what I was prepared to say to him. He placed a halting finger over my lips, sensing my inner struggle. He smiled, took my hand, and kissed it, making me want him even more. Then he pulled me outside, flagged a cab, and we departed the hotel laughing like teenagers as we headed to the convention venue.

As guests and speakers began arriving, one of the most surprising aspects of the Business Leaders of the World Convention was the number of celebrities and government officials that were in attendance. I met the Canadian Prime Minister and the German Chancellor! We were both starstruck as we wandered about the displays and discussion groups.

Finally, the lights dimmed, a signal that everyone was supposed to take their seats in the main auditorium. Seats were assigned and I was surprised that Mobley and I were up on the front row among the VIPs.

"I had no idea! This is like… a big deal!" Mobley commented loudly, noticing that he recognized numerous famous people nearby. Looking directly at the person seated to his left, he was shocked to see that it was the famed CEO of a huge tech company. His mouth dropped, and I nudged him in the ribs with a laugh.

"Mobley. Shhhh. Don't make such a ruckus. They'll realize we are just commoners and make us move to the back. Or throw us out!"

As I was laughing, the person to my right extended their hand. I shook it, trying to make out who it was in the low light of the auditorium. After an introduction, I learned she was the United States Secretary of Commerce. "Oh!" I blurted out loud as Mobley had, then instantly laughed. She smiled, visibly amused at my reaction, as were others sitting nearby.

I leaned over to Mobley and whispered, unable to contain myself. "I think we have good seats, Mr. Mobley."

"I would agree!"

"Okay, shhhhhhhh!" I jokingly scolded Mobley. "We have to be quiet now." Mobley pretended to zip his lips.

The conference began with numerous speakers, all recognizable as leaders in world commerce and business. Eventually, the speakers began giving out various awards against the backdrop of a huge onstage screen that played videos and images of various subjects related to those receiving recognition.

Mobley leaned over. "Wow. Will you have to go up there?" he whispered. "If you do, better you than me," he joked, giving me a devilish glance.

"No. I'm sure not," I replied. "I'd just die. Look at this crowd! There are even news cameras in the back. No one ever said anything about it to me, thank gawd. I think these are the big, majorish awards. I'm probably just mentioned somewhere in the brochure or something."

"Ah," he acknowledged.

The president of the European Council of Outstanding Business Leaders strode to the podium amidst great applause and began speaking to the crowd. After recognizing several notable attendees, my heart nearly froze as I began seeing images of Stoney Brook flash up on the screen.

I began to get a queasy feeling as he started giving a description of my plantation back in the Caribbean. How could I be of any notable mention to this important, huge crowd? Mobley visibly swallowed and looked over at me. "Oh nooo," I mumbled. Photos showing me at Stoney Brook began to play on the large back screen.

"Our next recognition is of a truly remarkable woman that exemplifies the finest of rising stars that are private owners of businesses that have been grown from the ashes up. I'll explain. Coming from a modest background of running a small coffee shop in Montreal, Canada, she was surprised one day, several years ago, to learn that she was to inherit a decrepit sugar plantation that was established by her ancestors, the proud Scottish family of McCaskill. Keeping it even marginally running wasn't a sure thing.

This plantation, located on a remote Caribbean island and as beautiful as it was, was not much of a prize, as it turns out. It was broken. Run down. In disrepair. It was nearly bankrupt. What little recurring income there was, mostly went into the labor costs of maintaining a mildly profitable sugar cane production operation."

A camera somewhere panned on me and just like that, I was projected up on the screen. Wincing and probably looking like a little kid, I instinctively began sliding down lower and lower in my seat. A man and woman behind me laughed, amused at my futile attempt of anonymity. The nearby audience watched the speaker, enthralled.

Morgan leaned over. "It'll be okay!" he encouraged, laughing at my nearly reclining position. "C'mon. Courage!" He pulled me up to a straight sitting position.

"That's easy for you to say," I whispered back, so nervous that my throat was going dry.

The speaker continued. "After beginning a coconut oil production venture, revenue began to slowly roll in. Contracts began to grow. The workforce began to grow. Then, after a complete and successful restoration of the entire estate of Stoney Brook, the business further ventured out, even making a new worldwide favorite to coffee shops everywhere, an economical and effective alternative to plastics... small stirrers made from sugar cane. The estate was opened as a luxury resort that now boasts five-stars by major reviews. The business is a model for outstanding environmental stewardship and ecological conservation. Now, only a mere two years after she accepted ownership, Stoney Brook has gone from nearly broke to being one among the most profitable privately owned businesses in the Caribbean and Central America region. I would like to introduce you to one of our most dramatic success stories. Of the Caribbean resort, the Stoney Brook Plantation. Ladies and gentlemen, our recipient for Businesswoman of the Year, Stefany Michaels."

The president came to the front of the stage and held his hand out towards me.

The crowd erupted into loud applause - I was horrified.

"Please come up."

In a panic, I looked pleadingly at Mobley. "No! Mobley!"

"It's okay! You'll be fine. Just go up," he said as he stood, coaxing me up. "You'll knock 'em dead!"

I was numb with fright. Wondering if the crowd could see me trembling beneath my dress, I approached the stairs where the other award winners had mounted the stage. I visibly wobbled in the heels. Nearly losing my balance, a steward took my hand, helping me up the final few steps.

Approaching the podium, I nervously shook hands with the president who then handed me a crystal and gold award. Placing his hand behind my back, he encouraged me to say something at the mic. This was something I had not anticipated and assumed this was only going to be a minor thing. Overwhelmed, my mind whirled with what I could possibly say.

Fumbling with the mic, I finally adjusted it to my considerably shorter height. "Um. Hi," I began, shocked at how loud - and strange - my voice sounded in the auditorium. I laughed uncontrollably aloud at this, the audience laughing with me.

"Wow. I'm really honored…" The mic dropped suddenly, and I had to readjust it. "Honored… to be the recipient of this award. I wasn't sure of what it was... actually." The audience again laughed.

"So. Um. I thank you for this," I said, hoping to be finished. I held up the award to loud applause.

The president raised his hand to silence the auditorium. "Miss Michaels," he began. "Please give us a few words to women out there that are considering starting up a business venture."

I blinked, trying to think. Shit.

A long, uncomfortable pause ensued as I stood there looking into the shadows of countless faces before me. It was so quiet, I could even hear a cough from the very back. A few in the audience shouted encouragements or whistled. My eyes fell on Mobley in the front row. He smiled and gave me a hearty thumbs up. The president, perhaps sensing that I was mute and dumbstruck, took a step towards me and hesitated.

"If there's anything I can say," I began uncertainly, "It is that I'm living proof that dreams can come true. It takes a lot of hard work. Some luck." The audience stared up at me in silence. "You can't do it alone. You need people. Strong people that can hold you up in the worst of times. I have good people with me. And I have one that is especially my strength. My estate manager. He's the guy that rebuilt Stoney Brook for me and his amazing ideas that kept us going. He's made me everything I am today. And he deserves this award more than I do. He is Morgan Mobley," I said, pointing at him. The shoe was on the other foot now, and he grimaced at the sudden attention. The president indicated to Mobley that he should stand as the audience clapped wildly.

The president gestured towards the mic. "Please. Continue."

"Well. Okay. I'll be honest," I continued at his urging. "There were times I didn't think I would make it… in being successful with what I was trying to build. I told myself, if I'm going to fail, then by damned, I'm going to go down hard.

"Just as I thought it was over, things did turn around. It was a lesson I'll never forget. So, what I want to say to people everywhere… not just young women, is no one worth their salt has everything given to them. You are what you build. Success is an achievement, not a gift - it's not a birthright. That means you will have to fight through the setbacks. Fight through your self-doubt - because you'll have it as sure as the sun rises. Start again if you need to. Reinvent yourself. Adapt. Evolve. Be there that next, wonderful day. Back in the fray. This struggle… of finding success… is what defines our enduring humanity. It's what gives us purpose. When you are knocked down – and you most certainly will be – you get back up. You stand firmly in the breech of this life we've been given, and you *never* give up on your dreams."

With this, I was shocked that the rest of the auditorium gave us both a standing ovation. He spoke to me as he escorted me to the stairs. I couldn't hear a word he said. Grateful I didn't trip, I was met by a barrage of handshakes and hugs from people I didn't even know. When I finally was able to take my seat, I gave the award to Mobley. I then leaned over and kissed him on the cheek.

The swarming attention after the awards ceremony was overwhelming. Besieged at every turn by innumerable handshakes, questions, and even news interviews, I felt sorry for Mobley who went largely unnoticed. Whenever I tried to pull him into these circles of activity, he resisted, preferring to watch from the distance.

Finally getting a break, I yanked Mobley into a quiet corner. "I'm sorry they are ignoring you," I told him. "I want you to be part of this. This is your success as well as mine."

"It's okay." He hugged me. "You are a much more attractive target for the cameras. This is your moment. You deserve it and I am so proud of you."

"You are the rock of my foundation, Mobley," I said, looking up at him. "But I've had enough. What say we get out of here? Go take in Paris?"

"I think that's a fabulous plan," he agreed with a broad smile, taking my hand to lead me through the crowd.

Having thoroughly enjoyed ourselves seeing the sights, sounds, and tastes of Paris, Mobley closed our hotel room door behind us. Smiling, he kissed me to the point of nearly making me melt.

Dropping to his knees, he took one of my hands and kissed it. Then, parting the slit in my dress, he kissed each of my legs as he looked up at me.

"And what shall be your pleasure this evening? Paris may have great restaurants, but the finest meal is in this room," he said, half-joking, but mostly serious. He planted several soft kisses further up on the insides of my thighs, stopping just at the edge of my white lace panties. Having me balance with a hand on his shoulder, he removed my shoes. A warm, burning flame that I had suppressed for two days erupted through my core. "Damn, Mobley. I want you. Hard."

"And hard is what you shall have, my lady," he said as I combed my fingers through his blond locks. "I doubt you brought the riding crop. So, you may have to do with a rolled-up paper," he joked. "I want to be your bad puppy."

I didn't laugh.

"What?" he asked, sensing my change of mood and increasingly curious with where my intentions lay.

Taking a deep breath, I pulled him up. This wasn't the standard procedure of the initial floor duty he was used to. He looked at me, intrigued as to where this was going.

"Look, Mobley. You know me now; my history, everything that's happened to me. I suppose Leanne has told you all about it. The years Miles beat the shit out of me. The shitty boyfriends I had in the past that did the same. I've been subjugated to men all my life. In ways that were not good."

"Yes," he acknowledged solemnly.

"This whole dominant and slave thing, you obviously know it has been weirdly liberating for me. Not counting my recent life at Stoney Brook, I've never been in charge of anything, really. My life. Events. And before you, certainly not sex."

I ran a finger slowly down his lips. "You let me be in charge. But more importantly, I'm *safe* to be in charge. You have allowed me to discover myself and grow. It's not just the sex. You see what I'm saying?"

"I do."

I walked over to the closet where I kept my two suitcases. As I went, I unzipped the back of my dress and slipped it off. Similarly, I unsnapped my bra then flung it on the bed. Pushing my panties down, I let them drop around my feet, watching Mobley's eyes widen.

Naked, I reached into my suitcase and pulled out four pieces of soft cotton rope. I walked back to stand in front of him. Never in my life was I more confident than I was at this moment.

Thinking I wanted to tie him up, he smiled and held his wrists out.

"No. Not this time," I told him. "These aren't for you." He blinked, confused.

"There isn't another person I trust more than you," I admitted to him. His puzzled expression deepened.

I leaned into him, kissing him. Placing the ropes in his hand, I closed his fingers over them. I relished the sweet confusion in his eyes.

"Tonight," I told him, "I want to experience the other side. I want to be controlled. Bound. Used. Made to taste. Teased. Consumed. Not like I was in the past - with a fist and blackened eyes. But with you - my best friend that knows well my many faults. My lover who knows my deepest desires."

Understanding sank in, finally. Taking the ropes, he slipped a hand around my neck and kissed me softly. I ran my fingers along his finely muscled sides as I slid down to my knees. Slowly unbuckling his belt, I then undid the waist snap, ran the zipper down, and pulled his pants with his underwear down to his ankles. Dropping back to sit on my heels, I bit one side of my lower lip and looked up at him.

"Okay," he whispered, caressing my face. He ran his fingers into my hair behind my head. Then he pulled me into him.

We walked along the Seine River, enjoying the afternoon views of Paris. The previous day – and evening with Mobley – had been a flaming conflagration of heated sex. Mobley had been gentle, soft, just rough enough. He was perfect with me, no more than I could take, but enough to take me to the edge. He had tied me up to all four corners of the bed with the cotton ropes. After that, the evening was a blur of intense sensations.

The dominant, such as I have been with Mobley, seems to be the usual, rightful recipient of things oral. Last night was no exception although that was certainly not the only thing we enjoyed together. Mobley took full advantage of his status as the dominant. In the course of the evening, he had no problem taking care of me too, and as usual, we both were left exhausted by the time we finally stepped out of the shower and dropped back into bed. I had slept in his arms amid the petals of a red rose.

Deep into the thought of these memories, I stopped, leaned against the protective railing, and pulled Mobley back into me. "Last night, Mobley. Wow. That's all I can say." He stood in close, and I wrapped my arms around his waist.

"Yeah. Me too. We just keep topping ourselves," he said with a laugh.

"What fun. I had no idea I would even like it, reversing roles as we did. You know what that's called?"

"No, what?"

"It's called going *switch*. It means you can enjoy being both dominant and submissive. Yet another thing I learned in Leanne's BDSM book."

He nodded with a chuckle. "Ah. I presume that we are both switches, then?"

"I think you presume correctly," I joked. I slipped my hand into his and we resumed our walk.

A taxicab slowly approached us, the driver probably wondering if we needed a ride. The heavily bearded man, behind large sunglasses and a ball cap, said something to us in French through the passenger window that we didn't understand. Mobley gave him a dismissive wave and the taxi drove on.

"Mobley. What if we get tired of it all?"

"Tired?"

"Yeah. I mean, we just keep moving the dial up. Like last night. How can we keep that up? Will we get tired of it? Will we get burned out?" It was an honest question.

"I will never get tired of you, no matter what," he told me, dead serious. He kissed me again for the umpteenth time that day. "Will you tire of me?"

Patting his cheek, I laughed. "No."

"Promise?" he asked, serious.

I thought about this for a moment, wondering if I could make such a pledge truthfully. Promises, in what I had experienced in my life, were made to be broken. Seeing the growing concern in his eyes, I slipped my hands into his back pockets. "Let's not talk about problems we don't even have. I shouldn't have brought it up." Giving him a squeeze, I urged him to continue walking with me and drop the subject. He stopped abruptly and turned me to face him again.

"Will you?" he asked, having sensed my conflicted thoughts.

"Will I what?" I countered.

"Promise me. You won't tire of me."

"Mobley. Sometimes, a broken promise can shield a broken heart."

We both stood staring into each other's eyes for a moment, and I wondered why I would say such a thing. Was it the result of my cynical past coming back to haunt me? Mobley looked sad for a moment but he did not press me further. Perhaps, like me, he was realizing we were at the apex of our relationship. Where else could it go? We both turned, resuming our walk together in silence towards a row of shops.

"There's that bakery we wanted to try!" I blurted excitedly, eager to reclaim our prior cheerful mood. We had both wanted to sample the bread of an artisan bakery we noticed the previous evening. Stepping into the entry way, Mobley held the door open for me and I started through amid the enticing smell of fresh bread and pastries.

Behind us on the road, something crashed loudly. Tires squealed and we both turned. A taxicab had just burst through a vender's cart on the sidewalk, sending drinks, food, and the unfortunate vendor careening into the air. We both recognized the face behind the wheel of the vehicle. It was the same driver that had previously slowed his taxicab along the river.

Mobley forcibly shoved me through the door backward. "Everyone look out!" He pressed deeper into the bakery pushing me over a table. We both went over the top, ending up on the floor.

The cab came in at a high rate of speed, struck the inside of the sturdy door jamb, shattering glass, brick, and mortar. The sudden impact into the door and supporting heavy brick wall brought the cab to a crunching halt. So violent was the sudden stop, the back end of the taxicab lifted into the air and swung around, the momentum then smashing it into the front glass windows of the bakery.

The cab driver, uninjured, exited the cab and I could see from my angle on the floor he was carrying an automatic rifle. Mobley pushed me down behind the overturned table. He ducked in over the top of me as we could hear the gun firing. Bullets snapped all around us, breaking off pieces of the table and hitting the wall behind us. The firing stopped.

Seeming to be uninjured, we both peered over the top of the table to see the taxicab driver trying to reload his rifle – or perhaps it was jammed. Mobley grabbed a plate on the floor, stood suddenly and threw it like a frisbee. It hit the driver hard, striking him square in the chest. Mobley jumped over the table and lunged at the driver and the two rolled about the debris on the floor. The assailant, now without his rifle, managed to break free of the struggle. Mobley just missed grabbing him with an outstretched hand from the floor. The man sprinted around the corner.

Mobley, now sporting a number of small glass cuts, stumbled over the broken chairs and tables back to me.

"Stefany! Are you ok?" He pulled me to my feet as the crowd of onlookers began gathering.

"I'm okay." I dusted bits of broken glass and pieces of splintered wood off my clothes. "But you? You are cut!"

"It's not too bad."

"What the hell just happened?"

Mobley pulled me into him protectively and looked uncertainly about, unable to formulate an answer. Bystanders were attending to the street vendor who had seemingly escaped with minor injuries. The scene quickly became congested with people standing about surveying the damage, speaking excitedly in French.

After spending a day fighting jittery nerves back at the hotel, we heard a knock on our door. Mobley opened it, letting in the Paris detective that had been handling our case.

Following a series of polite but uncomfortable small talk, he finally explained what he knew. "We still have not identified the suspect, even though we have examined various security cameras in the area. As you know, he fled the scene, and as of now, we do not know where he is. The rifle seems to have been smuggled in from outside of France. The cab was stolen. The real cab driver was found unharmed, bound in an alley on the north side of the city."

I shrugged. "So. What does this all mean? Was he trying to kill everyone? Was this a terrorist attack?"

"Ms. Michaels. He seemed to be firing specifically at you and your companion, Mr. Mobley. There does not seem to be any other intended victims in this attack."

"Just us?" I asked incredulously.

"Yes. It is one or both of you, it seems. The attacker intentionally tried to run you down with the cab," he clarified to eliminate any doubt. "Then tried to shoot one or both of you for reasons that we have been unable to yet determine. The investigation is ongoing. We are aware of the prior incidents of attempted murder at your home, and we are looking at the possibility they could be related. We are coordinating our efforts with the authorities of your island. If there are any further developments, we will contact you. For your own safety, we would like you to return to your home immediately. If you are agreeable, we have arranged a flight that leaves in an hour. We have two agents just outside your door that will escort you to the airport."

"Okay," Mobley said, sounding distant.

I nodded in agreement. "We'll be ready, shortly."

CHAPTER 19
THE DARK STORM OF A DARK NIGHT

Morgan: Much like the cops we've dealt with so far here on the island, Paris law enforcement doesn't have any answers except they 'think' it was directed at us. The taxi that tried to hit us was the same one that trolled us as we were walking by the Seine. I can't help but think that this is but another attempt by the same person or group that has previously tried to harm Stefany and me. This time, they've gone beyond the island, and it seems they will stop at nothing to kill us, not even international travel.

Notwithstanding an arrested suspect, I'm glad to be back on the island. At least here I feel somewhat in control of what we can do to protect ourselves. We've been incredibly lucky. All we can do is remain vigilant and be careful.

~~~~~~~

I've experienced many days of rain here on the island and seen my share of thunderstorms. And we've even been on the edges of some big hurricanes - we have yet to be right in the crosshairs of one of these big storms. That all looks like it's going to change. The weather forecast now has us sitting right in the middle of the path of a hurricane, set to arrive in about a week. It's said we can expect winds up to 130 miles per hour, perhaps stronger. When it begins to rain, we could be in it for days and get several feet of water dumped on us. Help from the outside world may be slow in coming, and honestly, we can't expect much in the way of supplies or financial aid with us being an independently governed island.

I don't think one can prepare enough for something like getting hit by a hurricane. And since I've never done it before, I must rely on the experiences of islanders who have gone through these many times before.

Stefany has closed Stoney Brook and the Mill Property to the public and canceled all stays during the storm and afterwards for several weeks in anticipation of the probable damage we'll have.

I'd be lying if I said I wasn't worried about Stoney Brook and the Mill Property. They've been around for hundreds of years, so I know they are built sturdy. Yet, all it takes is a bit of poor luck. In the past there has undoubtedly been wind damage to Stoney Brook, it's just been repaired following each storm, much as we'll likely have to do this time. As for how much damage we'll get, I have no idea.

I have all the estate windows secured with plywood covers. To try and help shore up the old barn, the boys and I strung a series of cross-lattice cables from rafters and beams tied into ground anchors outside to give it some extra stability. I hope it's all enough.

Cupping my hands around my eyes to attempt to better see the clouds in the distance, I wondered what exactly we were in for with this oncoming storm. For several days, the island experienced what I could only call a deathly calm. The skies were clear and there was not an ounce of a breeze. This morning, however, revealed a long bank of threatening clouds on the horizon of the ocean to the southeast. Now, a slight breeze wound its way steadily across the beaches and through the jungles, a hint at more to come.

"Mr. Mobley?" Stefany began amidst the managers and staff of Stoney Brook, all meeting out in the circle drive of the estate. "How are we set for fire safety? If we end up with the kind of winds the weather service is predicting, I wouldn't want to have a fire start in the middle of trying to get through this storm and not be prepared."

That was very forward-thinking, I thought, realizing that a fire threat had been the least of my worries in preparing for a hurricane. All the windows of Stoney Brook and the Mill Property were boarded and secured. Everything that wasn't already securely lashed down was stored away or tied to something else. We were prepared as well as we could be. But for fire?

Recalling my first few months of employment at Stoney Brook, I was pleased that I had addressed this very issue, back when I still thought of Stefany Michaels as a bitchy, harping shrew. Peering into her beautiful eyes as these memories flooded back, I was astounded in how far we had both come. In retrospect, I knew I was unconsciously in love with her back then, even though I detested her.

"Almost two years ago, the storage barn, mansion, big barn, and Mill Property were all fitted out with overhead fire suppression. Only the storage warehouse doesn't have this system. But there are numerous fire extinguishers throughout the building."

Stefany nodded with a hint of amusement. "Oh, yes. If I recall, I was rather upset at you when you surprised me after the fact with the unplanned expense of a modern fire suppression system."

"Um. Right," I confirmed, feeling Miles glaring at me from behind my back.

"You were right then, and I was unappreciative. In hindsight, I'm sorry I gave you grief. Well done, Mr. Mobley."

"Thank you." She then shot me a glance that told me she would think of ways of repaying me later.

"Like that's some great feat," Miles blurted. "It was mostly installed by the company contractor. And let's not forget, Stefany - you had a limited budget at the time, and that project alone put you in the red. The bungling and incompetent Morgan Mobley in charge of security and fire safety. What a joke."

My teeth clenched as I tried to maintain self-control. Saying such a thing in front of the entire Stoney Brook staff was galling, to say the least. Several of the staff snickered and chuckled.

"Miles, please," Stefany objected. "That's very inappropriate and we don't need sniping at this point. Mobley saved Stoney Brook with his ideas and management. And in doing so, everyone's job."

"He's a real hero, Mobley is. I think I've heard enough of those stories to last a lifetime, no thank you," Miles bitterly replied in a low tone.

The meeting continued without further contention, despite my desire to wring Mile's neck, and Stefany dismissed the entire staff to return to their homes and seek safety. Miles departed with his senior manager to the Mill Property, where they would stay and monitor from there. I momentarily fantasized about Miles hugging a harbor buoy after the storm washed him out to sea.

Leanne, Heidi, and Joe had left for Costa Rica. And with all the guests having been sent away, the only people left at Stoney Brook to hold the place down amid an onrushing hurricane would be Stefany and me. I couldn't be happier. As if on cue, a gust of dusty wind enveloped us as we jogged back to the security of the front doors.

All the island inhabitants by now were away from low lying beach areas and were in secure shelters, such as those of the several schools and government building with solid concrete foundations and basements.

For hours into the afternoon, Stefany and I went about Stoney Brook, double-checking that we had taken every possible preparation. The island authorities anticipated that the fragile electrical grid would be down perhaps an hour into the storm. Stoney Brook and the Mill Property had stout electrical generator backups, and these were all ready for service. All phone service, landlines, and mobile alike, would likely be out soon.

The wind picked up speed, causing an occasional ghostly whistle, finding a discreet entry around a window or door. By late afternoon, it was slamming into the sides of the estate in loud, violent gusts.

As we prepared to hole up in the lobby, Stefany looked nervous and on edge. I pulled her into a tight hug and kissed her. "We have this whole place to ourselves. Maybe you should break out a new assignment for me," I only half joked, hoping she would take me up on this idea.

"That's a very enticing thought. I just can't tonight, Mobley. I hate to admit, but I'm very worried about all of this."

"Stefany. This old gal, Stoney Brook, has been through quite a few of these storms in her history. I'm sure she'll be up for this one."

"I wish I shared your confidence."

"It will be okay. What say we go to the bar and have a drink? Take the edge off."

She thought about this for a moment. "No. Maybe later. I really think we should keep a lookout. Don't you? Can we uncover one of these windows? So, we can see what's going on?"

"I'm not sure that's wise. It could break if the wind kicks something up and hits it. Even if it is modern, tempered storm glass."

"Please? I need to see."

Reluctantly, I retrieved a cordless drill from beneath the front desk, went outside, and removed one sheet of protective plywood from a front window. About getting blown off the deck while handling the plywood and the drill, I wrestled it into the front doors and closed them behind me. If the window did break, I could probably reinstall the plywood from the inside.

"As you wish, my lady. A portal out into the storm." I motioned with my hand towards the window. "No rain yet. We'll get that a little later, according to the forecast." The lightning now was spectacular, streaking through the sky in multiple arcs at a nearly continuous pace, casting an odd, ghostly pallor across the front grounds of the estate.

Looking like a scared kitten, Stefany stared out, transfixed by the light show. Admiring her in her casual work jeans, I walked up behind her to place my hands on her hips. She straightened against me, and I kissed her neck just as the power failed and Stoney Brook went completely dark. In a far corner of the building, we heard the faint sound of diesel engines starting. The lights flicked back to life. I pulled her back and away from the window a few feet just in case.

"It will be okay. I'm with you. I won't let anything hurt you." At that moment, I thought about finally telling her I loved her. And yet again, like so many times in the past months when I thought I had the courage to tell her, I swallowed the long-suffering sentiment down. It could wait. For another time. Could it?

"You are my rock, Mobley." She turned, kissing me softly.

The lightning momentarily illuminated flying pieces of palm trees. Immediately following the lightning strikes, the sky was of such a pure black it seemed to be a solid mass, impenetrable beyond the window. When the sky was alight, we could see building debris from who-knew-where blow about the estate grounds in a macabre dance.

"What's that?" Stefany asked as we stood together.

I peered out, trying to discern what she was seeing amidst the lightning. In a far sugar cane field, nearly out of sight in the distance, I could make out a pair of headlights. The driver was taking the vehicle right through a full-grown crop of our cane. The more I stared, the more detail I could see - the running lights of what was evidently a full-sized eighteen-wheeler.

"It's a large truck and trailer," I answered, perplexed. "That's damned odd."

"Is it one of ours?" Stefany asked.

"No. It looks like a big transport trailer of some kind. I can't make it out."

It was very much out of place. "It doesn't make sense to park a big rig in the east field like that. It's more exposed there. And it looks like its parked broadside to the wind."

After a moment, the truck lights shut off and we stood there, wondering who in their right mind would do such a thing. Traffic on the island roads had been cleared for hours, and this driver should have been hunkered down somewhere more sheltered by now - not in an open sugar cane field, of all places.

"Stefany. I've got to go out there and see what gives. And whoever that is, should be brought in out of danger."

"What? No, Mobley. I don't think it's a good idea! Look at it out there."

"I'll be okay. I better go." I reluctantly unwrapped my arms from around her and went to the front desk to retrieve a flashlight.

Giving her a last reassuring kiss, I forced a front door open against the wind and securely closed it behind me. The wind was squarely in my face and making headway was difficult at best. Making my way down off the porch, I struggled through the courtyard and onward towards the main road, spitting pieces of grass and plants from my mouth as I went. After several minutes, I finally reached the edge of the sugar cane field. The truck was still out of my sight due to the height of the crop, so I walked up along the edge to where the truck left the road and drove through the cane.

Walking over the crushed cane, I approached the rear of the trailer. The shock spread over my body as I realized the large trailer was a transport tank for liquefied petroleum gas. Walking towards the cab, I could see the company name in large letters on the side of the tank: Unified Island Gas.

Pulling myself up on the cab, I pried open one of the doors. It was abandoned. And there weren't any keys, I noted.

"Hello!" Walking towards the front of the truck, I again shouted, hopeful to get the attention of anyone that could still be around. "Hello, is there anyone here!?"

Hearing no answer, and not sure I could hear one in the roaring wind, I turned and began walking back on the crushed cane trail, ready to give up my search. Off further to the east of the field, I noticed a rising glow in the dark night - it chilled my blood. It was a fire. And it was spreading at incredible speeds through the dry cane, lashed forward by the wind.

My mind rolled over the possibilities. Lightning? I hadn't seen any strikes directly on the estate property. What could have caused it?

My thoughts then turned back to the gas tanker. The fire was heading directly towards it! Full, or partly full, it could catch on fire and end up blowing Stoney Brook up in a monumental explosion. Even in the confusion and hesitation of the moment, it suddenly occurred to me that this was all intentional! Someone had brought the truck with the tank intentionally - abandoning it close enough to blow the estate to pieces.

The fire was a full-blown inferno now, with blown embers dancing on the ground between my legs. Several landed on my shirt, causing me to swat at them as they burned through my shirt to my skin. Would the fire take the barn? The edges of the fields had plowed borders of about 60 feet for emergency fire breaks, which was a standard precaution. But that was under normal conditions! Would these thin strips of bare soil serve to stop this fire? Winds were probably already gusting up to 50 miles per hour.

The fire quickly reached the truck and trailer, burning around it and beginning to ignite the tires. I ran towards the entry road, unsure of what to do. I needed to get Stefanie away from Stoney Brook. Or. Should I try and move the trailer somehow? The possible courses of action blurred in my mind as I ran back towards the manor, now with the wind at my back and threatening to topple me over as I struggled to keep up with my own legs. Falling several times onto the gravel road, the skin on the palms of my hands became raw.

What if I took Stefany and tried to run away towards the other side of the manor? Would that even be far enough away from an exploding tank of gas? Would we even make it far enough away in time?

Another possibility crossed my mind as I approached the equipment shed. What if I took one of the large tractors and pulled the truck and tank out of the burning field? Perhaps I could put the fire out?

There was no time - I decided on the tractor option. I forced my way into the door of the equipment shed and quickly grabbed one of the large yellow tow straps hanging on the sidewall. Carrying the strap over my shoulder, I ran towards the nearest large tractor, a front-end loader, parked near one of the overhead doors. Throwing the strap to the floor of the cab, I jumped in, slammed the door shut and was ecstatic to see the keys were in the ignition. Shoving the clutch in, I turned the motor over and it started immediately. Putting it in high gear, I didn't wait to open the overhead door. I floored the accelerator and drove the loader bucket and tractor straight through and over the door, flicking on the road lights as I went. The mangled pieces of the overhead door were immediately caught up in the wind and swept away towards the north side of the manor.

As I approached the smashed cane entry point, the whole field was fully engulfed in fire. It was easy to see the tank truck was equally in flames. Still uncertain as to my course of action, I pulled off the road and drove into the field, the flames licking at the tires as I drove. Reaching the tanker, I wondered if this would be my end; in an immense explosion, where a medical team would later scour the burnt field for tiny parts of me that could be thrown in a box for a hasty funeral.

It was no matter now. I was committed. And if I were to have even a small chance at surviving the evening, every second counted. I parked at the back end of the tank just as large drops of rain began slamming into the cab of the tractor. Maybe this was a good thing, and just in time. I grabbed the tow strap and jumped down and made my way to the back of the tank trailer. The cane around the tanker may have nearly burned out, but the tires of the trailer were hot sheets of flame, extending at least 10 feet, sideways in the wind. A tire gave way and exploded, signaling what was to come soon if I didn't get moving.

Stomping the flames that were licking at my legs, I lashed the tow strap several times over the rear bumper of the trailer and then around the large bucket of the loader. The bottoms of my pants were burned nearly to my knees, and the resulting embers painfully singed my exposed skin from the tops of my socks up. Jumping back in the cab, I wasted no time and threw the tractor into reverse, gently engaging the accelerator to see if it could pull the rig.

Thankfully, the tractor began inching backwards. Barely able to see where I was going, I craned my neck to look out the back window of the cab. Increasing my speed, I realized I was towing the largest bomb that the island would ever see. *If* it went off.

Reaching the entry road and still in reverse, I pulled the rig away from Stoney Brook as fast as I could without losing control. The tires of the tank truck remained in flames, as did the cab of the truck and various lower parts of the trailer. How it hadn't blown up yet, I didn't know. Another trailer tire exploded, nearly giving me a heart attack. Another followed in quick succession. The only redeeming factor currently was the ever-increasing rain, which by now was coming down and blowing in horizontal sheets, smacking against the cab of the tractor in a loud popping rumble.

Now on the road near the farthest corner of the field, I continued pulling the tanker, not sure of my next course of action. Would the rain put out the remaining fire? What would I do now?

Pulling the tanker to the side of the road, the tractor tires nearly went off into a deep drainage ditch. I narrowly avoided driving off the edge only by inches after throwing on the brakes. The weight and load of the tanker had helped me stop.

I had forgotten about the ditch. What if I push the trailer into the ditch? Was it deep enough to retain most of the blast if the tank exploded?

Jumping out of the cab, I ran to the loader bucket to unhook the tow strap, throwing it out of the way. Getting back into the cab, I threw the tractor into gear and quickly drove to the side of the trailer. Positioning the bucket beneath the flaming tires of the trailer, I pushed it towards the edge of the ditch, repeating this maneuver until the whole rig was positioned. With a slight nudge of the bucket, the whole rig rolled over, ending up in the ditch upside down. Another tire blew up. I wasted no time in aiming my tractor back towards Stoney Brook in the highest gear, the rain and wind sweeping right along with me.

I was halfway back to the manor when the tanker exploded. The light from the blast reached me before the impact, completely illuminating everything around me for as far as I could see. A sledgehammer of a shockwave struck the tractor, blasting out the rear window. Covered in tiny shards of broken glass, disoriented and stunned, my ears were ringing as I vaguely became aware of flames engulfing everything, including me.

Then, just as quickly as it happened, it was over. I kicked open the mangled cab door and clambered over the wreckage of the tractor, which had been blasted onto its side. Dropping onto the road, I immediately fell to my knees, finding that my legs would not hold me. I sat like this, unaware of time, the rain and wind flowing over my singed and battered body. Finally regaining my senses, I struggled to my feet and managed to stand, patting my body to see what I might be missing. I was amazed I had survived – and with no missing or severely injured limbs. My whole body was singed and smoking, but the tractor cab and my clothes seemed to have protected me from the flying glass and flames for the most part. My scalp felt thoroughly singed and I was likely bald at this point.

The one thought on my mind was Stefany and getting to her as quickly as I could. Staggering back towards the manor, pieces of my tattered clothes were streaming away from me like pennants. The barn had not been toppled, but it had endured severe damage. The large sliding doors were off, as were numerous pieces of siding and the roof.

But what of Stoney Brook? Had it survived? Was Stefany alive? Or was she hurt? As I drew nearer, through the periodic flashes of lightning, I could see the manor had not come through unscathed. The damage was severe - not even the emergency lights were on. As I approached closer, I was disheartened to see the front portico collapsed against the manor, the ancient columns smashed inwards. This wreckage was now blocking the very window I had opened for Stefany to watch the storm. Most of the covers for the windows on the east side had been blown away, the windows completely gone. Tree branches were down everywhere, now with some trees no more than large sticks. Large sections of the roof tiles were missing. Stoney Brook was now a shell... dark, foreboding - broken. I felt a tear mix with the rain and soot on my face.

"Stefany!"

Even in my beaten state, I noticed the lone figure emerge from the north forest, briefly illuminated by lightning. I was not that close, yet I knew it was a man. He crept along against the wind, much as I was doing. He entered into the kitchen, through a hole where twin doors once hung, disappearing into the dark, black interior of Stoney Brook.

Stefany: The hurricane is soon to arrive, and I have no small degree of anxiety. After nearly getting killed by a taxi crash and shooting in Paris, I feel like I'm lately just moving from one catastrophe to the next. I've not been through one of the big storms here. But that's about to change. Most of the island's inhabitants have been busily preparing to hole up in some of the few safe areas like schools or government buildings in the village. Most of the boats have been pulled from the docks and are secured to the best degree possible.

Stoney Brook has been here for centuries and somehow survived big storms. But will it this  time? It has become so much a part of me, I don't think I could make it if it were destroyed. What would I do? Rebuild? How can one rebuild such history? Have I come all this way, only to have Stoney Brook destroyed in some huge storm? It is said that wind gusts may approach 130 miles per hour! How can anything withstand that? All I can do is hope it doesn't get that bad.

~~~~~

All the guests are gone, for over a week now. As soon as the possibility of the storm became more real, I discontinued bookings. That's probably a good thing because now, the island is squarely in the path of the storm. Leanne is long gone as well, quite disappointed in me, I might add, that I didn't go with her as she insisted. My place is here.

I dismissed all the staff as well, so they have time to go make safe preparations with their families. Miles is headed to the Mill Property with a senior manager. I'm not as concerned for that part of the island because the mountains are much more of a shield against the winds.

I won't leave Stoney Brook, despite Miles threatening to pick me up and haul me to the village courthouse. That was quite the argument - more stress exactly when I don't need it. His concern is quite insincere.

Whatever happens, I'll be here to see it through with Mobley. He refuses to leave - even when I threatened with firing him. He ignored me and has vowed to stay. How can he do any more for me than he has already done?

Writing this now, before the storm gets here, I say this in all sincerity - as much as I adore and enjoy him, Mobley deserves better than me.

Mobley tried to be comforting before he left. Why a large truck would be parking in the east sugar cane field was beyond me. It was odd and alarming at the same time. Did the driver need help? I was fearful for Mobley out in the wind with debris blowing about.

The winds became so strong, I wondered how they could get worse. Yet, they kept growing in fearsome intensity. Things did indeed get worse. A faint glow began to erupt on the far side of the same sugar cane field that the truck – and Mobley – were in. It was my worst nightmare in these winds - a fire. Somehow, a fire started in the field across a broad front of the east side, and now was blasting towards the strange truck, and Stoney Brook.

Recalling the public service announcement that all phone service would be interrupted as the storm gained strength, I nevertheless resolved to try and call the fire station in the village. And perhaps they wouldn't even be able to come out! But I had to try and at least let someone know we had a runaway fire on our hands at Stoney Brook.

Racing to the front desk, I pulled the landline phone out and was encouraged to hear a dial tone. I began frantically calling the emergency number.

"Island Station Number 1. Please state the nature of your emergency," said the voice on the other end of the line.

"This is Stephanie Michaels out at Stoney Brook."

"Yes, Ms. Michaels. What's going on?"

"We have a cane field fire! I don't know how it started, but it's out of control and heading quickly towards us here!"

"Ms. Michaels, we are in the beginning stages of a hurricane. Wind gusts are already approaching 70 miles per hour. All of our trucks have been grounded and secured in all of the stations until the winds and dangerous conditions subside."

"But there's nothing you can do? I'm helpless here! My estate manager is out in the storm trying to help a truck driver. I'm afraid he is getting caught in the fire!"

"Look, Ms. Michaels. Tell those people to get back into cover as soon as possible. I'm sorry, but there's nothing we can do right now. It may be twelve hours or more before there's a lull in the storm. If you think Stoney Brook is in danger of burning, get out and find alternative shelter elsewhere quickly. Keep me informed if you can. All wireless communications are down, and landlines will likely follow soon. Get to safety, okay?"

"Okay," I meekly answered, feeling sick to my stomach. I tentatively hung up the phone, feeling totally helpless and in fear of Mobley's life.

Returning to the window, I could see the fire had gained strength and was quickly consuming the sugar cane field, blasting through horizontally in big chunks at a time. It would soon be entirely on fire and the truck that had parked in the middle of it was already facing the flames.

Suddenly, through the gloom of the blowing dust, I could see one of our field tractors racing towards the flames. It must have been Mobley, taking a tractor and hoping to do… what? As the tractor lights faded in the distance, I could see he was headed through the fire towards the truck. After several minutes, I was relieved to see the tractor pulling it out of the field amid the flames. Squinting to see through the smoke and debris, I could now see that the truck was a liquid cargo tanker. Whatever it was intended to carry, it was all a raging inferno as Mobley towed it back up to the entry road. What did he hope to gain by dragging it out of the field? At this point, he should have just let it burn up, I thought. Why would he take the time to pull out an already lost cause? My emotions coursed between helpless frustration and worry for Mobley getting out of this in one piece.

The flames were now blowing furiously towards several of the field storage sheds, sending them up into flames. Balls of burning debris scattered along the roadway, even making it to the courtyard and blowing onto the porch. Fortunately, the rain had also started, and these dangerous harbingers of flame were being extinguished as quickly as they appeared. The fire in the cane field decreased in intensity, but I could no longer see Mobley nor the tractor or truck.

I ran back to the front desk to again call the fires station. My fingers fumbled for the emergency number.

"Island Station Number 1. Ms. Michaels? Is that you?"

"Yes! The fire has died down a bit. It looked like it was going to blow the flames right into the estate manor, but the rains have come now."

"That's what we've noticed as well. So your situation has improved, yes?"

"Definitely! We may yet get out of this in one piece."

"Don't let your guard down. Watch the situation, be vigilant and remain safe. Okay, Ms. Michaels?"

Just as I began to reply, the entire lobby flashed white light, followed by a violent impact that lifted me into the air, throwing me across the lobby and against a sofa. All the lights went dark, and I could feel thousands of shards of glass spray painfully across my back. Pieces of wood and window frames smashed into the walls above my head. As I struggled to remain conscious, I was vaguely aware all the windows and the front doors had been blown completely open. The front desk I had just been at was in pieces around me, along with many of the other furnishings that were towards the front of the lobby. Everything was now unrecognizable dark heaps of debris. The wind crashed through Stoney Brook, so strong that it was driving the rain nearly sideways through the lobby. What had happened? I knew this was something catastrophic beyond the hurricane.

A jagged shard of splintered wood of about 7 inches in length, protruded from my left arm. Self-aware that I was still in shock, I pulled the fragment out, thinking it was much like an arrow. The driving wind continued to blast me, shooting me with glass and sharp splinters of wood. I wiped tiny pieces of tempered glass from the corners of my eyes. The rain stinging my face gradually brought me to my senses.

Lightning flashed and from the empty hole in the wall that was once a window, I could see a large chunk of something that looked like autobody steel flying in midair. I heard it crash into the building on an upper floor. I peered out into the blackness and could tell the front columns of the porch had given way. The whole porch had collapsed and now partially buried the front doors and several windows.

Whatever had happened, I was alive at least. But Stoney Brook had been smashed into pieces. I finally made it to my feet. Had Mobley survived? Meandering down the main hallway, my heart was broken to see most of the doors completely blown off their hinges, laying at odd angles in the hall, rain driving into the building.

Making it to the kitchen, it was in no better shape. The windows and doors were similarly blown inwards, and debris was everywhere. What looked like a nearly intact palm tree had been rammed clear through the kitchen, the roots dangling over the service counter. Walking towards the gaping opening in the wall where the twin doors should have been, I braced myself against the full force of the driving rain and wind, determined to find Mobley. Or what was left of him.

Running out into the wind, I struggled to head towards the cane field, which by now only had small pockets of glowing embers remaining. The heavy rain was making short work of any remaining flames from the fire, which was just about the only good news of the evening.

I was astounded by the debris. Ducking, a piece of tin shot past my head from the dark.

"Mobley!"

Nearly at the same time as I yelled for his name, he was there, fifteen feet in front of me, yelling my name.

"Stefany!"

I ran into his open arms, and he pulled me tight. He looked awful. Half of his shirt was torn away, and his exposed chest looked scorched and blackened. His hair was a wild mess and much of it looked to have been burnt away. There was no use trying to talk in the roar of the wind, not to mention all the dangerous debris flying about. I pulled him by the hand back into the shattered kitchen and moved to try and take shelter against a wall.

"Oh my god, Mobley! You are hurt!"

"I'm okay. I think. The question is, are you okay?"

"Yes. But what the hell happened?"

"It was a propane gas tanker truck. Full of fuel. And someone intentionally lit the field on fire to blow it up. And us." He took me by my arms to emphasize his point. "I saw him. He's in here with us."

My mouth dropped, wondering how much worse the evening could get.

"And now, I'm finally going to finish this," a gruff male voice announced through the wind. A loud popping noise rang out and Mobley slumped against the wall holding his arm. Turning towards the sound of what had to be a gunshot, a clattering piece of debris slammed into the window next to the assailant, providing a lucky but temporary distraction.

Mobley had been shot in the arm. There was no time to examine the wound in any detail. I pulled him through to the back of the kitchen and along the hallway. Another shot rang out, and this time the bullet hit the wall just to the side of my head.

Taking the basement stairs, I pulled Mobley down into the pitch-black depths with me, hoping we could evade or hide from the shooter trying to kill us. This again? Why was this person trying to kill us? Why did he try to destroy Stoney Brook? Amidst the fear, I felt pangs of anger growing. This was getting old, being targeted. And now? Mobley was gravely injured, and Stoney Brook was a broken disaster. I grit my teeth, resolved to bring both of us out of the evening alive. With these emotions, there was something else I wanted - vengeance.

Had the assailant seen us go down the basement stairs? Feeling our way along the corridor, we passed the wine storage rooms. I considered hiding in one of these, but there was no cover. If we were discovered, we would be sitting ducks. We went further, finally ending up in the museum section. I crouched with Mobley behind a display case, trying to see if anyone was pursuing us back in the corridor. I couldn't even see my own hand in front of my face. But at least we were out of the ferocious wind.

"Mobley," I whispered. "Are you badly injured?" He didn't answer but I could hear his breathing. It sounded increasingly labored and wheezing. It was nearly sending me into a panic.

"Mobley!"

"I… I think I am shot through the right arm," he finally answered.

Reaching for his arm, my fingers softly tried to discern his injury. What was left of his shirt was warm and wet. He was bleeding. I could feel the wound, which seemed to have gone all the way through his arm. I carefully felt for the tatters of his shirt and pulled the remaining piece off. I tied this around the wound as a tourniquet to stop the bleeding. Mobley winced.

"I'm sorry, Mobley. I've got to stop the bleeding and it has to be tight. We'll get it fixed up later."

At that moment, a flashlight beam arced down the corridor. The attacker was approaching, evidently having guessed we had gone in the basement. Now what would I do, I asked myself, trying to remain calm.

Mobley moaned again, but softly. "Whoever it is, they are coming. I'll go. You stay here and keep hidden," he tried to say with authority. "I'll handle this."

"No," I told him firmly. "You are weak as a lamb now and will just get shot. Then we'll both be toast. Just stay still. Be quiet."

He reluctantly complied as he had no choice at this point. We watched the flashlight work its way through all the wine storage rooms, one by one. Continually moving forward toward us, it finally stopped at the entrance of the museum room. The light swept the room, once. Twice. Then again. This time it paused on our display we were hidden behind. We were discovered. Somehow.

A shot rang out and the display case glass shattered all over us. Another shot slammed into the wooden casework. Then suddenly, the shooter was over us. His pistol was aimed squarely at my head. I knew this would be the end.

Mobley suddenly sprang up, despite his injuries, wrapping both his arms around the waist of the attacker and driving him towards the back wall of the museum. The flashlight fell to the floor, and I struggled to my feet to try and help Mobley.

As I tried to steady myself, my hand ended up in the broken glass of the display case. Warm with blood from the glass cuts I just gave myself, my fingers closed on a cold piece of flat steel. It was the ancient McCaskill Claymore sword. That was something I could use, I determined quickly to myself. It was the only thing I had; it would have to do.

Holding the sword in front of me, I ran towards the sound of Mobley wrestling with the assailant. In the dark, illuminated only by the flashlight that was on the floor, I misjudged the floor and stepped into the stairwell that led down to the subterranean cave. Instinctively, I screamed as I painfully tumbled down the stairs, the Claymore sword clattering loudly along with me. I landed with a thud on my back against the moist, cool floor of the cave, wondering how many bones I had just broken. The sword lay flat across my chest. Wrapping my bloody fingers around the pommel, I wondered how many had died at the hands of my ancestors with this very sword. And now, it was completely useless against a semi-automatic pistol - not that I would know how to use it anyway. Without knowing why, I laughed softly to myself and held the sword up, the madness of it all now seeming comical to me. Perhaps it was fitting.

The assailant had recovered the flashlight, and I could see him savagely smash it across Mobley's face. Mobley fell onto the floor near the top of the stairs, limp.

The flashlight beam fell on me now at the bottom of the cave steps. It was all over, I figured. I had given it my all. I had enjoyed extraordinary luck these past few months and become a successful, independent businesswoman. Stoney Brook had made a splendid return. I had Mobley, who was my best friend - and fun sexual plaything… the only man in my life I ever cared about. It was all slipping through my fingers now. It just wasn't meant to be.

The face of the assailant was clear now from the top of the steps, in the reflected glow of the flashlight.

"Constable Fillmore?! But. Why?" I asked him, incredulous, hoping for some final explanation for this betrayal.

"A cop's retirement pension isn't shit, as you can imagine. I spent years being the good guy back in the states. And got no appreciation."

"But you make money here. You're the head of the police force!"

"What, that? I can't even afford the rent on my house. This is nothing personal. It's just business."

"Business? For whom?"

"Whoever pays me the most to get rid of you. And your meddlesome estate manager here."

"Is he dead," I asked, tearfully, now openly crying.

"If he's not, he will be, just as soon as I finish with my priority - you."

"You were the one, this whole time that was trying to kill us."

"Well. Not just me. I tried to subcontract. That didn't work. This storm was a great opportunity. But even with it, this idiot here managed to mess that up by moving the gas truck too far away. Any closer when it had gone up and it would have brought this place down around your ears. I'll have to cook the scene a bit. I had hoped the tanker would take care of you two, but this job is something I'll have to do face-to-face, it seems."

"Can't we work something out? I'll pay you more!"

He evidently decided there would be no profit in any further negotiations with a dead woman. He began to take the first step on the top of the stairs towards me, the gun steadying at the end of his arm, pointing right at my face. This was going to be concluded up close and he was going to be sure of his kill this time. Of all things at this time to enter my mind, I thought about the Voodoo protection talisman up on my office desk that Marisha Neita had given me. What would be her explanation for this evening's events that was going to end with my death? My death, in the very cave where Seumas McCaskill left five of his old pirate shipmates to rot? What was I being protected against? Living? Sweet as the sentiment was, I would have loved to have heard her discuss that. Perhaps I could appear to her as a ghost and ask.

It all happened in a split second, yet I watched it unfold in incredibly slow motion. Mobley, not quite so out of it as he had seemed, surprised Fillmore by suddenly grabbing his back leg and thrusting him forward. I should have known; battered as he was - never count Mobley out.

Fillmore lost his balance… his tumbling body heading straight for me. I held my hands up defensively, knowing he would land right on top of me. On his way down, the gun fell from his grip. I distinctly heard his skull smack flatly on a step. The flashlight was next, the lens breaking and going dark. It was a long series of steps, as I knew all too well. Fillmore groaned and grunted all the way down, taking a hard beating with his descent on the unforgiving stone.

In the blinding darkness of the entrance to the subterranean cave, Fillmore's body landed heavily on top of mine, his chest against mine, causing the air to heave from my lungs. I felt his hot breath exhale long and deeply against my neck as the storm outside whistled and raged on, audible even from down here. I waited for the coming struggle of which I could only offer feeble resistance.

He remained motionless. His breathing stopped. A warm liquid ran over my hand and saturated my shirt over my stomach. Awareness slowly dawned. I then realized I had still been holding the Claymore.

CHAPTER 20

AMID THE RUINS

Stefany: Well, this feels different; writing in my diary in what's left of my office. The hurricane was bad enough. But we also had to endure the tanker truck blowing up, which seems to have caused the most damage. The rest of the island suffered, there is no doubt about that. But the damage to Stoney Brook was severe in comparison to other large structures.

There are no windows, we have standing water in many of the rooms, and all the furniture is strewn about, much of it ruined. Some of the men hauled out the area rugs to try and dry the place with

fans and water vacuums. It's going to be a struggle to stop the mold. We are still hauling debris, leaves, and branches out of the building and cleaning up. The pool gazebos were leveled to the ground. Two storage buildings were burned, and half the roof and the doors are off the big barn. All the pieces of the front portico have been removed except for the columns and the main support beams, which we can hopefully restore into their original location. The historic front doors are sitting on stands awaiting repairs and re-hanging. Such is the dire picture I have as I write this. Stoney Brook is a smashed ruin.

The jungles have been shredded about the island. All the trees were damaged, some completely uprooted, most without any leaves. I was sad to see that a tropical tulip tree that I had planted in the front courtyard was broken off. Very little of anything is left without damage. Oddly, the historic slave quarters escaped nearly any damage, and they seem to stand in silent defiance.

The Mill Property had relatively minor damage. Several of the bungalows will need some repair work. The boat dock is gone, as is the Woods Hole science ship, that I'm told is now about a mile offshore and barely afloat. Another large ship that was at the dock was severely damaged because the hull was smashed upon several broken support pylons.

The coconut groves didn't fare too badly, surprisingly. Many of the trees were entirely stripped of their fronds but I am told they should grow back. The estimate is, 25% of the trees are badly damaged, about 5% severely and will require replanting. About 65% of the current crop was ruined. All in all, it could have been worse I suppose. The ridges that surround the groves protected them.

I do have insurance on everything and am still in the process of seeing what they will cover. They are haggling, of course, over what damage was incurred at Stoney Brook due to the tanker truck explosion versus the storm. Does it matter??? They are saying they do not cover acts of terrorism. They are slimy, greedy shit-fucks but I must be nice to them, Leanne keeps reminding me.

The village suffered minor damage, which is surprising, considering the size of the storm we endured. The Blue Calypso lost its roof but can probably be repaired. There were a lot of boats that were damaged or sunk though. The docks will need a lot of work. Marisha tells me her Island Historical Society building made it through the storm okay, and I was very happy to hear that.

Speaking of Marisha, her Voodoo talisman survived the destruction in my office. It sits right next to my diary as I write this. Honestly, I'm no believer in such things. Yet, I am alive now. At the very least, I have Marisha to thank for her nice, sweet sentiment of "sending me good vibes." These past few days, I'm walking in a hazy dream, it seems. So much has happened since my last entry and it's only just recently becoming clear. Much of it seems dreamlike.

Can I bring Stoney Brook back to life after all this? I don't know. Can I even fix ~me~? I have nightmares about Fillmore. Him

A VERY BAD MAN

shooting Mobley then going after me. Him falling down the steps. Him landing on me. It's all coming back to me in horrific detail. The feeling of the sword pommel vibrating through my hands... The squishy sound of the blade pushing through vital organs... The slight feeling of resistance as the Claymore split ribs and burst through Fillmore's spinal column. The fluids, the blood, his saliva, his bowels releasing... all leaking down on me while I was pinned beneath him at the bottom of the cave stairs. His ghastly eyes, open wide with shock, as revealed when I could finally crawl out from beneath him and get an emergency light to help Mobley. I've thrown up numerous times when I can't quit thinking about it. The whole incident has ended up in the global press. I now have the unwanted distinction of being one of the few women in history to have skewered a man all the way to the hilt with a Claymore sword. And I must say, it is quite disturbing to me. Even if it was an accident. The irony of the whole thing is not lost to me.

People try to assuage my guilt, saying Fillmore would have killed me - and

Mobley. It was self-defense they say. Yes, it was an accident, although no one wants to hear that. I had no idea what I was doing and had just been holding the sword out. Fillmore just happened to fall on it. Instead, people want to believe the narrative of the heroic and courageous McCaskill woman, fending off a vile aggressor using her ancestor's sword. Refuting it does no good. It has somehow made me even more of a celebrity.

The storm subsided, and of course, as soon as the roads were cleared, everyone converged on Stoney Brook. The whole island had felt the tanker truck explosion, even while enduring a hurricane. Even though Mobley pushed the tanker and the truck into the east field drainage ditch, the explosion gouged out a crater fifteen feet deep and 70 feet wide. Some of the investigators sent in from the main island said the truck being in the ditch absorbed much of the force. Stoney Brook would have probably been destroyed if the truck had been closer on flat ground.

The story of Constable Fillmore and his whole campaign of trying to kill Mobley and me is still just coming out. The frightening part of it all is, it's not over.

When it was discovered that Fillmore had attacked us and he was lying dead at the bottom of the steps of the cave, a whole series of events began to fall into place. The second in command of the Island Police Force had to take over. And since he was little more than a high school graduate with no investigator experience, other agencies were invited in, given the severe nature of what had happened.

Then the press got wind of it all. Then it all went viral. Then Interpol and others got involved. It's believed that this has an international crime syndicate connection, but they won't tell me anything more. They are still here, by the dozens. Even now, I am watching them mill about from the gap in the wall of my office that was once the main window. Other than a few of my workers' cars, the only vehicles at Stoney Brook are rentals, leased by visiting law enforcement.

A look into Fillmore's situation and history revealed that he had been paid one-hundred-fifty thousand U.S. dollars. Cash. This payment, it is believed, was for orchestrating killing me... or perhaps running me off. And by proxy, it also meant killing the man who ultimately helped me save Stoney Brook and make it successful - Mobley. I guess in terms of being an investment for some big-time crime syndicate, Stoney Brook was small potatoes. But it would be useful for a variety of things, I suppose. Tax shelters, havens for criminals, a distribution center out of the reach of international law perhaps. The possibilities are endless.

Fillmore, embittered over his meager retirement benefits after a lifetime of service, sold his soul to someone evil to make some real money. Someone hired him, paying him what was probably a down payment to murder me. He then "subcontracted" the job to some hapless petty criminal to keep himself looking clean as the island constable, hiring that guy to try and kill us at the Mill Property. Fillmore, it is believed, later killed the wanna-be hitman due to a blackmail threat, as evidenced by several notes found in Fillmore's desk at his office. Evidently, Fillmore didn't appreciate the effort.

Fillmore hired the two men to kidnap me and try to kill me out at sea. Fillmore was probably the man that took a shot at Mobley at the convenience station, the investigators are still trying to figure that one out. Fillmore is obviously suspected for hiring the hitman in Paris. It was Fillmore that stole a liquified petroleum tanker from the terminal at the village, then intended to blow up Stoney Brook with it and kill both Mobley and me in one easy move. Investigators found a car parked a mile away from Stoney Brook that they thought he was going to use to leave the scene after everything blew up.

But... who had hired Fillmore? And did he even know who was paying him?

So far, the money is trackless, the investigators tell me. Oh, there are suspects. The Russian businessmen that I met with before at The Blue Calypso. No one seems to know who they were. One investigator said it could possibly be competing corporations that have interests in Coconut products. Or perhaps relatives of mine that want me to fail. Or maybe my estranged asshole husband Miles. But there is nothing concrete. Even the motive is unclear. And with Fillmore dead, much of the unanswered questions died with him. So whoever wants me dead is still out there. And no one seems to know how to figure out who it is.

Poor Mobley. He is still in the hospital on St. Thomas. Leanne is staying with him, and I'm glad about that.

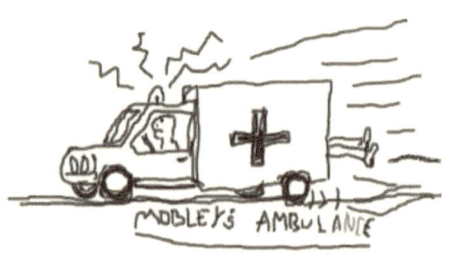

MOBLEY'S AMBULANCE

He's getting a lot of tests done and is under observation. The doctors are concerned for him, and how the blast may have damaged his internal organs. That and the burns, the cuts, his fractured jaw where Fillmore hit him with the flashlight. And being shot in the arm. What more can I say about Mobley. He again saved my life.

I think about him all the time. I think about his cute little mannerisms that used to irritate me... that I now adore. And of course, I think about the raw sexuality that I share with him.

Mobley has again ended up injured on my account. But I'm reminded every

day when I walk through the wreckage, whoever is responsible for hiring Fillmore and wanting Mobley and me dead is still out there. I'm still in danger. And so is Mobley.

I angrily crumpled up the letter confirming to me the Island Police will not be "charging" me in Fillmore's death. "That is very noble of them, indeed," I hissed under my breath, tossing the letter into the wastepaper basket with a spectacular across the room shot.

Several newly hired workers came in with plastic sheeting and staple guns, so they could secure the windows against future wind and rain. That was until the window replacements came in. In the next few rooms, I could hear another worker wet-vacuuming up the floor in my personal quarters. Fighting the mold was going to be a nightmare, I knew. Everything needed to get dry, then cleaned and fumigated. I wasn't even looking at replacement fixtures and furniture yet. Most of the furnishings that were damaged beyond repair were in a big pile in the middle of the courtyard along with all the broken glass, splintered wood and other debris awaiting disposal.

I opened one of my desk drawers to retrieve a pen to make a note to my lawyers, only to find a cute tree frog.

"Hey little fella," I cooed to it, grabbing it, and then letting it go out on the windowsill. I coaxed it along with a finger, sending it away from the soon to be plastic window covering that was moments from installation.

The lawyers I now have representing Stoney Brook are decidedly aggressive against some of the assertions by my insurance company. Much of the disagreement comes over the question of what caused the most damage at Stoney

Brook, the hurricane, or the tanker truck explosion? The insurance company is claiming it was mostly from the tanker truck in an act of terrorism, in which case, they will pay much less. My lawyers are arguing that it is irrelevant, the tanker truck explosion was a criminal act, not terrorism. I may not get a dime, who knows. If that's the case, it's the end of Stoney Brook.

"Hello, Ms. Michaels?" It was Lydia, from the front desk, peeking her head through the office doors.

"Yes, come in," I told her. The staff was walking on eggshells around me, acting like I was in a fragile emotional state or something. I was fine! But their codling of me was getting irritating.

Lydia approached my desk. "This is the mail for today, Ms. Michaels."

"Ah, thank you, Lydia," I replied, taking the mail then dismissing her.

I flipped through several notes, pieces of junk mail, then a couple of letters. The first letter was from my insurance company, no doubt confirming the damage list I sent them.

The next letter caught my eye, as it was addressed directly to me in a neat, printed type. The return address, I noted, was Stoney Brook, which was odd. I slipped a finger beneath the flap and opened it up. The letter, like the envelope, was neatly printed.

August 23
Hello Ms. Stefany Michaels,
You do not know who I am. You will never know who I am. But I know who you are. You are no doubt wondering why Fillmore did what he did and who put him up to it. That would be me. I am surprised that you are still alive. You are quite resilient.

I will leave it to you to guess why I did what I did. Again, you will never know

my motive. But I can tell you this. My purpose is simple. To get you to leave Stoney Brook and the island. I will not quit. You will hear from me again and I will kill you to accomplish my goals if necessary. And that goes for the meddler also, that guy you hired from the mainland U.S., Morgan Mobley. You are both on my "list."

No, the cops will not find out who I am. They have the whole world to look for me, and they won't even know where to start. There is no way they can. Even Fillmore didn't know who I was. I am very careful you see. They will find no traces of me with Fillmore. Or any of the others he hired to do his dirty work.

This letter will contain nothing of real use, forensically. But it doesn't stop me from having fun. It contains no trace of me. Nothing. No DNA, no fingerprints. When I do leave clues, they are intended to mislead. Oh sure, you'll find some things but none of it can be traced to me. Perhaps I'll leave a few grains of pollen from Madagascar. Or sand grains from the Mediterranean. Or a fingerprint from a merchant in China. Maybe I acquire the paper from a hotel in London. Use a pen from a hardware store in Indianapolis, Indiana. I love to play games. Give this to the cops if you want. It makes no difference to me.

You will never know when you will next hear from me. I do want you to know, if you continue to hang around, you are dying when the time comes. If you want to save yourself, leave.

Morgan: This entry is made on some scrap paper with a pen one of my nurses gave me. Being in the habit of writing in my journal and without it here, my thoughts can only roam about in my mind, it seems. I don't feel like writing much. My body is so sore, I can barely move. And it's been days.

~~~~~

Leanne has visited on numerous occasions. I am truly grateful for her friendship.

Stefany has not come to see me. She refuses my calls, or if she answers she makes excuses and must get off quickly. With texts, she is only brief. I don't know what's happened between us. I recall Leanne advising me that nothing lasts forever – all things must end. With this terrible sense of foreboding, I have a feeling the end is indeed close. I know I still love her. That will never change.

"It be a good Morning, Mr. Mobley," the nurse said in a cheery, thick Jamaican accent as she brought in a tray of breakfast. "How you feel today?"

"Good morning," I replied, looking over the offering on the tray. It wasn't too bad. Eggs, bacon, toast, milk, juice, coffee. My internal organs had healed enough I could handle that. "I feel fine," I lied. "Can I go?"

She laughed. "No. I'm afraid not. The doctors, they want ta keep you more I tink." The nurse set a small paper sack on my nightstand.

"What's that?" I asked.

"Dos are dee items that were wit you when you were life-flighted here. We safeguard your personal items since you can't be wearin' anytin' after being admitted." She set about checking the monitors and equipment in my room.

"Thanks," I said, taking the paper sack. I couldn't remember wearing anything except for my watch.

Taking a bit of toast and slug of coffee, I then dumped the contents of the bag out on the tray.

Amongst the items were my watch and wallet. There was also a pad of paper and a pen. The other item was strange to me yet looked vaguely familiar. It was a silver talisman on a chain. Holding it to my face, I examined it closely. The medallion was roughly cross shaped with two holes that looked like eyes at the top with a few small X's below, giving the overall look of an abstract skeleton figure. There were lines below on the bottom part of the figure that looked like they represented rope.

"Nurse? I'm fairly certain that this item is not mine." I held it out for her.

She picked it up, examining it. "Oh, yes sir, it be yours, all right. I was aworkin' dat night dey brought you in. I was dee one took dese tings for you. Dis was around your neck, Mr. Mobley. Yes, it be yours." She handed it back. "Very nice. Handcrafted, silver."

Again, I inspected the piece. Suddenly, it dawned on me. It was the talisman I had spotted laying on the ground at the convenience store when someone had shot at me. Seeing it, I had bent down, just missing the bullet that would have hit me in the head. Seeing only the rough shape, I had mistaken it for a cross, thinking it was a simple Christian religious medallion. In all the confusion, I never picked it up or saw it again. And now, this nurse was saying it was around my neck when I was brought into the hospital!

I rubbed the back, trying to make out a series of nearly illegible marks. There was a word; "Bowkee." If memory served, there was a cave artifact listed on the museum inventory as being associated with the word. Which artifact, I couldn't recall. I also seem to remember Stefany mentioning "Bowkee."

"Nurse? Do you know what this is?" I asked her, again letting her take it for a look.

"What, you no know what you own for yourself?" She laughed. "These mainland peoples like you, Mr. Mobley. You make me laugh."

"Why? What is it?" I asked again.

She let it spin in the air, examining it for different tool marks. "If you've a good heart, dis keep you safe. Dis is of Voodoo, Mr. Mobley. Bhoki, dee island slave witch. Very old magic."

CHAPTER 21
A BROKEN PROMISE CAN SHIELD A BROKEN HEART

Stefany: I gave the threatening letter to the investigators – as well as the next three that came in. They were all similarly worded, telling me to flat out just leave and abandon everything to save my life. Well, I've been through too much and come too far to give up now. I am not going anywhere.

Some of the cops are saying that the letter, although written to sound like one person, could be an organization, or many people. It matters not to me.

Leanne has been uncharacteristically without an opinion lately. All she will say is I need to be careful and go where my heart tells me. She wants me to be happy. She also knows how much Stoney Brook means to me and that I am not giving up. Without telling me, Leanne hired a handful of additional security officers for Stoney Brook and the Mill Property. While being opposed to this at first, there was no talking her out of it. Ultimately, I was able to at least convince her I should be the one paying for this, not her. In retrospect, having extra security is a wise decision.

Stoney Brook is once again beginning to show signs of life. What seems like an army of construction workers are busy, and what's best is they are all on the dime of the insurance companies after a small deductible, which I had no problem paying. It all worked out in court, and I am beginning to see how important it is to have a top-notch legal team.

Even the trees are beginning to come back. Stoney Brook is cleaned out and dry now. New windows are still going in. New furniture is on order and Leanne has been shopping for select antiques. We are going to build back and be better than even before.

Today for the first time since the storm, I took a swim in the pool which is now again operable. New gazebos are up, and the gardens are nearly back in shape. A new roof is nearly complete on the big barn, and the front columns, portico and doors are again up.

With all this new energy, I have no illusions that it could all come to an end. If I stay, will someone eventually kill me? Maybe so. At least I will have had my shot in this life. I'll stand my ground and I'll not be runoff by any cowardly shit-fuck hiding in the shadows.

Mobley is still in the hospital. He's been in there quite a while now and I feel bad for being so brief with him in his texts and with his calls. It hurts to do it. He no doubt is wondering what's going on. He's been in my thoughts every minute of every day, but I can't tell him that.

Today, I'll fly to St. Thomas with Leanne to see Mobley. I know what I must do and it's not going to be easy. Sometimes, a broken promise can shield a broken heart.

Leanne, standing with me in the Hospital lobby on St. Thomas Island, held a copy of the first threatening letter in trembling fingers.

"I'm glad you at least let me improve security," she said glumly.

"It was the right call. It's just good for business, anyway. Guests and tourists need to feel safe while staying at Stoney Brook. Security personnel will perform needed dual roles. Bartenders, gardeners, wherever they can. So, it's no big deal, really."

She peered at me over the top of the letter. "You are really going to go through with this?"

"What choice do I have? I mean, if you can figure out a different way, then tell me."

She gave a solemn nod. "If I were in your shoes, I would do the same thing. I just wish-"

"We've discussed this until we both know there's nothing left to consider." I put a hand on her shoulder. "I'm going to need your support. Now, more than ever. Please. I can't do this alone."

After a moment of hesitation, she seemed to steel herself. "I will. Of course." She accompanied me in silence up several floors to Mobley's room.

Arriving, we stood outside the closed door. "He will never agree to this unless it's an ultimatum," I declared.

"I know. That's why I suggested it," Leanne confirmed. "Just out of curiosity, when did you actually figure out I had agreed to pay him for his part in the sex slave agreement?"

"A long time ago," I admitted. "You once made an off-comment about him being well-compensated when I told you about him griping about getting cropped. I figured as much."

We both laughed for a moment, a welcome comedic relief from the dire circumstances of the prior two weeks.

"He tore the check into little pieces and gave it back to me a long time ago."

"He tore it up?" I asked, incredulous.

She forced an answer as a tear rolled down her cheek. "Yeah. I didn't tell you that part. He was insulted that I could ever think he wanted money when it came to you. Even if it was pay… in a most unusual context." Leanne paused a second while I felt my courage wane with this bit of news. "You know there is much more to this than just some business agreement for him? That's why he refused the money."

"Yes, yes," I said irritably. "You don't have to spell it out. I know he's in love with me. Saying it again doesn't make it any easier, you know."

"And you, Steph? What exactly do you feel for him? What will you be losing in all of this? I'm not asking that question to be cruel. For me, I well understand and know this is something we must do. I just want you to be prepared. Tomorrow, things will be different for you."

I shoved my face into my hands. The whole scheme was so harsh. I was pushing away the one person responsible for my very success. I was going to lose my best friend, my lover – and I was going to do it intentionally.

Leanne, seeing me waver, slipped her arm around me. "It's because you do care for him. You don't have any choice."

I could only nod silently.

"We have to assume the threats are valid now, after everything that has happened," Leanne explained. "You are both at risk. At least with you, it can be managed easier with good security measures. You know how he is. He's constantly out and about, exposed."

I again thought about the hateful words in the letter to strengthen my resolve. "I know. My own life is one thing. Me staying on to run Stoney Brook is my *own* risk. I am not going to risk Mobley's life."

I turned towards Leanne, looking for solace through bleary eyes. "He will hate me after this."

"Maybe. You can't think about that. You must be firm. He will never leave otherwise. You are doing the right thing." Leanne leaned in and kissed me on the cheek.

"Doing the right thing doesn't make this any easier. Let's just get this over with." I grasped the door handle and entered Mobley's room.

"Hello, Mobley," I said as Leanne closed the door after coming in behind me. "You are looking better!"

Mobley, hooked to an IV bag and dressed in a hospital gown, immediately brightened. He sat up with a broad grin. "Stefany!"

When I approached the bed, he took my hands, kissed them, then pulled me to him. He kissed my lips softly. I slowly withdrew. This was already getting out of hand. I sat on the edge of the bed and tried to remain strong.

"Ah, I've missed you. But I know you've been busy with Stoney Brook. I was hoping you could have visited earlier." He waved a hand towards Leanne. "Leanne would only tell me you were having difficulty with the insurance company." He pondered this for a moment, probably wondering if he should ask why. I grit my teeth, watching him try to read my expression.

"Yeah. Things are coming along. We are still cleaning up, that is going to go on a while. The repairs have started, so that's good. There are many construction workers on-site now, all hired by the insurance company. They are making good headway. It turns out attempted murder isn't necessarily an act of terrorism, as my lawyers so clearly pointed out in court."

"Well, that's great," he said.

Leanne wandered over to the window, her back to us, probably crying at this point.

"So how are you feeling, Mobley. They tell me you can leave this afternoon?"

"Yes. I am ready to leave, I'm fine. I'm ready to get back to work."

He picked up something in my expression that I was trying to hide.

"What? What's wrong?"

"Look. Mobley. I need to be straight up with you."

He blinked several times, his smile fading. "Okay. What is it?"

"I've hired another estate manager for Stoney Brook. An architect from Brussels."

After a long pause of this setting in, he finally spoke. "He... will be working with me?"

"No. I've decided he will take your place. I'm sorry, but... I'm letting you go." I felt my gut drop through the floor seeing the color drain from his face.

"But... why? I've done everything you have asked. And more. I... don't understand. After everything... we've-" He slowly withdrew his hand from mine. I wanted to cry.

"It's been time for a change, Mobley. And with our relationship... the way it's been, it's just time to stop. I'm sorry it's got to this point. The storm sort of made everything clearer. I have a business to run. You being at Stoney Brook has only given Miles ammunition to fight me in the divorce. So." It was getting harder by the moment to keep going with my lies. "I've had all your things boxed and shipped to the airport for storage until your flight."

"My flight?" He was in a state of shock now with the sudden transformation of our relationship.

"Yes. I've arranged for your transportation at the airport this afternoon. I'm handling all expenses, of course. Everything has been prepared for when you get out of here today. Your flight from here will take you to Miami, and then on to Chicago."

He leaned back heavily into his pillow, looking as if he had been shot. "There must be more to this? I can't believe you would just... let me go. We've built Stoney Brook from the ground up. Together. You and me. I've helped you. What else is it, Stefany? At least I deserve to know, don't I?"

It was time to put in the pinch hitter, I decided, noticing Leanne had not once turned around from the window.

"The payment, Mobley. I... know... um. About the money Leanne paid you to enter into the agreement with me."

"What? That?"

"Yes. The fact that you had to be paid to be with me. It changed everything. Frankly, I could never look at you again the same, knowing that. Much of it is my hang up, I know. But it is what it is." There, that was it. I had laid it on as thick as I could. I had unloaded every bullet I had into him, and I still didn't know if it would work.

"Stefany. I never wanted any money to be with you. I didn't accept that payment. Tell her, Leanne! I tore the check up!"

Refusing to turn around, Leanne stood frozen at the window. What a great help she was turning out to be.

"I understand that. I know you tore up the check. But you accepted it in the beginning as part of the bargain. At least initially, you kept it. I'm sorry, but I can't... don't... want to see you again." I stood, ready to leave my lies for the better good behind.

Mobley threw the sheets off, pulled the IV needle out of his arm and stood. Quite wobbly, he was still very weak, and he looked on the verge of collapse.

He placed his hands on both sides of my face. "No! Listen to me. I don't know what this is all about, this payment thing that never meant anything to me. You... are the only reason I went into Leanne's agreement. You. I would do anything for you then. And I would do anything for you now."

I couldn't look at him. I weakly tried to pull his hands away as I felt tears welling up in my eyes.

"I love you," he said, tearing my heart to pieces. "I've always loved you, from the moment I first saw you," he affirmed. "Don't do this."

With resolve, I pulled his hands down from my face, then I slipped an envelope out of my back pocket and sat it on the bed. "When you get back to Chicago and begin

630

making some decisions on what to do, open that envelope. It's a letter of recommendation and mentions all your work - all the things you have done to help Stoney Brook become successful. It will help you get back into school or maybe find a good job that you enjoy."

He looked at me curiously, trying to see behind my veil of pretense. "If you *truly* don't have any feelings for me... *none* whatsoever... then look me in the eyes, Stefany. Tell me to go. Say it. And I'll go."

I squared myself and stared into his blue eyes. "I... don't have any feelings for you. Sorry, but I don't. I want you to go. It's over." There was a long pause. In his expression, I watched Mobley disassemble, like a delicate vase falling from a pedestal and crashing to the floor.

He nodded, seeming to finally accept what I was telling him.

Even in the hospital, Mobley had a certain vitality that was hard to describe. He was undaunted by any setback that could befall him, it seemed. His confidence had always been his armor. But now, it was gone.

Throughout my life, I had been the one on the receiving end of a broken heart. For more times than I could count. It never occurred to me that I could ever be the cause of it to someone else.

I could only imagine the emotions crashing about in his head. He mostly looked confused, and I desperately wanted to take him in my arms. He wasn't angry, which was a surprise to me, given that it seemed to me that we were treating him quite unjustly. Perhaps he would be angry later. Angry for the betrayal. Angry for being used. I couldn't blame him in the least. I just didn't want to witness it.

"We'll be leaving now. I do hope you feel better when you get out. Goodbye... Mobley." Leanne walked with me to the door, silent, still refusing to look at him. Tears were streaming down her cheeks.

From the corner of my eye, I could see him sit heavily on the side of the bed, unsure of what to do. Bending slowly to pick up the envelope I left for him, he fingered an edge, lost in thought.

"Okay. Goodbye," he said, barely audible.

A concerned nurse rushed by, alarmed by the now bleeding IV bandage on his arm where he had pulled the needle out. She ushered him back into bed, giving us reproachful looks as we left, closing the door to his room, leaving us in the hallway to our thoughts. I braced myself with a hand against his closed door. "Morgan. I'm so sorry," I whispered. My strength to keep up the charade was gone. "I love you."

Morgan: My plane arrived in Chicago this morning after a stop in Miami. I am leaving Stoney Brook and Stefany with not much more than I arrived with; a sea bag full of my clothes, a backpack, one-hundred-seventy-three dollars (The Blue Calypso has the rest), two boxes with some of the things I ended up with from the island, and… this journal.

As promised, Stefany took care of all the plans and expenses in advance, even putting me up in a nice hotel in downtown Chicago for several days. I guess she knew I'd need some time to figure out where I'm going to go. Tomorrow, I've got to look at apartments near The University of Illinois at Chicago. Of course, I don't know how I'll pay for it. I'm going to have to live on credit for a while. I blame myself for it, as I

gambled much of my earnings away down at The Blue Calypso, even after being warned by Leanne and Stefany. I will need to find a job close to the university. Coffee barista sounds like a possibility, so I will hit those tomorrow.

The whole flight back to the mainland, I just couldn't get my head around why Stefany would shut me out so suddenly and send me away. I tried to call when I was discharged from the hospital, but she refused my calls. I think she blocked me from texting her as well. Leanne won't return my calls or texts either. The shutout is complete.

Seething anger has been boiling deep down inside me, but so far, I've been able to beat it back. There just isn't any way I can be mad at Stefany, even after what she has done to me. I do think she has taken quite a bit for granted.

I'm going to go down to the corner liquor store that's near this hotel and buy a bottle of whiskey with what little money I have. I'm going to peel down the covers on the bed, flip on the TV, throw a couple of ice cubes in a glass, and drink Stefany out of my mind tonight. Damn, I miss her.

My shoes landed in the corner of the room with a THUNK. Next was my pants and shirt, which I promptly threw on the floor. I didn't give a shit about anything anymore. The love of my life had literally sent me away right after saving her life, and maybe even Stoney Brook. And what did I get in return? She paid for my medical bills. I got a flight back. Some cab fare. A hotel.

I dropped onto the bed in my underwear and twisted the top off a beer. There would be no need to get anything to eat tonight, I would gain my sustenance through fluid means. A friend once told me that there was a sandwich in every beer. I would take that creed to heart.

I flipped through the tv channels, trying to find something suitable. A hockey game seemed like a good choice. Blackhawks versus the Vancouver Canucks. Perfect.

I loved that woman to the depths of my soul, I admitted. Stefany had been it for me; the perfect woman. Smiling, I thought about all the sexy escapades we had shared together. Initially shy and introverted, she had become a true sex freak.

There was no getting around it. She didn't even care for me enough to send me off at the St. Thomas Airport. No word, nothing. No goodbye kiss. I took a drink. It was my third beer, and I was feeling lightheaded already on an empty stomach. My lightweight status was official. Hunger was already sinking in, and I decided to change my mind on eating. Stefany was paying for it after all. She had even been thoughtful enough to cover some room service with the hotel. Maybe it was the least she could do, I thought bitterly.

Looking through the order-in menu I picked up from the nightstand table, I selected a steak; rare, baked potato, and mixed vegetables. After a call down on the phone to place the order, they confirmed 30 minutes. Great.

True to their word, a later knock on the door was right on time. After signing for the meal still in my underwear – and not caring - I returned to the bed with my meal in hand on a tray and dove in. It had been a long day and I was much hungrier than I previously thought.

My meal finished at about the same time as the hockey game. Canucks over the Blackhawks, 4 to 3. After opening another beer, I found a documentary on Frank Lloyd Wright, an early architect that I admired.

When I woke up, I rubbed my eyes, shocked that I had dozed off without even knowing it. I had missed the Wright documentary, falling asleep as soon as it had started. It was 3:11 in the morning. My body still ached from the beating I had taken when the tanker truck blew up. The doctors in the St. Thomas hospital had told me I was bruised through my entire body, and it was going to take time.

Again, my mind returned to Stefany. What was she doing? Was she sleeping? How were the repairs to Stoney Brook going? I walked to the bathroom to throw some cold water on my face. My hair was too long, I decided, upon closer inspection in the mirror. Growing back quickly after being singed in the explosion, it was well down my neck and curled up and over my ears. I would need to lose the tropical beach bum look and go for a more respectable approach if I wanted to get anywhere in Chicago.

My position was tenuous, even if Stefany had paid for my way back. Without an immediate job, I was on shaky ground. All I could think about was Stefany. And how tenderly she used to kiss me when sending me out of her room.

Gazing across the room, my eyes fell on a book I had brought from Stoney Brook. It was an engineering book about calculating load bearing weights for various materials. In the middle of it was the letter Stefany had given me at the hospital. She said it was a reference letter of recommendation listing my achievements at Stoney Brook.

"Ah, what the hell," I said to myself, trudging over to the book to retrieve the letter. "Let's see how well she talked me up for my next job." I sat back on the bed and ran a pen under the flap to open it.

A letter with an enclosed check floated down on my lap.

"Ah, so she gave me some severance pay, after all. Maybe now I can afford to-"

Picking it up, my mouth dropped open and I think my heart stopped in my chest. It was written for 6 million dollars. Surely that number of zeroes was a mistake. Or a joke. Or both. I returned to the letter.

Dear Morgan,

I know you are at a loss to understand what has happened and why I did what I did in having you leave. You are right to wonder, and I must think you are probably very bitter towards me at this point. I don't blame you a bit for feeling that way. After all, you have done more for me than I can ever recount in this letter.

If you are reading this, you are probably back in the states by now. This check I have enclosed; I want you to cash immediately. Please. Put it in a good savings account and invest well. All I can say is, you deserve this, and so much more than it's written for. I would have never made it without you.

Outside of the financial success you have made me, you have also made me a woman. For the first time in my life. I will cherish every moment we spent together. And I hope some of those moments bring you happiness and a smile, as they certainly always will for me.

As for why I sent you away, I am not going to say anything about that - except that it had to be that way. I only want you to know that it was never my intent to hurt you. Maybe someday, if we should meet again, I'll tell you more. But for now, I want you to continue your life and live it fully. Do what makes you happy, Morgan Mobley.

I will never forget you.
Stefany

I reread the letter several times, though it became increasingly difficult through watery eyes. She had her reasons for dismissing me, but maddeningly wouldn't elaborate. It was unlikely it was anger over Leanne's payment to me, that had been a ruse, evidently. She had been deeply appreciative of me as it turned out. She had paid me more than anyone could have ever imagined in their wildest dreams. Six million dollars. Holding the check in my fingers, I realized it was likely more money than I would ever have at one time in my life.

I tore the check in two and placed the pieces back inside the envelope with the letter. Bringing it to my lips, I kissed it and took a deep breath, wishing it were her warm, smooth skin.

CHAPTER 22
Hope Springs Eternal (From the Breast of Man)

Stefany: It's been five months since Mobley left. I miss him so much.

Today we began booking guests for the first time since before the storm. That's far beyond the two weeks I thought it would take, but it's good to get things back into working order, even if I am missing Mobley. Leanne tells me I have been in a tailspin. Somehow, I must pull myself out.

Miles is the main suspect in the hiring of Fillmore, no surprise there. But the investigators can't pin anything on him. Not a thing. Was he truly involved? Was he trying to kill me? Or was it someone else altogether??? Miles, of course, maintains that he is innocent and has only ever wanted to help me run Stoney Brook. Yeah, right. Whatever the truth is, I may never know. It is unsettling to know that there could still be someone out there trying to kill me.

~~~~~

My bank was able to contact Mobley. When they inquired as to why he hadn't cashed the check I sent with him, they said he was very grateful for the gesture, but had refused it. They explained it to me that he didn't feel right in taking it, after all the damage and expenses that I had after the storm. I was well insured, so Mobley, as usual, was just being a hard-headed idiot. While they couldn't tell me much more due to privacy rules, they did say he's back in school and working.

~~~~~

Marisha called. She has another installment of Seumas's ledger. She wouldn't tell me what was in it, but she seemed upset. "It's rather shocking," she had said in a trembling voice. She told me that I shouldn't let the contents sour our wonderful friendship. Today is a sunny and beautiful day on the plantation. I think I'll go for a swim and have a cocktail. Then I'll have one of the boys drive with me into the village so I can read what's in the ledger that has so upset Marisha.

Just as I rounded the corner of the lobby desk after checking on our guests, I saw Miles drive up in the circle drive and park. I walked out to the front steps to see what he wanted. He hadn't called or let me know of any issues at the Mill Property, so it piqued my interest, seeing he was coming unannounced.

"It's a beautiful day," he mentioned as he came up the steps to me, carrying a manila folder.

"Yes, it is," I agreed. "A tropical storm on the way in a few days, though," I added. "Is everything in order at the Mill?"

"It's fine, yes," he replied.

"So, what's up?" I asked. "You usually call ahead."

He handed the folder up to me. "A call for celebration. I have a surprise for you."

"Oh?" I muttered as I opened the folder. It was the divorce papers, all signed by Miles. My eyes widened in disbelief. "You are granting me the divorce?"

"I am. Yes," he confirmed without emotion. "With provisions."

I blinked. "Provisions? What provisions?"

"I've decided that simply managing part of Stoney Brook isn't in my blood and I'm ready to return to Montreal and continue my legal practice. Without you."

I stood in silence, waiting for more.

"As hard as it may be to believe, you are financially worth considerably more than me at this point. You've shown the world that any fool can make it if they are handed an inheritance on a silver platter." He eyed me with poorly concealed derision. "No matter how bereft of..." Here he paused, no doubt wanting me to fill in the blanks as he had often done in the past during his bouts of emotional abuse.

I helped him finish as I listed the top three on my fingers. "Intellect? Mental toughness? Business savvy?"

"Well," he shrugged and smiled, "you said it, not me. But more to the point at hand and in a stroke of irony, the legal divorce team you've put together these last few months more than rivals mine. They moved the court venue and changed the terms. As well as other things - which is why I had to relent. I don't have time for a costly court war. It's time. Lucky you."

"Yes. Lucky," I agreed.

"With the exception of the fact I own a condo here on the island and may see you in passing on occasion, I agree to be out of your life for good," he explained. "But, given your newfound success, I want a payout. If the situation had remained reversed, you would have been entitled to some of my net worth."

"You wanted me penniless and broken," I countered, feeling my anger rise. "You've only refused me a divorce because of what you could possibly get from Stoney Brook."

"Say what you will," he said with a dismissive wave of his hand. "We are now here in this moment. Frankly, I think Stoney Brook is going to have a hard time maintaining the level of profit it has enjoyed. But your success at this point is undeniable, and I'm prepared to leave you to whatever you make of it. So, a payoff is only fair."

"Ah. And just how much are you wanting, Miles?"

He squirmed for a moment, summoning the gall to speak. "Two million dollars."

"Two million?" I calmly asked to confirm. He nodded and smiled. His audacity and greed had long ago ceased to shock me.

At that moment, his past abuse all replayed itself in my mind. The broken bones. The smashed face. The bruises, cuts, and hospital stays. The sadistic denials and emotional torture he had put me through.

I had never thought of myself as a multi-millionaire. My income, investments, and just great luck - primarily due to Mobley - had put me in a place in my life I never imagined possible. I could meet his 2 mil demand and not blink an eye.

Pulling a pen out of his shirt pocket, I surprised him as I clicked it into action, quickly scribbling my signature through the divorce papers. This included the provision for paying him the settlement sum of two million dollars - which was to be deposited in an account of his choosing. How thoughtful.

I similarly signed my own copy. Closing the folder with his copy, I handed it back to him.

"I wasn't expecting you to be so… agreeable," he admitted.

"I'm just ready to get you out of my life, for good," I said, flatly.

"My representatives will be in touch, then," he finally said after a long pause.

"Wait," I said as he began to turn to leave. "Miles?"

"Yes? What?" he asked with a smug look as though he knew I would have regrets. "You've signed it, Stefany, it's done. There's no going back on it."

"No, I understand, Miles," I told him. "I just want to make sure you are paid in full."

He looked surprised. "Oh?"

"Yes," I confirmed with a smile.

With this, I punched Miles squarely in the jaw, knocking him backwards down the steps, surprising me at my own strength. It was a cathartic moment, despite the immediate pain in my right hand. The file folder flew from his hand as he landed awkwardly on his back, sending the divorce papers up into the air. Stoney Brook itself exacted a revenge of sorts as his head noticeably impacted on one of the stone steps, making me wonder if someone – other than myself - would need to arrange transport for him to the hospital. Tumbling, he ended up sprawled out at the bottom of the steps, one shoe off and his expensive suit and tie up over his head. He then rolled, first clutching at his head, then his ribs - then one of his knees. A satisfying low moan rose from his throat.

"Have a nice life. And Miles?" He blinked up at me just as his nose began to stream blood. "Get the hell off my property." I turned to walk back inside the front lobby to the wide eyes of the clapping staff and several guests.

Marisha's call had sounded urgent. Standing in her office, I again encouraged her to give me her latest transcription of the Seumas ledger.

"There are surprises this time, Stefany," Marisha said, thumbing through the pages.

"Hasn't there always been surprises?" I asked.

"Yes. But not like these. It is…" She hesitated.

"What?" I eagerly asked. "Is it that bad?"

"It is very *dark*," she finally admitted. "But also illuminating."

"Does it tell us what happened to Bhoki?" I eagerly asked. "And her child?"

"Yes," she solemnly admitted.

I reached for the transcript folder on her desk, but she placed a firm hand on top of it. "It will be okay," I implored. "Please. Let me read it, I can handle it, Marisha." She looked grim and uncertain.

After a long thoughtful pause, she finally relinquished and removed her hand. I picked up the transcript. "Very well. I'll leave you to it, then," she said, walking away. She turned in the doorway, looking back at me. "Please stay. You are welcome to read it in my office. We'll have tea afterwards."

"Thanks."

Taking a seat in the nearest chair, I opened the transcript and began reading.

The Ledger of Seumas Owen McCaskill
(continued)
October 8, 1625
"Nancy threatens to leave me unless I act against the slaves. Bhoki seems to clearly be leading them, urging them on with their

strange incantations and charms. I have been sick, and Nancy is certain that Bhoki is bewitching all of us, including our son.

November 12, 1625

"There have been two more revolts. Five particularly troublesome bucks were hung in the trees of the entry lane.

"It came a time here of reckoning to which I felt I had no choice. It were a hard standard, to be sure, and I believe I am dead for it as well as anyone. Darker days, there have not been.

January 23, 1626

"Bhoki gave birth to a girl, the name being Niesha, if I be honest, the lass is such a beautiful child, taken after her mother and gorgeous in every respect.

February 8, 1626

"Bhoki has all along loudly claimed to anyone within earshot it were I that sired the girl. She has seemed to dare me now, forcing an unprosperous end. How this set Nancy against me can no be conveyed accurately in this account. It is something that must only broach the lips of my household and at my own peril. As for Bhoki's child, it be easy to see the similarities and light complexion. I know 'tis true and yet can no allow my heart to take any joy in it – she is of my own flesh and blood.

"Nancy has sworn vengeance, upon me, Bhoki, and all the slaves. For my part, I have cast what doubt that I could that it weren't but a fault of my own blind heat and it were Bhoki's charms that led me astray. I asked forgiveness for sake of my marriage which I believe was not in heart given by

Nancy to full measure. Bhoki would be set apart and cause no further harm, I swore to no avail. Nancy has several time tried to kill the child by her own hand but were stopped. I forbade her touch the baby girl if she would have me punish Bhoki, which I have thus far stayed in favor of the word. Bhoki hates me now, after the stocks and the lash. I weep.

March 18, 1627

"The latest revolt has left a bloody path all the way to the village, and includes not just Stoney Brook, but has enveloped 5 other landowners about the island. Fire has damaged the main house and threatened to consume us all in our sleep. And even this as the symbols, blood markings, and dead things continuously placed about to stir fright. Bhoki seems to remain the center of this all, building rebellion wherever she goes or speaks. I were made to agree to finally punish Bhoki, not only by Nancy, but the other established families of the isle. I agreed to their desperate haste. I now do so with the full meaning of what this means for Bhoki as well as myself, and I wake each morning before the appointed date with dread in my heart. I too am condemned in my course, and well know my soul will not rest in heaven but shall be cast to the nether of hell. This agreement were made, and it be the devil's own. I can no spare her now. Nancy has left with young Arlon, swearing me to fulfill my word lest she never return.

April 13, 1627

"Bhoki begged that I spare the life of her daughter, our daughter, who is not two years old. It were always my intent to see them both happy but were neer accomplished to that avail. It all be of my own selfishness. The baby girl will be safe, but at the cost of my soul.

"On the execution morning, the wagons were loading of the full company of slaves and all other workers of the estate, and other landowners about, we made our way to the harbor. It was there I pronounced Bhoki the witch that she was, made list of her unnatural spells and magic, all to which she freely admitted. I then pronounced sentence of death. I, by myself rowed her out in longboat from the harbor shore. Twas there I attached a skiff anchor to her ankle chains. Given one last chance to say her final words, she said this to forever freeze my blood."

Send me on, then, if you've the courage. To the depths of the ocean which will be my loving blanket 'oer my soul. Know ye now, for the witch you say that I am, I damn you, and lay upon your uncertain brow a curse of eternal bitterness. It be upon you, Seumas McCaskill, and there shall be a youthful death of every one of your family's name in every generation - until such point as the blood of our daughter is redeemed as your own.

"With all the trepidations that gave me pause, I could not take her life, and set about telling her I would bring her back to shore and suffer my fate, knowing it were my lost nerve. This was all a failure of my own making. No one would lay a hand upon her or her daughter, and that be that. And it were now, she without warning picked up the anchor and stood amid the boat. She then hove herself over the side.

"As she escaped the light of the morning, I reached for her, seeing her face watch me until the black depth of the waters claimed her, which I know will haunt me in every shadow of night hereafter.

"Those landowners about on the shore were convinced it were all done by my own hand in search of a righteous justice. And so, I were of clear authority by their reckoning and again welcomed among them. It weren't so. I can no tell a soul, it was her - she cast herself asunder. The final plunge of her invisible knife into my heart were her last rebellious act. I know of no other with a hard courage such as Bhoki. It spoke of her notions of freedom and independence which she made me wish were borne of my own ideals - instead of hers. She knew in her action I shall no ever again have joy in my life.

April 29, 1629

"Bhoki has been gone now, two years, and I feel her presence still. After midnight, I often hear her shriek echoing through the halls, tearing us from our sleep and freezing our souls. I can no find the source, nor would it be explained away. Doors open and close of their own, and the house maids claim many an apparition is about, chief among them Bhoki's ghost. It be deep into the night I have thought to see her around corners but can no catch her. At the village, it is said that Bhoki rises from the black waters of the harbor at night, returning to walk the complete road back to Stoney Brook in search of her daughter. It are many a witness that in the morn sees her wet footprints upon the steps and walking planks. Aye, it is a frightening specter, I attest, as I too have witnessed her wet prints in the halls of Stoney Brook and about the grounds upon waking. And such is her continued torment.

June 7, 1629

"I awoke with Nancy this past day and were covered with bloody feathers lying about the bed, and with strange marks writ upon our bodies. I'm a light sleeper and know well that no person walking this earth could have done such without me waking. Nancy flew into fit, knowing that this were the work of Bhoki's spirit, come to take revenge, and the only way to stave off this curse would be to kill the daughter. I forbade her talk of this, as this will not happen, and never by my hand for certain if any sense could be made by arguing that this horrid act would only further anger the un-resting spirits that Bhoki has set loose upon us. There will not be a hand laid upon the child.

November 2, 1631

"Nancy died in childbirth. It has now been 4 years since Bhoki departed this world. I know that Bhoki's curse well covers my family like a black blanket. I am a broken man. As I write this, I have taken ill, and this be my last entry as my days are few now. Bhoki's daughter, Niesha, seems to be a happy young lass, running about, and at least with her I have kept my word. She be unharmed and I have made sure that she is cared for insofar as I am capable.

"In passing on the estate, I am having my legalist make assurance that for each successive generation of McCaskill, only one most direct heir may take possession. In this way, I hope that Stoney Brook may always remain in the family. If it ever be sold, may it not be for want. For now, I have passed on what I have to my son, Arlon Carrick, and hope and pray that he will not succumb to my same failures and the evil that has beset my namesake. And mainly, I pray that Bhoki's curse, a justice that should be mine alone, not hold fast to my family after my passing."

I closed the transcript. Sensing that I had finished, Marisha came back into the office.

"It would seem that the tragedy of my family is even greater than I imagined," I murmured weakly. "There's much more to Bhoki's story than I ever anticipated."

"Yes," she quietly agreed.

It was time to face the glaring reality of the transcript. A DNA test could confirm the obvious. Despite the dark history of the McCaskills, I was overjoyed with the revelation. "We both come from the same ancestor," I said. "Seumas. It would seem you and I are family, Marisha."

"It would seem so," Marisha whispered.

Morgan: **There hasn't been one day pass where I haven't thought about Stefany. It doesn't matter what I'm doing, she's right there - in my head. How is she doing? Is Stoney Brook completely up and running as it once was? I wish I could talk to her but know I can't.**

I flipped on the tv yesterday evening, and there was Stefany, a guest on one of the late-night talk shows and every bit the celebrity now. It seems so strange when thinking back to how she was when I first met her. She is a favorite for interviews about women in business and leadership roles. During the show last night, she said she was invited to play a cameo part in one of the upcoming superhero action movies. She said she also did a new photo spread for a swimsuit calendar to come out next year. Beauty and brains. I doubt I could find anyone to believe me if I told them I had been involved with her.

It pains me to write this, but I have either lost or misplaced the mysterious Bowkee talisman. The St. Thomas hospital nurse explained that I had come in wearing it when I was admitted there, but I think she was mistaken. She told me it was undoubtedly of Voodoo origin and associated with the island slave witch, Bhoki, a historical figure at Stoney Brook that is evidently known about the Caribbean! Stefany had casually mentioned the name to me several times and I am astounded. Incredibly, Bhoki would have been a contemporary of Seamus McCaskill. Likely a gift shop trinket, my talisman undoubtedly saved my life as I stooped to pick it up while being shot at back on the island. I am certain I had it in my backpack for the flight to Chicago, but it is gone.

~~~~~

Once again, I face the prospect of what it is to date. It is odd for me to jump back on the horse. There are several pretty candidates among my classes at the university. Yet I have failed to ask any of them out. Stefany destroyed any desire on my part to see another woman, it seems - at least for now.

~~~~~

Of all people, I ran into my ex-wife, Trisha, at my old favorite bar here in Chicago. In happier times of the past, we used to both go to the Top Hat Pub with friends every Friday night. I tried to avoid her, but she eventually noticed me. Her disdain was quite evident at first until further into the evening after she had the requisite number of drinks to ignore her boyfriend and cast her eyes about for other prospects - only to eventually fall upon me. Nope, not happening. She is a shallow, parasitic troll. I shudder to think of what she cost me. How I could have ever loved her is a mystery to me. I was polite, but I left the bar alone and without saying goodbye.

~~~~~

My cap and gown are laid out on the bed. I graduate today, and I can honestly say that I am going to be a "real" architect, with a degree and duly licensed. I'm starting out small, only as an apprentice at a firm here in Chicago. It's better than nothing. At least it will pay some rent and bills.

The graduation ceremonies over, several of my friends approached.

"Morgan! Congratulations, man!" We all shared a male suitable hug, not too long, and not too close.

"So, listen," one of my friends named Liam began. "We are getting together this evening, about 5:00. We'll go to Sam's place. Party, drinks. Everyone will be there. Those girls from Mabson's class. Morgan, you are in, right?"

"I don't know. Maybe."

Liam put his arm around my neck and shook me. "Maybe? Oh, no, bro. You are coming! Quit chumping us."

I looked about, admiring the lush green grass, gentle hills, and flower gardens of the Campus Commons. "Okay," easily relenting, but thinking to myself I could be lying. I may indeed be chumping - there was a great hockey game playing and I wanted to be alone.

Someone was trying to catch my attention, calling my name. Across the crowd, my eyes locked upon a familiar face, several yards away. For a moment, I was certain it was a case of mistaken identity. I quickly broke through the circle of my friends and ran to her. "Leanne!" Taking her up in my arms, I hugged her tightly.

"Ba-jeebus, Morgan," she squeaked from beneath my hold. "Don't break my ribs. I'm glad to see you too."

"I've missed you so much, Leanne. It's great to see you!"

"C'mon. I couldn't miss your graduation. I finally get to see you obtain some level of legitimacy. It warms my heart."

Ignoring her jab, I took her hand and drew her into my circle of friends, all of whom were admiring her and wondering how I had failed to mention knowing such a beautiful woman. "Hey everyone, I want you to meet a very good friend of mine, Leanne Tilden." Everyone took turns exchanging polite introductions.

Turning Leanne to face me, I took her by the shoulders. "Leanne. How is Stefany? Is she okay? What's happened at Stoney Brook?" I looked about anxiously. "Did she come too?"

"Everything is fine, Morgan. Stoney Brook is humming along, better than ever. But no, she couldn't come, I'm sorry to say."

The disappointment on my face must have evident. "I'm sorry," she said.

I felt a tap on my shoulder from behind. "Leanne's lying. Haven't you learned she will say anything for a reaction from you, Mobley." I turned to see Stefany, her eyes hidden behind dark sunglasses, resplendent and beautiful as ever. My friends blinked in disbelief.

She took off her sunglasses and peered at me as if searching for any changes I may have undertaken since last seeing me. Looking into her eyes, I knew I would be unable to restrain myself. I pulled her tightly into me, kissing her. No doubt shocked, she finally relented and cast aside her inhibitions, softly wrapping her arms around my head.

It was assuming, I knew. Especially with how things had ended at the hospital my last day. Besides that, she could be here with Miles - or a new boyfriend for all I knew. Gaining my sense of manners and propriety, I took a step back. "I probably shouldn't have done that. I… it's just that…"

"It's okay. I've missed you too," she replied, placing her hands softly on my chest.

A sudden quiet set upon us. "I think we have just witnessed a special moment," Leanne quipped, finally breaking the silence.

My friends all laughed then stood frozen. I tried to think of an explanation but decided to continue with introductions. "Everyone, this is Leanne's cousin, and *also* a very good friend of mine, Stefany Michaels."

"Actually, I've again taken my maiden name. It's Stefany McCaskill now."

"Hey, I've heard of you!" Liam said suddenly. "I've seen you! Is that *your* Caribbean plantation that Morgan used to work on? He never said he worked for a celebrity!"

"I'm... *not* a celebrity," Stefany countered, embarrassed.

"Yes, she is," Leanne said. "She is just too shy to admit it."

"Leanne. That is quite enough," Stefany scolded with no effect.

We all stood in a semi-circle with Stefany and Leanne meeting a barrage of questions. Each answer went contrary to my friends' perceived image of me as an aloof, solitary loner. Finally, polite manners were sufficiently expended - I wanted to see the women alone.

"Hey, guys. In all seriousness, could you give us a minute? I haven't seen them for quite a long time. I'd just like to catch up."

They agreed and reluctantly strolled away, but not without casting an occasional, awestruck look back over their shoulders.

"You know? I think I'll join them for a moment," Leanne said. "Maybe I can see what kind of company Morgan has been keeping here." She was trying to give us privacy, of course. I couldn't help but laugh as she soon found herself surrounded by my thirsty friends.

"How long can you stay?" I asked Stefany, hopeful.

"This was just a quick trip," she explained. "So we could see you graduate. It took a private detective to find out which program you were in. And where you were located."

Seeing my disappointment, she raised her hand, her fingers softly touching my cheek. "We have a flight out in several hours. We can't stay long, I'm sorry."

This hurt. I didn't know if I could let her out of my life again. In fact, I couldn't. Surely, I could do something. Anything. Make some sort of arrangement. "Can't you-"

"No. I can't." After letting the shock of the last few moments settle over me and reading my glum expression, she finally broke the silence, taking my hand. "This is great. You are graduating. I'm so proud of you. Do you have a job?"

"Yes. I took a beginning apprenticeship at a firm here in Chicago. It's a start." I hesitated. "Is Miles still on the island?"

"Yes," she answered gloomily. "He is living part-time at a condo he likes there. He is always parading some new girl around whenever I happen to see him on the island. But the good news is he finally granted me a divorce. And for the most part, he's out of my life and completely away from Stoney Brook. I'm Stefany McCaskill, glad to meet you," she joked extending a hand.

"It's a right proper Scottish name," I retorted, taking her hand in a mock shake. "A pirate's name, at that. Quite roguish. It's very appropriate for you." We both laughed.

"You recall Marisha was transcribing the Seumas McCaskill ledger?"

"Yes?"

"With Miles no longer managing the Mill Property, it was obvious I needed some help. I invited Marisha to come to live at the estate. I hired her as General Manager."

"Wow," I exclaimed. "I think she will be excellent in that job now that I think about it. But how did you come to focus on Marisha? I thought she was involved with the Island Historical Society."

"She still is," Stefany explained. "She is a natural-born leader. But I also found out she is my distant cousin. Seumas McCaskill is our common ancestor."

Stunned with this news, I blinked, trying to piece together all the implications - the descendants of both slave and master, related by blood, coming together to run Stoney Brook. Stefany was not so alone as she had believed.

"If she's anything like you," I said, "the world had better watch out."

"She is," Stefany confirmed with a smile. "Marisha is my business partner and we've grown quite close. She is like a sister to me. She is already invaluable to our operations."

I wanted to ask her about the guy she had hired as my replacement. Was he working out? Questions swirled about in my mind.

"And the Fillmore murder investigation?"

She hesitated, looking as if she had wanted to avoid this topic.

"Miles remains the primary suspect. He probably funded Fillmore and the attempts on our lives somehow. He knows how to hide things, many of his clients were and still are mobsters. But there is no proof he did it. So, the case remains open. He's out of my life for good now, so I don't think we'll ever know."

"You really think Miles organized it all?"

She shrugged. "Not one suspicious thing has happened since our divorce. It's very telling, I think." The glint in her eyes seemed to indicate there was a lot more to the story that she didn't want to share. Obviously wanting to change the subject, she playfully poked me in the ribs with a finger. "Why didn't you cash the severance check I gave you?"

"Because…" I tried to think of the actual answer. "What I did, wasn't for the money. I did it for you. And with how things ended, it just didn't seem right."

She blinked, her eyes watered, and I thought she might cry. "I paid you that because you earned it."

"We both know you didn't have to do that," I said firmly. "It was excessive. And with all the expenses after the hurricane-"

"I was nearly fully compensated through my insurance," she objected. "I am quite well off, I assure you." She playfully pushed my shoulder. "The former you, the *old* you would have cashed that check and headed out to the casino with a woman on each arm." We laughed at this, noting the irony in the realization we had both changed enormously since first meeting each other.

It was all I could do to keep from taking her hand and leading her away from everything. I wanted to tell her that I had never stopped loving her. I wanted to take her to where I could slip a ring on her finger - kiss her, uninterrupted, forever.

"So, about that check you tore up?"

I reluctantly returned to the subject. "Yes?"

"You know I'm a stubborn woman. And you know I like to get my way. In more ways than one."

"That I do know, yes," I agreed, laughing.

"Which is why I took the money – that is *yours* - and put it into a mutual funds account. It's been growing. It's completely in your name, I have nothing to do with it anymore. I insist that you take it. You can call it a graduation gift. From me to you." She took a paper from her back pocket and slipped it into my hand. "It will do no good to tear that up. It's only your account information and who you need to contact. You are truthfully worth far more than that to me. I won't be taking no for an answer."

If I were even half an idiot managing my finances, I would never need fear money problems again in my life.

"Stefany. I won't lose you again. Please."

She stepped into me, slipped her hand behind my head, and pulled me into a kiss. There was no hesitation on my part as I encircled her in my arms. I loved her more than ever. I had wished for this to the point of blowing my heart up. It was deep, meaningful, and sweetly lingering. Her fingers slipped up softly over my cheeks and into my hair.

"I'm sorry, Morgan." Breaking off, she stared into my eyes, perhaps hoping I would find deeper meaning in all of this. A tear slipped down her cheek, and I knew at that point she was struggling with this every bit as much as I was. She pushed her sunglasses back on, again hiding herself away from me. She stepped away and rejoined Leanne.

She had come back to me, making it the best day of my life – and now, she had made it the worst. "Can I come see you," I asked.

About twenty paces away, she paused to glance back at me thoughtfully over her shoulder. "To work?"

"Anything. Work, if that's what it takes."

She laughed, looked away, and resumed walking. "You are a glutton for punishment, Mr. Mobley. One of your most endearing qualities, I think. Send me a résumé. And a copy of your license. You should know I thoroughly check credentials now."

THE END

www.ingramcontent.com/pod-product-compliance
Lightning Source LLC
Chambersburg PA
CBHW030838030726
47495CB00005B/1276